Nothing in their lives had prepared
these men for motherhood

Mr. Mom

But now Caleb Jones, Matt Glass and
Flynn McCallister are learning to mix
formula, change diapers and do without
sleep. And each is well on his way to
becoming the perfect...

Mr. Mom

Relive the romance...

Three complete novels by three of
your favorite authors

CAROLE MORTIMER

began writing in 1978 and now has written more than ninety books for Harlequin Mills & Boon. This English-born author has four sons—Matthew, Joshua, Timothy and Peter—and a bearded collie named Merlyn. She lives on the Isle of Man with Peter senior, of whom she says, "We're best friends as well as lovers, which is probably the best recipe for a successful relationship."

SHARON BRONDOS

has always loved telling stories, so the move from telling to writing was an easy one. She sold her first romance novel to Harlequin Temptation in 1985. Since then she has written fourteen novels for Harlequin Superromance, as well as a Silhouette Shadows title and one for the Crystal Creek continuity series. Sharon lives in Wyoming with her husband, Gregory. The couple has three grown children.

DALLAS SCHULZE

loves books, old movies, her husband and her cat, not necessarily in that order. She has written over thirty books for Harlequin American Romance, Harlequin Historical and Silhouette Intimate Moments, and has a long list of awards to show for her hard work. She finds that her writing gives her an outlet for her imagination, and she hopes her readers have half as much fun with her books as she does!

Mr. Mom

Carole Mortimer
Sharon Brondos
Dallas Schulze

Harlequin Books

TORONTO • NEW YORK • LONDON
AMSTERDAM • PARIS • SYDNEY • HAMBURG
STOCKHOLM • ATHENS • TOKYO • MILAN
MADRID • WARSAW • BUDAPEST • AUCKLAND

HARLEQUIN BOOKS

by Request—Mr. Mom

Copyright © 1997 by Harlequin Books S.A.

ISBN 0-373-20136-2

The publisher acknowledges the copyright holders
of the individual works as follows:
MEMORIES OF THE PAST
Copyright © 1991 by Carole Mortimer
THE MARRIAGE TICKET
Copyright © 1993 by Sharon Brondos
TELL ME A STORY
Copyright © 1988 by Dallas Schulze

Printed in U.S.A.

CONTENTS

What does a tough, cynical businessman know about raising a child? *Absolutely nothing*, thinks Helen Foster—until she sees Caleb Jones and little Sam together.

MEMORIES OF THE PAST

Carole Mortimer

CHAPTER ONE

'I'M THINKING of selling Cherry Trees,' Helen's father had told her.

Sell Cherry Trees, the house she had been born in, her home until she was nineteen, the place where her mother had, sadly, spent so many months of illness, before finally succumbing to that illness eight years ago. Sell the home that had meant so much to them all over the years? Never!

Of course, she didn't need two guesses as to who had put the unheard of before idea into her father's head. Caleb Jones. The man who actually wanted to buy Cherry Trees.

She had heard nothing but 'Cal Jones' this and 'Cal Jones' that since the man had moved on to the old Rawlings Estate six months ago. Her father seemed to think he was wonderful, had spent many an evening playing chess with him over the months, and so, consequently, he had talked a lot about Mr Caleb Jones during her regular Sunday evening telephone calls to him.

And she had made her own enquiries about the man. What she had learnt certainly hadn't endeared him to her. Or rather, it was what she *hadn't* learnt about him that bothered her so much.

She wasn't interested in the personal life of the man, although according to her father Caleb Jones was a cross between a saint and the Good Fairy, having taken on the guardianship of his young nephew after his parents had died. And his business dealings seemed to be a closed book. Or too much of an open book.

As a highly placed accountant in London, she had enough contacts in the business world to enable her to discreetly obtain the information she wanted. Oh, there was information enough, but it was all just a little too neat and tidy as far as she was concerned, Caleb Jones was either exactly what he appeared to be, a financial genius, or he was a crook. Nothing but one of the two extremes could have made possible the meteoric rise to the successful millionaire businessman that Caleb Jones was at only thirty-nine. And, despite her father's admiration for the man, Helen didn't believe it was the former.

A man like that wasn't going to buy Cherry Trees if she could possibly prevent it.

Which was why she was driving down to her home on the Hampshire coast for the weekend to try and dissuade her father from the idea.

Sell Cherry Trees!

She still couldn't believe her father was even considering it!

Caleb Jones had to have exerted some pressure, even if it was only that of supposed friendship, to have got her father to go even that far; he had always claimed in the past that he would never leave the house which, although once the old gatehouse of the Rawlings Estate, had been his home since he'd married her mother thirty years ago.

It was only since Caleb Jones moved on to the estate and began to work on him that he had even contemplated changing his mind. Well, he was about to find out that David Foster's daughter wasn't as gullible to his ruthless charm.

Not far to go now. She had been aware of the freshness of the sea air for some miles, had her side-window down in the heat of the July day, knew that she was even now turning down the narrow hedge-sided lane that edged one side of the Rawlings Estate.

It was a vast estate, comprised of thousands of acres, covered all of the land between here and the sea, was one of the last big private estates left intact in England. And now it all belonged to Caleb Jones.

Except the rambling old house that had once been its gatehouse.

Caleb Jones. Even the man's name conjured up visions of a Godfather-like figure, sitting back smugly among the luxury of the earnings that, on the surface, seemed to have been acquired too cleanly. Not that one of the people she had spoken to about him had made one derogatory remark or cast one suspicion on him. But it was this very lack of open maliciousness that made her so wary; in a business world like London that just wasn't natural. Not natural at all...

What the—?

Her foot moved desperately to the brake pedal as something wandered across the lane in front of the car. Her panic turned to complete horror as she realised it wasn't a small animal as she had first suspected, but a very small *baby* toddling along on unsteady legs!

She turned the wheel sharply to the left, badly shaken as the car came to a shuddering halt on the grass verge, turning quickly in her seat to see the baby picking itself up after a slight stumble, completely unaware of the narrow escape it had just had if its proudly pleased smile was anything to go by.

Helen quickly released her seatbelt and scrambled out of the car, her only thought now to scoop the baby up out of harm's way before another vehicle came innocently around the corner and perhaps didn't manage to avoid hitting the tiny dungaree-clothed figure.

Dark blue eyes widened indignantly as Helen lifted the baby up, the pink rosebud of a mouth setting mutinously at what was obviously an unwanted interruption to what had been turning out to be a great adventure.

Once she reached the side of the lane Helen found herself

looking into a face so angelically beautiful that it gave her heart a jolt. Above the rose-bud mouth was a tiny button nose, and the dark blue eyes were fringed with long black lashes that fanned down against rosily healthy cheeks as the baby blinked up at her curiously.

Above the heart-shaped face was a riot of jet-black curls of such a length that it was difficult to tell whether the child was a boy or a girl. The dungarees were certainly no indication; children's clothes seemed to be unisex nowadays. And the parents could in no way be blamed for the indulgence of allowing the glossy black curls to grow so long even if it were a boy; it would be almost sacrilege even to think about cropping such a crowning glory.

But where *were* the parents? The child couldn't have walked that far on these unsteady little legs, and Helen knew from having lived here most of her life that there were no houses in the near vicinity. But she had to find the parents somehow, couldn't just drive off with the child and not—

'Sam? Sam! Lord, Sam, where the hell are you?'

Helen could hear the panic in the male voice, knew the still rebellious bundle squirming about in her arms had to be the missing 'Sam'.

'Over here,' she called out firmly, crossing the road in the direction of the voice.

The father. It had to be. The likeness between the two was unmistakable, the riotous dark curls, the dark blue eyes, the latter on the man anxious with the desperate worry he was obviously suffering at the disappearance of his child.

'Sam!' he gasped, having eyes for no one but the child. 'Thank heaven!' His face was pale, his hand shaking visibly as he ran it through his hair, running across the road, taking the eager child into his arms to bury his face in its throat, murmuring words of assurance and thanks for the baby's safe recovery.

Helen took advantage of these brief few minutes to take a closer look at the father. His hair was slightly wet to look at, the blue and black checked shirt he wore also appearing slightly damp, as if he had been exerting himself beneath the hot sun before the disappearance of his young child.

Well, whatever he had been doing at the time, he had no right to have been doing it when it had obviously distracted his attention from keeping the necessary watchful eye on his baby; she was still shaking from the horror of almost running the tiny child down!

The man, finally reassured that no bodily harm had befallen the child, looked up at Helen. 'I can't thank you enough—'

'Thank me!' Helen repeated harshly, breathing heavily in her agitation as delayed shock began to set in; she could have *killed* this adorable baby! 'What on earth were you doing allowing the child to wander off in that way?'

'Look, I understand you're upset—'

'Upset?' she cut in again, green eyes bright with anger. 'I don't think *upset* even begins to cover it,' she dismissed scathingly. 'I could have—could have—' She broke off shakily, breathing deeply. 'Don't you realise I actually had to swerve to avoid hitting the baby?' Her voice was slightly shrill.

The man paled again, turning slowly to look at her car parked at an awkward angle on the side of the road. 'I hadn't realised…'

'Obviously not,' she snapped.

'I was hedge-cutting when—'

'You had no right to bring a small child out here with you when you're working,' Helen reprimanded him incredulously, too disturbed herself at the moment to feel remorse for the way her bluntness had caused that almost grey tinge to the man's skin.

'I had him in a play-pen,' the man attempted to explain.

'Obviously not securely enough,' Helen bit out impatiently. 'And I'm sure your employer can't approve of your bringing such a young child to work with you.'

'I think I should explain, Miss—' Dark brows rose enquiringly over those deep blue eyes.

'Foster,' she supplied impatiently. 'Although I don't see what my name has to do with anything,' she dismissed coldly. 'I think your employer might be more interested to learn your name—'

'I should have realised immediately that you're David's daughter,' the man murmured thoughtfully, his eyes warm now. 'You have the same colouring, and he did mention that you might be coming down this—'

'The fact that you appear to have an acquaintanceship with my father doesn't alter for one moment the fact that I intend to see that nothing like this ever happens again.'

'You have to realise that it won't,' he protested cajolingly.

Helen's mouth firmed. 'I intend to see that it doesn't,' she told him coldly. 'You may be known to my father but so is Mr Jones—and I intend to inform him of your irresponsible behaviour at the earliest opportunity.'

'But—'

She held up one slender hand in a silencing movement. 'I don't want to hear any further excuses. For now I would suggest you take the baby home where it belongs, preferably leaving it with its mother, or at least someone with more sense than you appear to have—'

'But if you would just listen to me—'

'I don't think you have anything more to say that I would care to listen to,' she told him coldly. 'Now if you'll excuse me,' she added with haughty dismissal, 'I would like to complete my journey.' Her father was just expecting her some time today and wouldn't even realise she had experienced this delay, but she was feeling too sickened by the horrific accident that had almost occurred to want to talk to this man any more.

'Of course.' He nodded, looking more than abashed. 'I really am sorry for what happened. There must be a fault with the playpen—'

'I would say it's more probable that the baby managed to climb out of it in some way,' she said disparagingly, one glance at the mischievous smile on the baby's angelically innocent face telling her the child was more than capable of doing such a thing.

The man glanced down at the baby too, the fingers on one tiny hand pulling playfully at the dark hairs on his chest. 'You could be right,' he agreed frowningly. 'I hadn't noticed any fault on the pen itself earlier, I just assumed... I'm beginning to realise it doesn't pay to assume anything with you, you little monkey!' He tickled the baby's tummy as he spoke, its shrill giggles quickly filling the air.

'I'll be on my way,' Helen told him abruptly, turning on her heel.

A hand on her arm stopped her just as she reached the car, and she looked up at the man with coolly questioning eyes.

'I really am grateful,' he said gruffly. 'If anything had happened to Sam...' He repressed a shudder. 'I couldn't have lived with myself.' He shook his head.

He wouldn't have been able to live with himself! Dear lord, if she had harmed one hair on that baby's head...

'Just think yourself lucky that I don't drive on this road often enough to risk speeding along it, otherwise we might have been having a vastly different conversation from this one!' With that final verbal reprimand Helen got back into her car, firmly closing the door behind her to restart the engine, just wanting to be on her way now that the crisis was over.

She took one final glance at father and baby in her driving mirror before she turned the corner and they were no longer in view.

Irresponsible man, to let a young child wander off in that way.

She still hadn't found out his name, but there couldn't be that many men in this area that her father knew with those looks and an adorable baby like Sam. She wasn't normally a person who interfered in other people's lives, mainly because she never welcomed any intrusion into her own life, but what had happened this afternoon had been too serious to ignore, let alone forget.

She hadn't relaxed at all by the time she had driven the two miles further on to Cherry Trees, turning in at the driveway of the mellow-bricked house, taking a few minutes after parking to just sit and look at her childhood home.

She never ceased to feel a warm glow whenever she came back to this house, probably because it had always been so much more to them all: the haven for her parents' marriage, her own warm cocoon of childhood, the garden and surrounding trees that had given the house its name having been her own private playground.

The house itself was low and rambling, the bricks a mellow sandstone, the windows and twin balconies on the second storey, either side of the front porch, newly painted, she noted.

She had no doubt her father had done the painting himself, despite her request for him not to do so after the last time two years ago when he had fallen off the ladder and broken his ankle. Nagging him didn't seem to get her anywhere, but she would have to mention it to him again anyway. Maybe just for once he might listen. He wasn't getting any younger, for goodness' sake, and it was about time he realised it!

As if her thinking about him had alerted him of her arrival her father stepped out of the house into the sunshine, and it was difficult at that moment to think of him as anything but young. The sunlight glinted on hair as golden blond as her own, his face still handsome and reasonably unlined despite his fifty-five years, his step jaunty, his body having retained the litheness of his youth.

'Going to sit out here all day?' he teased lightly, bending down to her open window. 'I saw you from the balcony in my bedroom,' he explained, frowning suddenly as he looked at her. 'How long have you been wearing your hair like that?'

Helen could hear the censure in his voice, one hand moving up instinctively to smooth the neat plait that reached halfway down her back, a feathered fringe lightly brushing her brow. With this coupled with her tailored navy-blue skirt and neat white blouse, she knew she looked very businesslike. But that had been exactly how she had wanted to look when she'd got ready this morning. That her father didn't like it she was left in no doubt.

'A few months,' she said dismissively, getting out of the car. 'The house is looking marvellous, you must—'

'I wish the same could be said for you,' her father cut in bluntly. 'You've lost even more weight. It isn't attractive, Helen.'

'Stop changing the subject, Daddy,' she reproved impatiently, knowing exactly what he was doing. 'You've been working on the house again when I specifically asked you not—'

'Cal had someone come over and do it,' he interrupted with steady patience.

Rather than being reassured by that information, Helen bristled resentfully. Oh, she was glad enough that her father hadn't done the painting after all, but that Caleb Jones should have had a hand in it...

'You should have told me it needed doing,' she said shortly. 'I would have arranged for someone to come in and do it.'

'I told you, there was no need to trouble you. Cal—'

'Caleb Jones obviously has his own reasons for wanting to keep this house up to a certain standard,' she bit out curtly, her eyes flashing. 'Which is precisely why I'm here, you know that.' She swung her case out of the boot of the car, her movements very precise in her agitation.

'And I thought you had come to see me,' her father said self-derisively.

She straightened abruptly, sighing her disapproval of his levity as she saw his eyes twinkling with amusement. 'This isn't a laughing matter, Daddy.' She shook her head.

'I couldn't agree more,' he grimaced. 'I haven't even had my kiss hello yet!'

Her cheeks coloured hotly at the gentle reprimand. 'I'm sorry, Daddy.' She kissed him warmly on the cheek. 'I had a horrible experience not fifteen minutes ago, and I don't think I can be thinking straight yet.'

Her father immediately looked concerned, demanding to know the full story, waiting until they were seated in the comfort of the lounge drinking a much-needed cup of tea. She could see her father was as horrified as she over what had almost occurred.

He looked disturbed. 'And the child's name was Sam, you say?'

'Mm,' she nodded, shrugging. 'I couldn't tell if it was a boy or a girl, only that it was adorable.' Her expression softened slightly at the thought of the tiny child.

'He's a cute little imp, all right,' her father mused. 'A real handful.'

Her eyes widened. 'You do recognise who I'm talking about, then?'

'Oh, yes.' He nodded, looking at her closely. 'Sam reminds me a little bit of Ben,' he said softly, the statement almost a query.

Helen felt herself stiffen. It was purely instinctive, and yet she couldn't help herself. Ben had been a long time ago. And yet she still couldn't talk about him, not naturally, the way that her father now could.

'Perhaps,' she dismissed tightly. 'But at the moment I'm more concerned with speaking to Mr Jones and making sure an incident like today never happens again.' She knew she sounded pompous and prim, but the incident had been too serious to simply ignore and try to forget about.

Her father nodded thoughtfully. 'Speaking to Cal should definitely ensure that,'

Helen looked at him frowningly, a little disturbed about the way he said that. 'I don't want to get this man into trouble, or anything like that. But you have to realise how dangerous his behaviour could have been.'

'Of course I can,' he agreed unhesitatingly. 'Cal will too.'

She didn't feel at all reassured by her father's attitude. 'He won't sack the man, will he?'

Her father raised blond brows. 'Would it bother you if he did?'

'Well, of course it would,' she snapped irritably. 'Jobs aren't all that easy to come by in this area, and the man obviously has a young family to support and look after.'

'He only has Sam,' her father put in quietly.

'Even so—'

'Cal will give him the roasting he deserves,' he said with certainty.

She had already done that, in no uncertain terms, and jobs *weren't* plentiful in this particular area. Besides, she could still see that adorable little face looking up at its father so trustingly...

After all, she had already told the man exactly what she had thought of the whole incident, and she could tell by the stricken look on his face how affected he had been by it all, so surely that constant memory of what might have happened was enough. It certainly wasn't likely to happen again, she was sure of it.

'Perhaps it isn't necessary to discuss it with Mr Jones after all,' she said lightly. After all, she had plenty of other things she needed to talk to Caleb Jones about—talking about today's incident would only confuse things! 'He doesn't really need to know about it,' she decided with finality.

'Hm,' her father said thoughtfully. 'There's only one thing wrong with that, darling.'

'Yes?' she prompted sharply, not seeing what the complication was at all.

He nodded. 'Cal already knows what happened this afternoon.'

'You mean the man will have told him about it himself?' Helen frowned at the thought of the man's having gone to him so quickly.

'Cal *is* the man, darling,' her father explained huskily. 'Sam is the nephew I told you about, the one he's become guardian to. And I've invited Cal over to dinner tonight, so I'm sure he will want to talk to you again about what happened.'

CHAPTER TWO

CALEB JONES. How on earth could Helen have guessed *that* was Caleb Jones?

She had questioned her father's certainty on the man she had met at the roadside's possibly being Caleb Jones, describing him in great detail, only to have her father insist it had been him, that the adorable toddler was definitely the nephew he was guardian to.

The man she had met hadn't looked thirty-nine, early thirties at the most, and he hadn't appeared anything like the cynically hardened businessman she had expected. She couldn't even imagine him in a suit and tie, and his hair was far too long to be considered 'respectable'! But he had been resident on the estate most of the last six months, so that could possibly account for the untidiness of the latter.

But even so, it was hard to imagine that man with the overlong black hair, unlined face and muscled body as anything but the labourer she had first taken him to be.

And he was coming here to dinner tonight, before she had even had the chance to talk to her father about his idea of selling Cherry Trees!

Not that she doubted for a moment that the ploy had been deliberate on her father's part, at least. He had been deliberately evasive on the subject since her arrival, carrying her case upstairs for her and insisting she must feel in need of a shower after her journey. She did feel hot and sticky, but the shower could have waited for a while, except that her father obviously had other ideas.

She could already tell he was going to be at his most stubborn this weekend!

21

Which was precisely why she had got herself ready for dinner early; she was determined she would talk to her father about selling the house before Caleb Jones arrived.

He was in the lounge pouring himself a pre-dinner drink when she got downstairs, as she had known he would be. There was nothing her father enjoyed more than half an hour or so's leisurely relaxation with a glass of good whisky before he was due to eat.

He looked surprised to see Helen down so early, although there was none of the censure in his eyes for what she was wearing that there had been earlier. The classic plain black dress that moved silkily about her body as she walked was one of her father's favourites. And she knew that, but if he wanted to play at being devious so would she!

She had styled her hair in a much softer style for him too, soft curls piled loosely on top of her head, several loose tendrils on her forehead and cheeks framing her face.

'A definite improvement.' He stood up to pour Helen a sherry, eyeing her mischievously. 'Cal will like the change too, I'm sure.'

She bristled angrily. 'I really don't care what Mr Jones likes, as I'm sure you well know,' she reproved, accepting her sherry and sitting down in an armchair. 'And the reason I looked the way that I did when I arrived was because I had been to work this morning and drove straight down here from the office.' And her father was one of the few people she would ever have bothered to explain herself to in this way.

But then, he had obviously known her all her life, and it was a little difficult to stand on your dignity with someone who had changed your nappies for you as a baby, seen you with your two front teeth missing, reassured you that those detested freckles on your nose would disappear one day—

although he had been wrong about that—comforted you through your first bout of unrequited love!

He made himself comfortable in the chair opposite her. 'How is the big city?' he drawled, his eyes still twinkling, not the clear green of Helen's but a marvellous hazel colour that made them change from brown to green to blue. Though he was in his mid-fifties, and despite the devastating sadness of losing Helen's mother so early in their lives together, they hadn't lost any of their glow.

Helen eyed him derisively, not fooled for a minute. 'The "big city" is fine,' she returned drily. 'And stop being evasive.'

'Evasive?' His eyes widened innocently. 'Me? I don't know what you mean.'

'Oh, Daddy,' she smiled wryly, 'you really are a terrible liar.'

He gave a deep sigh, giving up all pretence. 'It's my house, Helen—'

'But it's my home,' she cut in protestingly.

He gave her a chiding look. 'It's seven years since you left here; London is your home now.'

She shook her head firmly. 'I always think of Cherry Trees as my home.'

'Really?' he returned drily. 'And how many times have you visited the place during the last year, the last six months, in fact?' His brows were raised questioningly.

Colour heightened her cheeks at the softly spoken reprimand. She had been down to the house twice in the last year, the last time being at Christmas seven months ago; if she had been here during the last six months she would have recognised the danger of Caleb Jones earlier, and perhaps have been able to put a stop to it before it got this far!

'It's still home, Daddy—'

'It's a big, rambling old house with lots of memories and

the hunger for children's laughter to fill the rooms once again,' he cut in harshly. 'And, as you've assured me on several occasions that you'll never move from London now because it's where your work is, that you have no intention of marrying or having children, the likelihood of your one day being able to bring my grandchildren down to visit me sometimes seems very remote!'

Helen flinched at the hard accusation in his voice. She knew her father didn't mean to be deliberately cruel, but nevertheless his words cut into her like a barb.

'It's your *home*,' she began firmly.

'Cal has promised me a cottage on the estate so that I can still stay in the area,' her father dismissed that problem.

'*Cal* seems to have thought of everything, doesn't he?' she said tautly.

'It's only logical—'

'As far as *he's* concerned it's only logical,' Helen cut in scathingly. 'But at the end of the day our home will have been sold and Caleb Jones will own it! It's all very neat and tidy—in his favour.'

Her father sighed. 'I've already explained that the arrangement suits me too.'

Well, it didn't suit her! As far as she was concerned Caleb Jones had used his friendship with her father—if indeed that was really what it was—to talk him into something that would, in the long run she was sure, be completely wrong for him. Her father loved this house, and she knew he would regret leaving it almost as soon as the deed had been done.

'We'll see,' she bit out tightly.

'There's nothing to see, Helen.' He shook his head. 'I've already made my mind up to sell the house.'

And she was here to undo it. He was being influenced by his feelings of good will towards Caleb Jones, and the other man was obviously taking advantage of that. Caleb

Jones might not look like a cynically hardened businessman, but he obviously knew how to behave like one! Maybe it was that very contradiction that had made it possible for him to be so successful!

'That will be Cal now.' Her father beamed his pleasure as he stood up to answer the ring of the doorbell. He paused at the door. 'I hope this is going to be a pleasant evening, Helen.'

She wished she could assure him that it would be, but they must all be aware that at best it was going to be a strain, at worst impossible. And with her father thinking so highly of Caleb Jones, and her own suspicions about the other man, it could so easily become the latter.

She could hear the murmur of the two men's conversation out in the hallway as her father brought the other man through to the lounge, deciding she would be at less of a disadvantage if she stood up to greet their guest; she really wasn't that tall, only five feet five inches, but the tailored clothes and neat hairstyle she wore for work gave the impression that she was much more imposing than she was. Tonight she only had the advantage of two-inch heels on her shoes, and as Caleb Jones was well over six feet tall he would still dwarf her.

She stood over by the patio doors that led out into the garden, knowing that from this position she had a clear view of Caleb Jones as he entered the room, but that the shadows in this alcove in early evening would mean it took him a few seconds to locate her.

It seemed a slightly childish move on her part, and yet as Caleb Jones stepped into the lounge ahead of her father she was glad she had taken it. The man looked devastatingly attractive in a dark lounge suit and the palest of green shirts, his dark hair brushed into some sort of order this evening, although it was still too long to be considered fashionable.

But with presence such as this man had he didn't need to be fashionable! She could recognise that air of authority for what it was now, although she doubted that in his privileged position he very often needed to enforce it.

He came towards her unhesitatingly, not seeming to have needed to have sought her out at all, knowing where she was instinctively. 'Miss Foster.' He held out his hand.

'Her name is Helen, and yours is Cal,' her father cut in firmly.

'Yes, please do call me Helen,' she invited, revealing none of the disturbance she felt as her hand was taken firmly in Caleb Jones's much larger one. His grip was firm and cool, and just long enough to be remembered. 'May I say you're looking slightly better now than you did this afternoon?' she added with a softness that was designed to take some of the sting out of her words.

The man in front of her didn't even blink at her deliberate reminder of their first meeting. 'I feel a lot better than I did this afternoon,' he returned evenly.

He knew of her antagonism, Helen could tell that as surely as if the words had already been spoken between them. As they surely must be some time very soon. But not in front of her father; she could already sense that this man had already decided that whatever the problem was it would be kept strictly between themselves. And that suited her just fine; she didn't want her father upset unduly unless she could help it either.

'And Sam?' her father put in affectionately. 'How is he?'

Caleb Jones's expression softened at the mention of the baby. 'The same little devil as usual,' he mused. 'He isn't even aware of the near catastrophe he caused.' He turned back to Helen. 'You were right about "the great escape", by the way. The little devil had piled his toys up in one end of his play-pen and used them to climb over the side,' he explained.

'He's very bright for his age.' Helen's father shook his head ruefully.

And so like Caleb Jones to look at—the thought popped unbidden into Helen's mind. And she instantly questioned it. Of course if Sam was his nephew that would explain their similarity, but there could also be a more obvious explanation. This second explanation might also explain why Caleb Jones had chosen to buy the estate in the first place and bury himself down here far away from London where his offices were. She didn't usually have such a suspicious mind, but her ambivalent feelings towards Caleb Jones had been aroused from the first.

It would also be much easier to understand his taking on the guardianship of such a young baby if the child were his own.

She hadn't taken too much interest in his private life when she had been making enquiries about him, except to know that he was unmarried. But that didn't preclude his having a child, a child that he might want to protect from the public eye. Not that it was really anyone's business but his own, and Sam *was* adorable...

'Very,' Caleb Jones agreed with her father indulgently. 'Too bright for his own good sometimes,' he grimaced. 'I'm beginning to wonder which one of us is in control of the situation.'

Helen's father chuckled. 'Why Sam is, of course. All children are. The secret is not to let them ever realise that. I remember when Helen and—'

'Daddy, shouldn't you be checking on dinner?' she cut in pointedly; the last thing she needed was her father reminiscing to this man about her childhood!

Her father gave her a knowing look, but his answer was directed towards the other man. 'Never become a father, Cal,' he said self-derisively, moving to the door. 'They grow up and start treating you as if *you're* the child!'

'I think it's a bit late for me to worry about that,' Caleb Jones said ruefully. 'Sam already has me taped.'

His beautiful mischievous nephew was another subject Helen would have preferred not to discuss if she could avoid it. But as her father left the room to check on their meal she knew their conversation was rather limited!

'Would you like a drink, Mr Jones?' she offered politely.

'A small whisky would be fine,' he accepted just as politely.

She moved smoothly across the room to pour the alcohol into a glass for him.

'Are you not joining me?' He raised dark brows enquiringly.

'I only drink wine,' she explained coolly. 'And I prefer to wait until we have our meal.'

Caleb Jones lowered his long length into an armchair before taking an appreciative sip of the neat alcohol. 'I've heard such a lot about you from David,' he explained. 'It's good to finally meet you at last.'

Helen looked at him scathingly. 'Is it?'

He didn't appear in the least perturbed by her manner. 'David obviously misses you very much,' he nodded.

She bristled angrily at what she sensed was a softly spoken reprimand. 'All children leave home to make a life for themselves at some time, Mr Jones,' she snapped.

'True,' he acknowledged without rancour.

Helen felt extremely irritated by the way he had made her feel guilty and then dropped the subject as if it were of no real importance. And it had been too smoothly done not to have been deliberate. Those innocently wide blue eyes were definitely deceptive, and she was more sure than ever that her preconceived idea of this man as being shrewdly clever was correct.

'How do you like—?'

'Could we dispense with the polite conversation when

my father isn't around, Mr Jones?' she cut in caustically. 'We both know the reason I'm here, and polite chit-chat isn't going to gloss over that.'

He arched dark brows. 'I thought you were here to visit your father.'

'And I have already had this conversation with him earlier,' she snapped. 'With much more effect, believe me,' she added scornfully.

He gave an inclination of his head. 'I'm glad to hear it.'

She drew in a controlling breath at the censure in his voice. He least of all had the right to stand in judgement of her behaviour. 'At least my affection for my father is genuine,' she challenged softly.

He didn't move, not so much as a muscle, and yet Helen could feel the anger emanating from him. 'Implying?' he prompted tautly.

'Implying that—'

'Dinner is served,' her father announced lightly as he came back into the room, his eyes narrowing shrewdly as he sensed the antagonism flowing between his daughter and his friend. 'Let's go and eat before it all spoils,' he added distractedly.

He was upset by the tension between herself and the man he considered a close personal friend, Helen could tell that, and yet she couldn't do or say anything to put his mind at rest. She didn't trust Caleb Jones, and there was no use pretending, not even for one evening, that she did.

It couldn't be of any comfort to her father now, but he was actually the one who had always told her to be honest in her dealings with people, polite but honest. And that was exactly what she intended being with Caleb Jones.

'You don't cook, Helen?' a lightly mocking voice enquired as they all went through to the dining-room.

Her father chuckled his enjoyment, eyeing her teasingly.

'Yes, I cook, Caleb.' She knew the complete formality

of 'Mr Jones' was out now that her father was back with them, but she stubbornly refused to call this man 'Cal'. 'But when I'm home my father insists on feeding me up; he doesn't think I look after myself properly in London,' she added drily.

'And do you?' the other man challenged softly.

Her mouth firmed. 'As well as any person living alone,' she bit out.

Caleb Jones nodded. 'I've lived alone in London myself—it's far from being an ideal situation.'

Helen couldn't help wondering just how often he had actually 'lived alone'.

But she couldn't help sensing yet another underlying criticism. 'It may have escaped your notice, Caleb,' she snapped, 'But there aren't too many vacancies for accountants in a rural area like this one!'

Once again he appeared unruffled by her vehemence. 'Strange you should mention that...' he murmured thoughtfully.

Helen didn't see anything in the least strange about it. This was a country area, with one or two small towns nearby, but none of them possessed the sort of company she wanted to be associated with. Up until now her father had always accepted that the move to London was necessary for the advancement of her career. She would not appreciate it if this man had been putting other ideas into his mind!

Her eyes flashed her anger. 'I don't see anything strange about it—'

'Oh, I didn't mean strangely odd,' Caleb Jones cut in smoothly. 'I meant what a strange coincidence; I'm looking for an accountant at the moment—in fact I'm going to start seeing people concerning that this week.'

Helen stared at him. 'You want an accountant working down here with you?'

He nodded. 'I spend most of my time here now, and rather than move all my staff and offices down here—which wouldn't please them, I'm sure—I thought a personal-assistant-cum-accountant liaising between here and London would be the perfect answer to the problem,' he explained lightly.

Helen had become more and more tense as he spoke, turning slowly now to look at her father, sure from his innocent expression—and his friendship with Caleb Jones—that he had known of the vacancy long before now.

And that too-innocent expression gave her a deep feeling of unease.

Surely her father hadn't expected her to be interested in applying for the job!

CHAPTER THREE

'YOU can't have been serious, Daddy,' Helen complained incredulously.

Dinner was long over, Caleb Jones had taken his leave a short time ago, and the two of them were enjoying a cup of coffee before going to bed.

Helen had lost her equilibrium somewhat after she had realised her father had seriously contemplated the idea of her working for Caleb Jones.

At the time she had passed the moment off with a flippant comment about liking her job in London, but she had known from her father's expression that he intended to pursue the subject once they were alone. Helen had decided that attack was the better form of defence!

Her father didn't appear in the least perturbed. 'It's an ideal step up the ladder for someone in your position,' he reasoned lightly.

'It's a leap,' she acknowledged self-derisively.

'Well, then—'

'Too much of a leap, Daddy,' she derided.

'I'm sure Cal would—'

'I certainly don't want any favouritism from him, thank you,' she snapped.

Her father looked annoyed by her outburst. 'I wasn't talking about favouritism, damn it—'

'Then what else would you call it?' she challenged, her cheeks red.

He drew in a controlling breath. 'Cal would merely consider your application as fairly as any others he receives.'

'I don't want to be "considered"—'

32

'I wish you would forget your prejudice of the man, and think what a really good opportunity it would be for you to work for him—'

'I don't *want* to work for him!' she cut in exasperatedly. 'I find the man totally obnoxious, and on top of that I question his ethics.'

'Helen!'

She had gone too far with her last remark as far as her father was concerned, she could see that, and yet it wasn't just Caleb Jones's underhand dealings over Cherry Trees that bothered her about the man; she still didn't know enough about him professionally to trust him completely in that area either.

'The City is suspiciously quiet about him,' she insisted. 'I would need to know a lot more about him than I do now before I would even consider working for him.'

'Don't let one bad experience sour you, Helen,' her father advised softly.

Colour warmed her cheeks at this gentle reminder of her youthful folly.

She had been extremely vulnerable when she'd first moved to London, had kept herself very much to herself during those first few years, so that by the time she'd taken up her position as a junior accountant in one of the larger firms she had been ripe for the attentions of a more senior accountant with the company.

It had taken her several months to realise that, while Daniel's personal investments weren't exactly illegal, they were at the very least unorthodox. And she had only found that out because by this time he had believed them to be close enough for her to be taken partly into his confidence, to suggest that she might like to supplement her own income in the same way.

It had been the end of what she had believed to be a promising relationship, and also the last time she had dated anyone in her own profession. The last time she had dated anyone at all, her father would have accused, but that wasn't strictly accurate; she did occasionally go out to dinner or the theatre if she met anyone she thought might be interesting to spend an evening with. But she had to admit those times were few and far between, and she rarely repeated the experience.

'I haven't, Daddy,' she assured him softly. 'I just find more satisfaction from my career than I do in a relationship with a man.'

'That's simply because you haven't met the right man yet,' he insisted.

'And have no interest in doing so for some time. If ever!'

'Then you should at least be interested in this position with Cal,' he reasoned.

Professionally she knew that she should, that she was, but personally she knew she would never be able to work for Caleb Jones. And besides, she hadn't just been making excuses when she'd said it was too big a leap for her professionally; Caleb Jones would need a very senior accountant indeed to handle the job he was talking of.

'It would have meant you could move back here,' her father put in pointedly.

And he would have no reason to sell Cherry Trees; she had already realised that. But she knew, even if her father didn't, that that had to be the last thing Caleb Jones wanted. Which meant her chances of getting the job were nil before she even started. She wouldn't humiliate herself by even trying!

'I enjoy my work in London, Daddy,' she told him firmly. 'I have no intention of leaving it.'

'I see,' he said flatly.

Helen sighed. 'No, you don't, but then you don't want to.'

'I just want— Oh, never mind what I want,' he dismissed irritably. 'I can see I'm just wasting my breath.'

'Playing the martyr doesn't suit you, Daddy,' she told him drily.

An unaccustomed flash of anger darkened his eyes. 'You are the most stubborn, annoying—I can't believe you're a child of mine!'

She chuckled as she stood up. 'Strange—everyone, including you, has always said I'm exactly like you.'

He gave her a glowering look. 'Don't be so damned facetious!'

She grinned at him, her eyes glowing deeply green in her amusement. 'And I'm too old for that to work any more either!'

'More's the pity,' he mumbled, disgruntled.

Helen gave a leisurely stretch. 'Why don't we talk about all this again in the morning? It's been a long day and it's late.'

'And nothing will have changed by tomorrow,' he said ruefully. 'But I see your point about the time.' He stood up with a sigh. 'I'm feeling a little tired myself.'

In truth he did look slightly strained; he had lines about his eyes and mouth that she hadn't noticed earlier. Could it be that her father was finally beginning to show his years? Or was it something more than that? She felt pangs of guilt for not noticing the subtle changes earlier. And were they changes that Caleb Jones had seen and recognised? If they were he was being doubly underhand!

She looked at her father with concern. 'Are you feeling all right, Daddy?'

His ready smile erased the lines of strain, making Helen wonder if she could have merely imagined they were there at all. Her father was probably just tired after all.

'Never felt better,' he assured her. 'I always feel more cheerful when you come home for the weekend.'

'Daddy!' she reproved ruefully. Would he never give up?

He grinned. 'I've never claimed to be anything but a devious old devil.'

No, he hadn't, Helen mused as she prepared for bed. But he had overstepped his limitations this time. There was no way she was going to give up her job in London and come back down here to live. Maybe she was being selfish, but it was no use pretending she felt any differently.

She certainly wouldn't want to live permanently anywhere near Caleb Jones!

'Restful, isn't it?'

Helen turned sharply at the sound of that softly spoken voice.

Her father had gone off into town on some errand or other, and she had taken the opportunity to stroll along the beach near the estate; it had once been a place she had spent many soothing and calming hours.

And it had, in recent years, always been somewhere she had come to alone...

Caleb Jones standing several feet away, his bare feet planted firmly in the golden sand, bronzed legs revealed by the white shorts, a pale blue short-sleeved shirt completely unbuttoned down the front showing a chest that was just as tanned, was not a welcome intrusion into her solitude.

Far from it!

'I always thought so,' she replied pointedly.

In fact she had been immensely enjoying the gentle lap of the waves on the sand, her feet bare as she enjoyed the latter's coolness near the water's edge.

The local people from the village rarely used this beach, a much more popular one, with a few amenities like a small café, situated just around the bay. It shouldn't have surprised her in the least that Caleb Jones had discovered and invaded this quiet stretch of water; he seemed to have intruded on several other important parts of her life too!

His mouth quirked into a half-smile, and Helen was sure he knew exactly what she was thinking. His next words confirmed it. 'I always come here when I feel like being alone,' he drawled.

'No Sam today?' she challenged.

Caleb shrugged. 'He's taking a nap. His idea of the start of day is daybreak, so by this time he's ready for a sleep. So am I, come to that,' he added self-derisively.

'Don't you have him trained not to wake you yet?' Helen couldn't help her curiosity about the child she had met so precipitately.

He grimaced. 'That's a little difficult; his nursery is right next to my bedroom. And playing in his cot only lasts for a few minutes once he's woken up. After the last episode I'm loath to leave him anywhere on his own too long; lord knows what he would get up to!'

Helen frowned. 'Doesn't his nanny—?'

'I don't have a nanny for Sam,' he cut in quietly, bending down to pick up a pebble and skim it across the clear water in front of them.

His action gave Helen a few seconds to take in his surprising statement. If he didn't have a nanny for the little boy then that must mean... Good grief, wasn't that taking his guardianship of Sam just a little too far? After all, there couldn't be many men in his financial position who would even think of doing such a thing, let alone carry it out.

'That seems a little—ambitious,' she dismissed coolly.

No wonder he rarely spent time in London any more if he had taken on the full-time care of a very young child!

He raised dark brows mockingly. 'Because I'm a man?'

Her cheeks warmed at his taunting tone. 'Not necessarily,' she answered defensively. 'Bringing up a child is difficult for anyone, but for a man alone, a man with a full-time career to think of, I would have thought it was virtually impossible.'

'It's—hard, at times,' Caleb admitted. 'Hence the need for the PA.'

Helen stiffened, at once wary. 'Wouldn't it have just been easier to engage a nanny for the baby?'

'Easier, perhaps,' he conceded consideringly. 'But not half as much fun!'

He sounded as if he was really enjoying caring for the baby, and she had no reason to think otherwise; after all, he did seem to have changed his whole lifestyle to suit his new responsibilities. But even so, she still found it an odd thing for him to have done, especially when the child supposedly wasn't even his own.

'I wish you luck with your other venture,' she told him dismissively, hoping he would go away and she could be left alone to her thoughts—and the privacy of the beach!

He gave her a sideways glance, standing next to her now. 'Not thinking of applying yourself?'

She gave him a knowing look. 'There wouldn't be much point, would there?'

'No?'

He didn't give anything away, she would give him that! 'No,' she drawled derisively.

'Your father would like it.'

Her mouth twisted. 'But you and I know it's a foregone conclusion that it will never happen.'

'We do?'

'Of course,' she snapped, impatient with his evasive tactics. 'If you gave me the job it would mean my father wouldn't sell Cherry Trees to you.'

'Yes?'

'Well, we both know you don't want that to happen.' Her eyes flashed.

'Do we?'

'Don't start playing games with me, Mr Jones,' she bit out disgustedly. 'We both know that, for reasons of your own, you have decided to have Cherry Trees back as part of the estate, and my moving back here to live would certainly defeat that objective.'

He nodded slowly. 'Yes, I can see that it would,' he said thoughtfully.

His calm dismissal of the subject annoyed her even more. 'I think you should know right now that I have every intention of stopping you from ever having Cherry Trees!' Angry colour burned her cheeks. 'It's my family home; you don't need it for your damned estate.'

Dark blue eyes looked at her coolly. 'It was part of the original estate.'

'That doesn't mean it has to revert back to it,' she said heatedly.

'Your father seems to feel differently,' he pointed out calmly.

'My father is influenced by your supposed friendship,' she scorned. 'I'm not taken in so easily.'

Caleb gave her a long considering look. 'No,' he finally replied. 'I don't think that you are.'

'Believe it,' she snapped. 'I intend to stay down here for as long as it takes to convince my father he is making a mistake.'

'Oh?' He looked surprised. 'I thought you were only down for the weekend.'

'I can easily arrange to stay for longer,' she bit out.

In fact, she hadn't intended anything of the sort when she'd first come down, but after meeting Caleb Jones, and talking to her father, she had a feeling it was going to take much longer than the weekend to make her father see sense.

Caleb didn't look concerned. 'I'm sure your father will like that.' He nodded distractedly, glancing at his wristwatch. 'I'd like to continue this conversation, Helen,' he smiled, humour giving his eyes a dark glow, 'but I'm afraid I'm expecting Sam's grandparents down for the day,' the smile disappeared, his eyes grim, 'and it wouldn't do to be late for their arrival.'

Helen looked at him closely. He didn't sound at all thrilled about having his parents visit. Maybe they didn't approve of him either!

'Don't let me keep you,' she mocked.

He nodded. 'I expect I'll see you again soon.'

She expected he would. She would have to return to London for a couple of days, of course, but she was due some holiday so she intended being back as soon as possible. It would just be a case of persuading her father not to do anything until she came back. *Just* a case? He could be so stubborn and headstrong when he felt like it!

'Enjoy your weekend,' Caleb added softly, turning to leave.

Before battle commences, Helen silently added. Because a battle it most certainly would be.

Odd, but she felt strangely elated at the thought of it.

CHAPTER FOUR

'SOMETHING wrong, love?'

A ghost from the past.

But it couldn't have been, Helen instantly dismissed. She had to have imagined the familiarity of that handsome face of the driver of the sports car she had just passed in the lane on her way to Cherry Trees; Daniel believed the countryside was at the very least an alien planet!

Helen smiled brightly at her father as she got out of the car. It had taken her longer than she had thought to organise the breathing space she felt was necessary to sort out the problem of her father's decision to sell Cherry Trees. So it was now almost two weeks later—and a promise from her father not to do anything rash in her absence!—that she had managed to return home with the knowledge of two clear weeks' holiday in front of her. Surely two weeks would be long enough to persuade her father not to sell, and, more important than that, to convince Caleb Jones that her father *wouldn't* sell.

'It's good to be home,' she told her father with genuine warmth.

He grinned at her. 'Starting your campaign already?'

She moved briskly around the car to take her luggage from the boot. 'Not at all,' she dismissed. 'How is our esteemed neighbour?'

'Cal?' Her father sobered a little. 'He's all right, I suppose.'

Helen looked up at him searchingly. 'What's that supposed to mean?'

Her father shrugged. 'Nothing, really. Come on, let's go

41

inside. It will be like old times, having you here again for a while.'

That was what she was hoping for. And she was more ' than willing to drop the subject of Caleb Jones for the moment, still shaken by that driver's resemblance earlier to Daniel. She hadn't seen him for years, their lifestyles completely different, but she still couldn't help shuddering every time she realised the narrow escape she had had with him. Every blond-haired Adonis was apt to remind her of what a fool she had been for the few months she had imagined herself in love with him.

'Starting *your* campaign already?' she returned just as mischievously as he had a few minutes earlier.

He raised blond brows. 'Well, at least this time you came home dressed for the occasion.' He looked appreciatively at the casual white trousers and white T-shirt she wore, her hair secured loosely at her nape.

The ploy had been deliberate, Helen had to acknowledge mentally. She was genuinely looking forward to this visit with her father, but she also wanted it to go well for purely selfish reasons. No, they weren't selfish, she really believed her father would be unhappy living anywhere else but Cherry Trees. It was up to her to help him to realise that.

'I'm on holiday,' she dismissed lightly.

'You're at home while you have time off work,' her father corrected reprovingly. 'One hardly goes home for a holiday,' he derided drily.

She raised her eyes heavenwards, her mouth twisting wryly. 'That's very good, Daddy,' she taunted. 'But I merely meant I have time away from work to do as I please.'

'Of course you did,' he mocked.

'Daddy,' Helen sobered, 'I hope we aren't going to keep sparring like this the whole time I'm here—'

'Why not?' He grinned. 'I find it quite entertaining.'

'But very tiring.'

He shrugged. 'It makes life a lot more interesting, though.'

'If you say so,' she grimaced. 'But I don't intend giving you the satisfaction of baiting me every five minutes or so.'

'Oh, well,' he dismissed. 'It was fun while it lasted.'

And it was far from over, despite what she had said, and they both knew that!

'Anyway, you'll have someone else to "spar" with this evening.' He gave her a sideways glance.

Helen gave him a considering look; he was about as subtle as a blow between the eyes! 'Expecting a visitor tonight, are you?' she said as casually as she was able. Really, her father wasn't even waiting for her to get settled in before challenging her with Caleb Jones's presence in the house!

He shrugged. 'Only Cal for our usual Friday night game of chess. We cancelled the chess in favour of dinner the last time you were here out of consideration for you,' he explained lightly.

'How nice,' she said with saccharine sweetness.

'I thought so.' Her father grinned, not fooled for a moment.

He was impossible! But more like his old self this visit, Helen decided as they lingered over a meal of salad and fresh fruit. The lines of strain seemed less about his eyes and mouth today, the former having most of their usual mischievous glow.

But, despite her ready acceptance of Caleb Jones's expected arrival here tonight when she had only just arrived, it was really just another reminder of how close the two men had become these last months. And of how difficult it was going to be to place the wedge in the relationship that was going to be necessary to persuade her father just how deviously the other man was behaving.

Considering how warmly the two men greeted each other later that evening, that wasn't going to be easy to do!

'Nice to see you again, Helen.' Cal held out his hand in friendly greeting.

Tonight he was dressed in fitted denims that showed the narrowness of his hips and thighs, and a loose short-sleeved shirt of the same shade of blue as his eyes. With his over-long dark hair slightly wind-swept by the light breeze outside, and his eyes warmly smiling, he looked devastatingly attractive. As attractive as he had the first time she had seen him, before her knowledge of his identity had put her on her guard.

Remembering the last time she had seen him, she couldn't help thinking of the beautiful baby he had in his care.

'...doesn't bite, you know, Helen,' she heard her father mock lightly.

She blinked at him questioningly, blushing furiously as she realised Cal still had his hand extended in greeting, and she had been so lost in her own thoughts she hadn't even noticed it!

'I was wondering how your nephew is,' she said briskly as she lightly brushed her hand against his. Even that contact felt like too much, her hand seeming to burn where they had touched. She didn't need a complication like that, certainly not with this man!

She couldn't remember the last time she had been physically attracted to a man—yes, she could, and look at the chaos Daniel had almost caused in her life. Caleb Jones could wreak absolute havoc! She must be having a brainstorm to have even been thinking of him in that way, must need this holiday more than she had realised. She would *not* fall for this man's charm, as others seemed to do so easily.

'Have you left him in the care of the maid again?' she added caustically, meeting his gaze with defiant challenge.

His mouth tightened, his eyes taking on a grim look. 'As a matter of fact—'

'Helen, how about making a drink for Cal and me?' her father interrupted, his brows raised warningly as she opened her mouth to protest at this abrupt interruption to her conversation with Cal.

She glanced back questioningly at Caleb Jones. He did look rather grimmer than the question had merited, but even so...

'I like slightly more water in my whisky than Cal,' her father added firmly, glaring at her pointedly.

What had she said, for goodness' sake? Her father seemed almost angry, and yet she was sure her remark hadn't been that insulting. In fact, it had been tame compared to what she would have liked to have said!

'Helen!' her father prompted again, even more sharply this time.

He really was agitated; Helen frowned. Not that Caleb seemed too aware of their tension, looking very distracted.

'Sam?' she questioned her father with sudden alarm, vividly remembering the determined expression on that cherubic face two weeks ago when Sam had made his escape from his play-pen to stumble across the road in front of her car. Surely Sam hadn't made good another escape, this time with more serious consequences?

Her concern broke through Caleb's preoccupation. 'He's fine, Helen. Really,' he assured her with a strained smile. 'Actually, his grandparents are visiting him again this weekend,' he added tautly.

Then what was he doing here? The question came instantly to mind. But a single casual glance at her father's fiercely warning expression had strangulated the question unasked in her throat. For some reason, and she would question her father on it later, he didn't want her to pursue the subject of this visit of Cal's parents to his home. There was definitely some sort of friction there, and maybe this guessed-at animosity of Cal's own parents towards him would give her an advantage against him she hadn't expected to find.

'I'll get your drinks,' she complied briskly. But her curiosity had been aroused now, and she would make sure she had the answer to a few questions before very long had passed.

The two men were already seated on either side of the chess-board by the time she returned with their drinks, and from the intent expressions on their faces, and their almost absent-minded acknowledgements of the glasses being placed beside them, she knew that they were already so engrossed by the challenge ahead of them that they were barely aware of her presence.

She moved quietly across the room, picking up the book she had brought with her, to sit down in an armchair.

But she didn't find the gentle ticking of the clock, the only sound in the room other than the soft thud of the pieces being moved about the chess-board, in the least restful. The story-line that had held her attention with ease during her hours of relaxation in London now held little appeal for her, and she found her attention wandering constantly to the two men seated across the room.

Cal was concentrating as hard as her father, and yet she knew enough about the game to realise that the younger man was losing badly. She had thought the two men would be evenly matched, and yet she could see that tonight Cal was very distracted. She could also see his impatience with himself as he easily lost the first game.

Her father looked concerned, attempting a teasing smile as they set up the board for another game. 'Feel like a breather before we play again? Or a top up?' He held up their almost empty glasses.

Cal relaxed back in his chair, flexing his shoulders tiredly. 'Yes to both, thanks.' He gave a rueful smile and turned to Helen conversationally. 'Let's hope the weather stays fine for your holiday.'

She bristled resentfully; this man did have a way of saying the wrong thing. Unless it was deliberate? 'I'm not on holiday,' she snapped, feeling none of the indulgence towards him for the remark that she had felt for her father earlier.

'Helen,' her father reproved wearily. 'Stop being so touchy.' He frowned. Now is not the time, he seemed to add silently.

She frowned questioningly, but he shook his head warningly. Lord, what was so sensitive about Cal's parents visiting him? Only they weren't visiting *him*, were they? It was Sam they had obviously come to see. She really would have to talk to her father later. Perhaps, without being too nasty about it, she could point out to her father that Cal might not be quite the nice man he thought he was when his own parents treated him so suspiciously.

Whatever it was about his parents' visit that was bothering Cal, it had really got to him, and he lost the next two games of chess to her father with little resistance. He sat back with a rueful sigh. 'It's not my night tonight, I'm afraid,' he grimaced.

'Another whisky?' Helen's father prompted lightly.

Cal looked down consideringly at his empty glass. 'I don't think I'd better...' he said reluctantly, obviously in no hurry to leave.

'Coffee, then,' her father decided firmly. 'You two have a chat while I go and get it ready.'

Helen glared at him as he left the room with a mischievous wink in her direction. The old devil, he was enjoying this situation altogether too much for her liking.

'Good book?' Cal stood up, stretching stiffly.

She hadn't read a single page since she'd sat down, had spent the entire time watching the two men, fascinated by the intensity of their game! But she wasn't about to admit that! 'Not bad,' she dismissed with a shrug. 'A bit like her others.' She had read enough of the book while in London to be able to say that with complete authority. But it was a safe read, with a predictable ending, and it didn't need too much concentration to read it.

Lord, he did look tired, she realised with a frown. 'How did the interviews go?' she prompted lightly.

He brightened a little. 'Very well, actually. I have someone starting who seems very competent.'

'That will relieve some of the pressure,' she nodded.

'Let's hope so.' He still seemed distracted.

'Does Sam not get on with his grandparents?' She frowned; all the more reason for Cal *not* to be here tonight if that was the case!

'Reasonably well,' he replied.

Then what was the problem? Because there certainly was one. 'I'm sure my father wouldn't have minded if you had missed your game of chess for one week,' Helen said softly.

'What...? Oh,' his brow cleared. 'No, I can assure you that I'm not necessary at the house tonight,' he added grimly.

He *didn't* get on with Sam's grandparents. Curiouser and curiouser—as the saying went. She could hardly wait to talk to her father alone.

But the two men seemed in no hurry to bring the evening to a close, relaxing back in a couple of armchairs to talk lightly as they enjoyed their coffee.

Helen studied Caleb Jones again, wondering at her earlier reaction to him. Oh, he was handsome enough, rakishly so, but that very fact should have been enough to repulse her; she had learnt the hard way that dangerously attractive men were selfishly obsessed with having life their own way. Caleb Jones had done little, so far, to disabuse her of that belief!

Besides, she had more sense than to ever let personal feelings towards a man interfere with her life a second time!

She stood up determinedly. 'I think I'd better go to bed.'

Caleb frowned, glancing down at his watch. 'I suppose I'd better be on my way.' But he didn't sound in the least anxious to go.

'There's no need to do that just because I'm going to bed,' Helen dismissed briskly. 'Stay and have another drink with my father.'

Caleb stood up too. 'I'm sure I'll see you again soon.'

So was she, but she had accepted that such meetings were unavoidable before she came down here!

He chuckled softly at the revealing expression on her face. 'Your enthusiasm for that idea is overwhelming!'

She blushed at the amused sarcasm in his voice, looking reluctantly at her father, expecting censure in his face but finding the other man's humour reflected there. The *two* of them were actually enjoying her discomfort now!

'Goodnight, Mr Jones,' she said with as much dignity as she could muster. 'Daddy,' she kissed him with a warmth that was accompanied by a saccharine-sweet smile, the look in her eyes promising further comment on his behaviour when they were alone.

Whether Caleb took up her suggestion or not, he stayed downstairs talking with her father for at least another half-hour after she had gone up to her bedroom. She became aware of the sound of his car leaving as she came through from taking her shower, strolling over to the window to watch his tail-lights disappearing in the direction of the main house, absently drying her hair with a towel as she wondered what sort of reception awaited him. It was his home, and yet she knew it was the last place he wanted to be tonight.

Her father was still seated in the lounge when she got downstairs, his expression pensive, although he brightened somewhat as she came into the room.

'I thought you would have been asleep long ago,' he said with a smile.

She shrugged. 'I needed a shower. And I thought perhaps Caleb wanted to talk to you alone for a while,' she added.

Her father grimaced. 'It isn't an easy situation for him.'

'But he must have realised that when he first took Sam on.' She frowned. 'And he could make things a lot easier for himself if he employed a nanny to help out.'

'Oh, it isn't caring for Sam that's the problem,' her father dismissed impatiently.

Helen looked at him questioningly, but he seemed lost in his own thoughts, and after a couple of minutes' silence from him she realised he wasn't about to explain himself.

'Then what is?' she prompted softly, her eyes narrowed thoughtfully.

'Sam's grandparents,' he said heavily.

The subject she had been longing to get back to all evening!

'What about them?' she voiced as casually as she was able.

'Oh, they mean well, I suppose,' her father sighed. 'And I'm sure they love Sam and want what's best for him, but...' He trailed off with a sigh.

'But?' she said gently.

'Sam loves Cal very much; they're great together.' He frowned.

'And?' Helen looked at him expectantly.

Her father stood up, moving to pour himself a cup of what must be lukewarm coffee by now. 'It's always a messy business when children are involved in a custody wrangle.' He shook his head.

'Cal's *own* parents are fighting him for the custody of Sam?' she gasped. Lord, this was worse than she had thought! Cal must have done something really outrageous for his own parents to think him unsuitable to bring Sam up. She couldn't even begin to guess what it might have been.

'Of course not,' her father denied censoriously.

'But—'

'The grandparents visiting Sam at the moment are the parents of Sam's mother,' her father said impatiently, as if that explained everything.

And maybe it did to a certain extent, although certainly not completely. Sam's father must obviously have been Cal's brother, but that didn't tell her why the baby's maternal grandparents were so against Cal's having custody of him.

Her father gave an irritated sigh. 'When Sam's parents were killed in a car accident both Cal and Susan's parents were left as guardians of the baby, with Cal having actual custody of him.'

'That seems clear enough.' Helen nodded slowly.

'Possibly,' her father acknowledged tersely. 'At least, you would think it was. But the grandparents were never happy about the situation, claiming that it would be best for Sam to grow up in a normal family atmosphere—that is with both a man and a woman to care for him. Namely themselves,' he added grimly. 'In the last few months they have been putting great pressure on Cal to let them have Sam.'

'And he doesn't agree?' Helen said softly.

'Well of course he doesn't!' her father snapped.

Helen shrugged. 'But maybe they do have a point, maybe Sam would be better off with them—'

'You know something, Helen,' her father cut in with cold anger, 'I sometimes wonder if you can possibly be my daughter after all.' He turned and strode furiously from the room.

Helen looked after him with dismay; her father had never spoken to her with that flat disappointment in his voice before.

CHAPTER FIVE

DAMN Caleb Jones and the trouble he was causing Helen!

By the time morning came, following that disagreement with her father over the custody of Sam, Helen had decided it was all Caleb Jones's fault. If he weren't their intrusive neighbour now, none of last night's conversation would have taken place. Certainly she and her father would never have argued in that way.

She knew her father was still displeased with her when she came downstairs to find a brief note in the kitchen from him telling her he had gone to the golf-course for the day. Normally he would have asked her to go with him, but obviously he was still so disgusted with her that he didn't even want to be in her company.

She still couldn't see what was so wrong about her comment that perhaps Sam would be better off with his grandparents. Obviously Cal was a friend of her father's, and his loyalty lay with the other man, but surely Sam's grandparents couldn't be such ogres that they shouldn't be considered even more suitable as stand-in parents for Sam rather than a man on his own. Especially when that man was as rakishly good-looking as Cal Jones was; poor Sam could live the rest of his life having a succession of 'aunties'!

Nevertheless, she could understand her father's sympathy with the other man's feelings, and cursed herself for being so insensitive. Hopefully her father would have mellowed after a day playing golf, and would be willing to accept her apology. Although she wouldn't count on it; her father could be more stubborn than her on occasion. That was where she had got that stubborn streak from in the first place!

As an added apology Helen prepared a curry ready for their dinner later in the day, knowing it was one of her father's favourite meals, but at the same time one he very rarely bothered to make just for himself. He would know the meal was something of a peace-offering, but that didn't matter.

The curry was bubbling away nicely when the telephone rang, and she groaned as she moved to answer it; it was just like her father to realise what she would do and be ringing to tell her he was out to dinner!

'Good morning, Helen,' Cal Jones's deeply attractive voice greeted confidently. 'Could I speak to your father, please?'

Helen frowned her agitation with having to talk to this man who was starting to become a permanent thorn in her side. 'I'm afraid he isn't here,' she said with a certain amount of satisfaction.

'Oh, damn,' she heard him mutter distractedly.

'Is there something wrong?' Helen couldn't help her curiosity.

'No, not really— Hell, yes,' he amended with a groan. 'I'm determined to have this thing out with Sam's grandparents once and for all, and I didn't want Sam around while we did it. He's very sensitive to the atmosphere which exists between the three of us, which was another reason I decided to make myself scarce last night,' he added grimly, and Helen could clearly picture the worry on that handsome face. 'He and your father get on really well together, and I was going to ask David if he would mind having Sam for the afternoon.'

'I'll have him,' Helen heard herself say, instantly wanting to retract the statement, opening her mouth to do so.

But the words wouldn't come, her tongue seeming to be stuck to the roof of her mouth.

The last thing she wanted was to be in the company of that mischievously beautiful child for any length of time. But the words of denial still wouldn't come, even though she could feel her own panic rising within her.

'I couldn't put on you like that.' Cal's frown could be heard in his voice.

Now was the time to agree with him, to give the impression her offer had only been made out of politeness!

But the words seemed to be stuck in her throat. 'You wouldn't be putting on me,' she told him briskly, all the time her brain screaming at her to agree with him, anything to keep her from having to spend time with the baby. 'I have the afternoon free anyway,' she heard herself add persuasively.

'If you're sure…?'

Of course she wasn't sure; she didn't *want* to look after Sam!

'I'm sure,' she said firmly. 'I'll come over and get him around two o'clock, if that's OK?'

'I could drive him over for you,' Cal offered, still sounding distracted.

'No, I'll come and pick him up, I might take him shopping straight after that.' What on earth was she doing? It was bad enough that she had offered to look after Sam at all, but she didn't have to add to the mistake by appearing in public with a baby that would be taken as her own as she walked along with him in his pushchair!

'OK, two o'clock, then. I really do appreciate this, Helen,' Cal added warmly.

She didn't want his gratitude, for goodness' sake—didn't want to be looking after Sam at all.

She was shaking as she replaced the telephone after saying goodbye to Cal. Sam to look after all afternoon… What had she been thinking of? She hadn't been thinking at all! At least, nothing that had passed from her brain to her tongue.

What was she going to do with a year-old baby for the afternoon?

Oh, this was ridiculous; she should just ring Cal back and tell him she had made a mistake, that she had something else to do this afternoon after all. But pride wouldn't let her do that, to telephone Cal and give the impression she was incapable of looking after Sam. Even if, emotionally, that was just how she felt.

She was too upset to eat any lunch, had almost burnt the curry by leaving it on too high a heat rather than letting the flavour be enhanced by leaving it to gently simmer, and she left the house to collect Sam with the feeling of a heavy weight having been put on her shoulders.

Her trepidation grew as she drove nearer to the manor house, vaguely noticing the improvements Cal had made to the garden since he had taken over the estate, her feet crunching on the gravel as she got out of the car.

'Helen!'

She turned guiltily, having almost given in to the temptation to get back in her car and drive off again, afraid that emotion might show in her face as she turned to look at Cal striding across the lawn towards her, Sam held in his arms.

She was struck once again by the likeness between the two of them, the same coal-black hair, the same navy-blue eyes, even their smiles similar as Sam laughed up into his uncle's face, his eyes glowing with good health—and mischief. He wasn't the sort of little boy who would ever be cowed by anything, completely happy in his environment. Which somehow made it all the more poignant that he didn't have his parents to share in his happiness. What a lot of pleasure this little boy would have brought into his parents' lives; she could see why Cal was loath to part with him. But at the same time, whatever decisions were made had to be in Sam's favour, and no one else's. And she was sure Cal was all too aware of that, which might, or might not, explain his strain over the situation.

'Two o'clock, as requested,' she said in a stilted voice.

Cal looked at her searchingly. 'You're sure you want to do this? Sam is usually good, but nevertheless it's an imposition,' he grimaced.

She was no more sure now than she had been this morning when she had so recklessly agreed to take care of Sam, but it was far too late to change her mind now.

'I have to go into town shopping anyway,' she dismissed carelessly—hoping *her own* strain wasn't too obvious. 'I can do that just as easily with Sam as without him.' Although she very much doubted that was true—a pushchair was an encumbrance few mothers managed to overcome!

'Shide, Unc Cal,' Sam cried excitedly.

'When you get back,' Cal told him indulgently. 'We were playing on the slide beside the house when you arrived,' he explained to Helen.

'Shide gen, Unc Cal,' Sam repeated mutinously.

'I'll take him back on the slide while you get his pushchair—and anything else you think I might need this afternoon,' Helen added heavily, holding out her arms for Sam. To her surprise he came to her without hesitation.

Cal gave a rueful smile. 'I hate to sound depressing, but he'll go to anyone who will take him on the slide!'

'Thanks!' she grimaced, turning to walk towards the side of the house.

Sam felt just as soft and cuddly as the last time she had held him, with that uniquely baby smell that was so unmistakable.

It was impossible not to join in his joy as he came down the tiny slide that had been erected in part of the garden obviously fenced off just for Sam's use, a sand-pit and small swing also available for his pleasure, although the slide was obviously his favourite as he went down it time and time again, with help from her to get up the two steps to the top of the slide.

'Enjoying yourself, Sam?'

Helen turned with widened eyes, the male voice not a familiar one to her, although it was obvious as she looked at the middle-aged couple who had come to stand outside the fenced-off area that this must be Sam's grandparents. Sam bore no likeness to either the short balding man or the taller blonde-haired woman, but nevertheless Helen didn't think they could be anyone else.

'I don't think he should be on that slide, Henry,' the woman said waspishly. 'He could fall and hurt himself.'

The likelihood of Sam's doing that seemed very remote to Helen, the slide only a couple of feet high, with the soft landing of lush grass if he should topple over. Although with someone having to help him up the steps in the first place this seemed highly unlikely at all.

'I doubt that, dear,' the man replied drily, giving Helen a friendly smile. 'I'm sorry, we haven't introduced ourselves. I'm Henry Carter, and this is my wife, Enid. We're Sam's grandparents.'

'I'm Helen Foster, a—a friend of Cal's.' She had been going to say 'a neighbour' of Cal's, but considering she was taking this couple's grandson off for the afternoon she thought she ought to at least be a friend of the family!

'Are you—?'

'Enid, Henry, I wondered where you had got to!' Cal strode across the lawn towards them all, his voice light, although his tone was belied by the worried expression in his eyes as he looked at them searchingly. 'Have you all introduced yourselves?' He arched questioning brows as he joined them.

'Yes, thank you.' Enid Carter spoke tartly, her back ramrod straight. 'Sam, come down off that slide at once,' she instructed the little boy as Helen helped him up the steps once again.

Sam hesitated for a moment, his expression one of confusion, before his eyes filled up with tears and he held out his arms towards Helen to be picked up, burying his face in her neck to hide the tears, his little body shaking with the emotion.

Helen looked at Cal for support, not in any position to deal with the older woman herself, but feeling the injustice of the instruction on Sam's behalf. There was sensible protection of a small child, and *over*-protection, and it seemed to her that Enid Carter was indulging in the latter. But that wasn't for her to say so.

Cal looked at Helen, speaking volumes with his eyes. 'I've put the pushchair and a few of Sam's favourite toys next to your car,' he told her softly, at the same time his expression pleading for her understanding of the situation.

And in a small way she was starting to understand his dilemma; Enid Carter could, if allowed to dominate Sam on a permanent basis, dampen all the spirit that made him such an enchanting child. Although she could be misjudging the other woman, Helen reproved herself; concern for the child's well-being had to be a good thing. And Sam's grandmother might just be over-protective of him because she had so recently lost her daughter. Who was she, Helen, to judge the other woman on such short acquaintance? Besides, from the few occasions she had had to see Sam with Cal Jones she didn't have any reason to suppose he was any better for the child.

But she took his hint for her to leave with Sam, holding the little boy tightly against her, an unwanted feeling of compassion for the dilemma of his future making her want to take him right away from the conflict.

'Do you like the zoo, Sam?' she asked him softly as she left his play area, not sparing another glance for the other adults present. They were old enough to sort out their own problems; Sam was the one who was important now. She just hoped they resolved this problem quickly, and that the conflict stopped, although from the tight-lipped expression on Enid Carter's face she thought it would take a lot for her to do that. Possibly only complete victory on her part.

Sam's face came out of her neck at the word 'zoo', his eyes glowing. 'Anmals?' he said hopefully.

Lord, he was adorable, she acknowledged achingly. By the end of this afternoon she was going to be his slave for life; she had already forgone the thought of shopping in the hope of pleasing him!

He seemed totally happy going out with her in the car, his seat, and him, easily strapped into the back seat, his gaze flashing everywhere as he looked about them interestedly. It took all of Helen's concentration to keep her attention on the road in front of them and not keep indulging in glances at Sam in her driving mirror.

Away from a situation that was obviously causing him unhappiness, Sam blossomed, completely forgetting the few words he did know as he talked to each animal at the zoo in turn in his baby gibberish. Not that the animals seemed to mind, sensing from the tone of his voice the sheer joy he felt in looking at them, several of the monkeys coming to the sides of their penned area to talk gibberish back to him!

It was an afternoon of complete pleasure for Helen. Sam needed a sharp eye kept on him at all times, but was still a delight to be with. He was completely without guile, stubborn but not deliberately wilful.

And by the end of the afternoon in his company Helen could more than understand why it was that Cal was so reluctant to part with him. Even if it was to the child's advantage. But that was still debatable, in the face of Enid Carter's over-protective manner. Helen could just imagine the other woman being completely horrified at the thought of Sam even being near the 'smelly animals', as she was sure the other woman would consider them.

Although that was jumping to conclusions, she mentally rebuked herself. But, sadly, she had a feeling that was exactly the way Enid Carter would feel.

'Unc Cal?' Sam said hopefully as Helen belted him back into the car for their homeward journey.

'Unc Cal.' She nodded, knowing the desire to see his uncle again was no reflection on the time they had just spent together; Sam had enjoyed himself at the zoo, of that she had no doubt. That he might have enjoyed it more if his uncle had been present was possible, but on the whole she would say it had been a successful afternoon.

But she could feel her own tension grow as they approached the estate; what if Cal and the Carters were still arguing?

Well, she would just have to take Sam home with her for a while, she decided firmly. Arguments of that kind were not suitable for a small child to hear; even one as young as Sam would pick up the tension in the atmosphere.

All seemed quiet when she and Sam were let into the house some time later by the young maid, although from the little she had come to know of Cal during their short acquaintance she didn't think he was the type to scream and shout to achieve putting over his point anyway.

'Mr Jones and his guests are in the sitting-room,' the maid informed her before quietly disappearing into the depths of the house.

It was the first time Helen had been into the house since Cal Jones had taken it over, and she had to admit, even if a little reluctantly, that the changes he had made were for the better. The house, which had once seemed so cold and formal, was now warm and welcoming, with an untidy elegance that allowed for the children's toys scattered about the entrance hall, obviously left there earlier by Sam, a Sam who now squirmed in her arms to be let down to play with them again.

Helen put him down, after first checking that there was no way the little boy could make an escape up the wide staircase that led up to the wide open gallery before leading to the many bedrooms. A specially built gate, little-finger-proof, had been put in at the bottom of the stairs to achieve avoiding just such an occurrence.

To give Cal Jones his due, she allowed grudgingly, he had done everything that he could to assure the safety of the adorable child in his care.

She left Sam playing on the carpet with a fire-engine and several large cars, knocking softly on the door of the room the maid had pointed out as the room Cal occupied with his guests, choosing to announce her own presence.

She was completely unprepared for the door being wrenched open mid-knock as Enid Carter stormed out of the room! The other woman had two red spots of anger on her cheeks, her pale blue eyes blazing with unsuppressed fury.

She turned angrily on Helen as she saw her standing there. 'It's only natural that I should want my grandson with me!'

'Er—well—yes...' Helen answered lamely, completely taken aback by the attack.

'Enid—'

'Be quiet, Henry,' his wife snapped harshly, turning to Cal with flashing eyes. 'I don't care how far you're prepared to go in your effort at respectability, I won't rest until I have Sam living with me!'

'Enid, we keep going round and round this situation until I start to feel giddy,' Cal answered wearily, obviously having spent most of his afternoon going over the same arguments—and getting absolutely nowhere.

Helen felt embarrassed at being caught in the middle of it all, had felt sure this conversation would have been over long ago, otherwise she wouldn't have brought Sam back when she had.

'Graham and Susan wanted Sam to live with me,' Cal continued gently. 'Doesn't that count for anything?' he reasoned softly.

'When Graham and Susan made that condition they hardly thought the two of them would be dead within a year,' Enid Carter snapped. 'It's only natural for them to have assumed that Henry and I would either be already dead or at least far too old to take on the care of a child if the situation had arisen that both of *them* would be dead. That only left them with the one choice, unsuitable as that one is,' she added coldly.

Helen heard Cal's angry intake of breath, wishing herself anywhere but in the midst of this very private conversation. She waited anxiously for Cal's explosion, eyeing him nervously.

'Enid, I've done everything within my power to make a stable life for Sam,' Cal finally said quietly, his own anger firmly under control, although it hadn't been easy for him to achieve, by the impatient fury in his eyes. 'No one, not even you,' he assured the older woman firmly, 'could have done more for him than I have.' He looked at her challengingly, although the stress of the last few hours was starting to show in the strain about his eyes and mouth and the slight pallor to his skin.

'Money can achieve a lot,' Enid Carter acknowledged bitterly. 'But then you and your brother have always been aware of that!'

Cal's mouth tightened. 'I don't think bringing the past into this is going to help the situation in the—'

'*Help* the situation?' the middle-aged woman echoed shrilly. 'If your brother hadn't dazzled my daughter with his wealth and charm none of this would have happened in the first place, because Susan would never have been married to him!' she said accusingly. 'Susan was engaged to a *nice* young man when your brother forced his way into her life—'

'Susan and Graham loved each other very much,' Cal began with careful deliberation, as if controlling his anger with extreme difficulty now.

As, indeed, Helen could quite believe he was! Enid Carter obviously had a lot of old bitterness that still pained her deeply, and although some of the accusations she was levelling at Cal, the ones about money in particular, weren't so different from what Helen herself had been saying, she still wished herself anywhere but witnessing this highly personal conversation.

'Susan was overwhelmed by the attentions of a rich and experienced man,' her mother said with contempt for the man who had become her son-in-law.

'Enid,' her husband began reasoningly.

'You and your brother believe you can buy anything.' She completely ignored the interruption. 'Even women.' She looked accusingly at Helen now.

Helen's eyes widened at this fresh attack on her, more personal this time.

'Enid, I believe that's enough,' Cal told her with quiet intensity. 'Attacks on me are one thing, but I won't have Helen involved in this.'

The older woman's mouth twisted disdainfully. 'I would say she is already very much involved,' she snapped. 'The two of you are—*friends*, didn't you say?' She looked challengingly at Helen.

Hot colour flooded her cheeks. 'Yes, I did, But—'

'*Good* friends, I would say,' the other woman scorned.

'Enid!' Cal rasped harshly. 'Our relationship isn't in the least like the one you are implying!'

Enid Carter recoiled as if he had struck her. 'You don't mean the two of you are getting *married*?' she gasped. 'Don't you believe that is going a little too far in your bid for respectability?' she added accusingly.

Now it was Helen's turn to gasp; she had gone from offering, recklessly, to help Cal out with Sam for the afternoon, to bluntly being accused of marrying Cal for his money. *Marrying* the man? The idea was ludicrous. Ridiculous. Laughable. Although *nothing* about this conversation was really funny.

'Enid,' Cal spoke softly, but the cold fury was there none the less, 'Helen is a friend who has very kindly helped me out today. I will not have her insulted, by you or anyone else.'

Helen looked at him. After the things *she* had accused him of, he could still champion her in this way? Although, she had to admit, their own difference of opinion had nothing to do with this situation.

'If she marries you she will have my *pity*, not my insults,' Enid Carter scorned. 'Come along, Henry,' she instructed arrogantly. 'I don't think there is anything to be gained by continuing this conversation.' She walked out of the room without waiting to see if her husband complied with her order, seeming to know that he would do so without her having to repeat it a second time.

And who could blame the poor man? Helen mentally sympathised; Enid Carter in full flow was a force to be reckoned with. Although she had to admit that Cal had more than held his own against the other woman.

Henry Carter made a move towards the door, and hesitated, before turning back to the two of them. 'I really am sorry about this.' He shook his head worriedly. 'I know you're only doing what you think is best, Cal.' He gave a helpless shrug.

Cal gave a wry grimace. 'Try and convince Enid of that, will you?'

The other man sighed. 'Susan was our only child,' he answered, as if that explained everything.

And perhaps it did. Sam was all this couple had left of their daughter. Although Helen didn't think Cal had much family to talk of either, so perhaps the same was true for him about his brother. It really was a difficult situation, for all concerned.

But at the end of the day it was really Sam's welfare they all had to think of, and, much as Helen found it hard to admit, if she were truthful, and from what she had seen today, Cal Jones was the right person to bring Sam up. Sadly, she was sure Henry Carter knew that too, although his loyalty obviously had to remain with his wife. Perhaps even Enid Carter knew the truth of that too, and that was why her reaction against it was so strong. After all, the other woman was in her sixties, and the responsibility of taking on a child of Sam's age at this stage in her life would be a great one. Guilt could be as much of an incentive to anger as anything else.

And Helen should know. It was her own guilt at not being with her father enough over the last seven months to know what was going on in his life that had made her so angry with herself the last couple of weeks.

But whatever the reason for Enid Carter's fury it was very real none the less, and could have serious consequences for all concerned.

'I know.' Cal squeezed the other man's arm reassuringly. 'But we all want what's best for Sam, don't we?'

The older man sighed at the truth of that. 'I'll try and talk Enid into seeing sense,' he offered, but his weary expression didn't hold out much hope of his doing that. He turned to Helen. 'I'm sorry you had to get caught up in this, Miss Foster.' He shook his head at the hopelessness of the situation.

'That's all right.' Helen gave him a reassuring smile, knowing her involvement had been purely incidental; anyone walking in on that fraught situation would have been likely to have been drawn into it, no matter how much they might have wished they wouldn't be.

He turned back to Cal once more. 'I really am sorry.' His expression became even more worried as he followed his wife out of the room.

Cal let out a deep sigh in an effort to relieve some of his tension, his hand shaking slightly as he ran it through his already tousled hair, as if it was far from the first time he had made the action this afternoon.

Helen could only guess at the tension of the conversation before she had come back, although if it had been anything like what she *had* heard it was enough to make Cal want to pull his hair out, not just tousle it!

'I can see now why you wanted Sam away from the house this afternoon,' she said ruefully, giving a quick glance out into the entrance hall to check that he was still playing with his toys. The events of the last half-hour had completely gone over his tiny little head as he concentrated on putting out imaginary fires in the cars.

Cal shook his head wearily. 'This battle has been going on for months now, and quite honestly I'm coming to the end of my patience.'

'It can't be good for Sam,' she sympathised softly.

He sighed. 'For the main part I've tried to keep him away from it, but children his age are quick to pick up tension, and that's the least of my emotions when Enid chooses to descend on us at the weekends!'

If they had this battle every weekend she wasn't surprised. No wonder he felt the need to escape from his own

home on Friday evenings to enjoy the lull of those few
hours spent in relaxation with her father before the storm
of the weekend began!

'I'm sorry you were drawn into it the way you were.'
He looked at her anxiously.

'It wasn't your fault,' she shrugged, although her cheeks
burnt from the accusations the other woman had made concerning the two of them.

And how would she have felt about the conversation if
she really were a special friend of Cal's? It would have
been devastating to have such remarks made about their
relationship.

'The really sad part of all this is that Enid knows how
much Graham loved Susan, he just wasn't her idea of a
son-in-law,' he added ruefully. 'That "nice" young man
Enid referred to whom Susan was going to marry was the
type that Enid would have been able to dominate, and so
not really lose her influence over Susan.' He shook his
head. 'Marrying Graham against her mother's wishes was
the one and only open act of defiance that Susan ever committed. And Enid never let her forget it,' he said grimly.

Or her dislike of the man her daughter had married, if
her comments a few minutes ago were anything to go by!
It was far from the ideal way to begin a marriage.

'I say "open" act of defiance because if Enid only
knew...' Cal gave a pained groan.

'Yes?' Helen couldn't help prompting, felt as if she had
just read a book only to get to the last page and find it was
missing. As indeed she now felt it was. And it was in Cal's
possession.

He drew in a ragged breath, visibly shaken now by the
scene that had just transpired. 'I wish Enid would just let
up on the pressure, because one of these days I'm not going
to be able to restrain myself... And if that happens I'm

going to do something unforgivable.' He shook his head again.

She could see his anguish at the very idea of it, could only guess at the effort it cost him to restrain himself from dealing with Enid Carter once and for all.

Cal looked at her with pained eyes. 'I'm not a deliberately cruel man.' His mouth twisted ruefully. 'No matter what you might think to the contrary...'

If she was honest she didn't really know what she thought any more. She hated it when the so-called heroines of television programmes came out with that hackneyed old line 'I'm so confused', but at this moment that was exactly what she was! Cal's dealings with her father over Cherry Trees seemed underhand to her, and yet his control with Enid Carter, gentleness almost, in the face of constant insults, spoke of a completely different sort of man from the one she had imagined him to be.

She put her hand on his arm, her eyes widening in alarm when he turned to her with a groan, gathering her into his arms to bury his face against her throat.

Her alarm turned to panic as she realised how right it felt to be held against him like this, Enid Carter and the previous tension forgotten as she raised her face to Cal's.

Dark blue eyes devoured the paleness of her face before he slowly lowered his head and claimed her lips with his own. Liquid warmth flowed through her veins as his mouth moved sensuously against hers, his hands cupping her face now as he held her lips up for the slow, searching kiss that made her legs tremble and her body shake. His shoulders felt muscled beneath her supporting hands, his body hard against hers, as the kiss went on and on, searching and tormenting at the same time, Helen's whole body on fire for a deepening of the caress.

'Sam kiss.'

Helen pulled back in horror to look down at the little boy pulling on her skirt for attention. He needn't worry, he had her full attention—she dared not even look at Cal!

CHAPTER SIX

'CAL'S on the phone. For you,' her father added softly.

Helen's pulse jumped tensely at the mention of the other man's name, but she could feel it beating a nervous tattoo at her temple when her father told her the call from him was for her.

She stood up disjointedly, unable to stand her father's knowing gaze a moment longer. 'He probably just wants to thank me again for taking Sam out for him yesterday afternoon,' she said sharply, smoothing her skirt agitatedly.

Her father watched the movement with an amused twist to his lips. 'Yes, you're probably right,' he replied without sincerity, his eyes twinkling with merry humour.

Not that Helen could altogether blame him. By the time she had arrived home yesterday evening her nerves hadn't settled down at all after that unexpected kiss from Cal and its abrupt, and embarrassing, ending, and she had walked in to find her father had got home before her. Her flushed cheeks and over-bright eyes could have been attributed to anger or inner turmoil, and she had known within a few minutes that her father had drawn the right conclusion. He had been eyeing her with that knowing amusement ever since!

It had been embarrassing enough to have Sam witness that kiss between his uncle and herself. She had hastily pulled out of Cal's arms, keeping her face averted from his searching gaze as she'd bent down to talk to the little boy. By the time she had stood up again she had been slightly more under control, although her gaze still hadn't quite been able to meet Cal's as she'd made her excuses to leave.

Her agitation had returned in full force when he had accompanied her to the door to take her hand in his. She had been unable to do anything else but look at him then, and the tenderness in his eyes had almost been her undoing, her natural instinct being to move back into the warm security of his arms.

But she had resisted the temptation, snatching her hand out of his as she had mumbled her goodbyes and fled out of the house into the sunshine.

She still didn't quite know what had happened between them yesterday. The shadows under her eyes were evidence of the sleepless night she had spent wondering how one moment she could have been talking to Cal quite sensibly and the next moment be in his arms returning his kisses. It was so completely out of character for her, and the knowledge of how desperately she had wanted the kisses to continue terrified the life out of her.

What on earth could he want to talk to her about now?

Maybe she was right, maybe he did just want to thank her again for taking Sam yesterday. Although somehow she doubted it; she knew *he* hadn't wanted the kisses to stop yesterday either!

'Yes?' Her voice was restrained, and yet slightly breathless, a churning sensation in her stomach as she clutched the receiver in her hand.

'Helen.'

Just the sound of her name on his lips was enough to tell her that no time might have elapsed since she had been in his arms, that the distance between them didn't exist, that the telephone was no barrier to the desire he still felt for her!

She moistened her lips with the tip of her tongue, almost able to taste him there. This was madness, a mere flight of the senses, and yet it was real, so very real.

'I have to see you—'

'No!' she protested sharply, taking a calming breath, knowing she was over-reacting, clearly revealing her confusion over the situation. 'I don't think that would be a good idea,' she amended distantly.

There was silence for several long seconds, and when Cal spoke again it was in a briskly businesslike tone, all huskiness gone from his voice. 'I'd like to take you out to dinner as a thank-you for—'

'I would rather not,' she cut in abruptly. 'I—I'm busy,' she added shortly.

'You don't know which evening I was asking you yet,' Cal returned a little mockingly.

Fool, she chastised herself. What had happened to the cool-headed, sensible person she usually was? If she had been that person yesterday, none of this conversation would be taking place!

'I'm here to spend time with my father,' she told him tartly.

'I'm sure David can spare your company for one night,' he drawled derisively.

She was sure he could too, if it was to spend time with Cal Jones. But she had no intention of telling her father of the invitation.

'Tomorrow night will be fine,' David Foster remarked behind her.

Helen spun round, glaring at her father accusingly for listening in on her side of the telephone conversation, at least.

'Did David say tomorrow night?' Cal prompted with mocking humour.

She gave her father one last glare of censure before pointedly turning her back on him. 'What my father says really has nothing to do with it—'

'But a few minutes ago you said that it did,' Cal reminded teasingly.

'I was trying to refuse you politely!' she snapped impatiently. Really, these two were like a comedy act, and she was their 'straight man'! She would swear Cal had put her father up to this, if she didn't know better; her father needed no encouragement to be interfering where he thought it was for her own good. But he couldn't possibly know how fraught with possibilities her seeing Cal Jones could be.

'Try impolitely,' Cal drawled challengingly. 'Otherwise I might keep asking you.'

'I don't want to have dinner with you, tomorrow or any other night,' she said irritably.

'I'm sure you can do better than that, Helen,' he mocked.

'Surely I was explicit enough?' Her impatience deepened.

'Explicit, yes,' he acknowledged. 'But your refusal leaves a little room for doubt.'

'What doubt?' she said incredulously. 'Surely a refusal is a refusal, no matter how it's put?'

'"You lousy swine" on the end of it might be more convincing,' Cal teased.

She wasn't sure she thought of him as a 'lousy swine' any more. In fact, she had been trying not to think of him at all today, although it had been proving a little difficult.

'Oh, go on, Helen,' her father cajoled. 'Say yes to the man.'

She wasn't sure what she was saying yes to, that was the trouble! Her reasons for being wary of Cal Jones seemed to have changed drastically during the last twenty-four hours.

Which was ridiculous. She wasn't frightened of any man, especially the sort of man she believed Cal Jones to be. She completely ignored that nagging little voice at the back of her mind that told her she wasn't sure about *that* any more either. 'All right,' she sighed. 'Dinner tomorrow. But on the strict understanding it's only as a thank-you for taking Sam out,' she warned.

'As if I would think it was for anything else,' Cal drawled.

'As if,' her father murmured tauntingly very close to her ear.

Helen rounded on him. 'Will you just go away?' She glared at him.

'If you insist,' Cal drawled. 'But—'

'Not you,' she told him impatiently, furious with her father. But he just grinned back at her, unrepentant. 'I was talking to my father,' she crossly explained to Cal. 'He seems to have forgotten that it's rude to listen in on other people's conversations,' she added pointedly, still glaring warningly at her father as he made no effort to leave her in privacy.

'It's my house,' he said blandly.

'But my call— Oh, damn,' she swore as she realised Cal was still listening in on this exchange, almost able to picture his amusement—at her expense. 'I'll see you tomorrow,' she told him abruptly, ringing off to look at her father in challenging reproval.

He didn't look in the least concerned by her anger. 'I wonder where he'll take you,' he mused thoughtfully.

'None of your business.' She gave an irritated sigh. 'I didn't want to go in the first place!'

'That was obvious,' he grimaced.

'Then why did you—? Oh, never mind,' she dismissed impatiently. 'I'll go and finish cooking lunch.' She went off to the kitchen before her father could say any more.

Dinner with Cal Jones tomorrow night.

How did she get herself into these situations? The answer to that was all too obvious; her father was the main reason she had helped Cal out with Sam yesterday afternoon, and he was also the reason she had been press-ganged into having dinner with the other man tomorrow evening. If her father hadn't joined in the conversation there was no way she would have allowed herself to be talked into agreeing to the invitation.

She didn't want to spend an evening alone with Cal Jones.

She hadn't been this affected by a man since—well, since Daniel.

She hated to admit it, but being in Cal Jones's arms had frightened her in a way being with Daniel never had. Because she had ached with wanting more than just being in his arms.

And she was terrified of that happening again.

This attraction she felt for Cal made her feel out of control, and it wasn't a feeling she was at all comfortable with. She had survived her years in London by being completely in control; a few days back here and her life was in turmoil. And she had a feeling it was going to get worse rather than better.

The rest of the day was spent with her suffering the smug expression of her father every time she dared a glance at him, his anger with her on Friday night completely forgotten in the face of this new development.

He might well look pleased with himself; he couldn't have been happier if he had arranged the whole thing himself!

'Do you want to order now or have a drink first?' Cal looked at her enquiringly.

She wanted to get the evening over with as soon as possible!

Her father's knowing looks as she had joined the two men in the lounge earlier had been enough to turn her tension into teeth-grating anger.

She had dressed for the evening ahead with great care,

the deep green dress fitted at the bodice but flowing silkily about her long legs, its style smart rather than provocative. Her hair she had compromised on, securing it back on either side from her face with two ornate combs, but leaving it flowing loosely down her spine. Her appearance wasn't severe enough to incur her father's critisism, but it was enough for her to feel comfortable. Or as comfortable as she could when she was spending the evening with a man she would rather avoid.

Cal's appearance had taken her breath away, the dark grey suit tailored to him perfectly, the white shirt and light grey tie obviously both made of silk. His hair was brushed into some semblance of neatness tonight, but it was still too long, and even as Helen looked across the table from him now her fingers itched to reach out and smooth the waving darkness off his forehead.

Heaven knew what he would make of it if she didn't resist the impulse!

The memory of the kiss they had shared was in the dark blue of his eyes every time she looked at him, her heart beating a wild tattoo in her chest, her nerve-endings jangling warningly.

As if she needed any warning of the danger this man represented to her peace of mind!

'I'd like to order,' she bit out abruptly.

Cal gave a half-smile. 'Get it over with as quickly as you can, hm?'

Colour warmed her cheeks. 'I didn't want to be here in the first place, you know that,' she told him sharply, giving her own order to the waiter as he came to the table, keeping her face averted as Cal smoothly ordered his meal after her.

How on earth was she going to get through an entire evening with this man?

'Helen.'

There it was again, that gentle command in just the sound of her name, and she raised her eyes to his reluctantly.

'Let's just enjoy our meal, hmm?' he suggested softly. 'We can talk about Sam, if you like—he's a pretty neutral subject.'

As long as they kept off the subject of the little boy's grandparents; Helen didn't want to become any more involved in that situation than she already had been.

Talking about Sam turned out to be easier than she had thought, the little boy having crept into her affections on their brief acquaintance without her actually being aware of it. But she realised what had happened as she talked to Cal, could only silently regret that it *had* happened, knowing it would ultimately cause her pain.

It was a more relaxing evening than she had expected it to be, Cal deliberately setting out to put her at her ease, she was sure. And he succeeded, the two of them talking easily together as they left the restaurant a couple of hours later, Helen's defences down so much that she accepted when Cal offered her a drink at the main house.

It was only as they approached the house that Helen questioned the sense of her actions. She really shouldn't spend any time alone with Cal; it could be her undoing.

She knew it was even more of a mistake when Cal suggested she go with him to Sam's bedroom to check on the little boy. Sam lay on his back in the cot, spread-eagled on the mattress, his curls dark against the whiteness of the sheet beneath him, his lashes long and silky against his cheeks, his little pink rose-bud of a mouth falling open slackly as he breathed gently.

Helen's heart ached at the sight of him, and she turned away with a choked sob, attempting to cover the emotion with a low cough, excusing herself from the room as Cal looked at her concernedly.

'I don't want to wake him,' she whispered hurriedly before escaping from the nursery.

She leant weakly on the wall outside the room, drawing in deep, controlling breaths, flatly denying entry into her mind the memories seeing Sam like that had evoked.

'Are you all right?' Cal stood in front of her, his eyes dark with concern.

Helen took in a shuddering breath, looking up at him with shuttered eyes, although she still leant on the wall behind her for support, her legs feeling decidedly shaky. 'I—it was very hot in the nursery,' she excused firmly.

'Yes,' Cal agreed, although he didn't look convinced, watching her frowningly. 'Let's go down and have that drink,' he suggested lightly as she made no effort to add anything to her earlier statement.

She had intended having a coffee and then leaving, but the brandy Cal suggested once they got down to the sitting-room seemed much more appropriate, the first few sips going a long way to settling her frayed nerves. Lord, she was becoming a nervous wreck in just a few days!

'Better?' he prompted as he watched the colour returning to her cheeks.

She swallowed hard. 'Much. Thanks.'

'I can't imagine my life without him now,' Cal said softly.

Helen felt her cheeks drain of colour again. 'No,' she agreed hollowly.

Cal grimaced. 'They're so dependent on us at that age.'

'Yes.'

'I don't suppose—'

'Cal, could we talk about something else?' she cut in sharply, her movements agitated.

He hesitated for a moment, and then he relaxed slightly. 'I suppose I do sound a bit like a doting father,' he dismissed self-derisively. 'I've enjoyed our dinner tonight,

Helen,' he told her softly, his gaze compelling her to look up at him.

It was an impulse impossible to resist, and she instantly found herself drowning in a sea of dark blue.

'So have I.' It was impossible to lie to him when he held her gaze so easily.

'On Saturday—'

'You do seem to hit on subjects I would rather not go into,' she interrupted tautly.

'We can't just pretend it didn't happen.' He shrugged broad shoulders.

Helen looked at him challengingly. 'Why can't we?'

His mouth quirked. 'Can we?' he prompted sceptically.

'I can.' She lied without hesitation this time, knowing she had no choice; she didn't want to talk about what had happened between them on Saturday, didn't even want to think about it.

He shrugged. 'Then you're having better luck than I have; I can't seem to get it out of my mind.'

'Maybe you need to spend some time in London,' she scorned defensively. 'You're obviously missing the—companionship you can find there.'

'Does this usually work?'

Helen looked at him sharply. 'Does what usually work?' she echoed challengingly.

His mouth quirked; he was not in the least perturbed by the insult she had just given him. 'It must do.' He spoke almost to himself. 'Otherwise you wouldn't still be using it,' he mused.

'What are you talking about?' she said irritably.

'Attack being the best form of defence,' he drawled.

Her gaze wavered and fell guiltily away from his; she wasn't going to win with this man, she knew she wasn't.

'Helen,' he stood directly in front of her now, one hand moving under her chin to tilt her face up towards his, 'I am not in the habit of seeking—companionship, anywhere.' A gently teasing smile curved his lips. 'I am of an age where I'm looking for more than you are implying.' His smile became more intimate. 'Actually, I wasn't looking at all, had decided my own life could go on a back-burner for a while, or at least until Sam is completely settled with me. And now, here you are.' He shrugged at the mystery of life.

'I'll soon be gone again,' she reminded sharply, unsure of what he was saying, but knowing she had to dispel any doubts he might have to the contrary.

'Not for a couple of weeks.' He tapped her cheek in playful reproval. 'A lot can happen in two weeks.'

Not to her. Never to her.

'I don't think so,' she told him hardly.

'I don't think *either* of us should think at all for the moment,' Cal said briskly. 'I had heard so much about you from your father, had even seen photographs of you.' He shook his head. 'But I wasn't prepared for the flesh and blood you, hadn't expected this.'

'This?' she echoed impatiently.

'This.' He nodded, lowering his head to hers.

It was what she had been waiting for—and fearing—all evening, Helen knew that as her body curved snugly into the hardness of his.

Just as if it was where she was meant to be.

The hours that had elapsed since she had last been in his arms might never have been; her arms curved about his neck as their mouths fused together. His hands cupped either side of her face, tasting her lips slowly before claiming them with an agonised groan. His arms enfolded Helen against him, his hands caressing the length of her body, sending shivers of sensation wherever he touched.

Helen trembled with reaction, never having known this

mindless desire, wanting to be closer to him, so close she didn't know where her body began and Cal's ended.

Her hands were entwined in the thick darkness of his hair, loving its silky softness, his body sensual to the touch, aware of her own effect on him as he quivered against her.

'Maybe I shouldn't have started this,' he groaned against her throat. 'But now that I have, I don't want it to stop!'

Neither did she, raising no objection as Cal gently removed the combs from her hair, framing her face with the loose blonde waves as he looked deeply into her eyes.

'Helen!' he said achingly as he saw his own desire reflected there, claiming her mouth tenderly now, in no hurry to rush the loving they knew they both wanted.

Helen returned his kisses, her whole body shaking with need, a need that was inevitable, had been from the moment they had first kissed.

This was what she had been trying to run away from since Saturday!

A warm lethargy entered her limbs, but at the same time her body was taut with wanting, her breath catching in her throat as Cal's hands caressed down the sides of her body, fingertips lightly brushing the tips of her breasts, her nipples hard with desire, red-hot pleasure coursing through her body as he repeated the caress again and again.

Helen had never known anything like this in her life before, knew that she was no longer in control, that desire had taken over, a desire that wouldn't be denied. It was the same for Cal, she knew that, could feel the hardness of his body against her as he made no effort to hide his need from her.

He raised his head, looking down at her with dark blue eyes. 'Helen?'

She knew what he was asking of her, knew he wouldn't take advantage of the desire between them if it wasn't what she wanted too.

She opened her mouth to speak. 'I—'

'Cal, I wondered if—' A brief knock had heralded the arrival of the man who now stood framed in the doorway, breaking off what he had been about to say as he realised he had interrupted them.

Helen couldn't see the man's face properly in the half-light of the hallway behind him, the lounge itself lit only by a small table-lamp some distance away from the door—and yet she had recognised the voice instantly.

The man standing in the doorway was Daniel Scott!

CHAPTER SEVEN

DANIEL'S presence here was enough to tell Helen she hadn't been mistaken on Friday at all, that it had been him she had seen driving down the lane near Cherry Trees after all.

And she didn't need to be a mathematician to work out that Daniel had to be the personal assistant/accountant that Cal had taken on to help him.

Daniel, of all people!

She had stepped back from Cal the moment the other man had knocked so briefly on the door, but she moved even further away from him now as Daniel eyed them speculatively.

Daniel had changed little since she had last been in his presence, still the handsome devil who had impressed her so easily six years ago, his hair thick and golden, brushed lightly back from his too-handsome face, the features almost too perfect; his eyes so light a blue they were almost grey, fringed by long dark lashes; his nose short and straight, with a sculptured mouth and strong determined jaw. He was wearing a loose grey sweater and fitted denims, the latter emphasising the muscled strength of his body.

He had a handsomeness that only seemed to increase with the years, thirty-five now. And yet Helen wasn't in the least impressed by him, not any more, knew him too well for that.

'I'm so sorry,' he apologised to Cal as he moved further into the room. 'I didn't realise you weren't alone.' The smile he gave Helen was speculative, to say the least.

Cal had recovered his composure quicker than Helen, and was in complete control again now, any irritation he might have felt at the interruption quickly masked, although his smile was a little strained.

'Helen, this is Daniel Scott, my new assistant,' he introduced smoothly. 'Daniel, this is Helen Foster, a friend of mine.'

Daniel thrust out his hand confidently. 'Miss Foster,' he acknowledged softly.

'Mr Scott.' She swallowed hard, touching his hand as briefly as good manners would allow.

A *friend*, hmm? Daniel's mocking gaze seemed to say as Helen continued to look at him with distaste.

Why did he have to judge everyone by his own standards? she fumed silently. Just because he had walked in and found her in Cal's arms it was no reason to jump to conclusions concerning their relationship. But that was typical of Daniel, as she well knew.

'What did you want to see me about?' Cal prompted with a politeness that was slightly belied by the irritation in his gaze.

'I had some papers here I wasn't too sure of.' Daniel indicated the sheets of paper in his hand. 'But they can wait until morning,' he dismissed with a shrug.

'Please, don't let me stop you,' Helen spoke directly to Cal, not wanting even to look at Daniel again, knowing what she would see in his eyes. And she had no intention of feeling self-conscious about something that was none of his business. 'I have to go now anyway.'

The moment between them had gone, they both knew that, and yet Cal looked as if he would like to ask her to stay, at least until Daniel had gone and they could say goodnight in private.

But Helen just wanted to get away, from both men, and

regain her composure in peace. 'I really do have to go,' she said firmly before he could object. 'It's very late.'

And the question of time hadn't arisen until they had been so rudely interrupted, they both knew that. But Cal seemed to take one look at the determination on her face and decide not to argue with her.

'I'll walk to the door with you.' His tone brooked no argument to this suggestion.

Helen moved to the door, her movements disjointed, just wanting to escape now from what had become a very embarrassing situation.

'Goodnight, Miss Foster,' Daniel called softly from behind her.

She turned sharply at the mockery in his voice, her eyes flashing her dislike. 'Goodnight, Mr Scott,' she bit out tautly.

He nodded. 'I have no doubt we will meet again,' he said pleasantly enough, although Helen could clearly see the challenge in his eyes.

'No doubt,' she echoed sharply.

Cal closed the lounge door behind them, following closely behind Helen as she all but marched to the front door in her need to escape.

She turned as she reached the door. 'Thank you for dinner. It was—'

'Why so formal, Helen?' Cal looked puzzled. 'I realise it was a little embarrassing just now, but even so, I think we're past the stage where we have to be so distantly polite to each other.'

His gentle teasing did nothing to relax her; she just wanted to get away from here!

'I suppose so,' she acknowledged distractedly. 'But I really do have to go now.'

'Helen?' The soft query of her name made her look up at him with vague eyes. He looked at her searchingly for several seconds before giving a resigned sigh. 'I'll call you tomorrow, OK?' His gaze compelled her to answer in the affirmative.

A telephone call couldn't do any harm. Besides, she had a feeling that if she didn't let him call her he would come round to the house, and she could refuse him all the more easily over the telephone. Because she had no intention of going out with him again. It had been bad enough before she knew of Daniel's presence in Cal's house, but now it was impossible!

'All right,' she nodded abruptly. 'Tomorrow,' she accepted.

His hand under her chin gently raised her face to his. 'Drive carefully,' he murmured against her mouth before his lips softly touched hers.

She didn't feel like driving at all once she had got behind the wheel of her car, reaction beginning to set in in earnest now.

Daniel of all people, *here*.

He was the last person she would ever have imagined moving to the country. And now that he had she wished it could have been anywhere but near her home.

The less she saw of him, the better!

'That was Cal again.' Her father looked at her reprovingly. 'I can't keep telling him you're out,' he added irritably.

It was the third time Cal had telephoned today, she knew, and yet she just didn't want to talk to him.

Shocked reaction had set in after seeing Daniel again after all this time, and she needed to be left in peace to sort out her confused thoughts. Most of all she needed to stay away from anything that reminded her Daniel was in the neighbourhood at all, and Cal could do that all too easily. After all, if it weren't for him Daniel wouldn't be in the area.

Worst of all, she felt conscience-bound to warn Cal about Daniel, and yet how to do it, that was her worry now. She certainly couldn't pretend she didn't know anything about his background; it might not be exactly black, but it was certainly shaded in grey! And she had a feeling Cal wouldn't want a man like that working for him.

Or would he? The man she had thought him to be two weeks ago wouldn't have been in the least concerned by an employee's shady past, as long as it was now working in his favour; had she really changed her mind about him so much that she no longer believed that to be true? As far as Daniel and his working for Cal went, she knew the answer to that was yes, but she still thought he had been underhand about his dealings with her father over Cherry Trees.

But none of that solved her problem here and now of Cal's third telephone call today.

She came to a decision. 'Well, if he calls again you won't be telling a lie,' she said firmly. 'Because I am going out!'

'Helen—'

'Not now, Daddy,' she warned tautly, her emotions fraught with tension.

'But, darling—'

'I'll talk to you later.' Her voice gentled slightly. 'I promise.'

She couldn't tell even him all of what had taken place last night; although after Cal's telephone calls today he must already have a pretty good idea!

She would have to tell her father of Daniel's presence at Cal's house; knowing, as her father did, of her involvement with the other man in the past, it would be awful if her father should meet him by chance and realise exactly who he was. Especially if she hadn't yet told Cal!

'All right,' her father sighed. 'But I must say you're acting very oddly.'

She knew he meant out of character, her usual cool calm completely absent today. But she had been so completely shaken by what had happened last night, and of the abrupt ending to the evening.

She still couldn't quite believe the cruelty of fate that had thrown Daniel into her life once again. Her avoidance of him these last few years, while it hadn't been exactly deliberate, hadn't been unplanned either. It had been all too easy not to frequent the places she knew he would choose to spend his evenings, and on a professional level she hadn't cared whether their paths had crossed or not, knowing, as she did, that her personal integrity far outweighed any success he might appear to have made. By some lucky quirk Helen had managed not to see him for the last six years. Now, with his proximity, it was going to take all of her ingenuity *not* to see him!

Her favourite cove was out of the question for her worried wanderings today, as she remembered all too well how Cal had so easily found her there last time. Remembering that, he might try to locate her there again today.

But she needed to be near the sea, its deliberate inevitability a balm to her frayed nerves.

Nothing about her own life these last few weeks had seemed inevitable; she had been sure that without too much effort on her part she need never see Daniel Scott again, had been even more sure that a man like Caleb Jones had appeared to be could never affect her deepest emotions in any way.

She had been wrong on both counts.

Oh, this unexpected meeting with Daniel again after all this time was disquieting enough, but to acknowledge, even to herself, the growing attraction she felt towards Cal was totally devastating. She had at least thought she liked Daniel before believing herself in love with him; she still wasn't sure she actually liked Cal, only that he affected her more than any other man she had ever known.

The cove she finally found was even more private than her usual refuge, and as she clambered down among the rocks she felt a sense of peace washing over her, the complications of her life unimportant for the couple of hours she spent there just enjoying the gentle uprush and ebb of the grey-blue water.

Nothing had really changed about her purpose here, she realised; she still had to persuade her father that Cherry Trees was their family home, and should remain that way. Oh, Daniel's presence here was a complication she hadn't expected, but she had no reason to suppose he was any more eager to see her again than she was him. As for this attraction that seemed to have sprung up between Cal and herself... She was a grown woman, wasn't she, quite capable of dealing with that complication? She and Cal were completely unsuited as a couple, and a purely physical relationship had never appealed to her. Those decisions made, she returned home with a determined resolve.

She was quite unprepared for Cal's presence in the garden with her father, Sam playing happily at their feet as they enjoyed an early evening drink together!

Dark blue eyes studied her guardedly as she strode purposefully across the lawn towards them, only a slight, but brief, hesitancy in her step showing she was in the least disconcerted by his presence here, before she continued her progress across the garden bathed in early evening sunshine.

Sam looked up from his digging of the flowerbed as he sensed her presence, his face instantly lighting up with pleasure. 'Lennie!' he cried gleefully, raising his arms towards her to be picked up.

Only the hardest of hearts could remain unmoved by such spontaneity, and, although Helen knew she shielded her emotions from hurt, she couldn't remain immune to the happiness in those baby-blue eyes, bending down to pick the little boy up, giving a tearful smile as he planted a shy kiss on her cheek.

'Nothing but seeing you again would do.' Cal had stood up to move to her side, talking softly as Sam buried his face shyly against her neck. 'He's talked of nothing else but you since Saturday.'

She felt sure that had pleased the little boy's grandparents, at least his grandmother! They couldn't possibly realise from that what little real significance she had in Sam's life.

'Only because I took him to see the animals at the zoo.' She tickled the little boy in her arms until he squirmed amid giggles of laughter. 'Sam's as mercenary as the next child, aren't you, baby?' she teased him. 'He's hoping I'll take him there again.'

'Maybe,' Cal acknowledged a little sheepishly. 'Although he has genuinely taken a liking to you,' he added seriously.

'And I like you too, little man.' She held the baby close against her, fighting off the pain of familiarity as memories washed over her. The smile she bestowed on the child was a little more strained now. 'Has anyone thought to offer you a drink, I wonder?' she drily rebuked the two men, with their long, cooling glasses of whisky and water.

'He's already drunk all of his lemonade.' Her father held up the empty feeding cup with knowing satisfaction. 'But if you're hinting you would like a drink I'll go into the house and get you some fresh orange.' He stood up.

The last thing Helen wanted was to be left alone with Cal, but a refusal of the offered drink would show that all too obviously. And she was supposed to be a mature woman of twenty-six, and surely past the stage of resisting being alone with any man!

'Lovely,' she accepted with a tight smile in her father's direction, all the more annoyed because he knew exactly what he was doing.

Cal took a step closer to her as her father entered the house. 'You wouldn't take my calls.' It was a statement rather than an accusation.

She didn't look up at him. 'I've been out,' she returned softly, all the time smiling at Sam.

'Not all day,' he rebuked gently.

Helen's eyes flashed deeply green as she glared up at him. 'Part of it,' she defended.

'After my calls became impossible to ignore,' he said drily.

'I don't have to explain myself to you,' she flared.

He looked at her consideringly for several seconds, before nodding slowly. 'No, you don't,' he acknowledged softly. 'But you did say I could call you,' he reminded her.

Her cheeks became flushed. She had accepted the possibility of his telephoning her before she had spent a night telling herself how impossible the situation was. Daniel's presence here was merely a complication to a situation she already knew was fast hurtling out of control. Daniel was just a very timely reminder of how becoming emotionally involved with people became a very painful experience. And falling for a man like Cal could be even more devastating than believing herself in love with Daniel had proved to be all those years ago; Cal had the added complication of Sam for her to deal with.

She shrugged dismissively. 'So I changed my mind,' she challenged.

Cal looked as if he would like to lean forward and shake her, but he instantly resisted the temptation, his gaze resting on Sam as he sat so confidently in her arms.

'So you did,' Cal said heavily. 'Running away from our

emotions is never the answer, you know, Helen,' he added softly.

Her mouth set angrily, two vivid spots of colour in her cheeks now. 'You don't know what you're talking about,' she snapped. He couldn't know about Daniel, he just couldn't! Unless her father—? But no, he didn't know yet that Daniel was working for the other man. At least, she hadn't told him... 'Has my father said something to you?' she demanded sharply, her eyes narrowed.

Cal shrugged. 'Some things don't need to be said. I'm sorry that you had to go through something like that, but you can't let it colour your whole life.'

He didn't know about Daniel specifically, but he knew enough to realise someone had hurt her very badly in the past!

'How I deal with the pain in my life is my business,' she bit out tautly.

'Not if it affects what's between us.' He shook his head.

Helen looked at him scathingly, her guard well back in place now. 'There's nothing between us,' she snapped. 'Physical attraction—'

'There's more to it than that and you know it,' Cal cut in determinedly.

'I don't know any— Oh, look, Sam, here comes Uncle David with my orange juice.' She quickly changed her angry denial as her father came out of the house, dampening down the emotion with effort. 'Thanks.' She accepted the glass of juice, deftly avoiding meeting her father's searching gaze. He had already played too big a part in involving her in this situation, and it had to stop. Now. 'I have to go in and wash my hair,' she excused herself firmly, handing Sam back to Cal, deftly avoiding too much contact with him as she did so, although she could see by the knowing look in those dark blue eyes that he was completely aware of what she had done. But that didn't matter; the sooner he accepted the situation, the better, as far as she was concerned.

'Couldn't that wait until later?' her father prompted hardly, a reproving look on his face.

Helen ignored that look; Cal was his guest, not hers! 'You know how long it takes for me to dry my hair,' she insisted lightly.

'Sam.' The little boy held out his arms towards her.

'I think he wants to come and watch,' Cal explained drily.

'I don't—I—' She became flustered in the warmth of Cal's gaze as he told her without words that he clearly remembered last night when her hair had been loose about her shoulders, his hands buried in its thickness as he kissed her. It was scraped back today in the severe plait down her spine that her father so hated, and she could see Cal felt the same way about it as his gaze lingered on the blonde tresses.

'Sam,' the little boy said again, more firmly this time.

'By coincidence I was reading him the story of Rapunzel last night when I put him to bed,' Cal murmured softly. 'He doesn't really take in the stories, but he's obviously remembered enough of this one to be interested in the letting down of your hair.'

'It isn't long enough for anyone to climb up,' she returned tautly, taking Sam into her arms.

Only long enough for him to bury his face in its scented thickness, Cal's warm gaze seemed to say.

She turned away abruptly, knowing she was once again becoming seduced by those deep blue eyes. It just wasn't fair after all the arguments she had given herself today for not becoming involved with him!

'Excuse us.' She spoke to neither man in particular, talking softly to Sam as they went into the house.

The telephone was ringing as she walked through the

hallway, and she picked up the receiver with an apologetic smile at Sam as she put him down on the floor. At least she knew it couldn't be Cal calling once again to disturb her calm existence.

She recited the telephone number automatically, keeping a close eye on Sam as he wandered off into the lounge.

'Hello, Helen,' greeted an all too familiar voice. 'I think we should meet, don't you?'

Daniel, she realised instantly.

Here was someone else who had the power to shake up her ordered world!

CHAPTER EIGHT

HELEN'S hand tightly gripped the receiver, her fingernails digging into her palm where she held it so firmly.

How dared he call her here? was her instant reaction. Discounting the fact that he had acquired her telephone number at all, he had no right to call her at her father's home. No matter what he felt the urgency to be.

Although he didn't sound as if he had been at all disturbed by her presence here. But remembering his cool self-confidence of the past she thought that was probably true.

All the more reason to give the impression it was of no importance to her either. 'I can't imagine why you should think that,' she returned coolly, 'when I've had nothing to say to you for almost six years.'

'I'm flattered you should remember how long ago it is since we last met,' he murmured softly.

He wasn't flattered at all, knew she had good reason never to forget his part in her life! 'I thought you would have gone much further up the professional ladder during that time than you actually have,' she said challengingly.

'I wouldn't have thought PA to a man like Caleb Jones was backsliding,' Daniel bit back tautly, obviously stung by the taunt.

'It's a good job,' she granted dismissively. 'But I would have thought you would have your own accountancy firm by now.'

'Maybe I don't care for the responsibility,' he rasped.

And maybe things weren't going quite so well for him now as they had been all those years ago. She hadn't particularly been aware of any talk of him among her colleagues, but it soon became known in that tight circle which of them it might be best to avoid employing. It would also go a long way to explaining his presence here in the countryside, when he had always professed to hate it so much.

'I have nothing to say to you, Daniel.' She sighed at the waste he had made of his undoubted talents.

'I believe it might be in the best interests of both of us if we did meet,' he said insistently.

Helen frowned; what could he possibly mean by that remark?

'Let's meet and discuss it,' he told her when she voiced her concern.

'Discuss what?' she prompted irritably.

'Not over the telephone, Helen,' he returned briskly. 'Perhaps I could meet you for dinner tomorrow evening? Or will you be seeing Cal then?' he added mockingly.

'None of your damned business!' she snapped. 'I—' She broke off as a crash sounded in the lounge. Oh, lord, *Sam*! She had forgotten all about the wandering baby in her agitation, and she had had the nerve to rebuke Cal for his negligence of the little boy the first time they had met; she was no better when the provocation was deep enough. 'I have to go,' she told Daniel abruptly.

'Dinner, tomorrow, eight o'clock, at the Bowling Green Inn,' he managed to say quickly before she put the receiver down to go to Sam.

The baby was standing in front of the fireplace with a guilty look on his face as he looked up at her, tears balanced on the edge of his long lashes ready to fall, an ornamental china robin in two pieces on the fireplace at his feet.

It didn't take much imagination to realise that Sam had reached up on to the high mantel for the robin, lost his balance and somehow dropped the treasured bird.

'It's all right, Sam,' Helen instantly reassured him as his

bottom lip trembled precariously, going down on her haunches so that she was on the same level as him. 'A bit of glue and the robin will be as good as new.' She smiled at him.

'Sam notty.' He still looked forlorn, his head hung in shame.

Helen had to bite her lip to stop herself laughing at Sam's accurate description of himself as 'naughty'; it was obviously an expression he had heard about himself many times before! And no doubt his action was a little naughty, for the little boy was obviously aware that he shouldn't have touched the ornament at all, but who could possibly be cross with him when he looked so adorable in his contrition? Certainly not her.

'A little bit,' she admitted consideringly. 'But you won't do it again, will you?'

He shook his head gravely, the incident forgotten as far as he was concerned as she suggested they go upstairs and wash her hair now.

It was obvious from his curiosity that he had never been upstairs in the house before, going from room to room in open nosiness once they were upstairs.

As soon as they reached Helen's bathroom it became clear he had lost all interest in watching her wash her hair, pulling at his clothes with the intention of taking a bath.

Helen laughed softly in defeat of his determination as she ran the bath water for him; there was obviously a lot of his uncle in the little boy!

She sobered slightly as she thought of Cal's own stubbornness. Now, more than ever, with Daniel being awkward, she didn't want to become involved with the other man, felt threatened by one and deeply disturbed by the other, and neither emotion was a comfortable one.

*   *   *

'I'm so glad you decided to come after all,' Daniel said smoothly from across the table in the restaurant booth.

It hadn't been a question of *'deciding'* anything; she hadn't had any choice but to come here this evening. If she hadn't turned up at all she knew Daniel well enough to realise he would make trouble over it. And she hadn't been able to telephone the house to tell him she wouldn't be coming because Cal might have taken the call. And Daniel had been well aware of that.

'What do you want, Daniel?' she said wearily, not prepared to play games with him.

'Shall we order?' he returned lightly.

'I didn't come here to eat—'

'It is a restaurant,' he mocked, grey-blue eyes dancing with mischief.

He was still so handsome, even more so in the dark suit and pale grey shirt he wore tonight. But Helen was unmoved as she looked at him, knew that this outward charm was a deceit, not fooled for a moment by the warmth of his smile.

'I'm not hungry,' she snapped impatiently. 'Now what do you want to talk to me about?'

He turned the charm of his smile on the waitress as she appeared at the side of their table. 'Yes, we're ready to order now,' he said smoothly. 'Prawns Marie-Rose and a crispy duck with salad to follow for the lady,' he ordered over Helen's gasp at his audacity. She didn't hear what he ordered for himself in her amazement that he had remembered her own preferences after all this time. 'You do still like prawns and duck, I hope?' he murmured huskily once the waitress had gone.

'Yes...' She shook her head irritably. 'That isn't the point—'

'I can order you something else if you would prefer it,' he put in calmly, looking at her enquiringly.

'I would *prefer* it if we weren't having this conversation at all!' She glared at him.

He sobered, his expression suddenly one of anger rather than the amused indulgence with her discomfort he had been displaying since she had arrived at the restaurant ten minutes earlier. Daniel had already been seated at the table when she had arrived, and she had sat down only long enough to tell him she wouldn't be staying, wasn't even dressed for an evening out, her trousers and deep green blouse smart but certainly not suitable for dining out in. He had somehow managed to manoeuvre it so that their meal was ordered, and a bottle of wine was already being opened beside their table.

'I would prefer it too,' he rasped once the wine waiter had gone. 'But I'm sure you'll agree we have to talk.'

'I can't think what about,' Helen snapped. 'I said all I had to say to you almost six years ago!'

'And it's concerning that very thing that we have to talk now.' He nodded curtly, his nostrils flared in anger.

Helen frowned. Maybe she was a little dense tonight; she had slept badly the night before, had been sleeping badly since her arrival actually, and she had felt uncomfortable lying to her father earlier when she had told him she was going out for a drive; she certainly had no idea what Daniel and she could possibly have left to talk about!

'I think the past is best left forgotten,' she told him abruptly, not wanting to dwell on her past humiliation; it had taken her most of the last five and a half years to try and get over that.

'My feelings exactly.' Daniel nodded determinedly, his expression grim.

She frowned her puzzlement. 'Then—'

'Completely forgotten,' he added pointedly.

'You're the one who keeps bringing it up,' she pointed out impatiently.

'I mean all of it, Helen,' he bit out coldly, all the smooth charm gone now. 'Not just our past relationship.'

Her brow cleared as she at last realised what he meant. She had as much as decided, out of loyalty for her father's friendship with Cal, that she would have to say something to Cal about what she knew concerning Daniel's past dealings. How to approach the subject, without mentioning her own involvement with Daniel, had been her main problem. She could see from Daniel's expression that he was very worried about her doing just that.

She shook her head. 'I don't think I can do that,' she shrugged ruefully.

'Why the hell not?' he rasped, his eyes narrowed with fury.

'Cal has a right to know—'

'I did nothing illegal,' Daniel cut in forcefully.

'It was immoral!' she insisted firmly.

'That doesn't necessarily mean it was a crime,' he scorned.

She was well aware of the fact that nothing he had done had been a criminal offence; if it had been she would have done something about it.

'Cal—'

'Just how close *are* you and Cal?' he interrupted speculatively.

'None of your damned business!' Her cheeks were flushed with anger.

'You looked close enough to me the other night,' Daniel taunted.

'I told you,' she said in an evenly controlled voice. 'My relationship with Cal is none of your business.'

'Oh, but I think it is.' Some of his anger had faded now, and he was back in control again.

Her mouth tightened. 'If you think our past relationship—'

'Oh, that has only a little to do with it,' he mocked. 'It's the relationship we have now that is important.'

'We don't have a relationship now,' she denied vehemently.

'Exactly,' Daniel taunted.

Helen gave an impatient sigh. 'What *are* you talking about?' She gave the waitress an irritated frown as she placed their starters on the table in front of them, the other woman scuttling away timidly in the face of such vehement displeasure. Helen gave Daniel a scathing look. 'Could we just get this over with so that I can leave? I certainly have no intention of eating this meal!'

'Please yourself.' He shrugged unconcernedly, relaxing back on his side of the booth. 'You see, Helen, after the other night we don't even know each other.'

'Daniel—'

'The moment you returned my formal greeting as if we had only just met for the first time you made it virtually impossible to ever admit to knowing me six years ago.' His head went back in triumph, challenging her to dispute his claim. 'If you try to tell Cal any differently now he's going to wonder why you didn't come straight out with the truth the other evening, will probably think that you were involved in those past deals too.'

Helen paled, realising just how easily she had played into this man's hands.

She stood up abruptly.

Daniel's eyes narrowed as she picked up her bag. 'What are you doing?'

She didn't even bother to answer him, walking out of the restaurant, ignoring the waitress's worried look in her direction as she went out of the door; let Daniel explain— if he could!—her reasons for leaving.

She felt sick, knowing that the situation was of her own making. But she had been so surprised to see Daniel at

Cal's the other evening that her responses to him had been mechanical rather than devised.

But it was just like Daniel to want to take advantage of her disconcertion. He had always been one to recognise the best and easiest way out for himself.

Her father gave her a piercing look as she let herself back into the house, putting down his newspaper as she seemed preoccupied and ill at ease. 'Have you been to see Cal?' he queried softly.

She looked at him sharply. 'Cal?' she echoed in a puzzled voice; she had avoided being alone with the other man last night, until he had finally had to give in and leave with Sam, the little boy tired out. The telephone had been noticeably silent all day, so it seemed Cal had taken the hint that she didn't even want to talk to him. 'Why on earth should you think I've been to see Cal?' She frowned at her father.

He gave a wry smile. 'Because you always have that harassed look when you've been talking to him.'

She sighed at the truth of that; her father couldn't possibly know there was now someone else in the area who could upset her even more than Cal did, in a completely different way.

'No,' she said heavily. 'I haven't seen Cal tonight.'

He looked at her consideringly. 'Then what has upset you?'

Her father was too astute, knew her far too well, to be fobbed off with a half-hearted explanation. Besides, he would have to know about Daniel's being here sooner or later... The only consolation to telling her father was that he didn't know the full story of her break-up with Daniel; he hadn't been in any sort of emotional state himself at the time to be burdened with her humiliating misjudgement as well as her heartache over loving a man who had let her down. Her father had believed then, and still believed, that

Daniel had callously ended their relationship because he was no longer interested in her, and had no idea she had been the one to tell Daniel she no longer wanted any part of his life.

The expression on her father's face darkened when she told him about the other man now working for Cal.

'It was just a surprise to see him again,' she dismissed abruptly. 'The other stupidity is just an embarrassment.' She had told her father of her initial reaction of acting as if she had never met Daniel before. 'I would just feel such a fool admitting the truth to Cal now.' She shrugged with more calm than she felt; Daniel could make her look more than a fool if he was crossed. Lord, how she had ever thought herself in love with such a man was beyond her. Her only possible excuse was that, like her father, she had been vulnerable at that time in her life. And that wasn't really any excuse for being taken in by a man like Daniel had turned out to be.

'Well, if Daniel is happy not to admit to the relationship too, it shouldn't prove a problem.' Her father shrugged, although he didn't look very happy about the situation himself.

Daniel was more than happy not to admit to the relationship!

'I feel uncomfortable about it.' She made a face.

'So do I,' he admitted needlessly. 'But I don't suppose it's necessary for Cal to know...'

Now she had put her father in an awkward position too! 'If you would rather I told him—'

'No,' he cut in abruptly, standing up. 'But I just hope Scott stays out of my way,' he said grimly. 'I remember what you were like six years ago after he had let you down, and—' He broke off as the doorbell rang. 'I wonder who that is,' he muttered vaguely as he went to answer the door.

Cal. She knew it instinctively.

She met his gaze unflinchingly as he came into the room ahead of her father, although she felt as if her duplicity were stamped all over her face.

He looked breathtakingly handsome in a light blue shirt worn beneath a checked jacket, his denims faded from wear rather then affectation, his dark hair once again ruffled from the light breeeze outside.

'I wondered if you would care to come out for a drink.' He came straight to the point, probably sensing that her mood was not a patient one.

On top of her empty stomach—she hadn't been able to eat before she went out to meet Daniel either!—it would probably make her ill. And yet she somehow felt the need to be with him, felt as if she had a heavy weight hanging over her head just waiting to fall on her. And once it did she knew there would be no more invitations like this one. Far from her wanting to stay away from Cal, Daniel's threat to her now made her realise how much she really wanted to do the opposite. This incomprehensible desire for Cal was even more ridiculous than the way she had once felt about Daniel, and yet to have her relationship with Cal threatened by the other man took all the fight against the relationship out of her.

'I'd like that,' she accepted huskily.

She didn't know who was more surprised by her easy acquiescence, her father or Cal!

'If you could see your faces,' she mocked.

'Take her out before she changes her mind,' her father advised Cal.

'I intend to.' Cal grasped hold of her arm and led her out of the house, hardly able to believe his luck.

'There's no rush,' she laughed as he bundled her into the Range Rover he had driven over in.

His gaze was dark. 'How do you know?'

She blushed at the desire in his eyes, his meaning obvious. For once she offered no argument, warmed by her own need to be in his arms.

It was ridiculous, totally illogical after the way she had been fighting against him, and yet she knew that of the two men Daniel was by far the most destructive and selfish. She wasn't sure how she felt about Cal any more.

But being in his arms proved more difficult tonight than at any other time! Cal actually did want to take her out for a drink, choosing a quiet little inn about ten miles drive away. The evening was still clear and warm, and they decided to take their second round of drinks out into the garden.

Cal gave a sigh of satisfaction as they seated themselves opposite each other around a table shaded by a multi-coloured umbrella. 'I can't remember the last time I felt relaxed enough to do this.' He took a thirst-quenching sip of his beer.

'Drink warm beer and swat gnats away before they bite you?' she teased, sipping her own fruit juice with only slightly less relish; it was turning out to be one of the hottest summers they had had for a long time.

He gave her a reproving look. 'The beer is deliciously cold,' he drawled contradictorily. 'And I'm rarely troubled with gnat bites.'

'But I am!' She swatted ineffectually at one of the insects, knowing that, no matter how hard she tried to keep them off her, later tonight she would find her skin speckled with their bites. 'I just seem to attract them,' she said disgustedly.

Cal looked concerned. 'We can sit inside, if you would prefer it?'

'No, of course not.' She smiled. 'Why should I deprive the gnats of the feast they are obviously promising themselves right now?' she added ruefully.

He laughed softly. 'Any comment I make to follow that remark would only be misconstrued!'

Warmth coloured her cheeks. He might not have taken her into his arms yet, but he obviously wanted to. It gave her a sense of anticipation as they continued to laze in the late evening sunshine.

'I'm hoping to have quite a lot of the pressure taken off me in the next few weeks,' Cal said with pleasure. 'The man I've taken on to help me out seems to be quite capable. But of course, you've met him, haven't you?' He raised dark brows.

All thoughts of relaxing instantly deserted Helen, and she sat up stiffly. 'Have I?' she said sharply.

Cal's mouth quirked. 'I remember his interruption of the other evening only too well,' he reminded self-derisively.

'Oh, that,' she realised with some relief, although she didn't relax. Was that really what Cal meant, or was he testing her in some way? He couldn't know about Daniel, could he?

His mouth twisted ruefully. 'I wish I could dismiss it so easily; at the time I felt slightly murderous towards him!'

'It didn't show,' she said almost coyly. Coyly? Her? She didn't remember ever being *coy*! But then she had never met anyone quite like Cal before, she acknowledged reluctantly.

Cal shrugged. 'The man had only been working for me a day; I thought I should allow him a little more time to appreciate what is important to me before bawling him out for it.' He gave a rueful grimace.

Important to him? Was she?

'How is he working out?' She forced a casualness into her voice that wasn't really there; it would solve a lot of problems if Daniel was to prove unsuitable for Cal.

'He seems OK so far,' Cal dismissed. 'Only time will really tell if Daniel can adapt to our unusual working conditions. He's been used to working in the city, to normal office hours; he's going to find it very different working for me.'

She should have known that Daniel's work would be up to standard. There could be no doubt about his professional skills; it was his professional *ethics* that she had questioned. All that she could hope for was that his natural aversion to being in the countryside would eventually take precedence. Otherwise she was going to feel very uncomfortable every time she came home to see her father.

'I wish you had been willing to consider the job.' Cal looked at her ruefully.

'I still don't think that would have been a good idea.' But for different reasons now! The way their relationship was developing, it wouldn't have been wise for them to work together too.

'Possibly not,' he considered, his eyes warm. 'Are you ready to leave?'

She had been ready for the last hour! Although it had been pleasant enough, dangerously so; she hadn't wanted to argue with him once!

The silence between them in the Range Rover was companionable on the drive back rather than awkward, although Helen could feel her anticipation rising as they neared home.

'Care for a nightcap?' Cal asked huskily.

Remembering what had happened last time she went to his home, Helen knew she didn't want a repeat of that. She wanted to avoid seeing Daniel again at all if she could.

'Let's go to Cherry Trees,' she suggested lightly. 'Daddy can join us too then.'

Cal gave her a searching look in the last of the day's light, as if looking for a reluctance on her part to spend time alone with him. He seemed satisfied with what he read in her face, nodding agreement.

The lights were still on in the house when they got there, although Helen knew as soon as she went inside that her father had already gone to bed, the television silent, the lights only left on for her return.

'Coffee? Or something stronger?' She looked at Cal enquiringly.

'Actually, I'm not worried about either.' He smiled. 'Unless you would like something?'

She wasn't particularly worried about a drink either, but it was a little ridiculous neither of them wanting one when that was supposed to be the reason they were here at all!

She shook her head, suddenly feeling very self-conscious. 'I won't bother,' she said abruptly.

'But if you would like—'

'Really, Cal,' she laughed. 'Stop being so polite, I'm not used to it!'

He grinned. 'As I remember it, you were usually the one who was impolite.'

Her smile faded. 'I had good reason—'

'You think you had.' He moved across the room to tap her lightly on the nose. 'Things aren't always what they appear.'

No, she had realised that concerning her ideas about Sam's possibly being Cal's son. She knew now that wasn't true, but from initial appearances it had seemed a possibility to her. Could she be just as wrong about his plans concerning Cherry Trees? But she didn't see how she could be when her father seemed intent on selling and Cal seemed just as keen to buy the house.

Cal had watched the emotions flickering across her face, giving a rueful sigh. 'Could we not talk about that just now?'

'We have to talk about it some time,' she reminded herself as much as him; it was the reason she was here, after all.

'But not now,' Cal insisted firmly, caressing the side of her face with his thumbtip.

No, not now, she accepted achingly, moving willingly into his arms, her face raised to his as she returned his kiss. If anything she was more deeply affected than the last time she had been in his arms; the movement of his lips against hers was sweet torture.

Cal raised his head with a husky laugh. 'David is probably imagining all sorts of things going on down here now that it's gone quiet.'

Helen couldn't help smiling herself; it was like being two teenagers stealing illicit time together. 'It's more likely he's gone to sleep with a smug smile on his face,' she said drily.

'Or that he's resting himself ready for tomorrow,' Cal murmured indulgently, his arm resting along the back of the sofa behind her as they sat down.

She looked up at him enquiringly. 'Tomorrow?'

'Believe it or not, I used to weigh a stone more than I do now,' he grimaced.

'Yes?' Helen frowned her puzzlement with the statement.

'Your father will probably have lost weight too after running around after Sam for a couple of days,' he said with a shrug.

Helen stiffened. What did he mean by that remark?

Cal turned to her enquiringly at her prolonged silence, frowning a little at the incomprehension on her face. 'He didn't tell you?' he said slowly.

She was so tense now she felt as if she might break, the pleasant interlude in his arms over in the face of this new threat to her peace of mind. 'Tell me what?' she pushed tautly. But she knew. She *knew*.

Cal sat forward on the sofa as she stood up restlessly, his elbows resting on his knees as he looked up at her with concern. 'I have to go to London for a few days, a legal matter, and David has offered to have Sam here while I'm away,' he explained almost reluctantly.

Exactly what she had thought he meant! Sam here, in this house, playing, sleeping, just being here. She didn't know if she would be able to bear it.

Cal stood up and came across the room to her, grasping her shoulders. 'David said it would be all right,' he muttered almost to himself. 'But it isn't, is it?' he said heavily. 'Damn it, I had no idea it would affect you like this, or I would never have asked... I should have realised it might be too much for you.' He shook his head in self-disgust at his thoughtlessness.

Helen looked at him sharply. 'What do you mean?'

Her heart was beating a wild tattoo in her chest; her hands felt clammy and yet cold at the same time.

Cal gave a deep sigh, as if regretting what he was about to say, and yet knowing he had to say it none the less. 'I know about Ben, Helen,' he told her gently. 'David told me about him months ago.'

Ben. Oh, lord, how just the mention of his name could still hurt her!

Ben. As beautiful as Sam, but fated to die despite all her efforts for it to be otherwise. A precious child who hadn't lived to see his first birthday.

CHAPTER NINE

HELEN moved abruptly away from Cal, putting some distance between them as she went to stand in front of the window, staring out with sightless eyes, her hands twisting together in her agitation.

She put her head back, stiffening her shoulders, although she couldn't turn and look at Cal, her eyes filled with unshed tears, even now, after all these years.

'What did my father tell you?' she asked flatly.

Cal seemed to sense that she wouldn't let him near her, standing where she had left him. 'I had to know, Helen, otherwise I might have said or done something unthinkingly that would have hurt David in a way I wouldn't have been able to understand.'

She closed her eyes, swallowing hard. 'Yes,' she finally managed to choke out.

'Helen—'

'Please *don't*!' she almost shouted, her hands held up defensively as he would have come to her. She couldn't bear for him to touch her, would have broken down if he did. 'That year—it was the worst time I've ever known in my life,' she said shakily.

Much worse than anything Daniel could ever have done to her, touching her in a way that Daniel never could, although she acknowledged that it was because she had already been hurting so much that Daniel had been able to reach her in the way that he had. Maybe if she hadn't already been in such pain she would have been able to see through him from the first.

112

Cal drew in a ragged breath. 'In a way I can understand, although I was lucky, I still have Sam,' he said thankfully.

Of course. He had lost his brother and his brother's wife. Suddenly. With no warning at all. They hadn't really known what would happen, but she and her father had had more warning of what was to come than Cal could have done.

'I'm sorry,' she trembled. 'I didn't think.'

'As I said,' he shrugged, 'I was luckier than you and David, I still have Sam.'

And they had had Ben for almost a year. A year when they had almost lost him several times. But he had fought back, until that fateful day only eleven months after his birth when he hadn't been able to fight any more. It had broken Helen's heart to sit and watch him die.

'You were very close to your mother?'

She closed her eyes as fresh pain washed over her, taking her breath away.

Her mother. Tall and beautiful, her hair still naturally blonde, green eyes full of laughter, of a love of life. But she had lost that life giving birth to the son she and Helen's father had longed for for so long.

The pregnancy had been so unexpected, a complete surprise in her mother's fortieth year, none of them believing there would be another child after all these years; after all, Helen had been over eighteen by this time. The excitement for all of them when what Elizabeth Foster had believed to be an early 'change of life' had turned out to be a pregnancy!

It had been such an easy pregnancy too, closely monitored because of her mother's age, but there had been nothing to warn them of her mother's heart defect that only showed itself at the height of labour, causing her heart to stop and never begin beating again; no warning either that Ben would have that same heart defect, except to a greater degree. The double tragedy had been all the harder to bear because the problem had never shown itself before, Helen born a normal, healthy child after a relatively easy labour.

But it wasn't to be a second time—her mother's heart had been strained too much, although she had never known that her son would only live another eleven months before he too died.

Helen's father had been devastated by his wife's death, theirs a marriage of love and laughter, and Helen's grief had only been slightly less because her time was so occupied with taking care of a very sick baby.

With her father unable to deal with the baby at all for the first few weeks of Ben's life, his desolation at losing her mother almost crippling him, Helen's closeness to Ben had been complete. She had fought so hard to keep him alive. But it had been a fight that the doctors and specialists had warned her she was destined to lose. Although it hadn't stopped her trying to win.

Her heartbreak at Ben's death had been so deep that she'd had to get away, completely away from anything that reminded her of him and the happy family she had once known, which was why she had originally gone to London. Where she had ultimately met Daniel and been hurt all over again.

'Yes,' she said heavily. 'I was very close to my mother.'

Cal shook his head. 'David told me how you bore the responsibility of Ben when he was too broken to cope with anything.'

She swallowed hard. 'Could we talk about something else?'

She hadn't realised Cal had moved until she felt his hands on her shoulders turning her towards him. But at his first touch her control broke and she buried her face against his chest, clinging to him as the sobs racked her body.

'Oh, lord, I didn't mean to upset you,' Cal groaned, holding her tightly against him. 'Helen, I'm sorry, so sorry.'

She wasn't, not really, Ben just something else that had stood between them. She had loved her brother dearly, had been more like the mother to him that he had never known, and she had found it impossible over the years to talk about him with anyone, even her father. *Especially* her father—both of them were too close to Ben. But she had known how much her father needed to talk of the baby they had lost, had regretted not being able to share that with him, even in words, knew that he had recognised an affinity in Cal that made it possible for him to talk to the younger man.

Helen now knew that same affinity.

She regained some control, shaking her head. 'It was so long ago.'

'That doesn't lessen the pain,' Cal said understandingly.

'It should have dulled it,' she returned firmly.

'You had a double tragedy of the magnitude most people couldn't even begin to imagine,' he soothed gruffly.

And he understood all too well what she had been through. In a way she had always known that he would, had feared even that closeness between them, could feel the tendrils of that known affinity wrapping themselves around her heart. She knew, and in a way, accepted, her physical attraction towards this man, but she didn't want to care for him any more deeply than that, was afraid to care for anyone in that way. And yet she knew that with this man she was dangerously close to doing just that.

She pulled out of his arms, making an obvious move away from him. 'It was all a long time ago,' she repeated firmly. 'So Daddy has offered to have Sam here while you're away?' she added briskly, the distance she had deliberately put between them not just one of proximity.

Cal looked as if he would have liked to have said more

on the subject of Ben and her mother, but he could obviously tell by her expression that she wouldn't welcome any further intrusion upon her battered emotions.

'Yes,' he confirmed heavily. 'But if it's going to upset you…?'

'Of course not,' she denied offhandedly, having no real idea just how Sam being in the house would affect her. 'I'm sure we'll cope very well. I can take him down on the beach during the day, I'm sure he would like that.'

'Yes,' Cal agreed distractedly. 'I'm going to sort out things with Enid and Henry once and for all, legally, if possible.'

After the other day Helen had a feeling that might be the only way he could stop the arguments! 'Poor Sam,' she sighed.

'I don't know what else to do to put a stop to all this,' Cal confided sadly. 'I do have an alternative, but— Well, it isn't one I could ever use,' he dismissed hardly. 'Susan wouldn't have wanted me to do that. They left me a letter, you see,' he agitatedly paced the room. 'Explaining why it had to be me who had Sam.'

Helen had sensed there was something he was keeping to himself, felt uncomfortable at having him confide in her in this way, felt those tendrils about her emotions drawing in tighter.

'Susan loved her parents,' Cal continued heavily. 'But she knew they were the last people to bring up Sam. Susan was born to them late in life, was almost suffocated by them during her childhood; she couldn't bear the thought, much as she loved them, of their putting those same restrictions on Sam's life.'

So this was that other 'act of defiance' that Susan had committed, not openly as her marriage to Graham had needed to be, but quietly, privately, with the man they had entrusted their son's life to. It just made Helen feel all the worse for all the awful thoughts she had had of Cal since before she even arrived here a couple of weeks ago.

Was it really only two and a half weeks since she had first met this man? She was beginning to feel as if she had known him a lifetime!

And what she had just learnt of the trust that had been placed in Cal made a nonsense of all the bad things she had been imagining of him. And she could only admire him more for the restraint he was exercising concerning Enid Carter; it must be so tempting for him to just show the other woman the letter and stop her insults once and for all, and yet she knew Cal would never do that, that he would try to maintain the love the Carters had for their daughter no matter what the cost might be to himself. Although Helen was equally convinced that he wouldn't exercise that same constraint if Sam's welfare was to become really threatened.

It was a terrible, if necessary, burden that had been placed on him. And he had chosen to share that burden with her...

'I'd better go,' Cal decided suddenly, as if he too was slightly taken aback at having confided in her the way that he had. 'I'll be over early tomorrow with Sam. Is that going to be all right with you?' He looked at her anxiously.

She shrugged with much more nonchalance than she actually felt. 'It really isn't my decision; as my father is fond of pointing out, this is his house, not mine,' she said ruefully.

'Helen—'

'Cal, it will be all right,' she cut in tautly, her cheeks colouring slightly as she realised she had used that shortened version of his name for the first time. But then, their relationship had changed so drastically in the course of just one short evening that it wasn't surprising she was slightly off balance! 'It *will* be all right,' she repeated firmly.

He looked as if he would have liked to say more but restrained himself with effort. 'I'll see you in the morning, then,' he told her gruffly.

'Yes,' she acknowledged abruptly, walking out to the door, looking at him expectantly as he seemed reluctant to leave. 'I had better get some rest too if I'm to chase after Sam the next few days,' she said lightly. 'I'm sure that's what Daddy really had in mind when he made the offer!'

Cal seemed relieved that the tension had been lifted, smiling down at her. 'I wouldn't be at all surprised, although the two of them do get on well together.'

She sobered a little, knowing how much her father had regretted the fact that Ben had rarely been well enough to play with, let alone get into mischief the way Sam did. 'I'm sure.' She nodded curtly.

'Helen?'

She looked up at Cal warily. Her emotions were too ragged already; she couldn't stand much more tonight!

'Goodnight.' His lips lightly brushed her own before he left, seeming to sense her vulnerability and not want to take advantage of it.

Helen stayed in the lounge a long time after he had gone, tired and yet not sleepy, knowing that the next few days were going to be a severe strain on her emotions.

'Asleep?' her father asked indulgently as she came down the stairs.

She had just fed Sam his tea, bathed him, put him to bed, and read him a story, which he had fallen asleep halfway through. So much for that story of Rapunzel that Cal had said he liked; she had a feeling Cal enjoyed that story more than the baby did!

As she had thought would happen, she had looked after Sam more than her father had, her father seeming to think he only had to play with the little boy a couple of times a day and that he would amuse and look after himself the rest of the time. Admittedly it was a long time since her father had had a young child in the house, but he seemed to have forgotten all the other things there were to taking care of one! If he had ever known. Helen seemed to recall that her mother had done most of the looking after when she was young; before his early retirement last year her father had been kept busy with the clothing store he had owned and run in the nearby town.

After only three days of running about after Sam Helen was exhausted, dropping down tiredly into one of the armchairs.

'Yes, he is, thank good—' She broke off as the telephone rang, groaning at the thought of getting up to answer it. 'Would you?' she asked her father wearily.

He glanced at his wristwatch. 'It will only be for you,' he said derisively.

If one of them didn't answer it soon then neither of them would need to!

'It's eight o'clock,' her father added pointedly, teasing humour in his eyes.

She stood up with an impatient frown in her father's direction.

'Cal doesn't telephone at eight o'clock every night to talk to me,' her father taunted as she went out into the hallway to answer the still ringing telephone.

'He's checking on Sam,' she turned briefly to snap irritably.

'Of course he is,' came her father's taunting reply as Helen picked up the receiver.

'Everything all right?' came Cal's anxious voice down the line.

Her father was right about these calls; they had come regularly at this time for the previous two evenings too. He was also right that Cal didn't call to talk to him; he always enquired after Sam in great detail, but he also made it obvious that he wanted to hear her voice too.

'Fine,' she answered lightly, going on in some detail about the events of Sam's day. 'He wants to know when you're coming home.' Those deep blue eyes had filled up with tears today when Sam had asked where his uncle was. And she had to admit, though not because she was tired of looking after Sam, that she would be interested in knowing herself when Cal intended coming back. Much as she hated to admit it, she had missed him.

'Tomorrow,' Cal answered with some relief. 'I'm not absolutely sure what time. But everything is sorted out with Enid and Henry at last.'

'Without—'

'Yes, without that,' Cal confirmed dismissively. 'Enid has been suffering with her nerves for some time, and I finally managed to persuade Henry to get her doctor to advise her that rest and no pressure are what she needs now. Henry has never wanted to interfere in Sam's custody anyway, so he was only too pleased to try and calm the situation down; it was just a question of seeing him on my own for a time and sorting out a plan of action. I'm not saying Enid won't still be a pain, but I think she's finally been convinced that she isn't strong enough to take care of a very young child.'

It also meant that Enid Carter had a very valid excuse, for herself as much as anyone else, for not pressing to have Sam with her. None of that really mattered as long as Sam could now be left in peace to settle down to life with the uncle he obviously adored.

'I'm glad.' And they both knew she didn't just mean the custody of Sam, that she was also relieved that it hadn't been necessary to use Susan's letter to achieve the armed truce that now existed between Cal and Sam's grandparents.

'Can you take Sam back to the house tomorrow?' Cal's voice was husky, knowing exactly what she had meant by her statement.

Daniel was at the house. She had seen him about the estate several times when she'd taken Sam down to the beach, had studiously avoided actually being close enough to have to acknowledge him.

'Couldn't you pick him up from here?' she suggested tautly.

'I'm really not sure how early or late I'll be,' Cal answered in a preoccupied voice. 'But if there's a problem with your going to the house—'

'There's no problem,' she cut in sharply. 'As long as you make sure we're expected.' The last thing she wanted was to run into Daniel unexpectedly; there was no telling what his reaction to seeing her again might be, and it might be done in front of witnesses!

'I'll ring the housekeeper and confirm that with her,' Cal instantly assured her. 'How are you?' His voice was husky now.

Her cheeks felt hot. 'Very well.' Better than she had expected, actually; Sam was a joy to have around rather than a constant reminder of Ben, as she had thought he might be. Sam brought with him only joy and laughter, whereas any joy and laughter she had known with Ben had been tinged with the knowledge that he would be with them for only a short time; Sam was bright sunshine, whereas Ben had been like a bright star in the sky. There *was* no comparison.

'I'm glad,' Cal said softly. 'Will you have dinner at the house with me tomorrow night?'

Daniel was there, she reminded herself once again, although the hunger to be with Cal again warred with that knowledge.

'There won't be anyone there but the two of us.' Cal

seemed to guess—if not necessarily for the right reason!—
her reluctance to see Daniel at the house again. 'Daniel isn't
returning from town until Monday morning.'

Daniel hadn't gone to London with Cal, but he must have
returned there for his weekend off. His absence took away
any last lingering doubt she might have had about having
dinner with Cal.

'I'd like that,' she accepted softly.

'I've missed you, Helen,' he told her huskily.

She had missed him too, although there was no way she
was going to admit as much, even if he couldn't actually
see the blush to her cheeks. 'I'll see you tomorrow some
time,' she answered briskly.

Cal gave a husky laugh, seeming to guess how she felt
without her actually having to speak a word. 'Give Sam a
kiss for me,' he said lightly. 'And take one for yourself
too,' he added softly before ringing off.

'Cal OK?' her father looked up from the newspaper to
enquire.

'Did I say the call was from him?' She hadn't forgiven
him for his earlier teasing yet!

'Only one person I know can bring that flush to your
cheeks,' he mocked with affection.

Helen gave an impatient sigh. 'You'll be pleased to know
that Cal is coming home tomorrow.'

'And are you pleased?'

'Daddy—'

'Strike that question.' He put the newspaper down to
hold up his hands defensively. 'I can tell by your face that
you're pleased,' he added teasingly, giving her a cheeky
grin as she threw a cushion at him, catching it neatly in his
hands. 'I'm pleased the two of you are getting on so much
better.' He sobered, putting the cushion down. 'It was what
I had hoped for.'

Helen gave him a considering look. 'What do you mean, it was what you had hoped for?' she questioned slowly.

He shrugged. 'I thought the two of you would get on together.'

'Yes?' She was very still now.

'There's nothing wrong with that,' he said defensively at her accusing look. 'You're my only daughter, and I happen to like Cal very much.'

'Yes?' she prompted again, more than a little wary now.

'Nothing else.' He stood up agitatedly. 'I just wanted the two of you to like each other.'

'We like each other,' she admitted slowly, a suspicion suddenly hitting her. 'Daddy—'

'That's good then, isn't it?' he dismissed lightly.

'That depends,' Helen said consideringly.

Her father was starting to look uncomfortable. 'I don't know—'

'Just how far were you prepared to go in order for Cal and I to "get on"?' she cut in in a hard voice.

'Helen—'

'How far, Daddy?' she repeated with firm determination.

He stood up agitatedly, pacing the room, not at all happy with the turn the conversation had taken.

'Daddy—'

'Oh, all right,' he snapped impatiently. 'So I exaggerated a little about wanting to sell Cherry Trees to Cal, but it turned out all right in the end, didn't it?' He faced her defiantly.

She couldn't believe he had done this to her, didn't want to believe he was capable of such a thing, and yet she knew that he was.

No wonder Cal was so stunned by her attacks on him for wanting to buy this house; the sale hadn't been his idea at all, he hadn't really been interested in buying it!

She could see it all now, knew exactly what her father

had done, realised that he had brought her down here in
the first place under false pretences, in anger if that was
the only way to achieve his objective; he had wanted her
and Cal to 'get on'. But for what purpose?

'Did it?' she rasped hardly.

'Now look, Helen—'

'I'm trying to, Daddy.' She nodded slowly.

'Cal's a good man,' he defended stubbornly.

She had come round to that idea herself, even more so
since she had realised the lengths he was prepared to go
to, the insults he had been willing to put up with, in order
to avoid hurting Enid Carter. The man she had first thought
Cal to be wouldn't have cared whom he hurt as long as he
achieved his objective.

Cal hadn't said a word either to disabuse her of her belief
that he was after Cherry Trees in an underhand way, by
using his friendship with her father. Now it turned out that
her *father* had been using the friendship to try and match-
make between the two of them.

Had Cal realised that?

If he had, why hadn't he put her firmly in her place when
she had begun to insult him?

She remembered the things he had said to her earlier, the
times she had been in his arms. What did it all mean?

She was afraid to hope.

'I'm just beginning to realise how good,' she reproved
her father. 'He must have realised long ago what you were
up to.' She shook her head disgustedly.

'It didn't put him off, did it?' he said with satisfaction.
'On the contrary,' he added pointedly.

'Well, now that we *both* know what you've been up to
you can just stop it,' she snapped in her agitation. 'Forget
about selling Cherry Trees and just stop your interfering,'
she said warningly.

'I was only thinking of you, Helen—'

'Were you?' she cut in derisively.

He had the grace to look slightly uncomfortable. 'Maybe not completely,' he admitted ruefully. 'Maybe I am being selfish in wanting you to be happy, with a family of your own. But I wanted it for you as much as for me.'

'You're assuming rather a lot.' Her cheeks were hot with embarrassment.

'You can't blame me for trying,' he reasoned imploringly.

No, maybe she couldn't blame him for that. She just wished she had been more aware of what he had been up to from the first, then she possibly wouldn't have made such a fool of herself over Cherry Trees. Cal must think she was a shrew.

But that *hadn't* stopped him wanting to be with her, taking her in his arms, that little voice in her brain kept persisting.

'Couldn't you have just introduced the two of us and left the rest to chance?' she sighed.

'You're always so defensive with men, keep them at such a distance, that Cal would probably never have got past that wall you put up around yourself,' her father explained. 'This way, you were both thrown slightly off guard.'

He was right; she knew he was right. But even so...

'Just don't ever do anything like this again,' she cautioned.

He eyed her speculatively. 'Will I need to?'

Helen didn't even bother to answer him, starting to collect up Sam's toys ready to take him home tomorrow.

Would he need to?

'Well, well, well,' drawled a mocking voice. 'So you've brought the little cherub back, have you?'

Helen spun round from unpacking Sam's toys in the

nursery—the baby was asleep in the adjoining bedroom—
getting up to gently close the door between the two rooms
before answering Daniel's taunting remark.

She had returned to the house mid-morning, having
lunch with Sam downstairs before putting him down for his
afternoon nap. Daniel had obviously returned from London
earlier than Cal had expected!

He seemed to be working, dressed in a suit and pristine
white shirt, his golden hair meticulous. He left Helen cold.

'Sam is back home, yes,' she replied in a controlled
voice.

Daniel strolled further into the room, his gaze flickering
over her insolently, the pale yellow sun-dress she wore and
her loosened hair obviously finding approval as his gaze
warmed speculatively.

'I must say you're a dark horse, Helen,' he taunted. 'No
wonder I didn't get very far with you—you were saving
yourself for a much bigger fish!'

Two spots of angry colour darkened her cheeks. 'Don't
judge everyone by your own standards! It's almost six years
since I knew you; if I were as mercenary as you're implying
I would have found someone rich by now!'

Daniel shrugged, strolling carelessly round the room.
'Maybe you weren't in a hurry.'

'And maybe I wasn't looking for anyone rich at all!' she
snapped contemptuously.

'But you seem to have found him,' Daniel drawled pointedly.

'Cal is a friend of my father's—'

'Oh, come on, Helen,' Daniel scoffed. 'I saw the two of
you together the other evening.'

'You didn't see anything,' she dismissed hardly.

He shrugged. 'Maybe if I had delayed my entrance a
little longer I might have done!'

'That's disgusting!' she gasped with distaste for the unpleasantness of this man's mind. Had she really once found him attractive? She found that impossible to believe now, although she hadn't really seen this side of him until she had thwarted his intentions towards her almost six years ago—up until that moment he had been nothing but charm and warmth.

'Oh, don't be such a prude, Helen,' he derided impatiently. 'We don't have to play games any more; you're out for what you can get out of life and so am I.' He shrugged. 'I have a healthy respect for anyone who doesn't mind admitting that.'

Helen eyed him with dislike. 'There's nothing healthy about having that attitude towards people,' she scorned.

'I told you, you don't have to play games any more,' he chided softly. 'And who knows, maybe we can have a little fun together as well?'

She stiffened. 'What do you mean?'

'You can't be that näive,' he mocked, moving towards her, taking her into his arms. 'I always wanted you, Helen.' His arms tightened as she struggled against him. 'I think it's all this cool "don't touch me!" beauty that does it,' he added appreciatively.

'Let go of me!' She pushed against his chest. How dared he touch her in this way?

'I told you,' he murmured softly. 'You don't have to pretend any more.'

'I'm not *pretending* the disgust I feel for you!' She still pushed against his chest, although couldn't manage to free herself completely.

His face hardened. 'Let's put it another way, Helen,' he said with soft menace. 'Neither of us wants Cal to realise we knew each other six years ago, but *I* only have a job to lose...'

Helen became very still, looking up at him disbelievingly. 'Are you trying to blackmail me into going to bed with you?' She was incredulous at the idea of it.

'Blackmail is a little too strong a word,' he dismissed lightly. 'I—'

'I don't think it's too strong at all,' rasped a familiar voice from the open doorway into the hallway.

Helen turned to look at Cal with open horror, not having been aware of his presence in the house because of her argument with Daniel.

CHAPTER TEN

BY THE time Cal had come further into the room, his eyes a cold metallic blue in his anger, Helen had released herself and moved as far away from Daniel as she could possibly get, her legs trembling, her hands shaking.

She couldn't believe this was happening. *Could* it really be?

Cal glared at the other man with cold fury. 'I want your things packed and you out of my house in half an hour.'

'Half an hour?' Daniel gasped indignantly. 'But—'

'Think yourself lucky I'm giving you that long,' Cal bit out tautly, obviously controlling himself with effort. 'If it weren't for the fact that I don't want any reminder of you left in the house I'd make you go right now and send your things on to you.'

'Look, Cal—'

'Will you just go?' he rasped. 'Before I do something you'll regret.' The physical threat was obvious. Cal looked at the other man with open contempt. '*I* certainly wouldn't regret it.'

'Helen and I are old friends,' Daniel persisted cajolingly, ignoring her outraged gasp as he looked at the other man for understanding, finding only a cold stare in return. 'I realise it must have sounded bad to you when you arrived, but—'

'It didn't sound bad, Scott,' Cal bit out between clenched teeth. 'It sounded exactly what it was, and I don't even begin to deal with blackmailers. Now get out.'

Daniel looked at the other man for several seconds, finally realising that he wasn't going to get anywhere with

129

him, throwing Helen a vindictive look before turning back
to Cal. 'Helen and I were lovers long ago—'

'That isn't true!' she cried out desperately, looking to
Cal to believe her. He still looked at Daniel, his expression
enigmatic. 'It isn't true,' she repeated lamely. 'We did
know each other, but—'

'Would you leave, Helen?' Cal instructed in an even
voice, still not looking at her.

He didn't believe her. Oh, lord, this couldn't be happening!

'Cal, please,' she choked, looking at him imploringly.

'Helen, leave,' he told her through gritted teeth.

She felt sick, running from the room with a choked cry.

She had known, the moment she first saw him in the
nursery doorway, that she had fallen irrevocably in love
with Caleb Jones!

'Love, wouldn't it help to talk about it?' her father
prompted gently.

She had stopped crying now, just felt completely numb,
sitting on the edge of her bed, her face as white as the
sheets she sat on.

She was too numbed to talk, her emotions a vacuum.

'Helen?' he prompted again, his arms about her shoulders, looking at her with worried concern.

She shook her head. 'It's—it's too awful.' She swallowed hard, the nausea having got worse, not better.

'Tell me.'

She still couldn't talk about that awful scene at Cal's
house, didn't even know how she had got home or up to
her bedroom. She had just wanted to be alone with her pain.

Her father had followed her up the stairs, had sat beside
her with worried concern while she cried as if she would
never stop. But she had to stop eventually and when she

did her father was still there, waiting to be of what comfort to her that he could.

She loved Cal.

It was fact, indisputable; she had known it the moment she'd realised he was standing in the doorway looking at her in Daniel's arms.

And he didn't even want her in the same house as him, had just wanted her away from him as quickly as possible.

She couldn't tell her father about that, couldn't bear him to know of Cal's disgust with her.

'It might help to talk about it,' her father encouraged.

The old, well-worn platitude. As if it ever really did help in a situation like this. It couldn't make Cal's disgust with her go away.

'No,' she said flatly.

'Helen—' He broke off as the doorbell rang. 'Damn,' he muttered as he stood up. 'I'll be back as soon as I can,' he promised concernedly.

If that was Daniel come to gloat because he had managed to ruin her life once again she didn't think she would be answerable for the consequences!

She could hear the door being opened, the murmur of voices, the door closing again, then silence.

At least it wasn't Daniel—it couldn't have been or her father would have been more heated than he had been.

She turned back into her bedroom, her movements heavy with despair.

'Helen.'

She turned sharply at the sound of Cal's voice. What did he want? Had he come here to tell her exactly what he thought of her and her past association with Daniel? But it hadn't been what he thought it was! Not that that would make much difference, she had still deceived him about not knowing Daniel at all.

He looked at her closely. 'Your father said you're upset.'

'I—' She swallowed hard. 'I'm all right now,' she lied; she didn't think she would ever be all right again.

'I'm sorry all that, at the house, had to happen,' Cal sighed.

'So am I.' She nodded.

How could she have ever thought she disliked this man? How could she ever have mistrusted him? He was now more dear to her, more important than anything else in her life had ever been. And it was too late. Just too damned late.

'Scott is a very unpleasant man,' Cal said with distaste. 'I don't know how I could ever have been fooled by him for a moment.' He shook his head with self-disgust.

'Nor I,' Helen said heavily.

'I doubt either of us will ever see him again,' Cal told her with satisfaction, his expression grim. 'I made my opinion of him pretty clear after you had gone.'

She moistened dry lips, nodding. 'I see.'

Had he come here to do the same to her? She didn't think she could bear it, even if the attack was perfectly justifiable, if he was to tell her exactly what he thought of her too!

'Helen, I know all that was—unpleasant, for you, but it's over now. There's no use upsetting yourself about it any more,' he calmed gently.

She swallowed hard. 'I couldn't believe it when I discovered he was the man you had taken on.'

'No,' Cal grimaced. 'It must have been a shock for you.'

Helen looked at him with pained green eyes. 'I don't know what he told you about our relationship in the past but I can assure you I wanted nothing more to do with him once I realised how underhand his dealings were.' She had to at least disabuse him of that point.

'He tried to tell a different tale.' Cal nodded. 'But I wasn't going to fall for that.'

'You weren't?' She looked at him in sudden hope.

'Of course not,' he denied contemptuously. 'I know you, Helen, you aren't that sort of person at all. Lord, woman,' a sudden thought seemed to have occurred to him, 'you didn't think I actually believed the man, did you?'

'You seemed—um—you didn't want me near you,' she reminded shakily, remembering the pain of that moment.

'I wanted you away from there before I began to pull Scott apart limb from limb!' he corrected incredulously. 'You didn't really believe I asked you to leave because I couldn't bear you near me?' he gasped disbelievingly. 'Oh, Helen, I've never wanted to hold you more, to be with you more; I missed you like hell while I was away. But I had to deal with Scott, and if he had said much more about you while you had to stand there listening to the lies I would have hit him then and there!'

'You would?' she gasped.

'I would,' he confirmed teasingly, crossing the room to her side.

Helen looked up at him with wide eyes. 'How do you know they were lies?'

Cal gave her a reproving look. 'I'm not even going to acknowledge the stupidity of that question by answering it,' he dismissed firmly.

'But—'

'Helen, all the way back from London today I was thinking about kissing you.' His gaze on her lips was almost like a caress. 'Nothing else, just kissing you.'

Her breath seemed caught in her throat. 'Cal—'

'Nothing else, Helen,' he repeated, his arms closing firmly about her. 'Not Sam. Not the estate. Not work. Just kissing you.'

She didn't want to argue with that, just wanted to be in his arms, returning that kiss he seemed to want so badly.

It didn't seem possible, after what she had believed earlier, but if Cal said it was so then it was.

'Please—kiss me,' she groaned her own need, her body curved into his.

They were both desperate for the contact, their days apart, plus that awful scene earlier, having heightened their need of each other. The kiss went on and on, neither wanting it to end.

Cal finally pulled back with a husky laugh. 'This had better stop, or we'll have David coming upstairs to break us apart.'

Helen shakily returned his smile, knowing that if he hadn't stopped then she wouldn't have cared whether her father had interrupted them or not. Although he was probably consumed with curiosity as he waited downstairs!

'I love you, Helen,' Cal told her gruffly.

She swallowed hard. 'But—you hardly know me,' she said breathlessly, hardly able to believe this was happening to her.

'All the details can wait,' he dismissed indulgently. 'I love *you*, the person I know you to be, the woman who allowed Sam into her life despite the pain it caused you.' They sat down on the bed, Cal's arm about her shoulder. 'I knew from the very first moment I realised you were David's daughter how deeply being with Sam affected you. Just as I knew I wanted you in my life,' he added softly.

'I was rude and arrogant at our first meeting,' she said disbelievingly.

'With good reason,' he defended. 'I still get the shakes when I think of what might have happened. And I know that it was just as traumatic for you.'

Oh, it had been. The whole incident could have had tragic consequences.

'I do love you, Helen,' Cal turned to her intensely, instantly banishing the memory of that near disaster when they had first met. 'I love you and I want to marry you. If you'll have me.'

'What?' she gasped.

'I want you as my wife, Helen,' he told her deeply. 'If you could learn to love me. Hell, even if you can't love me,' he added desperately. 'We could have a good life together, Helen. And you do respond to me, that's enough to be going on with.'

She drew in a steadying breath. 'If this is for Sam's sake—'

'It's for *my* sake,' he cut in with impatient anger. 'Haven't you listened to a word I've been saying? I love you; I want to marry you. I've lived thirty-nine years without feeling the emotion; give me the credit of being able to recognise it when it at last comes into my life! And yes, it would be nice for Sam to have a mother figure in his life, but it isn't going to be the end of the world if he doesn't. I don't want to marry you for Sam, I want to marry you because, quite honestly, the thought of having to live without you now is a desperate one!'

She had to believe him, could see the naked pain in those dark blue eyes. 'I love you too,' she choked. 'I didn't want to—'

'I would never have guessed that!' Cal murmured affectionately.

'It hurts too much to love, Cal.' She swallowed hard.

'But it gives much more than it takes away,' he encouraged eagerly. 'Yes, we'll argue. Yes, we'll probably hurt each other. But at the end of all that we'll still have each other and the love we feel for each other. I still can't believe you feel the same way I do!' He shook his head dazedly.

How could she not have loved this man? She had been sure to lose this battle from the first, and should have realised that. But if she had she would never have gone near him, and the thought now of living without this burning excitement of loving him and being loved in return was a devastating one.

'Daddy planned for this to happen, you know,' she felt bound to say.

'I knew that,' Cal nodded ruefully. 'And at first his matchmaking amused me. I had no intention of buying Cherry Trees from him until he brought the subject up—'

'Oh, I realise that.' She sighed at her father's duplicity.

'But I only had to meet you the once to decide his matchmaking was a good idea.' He grinned. 'There's nothing like having a father's approval before you've even met the lady concerned!'

'He's incorrigible!' Her cheeks were flushed with embarrassment. 'If I had known what he was up to in the beginning I never would have come down here.'

'And that would have been a tragedy,' Cal said heavily.

Yes, it would. But even so... 'You do realise that he'll be interfering like this for the rest of our lives,' she cautioned.

'"Rest of our lives"?' Cal looked at her with a burning hunger in his eyes.

Her heart beat a wild tattoo in her chest, her pulse racing. 'I never thought I would say this to anyone,' she could barely speak now for nerves, 'but I would love to marry you.'

'I have a ready-made family,' he pointed out reluctantly. 'Not many women would want to take that on.' He looked at her anxiously.

Helen gave a choked laugh. 'I would want to marry you if you had half a dozen children already—as long as they were all as adorable as Sam!'

His arms tightened about her, his face buried in her hair.

'*Our* children will be as adorable as Sam. More so probably, with the beautiful mother they are going to have.'

Their children.

Even in her wildest imaginings that was something she had never dreamt of.

'Shh, you have to be very quiet.' She could hear Cal whispering to Sam, smiling dreamily to herself as she pictured them creeping into the room so that they shouldn't disturb her.

She opened one eye in the semi-darkness, watching them as they crossed the room to her bedside, the tall strong man and the sturdy three-year-old at his side.

Sam had grown a lot the last two years, looking even more like Cal as he matured, taking on a lot of his uncle's characteristics too as he copied the man he adored.

He peered now over the side of the crib that stood at Helen's bedside, frowning deeply. 'She's very small, Uncle Cal.'

Cal gave a throaty laugh, ruffling the little boy's hair. 'You were that small once, Sam.'

Sam gave him a scoffing look that clearly doubted that, before turning back to the crib. 'I can't see her properly; is she pretty?'

'Not as pretty as her mother—'

'Flattery will get you everywhere, Cal Jones.' Helen laughed softly as she sat up in the bed and switched on the bedside lamp, blushing at the unashamed adoration in Cal's eyes as he looked down at her.

In the early hours of that morning they had shared the experience of seeing their daughter come into the world, her thick blonde hair the same colour as her mother's, the eyes looking as if they would stay the deep blue of her father's. No couple could share a more beautiful moment than seeing their child born.

'We didn't wake you?' Cal leant down to brush his lips against her, his gaze full of tenderness.

She shook her head. 'I was only dozing. So what do you think of her, Sam?' she prompted teasingly.

He gave the baby a considering look as she lay so peacefully asleep, long dark lashes fanned out across her peachy cream cheeks; after all the warnings she had had of babies looking all red and wrinkled, little Elizabeth was the most beautiful baby Helen could ever have imagined.

'I thought I'd be able to play with her,' he voiced his main disappointment.

'You will, when she's older.' Helen gave Cal a conspiratorial smile before turning her attention back on the little boy. 'I did try to explain that to you, Sam, before she was born.'

'Yes.' But he sounded as if he had hoped she might be mistaken about it, and now that he had seen the baby his worst fears had been confirmed.

Cal laughed softly, swinging Sam up into his arms, looking nothing at all like a man who had spent most of the night holding Helen's hand through the labour of birth, euphoria making him look years younger. 'She'll get bigger, Sam,' he consoled the little boy.

Sam didn't look very convinced about that, but now that he had seen how boring the baby was going to be he decided he would explore Helen's hospital room, asking to be put down before wandering off.

Cal sat on the side of the bed. 'How are you feeling?' Concern for her darkened his eyes.

'Wonderful!' she assured him warmly, clasping his hand in hers.

'David can hardly wait to see her,' Cal told her ruefully. 'He should be along later.'

She smiled indulgently, knowing how pleased her father would be that they had named the baby after her mother.

The last two years had been the happiest Helen had ever known, happiness beyond her imagining. As Cal had predicted, they did have their arguments, but the making up had always been worth it!

And now they had a daughter to complete their happiness; Sam was already like a son to them both, so Elizabeth had been like a completion of their family unit.

Helen sat up with a smile as the baby began to stir, wondering what Sam was going to make of her feeding the baby herself.

Cal bent down to pick the baby up, the hard planes of his face softened with tenderness for his little daughter. 'I'm not going to stand a chance with two of you in the house,' he said ruefully, placing the baby in her waiting arms. 'Sam and I will have to try very hard to resist the pair of you!'

Helen touched the tiny hand that lay so trustingly against her breast, her eyes full of unshed tears as she looked at Cal. 'I love you very much, my darling. Thank you so much for loving me.'

'Thank *you*,' he said gruffly, as moved by the moment as she was.

Sam climbed up on the bed with them, watching the baby with more interest now.

As she looked at her family all around her Helen knew she had never known a moment of such sheer happiness before. She didn't doubt for a single second that the happiness would continue...

Matt's courage is legendary. But is he brave enough to take on the role of daddy to his recently orphaned niece?

THE MARRIAGE TICKET

Sharon Brondos

CHAPTER ONE

ALLISON FORD slowed her shopping cart to a crawl, matching the snail's pace of the cart in front of her. Safeway wasn't crowded this early in the day. It was summertime and housewife shoppers weren't trying to work around school hours. She could have quite easily moved faster. She smiled at her unusual behavior.

Ordinarily, she raced through the grocery store, attempting each time to beat her record from the previous time. She hated grocery shopping with the kind of passion only those who had done it with regular, unavoidable, mind-numbing regularity could appreciate. It was a necessary, but boring part of life. Today, however, she found herself intrigued by the man and child using the cart ahead of her. They were quite a pair.

The child was just a baby, really. Barely two, Allie figured. A blond-haired, blue-eyed Kewpie of a kid. Hard to tell what sex. The clothing offered no clues. The outfit, completely mismatched, had obviously been selected without any eye to style. The kid looked as if she/he'd been dressed in whatever had come to hand. The little round face and chubby arms reminded Allie of Sally and Sam at that age. Though, of course, this was only one child, and at that age, her twins had seemed like seven or eight of them all at once.

Allie sighed, her mind hearing the peaceful, lonely silence in her house that would last for another two months—the rest of June, all of July and most of August, while the ten-year-old twins spent their summer vacation with their grandparents in Montana. Lonely, lovely silence…

The kid in the grocery cart was *not* being silent. Allie remembered that kind of behavior only too well. How, when the twins were small, she would push the cart through the aisles, back stiff, shoulders squared, pretending everything was normal, gathering up the food for the week, while her offspring yowled and howled. People had stared then, even as they were staring now at the lone squaller. Sally and Sam had dueted, but even together they'd made less noise than the blond banshee yodeling displeasure at his or her father this morning. From what Allie could tell, the man was taking it all with the patience of a saint. She studied him from behind.

He wasn't dressed like a local. Guys in Linville Springs, Wyoming, rarely wore outfits that made them look like extras in grade-C African safari movies. He was in desert khaki from head to toe. Short-sleeve shirt, tan trousers with a bunch of pockets. Short-topped, desert-style boots, rather than the more familiar cowboy ones. His hat, also not a cowboy-style, more like an Australian outbacker's, was crushed to damp shapelessness in his kid's hands. He had dark blond hair, slightly wavy and just long enough to curl over the collar of his shirt. It looked styled, not just cut. Like the man was maintaining an image of some kind. Odd. And interesting.

Allie couldn't be certain, since she was behind him, but something about the way he carried himself made her think he was probably handsome. There was a confidence and pride in his carriage that was at serious odds with his undignified circumstances.

Or maybe it was the way the women shoppers coming the other way all gave him a double take. At first, she thought the reason for their stares was the screaming kid.

Now, she decided it might be the result of a combination of factors, including masculine good looks.

She smiled again as she watched him walk. Some woman was sure lucky to have a husband like that. Not only did he take the kid to the store, but he had a good body and excellent moves. Yeah, some women were lucky in the husband game, she guessed.

Not that it should matter to her. Once in the husband game as a loser, she was out of it for all time. She had sense enough now to know what she was good at and what she wasn't. As a mom, she was apparently okay. The twins were growing up all right. As a wife...well, she'd never had much of a chance with that. Nor was she interested in taking a chance again.

Allie reached for a box of cereal and had put it in her cart before she remembered she needed no cold cereal this week. Without the twin food-vacuums, she could make a box last for a month. Maybe more. Breakfast was not exactly a big meal for her. She'd spent too many years eating it on the run after making certain the children had plenty and were set for daycare or school.

So the cereal wasn't necessary. Bread was. She wouldn't be eating lunch out with clients seeking her financial advice much during the summer months. Soup and a sandwich in front of the computer was her standard fare when she ate at home in her office. She started to move around the man and his child to get to the bread aisle. The baby reached out and grabbed her sleeve. "Mmmaaamma!" she/he screamed.

Allie stopped. The kid had an iron grip on her shirt, and if Allie kept on moving, she was liable to pull the poor little thing right out of the cart. She didn't look at the father, who had also stopped, but at the baby, whose face was suddenly sunny and smiley. "Momma," the child cooed.

The other tiny hand grasped her arm, pinching her skin. "Momma!"

Unable to resist, Allie slid her hands under the baby's arms. She didn't lift, though, and the little one frowned. "No, honey," Allie said. "I'm not your momma." She smiled and the child stopped frowning and grinned happily. The small hands released her sleeve. They reached for her embrace. Allie turned a rueful look and an apologetic smile on the father. He probably wouldn't appreciate a stranger touching his child. "Sorry, I…" she began to say, pulling away from the baby. Then the words faded.

The man looked as if he was in the grip of some strong, deep emotion. *Sorrow,* it was sorrow, she realized with a sudden sick feeling that startled her. He cleared his throat and lifted the child in his arms. He handled his burden carefully, but awkwardly. The baby instantly started screaming again.

"No need to apologize," he said, his voice loud enough for her to hear its huskiness over the shrieking. Huskiness and an odd sort of accent. One Allie couldn't place. "She does that with every woman who looks the least bit like her mother did. You've got the same length blond hair, and she's partial to blondes." He patted the little head that was now buried in his shoulder. "Drove me crazy at first. But I'm used to it, now." He kissed the child's fair hair and spoke soothingly to her.

Allie swallowed. She'd apparently stumbled onto a tragedy that was a mirror image of her own. Past tense. The little girl's mother, this man's wife, was dead. Tears stung Allie's eyes. "Would you mind if I did hold her?" she asked, hoping she wasn't intruding on his grief. "Maybe she'd calm down."

The man handed the child over, relief transforming his features. "Thanks," he said. "At this point, I'm willing to try anything. This is our first big grocery outing together.

We've been getting along so well, I didn't expect her to act up. She's tolerated the quick trips with no problem, so I figured she'd be fine on a longer one. Maybe a little fussy, but I can deal with that. Never thought it would be like this.''

Allie cuddled the baby, who immediately wrapped her arms tightly around Allie's neck. Memory flooded her at the sensation. It had been like that with Sally and Sam. So much need for love! So much she wanted to give... Only, she'd never been able to hold one without the other clamoring for equal attention. She remembered the constant state of exhaustion she had lived in while they were small. She'd had no one to help her. Still, it had been so wonderful to be so needed. She shut her eyes, not caring if the man saw the tears she felt falling down her cheeks.

"I know something of how you must feel," she said. "I lost my husband even before my kids were born."

Her words clearly took him by surprise, and he didn't seem to know how to respond. He smiled, frowned, then smiled again. Sympathy shone in his brown eyes, and the smile was a sad one. "I can't quite trade on your pain, ma'am," he said. "I didn't lose a wife, you see." He touched the baby's hair. "I lost my sister. Laurel's my niece."

"Oh?" Allie felt something stirring in her mind. A vague memory. Some bit of knowledge hovered just out of view.

"Her mother was my sister," the man repeated. "My twin, actually, but now it's just the kid and I. We'll make it, though, won't we, Laurel?"

Laurel turned around in Allie's arms and reached for her uncle. He took her, hugged her for a second, then placed her back in the cart. "Thanks," he said. "I think she's got the crying out of her system now," he added. "I'd better get going while she's in a good mood."

"Good luck," Allie said. Laurel stared up at her, tiny

chin quivering. But she didn't cry as her uncle pushed the cart away, leaving Allie standing alone.

She took a deep breath. Only now did it register on her that the man was, indeed, good-looking. Maybe not exactly classically handsome, but definitely interesting. Square chin, firm jawline, smooth tanned skin. Warm brown eyes. Character lines etched lightly in that skin... Odd that she'd noticed all that. She had been so absorbed in emotions, she hadn't even tried to get his name. She knew something about this man, however, she was sure. But she just couldn't remember...

"I see you met our local celebrity, Allie."

The voice startled her. But she recovered her composure almost immediately. June Watson had brought the front of her shopping cart within inches of Allie's heels, and Allie hadn't heard a thing until the woman spoke. "Celebrity?" Allie asked, turning and looking at June.

"Uh-huh." June nodded, waiting. She wasn't a fat woman exactly, but she had a hefty look about her that made her seem oversized. Long ago, Allie decided that came from all the gossip June absorbed. It bloated her like a balloon. She devoured it like candy.

But didn't everyone need a bit of candy, now and then?

"All right, June," she said. "You've got me. I haven't a clue who he is."

June giggled. Her painted-on black eyebrows rose a good inch. She eased closer, lowering her voice. "Not a clue? Well, let me fill you in on..." Her slide into informational mode was cut off by a crash and a yell, followed by a bawl. It was a series of sounds that Allie recognized only too well.

"Whoever he is," she said, "it sounds like he's in trouble. I'll be right back," she added. June seemed rooted to the spot, her mouth forming an O.

The scene that met Allie's gaze when she rounded the

corner of the next aisle was no surprise. How many times had she been the one standing guiltily next to a pile of cans or cartons that one or both kids had managed to pull down. Unfortunately for Laurel's uncle, the child had gone for the big-time in grocery disaster. The display she had destroyed was made—*had been made*—of glass jars. Jelly jars.

Laurel's uncle's hat lay in the middle of the glass and goo. The man was staring at the floor, apparently unable to believe what had just happened.

Allie walked up to him and touched his arm. "Don't get upset," she said, when he looked at her. "It happens all the time. Did to me, anyway."

He stared at her now. "I...I just turned away for a second. How could she...?" Behind him, Laurel cooed and giggled. She had jelly smeared on one cheek. "I...I let her have a little taste of the jelly I was buying," he said. "She liked it. I guess she wanted more."

"I guess so." Out of the corner of her eye, Allie saw the store manager approaching. "Look, let me take her while you settle this with Tim."

"Tim?" The man ran his hand over his hair, leaving a smear of jelly in the blond strands. Laurel whooped with laughter.

"Tim Swenson's the store manager," Allie said, lifting the child from the cart. Laurel wrapped her arms tightly around Allie. She felt stickiness on the back of her neck. Laurel wiggled, jamming her knees into Allie's midsection. She gasped and shifted the child's position. "Don't worry," she added. "He's a reasonable guy."

Laurel's uncle looked at her. "You," he said, "are either crazy or a saint, coming to my rescue like this. Thanks, from the bottom of my heart, friend." He smiled and really looked at her, and she realized he was actually seeing her for the first time.

And she was really seeing him. He was not just handsome; he was gorgeous! The smile did it. The gaze that he directed right into her eyes transformed him. For a fraction of a second, she felt a little dizzy.

"Um, excuse me." Tim circled the mess on the floor. "Um, hi, Allie. This guy a friend of yours?"

"It was an accident," Allie said, recovering herself. "Tim, you know you shouldn't put those breakable displays where kids can get their hands on them." Laurel cooed and slapped her little hands on Allie's shoulder, bouncing her knees at the same time. The fabric of her blouse stuck to the child's palms for a second.

"I know." Tim eyed the mess ruefully. "We've got a new display person. He thinks he's some kind of artist."

"I'll pay for this," Laurel's uncle said, reaching for his wallet. "It was my fault for not watching Laurel close enough." He opened the wallet. "How much?"

Allie nearly gasped aloud. He had a wad of bills in his hand, and from the denominations she could see, it was close to a thousand dollars. For grocery shopping? What would he do if he were really on a spending spree?

Tim's brown eyebrows jumped up into his receding hair line. "Put your money away, mister," he said, dropping his voice and looking around to see if anyone else had seen the wad of bills.

"But...?" The man seemed confused.

"I don't want you to pay for the jelly," Tim said. "I was just making sure no one was hurt."

Allie watched the money disappear. The man had a puzzled look on his face. "I ruined all that stuff, and you won't take payment?" he asked, glancing over at her and the baby, then back to Tim. "Why?"

Tim looked uncomfortable. "Store policy. The display was set up wrong."

"But I should have kept my kid under closer control."

"You don't know how," Allie said, unable to keep from

blurting out the unvarnished truth. "The two of you were a disaster looking for a place to happen. I could have predicted this. It's just lucky she wasn't hurt."

The man said nothing. He just looked at her. The child said, "Momma," again and gave her a hug. Then she turned and reached for her uncle. "Daddy!" she cried out, smiling.

He took her from Allie. "Look," he said, his tone suddenly chilly. "Thanks to you both, but I can manage on my own. I don't need help, and I don't need my mistakes excused. They're mine, and I'm quite aware of them without having them pointed out to me."

He fumbled in his pocket and pulled out two wadded bills. Pressing them into Tim's hand, he said, "Take this for the jelly and as a down payment for any other disasters we may cause in the future. Don't argue."

He handed Allie another bill. When she started to protest, he said, "This is for dry-cleaning your clothes. Please, let me do this." He gave her a look that ranged somewhere between angry, proud and sorrowful. Then he hefted Laurel onto his lean hip, bent over to pick up his hat from the jelly puddle and maneuvered his cart down the aisle.

No way, Allie thought, could she refuse the money. It would be a direct attack on his dignity. Bad enough she'd shot her mouth off and criticized him. "Okay," she said, mostly to herself, but including Tim. "I can take a hint. He's on his own. I'll stick to my business and keep out of his." She brushed at the back of her blouse. Jelly stains in the form of little handprints dotted the area of her shoulders. "I'm too busy for this, anyway. Now, I've got to run home and change clothes."

Tim laughed, sounding nervous and self-conscious. "I guess you will," he said. "It looks like the kid got a good half jar of jelly on you."

Allie tried to look at her back. "Reminds me of old

times," she said. "This blouse is cotton. I don't need to have it dry-cleaned, but I'll have to get some strong stain remover for the wash. It's been a long while since I needed that. At least for my own clothes."

Tim looked down at the money in his hand. "Go ahead and pick up whatever you need. It's on the house." He showed her the hundred dollar bill the stranger had given him.

Allie looked at her bill and gasped, horrified that she, too, held a "century" in her hand. She'd have to figure out some way to give it back, she decided. This was too much money! "I guess it is. You ought to give him grocery credit for at least one of those bills. He didn't break two hundred dollars worth of jelly, for goodness sake."

"I should. But I'm kind of afraid to. You know, a guy like that. You don't want to go around offending him. Think I'll give the money to the Boy Scouts or something. Donate it in his sister's name or something. Maybe the Girl Scouts…"

"A guy like what? You know who he is?" Allie felt her curiosity growing. Tim seemed somewhat intimidated by the man. Why? Ordinarily, he'd have joked about the mess. "June indicated he was a celebrity, but I don't recognize him."

"That's because you never buy the gossip tabloids at the checkout counter."

"He's not a movie star, is he?" She was fairly sure of that. Allie went to the movies regularly. It was one way of bringing adventure and romance into her life without any of the risks. Plunk a few dollars down and escape from reality for a while. Her reality. A reality that was simple and clean, uncluttered with dreams like those on the silver screen.

"Nope. He's not an actor. Just one of those guys who go to places nobody in their right mind would think of going.'' Tim managed to grin and look macho and sheepish at the same time, seemingly proud to be of the same sex as the stranger. ''You know, tough guys. Actual, not pretend. Real-life stuff. Risks his life for a living. He's some kind of professional adventurer.''

Allie thought of the emotion he'd shown when he'd mentioned his twin sister and the tender way he had handled his niece. Some tough guy, all right. ''Oh,'' she said.

''He was the guy who pulled off the rescue of that entire movie company a year or so ago. Remember, the bunch of actors and folks that got kidnapped down in South America?''

''No.''

''Well, it made the news, let me tell you. The bigwigs at the studio hired him to rescue their people, 'cause the government wouldn't or couldn't. He found 'em all in the middle of the jungle and saved every single person. Since then, he's been a real celebrity out in Hollywood. He's dated a lot of that flashy movie star kind of woman,'' Tim explained. ''That's how come he's been in the tabloids. I guess you don't even look at them when you're waiting in the checkout line.'' He signaled for a boy with a mop, a bucket and metal dustpan to start cleaning up the jelly mess. ''Most folks do,'' he added.

Allie had no reply for that. She usually spent her time in the line figuring out how her clients could best invest their dollars or, lately, how her own political ambitions could be fulfilled, not reading headlines about Elvis sightings or aliens. But, then, she reasoned, it took all kinds of people to keep a grocery store in business.

''How's your campaign going?'' Tim asked, changing the subject. ''If you want to put some posters up here, you know you're welcome to do it. Come in and campaign some, talk to folks if you want, too. A lot of us are real happy you're taking on the big politicos. You know that.

My wife thinks you're the next best thing to sliced bread, on account of your taking on women's issues specially. She's helped me understand how it'll help all of us for you to be down in Cheyenne next year.''

"Thanks. I'm glad to hear that. Campaigning is new for me, so I'm not at all sure how I stand right now." Allie felt grateful the topic had turned back to something she was familiar with.

"But I guess it's going all right," she continued. "Actually, I've got to go back to my office and call my campaign manager. I had a message that he needed to speak to me. So, I'd better get cracking. Thanks for the offer. I'll probably take you up on it, come fall. At least I know enough to realize I'll have to hit it hard closer to election time."

Tim nodded. "Remember, though. I mean it," he said. He was watching the cleanup process with a careful eye. Allie left him, thinking she really ought to hurry on and not give in to her natural tendency to visit with folks. Even handsome, adventurous, mysterious strange folks...

Speaking of which...

June appeared around the corner, her shopping cart filled to the brim. When she saw Allie, her expression turned gleeful. Clearly, she wanted to continue their conversation and find out what had happened with the celebrity and the jelly jars. She also would undoubtedly be more than willing to fill in any gaps in Allie's knowledge file about that particular celebrity. Was it worth it?

No. Allie decided that satisfying her curiosity was not worth the time she would have to spend listening to everything else June had to offer. It could go on for a good while. A while she couldn't afford today.

So, she waved, smiled brightly, then turned tail and ran for the check-out line. Laurel's uncle had stirred her interest, but not all that much. Besides, she'd rubbed him the wrong way with her comments about his inability to care for the little girl. She felt badly about that. She should have known better. As she set her purchases up on the counter at the express lane, she thought back.

How well she remembered resenting even well-meaning criticism. Hadn't she reacted in exactly the same way as Laurel's uncle to helpful comments from friends years ago? You had to respect a person's privacy in grief, *and* their right to make their own mistakes, she believed.

When she got out to the parking lot with the two small bags of groceries, however, she saw he was still there and in trouble. Or rather, in the middle of a new muddle.

Laurel was yelling at the top of her lungs again, and Allie didn't much blame her. He had her strapped into a strange wooden contraption in the back seat of a truly battered old Jeep. Roll bar, but no top. Laurel looked safe enough—the makeshift car seat was likely to withstand an accident better than the vehicle, but the child was not happy about it. Allie knew she ought to pass by without saying a word, but her car was parked right next to his. She couldn't avoid him if she tried.

The man looked up as she came near. "I know what you're thinking about this," he said, his tone sour. "This is just a temporary thing. I'm going to get her a regular car seat," he explained, his tone and expression defensive. "I know her parents had one, but I can't find it."

Allie eyed Laurel. "She looks safe."

"Safe, but not happy."

"Well, isn't that the way it is sometimes for all of us?" Allie tried to sound unconcerned, but the child's cries were tugging hard at her. "Sooner she learns that, the better, isn't it?"

He seemed to be considering that wisdom for a moment. "I'm sorry I snapped at you in there," he said, not looking at her. "I had no right to do that." He patted Laurel's head.

She was no longer wailing, but was sobbing softly. "You were just trying to help," he added. "God knows I probably looked like I needed it."

He sounded contrite, unhappy and at a real loss. Allie thought about it all for less than a second. "Get in your Jeep and follow me," she said, setting her groceries on the back seat of her car. She slid onto the driver's seat. "What's your name? I can't go on calling you 'Laurel's uncle,' now can I?"

"Huh?"

She shut the door and leaned out the open window. "I'm going to take you to a store for kiddie gear. If you don't have a decent car seat, it's a good bet you're missing some other things, as well. Come on. We can use some of the hundred you shoved at me for dry cleaning. It was far too much."

"Keep the money, please. I have enough of that. And I don't really need your help. I've made do." He looked angry and defensive again. "Laurel and I, we've gotten by."

"I see." Allie tapped her fingers on the car door. "And is she taking John Wayne lessons, too? I mean, a girl can't be too tough these days, ya know," she added, in exaggerated imitation of the classic style.

He looked even angrier for a moment. Then, he laughed. "Okay," he said, extending his hand to her. "I should accept your offer. I will admit I need some advice. I don't even know where there's a store that carries the kind of stuff she needs. My name's Matt. Matt Glass."

Allie shook his hand. His name meant nothing to her, not even coupled with the information Tim had provided. So why, she wondered, were little bells of recognition still going off in her head? Why did he trigger some mental path that wouldn't quite connect? "And I'm Allison Ford," she said. His handshake was gentle, but the skin on his palm was so hard, it was like touching warm wood. Warm oak with a kind of electric current running through it...

"Hi, Allison." He smiled, and she saw a glimmer of interest in his eyes. Then Laurel announced her displeasure by crying again. Whimpering tiredly, she squirmed in her seat. "Um," he said, releasing Allie's hand and turning back to the baby. "Maybe I'd better take a rain check. She's really cranky this afternoon."

"When does she nap?"

"Nap?" He looked back at Allie, his expression blank. "Oh, I don't know. Whenever. She usually just falls asleep wherever she is while I..."

"You don't have her on a schedule?"

"No." He looked worried. "I didn't know I was supposed to."

"First helpful hint of the day—schedules keep things from getting out of hand." She started her car. "Trust me, I know." She glanced at him and saw from his face that he was still doubtful. "Come on, I'm not trying to butt in. I'm just trying to help."

He stuck his hands in his pockets and regarded her. "Why? Why would you want to help me? I'm a complete stranger to you, aren't I?"

"Sort of."

He frowned.

"I've been informed by a reliable source that you've shown up on the front pages of the supermarket tabloids, but aside from that, I don't know you from the next stranger. As to why I want to help? I actually have no idea. Maybe it's just the way I was raised. Maybe I feel an affinity for your situation. Maybe, I..."

"Maybe you could just tell me where the store is," he said, his expression remote again. "If I can find it, I can get what I need." He paused. Then added, "I'm sure you have other things to do."

"As a matter of fact, I do." She set her hands on the wheel and remembered Ned's call. She needed to get in touch with her campaign manager soon. So, best to just give this man directions and let him go on his way. "The place to start is at the Target store up in the mall." She pointed up the hill toward the one big shopping mall Linville Springs had to offer. The East Mountain Mall complex sprawled over the top of a bluff overlooking the Safeway parking lot and much of the city below. "Go now before it gets crowded with afternoon shoppers. You won't want to stand in the line with her so tired and crabby."

Matt Glass squinted against the late-morning sun and looked up the hill. "I honestly never even noticed that place," he said, his tone bewildered. He rubbed his face. "What the hell kind of fog have I been in, anyway?" he asked, speaking to himself, not to her.

Allie said nothing. She knew exactly what he was talking about. It was the fog of grief and disbelief that had enveloped him. She knew it only too well.

Laurel, who had been dozing, suddenly came awake with a yowl. "Mmmaaamma!" she cried. "Daaaddyyyy."

Matt turned away from Allie and reached to comfort his niece. "Hush, honey," he said, softly. "I'm right here. We're going home now." He looked back over his shoulder. "Thanks for the information, Allison," he said. "I'll get to it when I can."

"Okay. Glad to help." She let off the brake and eased out of the parking place. He might be in over his head, but he really didn't want help, she decided. Whoever he was, he was used to doing things by himself. She could relate to that and respect it in someone else.

Besides, if she gave up the time to go shopping with an attractive, appealing stranger, she might as well hang up her political hat. Time was more valuable than money to her right now. She had to be selfish these days if she was going to succeed.

Hadn't she been told that a time or two?

Yeah, she had been. So, do it! she scolded herself. She drove away without looking back.

MATT GLASS SAT in the driver's seat of his Jeep and watched the woman's car as it disappeared up the hill. Why had he been so brusque with her? She had only been trying to help. He looked at Laurel who was asleep again. The baby's skin was sweaty. That wasn't good. He was an idiot to turn away from an honest, concerned offer. He could sure use a woman who knew about kids right now…

Besides, she was the prettiest woman he'd seen in this town and she wasn't married. *Forget it.* He smiled at himself, wryly. Old habits died hard. *Get it out of your head, Glass.* He was a family man, a father now, in fact if not in name. A man with responsibilities and an obligation to set a good example to a small girl. It wouldn't do to go chasing after a strange, though attractive woman as he would have in the past. No, indeed.

His tomcatting days were over. He set the Jeep in gear and checked Laurel once more before pulling out of the lot. She was still sound asleep. Innocent as a lamb, with jelly smeared all over her hands and sweaty face. Matt felt a rush of that strange emotion he'd come to recognize as parental love for this little bit of humanity.

What a surprise, he thought, heading toward home. He, Matt Glass, of all people. Turning down time with a beautiful woman. Driving home alone with a little kid. Still grieving about his dead sister, for sure. Still angry about the accident that had claimed her life. But somehow happier than he'd been in a long time… Confused as all hell, but happy! Maybe even…content?

What a surprise…

CHAPTER TWO

FROM THE GARAGE Allie pushed open the kitchen door with her hip, grocery bags in her arms. Immediately, Fred, her little poodle came dashing to greet her. Behind Fred wandered Tom, Dick and Harry, the cats. Their sedate pace belied the fact that they were immensely relieved as usual that she was back to referee their ongoing conflict with Fred. She set the bags down on the table and knelt to administer love.

Fred rolled over to have her tummy scratched. The cats strolled by, one at a time, for an ear rub. Allie cooed and greeted. All were female, despite their names. And, in typical cat style, once assured of her return and continued affection, they left her alone. Not so Fred, who remained to see what kind of goodies were in the sacks.

"Nothing for you today, girl," Allie said. "You have plenty of biscuits. I know, because I checked. I'll take you for a walk later, and we can do a deal for a treat if you do your duty. Understand?"

Fred did. She wagged her tail and went over to lie down in a patch of sunlight.

Allie unloaded the food, put it away and went downstairs to the laundry room. She stripped off the sticky, dirty blouse and stuck it in the machine. Sorting through a pile of clean clothes, she found an old, comfortable T-shirt and slipped it on. Then, moving past the washer and dryer, she entered the section of the utility room that was her private, personal space...

And her office. Her *real* office.

The office where she greeted and dealt with her financial planning clients was upstairs in a small converted bedroom. But the heavy-duty work, she did down here, in the depths of her home where there was no window, no view, no distraction to take her mind away from the task at hand. She flicked on the overhead lights and went to her desk.

ALLISON FORD FOR HOUSE. The poster lay on a pile of papers, and her own face smiled up at her from the black-and-white photograph topping the statement. Allie touched it and smiled back at herself. She was probably out of her mind to try running for the legislature, but she would be as crazy not to, she had decided. The traditional political parties and mostly male candidates weren't helping very much with issues that concerned her friends and clients. It was time for an independent like herself to make an impact. There were nine legislative slots to fill this election from her county, and she intended to get one of them. She had the fire, the intense desire to run, win and serve, and the twins were old enough to deal with her being gone from home some of the time. She picked up the poster and set it aside. Time to work.

She dialed her manager's office number, curious to know what it was that Ned thought was so important. He wasn't in, so she left her name on his answering machine. That was strange, she thought. This was the second time today she'd tried to reach him. He'd sounded extremely anxious early this morning when she had found a message from him on her own machine. Since she routinely rose at sunrise and jogged a few blocks, anyone calling before seven in the morning had to talk to the mechanical secretary.

She sorted mail, noting with some satisfaction that she was already receiving letters of encouragement. Money had trickled in, as well. Not much, but enough to give her hope. Even a small campaign these days was a great expense, if you had to do it out-of-pocket. If she didn't get more support, though, she would be in some trouble.

Her personal budget was run on a tightrope at all times, especially as the twins got older and needed more things. They ate as if there was never going to be another bite of food for them, and they outgrew their clothes at an alarming rate. She could take the risk of dipping into the special funds she had set aside for the kids' education and for emergencies, but she was extremely reluctant to do that. Only as a last resort, she had promised herself when she decided to run.

But it was, after all, still early. Few folks thought about the November elections in June. Particularly in an election year when there wasn't a presidential race. The crunch would start in August, increase in September, reach a fever pitch in October...

And all be over, one way or another, in November.

Her computer was already turned on—she had been at work earlier that day, so she took a few minutes to log in the checks and file them in an envelope to give to Ned for her campaign fund. Meticulous record-keeping was a deeply ingrained habit that came from having to survive a financial disaster ten years earlier. She turned her thoughts away from that and ran a budget program. Her own, this time.

It wasn't comforting. If she didn't get more support for her campaign soon, she was going to have to dip into personal funds beyond the point where she felt safe. Allie frowned and pushed back from the desk. She needed some help and advice. There must be something she could do to generate contributions now. Ned should be calling her back. Maybe, he had some good news. She could use it.

She got up and went upstairs, forcing herself to remain calm. Her palms were sweaty and her stomach churned— her usual response to money problems. She couldn't help her reaction, but she could control it. "Hey, Fred," she called. "Want to take a walk?" The little gray dog came scampering, wiggling with joy at the prospect.

The long walk calmed her. Fred did her business dutifully, then spent the rest of the excursion exploring the delights of nature along the path they took. The day wasn't too hot, though the sun was almost uncomfortably warm on Allie's skin. Real summer heat wouldn't set in until later in the month. Even then, it would cool off pleasantly at night. Wyoming's high desert climate was harsh during the winter months, but lovely most of the summer. She felt much better when they returned home.

Until she played back her telephone messages.

MATT GLASS SAT backward in the kitchen chair while he fed Laurel dinner that evening. Or, rather, while he supervised thirty minutes of a food fight that outdid any slapstick comedy version of that sport. It was dramatic and extremely messy. Laurel loved it. Actually, he had come to the point where he was sort of enjoying it himself.

Providing he remembered to wear the proper armor—old sweats and a shower cap. Otherwise, he ended up having to bathe himself three times a days as well as rinse off the little angel. This evening, however, the angel was relatively neat.

"Maybe," Matt commented as he scraped some mashed sweet potatoes off the edge of the high chair, "you got it all out of your system in the store. Trashing the jelly was certainly enough accomplishment for one day, babe."

"Jelly!" crowed Laurel. "Mmmaaamma."

Matt didn't reply. Bad enough Laurel had made a solid connection between that pretty blond woman and her own mother. He knew it would make matters worse if he tried to correct the child. He took the washcloth and wiped her face gently.

"Mmmaaamma," Laurel repeated, her tiny eyebrows drawing together.

Matt forced himself to smile. "Okay. Eat your peas, sweetheart. All gone. Then, you get a cookie. Okay?"

His niece looked at him. He could almost see the little wheels turning behind her blue eyes. "No peas," she stated, scowling. "Cookie!"

He sighed, picked up a spoon and started shoveling. The food fight became a war. There had to be an easier way, he thought. Just had to be! Women wouldn't have done this for millennia without having figured out an easier way. Would they? Too bad he didn't know an experienced one he could ask.

He sighed again, wearily. He'd forged rivers, crossed deserts and climbed mountains that were less of a challenge than this little person.

Both Matt Glass and Laurel Essex were sound asleep before the sun was fully gone from the Wyoming sky that evening. It was a toss-up as to which one of them was more tired.

"I CAN'T BELIEVE he did this to me!" Allie wailed. She ignored her mug of beer and put her head down on her arms, which rested on the dark wood table. "Cannot believe it."

They sat and drank their beers silently for a while. The bar was a neighborhood watering hole, quiet and clean. Dark enough for privacy and conversation. When Allie had heard on her answering machine tape that her manager had not only deserted her, but had actually gone over to her primary rival, Rita Morely, she had called M.J. who had suggested she needed more than a sympathetic ear to listen to her troubles. She needed an attitude adjustment, he advised, and had invited her to meet him at Shady's Spot.

"Believe it, darlin'." Her cousin, M. J. Nichols, patted

her hand consolingly and lifted his own mug. He took a hearty drink. "The man's a snake. To desert you like that. Showed his true colors. He always was Rita's man, or at least a regular party man. You're better off without him since you're determined to run as an independent."

"Maybe so." Allie sat up. "But with Ned's departure comes a host of trouble, and you know it or you wouldn't have suggested I go out drinking with you, you sweet-talking jerk! You want me to forget my problems for a while, don't you."

"Don't insult me, cousin." M.J. smiled. The expression affected all the muscles in his round, pleasantly handsome face. He ran a hand over his thinning, dark hair. "I'm one of the few counselors you have you can really trust."

"Hell with you," she replied, but with a bit more cheer in her tone. "So, what's your counsel, Counselor?"

M.J. sobered. "You do have a problem, Allie. I won't fool around with that. Most candidates have thrown their hats in the ring and acquired their managers by now, even if they haven't been loud about it. There aren't too many folks left out who have any experience."

"And Ned went over to the enemy camp." She groaned again. "What in the world was wrong with me that he did that? Is Rita such a sure winner? Should I bow out now before I get in debt up to my eyeballs."

M.J. regarded her. She was his only relative here in Linville Springs, and they were close as brother and sister. They had shared confidences for years. Helped each other through good times and bad. But tonight he didn't know what to say. "I'd take your show on myself—" he began.

"No. We've been over this before, M.J. You're a trial lawyer, not a PR man. I've got to find someone who knows the political ropes and is willing to work for nothing but future hope. Rita Morely's gonna kill. me, otherwise. I'm not a good sport about this. I'll mind losing terribly, but I will *hate* to lose by a wide margin.''

"Don't talk of losing. Rita's got the brains of a ground squirrel. The county needs you in the House, not her. She may have the party backing, but she's not the person we need. She's just doing it because it's traditional for a Morely to be in public office.''

"She could run for dogcatcher.''

"Be nice, Allie.''

Allie pulled a face and then changed the subject. "I ran into an interesting guy today,'' she said, changing the subject. "At the grocery store. He was not your average homeparent type. And he was very good-looking.'' She paused, wondering if she should go on and recite the interesting gossip she'd heard about the stranger. But M.J. wasn't paying much attention to her chatter. He was apparently thinking about her problem.

"Have you thought about Josh?'' he asked, changing the subject back.

"Josh?'' Allie grinned. "For what?''

"For the job. Josh Henderson isn't the brightest guy in the city, but he's done some serious campaign management in his time. He doesn't need the money, so he might be content to work for the promise of a staff job if you make it big eventually.''

"I considered him first when I started looking. He's done two sheriffs' races in a row and lost them both. I just don't much feel like hitching up with a known loser. It's not good precedent. Besides, he's not likely to want to help an independent, either. He's always worked for a party candidate, hasn't he?''

"You're right. But you might have to modify your standards, you know.'' M.J. moved his beer mug on the table, creating small, wet rings. "There is this guy from California I heard about. A colleague of mine who's dealing with some estate work for him mentioned in passing that he'd had some experience in political campaign management. I guess she said it because she knew I'm related to you. He's supposed to be pretty good."

"He won't want to work for nothing, if he's used to pay. Which he probably is, if he's from there. Anyway, I don't want to hire out-of-state. You know how that goes over in this kind of economic environment. Everybody who hires from outside gets a black mark against their name."

"I said he's *from* California. Apparently, he lives here now. At least the estate is here, as I recall."

"Oh."

"Don't know much else. But it wouldn't hurt to call him and talk."

"I guess not."

M.J. took a napkin and scribbled some notes on it. "Here's his name. And Josh's and a few others. Give 'em all a try, Allie."

"Thanks." She took the napkin and stuck it in her purse. "I really appreciate this. And the beer, too."

"Kids okay?"

"Sure. They love it up at the ranch. I think sometimes I was crazy not to go back. Sticking it out on my own here alone? I should have my head examined."

"Nice words for a woman who's done some serious overcoming. Come on. Is this you talking? The woman who can leap tall financial columns with a single bound? Give up and go home to Mom and Dad?"

"Sometime, M.J., even us superwomen get real darn tired of overcoming." Allie sighed. "How have men managed to do it all these years without cracking up?" She grinned. "Maybe I need a wife."

"Funny. Funny." M.J. drained his beer. "I don't have one, either, and I get along just fine. You sound cheered up enough. And I've got court tomorrow. You going to stay?'' He put down money for the drinks and included a generous tip.

"No,'' she replied. "I think I'll mosey home, as well. Fred will need to go out, anyway.''

"You treat that damn dog like she was a kid.''

"Better than I would a kid. She doesn't have to grow up and face the cold cruel world. Fred and the cats, I can spoil. Sally and Sam, I don't dare. For their sakes.''

M.J. stood up. "You're a wise woman, Al. You'll find a new manager, and you'll win this race. You'll kick Morely's aristocratic behind.'' He gave her a hug. "And someday, I'll be cousin to the governor of the great state of Wyoming.''

"In your dreams, M.J.! In your dreams!''

THE NEXT MORNING, Allie woke up early, jogged, showered, ministered to her pets, ate breakfast and then went downstairs to deal with her main problem.

Her dream.

She had teased M.J. for dreaming about being related to the future governor of the state, but she was dead serious about her own ambitions to try for the state's highest office someday. She did have an agenda, and the governor's office would be the best place to execute that agenda.

Someday. For now, she simply had to get a manager. No way could she continue her business, take care of her kids, run for the legislature *and* manage her own campaign. She was only human. She needed to hire a new manager.

She made phone calls for an hour before she gave up on her own list. All the people she spoke to were sympathetic to her problem, but unwilling to pick up responsibility for her political race. She was a virtual unknown outside the city limits. Although she'd served on the school board for three years and finished a term for an ill member of the city council, that didn't give her the name recognition necessary for a county election to a state office, one former politician told her bluntly. She ought to just stick to running her business and raising her kids, he said. Allie hung up the phone, her face burning with anger, her mind filled with frustration.

So, she called Josh Henderson.

"Well, Mrs. Ford," he said, slowly. "I don't know. I...I'll have to give it some thought, you understand."

"Sure, Josh," she said. "I know this is short notice. I'd counted on Ned to carry me through November, but..."

"Well, Mrs. Ford, you know Ned is interested in his own political life. Moving to Mrs. Morely's campaign does make sense."

"It does not make me think much of his integrity."

"Well, that may be, but..."

"Look, Josh. Why don't you think about my offer and let me know your decision by, say, this evening. I really do need to get things back on track right away."

"That's true." A pause. "All right. I'll think on it and call you tonight."

Allie thanked him and hung up, again. Josh was a nice guy, she thought. Nice and polite. But no intensity. He had money from his family and a degree in geology that he'd used to open a small consulting business. It was rumored he worked only when he absolutely had to. She believed he was intelligent enough, but lazy at heart, and she worried about his potential commitment to her political career. He might help, but he'd never light any fires.

And, she needed a bonfire! Maybe...

She picked up the napkin M.J. had scribbled on the night before. Hard to read his writing, especially the name of that California guy. Glore. Blane. Gla...

Glass. She opened up the telephone directory. Scanning the residential section, she found two numbers with that surname. She called. At one home, no one answered. At the other, the wife did, and she said her husband was an auto mechanic. Not at all interested in politics. Allie hung up and sat back.

Who the heck had M.J. meant?

Then, it hit her.

Matt Glass. Of course! He was the guy from the grocery store. Well, there was one person she knew could supply the necessary information she needed now. She dialed June Watson's number from memory. June would have read those tabloids and would know all!

MATT MANAGED to grab Laurel and the telephone at the same time. She had been on her way to exploring, by way of overturning, a full pitcher of lemonade, and he had barely stopped her agile little hands in time to prevent total disaster. Frustrated in her purpose, she squalled lustily while she dangled from his arm. He bumped his temple with the receiver. "Yeah? What do you want?" he snarled into the mouthpiece.

"Mr. Glass?"

Matt struggled while Laurel wriggled and howled. "Yeah. This is Glass. Listen, speak up, please. I can't hear you." He sat down on the floor, trying to hold and soothe the child and talk at the same time. The voice on the phone was female and softly modulated. Kind of sexy, too.

"I can't imagine why," the voice said, dryly. "Is Laurel okay?" No, not sexy...sarcastic.

"She's fine. Just yelling. Who is this? If this isn't important, mind calling back? I've got kind of a crisis here."

"Okay. This is Allison Ford. We met at Safeway yesterday. Over the jelly jars. I'm in the book. Give me a call back when you can."

"Safeway?" Ah, the grocery store...

"I'm the lady with the jelly on her blouse. I'd like to talk to you about managing a political campaign for me. I

need help. Please call me back. Allison Ford. Okay?'' She
hung up.

Matt stared at the receiver. Yeah, he did remember. She
was a difficult woman to forget. He reached for a pencil
and a notepad and jotted down the name. Allison…Ford.
Like the car. He regarded the name, thinking about what
she had said. Slipping into a reverie was a big mistake.

He allowed Laurel to crawl out of his grasp while he
reflected. Moments later, the pitcher of cold, sweet, sticky
lemonade cascaded down on his head and shoulders. Matt
roared with surprise, then collapsed in helpless laughter.
Laurel, giggling happily, crawled back onto his lap. He
wrapped his wet arms around her. ''I give up,'' he declared.
''Ready for another bath, sweetheart?'' he asked. ''I should
invest in soap futures, I think.''

''Daddy,'' Laurel crooned. And Matt lost his heart for
the hundredth time that crazy day.

ALLIE STOOD at the front door and eyed the doorbell. He'd
called and asked her to come over about thirty minutes ago.
Matt Glass lived in the house that had belonged to Laurel's
parents, Martha and John Essex. It was a mansion, really.
Huge wood-and-stone thing. John Essex had been wildly
successful in the minerals market in Wyoming and when
prices took a nosedive, had invested his money well to
cushion his family against hard times. But that cushion
hadn't saved him and his wife from perishing in a private
plane wreck several months ago.

She remembered it all, now. With June's prompting, it
had all come back to her. She realized why Matt had trig-
gered some memory tingle in her. It wasn't really the man,
it was the child. She remembered hearing of the Essex tragedy and aching for the little one left behind. She knew only
too well what it was like to be alone when you felt lost
and afraid. And she'd been an adult when it had happened

to her... She could only imagine the pain, confusion and suffering that small child was going through!

Well, Laurel Essex wasn't alone, now, clearly. Though to judge from what she'd heard on the phone an hour before, the little girl was living in chaotic conditions. Allie rang the bell.

Matt Glass opened the door almost immediately. "Hi," he said, smiling broadly. "Come on in. Uh, Ms. Ford, right? Glad to see you. Keep it down, if you don't mind. She's asleep, finally. We had a bit of an accident."

"Is she okay?"

"Laurel is indestructible." He shut the big front door. "I can't say the same for myself or the house."

Allie noted his hair. It was damp, as if he'd just got out of the shower. "Keeping you hopping, is she?"

"That's an understatement. Come on in the den. Want some coffee? I keep a pot up on top of the refrigerator. That way, I..."

"Can get it when you need it, but she can't." Allie laughed. "I remember what it was like!"

"And you had two of them." He regarded her with awe. "And you're still walking around sane."

"It can be done." She moved past him into the den. It was a room that matched the general comfortable grandeur of the house. Wood paneling that gleamed softly. Leather upholstery on the chairs and couch. A large oak desk. English hunt prints on the walls. Allie selected a chair and sat. "You just have to know your subject."

"I guess." Matt Glass rubbed the back of his neck and took the other chair. "And I guess I don't know the subject of kiddie care yet." He rubbed his eyes. It was only three in the afternoon, and he was already exhausted.

"But you have had experience running political campaigns."

"Yes. Limited."

Allie studied him. It looked as if he'd been reduced to the last of his wardrobe. One pocket on the wrinkled shirt was torn and a button was missing. The pants looked as if they'd been taken right from the dryer. His feet were bare, and he hadn't shaved.

With the damp hair, the dirty-blond stubble and the old, go-to-hell clothes, he looked far more like the adventurer he was rumored to be than a father-in-training or a political advisor. She looked away and tried to visualize him in a three-piece suit. Running a civilized political campaign…

Impossible.

"I was given your name by a friend," she said, opening a legal pad folder. "This person understood you had managed a few campaigns out in California."

"For friends. The offices were minor ones. County level only. I…I don't pretend to be a professional manager."

"But your people won."

"They did." He rested his ankle on his knee, apparently oblivious of his bare foot. He folded his hands together and placed them against his chin.

And he stared directly at her.

"You're being too modest, Mr. Glass. I checked." Allie looked down at her notes. His gaze was making her a little nervous. "According to my sources, your candidate for sheriff won against an incumbent and in a district where her political party was seriously on the outs. Your…"

"What sources?" He had steepled his two index fingers together and was covering his lips with them. Body language of caution.

"Will you work for me?"

"No. I can't."

"Then, I can't tell you who told me." She stood up. "I must say, I'm not really surprised at your refusal. You're new here. You have a handful with Laurel, and…"

"Sit down." He pointed to the chair with both fingers still steepled. "Please."

Allie sat.

"You're a very attractive woman, Ms. Ford," he said, relaxing back into his chair. "You're obviously intelligent and quick to make decisions. You'd be a breeze to manage, if you can follow instructions as well as you seem to do everything else."

Allie felt herself blushing. But she said nothing.

"I can't take your job, and I regret it. But I'd do you more harm than good, if I did. As you say, I don't know the lay of the land around here. And I honestly don't know how long Laurel and I will stay. You see…"

"You're leaving?" She felt unaccountably disappointed. "Well, I guess this isn't your home. I suppose you…"

"It's Laurel's home. I have a house and a business in California. I own an adventure-tour company, Glass Attacks, Ltd. Specialty stuff that caters to the kind of vacationer who wants a taste of danger in their recreation. I've delegated work to my staff, of course. I had no idea what I'd find when I came here. How long I'd have to stay. But that's where I live. Laurel will move there with me, when I think she's ready." He lingered over the last words, clearly giving them emphasis for himself as well as for her.

"How is she doing?" Allie leaned forward. "I know she's young, but it must be strange for her to suddenly…I mean…you know…"

"I know." Matt stood up. He walked over to the desk. "She had everything here, and it was taken away in an instant." His fist hit the top of the desk. "An accident! Why?"

"No answers for that."

His shoulders slumped. "No, there's not. You should know, since you lost your husband. Was his death accidental, too?"

Allie hesitated. "I...I don't know."

He turned around. Looked at her. But he didn't ask any questions. "I wish I could help you," was all he said. It could have meant a number of things.

"It's okay. I talked to a local guy before I called you. He's no great shakes, but I think he'll take me on."

"Well, then..." He made a gesture of dismissal with his hands.

She stood up. "Don't get the wrong idea. I didn't come here already knowing I had the job filled."

"I didn't mean..."

She held up a hand. "Josh Henderson isn't my ideal choice. I wanted to hear what you might say. I have. Thanks for your time. Sorry to bother you."

"It's no..."

"I'd better get on back home. Josh said he'd call this evening with his answer. I don't want to miss the call. Good luck, Mr. Glass." She closed her folder and gathered her purse under her arm.

"Thanks, I..." He took a step toward her. "Call me Matt, for goodness sake. Not even my father's called *Mr. Glass.*"

"I'm Allie." She laughed, hearing the sound as nervous and awkward. "'Ms. Ford' makes me sound like a new line of car."

He grinned. "Well, you don't look anything like one."

"Thanks, I think." She felt completely at a loss for something to say. She had to leave. She wanted to stay. And all he was doing was standing there, watching her, not making it any easier for her. "Um, did you get a car seat?" she asked.

"Found hers. It was out in the garage."

"Oh. Good."

"But thanks for telling me about the store. I'll get up there by and by."

She made herself glance at her watch. "I'd better go."

"I'll see you to the door."

"This is a beautiful house," she said as they walked back to the front hall. "I understand your sister's husband built it."

"He did. But I'll try to sell it once Laurel and I move back to California. I feel uncomfortable surrounded by their things. Like I'm still just a guest. Anyway, it's far too big for just two people."

"I suppose it is. If I had that kind of money, I might even consider buying it from you." She paused by the door and smiled at him. "My place is fine for just me, but with the twins growing like weeds, it seems small when they're home. And then, there's the rest of the family."

"Who...?"

"I have a dog and some cats. They're family, too." She reached for the doorknob. "Thanks again, Matt. Good luck with the parenting. See you around." She opened the door and was gone.

Only after the big door closed behind her and he heard the sound of her car moving out of the driveway did Matt realize she had left before he had even gotten around to giving her the coffee he'd promised.

You jerk, he thought. He looked in the direction of Laurel's room. Was this what having a kid did to a guy? Make him lose his mind entirely?

Or was this special? Would he have acted as stupidly, regardless? Because he found Ms. Allison Ford extremely appealing, and he knew he could do absolutely nothing about that. There was no reason for him to seek her out, or for her to get in touch with him, now that he'd rejected her offer of a job. No reason for them to get together and see if his admiration for her might be returned...

Or, was there? Hey, his life wasn't over. He looked around his sister's big house. Right now, his energy might have to be devoted to Laurel's needs but that was no reason he couldn't enjoy himself anymore. Was it? Hell, no! Matt smiled.

Furthermore, she did seem to know about kids. So he had two motives going for him.

CHAPTER THREE

"WE'VE GOT to stop meeting like this. People will begin to talk, Allison Ford."

Allie looked behind her. Her heart did a little leap of pleasure, which surprised her. A smiling Matt Glass, his shopping cart filled with food, and no fussy kid on board, was right on her tail. "Hi, Matt," she said, casually. "Where's Laurel?"

"Home." His smile faded, and he looked glum. "I'm trying out sitter number...let's see. I think this is the tenth or eleventh this week.

"You're kidding?"

"No, I wish I were. Either the sitters are more interested in watching television than my kid, or Laurel takes an instant dislike to them, or they want...something more..." He looked extremely uncomfortable for a moment. Then, "The woman who was taking care of her when my sister died won't come anywhere near us. I think she's superstitious. It's like we have a curse on us or something. You don't happen to know anyone who cleans houses, do you? A reliable, steady kind of woman. Someone I can trust will behave herself and do a decent job."

Allie looked at him for a moment. He was asking honestly for help. "Come on out of the line of traffic," she said, pulling her cart to the side. "I think I understand your problem."

"You do?" He pulled over next to her, rested his forearms on the cart and regarded her with an expression of hope on his face. He was dressed neatly today. Almost in a normal Linville Saturday fashion with a navy blue polo shirt and tan slacks. Jeans would have been more the local style, but the pants were acceptable. Only the sandals were unusual. They looked handmade. Foreign... Exotic...

"I do," she said. "You're the nearest thing to a celebrity this town has seen for a while. Just how have you gone about getting help?"

"Well. I advertised in the paper..."

"And?"

"The results have been less than satisfactory."

Allie smiled. She could just imagine. Most of the job applicants had probably come on to him, rather than shown interest in his kid or his house. "What you need," she said, "is personal reference. You need to have people you trust recommend a sitter or a housekeeper they trust. Ones they know. Advertising is the last resort around here. Word-of-mouth is the way to go. People believe one another, here."

"Oh."

He looked forlorn and confused. Impulsively, she reached up and patted his cheek. "I'll see what I can do, okay, Laurel's uncle?" She started to move away. "I'll give you a call, if I think of someone."

"Wait." His hand settled on her arm. She felt warmth and reserved power in his grasp. Exciting warmth and strength... "Are you busy now?" he asked.

"I'm shopping, Matt."

"I mean after. How about lunch somewhere?" He grinned somewhat sheepishly. "I think I owe you at least a cup of coffee. The other day, I let you get out of the house without any. And I'd made the offer. Not very polite of me. Let me make it up to you."

Allie considered. This was a social move. Nothing more, nothing less. He didn't owe her a cup of coffee or anything else, for that matter. He wanted her company.

Hmm.

But...

"I can't," she said, feeling regret. "Josh Henderson is coming over this afternoon for some serious campaign battle strategy. I've already lost time I can't afford."

"So, your friend did take the job."

"He's not exactly a friend." They both wheeled out into the aisle and continued down the row while they talked. "But I've sort of known him a long time. I guess you'd have to call us acquaintances, rather than friends. We've both lived here a while, and it's a small town, really, so you know folks. And, yes, he did take the job."

"I'm glad. For you."

"Thanks. I'd better get back to my shopping."

"Me, too." He wheeled out behind her.

They didn't speak after that. Too many other people around.

But Allie felt him right behind her. Felt him watching her. Felt an unaccustomed warmth on her face... An odd set of sensations... She was rarely this self-conscious.

When she was finished shopping, she said goodbye over her shoulder, and he just smiled at her. Going through the checkout alone was a relief. It wasn't that she was unaccustomed to having a man look at her with interest. It was just that this one surprised her with his attention. She couldn't quite figure him out. Allie was not particularly comfortable with surprises. She'd had one too many bad ones in her adult life.

Out in the parking lot, she got another one. Summer brought out the party spirit in some of the younger, rowdier residents of Linville Springs, and right next to the Safeway was a large, discount liquor store where many stocked up on liquid refreshment. It was a favorite stop for groups on their way out to the big recreational grounds southwest of the city. Not all members of those groups were willing to

wait until they reached the park before sampling the goodies in their beer coolers.

"Heeyyyy, baby! Wanna party?" This from a boy in the
back of a pickup truck. He was one of about half-a-dozen
crammed in the back, and his buddies encouraged him by
whistling and hooting at her.

Allie didn't bother to look. The truck was over by the
liquor store, and the last thing she wanted to do was get
into a verbal fracas with some drunk kids. So she ignored
them. She unlocked the trunk and set the groceries down.

"Heeyyyy. I'm talking to *you*, sweetcheeks!"

A beer can bounced off the roof of her car. Another hit
her on the hip. Allie turned and glared. She could ignore
their yelling but she would not stand for their tossing cans
at her. She singled out the guilty individual by the wide
grin on his young face.

And she almost grinned, herself. He was the teenage son
of one of her clients. She knew him, and that meant he was
doomed. Never, ever, she had always warned her own kids,
fool around in Linville Springs. Someone, somewhere,
somehow will know you and tell on you! Small towns,
small cities are like that.

"Do your momma and daddy know where you are and
what you're doing, Kevin Warren?" she asked. The boy,
red in the face from drinking and sunburn, blanched. His
leering grin faded away entirely. "And does the manager
of the liquor store there know you're way under age?" she
added. The boy turned even grayer, looked close to tears.
He had no reply. But someone else did.

The driver of the truck leaned out the window. He was
older and had a tough, mean face. He wore no shirt, and
his arms were thick with muscles and bronzed with suntan.

"Listen, bitch," he snarled. "Mind your own business,
okay? And if you tell on the kid, you're gonna regret it,
understand me?"

Allie was about to react angrily, when she noted Matt strolling toward the truck. He had on dark glasses, so she couldn't see his expression. In the crook of his left arm, he carried a small grocery bag. His other hand was stuck in his pocket. She hoped he wasn't about to interfere, but it looked as if he was only heading for the liquor store. Maybe he hadn't heard the nasty exchange.

But he could hardly have helped it. Half the parking lot was watching the little drama, she realized, glancing quickly around. Now what was she supposed to do?

Exactly what she ought to do!

"Kevin's not old enough to drink legally," she replied loudly, directing her words to the driver, but really addressing the boy. Kevin had to see that she wouldn't be bullied by his companion with the muscles and the mouth. "He should know that his folks would be really disappointed if they…"

"You want disappointment?" The driver started to open the door of the truck. He grasped a tire iron in one meaty hand. Kevin, obviously frightened and aware he was in deep trouble, leaned over and spoke urgently to him. "Hell, no!" the driver said. "She asked for it, and I'm just the one to give her what she wants…"

"What did the lady ask for?" Matt had come up around the front of the truck while the driver's attention was on Kevin. He still held the groceries under his left arm. His right hand and arm were free. "Seems to me, she was just trying to help." His mouth was smiling. His eyes were hidden behind the dark glasses. The muscles in his neck and shoulders were tense, however. Allie could see that. She doubted the smile was in his eyes. A chill feeling settled over her and froze her in place for the moment. Long enough for Matt to act.

Allie saw the next part in slow motion. The liquor store manager, alert to trouble, had apparently notified the police of impending problems. A squad car slowly entered the parking lot from the east. She saw another one coming in from the southwest entrance. No one else seemed to notice the cops. They were all watching the two men. The driver of the truck looked at Matt, swore and swung open the door, his left fist balled and ready for battle, his right hand holding the tire iron aloft.

He didn't get out of the driver's seat. Matt stepped by the door, dropped his grocery sack and bent down to pick it up. Then, he stood. At the same time, his shoulder slammed into the door, trapping the driver's arms between frame and door. The man howled in rage and pain. The weapon clattered to the pavement. The ugly, metallic sound echoed in the hot summer air.

Matt straightened. Allie saw him remove his sunglasses, stare at the driver and speak. Their faces were inches apart. She couldn't hear the words, but their effect was plain to one and all.

The driver seemed to shrink where he sat. Matt opened the door and released his arms. The man bent over and hugged himself in obvious pain. Matt spoke again. The other man nodded. He didn't look at Matt.

The cops were now parked and getting out of their cars. Allie continued to watch. She recognized at least two of the officers. Matt slid on his glasses, tucked the grocery sack back under his arm and strolled away from the truck. Toward her. He was smiling and ignoring the police.

And they paid no attention to him. They surrounded the pickup, and she saw Kevin break into tears. The other youngsters in the back looked terrified. The driver, still hunched over in the front seat, didn't move until one of the officers helped him out of the vehicle. He stumbled and hid his face in his big hands.

Matt stopped in front of her. "You okay?" he asked, lifting his glasses and looking at her. "You look a bit upset.'' His brown eyes showed absolutely no emotion except mild concern.

"I'm fine.'' She put a hand over her eyes to shade them. Her fingers trembled. "That was real slick,'' she said, trying to sound casual.

"Thank you. I didn't want to make a scene.''

"But you handled a troublemaker before he was able to get started good. I admit I'm impressed.'' She put her hand down. "You've done things like that before.''

Matt just shrugged.

"Why did you do it? You could have been hurt, you know.''

"I didn't see that as much of a likelihood.'' He put his glasses back on. "Believe me, I wouldn't have done anything to provoke real violence. I'm a peace-loving man.''

Allie looked at him and raised one eyebrow. "Right,'' she said, remembering what Tim had told her about his rescuing those film people. Surely, there had to have been some violence associated with such an event. "'All's well that end's well?''' she quoted.

He nodded, ignoring or not noticing her sarcasm. "Is the kid you know liable to get in much trouble?''

"Yes.'' She glanced over at the scene. The cops were taking names, but nothing more. "Not from the police, but his folks will be called and he might as well kiss freedom goodbye. He'll be grounded until he's on social security. They're going to be pretty upset with him.''

"Too bad. He was only acting stupid. The older guy's the one to blame.'' A muscle tightened in the corner of his jaw. "Not only was he leading the kids astray, but he was looking for a fight. If you hadn't come along, he'd have picked on someone else. He was trying to scare you and was enjoying the hell out of it.''

"He succeeded,'' she admitted. "A big, mean guy with a tire iron in his hands has that effect on me. He didn't have to try very hard." She placed her hand on his arm. "Thanks. You saved me some serious embarrassment, at the very least. I owe you."

"Lunch?"

She laughed. "You're persistent, I'll give you that. No, I still can't do lunch. How about dinner?"

Matt looked interested, but before he could answer, one of the policemen came over. She smiled at him. He was a friend who went to the same church she attended. Touching the brim of his hat, the young cop nodded to Allie.

"Hi, Allie," he said. "You know this guy?" He looked at Matt.

"Yes. Walt, this is Mr. Glass. Matt Glass. Matt, Officer Walt Resner. Is there a problem, Walt?"

"Nope. Not unless Mr. Glass wants to make it one. He could press charges. Some folks might say Teddie Baker was out to bash him with that tire iron." He regarded Matt closely.

Matt shook his head. "Didn't seem like that to me. I just passed by, dropped some stuff and accidently hit the door when I stood up. Sorry if I bruised Mr. Baker any."

"Oh, he's bruised, all right," Walt said, clearly having difficulty hiding a grin. "Claims both his arms are broke. They ain't. But I think he's real mad 'cause you made him cry in front of the kids."

"I did?" Matt looked theatrically stunned. "Why, I had no such intention. I just suggested he might try improving his manners. That's all. I didn't mean to scare him."

"Right. Sure, you didn't." Now, Walt did grin. "But old Teddie ain't used to being taken down so quick and clean. Did his pride some serious harm."

"Sorry to hear that."

Walt studied him for a moment. "No, you ain't. No reason to be. Teddie's known for starting trouble. Usually, he manages to finish it before we can get on the scene. I admire what you did, Mr. Glass. As a matter of fact, you probably kept a situation from getting real nasty. But I got to warn you to watch yourself.''

"You mean, he's likely to have trouble from that man?" Allie asked. "Surely, Walt, you aren't criticizing what he did?"

"No. I mean, yes. I ain't criticizing, and yes, I'm warning him. You keep a lookout in your rearview mirror, Mr. Glass. For a while, anyways."

"Thanks." Matt didn't look worried. "I appreciate the advice."

After Walt left, Allie leaned back against her car. Her heart was beating too fast, and she realized for the first time that she had actually been frightened and not simply upset. Matt Glass had saved her from more than mere embarrassment.

"Did it all just hit you?" he asked, his voice soft and soothing. "You look kind of pale."

"Yes. I...I mean, no. I'm really fine. Nothing happened, thanks to you." She started to turn away.

"How about that dinner invitation?"

"Oh. Yes. Um. I'll call you and..."

"No, I'll pick you up about eight. Is that all right?"

"Eight? It's fine." Allie gave him her address.

"Good. I'll see you then." He touched his temple with his finger in a salute. Then, he turned away and sauntered back to his decrepit Jeep.

Allie got into her car and sat for a moment, thinking. While she was no longer overly upset at what had just happened, she was still stirred up inside. Her emotions were whirling. How did she feel about the incident? How did she really feel about the way Matt had handled it? And how did she feel about his taking her place in the confrontation with the driver of the pickup truck?

Because that was what he had done. In the heroic male

tradition, he'd taken her place on the firing line. Easily, naturally. And she hadn't uttered so much as a squeak of protest. Like it or not, she had just been rescued by a man she hardly knew. It would have been silly and ungrateful to have complained, she believed. She thought of the mean look on Teddie's face and the size of his muscles. The tire iron... The smooth, confident way Matt had stepped in and defused the situation...

She ran the rest of her errands with only part of her mind on business and arrived home just as Josh Henderson pulled up in front of her house. She looked at him as he got out of his car—a shiny new model that made Matt Glass's Jeep look like a piece of trash. Handsome and groomed as always, Josh was wearing a suit, even though it was Saturday and the meeting with her was an informal one.

She wondered if Matt even owned a suit.

She wondered how Josh would have handled the situation in the parking lot. Or how most of the men she knew would have behaved. Some of them certainly would have tried heroics, but she wondered if any would have been so smoothly successful as Matt Glass.

Matt was unusual, no doubt about it. Too bad she couldn't count on him for anything more than some interesting moments in her life. He was, she had seen for herself, a competent man. Sure of himself and capable of meeting life head-on.

MATT FELT totally out of control. The situation had gone rapidly from bad to worse, and he had no idea what to do. "Laurel," he said, staring at the smiling, angelic face of his niece. "What am I going to do with you?"

Laurel giggled.

Matt sighed. "I can't take you out to dinner," he said. "I think you might be a hazard to romance, my dear. You're sure a hazard to everything else around here."

She giggled again, then toddled off in search of some more fun. Matt sat on the floor of his bedroom and stared at the small hill made of his clothing. Every scrap he'd owned had been dragged from drawers and the closet. And nothing was clean any longer. Laurel had carefully doused the garments with water and soap. Lots of soap. "Washing for Daddy," she had cheerfully explained in her own charming way.

The sitter had claimed Laurel wasn't out of her sight more than two minutes. Matt put his head in his hands. It had taken considerably more than two minutes for even such a talent to accomplish this much mayhem. One more sitter scratched from the list. He heard the faint sound of childish laughter. Then, a crash.

"Laurel!" He rose to his feet and ran in the direction of the noise. "Oh, Laurel. No!"

THAT EVENING, he confessed. "I'm out of my depth," Matt said. He handed Allie a glass of wine. He had called and tried to cancel the dinner date until she realized what his problem was and volunteered to come over to his place. "I admit it. She's got me with my tail between my legs, and I'm running. What am I going to do? I need help."

Allie sipped. The wine was white, smooth, cold and refreshing. They were sitting in the living room. "You're only confronting the normal sorts of problems faced by every parent of a two-year-old," she replied. "In your case, it's worse, though, because Laurel hasn't had two years to train you."

"What?" He laughed. "Don't you mean *I* haven't had two years to train *her*?"

Resisting the urge to explain how, in her own experience, children and pets seemed to do the training of their personal adults, Allie looked beyond him to the view out of the big picture window. Although it was nearly nine in the evening, sunlight still struck the tops of the tall pine trees and glowed off the mountain in the distance.

"Either way," she said, "you're just not used to the pattern of her life, Matt. And she's probably doing some acting-out because she knows she's lost something very dear to her, though she's too young to know exactly what it is. I know you have trouble getting her to bed, since I watched the process tonight. Does she sleep at night without problems?"

"Not always. Sometimes she wakes up and yells and cries until I come in and talk to her for a while. Give her some comfort. Hold her until she drifts back off." He set his wine down. "You know, you are a good sport to come here for dinner instead of going out. I'm not much of a cook."

"Pizza and salad is fine with me. I understand your situation better than you might think." She took another sip. "When the twins were little, I was a hermit. No social life at all."

"And now?"

"Now? Of course, I go out when I want. But, I've got more important things to do than worry about my social life."

"How did your meeting with your manager go?"

She set her glass down. "All right, I guess."

"You guess?"

"It went fine," she replied, feeling defensive. "Josh is going to do a great job for me."

"I'm sure he will." Matt got up and refilled his wineglass. "Tell me why you're going into politics." He returned to his chair. "I'm really interested."

Allie studied him. "Because of the pain I went through when my husband deserted me." It was a simple answer and the most honest she could give.

Matt's eyes widened. He said nothing.

"Paul walked out when I was five months pregnant. Just left for the office one fine day and never showed up, never came back, never called, never wrote, never...nothing. He disappeared off the face of the earth, leaving me with all the debt he'd piled up in medical school and..."

"He was a doctor?"

"Yes. Just out of training. Just starting his practice. He had a few patients already. We not only had the education bills, he had also just bought and equipped an office. Do you have any idea how much something like that costs? And how difficult it is to unload?"

Matt shook his head.

"Well, I did unload it. Eventually. And I paid back every cent he owed, but..."

"Why? Weren't those his debts? You weren't responsible if he deserted you."

"It depended on who was doing the talking. I wasn't as assertive then as I am now. I didn't know what to do, except to pay back what we owed. It doesn't matter now. It's history. But it scarred me, and I swore I'd try to see to it that other women didn't suffer the same kind of pain. I worked in a bank when the kids were small, but now I run my own business. I advise women on finance. Exclusively female clientele. And, I concentrate on those who are married and are not the primary breadwinner. The dependent ones. They're the ones most likely to be done in by the system if they lose their husbands, one way or another."

"I see." He covered his mouth with his hand and leaned back in the chair.

Allie smiled. "And what, you're wondering, does this have to do with my decision to get into politics?"

Matt nodded. "I assume you're out to get all the men who..."

"No. Don't misunderstand me. I'm not after men or any particular group. I'm just after fair treatment for everyone.

A simple thing. I just want to see each person responsible for his or her own debts, and if one member of a team bugs out…"

"The other's not left holding the bag." He nodded. "It's a fair argument for justice."

"*Financial* justice. It goes deep into our cultural past. Women frequently got the short end of the stick when it came to money. So do children. Look at the problem of collecting child support money. Look at the incredible difficulties for women in sexual harassment cases. Lost work time, lost wages. I work now to see that doesn't happen to my clients. I'd like the opportunity to make legislative decisions that would create a fairer climate, as well. It's in process, of course, but it's not moving fast enough for me. I want to do something about that."

"I see." Matt got up again and went over to the window. Allie Ford was gorgeous, smart, articulate, motivated. All admirable qualities in a woman, especially one running for public office. But, she was basing it all on one thing—her man had run out on her. He remembered the reluctance with which she had met his offer of lunch that morning. How he'd had to practically stand on his head to get this dinner thing set up. She undoubtedly distrusted men, whether she admitted it or not.

Not the sort of woman he needed to get mixed up with.

"Have you any clue about your husband?" he asked.

"I know he's legally dead," she replied. "He's been gone long enough without word or contact. Long enough and then some. That's about it."

Matt turned around and looked at her. She was smiling, slightly. Unruffled. Calm. Not exactly a grieving wife. Of course, it had been years… "Make any attempts to find him?"

Now, she blushed and her eyes seemed to darken from sky blue to the color of midnight. "I turned the world upside down," she declared, gripping her wineglass. "I even hired private investigators after the cops gave up. But I couldn't afford to do that for long." She set the glass back down on the coffee table. "I finally gave up. If he'd wanted us, he would have found some way to let me know where he was."

"And, if he couldn't? If he was dead?"

"Then, there wasn't much point in my spending money I desperately needed for other things, was there?"

"I suppose not."

"I almost married again, once." She picked up the glass and rolled the stem between her hands. "He worked on a ranch up in Montana near my folks. But, it wouldn't have been right. I don't know if I'm free."

"Legally, you are, aren't you?"

"Sure." She shrugged. "But I just keep thinking about those stories where the husband disappears and has a good reason. Then, the wife falls in love again and marries, and then the first guy shows up and..."

Matt laughed. "That's fantasy. Look at you. I am surprised no one's talked you into making the trip to the altar. Or are you still in love with the one who left you?" he asked, seriously.

"No." She regarded him steadily. "I'm not. How about you? Ever marry?"

"No." He shook his head and sat back down. "Not me. Though I'm settled for now with Laurel in my life, I'm the original rolling stone. Just like my old man." He drained his glass. "He walked out on my mother, just like your husband walked out on you. But he didn't give her the grace of disappearing. He took me, and every so often we'd make a pass back through town to say hi to Mom. Keep her hoping, you see. Then, off we went again. She never knew where, when or for how long."

"That's awful!"

"Yes, it was. I was well into my late twenties before I realized how awful. That was when Mom died and Martha married John Essex. Now that I'm a mature man of thirty-four, I..." He let the words trail off. "I'll order the pizza now," he said. "It takes about twenty minutes for them to get here, and I'm hungry. How about you?"

"Sounds fine to me." She smiled, wryly. "We are a pair, aren't we?"

"Huh?"

"Look at us, Matt. I'm out to make my 'sisters' financially safe from the depredations of their unreliable mates, because of what happened to me. You're taking on your two-year-old niece by way of penance for what your father did and..."

"Laurel's no penance!"

"Hey, don't get angry. I just think..."

"You don't know me. I love that kid."

"Matt, I'm not denying you love her." Allie stood up and went over to him. "It's plain to see by the way you behave. Your concern for her is admirable. But..."

"But you don't think I'm competent?" He bit off the words, one by one. "I'm not fit to be her father?"

"I didn't come here to fight with you, Matt. I came to enjoy dinner in your company."

"Sorry." He looked away. "I had no call to get angry at you." He took a deep breath and blew it out. "I'm not used to feeling like this. At a loss, I mean. Over what to do with Laurel. I guess I'm lashing out."

"Has someone questioned your right to care for Laurel?"

He laughed, the sound bitter. "Would you believe her folks' lawyer? The woman as much as told me straight to my face I wasn't an appropriate guardian for the child. My sister left her affairs in order. Laurel inherits the whole kit-and-caboodle. But she neglected to name a guardian. So, I get the job, since I'm the nearest blood relative. That doesn't make the lawyer happy at all.''

"Maybe you need your own lawyer. My cousin is…''

"I don't need anyone. I have a right under the law to care for my niece.'' He paused, and Allie thought she saw deep emotion which he quickly buried. "She's all the family I've got now,'' he added.

"Your father…?''

"He's not family, Allie. He belongs to everyone and no one, least of all to me.'' He reached out and touched her face. "You don't know how lucky you are. Maybe your husband did leave you, but you have children. *Your* children, not his. And you have your parents. You have *people*. Family.''

She felt tears in her eyes. "So do you, now, Matt. Laurel's yours.''

"That's right.'' He clenched his fist. "And God help anyone who tries to take her away from me!''

His expression was so fierce it frightened her, and Allie remembered how easily he had handled the bully in the pickup truck. How just a few words had apparently intimidated the man to the point of tears. Matt Glass, she decided, was not just a nice guy, taking over for his deceased sister. He was a complicated man with some deep and serious anger. What did she really know about him? In spite of his tenderness toward Laurel, there was a hard edge to him.

And she needed to ask herself right now if she was willing to get involved with that sort of man. Right now, before the ground under her feet started to give way.

And, looking at the passion and fire in Matt Glass's handsome face, she decided if he directed that energy into a romantic relationship, the ground could give way real fast.

CHAPTER FOUR

MATT'S EMOTIONAL MOMENT had passed quickly, and they had finally settled down in the dining area with the freshly delivered pizza and the surprisingly good salad he had made. The wine he offered was outstanding, and the conversation had remained comfortable, if impersonal. Allie was feeling pleasantly relaxed.

Not for long.

Laurel's scream was so sudden and full of terror that Allie knocked over her wineglass. Matt was already on his way down the long hall to the baby's bedroom when she caught up with him.

"My God," she said. "I've never heard a child cry out like that. So much fear!"

"I know." Matt opened the door completely—it had been left ajar—and turned on the light. Little Laurel sat in her crib, the sheet twisted around her legs, her face red and her cheeks streaming with tears. He reached for her, and cuddled her straining body to his, holding her tight and telling her it was all okay.

Over the child's head, he gave Allie a look of total sorrow and helplessness. This, from the man who had so easily subdued a violent bully that morning. She felt her own eyes tearing. What her heart was doing was beyond her comprehension at the moment.

Finally, the baby's shrieks subsided to sobs, then to hiccups and then to babbling talk. She pulled away from Matt's tear-and-slobber-soaked shirt and looked around at

Allie. A big smile burst through the wetness on her face. "Momma!" she stated, reaching.

Allie took her. "I'm *Allie*," she said, stroking the soft head of hair. "Auntie Allie, okay?"

"Momma."

"She's elected you for the evening," Matt said, his tone rueful. "Believe me, when she gets that tone of voice, nothing will change her mind."

Allie laughed uneasily, her insides still quivering from the feeling of turmoil that the screams of the child and the sight of Matt's helpless expression had caused. "I don't believe you said that, Matt. Boy, does she ever have you wrapped around her little finger!"

"You try dealing with her. You'll see."

"All right." She regarded him, then Laurel. "I never could resist a challenge." She hoisted the baby onto her hip. "Hey, Laurel. How about getting some pizza with Auntie Allie?"

"Pizzzzaaa. Mmmaaamma." Gurgling laughter. A whoop and hiccup of happiness.

"See?" Matt turned back to the disarrayed crib. He stripped off the tangled sheet and blanket. "She's set on it, and you can't change her mind."

"'I have not yet begun to fight.'" Allie headed for the door. "But first, Laurel, would you like to go potty?"

"Pizza. Momma. No potty."

"I warned you," Matt declared, moving past her with an armload of bedding. "She's got a bladder like a camel when she wants."

"No child this age should be trusted right after they wake up." Allie eyed the sheets, felt Laurel's pajamas. "Unless she's already wet."

Matt sniffed. "Nope. She's pretty good about it. Got great control," he added proudly.

Allie considered this. If Laurel hadn't lost her toilet training, that was an excellent sign of emotional strength in so young a child. But right now, the strength did present a slight problem, since she was sure Laurel was just being stubborn. It came with two-year-old territory, and it didn't need special trauma to bring it on. "Laurel," she said. "*I* have to go potty. Will you come with me?"

"Pizza." Laurel stuck several fingers in her mouth and banged on Allie's shoulder with the other hand.

"After I go," Allie said. She carried the child into the bathroom and shut the door in Matt's face. "Girls only," she added.

Laurel thought this shared toilet experience was hysterically funny, and bolstered Allie's eroded confidence in her mothering abilities by performing, as well. In a few minutes, they were back out at the dining room table, dealing with the pizza.

"You should get a drop cloth for the floor," she suggested, watching the process of Laurel and Matt at work, eating. "Even though it's good hardwood, it's going to stain and cost a fortune to redo when you want to sell."

Matt caught a juicy section just before it hit the floor. "I expect at this rate, I'd probably do well just to have the place demolished and sell the empty land."

"Don't be a defeatist."

Laurel's milk glass tipped, sending white rivulets across the top of the polished wood table. Matt slapped a pizza-stained towel over the mess. "Why not, may I ask?" he asked. He sounded dead-tired and discouraged.

Allie got up. "Look. She's your kid. Your responsibility, and I hate to say anything, but you are doing it all wrong." She went over to Laurel and picked the child up. Laurel whined a protest that had all the signs of becoming a full-blown wail over being thwarted. "You can't let her stay in control. Mind if I try?" Allie asked.

"Be my guest." He waved his hand, put his fingers in his ears and shut his eyes.

"Okay, Missy Essex," Allie said, her tone firm but friendly. "Let's go into your eating room." She carried her into the kitchen and pulled out the high chair.

"No!" Laurel kicked.

Allie didn't say anything. She placed the now angrily complaining baby in the chair and pulled it up next to the kitchen table. Matt came in, carrying the remnants of the pizza. He put it on the table, as she directed.

"I don't know what you're planning," he said, "but I guarantee it'll never work. When she starts like this, she gets madder than an old-line Democrat at a present-day party caucus." Clearly, he anticipated her failure. He had a sad but smug smile on his face.

Which faded as Allie went into action. She sat down and placed the pizza in front of her. As long as Laurel howled, she did not look at the child. She placed her hands on the table and kept them still. After a few minutes, Laurel quieted. Allie picked up a small square of pizza. She turned and placed it on the high chair tray. "Here you go," she said. "You may eat now."

Laurel picked up the pizza and threw it on the floor. She started yelling again. Allie looked away, ignoring the deafening shrieks. Put her hands on the table and waited. She couldn't see Matt, but she sensed his bemused gaze on her.

It got quiet. Allie picked up another piece and handed it to Laurel. She repeated her instructions. "You may eat now." This time, the child ate.

When Allie smiled up at the dumbfounded Matt, she did her best not to look as smug as he had. She doubted that she'd succeeded, however.

An hour later, Laurel was cleaned up and back in her bed, asleep. Allie smoothed the covers over her one last time and turned from the crib. Matt was standing by her side. He bent over and kissed Laurel's curly little head. He and Allie walked from the room together.

"How often does she have nightmares like that?" Allie asked. They stood in the hall outside the bedroom, whispering. She had been unwilling to bring the topic up in front of Laurel. One never knew what a small child could understand.

Matt looked unhappy again. "Too often, in my book. Once, twice a night, sometimes. Some nights, of course, not at all. Sleeps like an angel. I asked the doctor about it. He was going to give her a sedative for the rough times. I didn't like that, so I never went back."

"Who was the doctor?"

Matt told her.

"There are are others in town who will be of more help," she said. "I'll see what I can do to get you..."

"Allie." He stopped and put his hand on her arm. "It's not your problem, it's mine. You have enough to do in your own life without worrying about us."

"I'm not worrying." She looked at him. "I'm just trying to help."

He touched her face, tracing the line of her cheek with his fingertips. "You'd better learn how to say no now, or you're going to be in a world of trouble that you won't believe."

"Because of you?"

"No, because of politics." He dropped his hand and looked away. "I was thinking of your dreams and ambitions. Others will take advantage of you. Use you for their own purposes. A politician has to be essentially selfish, no matter what public line he or she gives out. You have to learn to dance on the waters, Allie. Dance gracefully, but not sink. I wonder, really, if you can."

That made her angry. "I can do it. And I didn't ask you for advice."

He stepped back, put his hands in his pockets. "Yeah, I know. But I was giving it, anyway, wasn't I."

"Thanks, but…"

"Just like you gave it to me about Laurel." He started back down the hall toward the living room, his step suddenly full of energy again and his fingers snapping. "I have this thought, Allie…"

She followed him, but apart from offering her a drink, he didn't say anything more until he'd settled next to her on the big sofa and was sipping brandy from a snifter. Allie had declined, realizing how tired she was the moment she sat and knowing she had yet to drive home. Then, he spoke of what he had in mind.

"We need to share our experiences and knowledge," he said. "We each know things the other needs to know."

"Are you suggesting a brain trust?"

"Exactly. You give to me—I give to you. No money changes hands. No contracts, no specific commitments. Just a sharing. What do you think?"

Allie blinked. "It sounds to me like you just want to be friends."

He stared. Then, he chuckled. Then, real laughter rolled. "By God, you are quick. Put me right back in place, just like a pro." He took a deep swallow of the brandy and leaned back. "If you'd obey a canny and competent manager, you'd be well on your way to winning your election."

"Obey?"

"Yeah." Another swallow. "You know. Follow instructions. Do what you're told. Keep out of hot water in public confrontations. Lots of matters too detailed to list here. But obedience to the manager who knows what he or she is doing is the prime directive."

"Arf, arf," she said, putting her hands up like paws and panting.

Matt regarded her. She had misunderstood him. Thought

he intended her manager to be her boss. That wasn't what he meant at all. She and her manager would have to work together as a *team*. He made himself grin at her joke, though. What he was thinking right now wasn't exactly just friendly.

It was far more than that. She had touched something inside him. He *wanted* to be involved with her life and her dreams. He wanted to be involved with *her*.

He felt confused, suddenly. Confused and awkward. The damn brandy, probably. He set the snifter down. He was too tired to be drinking, his emotions too raw and close to the surface. He decided it was time to tell her some truth as he felt it. "I want to be friends with you, of course," he said, measuring his words. "But that's not all. I want more than just a casual friendship. I need you to be willing to be..."

"Involved?"

Matt sighed. "Yeah." Then, he leaned forward and kissed her lips. She didn't move away. "This surprises me somewhat," he said, softly. "How about you?" It was not just a comment. It was a sexual invitation, and they both knew it.

Allie sat very still, savoring the sensual feelings that rose in her body. It had been a long time since she'd felt this way. And it was his gentleness, his delicacy that caused it. Just touching her lips with his. Breathing on her cheek, the sweetish smell of the brandy in her nostrils. The warm sensation of his skin so near hers. The way the lamplight caught the dark gold in his hair... Allie pulled away and sat back on the sofa.

"I just can't get romantically involved right now," she said. "It wouldn't be fair to you, Matt."

He sat back, too, breathing deeply. "The hell with fair!"

"You know what I mean! You're emotionally tangled up because of Laurel. I'm in a political race. We..."

"We what? Because we have problems and difficulties, we can't explore this thing between us? Don't be ridiculous, Allie. You're the first woman in a long time who's set off my system like this, and I don't mind admitting it to you right here and now. I'm going to be honest. Maybe there's no future for us, but why can't we have the present?"

"Boy oh boy, is that a line!"

That hit him hard. "If you don't like it, I'm sorry. But, it's no line."

"Matt." Allie touched his hand. "Look at this. You're alone in a town where you have no friends, no support and you're dealing with a yardful of trouble unlike anything you've faced before. You are completely out of your depth with Laurel. I come along. I know about kids. You're looking for a friend. You see a potential lover. You're bored, socially and..."

"You really are cynical, aren't you." His eyes were narrowed now, regarding her coldly.

"I have reason to be." She stood up. "Thanks for dinner, but I think I ought to go."

"Allie, sit down. Please." He patted the sofa cushion. "Maybe you're right. Maybe we shouldn't get involved. But that doesn't change the fact we could stand to pool our resources, does it?"

She sat, gingerly. On the edge. Said nothing.

"Okay." He smiled wryly. "It's almost one in the morning. What with the wine and the brandy and the excitement of Laurel's bad dream, I'm a bit out of focus. I made a move I shouldn't have. But you can't tell me you didn't feel something, too, when we kissed."

She nodded. "I did."

"So...?"

"So, the idea's good, I guess. Of our pooling resources. Sharing knowledge, at least. For the other, I..."

His hand moved toward her, and his fingers lightly touched the fine, fair hair on her bare arm. "For the other, let's just see."

Allie felt something wonderful trying to rise to the surface from deep inside. But it was strange and unfamiliar and frightened her more than a little, so she just laughed. "I'd better get home," she said, standing again. "But if you mean it about our being friends, then how about a picnic tomorrow? The three of us."

"Sounds good." Matt didn't move, but he didn't look as if he was going to protest her departure, either. He looked exhausted.

And very sexy. Allie was sorely tempted to stay with him.

Soon after, however, she was on the road home, regretting her good sense in leaving him, but confident she'd made the right decision. Quick romance and sex was not her style, and would be political death if she indulged herself like that right now. All the voters needed to know about a candidate in their town was that that candidate led a scandalous private life. Just look at what it had done to some major national contenders in the last decade. Besides, this was essentially a small town, and you couldn't hide much for very long. Nothing was secret; nothing was sacred. Like it or not, that was the way things were.

She drove slowly down the mountain road, keeping an eye on the sides for deer. The Essex home was about one third of the way up Linville Mountain, and the deer browsed the land freely, as if cars had never been invented. Allie respected their right to be there. She would have driven off the road herself in order to avoid one, if it ever came to that. Besides, in her mind, only an idiot took the twisting mountain lane at any speed.

No deer interfered in her passage tonight, though she saw many out in the lush fields. But as she hit the straightaway down to the valley and town, she noted that hers was not the only vehicle on the mountain road at this late hour. Another car was following her, and the strange thing about it was that it had no headlights. Allie slowed, hoping the driver would pass her, and see that he or she had neglected to turn on lights.

But the other car slowed, too. Annoyed, she picked up speed. So did it.

A strange sense of dread fell on her. She thought of the altercation with the man in the parking lot that morning, and suddenly she was afraid. Matt's house was fairly isolated, being one of only four or five on the road.

And hadn't Walt warned him to watch his rearview mirror? A warning from a policeman carried some weight in her mind. And that Teddie whatever his name was would connect her to Matt, wouldn't he?

Fear combined with anger. Crime in Linville Springs was a rarity, compared to large urban centers, but it did happen.

But not this time. When Allie reached the bright orange arc lights of the main highway that led around the city, the other car switched on its lights and pulled off onto a residential road. Just a late-night driver who'd been unaware of his problem, she thought. She'd been silly to have had such wild thoughts.

She did, however, make a note in her mind of the license plate. She had been too far in front to read the number, but the plate was not from Wyoming. The car itself was boxy in shape. She noted that, too.

THE NEXT MORNING, she barely managed to drag herself up in time to get ready for church. She let Fred out into the backyard, apologizing for neglecting their standard early-morning walk. "It was a late night for me, girl," she said, letting Fred back into the kitchen after the little poodle had dutifully done her business. "I'm off schedule, I know, and I'm sorry."

Fred pouted, but ate a hearty breakfast anyway. By the time Allie left for church, Fred was back asleep on the unmade bed. *Lucky dog,* Allie thought, smiling to herself. Fred's worries were limited to a few issues like morning walks and whether or not her owner had restocked the doggie treat box.

Church failed to relax and restore her. Usually, it did. But today, anticipating the upcoming picnic with Matt, she couldn't concentrate on worship. She sat, distracted, through the familiar service and didn't linger over the fellowship-coffee hour afterward. Several friends asked if she was free for Sunday dinner, but she declined, saying she had plans. That brought some smiles and raised eyebrows, but she didn't elaborate.

It was no one's business, she figured.

Back at home, she prepared hurriedly for a picnic and then called Matt's number, figuring he, at least, had been able to sleep in. Laurel ought to have given him a break that morning, since the little one had been up so late herself. Allie stood there with the phone ringing, Fred barking for a walk and the three cats winding around her ankles, whining for kitty treats for some time before she decided he wasn't home.

Or wasn't answering.

She thought again of the car that had scared her the night before. What kind had it been? A boxy vehicle. Four-wheel drive kind of thing—a Bronco or Suburban, maybe. The one good glimpse she'd had under the lights had left her with that impression. That and the out-of-state license were the only bits of information she had. She tried to remember. Had it been behind her from Matt's house, or had it picked her up farther down the road. More important, had it been following her?

She didn't know.

Suddenly, Fred's barking tone changed. Instead of heckling her, the dog was sounding a warning: territorial invasion. The doorbell rang. She hung up the phone and went to the front door. She hesitated. Then, feeling silly, she opened it.

Matt and Laurel were there, clean and dressed in jeans with smiles on their faces. Fred danced, barking to high heaven.

"Doggie!" she squealed. "Wow-wow!" She leaned out of Matt's arms and reached for Fred, who decided to back away as quickly as her legs would carry her.

"Morning," Matt said. "Get my message? I said I'd be here an hour ago. We were a little slow getting in gear. Sorry."

"Morning." She stepped back, letting him in. "No, I didn't… Oh, I guess I didn't check my machine when I got back from church. It's okay that you're late though. I'm not quite ready, either. I went right to the kitchen and fixed lunch for us. Fred, be quiet." The dog had backed down the hallway and was yapping for all she was worth.

"Doggie," demanded Laurel. Then she spotted the three cats, who were lined up by the kitchen door, watching the show. "Doggie?" she asked.

"No," Allie said, picking up the nearest feline. "This is a cat, Laurel. Meeeooow. Cat. Her name's Tom. Kitty-cat."

"Kitty." Laurel gave Tom a quick touch, then pointed back to Fred, who had settled down a little and was only barking every twenty seconds. "Doggie!"

"This is quite a menagerie," Matt said. "Could I put her down? Will the dog bite?"

"Yes. No." Allie set Tom down, and the big calico raced for parts unknown. "Fred's all right, and she won't bite. She just doesn't see many kids quite this young, and you startled her. Just a minute." She called the dog and Fred approached, silent now. Belly to the floor. Eyes pleading. When she reached Allie, she went flat and rolled over, exposing her soft tummy. Allie picked her up. "Here, Laurel. Touch gentle, now. Gentle." Fred seemed to tremble with terror.

Laurel complied. Entranced, she stroked Fred's back. Fred relaxed and licked her hand. Laurel squealed, drew back, then giggled. "Soft," she said.

"She is," Allie agreed. She stood, watching carefully, but sensing the relationship between child and dog was all right. Harry, the most mellow of the cats, a part-Siamese, came over voluntarily to sniff Laurel and check her out. Amazed, Allie watched the child stroke the cat's head, leaving the tempting long tail alone. "Matt, she's so gentle. Like she understands the animals are skittish. You must think about getting her a pet."

"Just what I need." He looked impressed, however. "She is being good, isn't she," he added, pridefully.

"She is." Allie smiled. "I'll get the picnic lunch. Just a minute."

Matt knelt down by Laurel and Fred. "Take your time," he said, petting the poodle. Allie watched for a second, entranced.

They looked like a family. *Her* family. She shook her head, ridding her brain of the image and the words. They were strangers, friends at best. She had her own family, the twins, and her own life. That was what mattered.

Laurel and Fred persuaded her to let the dog go along on the outing. Both child and canine had looked so forlorn when she announced that Fred had to stay home, that she relented. And, to her amazement, Fred, who always sat on her lap when riding in a car, even when she drove, took position immediately in the back seat next to Laurel's car seat, remaining just close enough for an occasional pet or two from an obviously devoted little girl.

"I think you may have lost your dog," Matt confided, settling into the passenger seat after stowing the picnic basket in the trunk. "Or gained a kid."

"Thanks, but no." Allie started the engine. "Two's plenty for me, and Fred is only using this ploy to try to make me jealous. She's a natural schemer." She pulled out of the driveway and headed down the street. The warm June air blew in the window, making her loose hair tickle her skin. It felt good, so she left the window down.

"I don't believe you." He touched her shoulder, then her cheek, making her skin tingle even more. "I think you trained her to entice Laurel so that I'd have to spend all my time with you."

Allie glanced at him, saw he was teasing and smiled. "You really are smooth, Matt. No wonder you got to date all those gorgeous movie stars."

His smile faded. "Don't believe everything you read in the tabloids."

"I don't read them."

"Then, how...?"

"Everybody else in town seems to. I got the skinny on you from one June Watson. She's the resident authority on Hollywood gossip."

He covered his mouth with his hand and swore, softly. "That was a hell of a silly period in my life," he said. "I got kind of caught up in the glamour scene before I realized how insane and shallow it was."

"Hey." She reached over and slapped his leg. "Don't take it so seriously. I certainly don't. No movie stars here. Just us folks. This is Sunday. The day of rest. We are going on a picnic. You know? Have fun? Relax before hitting the rat race again tomorrow?"

"There is no rat race in Linville Springs, Wyoming," he intoned. "Trust me." He let his head fall back against the headrest. "I've never felt so wrapped in cotton in my life.

In spite of my worries about Her Majesty back there. This place should be renamed Valium City.''

"Maybe, it's just normal.''

"Do I detect defensiveness?''

"Well, I didn't make a nasty remark about your home.'' She turned the corner and headed for the highway out of town. "I'm not being defensive. Just protective.''

"Come on, Allie.'' His voice had an edge to it. "You've got to admit this is life in the stop lane compared to New York or Los Angeles. Or any world capital. I mean, if we were trying to go on a picnic in L.A., we'd have started hours ago, just to deal with the traffic.''

She laughed. "You might call that the fast lane. I call it suicidal.''

"Maybe.'' Now, *he* sounded defensive. "But that's where the opportunities are. That's where life's happening, my dear.''

"And here it's not?''

"I didn't say that.''

"No, maybe not exactly.'' She flashed him a challenging look and smiled. "But you sure implied it. Okay, Mr. Matthew Glass, I'm going to prove to you that life with a capital L is right here in Valium City, as you called it.''

"I can't wait. The anticipation is killing me.''

"Good.'' She grinned again. This time, wickedly. "It might save me the trouble.''

CHAPTER FIVE

THE LOCATION she had chosen for their picnic proved a good start to her campaign. Step one was to show him the countryside. Step two, she knew, would come later, when she introduced him to all the possibilities in Linville Springs itself: the cultural and sports events, the intellectual opportunities, and perhaps, more importantly, the quality of life that a "fast lane" city could never offer.

She smiled to herself. He had no idea! And, unlike a big city, everything was just about fifteen minutes away from your front door. No traffic to fight or hours of boring commuting.

Paradise!

They drove for a while down the I-25 and took a turnoff that led up into low mountains. The road became barely two-lane, and she noted that Matt gripped the "chicken" bar tightly from time to time as they made their way around tight hairpin turns. She was sure he'd been on worse roads in his time and decided he must not have faith in her driving skills. That, however, was his problem, not hers. She knew what she could handle.

Laurel and Fred were asleep, apparently lulled by the warmth of the day and the motion of the car. The poodle's head rested against the baby's leg. Odd, Allie thought. Fred was not a children-dog. She liked the twins well enough, but Sam and Sally went their way and Fred went hers, and she'd never cuddled with them like she was doing with Laurel.

Interesting. She drove on.

Because of the recent heavy rains and the high altitude, the wild flowers were still abundant, making the wide meadows look like the work of an impressionist who had reached for the outer limits. Blue, yellow, orange and red spangled in the sun. Even the wild grasses were multicolored, varying from deep greens to pale olives and even purples and gold. Matt regarded this rapturous scenery with no comment, but she could see the admiration in his expression.

"This is high desert country," she said. "When we get a lot of rain like we did this spring, it blooms like mad. Some years, this would all be dried grass, by now, burned brown and gold by the heat and dryness. No flowers left."

"Hard to visualize. It looks so lush."

"Trust me. This is hard country. Drought is more common than flooding. If the snowpack's not deep enough, the land just withers at the first sign of heat."

"How do things live, then?" He seemed interested at last.

"They've adapted. The antelope and deer will eat anything when they have to. I remember one year it was killing cold almost all January. I mean twenty, thirty below zero. The big herds lost all the weak animals. You'd see them just lying out in the snow. But the others survived by eating plants they wouldn't touch right now. It's amazing to observe the cycles. We're in a good one this year."

"I assume the antelope and deer are suitably grateful."

"I suppose."

He stared out the window. They drove through a wooded area by a narrow, rushing creek and small beaver ponds. She pointed out the dams and the gnawed tree stumps. "The beavers aren't out right now," she explained. "Too hot. But they'll be back at work again tonight. Chewing, mending, fixing, building and storing for the winter. They thrive if they're left alone."

"Predators?" he asked. "Natural ones?"

"A few left. Most have been killed off by men, of course. Some of that was necessary. Most of it wasn't."

"The history of our species. Tame it or kill it. Sometimes, both." His fingers tapped on the window.

"We are a pretty scary bunch. That's for sure. And you see it close up and personal out here."

"I don't know. Drive-by shootings in L.A. are pretty close up and personal. The rage factor on the freeways. Drugs."

"I though you were defending your neck of the woods. What's this?"

"Just speaking the truth. I didn't say it was safe there. I said, it was exciting. Dynamic. Central."

"Central to what?" she asked, turning off onto a dirt road that was more of a path than a drive. The spring rains hadn't done much for the dust along the trail, and it blew upward like grayish-white plumes behind them. "Armageddon?"

"Very funny." Matt held on to the door grip. "What's the purpose here? Demolition of my kidneys?"

"We're off-roading. I thought you were a great adventurer. Surely, you've been on rougher roads than this in your career."

"Not with a kid and a poodle and a picnic lunch, I haven't." He grinned, taking the sting out of his words. "And not with such a pretty driver, either. And you're good. I have to admit that."

"Thanks." She slowed and steered around a large rock in the middle of the road. "But flattering the driver won't make the journey any easier or shorter. It'll be worth it, though, believe me. I'm taking you and Laurel to a special place."

His fingers touched her cheek again, tracing the line of her jaw. "You already have," he said.

Allie shivered with pleasure and thought that, in a way, it was too bad they had the dog and child along. In other ways, it was a darn good thing!

The scenery went through another dramatic change as she neared her goal. The dirt road wound upward through the hills and rocks and past huge cliffs of white-gray stone and earth. Everywhere, the wild grass and flowers peppered the stony soil with color and life. By now, Matt had abandoned all pretense of disinterest and was staring and commenting openly on the beauty and grandeur around them.

"And this is, what, thirty or forty minutes from your front door?" he said. "And since we left the highway, we've seen no other vehicles."

"Wyoming has more cattle and sheep than people," she said. "You know we aren't even classified by the feds as a rural state. We're too sparsely populated. We're *frontier*. That's our official government status."

"I'd say it's appropriate," he said. "In California or Arizona, an area this beautiful would be overrun on the weekend. There'd be a theme park. And some New Age group would have set up a consciousness raising camp up there on the rocks. It'd be a real mess."

"Our saving grace is the climate," she admitted. "It's too harsh most of the year. Saves the beauty for those of us willing to put up with the hard times."

Matt was silent. He'd had no intention of being impressed, but she had managed to do it. This wasn't a soft, otherworldly land. In its way, he supposed, it was harsher than the urban morass he had left or some of the tropical jungles he'd explored. For all his travels and adventures, he was, essentially, a hot-weather man. A month of temperatures below zero! That was a serious hardship to contemplate!

"When it gets so cold," he said, finally, "what do you do? I mean, I'd understand outfitting an arctic expedition or an Everest climb, but regular people? Dealing with that kind of weather? How does a community keep running?"

She laughed. "Very carefully, believe me." She slowed as they crossed a tiny stream. It ran right through the dirt road. "Funny thing is it can be forty below and then just a few hours later, twenty or thirty above. The weather can change almost in a blink. When that happens, water pipes will burst. The plumbers do a landslide business then."

"Have you ever had pipes in your house go?"

She nodded. "Sure have. Right after I moved in. The kids were about Laurel's age. Maybe a little older. I was asleep. It was the middle of the night, and I woke up to the sound of a creek babbling. Only it wasn't a creek and it was babbling all over my basement. Fortunately, I hadn't started working for myself then, and there was no computer down there or..."

"What did you do? How did you cope?"

She shrugged. "I filled up everything I could find with water, including the tub, and then shut the water off. In the morning, I called a plumber. Very popular fellow that day, let me tell you. Pipes had burst all over town during the night. But he came out eventually. And after the pipes were all fixed and the mess cleaned up, I had the insulation on the house beefed up." She slowed the car to a halt. "Well, here we are. What do you think?"

Matt was silent. He wasn't sure whether to respond by saying what he thought of her or of the location.

Both were magnificent!

"It's great," he said. "Let's eat. I'm starved." He felt like a jerk after saying that and seeing the brief look of disappointment on her face, but he didn't trust himself to express his true feelings.

In fact, he wasn't even sure what they were. Just this

welling up of something deep inside. Something he'd never felt before.

Allie took his casual comment as a mild criticism. He was right. She had driven them much too far so near lunchtime. Poor judgment. But the place was worth it, even so. And Laurel had slept, hadn't fussed at missing the regulation noontime feed. She did start to fuss the moment she woke up, but the sight of Fred turned her whines to giggles.

Matt helped the child out of the car seat. They were parked in a narrow valley, filled with cottonwood trees and edged on one side by high, gray rock cliffs, which sported yellow wildflowers in crannies and one brave pine tree growing sideways out of a deep crack. On the other side, the land rose more gradually, finally spreading out into a wide, flower-strewn meadow about twenty feet in elevation from the valley floor. A tiny stream sang through the lowest part of the valley, and it was toward the stream that Allie indicated they were to go. She hefted the picnic basket, giving him no chance to offer help. Matt took Laurel's hand and followed Allie. Fred danced alongside.

He spotted their destination immediately. A huge flat rock by the water made a natural picnic table. Fred, obviously familiar with the location, ran ahead, chasing after invisible tracks of local creatures. The poodle ran into the stream and lapped the fresh running water, and Laurel giggled and strained to follow.

"Don't let Laurel drink the water," Allie warned. "It's probably pure, but nowadays, you can't take the chance. Fred's doggie system can handle it, though, and we could boil it if we needed." She set the basket down and took out a cold thermos and cups. "Here, Laurel," she said, pouring liquid into a cup. "Lemonade. Yum, yum." Laurel reached for the cup and drank thirstily, letting a goodly portion trickle down her front.

"Maybe she could take a bath in the stream," Matt commented.

"Maybe all of us will," Allie responded as Laurel almost threw the cup back at her, splashing the remaining lemonade on her jeans. "But that's what it's there for. The twins and I have skinny-dipped here for years. We build a little dam with rocks, just like the beavers, and splash away to our hearts' content." She turned away, setting out sandwiches, small bowls of potato salad, slaw and Jell-O, busying herself about the domestic business of feeding a man and child.

Matt laughed, uneasily, thinking of her taking off all her clothes and splashing around in the shallow water. The gentle breeze would stir her long blond hair... Sunlight would catch the drops of water on her bare skin, turning them gold against the ivory whiteness of her body... As she bathed, her pink nipples would pucker and tighten into hard little points... He cleared his throat, trying to shake off the erotic, romantic image.

But he couldn't. It was more than sexual. The maternal image was almost stronger, since he was seeing her with her children and not with him. Eternal mother—strong, young, at ease with nature and herself...

"Momma?" Laurel had been wandering around, checking out small details like a yellow flower, a gossamer insect and anything that interested Fred.

"What?" Allie answered without thinking.

"Dis?" Laurel pointed at a shiny flake of stone.

Allie got up and went over to the little girl. She knelt down and explained to her about the rock in very simple terms.

And Matt Glass felt his heart do some very strange things.

Eventually, they ate lunch. Fred, exhausted by her frantic initial bout of exploration, dozed in the dappled sunlight.

Laurel played for a while, getting messier by the moment, but eventually, she too slept on a blanket next to the dog. Birds chirped in the trees, a ground squirrel fussed and the wind sighed in the cottonwood branches. Matt also sighed.

"This has to be heaven," he said, lying back against the rock, using his shirt as a pillow. The day had grown hot, even at this altitude, and he'd taken the shirt off in order to enjoy the air and sunlight against his bare skin. "I'm relaxed as I can ever remember being."

"So nap." Allie smiled as she repacked the picnic remains. "That's what Sunday afternoons are for."

Matt closed his eyes. "Allison Ford, you live in the twilight zone. Sunday afternoons are for worrying about Monday mornings."

"Naaah. Not here."

Silver clinked, and he became aware that nothing she had brought along was disposable. Regular silverware, hard plastic plates that were meant for the dishwasher and years of reuse. Even the napkins were cloth. He approved, having seen enough ecological damage done to fragile environments to last him a lifetime. This environment, for all its toughness, was undoubtedly just as fragile as a rain forest. She was respecting the land she obviously loved. Matt thought about that...

And dozed.

Allie sat quietly, almost sleeping herself, and watched the man. Relaxed in sleep, he looked younger, kind of innocent and certainly more vulnerable. Most men did, she reflected, looking away. Had nothing to do with reality, just the result of relaxed muscles.

But he had something intriguing in his face that drew her attention back.

She studied him. He was undeniably handsome as all get out. Nothing plain or common about his features. They were charmingly, beautifully male with just enough ruggedness to make them interesting—make him seem a little tempting and deliciously dangerous. Now that she could see his bare upper torso, she knew the rest of him was just as appealing. She picked up a tiny pebble and tossed it into the creek. Fred's ears perked, but no one else moved.

If she and Matt did have a romance, she could keep it discreet. She'd done it before. She wasn't the kind of single mom who brought home "uncles" for the kids to deal with. The female needs she had were not driving her beyond her control and she could handle them, just as she always had. Physical drives were only as important as you let them be.

Matt sighed in his sleep and started to snore lightly. An oddly comforting sound. As if his trust in her was strong enough for him to relax completely. A large horsefly buzzed over his chest and she shooed it away, batting at it viciously as it passed over Laurel's slumbering form. Fred opened one eye. Then closed it again.

What would the twins think of Matt? Allie pondered that while keeping watch for the return of the fly. They had liked her Montana cowboy, but he was connected with the ranching life they had learned to love from her parents. Matt had no such connections. Actually, he was completely alien to all they were familiar with. *And* he came with an addition—another kid. How would that go over?

Well, it was silly to think about it right now. Nothing had happened between her and Matt other than a little kiss and some stirrings on her part. She had no idea what Matt's attitude toward her was, apart from the fact that he obviously enjoyed her company and seemed attracted to her, as well. He was probably bored in some ways, and she was a handy means of entertainment.

No, that was unfair. He was more decent than that.

But, stripped of all frills, wasn't that about it—she was convenient.

Well, so was he. Allie tossed another pebble. Watched

as it tumbled in the cold, clear water. She was not in any position to be making accusations about motives. She lay down. Just to rest a minute, she told herself. Overhead, the sky was clear, brilliant blue. Not a single cloud in sight. Typical Wyoming summer sky...

She relaxed, almost dozing.

Later, Matt, Laurel and Fred were busy in the creek, playing with the water and one another. Matt had discovered Fred's penchant for chasing small, smooth rocks, retrieving them and presenting them back for another toss. As usual, the little poodle performed this task without a sound. For Fred, rock-chasing was too serious a business to involve unnecessary barking.

Allie sat up. That odd feeling of family swept over her again. Matt, who was dividing his attention between Laurel's splashing in the inch-deep water and Fred, waved and grinned. "Hello, sleepyhead," he said. "Have sweet dreams?"

"No dreams." She stood, stretching. Looked up at the sky. "Uh-oh."

"What?"

She pointed. Since she'd been asleep, threatening clouds had gathered in the sky. They hovered at the horizon now, dark as night, and while overhead it was still clear, the wind had picked up and Allie could see that the storm front was moving quickly in their direction. "Time to bail out," she said. "Storms's coming in from the north."

Matt gathered up Laurel, ignoring the child's protests. "That's bad?"

Allie scooped up Fred. "It could be. I'd rather not be caught on the dirt road when it hits. So, let's shake it."

They did. Less than five minutes later, they were traveling along the dirt path at a bone-jarring pace. This time, Matt sat in back with Fred on his lap and his arm securing

Laurel in place in her car seat. He didn't totally trust the device, he explained.

Allie had a feeling he also still didn't totally trust her driving.

They were half a mile from the hard road when the rain and wind hit them. Matt, who had seen all kinds of tropical storms in his life, was astonished at the ferocity of the wind and hail and rain. "Stop!" he yelled over the almost-deafening thunder of hailstones on the roof of the car. "Find some shelter, quick!" He grabbed Fred and cradled Laurel.

"I got it!" Allie screamed. "Just about a hundred yards ahead." She bent down, peering through the gray sheeting of rain and hail. Slowing the car to a crawl, she watched for the turnoff she knew was just ahead.

"Just stop," Matt suggested, hollering over the din. "We'll be safer standing still."

"Trust me." The sudden humidity in the air from the rain had fogged the windshield on the inside, and she reached forward, swiping at the glass with her hand. "We're nearly there." She drove on, in spite of his continued objections. Fred was barking, a frantic, frightened sound, and Laurel was crying.

Allie reached the turnoff. She swung the vehicle, felt it hydroplane for a second, then the heavy tires caught in the mud and water. They moved slowly, ponderously, then freely and she drove under the shelter of a dense grove of cottonwoods. The battering of the hailstones ceased almost entirely, since the heavy branches full of summer leaves sheltered them.

"Whew." She leaned back and shut off the engine. "That was a little too much excitement for me." She turned around. "What about you guys?"

"We're all right." Matt had a lapful of upset dog and clinging child. Once the engine went off, Laurel had managed to scramble out of her seat and onto the security of his lap, sharing the space with Fred, who was shaking like a furry leaf. "Forget what I said about a Valium state of being. *I'm* wired. Especially when we almost went off the road back there."

"Nonsense. We were perfectly safe." She reached over to pet Fred, who was gradually calming down, but still pressing her little body tightly against Matt's chest. Laurel had already recovered her courage and was looking with wonder at the piles of hailstones just beyond the trees.

"Sure we were," he commented, skeptically. Then, he started to show Laurel how to draw on the misted window.

"I wonder if she remembers snow," Allie mused, resting her chin on her hand. "I wonder if she'll remember this? I hope she wasn't too scared."

Matt drew a Happy Face. Laurel giggled and poked her finger at the drawing. Fred bounced over and licked at it, her fears apparently forgotten.

"Probably not, and evidently not," he said. "She's tough and resilient, I believe. We all carry scars in this life, but we go on, anyway, don't we?" Then, he leaned forward and kissed Allie's cheek. The caress was light and quick, but there was promise behind it. "I've met a lot of people in my life," he added. "But no one quite like you. You keep surprising me. And that's good. You're some piece of work, you know that?"

"Not yet." She stared into his brown eyes. "But I'm willing to learn."

For a long moment, they gazed at each other, the sexual electricity building to an almost intolerable level, eclipsing all other sensations. Allie felt it coursing all through her body—that magical sense of closeness and desire.

Bam! Bam! A big fist hammering on the window by her head startled her out of her sensual reverie. Allie yelped. Matt shouted. Fred barked and Laurel screeched. A gruff voice hollered, "Hey, you people gonna sit out in the rain the rest of the day, or do ya wanna come inside?"

Allie rolled down her window. An old man, an old friend, actually, whom she recognized with a sense of relief, stood there, a smile on his face and a huge umbrella over his head. "Kelly McClean?" she asked. "Is that you?"

"None other, missy. You and your husband, your puppy and your kid come on inside the house, now. Lightning and such around yet. Gonna be a twister, too, 'less I miss my guess. Radio says so, anyways."

"Twister?" Allie felt her heart chill. She reached back for Fred. "Is there a warning or just a watch?"

"Warning." The old man's smile faded, and he looked deadly serious. "Best we all get inside and into the cellar."

"Is he talking about a tornado?" Matt asked, making sure Laurel was secure in his arms. "Here?"

"Just get out," Allie said. "And get inside. I'll explain once we're in the shelter."

They all bundled out, huddling under the big black umbrella and following the man into a house that Matt hadn't even noticed. It was scarcely more than a wooden shack, it seemed, hidden back in the trees. But once inside, with the door shut against the rising wind, he saw it was tight and cosy and surprisingly neat.

But he had no time to inspect the place. The old man led them to a trapdoor and down into a dark cellar. A kerosene lamp lit the small area and the smell of it, combined with the scent of earth, sent Matt back in time to a moment in his childhood when he and his father had once sought refuge in such a place.

But it was not the weather they'd hidden from then. It was from other men. Angry men who wanted to kill them for trespassing on territory forbidden to explorers. They had invaded a temple, the men had said, but Robert Glass had been certain that they had simply stumbled into a smuggler's nest. They had been in Central Asia; Matt was still in his teens. Just one of the many excursions that had led the two of them into deep trouble with local folks.

Matt held Laurel tighter. It was a wonder she still had one relative left alive, given the way he'd spent his childhood with her grandfather! For years, he'd believed being in danger was normal. Maybe that was why he found the calm pace of life around here so...different. *This* was normal, not the way he'd been raised... He let that thought wander around in his mind for a moment, then turned his attention to their host.

"It was King here let me know you was up there," the old man explained, gesturing toward a rising shape in the corner. "He musta heard you, 'cause he set up a howl until I went up to take a look. Good boy, King," he added. King, a big, rangy hound greeted them, sniffed at Fred and obviously found her acceptable.

Allie set Fred down. The two dogs exchanged canine greetings, tails awag. She turned to the old man. "Mr. McClean, I'm Allison Ford. We've met, but it's been a long, long time."

"I remember you, missy," McClean said. "You married that doctor fella that disappeared. The one was treatin' them important fellas like that politician. Dr. Paul was his name. He saw me once when I needed some doctorin' help, just like I was somebody important." He chuckled at the memory. Then he went on talking.

"I guess I've seen you a few times since, too. You was workin' at that bank in town. You had them two twin young'uns." He regarded Matt and Laurel. "This your new one?" he asked, not indicating whether he meant Matt or the little girl.

Allie didn't explain in clear detail. "This is my friend, Matt Glass, and his niece, Laurel Essex," she said. "We were picnicking up at the big flat rock and got caught by the weather. I wasn't keeping my eyes peeled."

Matt reached out and shook McClean's hand. It was like grasping leather and steel. "She was napping, sir," he said. "Laurel and I were playing with the dog, and we're kind of new to this part of the country. Tenderfeet or greenhorns, I guess you'd call us. Didn't know what the clouds could mean."

McClean nodded, as if that confession was exactly what he expected. "Name's Kelly McClean. Need to learn to read the skies out here, son," he said. "That's where the weather tells you what it's gonna do to you. Set yourselves down." He indicated a folding chair, several blankets and a bedroll. "I got a transistor radio we can listen to. Plenty of food and water if we need it. Make yourself to home."

They did. "A tornado warning is indicated when one's been seen nearby," Allie explained to Matt. "And nearby can be as much as eighty to a hundred miles away from the reporting site. A watch just means one's likely."

"They seen one about fifty mile out in the flats," Kelly informed them. "Don't think it'll come this far into the hills, but best to be safe about it." Everyone agreed. And so, for the next hour, Matt sat cross-legged on the hard-packed dirt floor with Laurel scampering around, playing with the two dogs, and listened to the story of a life. Kelly McClean's life. It was fascinating.

Allie positioned herself on a blanket and proceeded to draw Kelly McClean out. It wasn't difficult, since the old man loved to talk about himself. She'd heard parts of the tale from others, but wanted Matt to have the opportunity of listening to it from the source.

Kelly McClean was one of the last of the old-time cowhands. Retired long since, and living off royalties from a lucky piece of real estate investment that had turned out to hold oil. Even with the prices down, he could count on a

steady income, good enough to support him in the simple
style he preferred. "You live close to the land all your life,
son," he said, addressing Matt, "you don't want to go living in no fancy high-rise old folks home."

"There's a senior citizens' apartment complex in town,"
Allie explained. "Right near shopping and theaters. But it's
not for you, eh, Kelly?"

"Too damn many folks all crammed into a little space."
Kelly patted King. "And they wouldn't let me keep my
dog. Say he's too big for an apartment. So I stay out here."

He went on, telling about his years working in Colorado,
Wyoming and Montana. Riding fence, herding cattle,
breaking horses and training them. Matt realized he was
hearing living history. What he wouldn't have given for a
tape recorder at that moment! He also learned that the old
man had known Allie's husband fairly well. That they had
shared a dislike of what Kelly referred to as city-life. Allie
quickly changed the subject when Kelly seemed to want to
talk more about the missing doctor.

Interesting.

After a bit, Kelly slowed down and reached over to raise
the volume on the radio. The announcer made some state-
ments that Matt didn't quite get.

Both Allie and Kelly spoke at the same time. "Danger's
over," they said. King barked, and Fred joined in the chorus. "Let's go see what happened," she added.

They all went up the narrow ladder to find the day sunny
and bright again. Wind had blown several large branches
off the cottonwoods around the little house and the top of
Allie's Eagle was somewhat dented, but otherwise everything looked sparkling clean. Hailstones were piled almost
a foot deep in places.

Matt breathed deeply. The air smelled earthy, and the
contrast between the green summer foliage and the white
hailstones made the scene look like a fantasy set for some

high-budget movie. The two dogs immediately began running around, noses to wet ground, and Laurel whooped with delight when she touched a cold pile of melting hailstones.

"Wow," Matt said. "Next time I say this place is boring, you just give me a swift kick in the rear."

"All right." Allie reached over and patted his bottom. "I'll just do that," she promised.

And her eyes told him that she was interested in doing much, much more.

CHAPTER SIX

BUT AS SOON AS they returned to town, Matt noted that Allie's attitude underwent a radical change. Quiet on the drive back, once they reached her home, she became distant and distracted. As if she were consumed with disturbing thoughts. Almost as if she had become another person. He just couldn't figure out why. He wondered if the old cowboy's mentioning Paul Ford had anything to do with her mood. It didn't seem likely, since she'd been cheerful enough while they were all crammed into the little cellar. But, he filed away the idea for later inspection.

They had left Kelly McClean with effusive thanks for his hospitality and assistance and cheerful promises to return for another visit. Matt remembered that, as they said farewells, the old man had mistakenly referred to him as Allie's husband again, but he had dismissed that as a product of Kelly's age and social attitudes. A forgivable and understandable mistake on his part. She couldn't have taken offense at that. That couldn't be what she was pondering so darkly.

Could it?

She was certainly friendly enough as she helped him get Laurel's car seat back in his Jeep. "Look," she said. "We never did get much brain-trust work done this weekend. And I agree with you that it's a good idea to share our expertise on an informal basis. I'll call you, all right?"

"Sure." *Don't call us...*

Laurel fussed about leaving Fred for a few minutes, but

once they were on their way up the mountain to home and she recognized the passing scenery, she seemed to settle down and greet reality squarely.

Just as he had to do.

Fred wasn't hers.

Allie wasn't his.

He pulled into the driveway of his late sister's home. The afternoon storm had blown through here, too, scattering leaves and small branches, but doing no real harm.

Maybe that was the way his relationship-friendship with Allison Ford was supposed to be: a little clutter on the path of his life, a little excitement, a little calm romance, but nothing significant.

He pulled into the garage. "Okay, honey," he said, turning to his niece. "We're home, now."

"Mmmaaamma," Laurel demanded. "Wow-wow! Tred!" That was what she had started calling the little poodle. And she cried loudly now when he tried to explain that the dog and Allison were at their house and he and she were here, at theirs. Cried and exclaimed she wanted them both. "Momma *and* Tred!"

Matt sighed. Nothing significant?

Right.

ALLIE GREETED the cats and let Fred out into the backyard. The poodle dashed in a wide circle, going at what seemed to be nearly the speed of light. It was one of Fred's favorite forms of letting off steam and getting exercise. A much-deserved treat after the perfect behavior the dog had exhibited during the afternoon.

"Good girl, Fred," she said, clapping her hands and encouraging the little animal to run faster. "You are a gold-star dog. Big treat in the dinner dish tonight, girl."

Fred frisked, wagging her tail, eyes dancing with glints of mischief, well aware, it seemed, that she had done her job properly for the day. Allie let her into the house, and Fred abandoned all pretense of goodness, barking and taking off after the three cats, who clearly did not care to share her high spirits. Fur flew.

Ignoring the yipping and yowling, knowing they would all four stop short of actually drawing blood, Allie went downstairs to her office and checked the answering machine. Matt's message—the one she'd missed that morning—was first.

"Hi," his message said. "Haven't heard when you want us to show up, so we'll just arrive when we're ready. Looking forward to this, I have to say. I need you...your help." He'd stumbled a bit over that last phrase.

She let the tape move on to the next message.

It was from M.J. "Darlin' cousin, I take it you've forgotten the Greek dance entirely. It's next weekend, and as a political candidate, you'd be an idiot not to show up. I'm sure Josh hasn't thought of it. It's not his sort of thing, anyway. You can still order tickets, I think..."

Allie slapped her forehead as she listened to his instructions. The Greek Church in town had this festival every summer, and it was *de riguer* for politicians and candidates to go and be seen. Spread the old name around and hope people would still remember in November.

It was also a hell of a party.

But, she needed an escort. It was not the sort of event a woman went to unescorted, not even if she was a political candidate. M.J. would have offered, ordinarily. Even though they were cousins, it would be all right to show up together. But M.J. must have a date, himself. Allie needed to find a suitable man who wouldn't raise eyebrows or make gossips' tongues wag. She needed to think of her reputation as well as her image.

Especially since she was running for office. The Greek community was large, highly political and very conservative, for the most part. Family meant everything. Respectability ran a close second. She was far more acceptable as a widow, than she would have been as a divorcée, but she still needed a man's arm to...

Matt.

She reached for the phone. Heck. It would be fun for both of them. She sort of owed him that. Her mood on the ride back home had been strangely gloomy, and she knew he'd picked up on it. She'd let the fun dribble out of the afternoon by thinking about the future. Thinking about her political hopes. Thinking about Kelly McClean mistaking her and Matt for husband and wife. Wondering if she and Matt would ever become more than friends. Worrying about a kind of tomorrow that might never come. One that involved a relationship with him that would never have any permanence.

Darn it. She was borrowing trouble and making herself unhappy for no reason. She started to punch in his number.

Then, she set the phone down.

If she did show up on Matt Glass's arm, that could be a public statement in and of itself. A statement that they had something going. True or not, it would be quickly carried along the grapevine until everyone in the county would know about her and the handsome man from California. Would *think* they knew. Was she ready or willing to do that? Allie sat down.

She sure *wanted* to. But it was a terrible idea, given her political ambitions. Matt's reputation was public knowledge. As well, he'd made no secret about intending to leave Linville Springs. To be associated with him in any sort of romantic friendship would be detrimental to her future hopes. That was for certain.

Damn.

Fred came running downstairs, her little pink tongue hanging out. She flopped on her blanket beneath Allie's desk and sighed contentedly. Apparently, the fracas with the cats had gone to her satisfaction.

"If only life could be so simple for me," Allie said, glowering at the dog. Then, she bent down and stroked Fred's back. "But if it were, it'd be a dog's life, wouldn't it. And I'm a people, last time I checked." Fred grunted and rolled over for a tummy scratching. Allie obliged for a moment. Then, she straightened and picked up the phone again. There were times when acting on feelings the way Fred did seemed the only sensible way to go.

Matt answered after the seventh ring. He sounded out of breath. "Yeah?" he asked, curtly.

"Hi," she said. "It's Allie. Sorry to bother you, but I need a date for next Saturday night. Nothing personal exactly, but it's a big local function that's important politically. And it's a church-sponsored thing, so to be proper and acceptable, I do really need an escort. Single women are okay if they're with their extended families and are too old or too young for action, but the rest of us need our own man in tow. I know it sounds like a stodgy event, but I'm sure it will be fun. Would you mind?"

Matt stared at the wall in front of him. He had grabbed the phone in the kitchen and the wall he faced was decorated with his sister's family photographs. Mostly candid shots, they showed a life he had only imagined and dreamed about as a boy and younger man. Now, he was a shadowy part of that life—kind of a guardian angel, though certainly no angel—who had stepped in when the real parents' lives were erased. For some reason, this realization plus the breezy impersonalness of Allie's invitation made him feel a little sick inside. He was a substitute for Laurel and now, a substitute for Allie. It hurt, deeply, he suddenly realized. Cut right to the center of his pride and sense of self-worth. All his instincts screamed for him to run away. But something stronger kept him on the phone.

"Sure," he said, keeping all emotion from his voice. "I'd be happy to go. I said I'd help out with your campaign, didn't I?"

"Oh, great!" She grinned down at Fred, who was observing her with one dark little eye open. "Thank you, thank you, thank you! You don't know what a relief this is!" She hesitated for a moment. "I'll be proud to be seen there with you, Matt," she added.

He had no idea what she meant by that. "It's next Saturday night you say? I'll need to line up a baby-sitter."

"Oh, let me, please. This way, we'll be helping each other out. If the sitter works well for Laurel, then you're ahead on that part of your overall problem."

Matt had to smile at that. "Then, we have to work on a housekeeper, don't we?"

"I'll start making calls in the morning. I can do it between clients. Matt, I did have a terrific time today, and I'm sorry if I seemed a little withdrawn toward the end. I have a lot on my mind."

"I understand. But I could have used some help explaining to Laurel that Fred was staying with you once we actually got here. She pitched a fit."

"Oh, dear. Maybe we ought to…"

"Allie, I just told you that because I wanted you to know you and Fred have already become very important to her. I think I know what you're about to suggest, and I don't think it would be a good idea to get her used to the idea that Fred could come visit or she could come see you whenever she wants."

She was quiet for a moment. "You're right. She's already lost too much. She needs to get attached only to those people and things that she can count on." A sad little laugh, then: "I don't much see Fred as a rent-a-dog, anyway. She's happy enough away from home as long as I'm in sight-or-smelling distance. Otherwise, she gets extremely upset. One time, the kids tried to take her up to the ranch without me and…"

She babbled on, hearing herself sounding like an idiot, chattering away, but unable to stop. Her emotions were in such conflict that she had no clear way to express her feelings. She didn't even understand them herself.

Why was she being like this? It made no sense. None at all!

Finally, after promising to call him back tomorrow or Tuesday with a baby-sitter's name and number, she hung up. Touching her forehead, she found to her absolute amazement that she'd been sweating. "Fred?" she asked, looking down at the now-sleeping little dog. "Am I really going out of my mind?" Fred just huffed softly and turned over, seeking a more comfortable position on her blanket.

Allie smiled in spite of her concerns about her strange emotions. No help from Fred when it came to talking something out. Poodles and cats were a great source of creature comfort—"warm fuzzies" and such—but they couldn't do any giving and taking when intellectual input was needed. They were always a comfort, but no help. So, she picked up the phone again and dialed for help. She dialed her friend, confidant and cousin, M. J. Nichols, Esquire.

"YOU'RE IN LOVE, cousin," M.J. said, scooping a generous helping of Mongolian beef onto her plate and an even heftier one onto his own. They had agreed to meet in The Fragrant Cooking Pot, a favorite Chinese restaurant of theirs not too far from Allie's home. "It's that simple."

"Wrong." Allie sipped her Tsing-tao beer. "I hardly know the guy. I do not love him."

"I didn't say that. I said you are *in* love. A condition I recognize easily, having been there quite often myself."

"M.J. Please make sense to me. I feel all…twisted up

and turned around inside. I can't be *in* love, as you put it. I've barely kissed the guy.''

''Makes no difference.'' M.J. added a scoop of rice to his plate and went to work on the meal with skillfully applied chopsticks. ''Don't you remember hero worship or having a crush on someone in high school?''

''Sure, but...''

''Same thing.''

''No, it can't be!'' Allie slapped her hand down on the table. Several nearby diners glanced at her. She lowered her voice. ''I am no high schooler with dreamy notions of romance. I thought I had real love once, and it didn't work out for me.''

M.J., who had been teasing in his attitude up to now, turned serious. ''I know that, Allie. And it's made you both extremely careful and extremely vulnerable. I know this may sound a bit nineteenth century, but as your nearest male relative, geographically speaking, I want to meet this Matt Glass. Frankly, he sounds like he might be dangerous to you.''

''He's the sweetest man imaginable.''

''I don't mean physically, honey, and you know it. I'm talking about emotions. And I have an idea. I'm taking Miranda to the Greek dance. She's a natural mixer and wouldn't mind sharing me for a while with you two. Why don't we double-date?''

''Um.'' Allie sat back, considering. ''That's a generous offer. But, no thanks. I don't want to interfere with your love life just because I'm all messed up about mine.''

''See?'' Her cousin pointed at her with a chopstick. ''You just pleaded guilty. You confessed you were messed up about your love life. We double-date. Final word on it. The prosecution rests.''

''Damn.'' She grinned. ''I hate arguing with a lawyer. I never win.''

"Not with me, you don't." M.J. grinned back. "'Cause I'm so terrific."

"And modest!"

He preened, jokingly, mugging and brushing his hair with one hand. "Right. Don't forget modest." He sobered again. "Let's get back to your emotional life," he said. "Think about it logically."

"There's nothing logical about it. That's just the problem."

"Wrong. You're too close to see it, *that's* the problem. Look." He set down his chopsticks, and his tone became persuasive.

"You meet this guy under the most domestic of circumstances—in the grocery store with a little kid in tow. He's nice to the kid, even when the kid half destroys the store. He's attractive to you, socially and physically."

Allie frowned, trying to follow.

M.J. picked her confusion up and explained. "He behaves good, he looks good. And, there's more. The implied 'danger factor' that makes him fascinating to women. You find out by gossip and grapevine that he's some kind of adventurer-hero who's saved people's lives and who has now given up all that wild, exciting life for the sake of his orphaned little niece."

"Not just for her. What he used to do was a young man's game. He said so. And, he's getting older," Allie added.

"So are we all." M.J. swept that away with a wave of his hand. "But he hasn't quit being a hero. Not to you, anyway. Right there in front of the grocery store, he does his thing. He rescues you from an embarrassing scene with a tough-guy type, and from what I've heard about the incident, acts cool as..."

"That happened just yesterday, and you were in Denver." She shook her head. "How did you hear about it? You aren't keeping tabs on me again like you did when I was first on my own, are you? Because, much as I appreciate the thoughtfulness behind that, I do not need it anymore, and you know it.'' She put an edge in her tone, because she had a sudden suspicion. She remembered the car that had seemed to be following her when she'd left Matt's. Could that have been someone whom M.J. had asked to watch out for her?

However, the lawyer put her concerns to rest immediately. While he might be able to sway a jury with intellectual verbal gymnastics, he could never deal with her in any manner but honestly. She always saw right through him.

"No." He smiled, his expression full of love and respect. "I am not worried about you, and I wouldn't violate your privacy by keeping tabs, anyway. I know now that if you need help, you've sense enough to ask for it." The smile turned impish. "Like now."

"You're a sweetie," she said. "Now, where did you hear about Matt and the parking-lot cowboy?" She reached over and covered his hand with hers, a friendly gesture that was usual with them, but that caused a middle-aged couple sitting a few tables away to raise eyebrows. The woman, she noticed, was heavy and had black hair; the man thin and anxious looking. Funny, Allie thought, they seem to be watching us and listening to our conversation.

Well, no real wonder. She knew her own voice had been raised from time to time and that the topics she had mentioned were often somewhat spicy, and so she figured the pair were just interested in possible gossip. They were not, however, folks she recognized, and she put them from her mind. That was easy enough as they were relatively nondescript.

M.J. shrugged. "You know this town. Gossip gets good mileage when the story's even remotely Old West. From what I heard, it was right out of a classic bad guy-good guy scene with you as the damsel in distress. Walt and the other cop on the scene—I've forgotten his name—couldn't wait to spread the word about how smoothly your boyfriend handled…''

"He's *not* my…''

M.J. ignored her interruption. "So, then you go to his house and have a romantic dinner, alone. Then a picnic with a little more *safe* danger thrown in with the weather situation and…''

"This is ridiculous. Our dinner at his place was far from romantic. We ordered out for pizza. Laurel had a nightmare, and…''

"And don't tell me you didn't share some quiet, intimate moments. Oh, I don't mean sex, of course. Not time for that yet. But you got to know a little more about each other, felt a little more comfortable and trusting, and…'' He broke off and stared at Allie. "You're white as a sheet, Al! What's wrong?''

"I think I just had a sudden news flash," she said, grabbing her beer and taking a long swallow. "I think I know why I'm tied up in knots about this guy.''

"You agree with me?''

"Not exactly. See." She put down the beer and tapped her fingernail on the table. "Maybe I am terrified of what he represents to me subconsciously—a husband for me and a father for my children.''

"What? I can't follow you on this." M.J. looked totally incredulous. "Allie, you really have lost it, hon.''

"No. Listen. It makes perfect sense. If I was in love, as you put it, more would have to have happened between us sexually. I can't buy that at my age and level of romantic experience, I would just go gaga over a man without…''

"Road testing him?''

She laughed, then sobered. "Don't be crude. But, yes, that's right. So, see, what must be happening in my inner self is a fear that anyone I'm attracted to will turn out to be the same kind of man Paul was. A man who will make me love him, then leave me. It sounds silly, but I think it's possible that's what's eating at me, deep inside."

"I think you may be on to something there. About your feelings, at least." M.J.'s eyes narrowed. "But husband and father? That's a pretty heavy label to put on the man, isn't it? Even in the depths of your psyche?"

"He's pretending to be one. Trying to be a father to Laurel. Pretending, sort of, to be a husband to me. Oh, not consciously, of course. But, see? We have odd little meals together, tend the baby, talk and visit, but it's all rather domestic and friendly and impassive..." She broke off as another idea occurred to her.

"What? Now you look like you're on another track."

Allie shook her head. "I don't know. I'm still confused about my feelings. Maybe what I need is a real date with him. One where Laurel can't interrupt us or a storm can't drive us underground to hang out for hours with a neat old man who keeps calling Matt my husband or..."

"Or you can't use some excuse of your own making to avoid the attraction you feel for the guy." M.J. shifted in his seat. "I'm not all that comfortable advising you about sex, Al. But maybe, you just ought to go to bed with him and get the mystery out of the way."

She rested her chin on her hand. Looked off into the distance. Saw again that the strange couple were still staring. They couldn't have overheard the last part of the conversation, though, since she had consciously kept her voice low, so she went on talking. "Maybe," she said, "I should."

M.J. regarded her. Then, he pointed at her food. "Eat, then," he said. "You're going to need all your strength."

She ate, eventually. It took a while before she could, however. She was laughing too hard.

ON SATURDAY Matt found himself wound up to a fever pitch of what he could only describe as ridiculously adolescent anticipation and excitement. He hadn't been close to Allie in nearly a week, and he was eager as a teenager to see, touch, smell and talk to her again, face-to-face. He was also just as nervous as an inexperienced youth, and that amazed him!

In so many ways, the week, including last weekend, had been a good one, thanks to her. In other ways, it had been just shy of a nightmare, but that had nothing to do with Allie Ford. The young college woman Allie had suggested as a baby-sitter had been over twice already and had proven capable of handling Laurel reasonably well. Debbie Preston was a serious person with a quiet sense of humor, a student majoring in psychology and a woman able to sympathize with Laurel's situation. She was also engaged to a young man and had absolutely no interest in seducing Matt.

Things seemed to be falling into place.

The problem was, he didn't really know what that place was or what he wanted it to be. His feelings about Allie were clear enough in many ways; unclear in others. Did he really just want her as a friend and/or temporary lover? Did he have the right to become her lover, knowing her history, the way her husband had walked out on her, knowing he would be leaving her eventually, as well? With the messy way things were going over his guardianship of Laurel and the management of the Essex estate, he wanted to get out of this place just as soon as it was all settled.

Hell, why did it have to be so complicated? He checked his image in the mirror, briefly, nodding in self-approval at the conservative look of the dark suit and white shirt, the plain red-and-navy-striped tie. A church dance, she had said this would be. So, he'd dressed for church. He vaguely remembered her mentioning a specific ethnic group's religious organization, but had forgotten whether it was Italian or Greek or whatever. That didn't matter, either. The evening would be pleasant, but hardly wild, he was sure. What mattered was that he would be spending it with her.

ALLIE WAS just about ready when she heard the doorbell ring. She stopped for a moment, listening to Fred yap and realized she had neglected to tell Matt *anything* about the evening.

Including the fact that they were doubling with M.J. and Miranda. Well, he was supposed to be an adventurer. Now was his big chance to prove it. She put the hairbrush down and went down the hall, telling Fred to be quiet. She opened the door and smiled...

...Unable to say a word.

Matt Glass looked like a real movie star or a *GQ* model—cool, suave and groomed to the nth degree. He did not look like a rough-and-ready adventurer. Further, he didn't look like a harassed single parent of a feisty two-year-old girl. A big change had occurred in a small space of time, and she approved, wholeheartedly.

Since she had last seen him—a brief encounter up in the mall two days ago when Laurel was too much of a distraction for them to have a decent conversation—he'd had his hair cut and styled, and the usual endearing but grubby shadow of blond whisker was gone from his face. He looked smooth, tanned, sophisticated and expensive. The suit was obviously tailor-made.

"Uh, hi," she finally managed. "Come on in."

Matt did. Fred greeted him, enthusiastically, but as he bent down to pat the little animal, he had trouble tearing his gaze away from Fred's owner. When he'd first set eyes on Allison Ford, he remembered, he had thought that if she was fixed up properly, she could hold her own with the best of the beauties of Hollywood.

He'd been right. Tonight, she could hold her own anywhere. Her hair was curled and pulled up and back, giving her a glamourous look that enhanced her natural beauty. Makeup was minimal, but just right, and the blue silk dress was a natural match for her eyes. Whatever perfume she wore blended perfectly with her own sensual scent. He almost sighed aloud.

"I'm not quite ready," she said, still smiling in an uncharacteristically self-conscious way, as if she wasn't totally comfortable with being all dressed up. "And I forgot to tell you we're going with another couple."

"Oh?" Matt straighted. "Who?"

"My cousin, M. J. Nichols, and his date, Miranda Stamos. M.J.'s a lawyer."

Matt smiled. "I know there's a good lawyer joke in there somewhere but I just can't think of it right at the moment."

"You don't mind?"

"Of course not. In fact, I'd like to meet this lawyer cousin. If we hit it off, I might take some of my business problems over to his office. I'm beginning to think I need a personal attorney here, as well as the one I have in California. The Essex estate is getting more complicated than I thought it would be, and I'm really not at all happy with Martha's lawyer, nor, it would seem, is she with me. Of course, there's nothing I can do to change that, but..." He shrugged.

She put her hands on her hips. "Are you having trouble over the estate because your sister's lawyer doesn't *like* you?"

He held up his hands. "Let's not get into that tonight. Tonight is for relaxing and having fun." He put his hands on her bare shoulders. "And getting you political points, remember?"

She moved closer, and the temptation to kiss her became almost unbearable. But he had to resist. A kiss, an intimate touch, and he would be a lost man, he knew!

"There's something else you ought to be forewarned about tonight," she said, laughter in her tone, though her expression was serious.

"What's that?" He managed to speak normally, despite the strength of his desire.

"This town is unique in its social dress code. We are, as a group, unwilling to conform. Most events, you'll find folks dressed anywhere from a formal suit or a fancy dress to jeans. And you cannot tell who is who by what they wear. The most important person at an event could easily be one of the most casually dressed. Tonight'll be no exception."

"Am I overdressed?"

"No, you look great. A lot of men will have on nice suits. That's not the problem."

"What, then?"

"You're really going to regret wearing that red tie with a white shirt," she said, breaking into outright laughter.

CHAPTER SEVEN

SHE WAS RIGHT about the tie, of course. But Matt didn't find out why until later that night. It had nothing to do with formal or informal dress. The reason was far more entertaining...

About fifteen minutes after Matt arrived at her home, her cousin and his date showed up. Matt took an instant liking to M.J., though he also knew immediately that he was under censorious inspection by the man because of the lawyer's relationship to Allie. Clearly, M.J. cared a great deal for his cousin and watched out for her interests.

Nevertheless, Matt decided this was a guy who would be a friend one could trust with one's life. Matt's instincts for such good people rarely failed him and had kept him from disaster more than once during his years of risky living.

M.J.'s date, Miranda Stamos, who was dark-eyed and beautiful, flirted with Matt briefly when introduced, but she obviously did so out of habit rather than serious intent. All in all, Matt decided as they left Allie's house and piled into M.J.'s Saab, it was likely to be a pleasant evening, spent with pleasant people.

Miranda, M.J. and Allie chatted about local matters as M.J. drove them across the city to the only place large enough to cater for this sort of event. Allie explained to him, with occasional interruptions by M.J., how the Events Complex had been a political millstone around the neck of the last municipal administration until someone suggested making it more easily available to nonprofit private events as well as public ones. The financial problems had begun to turn around after that, Allie said.

Then, the conversation turned to Matt.

"I know M.J. says you're from California," Miranda said. "But somehow I get the feeling we've met somewhere before." She regarded Matt from over the back of the front seat, her dark eyes full of frank curiosity.

Matt slid his hand over to cover Allie's. "I don't think so," he replied, smiling. "I'd surely remember." He gave Allie's hand a squeeze. She responded, indicating she understood his flirting with Miranda was only out of good manners.

"No, you've got me wrong. I'm not coming on to you," Miranda said, frowning now. "I mean, I really do think I've seen you..."

"Miranda," M.J. interjected, laughing. "Give the guy a break. He just..."

"You're on TV!" Miranda turned almost all the way around in the seat belt and put her hands on the back of the seat, gripping the headrest. "I mean, not around here. But I've got one of those satellite dishes and I get channels from all over. And I've seen you..."

"I have an ad for my business on a local Los Angeles station," Matt admitted. "I run an adventure-tour company. That must be..."

"No." Miranda looked determined. "It was something else."

Allie watched and listened. Matt was uneasy and hiding something. Why? His hand was still over hers on the seat, and she had the urge to move away from him. But she decided to wait. To trust him a little longer.

"You might as well confess, Matt," M.J. said, glancing at them through the rearview mirror. "I neglected to explain that Miranda is not only a first-class beautiful woman who runs a first-class business, but that that business is a private detective agency. Best in the state. If you've got some deep dark secret, she'll ferret it out, make no mistake about that.''

"You're a P.I.?" Matt stared at the dark-haired beauty. Miranda grinned and nodded.

Allie made a funny sound. He couldn't tell if she was laughing or groaning.

"Okay," Matt said. "The truth is, I'm embarrassed as hell about it, but they've made a TV movie about me. That's what's clicking off the signals in your mind. It hasn't been aired yet, but they're already doing some promo material. I think it's scheduled for some time this fall. I intend to be out of the country when it happens. Far, far away! If you've been watching the L.A. channels, they've been covering the project pretty closely, since it involved important and popular people from the industry. Good press, you see."

Allie was stunned. "They did what? Made a movie? About you? Why?"

"Shoot, Allie," M.J. said. "Don't make it sound like the guy's not worth it. What did you do to deserve it, Matt?"

Before he could reply, Allie shouted out, "Oh!" Realization suddenly hit her. "That rescue thing. The movie people in the jungle. Right?"

"Right." Matt pulled at his shirt collar, clearly quite uncomfortable now. "And sometimes, I wish I'd just stayed home and left them out there in the damn jungle. They're more dangerous than half the wild animals there."

"What jungle?" Miranda was practically panting with curiosity at this point. "What movie people? What? What? What?"

As Allie listened, Matt gave a laconic, deliberately undramatic account of what had been a spectacularly dangerous and dramatic operation. Matt had rescued almost a hundred people who had been caught in the middle of a small uprising in a politically unstable country. He and a small group of specially trained men had gone into the area, created a diversion, which distracted the kidnappers, and then had led the movie people out to safety through a trackless area of jungle. An area not even the local soldiers dared to tackle. Though he glossed over the trek, she could tell it must have been a harrowing adventure. Everyone had survived and the injuries had been minimal. When Matt was done with the telling, there was silence for a few moments.

Then: "Wow," Miranda said.

"I'll second that," added M.J.

"All in favor..." Allie raised her hand.

"Allie." Matt sounded annoyed. Annoyed and concerned. "All of you, please listen. If this gets made too much of and heard of by the wrong people, it could do me more harm than good. It shows an image I'm trying to live down. A man who lives for danger. What kind of father is that? I'm through with that kind of life. I want to live safely and raise Laurel in a home where she'll have the kind of security I... Where she'll be secure and know it. So, I'd really appreciate it if you'd all try to keep a lid on this TV thing."

Allie said nothing, but she wondered just what lay beneath the surface of his insistence on safety and security and what he meant by the wrong people. Who in the world would care that he'd been a hero once, and was now ready to settle down to raising a child. It showed strong character, as far as she was concerned.

Didn't it?

M.J. turned off the highway onto the Events Center access road. "If you hated the idea so much, why'd you contract to let them tell your story in the first place."

"That was almost four years ago," Matt explained. "I was different. My life was different. I made a mistake and had no idea I was doing it, until recently. But, no one can read the future.''

"Well." Miranda reached back and patted his cheek. Then she settled down into her seat. "Don't worry about me, Matt. My business is keeping secrets."

"And I won't talk, either," M.J. said. "Don't let my much-maligned profession scare you."

"My lips are sealed," Allie added. "But once that show airs, with your name, you know you'll have to deal with the consequences."

"By then," Matt said, his tone strange, "I hope there'll be none." He stared out the window off into the gold light of the Wyoming summer evening.

Before Allie could pursue this, however, they had arrived at their destination. M.J. pulled into a parking space. "Here we are, folks. But before we bail out and start partying, who's volunteering to be Designate for the Night."

Matt raised an eyebrow and looked at Allie. "Does he mean designated driver? What for? I thought this was a church party."

After the laughter ceased, Allie explained. "It is. But it's also a total social blowout, complete with dedicated eating, drinking and dancing." She reached for the keys M.J. dangled in his hand. "I'll take the sober role tonight," she added. "Not only do I have to do some political glad-handing here, I'm heading up to the ranch on Wednesday, so I'm planning to get some work done on my real job tomorrow afternoon. Can't do that with an ouzo hangover. I'll be tired enough from all the dancing."

Matt slapped his forehead. "Ouzo! Greek! Dancing. I get it now. This is like a village festival." His grin was as wide and genuine as Allie had ever seen it. "Come on," he said, taking her hand and slipping his arm around her waist. "We are going to have one hell of a good time!" He pulled her out of the car and started sidestepping in a complex dance pattern, his free hand over his head, fingers snapping out a rhythm.

"Good grief!" Miranda watched, astonished. "He knows the steps. Like a native!" She turned to M.J. "Here moves an expert. Observe and learn, you Wasp barbarian."

"You know how to do this?" Allie stumbled and found herself pulled tightly against Matt's side. "Greek line dancing?"

"Learned it before I hit puberty," he said, releasing her with apparent reluctance. "My father and I spent winters in the Greek islands for a while. Before the Southeast Asia bug bit him, and we were off to Thailand and Singapore. Yes, I can dance quite a few standards." He gazed at her, an unreadable expression in his brown eyes. "I'm just delighted and astonished to find the opportunity here."

"In Valium City, you mean?"

He grinned. "I deserve that. And, I concede I was wrong. Let's party," he said.

And they did.

The dinner and dance were held in a large hall off to the side of the Events Complex. They were met at the door by teenagers, all dressed for the occasion. These kids, Allie explained, were the church's youth group, doing their part. The women did the organizing and special cooking, the youngsters did the decorating and manned the ticket tables. The men found and paid for the authentic band.

As they handed in their tickets, they were presented with round silver stickers declaring them Greek for a Day. The stickers were to be attached somewhere on clothing, so that party crashers would be detected.

Allie put hers on the top of her dress just below her right shoulder. "It'll stay, believe me," she said. "The stickum on these is incredible. I put one on my bathroom mirror once after one of these parties a few years ago—I was not very sober that night—and I'm still scraping little bits of it off when I clean the mirror.''

Matt attached his to his tie. Allie raised her eyebrows, but said nothing. She wondered if he'd noticed how few other men were wearing ties. Even M.J., usually conservative in his dress, had on a polo shirt.

They joined the throng and mingled. Matt found that, just as Allie had described, it was composed of people of all ages, extremes ranging from Greek great-grandparents whose English was still limited and heavily accented to young children who could fly from one language to the other without missing a beat. Many of the revellers, however, were not Greek but were local folk who came to enjoy this traditional fest with their ethnic neighbors. And clothing was as varied as she had predicted. Though she introduced him to everyone she spoke to, he held back, letting her dominate the conversations. These were her people, not his, and this was her night. He was only there to help her with her political ambitions, and for no other reason. He watched her lovely face and her sensual form as she smiled and moved.

No other reason. No selfish motives on his part...

Right.

To his great relief, no one gave any indication that they recognized him. He and Allie had already decided that he was only to be Matt Glass, my friend from California. Some women stared at him, but no one said anything.

During dinner, they sat with Miranda's family, a large convivial group, all of whom accepted Matt merely as Allie's friend. Not boyfriend or potential suitor.

Until he made the mistake of laughing at a joke delivered by an aged uncle. The joke was delivered entirely in idiomatic Greek. Silence fell.

"You understand?" Jason Stamos, Miranda's father, a proud, handsome man asked. "You got Uncle John's joke?'' He stared at Matt, his attitude toward the newcomer now obviously in flux. Every other Stamos at the table also stared intently.

Matt cursed himself. "I didn't mean to eavesdrop."

"No, no, no." Stamos spread out his hands. "You misunderstand. We are impressed and pleased." He indicated his family. "It's rare to have a…stranger who can converse with us in our language, much less get a joke. How long did you live in my country?"

Matt explained briefly about his childhood. His audience, Allie noted, was rapt, hanging on every word. "I never had trouble picking up languages," he said. "We lived in so many places that I just would learn on the street what I needed to make my way." He shrugged, plainly uncomfortable with the topics of his skills and his childhood.

"But your poppa?" Miranda's grandmother looked alarmed. "Was he not with you? Keeping you from trouble on those streets. A young boy should have a poppa to watch over him. To hug him when he is good. Punish him when he is bad."

"My…father was a busy man."

"But…"

"Grandmomma, I think Matt has told enough about his private life." Miranda turned to her uncle. "But you should also know that he can dance."

"Ahhhh!" The exclamation was collective.

From then on, Matt knew he'd changed status. The family was clearly fond of Allie, and now he met some strange standards of approval. In spite of Miranda and Allie's attempts to keep him off the griddle, pointed questions were fired at him concerning his past, his future and, particularly, his intentions toward Allie. With her help, he evaded as best he could. Then, he was saved. The music started.

Allie hadn't noticed the band setting up while they had been talking. She'd been too busy trying to protect Matt from the Stamos family who were most interested in him. But when the first notes of the Greek music wailed through the air, she found herself lifted out of her chair and led toward the wide, circular section set off for the dancing.

"Uh, I'm not all that familiar with the steps," she said, hesitating and pulling back. "Why don't you go on without me for a little while. It looks like mostly men out there now, anyway."

Matt paused. Holding her around the waist felt so good, he hadn't paid much attention to which dance was being played. "You're right," he said, smiling at her. "It is a men's dance. I was in too much of a hurry to get away from Great-grandmother and her questions. I'd like to do this, though. Mind?"

"Not at all." She indicated a large group of people gathering toward the back of the room. Political discussions were radiating from the bunch. "I have my work to do. You enjoy yourself."

"All right. But I won't let you work all night." He touched her face with his fingertips. "I'm sure once the men have had a chance to show off, they'll get into the village dances where everyone can join. The steps are not that hard to learn. If you've done it before, you'll remember, and I can teach you the easier ones with no trouble."

"I'm sure of that," she replied, wondering if either of them was talking about dancing now.

So, she left him, already moving to the rhythm of the music and shucking off his jacket. It was, however, difficult to tear her gaze from him, he made such a romantic picture as he moved in and joined the men in the line. His body picked up the rhythm and the step pattern immediately. The dance was elementally male without being overtly sexual at all. Showing off the men's strength... Their purposefulness... She could watch him all night...

No, she could not! Sighing, she reminded herself of her

real purpose for being there. She made a quick survey of the crowd and wandered over to the far side of the room where the biggest political guns were congregating.

Most of them around Rita Morely.

After greeting some friends and a few lesser local political lights and competitors, Allison approached, nerves on edge. She hadn't seen Rita tonight before this moment and had secretly hoped the other candidate had not realized the potential of this gathering or had not managed an invitation.

But, clearly, she had done both. And her escort was one of the great silver-haired foxes of Wyoming politics, David Benning, a former U.S. senator, a man who had retired ostensibly due to a heart condition. A consummate politician and wheeler-dealer, he was also known as a clever manipulator of other things besides politics, and that's what had supposedly led to his downfall. Allie had heard rumors about dear David cutting and running before some romantic scandal caught up to his coattails, but it was purely speculation and gossip, of course. What bothered her was the fact that he still had a fair degree of political clout.

And here he was with Rita, a widow, just as she was, on his arm. Allie pasted on a smile and moved in.

Rita saw her first. "Well, hello, if it isn't Allie Ford," the older woman said. She extended a perfectly manicured hand. "How are you tonight, dear? Really didn't expect to see you here. You're so busy with your family and your little business and all."

Allie touched hands. Her own nails were short and unpainted. "Oh? Why not, Rita?" she asked, looking up a little bit. Morely was taller by several inches, and her high pompadour of graying black hair made her seem even taller. She was also thin as a rail. "I always send the kids up to my parents' ranch for the summer, and I've adjusted my work to take in the time I need for campaigning. Besides, I wouldn't miss this party for anything," Allie added.

"But your escort?" Rita looked around. "I don't see you with a date. Don't tell me you came all by your lonesome self? How dreary for you, darling."

Here, David Benning broke into the conversation. "Haw, haw, haw," he said more than laughed. "No, Rita, honey, she did not get here by herself. Our Allie here has landed herself a fine catch of a man for tonight's festivities." His bushy white eyebrows rose. "Or, at least an exciting one, so I hear. Just her speed, if you ask me." His tone had some ice in it, despite his warm words. He bent down and gave Allie an unnecessarily long kiss on the cheek. "How are you, darlin'?" he asked.

"Fine, David, I..."

"What exciting man?" Rita interrupted. "Don't tell me that Josh Henderson got up enough nerve to take you out. Of course, I'd hardly call him exciting. Not in politics, anyway. But I suppose you already know that."

Allie bit her lip, determined to say nothing about Rita's stealing her former campaign director, Ned, and leaving her to manage with Josh. This could deteriorate to a catty snarling match if she wasn't careful.

"No," she replied. "I didn't bring Josh. I asked another man out tonight. Just a friend. He's not from around here. You wouldn't know him, Rita."

A carefully penciled eyebrow shot up. "Oh?" Rita looked unconvinced. "I thought I knew all the single..."

"Hey, they're playing our song, Allie." A warm hand settled on her shoulder and turned her around with gentle playfulness. Matt, in all his masculine glory, stood in front of her, blond hair blazing gold in the artificial light, his handsome face glowing with sweat and exertion, his smile broad, genuinely full of life and joy.

True to her prediction, his tie was gone, and the stains on his collar from where his sweating had caused the red dye to run onto his shirt were pinkish. He saw her notice, and he smiled even wider. "You were right about the tie," he said. "Should have listened to you, as usual."

Allie started to introduce him, but he pulled her away from the group. "Come on, darlin'. Dance with me!" he said. He nodded at the other people gathered there, but his eyes never left her face. The world of Ritas and Davids receded, and Matt became the center of her universe.

A sense that all was right with the world filled her.

"Okay," Allie said. "I'll try." She took his hand. The sense of harmony increased on contact. *This* was why she'd come to the dance, she realized as soon as they touched. Heat radiated from him, including her in the sweet warmth. The chill of the encounter with Rita Morely left her as she was led toward the dancers. He pulled her into the line, and in a few minutes, she was at ease with the simpler steps and moving smoothly and rhythmically with the music and the other dancers.

Especially, though, she moved easily and harmoniously with Matt Glass. It was as if they had been made to dance together, even in this unpartnered style. As if their bodies already knew how to move smoothly in concert.

For the rest of the evening, she danced with Matt next to her in the line, his hand in her hand, or his arm across her shoulders and her arm around his waist. It was an intimacy that teased by not being quite complete. Teased, but also promised delicious and wonderful things that no words could have done more eloquently.

Things Allie began to want very much as the minutes flew by on the notes of the music.

From time to time, when the band took a break or when the tempo and pattern of the particular dance was too difficult for her, she and Matt stood outside on the terrace overlooking the city in the cooler night air. It could have been a very romantic place. Oh well, she mused, at least if it wasn't so crowded with people it gave her a chance to visit and talk politics.

The view of Linville Springs was spectacular, bringing out local pride in almost everyone who gazed on the lights of the city. Rita's little entourage, Allie noticed, never left the back of the room. Never joined the dancing. Never came outside to chat with the people enjoying the fresh air. They huddled, talking with one another and speaking with any others who wandered over, but made no effort to share in the fun.

Their loss, she figured.

The only thing that bothered her was the venom in the other woman's stare when she caught her looking directly at her. David Benning also watched her. Matt, it seemed, however, came under a more calculating scrutiny from the older politician. Allie filed that for future reference, hoping that nothing would ever come of it, but beginning to wake up to the fact that she'd better be ready for anything.

And, she decided she ought to mention her concerns to Matt. Even though he was just a friend, an innocent bystander in her political business, some of the trouble might rub off in his direction if she made too much of their relationship. Rita was obviously angry and more than willing to play dirty.

Which, Allie realized when she thought about it, was actually a good sign, because it meant Rita was worried about her as an opponent. Allie clutched Matt's hand as they danced in the line, and she threw back her head and laughed for the sheer pleasure and joy of it. At that instant, her worries disappeared like dark smoke.

Matt felt her happiness go right through him like a jolt of electricity. Through their joined hands, he could almost experience her emotions directly. Right then, he wanted to escort her from the dance floor, find a secluded place and make love for the rest of the night.

It would be a night like no other for both of them, and he knew it in every atom of his being.

And, he also knew that if he did that, he'd be the biggest scoundrel in the history of romance. She was too vulnerable, and she would place far too much stock in what happened. Think he'd fallen in love with her. Think he'd be likely to stay with her. Which, no matter how much he wanted her right now, would never happen. It would be the same experience she'd had with her husband. Love and desertion. Betrayal, for whatever reason, was still betrayal.

He couldn't do it. It was not right! But there was no denying he wanted Allie. Desperately.

Fortunately, he was no randy teen, but a man experienced enough to hide his rampaging desires reasonably well. At least in public. What would happen when they finally were alone was anybody's guess.

Allie could sense that her friend was feeling far more than merely friendly. By the time the party was over at the traditional midnight hour, he seemed almost too hot to handle. His brown eyes had depths of desire in them beyond anything she'd ever seen before, and when he fixed his hungry, heated gaze on her, she felt herself respond, eagerly. Her body seemed to melt and swell and sink and rise, all at the same time. She knew the feelings, but it had been many years since they had come on her so strongly. Many, many years.

She wanted him. Wanted this man who had such strength and grace in his body, passion in his eyes and gentleness in his hands. Who was not hers to keep, but only to enjoy for a time.

And, she determined, she could do just that! She joined M.J. and Miranda, who were both feeling very little pain, and Matt, who still seemed relatively sober, and began to figure which home she and Matt should use for their first night together. Would his baby-sitter be willing to stay for the entire night at his house? Or should they just take a chance on Laurel's interrupting them with another nightmare... It was a dilemma, but one she could deal with, eventually.

But, as they were making their way toward the exit, Rita Morely and David Benning intercepted them. Rita was all smiles. David looked as if he was smiling at something no one else could see or appreciate. Allie suppressed a shiver when she saw the strange expression on the older man's face. He looked downright spooky. But she forgot about him when Rita spoke.

"I have finally found enough people with enough information to put it all together," she said, addressing Matt directly and not looking at anyone else. "*You're* the young man who came out when Martha Essex died and is *claiming* to be her brother." She stared rudely now, looking at him as if he were a bug on a glass slide. "My, my; my. Allison, you do manage to ally yourself with the *strangest* men. First, one that ran away from you, and now this." The words hung in the air like a bad smell. She gave the entire group another smile and swept past. David Benning had the good grace to try looking embarrassed as he followed her out the door.

Allie looked at Matt. *He* looked as if he were ready to take the world apart with his bare hands!

CHAPTER EIGHT

"CLAIMS to be Martha's brother?" Allie put her hand on Matt's arm. "Matt, what's she blithering about?"

"Nothing." His face was stone.

"Matt, what's the deal?" She shook him, gently. "What did Rita mean?"

"It's not your worry," he said, cold as ice. "I'd better get home. You ready to drive?"

"Hey, man." M.J. moved in. "You have a problem? You're with friends, remember."

"Not here." Miranda pushed at them all. "Let's wait until we're out in the car. Alone."

But once in the Saab, all Matt would say was that he was having some trouble with Martha's lawyer, Penny Jackson. "She's beating on the fact that Martha and I weren't brought up together. That we were essentially strangers. She doesn't see me as Laurel's proper guardian, that's all," he said. "It's a personality thing."

"The hell with that!" M.J. declared. "She has no legal right to decide on the basis of her likes and dislikes if your sister's will..."

"Well, my sister's will is one of the issues." Matt, who was sitting in the front passenger seat next to Allie, rubbed his eyes. "But as I said, it's not your problem. Please, forget it. I had a great time tonight, and so did the rest of you. Let's just go on home."

Allie made no move to start the car. "Is the lawyer ques-

tioning your qualifications as a parent, or is she worried you're after the estate money?''

Matt regarded her. No desire showed in his eyes now. Just anger and frustration. ''Oh, I'd say both.'' He looked away. ''And, she has some grounds. My past...''

''Is past!'' Allie touched his arm. ''You're the best guardian in the world for Laurel,'' she said. ''I've rarely seen such an attentive and concerned parent. I'd swear to it in any court of law in the nation. And even more important, Laurel depends on you and loves you. If she lost you, she...''

''She won't.'' Matt stared out the window. ''I don't give a damn about the estate. Not for myself. I'd hate to lose it for her, though. It's her birthright. But if it came to it, I'd...''

''You'd what?'' Allie felt hot anger. ''Cut and run? Hide with her? No, mister. You stay right here and fight for what's rightfully yours and Laurel's.''

''Allie, settle down,'' Miranda advised. ''You can't know what's on Matt's mind.''

''I know Jackson,'' M.J. said. ''This woman who doesn't like you has a reputation for being difficult. Maybe I...''

''I don't want to burden you people with this.'' Matt shook his head. ''I'll handle my own problems, thanks.''

''Maybe,'' Allie said, touching him again, ''we'd like to be burdened. You need friends if you're really facing a hard time, Matt. Don't shut me...don't shut us out.'' Suddenly, her feelings were as strong as they had been earlier, but now they were different. More grounded. She...*cared.*

No. No... She...loved him?

To hide her confusion and turmoil, Allie reached forward and started the engine. She could not be feeling this! Should not. Not for Matt Glass, a virtual stranger. A man whom she'd only known ten days and who'd be out of her life in a few months at the very latest. But what else could it be?

Still soft and tremulous, but real and getting more and more solid and undeniable.

"Look," she said, over the rumble of the motor. "It's late. Almost two in the morning now. We've all had a hard night of partying. There're four of us. I vote we get together tomorrow and talk. But, ultimately, it's up to you, Matt. Do you want our help?"

He was quiet for a long time, his profile etched against the night by the arc lights in the parking lot. "I think I do," he said, finally. "If it were just me, I'd slog it out, in my own way. But Laurel... I'll ask for help because of her. *We* need your help." His voice seemed close to breaking.

M.J. leaned forward and slapped his shoulder. "Don't worry, Matt. There are a fair number of good brains in this car, even if some are a little pickled tonight. We'll combine and conquer. Count on it!"

Allie saw Matt smile, but he said nothing. Just slouched down in the seat and folded his arms across his chest. She started out of the lot, and M.J. and Miranda fell silent also.

By the time she got back to her house, it was clear none of the others were in any shape to drive, and Allie was too tired to taxi them so she offered beds all around.

"I've plenty of room," she said. "Matt and M.J. can sleep downstairs in Sam's room on the twin beds and Miranda can bunk in Sally's queen-size."

"Oh, goodie," Miranda said, with a giggle. "A spend-the-night party."

"Sounds great to me," M.J. echoed her sentiment.

But Matt shook his head. "I can't leave Laurel all night. If she has a nightmare, I..."

"Matt, she knows the sitter now. Debbie's steady and reliable. You can't be with her twenty-four hours a day, seven days a week for the rest of your life."

He sighed. "I'm so tired and worried, I guess I can't think straight. You're right. And I did set it up in case I was out all night," he added, looking over at her. His face was expressionless. "Debbie planned to sleep over anyway, since we were getting back so late. And I admit I had some ideas about how I wanted to spend the rest of our date."

Allie smiled. "I'm flattered."

M.J. made some rude noises. "I think this is where I'm supposed to get into the act and be indignantly in defense of my cousin's honor, but frankly, I'd rather go to sleep." He opened the car door. "Coming, dear?" he asked, extending his hand to Miranda. "I'm afraid I have to confess that I don't even have the energy to make a decent pass at you tonight. Forgive me."

Miranda giggled again.

Allie got them all into the house, distributed fresh toothbrushes and showed them to their rooms. She was exhausted herself, and would have fallen right into bed but for the necessity of letting Fred outside for a few minutes. Feeling she needed some fresh air, herself, she went outside with the dog.

The night air was chilly and clear as crystal. While Fred sniffed around, Allie studied the stars, the hills behind the house and the alley that ran in back of her yard...

And the car parked down the alley. In just the right spot to have a clear view of her home. She shivered. Wondered who...?

Fred frisked at her feet, indicating it was time to go inside. Allie shrugged and followed the poodle. If the car was there in the morning, she'd report it. Glancing at the kitchen clock while she got Fred a treat from the pantry, she noted that morning wasn't far away. She pressed her fingers to her temples. Even without drinking, she'd managed to get a headache.

It was undoubtedly due to the cigarette smoke and the noise.

It could not have a thing to do with the crazy notion that

she might be in love with Matt Glass. And nothing at all to do with her frustrated lust for him. Not a thing! She checked on the cats, made sure they had enough food and water and shooed Fred into the bedroom. Time to sleep, she instructed herself.

But she did not get much rest, in spite of her exhaustion. Morning came far too soon, bringing with it birdsongs, Fred whining to go out again and the phone ringing. She was tempted to let the machine answer, but it was Sunday, and realizing it might well be her kids, she reached for the receiver.

She listened, and her heart froze. The voice was low, male and gravelly, and the insults and accusations that poured like acid into her ear were words that had never before been leveled at her. Indignation rose, along with bile.

Then, with a shiver of horror, she thought she knew who was talking. At first, she was too stunned to do anything but listen. Then, slowly, she replaced the receiver, the numbness of emotional shock threatening to make her drop it before it cradled. She got it in place, then just lay still.

The bedroom door opened. Fred barked once, then was silent when she saw who it was. Matt stood there, wearing only the pants from the suit he'd had on the night before. His hair was wet and slicked back as if he'd just stepped from the shower. He even looked clean-shaven.

"I heard," he said, his lips twisting in a strange expression. As if he was going to be sick. "Heard it all. I was in the kitchen and grabbed the phone without thinking. Figured it might be the sitter with a problem, and I didn't want to wake anyone else." He moved into the room and shut the door. Fred settled back on the bed, watching him. "Are you all right?"

"No."

"Any idea who?"

She shook her head, tears starting to trickle down the sides of her face. Her breathing became rapid. "It...it sounded like Paul." She gripped the sheet and summer blanket with clenched hands that trembled. "But he's..." Her voice rose to a treble level, almost like a child's cry.

Matt came around and pulled her up to him, embracing her tightly, not even noticing how little separated their bare skin right now. All that he thought of was how to soothe away her fear and horror. "It wasn't your husband, Allie. And it wasn't a ghost with an evil tongue. It was an enemy who's afraid of you. Keep *him* afraid. Don't let the fear turn onto you. You're safe. You're with me."

She tried to cling to the last shred of dignity she possessed, but the sobs came. She collapsed into his arms, and put her head on his shoulder and cried.

And she did feel safe. She felt safer than she ever had before. Safer than she'd felt with Paul, the man she had trusted to be with her for the rest of her life. Fred snuggled in, determined to be part of the moment, and that gesture of companionship from her pet made her cry all the harder.

Matt held her, reveling in the feelings roiling through him. Women had cried in bed with him before, but never had he responded with such tenderness. Her little dog looked up at him with dark brown eyes full of trust and concern. Matt thought he might cry himself in another moment. A quick, hard knock on the bedroom door jarred him out of that, however.

"What the hell's the matter?" The door opened again and M.J. and Miranda entered. Both looked dreadfully hung over and worried. "We heard the phone, then you walking down here and then Allie's crying," M.J. explained.

"The call. Bad news? Is somebody hurt?" Miranda asked.

Allie managed to get hold of her emotions. She wiped

her face with the sheet and pushed Matt back a little. "No," she said. "It was…"

"It was a poison-pen phone call," Matt explained. "Some bastard tried to scare her. That's all." He stood up, releasing Allie. Fred placed her front paws on his leg, and he picked her up. "If it happens again, we can get a special gadget that'll trace the caller."

"Scare *you?*" M.J. ran his hand over his face, making the dark bristle of his whiskers rasp. "Allie, you aren't afraid of the devil himself. So who could possibly put such a fright into you?"

"He hinted he was Paul. Back from the grave I'd put him in." She hiccuped, forcing back more sobs. "Said I'd killed him. Said I was…being unfaithful to his memory."

M.J. swore.

"That's the expurgated version?" Miranda asked, folding her arms over her chest. "I take it the real thing was more vitriolic?"

Allie nodded.

M.J cleared his throat. "I need coffee, some aspirin and a shower, and not necessarily in that order. Then, I say we hold a war council. We can deal with Matt's situation first."

"No." Matt stroked the poodle, calming her. "My problems can wait."

Allie reached for her bathrobe and pulled it on. "This may be an isolated incident. It may never happen again and it's no one's problem but mine," she said, getting up. "You all have homes to go to and things you need to do. I'll get some coffee perking, and…"

"My God!" Miranda exclaimed. "I don't know when I've seen two people more stubborn about getting help from willing friends." She put her hands on her head. "If my head didn't hurt so bad, I'd get mad at the both of you."

Allie reached for Fred. "Take a shower, Miranda," she

said. "Use my bathroom. Here's a clean robe. You'll feel much better, believe me." She walked out of the bedroom and headed down the hall.

Matt found himself staring at M.J. "She ever have a call like this before?"

The lawyer shook his head. "Not to my knowledge. And I think she'd have told me."

"Take a shower, yourself, M.J.," Miranda said. "We won't let her kick us out so easily. And Matt, if you want to go get your niece and bring her down here so your mind is at ease, do it."

Matt moved his gaze to the woman private investigator. "You think there's any connection between her problem and my situation?"

Miranda shrugged.

"Because if there is, I'll get out of her life. I'll take Laurel and…"

"You'll what?" Allie came back, hurriedly, Fred at her heels. "Leave town? Leave me? Oh, great. That'll be a big help." Her angry expression melted. "M.J., there's a strange car parked just down the alley. It was there last night, too. Gave me a funny feeling. Like someone was watching the house."

Matt looked at M.J. They both left the room at a run. Allie heard the back door slam. "They aren't wearing shoes," she said.

"Hell," Miranda commented. "M.J. doesn't have his pants on. Just underwear."

Their laughter was uneasy, but genuine.

A few minutes later, the two men came back inside to the kitchen. Allie had the coffee going, and Miranda was in the shower.

"We scared 'em off," M.J. announced. "Whoever they were, they saw us both coming and they peeled out fast, backward down the alley."

"I got the license number," Matt added. "But it's an out-of-state plate. Could be a rental, too."

Allie set out mugs, cream and sugar. "What kind of car do you think it was?"

"Toyota," Matt said.

"Land Cruiser," M.J. added.

Allie hesitated, then said "The other night, Matt, when I left your place, I thought someone was following me. It was a squarish kind of car. It could have been a Land Cruiser. I think there were two people inside, but it turned off once I hit the city limits, so I didn't get a chance to really see."

The men glanced at each other. M.J. took a mug and filled it with coffee. "Two people? That how you read it, Matt?"

"Yes." Matt filled another mug. "There were two people in the Toyota. I'd swear to it."

"I'm heading for the shower now," M.J. said, carrying his mug with him. "Don't make any rash moves or important decisions until I return." He left the room as Miranda walked into the kitchen, her hair wrapped in a towel.

"I'm going to get Laurel," Matt said. "All this is making me uneasy. I want her with me." He gulped his coffee. "You'll be all right with M.J. and Miranda here, won't you?" he asked, directing his question to Allie.

Allie stood with her mouth open. Under any other circumstances, she'd have been insulted at the inference that she was unable to care for her own safety. But for now she let it pass. "Yes," she replied. "I'll be all right with them here."

"Good." He nodded solemnly, clearly not seeing the irony in his level of concern for a woman who had managed to take good care of herself and her children for all of her adult life. Then, he went downstairs to get his shoes, shirt and car keys. A minute later, he was back upstairs and out the front door.

"Wow," Miranda whispered. She sipped coffee and studied Allie's expression.

"Yeah," Allie didn't meet her gaze directly. Tears stung her eyes, and she wasn't exactly sure why. "Give 'em an inch." She went over to the pantry to take out pancake mix. As she opened the pantry door, the three cats magically appeared. Sighing, she deposited a fresh scoop of dry cat food in their dishes. Then she took the batter to the counter. "Some men don't know how to stay out of a person's business, so they end up trying to boss everyone around."

"That's not what I mean, and you know it, Allison Ford." Miranda set her coffee mug down on the table and started to towel-dry her hair. "But if you want to play dumb, feel free."

Allie slapped bacon onto a flat iron skillet. "I'm not playing dumb. Just stating facts." She was uncomfortable discussing this with Miranda. They weren't really close friends.

"Right." Miranda got up and gathered one of the cats to her chest, patting the soft fur. "The man is in love with you, Allie. How do you feel about that?" She buried her face in the cat's fur. "Nice kitty," she murmured.

Allie didn't even bother to frame an answer.

IT HIT MATT halfway up the mountain, just as a pickup truck came around a curve in his direction. Last night he'd wanted to make love to Allie. Make love until they both nearly died of the pleasure of it. Today, without that ever happening, he loved her. *Loved* her! He blinked and let out a low whistle.

That changed to a yell of surprise and rage when he saw that the pickup intended either to plow right into him or force him off the side of the road and down the cliff. No mistaking the evil intention. Instinct took over, and he twisted the wheel hard to the left, bluffing the other driver into flinching.

And, instinctively, he glanced up into the rearview mirror to see what happened behind him as he rounded the curve. The sight of the pickup screeching at the edge of the drop was the last thing he saw before he saw the oncoming dump truck and was sent spinning into pain and then oblivion.

WHEN THE PHONE rang again, Allie shrank from it. M.J., clean but wearing the rumpled clothes from the night before, reached over and picked up the receiver. He spoke. His expression twisted, then leveled into unreadablity. "What's his condition, Phil?" he asked finally. His gaze fixed on Allie and didn't leave her.

Allie felt her heartbeat stop. Phil Jacobs was the chief physician in the emergency room at the hospital. "Who's ill?" she cried, grabbing the edge of the kitchen table. "M.J.! Who?"

M.J. hung up. "Matt Glass ran his Jeep into the side of a dump truck coming down the mountain about thirty minutes ago. The Jeep's totaled, and…"

"Matt!" The tears poured down Allie's face, but she had no idea she was crying. "He's dead. It's all happening again. Just like Paul…"

M.J. looked as if she'd cut his heart out. "No, darlin', he's not, and it is not the same. Matt's all right. He's banged up some, bruises and small cuts, but nothing serious. Phil says he's got a mild concussion, that he's mad as hell and raving about some maniac trying to run him off the road, but nothing's broken and…" He quit talking. Allie had fled from the room.

"Let her go," Miranda advised as he tried to follow.

"Give her a minute, M.J. I think she's in love with the guy."

"I know." M.J. settled back in his chair. Fred, upset by her mistress's sudden departure, jumped up on the most familiar lap and settled down, as well. M.J. stroked her little head and scratched her ears. "Miranda, how would you like to work for me?" he asked.

The P.I. smiled. "Investigating things for anyone I happen to know?"

"Uh-huh." M.J. nodded. "Two people who are too stubborn and self-reliant to ask for help on their own."

"You have an employee." She held out her hand.

M.J. shook it. Then he turned it over and kissed the palm.

"THE PICKUP CAME right at me," Matt stated, speaking to the policeman investigating his case. "It was a deliberate attempt to ram me or force me off the road and over the side of the cliff." Anger thrummed in his voice, but he spoke calmly.

Allie sat in a corner of the hospital room, listening and watching. She had raced to him, only to find him full of anger, not seeming to need her attention or comfort at all. Perhaps, not even wanting her there. She wasn't sure yet. She was still trying to read him. Phil and the other physician attending Matt had insisted he stay in the hospital for twenty-four hours observation, but it was clear that Matt Glass had no intention of obeying doctors' or anyone else's orders.

When she had entered the room, the cop was asking questions, so she had only made eye contact with Matt. It had been like looking into a furnace. The variety of emotions she saw both elated and terrified her. Matt was all right!

But he was killing mad!

"The pickup truck was Teddie Baker's?" The cop looked at his notes. "You're sure about that?"

Matt shook his head, wincing in pain as he did so. "No, I'm not. I only caught a glimpse of it, since I was concentrating on avoiding it and staying alive."

"There was no evidence of a pickup at the scene," the cop said. He was about forty, overweight with thinning sandy hair, and he looked mildly irritated as if this investigation had interrupted his plans for a quiet Sunday. "Just some skid marks on the side of the road, and they could have gotten there at any time. The driver of the dump truck didn't see any other..."

"The driver of the damn dump truck had been partying all night up at a cabin!" Matt put his hand to the sides of his head. His physical pain was obvious. "But you didn't test *his* blood. Just mine."

"You'd been partying, too," the cop commented. "We have witnesses who say you weren't in any shape to drive yourself last night."

"Witnesses?" Allie interrupted, now. "What witnesses? I thought..."

"They're accusing me," Matt said. "Of reckless driving." His eyes shone with a dark, dark gleam. "The dump truck driver says I came out of nowhere and blindsided him. No one else saw the pickup that tried to take me out. And the other guy has lots of friends around here."

Allie stood. "Well, so do you." She looked at the cop. "Mr. Glass's lawyer is outside. I suggest you hold off on any more questions until he is present."

The cop shrugged. "That's his right."

"My right," Matt said, quietly, "is to find Baker and get the truth out of him."

Allie made a decision then and there. "M.J. is going to stay here with you for a while," she said. "I'm going up to get Laurel. And you two are staying with me."

Matt frowned.

"No argument." She softened her expression. "Listen to reason for a change. How can you hope to keep up with her, feeling like you do? You're all bruised up, Matt. And I know your head must be nearly killing you. Let me do this. Please."

He shut his eyes. "If it puts you in danger, I..."

The cop raised his eyebrows, but said nothing. Plainly, he was curious, though.

"We can talk about that later," she said, going over to him and kissing him lightly. "Try to stay still and calm. I'll be back soon. M.J. will be right here." She left, after giving the cop a hard look.

Matt watched her go out the door. The cop was asking more questions, but he didn't hear a word. Something that had happened just before the crash tickled at his mind, but he could not for the life of him remember what it was. Something about Allie. He continued to ignore the cop while he played back the night and the morning right up to the time he'd left her house to go after Laurel. He remembered how much he'd wanted Allie. How his romantic plans hadn't worked out, although that had been acceptable, given the situation. Then, the morning had come all too soon, with the bad things happening. He remembered the horrible phone call she'd received. Remembered holding her and feeling... Feeling... What? Just out of reach, it hovered, teasing him...

"Mr. Glass, are you all right?" The cop was by the bed now. "Should I call a doctor?"

Matt rubbed his aching eyes. "Yeah. I mean, no. Don't call the doc. I'm all right. I had worse headaches from the altitude in the Himalayas."

The officer's eyes widened. "You climbed them mountains?"

Matt regarded the man. "I was on a few expeditions

when I was younger. When I could still tolerate the cold conditions. Never made it to the top, though. Why? You climb?''

Pride swelled the older man's face. ''I did the Grand up in Jackson Hole once. Greatest time of my life, let me tell you.'' He glanced down at his notebook. ''But I was younger, too. Look. I know you're hurting, so I won't keep at you. For now. But if that truck driver files charges, you…''

''He won't.'' M.J. came into the room. ''Officer, I think we have evidence of a conspiracy here to lay blame for the accident at my client's door, where it clearly does not belong.''

Matt blinked. Miraculously, M.J. had managed to transform himself from a Sunday-morning party wreck to a spiffy lawyer, complete with the three-piece suit. Just how much time had he lost, anyway? He tried to follow M.J.'s voice as the lawyer spoke to the cop, but his hearing faded, and he dozed. All he heard for certain was the phrase, ''Known acquaintance of one T. Baker.''

After that, he only saw darkness and heard the soft sound of Allie's voice echoing in the secret places of his mind and heart.

It was sufficient for him.

CHAPTER NINE

THE FOLLOWING FRIDAY, behind on her carefully planned business and political schedule and in turmoil regarding almost every single aspect of her private life, Allie drove up to Montana to spend the Fourth of July weekend and the following week with her parents and twins. After pulling out of her driveway, she looked back at her three passengers. "Everybody comfy?" she asked.

Matt and Laurel nodded and smiled. Fred didn't smile, but her tiny tail whopped the seat softly. Allie turned her face forward again. The tensions and fears of the last days faded. A sense of pleasure filled her.

She wasn't even worried about being behind. They all needed this trip. She had done the right thing.

The day after his accident, Matt had come home from the hospital to her house and Laurel had been there waiting for him. The child's delight at being reunited with her uncle was matched only by her continued pleasure in Fred's company and the fun though touchy work of getting friendly with the suspicious cats. To Allie and Matt's relief, Laurel did not seem to connect Matt's temporary disappearance with the loss of her parents. Her adjustment to the changes seemed excellent, in fact.

Allie set them both up in Sally's room, thinking that it would be better for Laurel to be as near Matt as possible. While Matt had rested at the hospital, and while M.J. and Miranda had worked on the case, Allie had rallied a few of her friends and had moved most of Laurel's baby equipment down the mountain to her house. If the arrangement had caused anyone moral or social problems, they had kept their opinions to themselves.

Which was undoubtedly wise. Allie would have taken off heads, if anyone had even snickered. She had many reasons to be sensitive about the subject.

Three more phone calls early on during the week from the mysterious "ghost" of Paul Ford had disturbed her deeply, making her even more careful about her behavior. Not that she believed the calls were from Paul, but the nasty, ugly words she heard just before slamming down the phone each time jarred her to her core and made her determined to demonstrate that she could be a friend to Matt without being a lover, as the caller so lasciviously implied. Her relationship with Matt was pure as snow. She was his friend, not his mistress or lover.

But she had enjoyed his company during the week they had lived under the same roof. She glanced back in the rearview mirror once more. He sat, relaxed, one arm around Laurel in her car seat and the other resting on Fred's back. He was watching the passing scenery, a faraway expression on his handsome face. If only he were a different man, she thought, she could watch him watching forever and be perfectly happy. And they hadn't even kissed. Really kissed. She imagined how *that* would be...

"This is incredible country," he said, interrupting her erotic musing. "Just goes on and on forever, doesn't it."

She smiled. "Seems that way. The local joke is you see more antelope and sagebrush than people on this highway." She glanced into the mirror again.

His smile was sad, almost wistful. "Seems that way," he said, repeating her words. Then that faraway look again.

What was he thinking?

All the time they'd been together this last week, he'd been distant. Friendly, of course. Pleasant. But distant, as if she were some stranger he didn't want to bother or offend. If he hadn't still been suffering headaches, she was sure she would have challenged him on his attitude, but it was too soon after his accident to upset him, she felt.

And, frankly, there was really too much going on for her to pursue her relationship or non-relationship with him. She hadn't questioned him on the custody case yet. She hadn't even talked to him about the phone calls. She didn't want him getting upset about the propriety of their living situation. She was sure he knew about the calls. He'd been there when they had come in and she couldn't disguise her disgust. Oh, he knew. But they didn't discuss them.

At Josh's suggestion, she had started doing some door-to-door campaigning. That had taken up the long summer evenings, leaving only time for brief conversation with Matt before she had headed, exhausted, to her solitary bed. Josh had also been working on setting up a public debate for her with Rita, but so far, timing was a problem. Rita's manager, the traitorous Ned, hadn't agreed to a date yet.

Allie had scheduled twice as many meetings with her clients, realizing that, as the fall neared and the campaign heated up, she would have even less time to spend advising them. Matt had stayed out of the way during the day when her clients came and went, but she knew *they* knew she had guests, one of them a handsome, mysterious male and the other a small child. The evidence that others were staying with her was there for anyone who cared to look. Laurel was a normal two-year-old and with her around, it was impossible to keep the house tidy. Toys lay here and there, no matter how well Matt kept after his little charge.

She was, however, according to Matt, less inclined to mess things up deliberately than she had been at her own home. They both found that interesting. Maybe, Allie reasoned, it was because she had the animals and two adults to amuse her and keep her mind off mischief.

And maybe, as M.J. suggested one evening, it was because the little girl felt really secure again. Allie had left that idea alone, afraid to pursue it.

"Think your kids are ready for us?" Matt's question, coming out of his long silence, pulled her back to the present. "Kind of a shock for Mom to be bringing up a guy and a baby. Especially since the guy and kid are living with her."

"They're ready," she assured him, not sure herself. "You two aren't the first stray cats I've adopted. How do you think we got Tom, Dick and Harry?"

Matt chuckled. He hadn't been laughing much recently, and the sound warmed her. "You kept them. Are you keeping us, too?"

Allie gripped the wheel. "Of course not. You don't belong to me, and you have your own homes. T., D. and H. did not. They simply saw a good thing and settled into it. Smart cats."

Matt didn't respond to that. Silence fell again. He crossed his arms and stared out the window. Allie looked in the mirror and saw his profile. His features were drawn hard, his mouth turned downward. It didn't make him any less handsome.

She wondered if he was thinking about the accident. He hadn't driven himself since it happened, due to the headaches he was still having. They made him moody, which she understood, apparently affected his vision and made him forgetful, he claimed. She wasn't sure what he meant by that, because he seemed sharp enough to her. The doctor hadn't said a word about memory problems, either. Phil had said that, except for the bruises and the lingering headaches, Matt was good as new.

He certainly had followed the orchestration of his defense closely enough to demonstrate mental acuity, Allie thought. He'd kept right up with everything M.J. and Miranda were doing in his behalf.

Miranda had discovered that the witnesses who told the police of Matt's intoxicated state the night before the crash were none other than Rita Morely and David Benning. Apparently, no one else at the dance was willing to say he'd been actually drunk. Of course, there were a number of folk who were in no condition to make such judgments that night, she realized.

The bad part was that there really was no evidence of Teddie Baker's pickup having been on the road. The driver of the dump truck that had actually hit Matt hadn't seen it. And Teddie, according to his cronies, had been down in Colorado that weekend, so he couldn't have been on the mountain road, as Matt claimed. Also, his truck was in the shop. Some kind of trouble with the fuel line. He'd had the engine steam-washed, too.

Matt had muttered something about all evidence being cleaned away by professionals and that Teddie's friends were lying. Miranda had agreed. If they had found the pickup and been able to match dirt on it with the dirt in the tire grooves along the side of the mountain road, they might have a case against Teddie. But now, they had nothing.

M.J., not one to be discouraged easily, had managed to find witnesses to the dump truck driver's revels of the night before. Just the fact that the man, one Gorden Hendry, could come up with no good reason why he'd been driving such a vehicle down the road on a Sunday morning was enough to cast some suspicion on his own sobriety. No criminal charges were laid. The event was simply labeled an accident with no one at fault. Hendry was certainly just an unlucky man who had happened into a collision with Matt.

But, rumors abounded. Gossip slithered. And Allie's reputation was on the line, because Matt was staying at her home. Allie had insisted. For Laurel's sake, if not for his own. They actually had a few hot words on the topic before he'd dropped it.

"Does Josh have you in the rodeo parade next month?" Matt asked, his voice again startling her out of her gloomy reverie. "I just read about it in the paper this morning."

She half turned and looked at him. The bruises on his face were fading, but he still looked as if he'd gone a full ten rounds with the dump truck itself. "What do you mean?"

"You need to ride in the parade. It's a great PR opportunity." Matt sat up. "Allie, I've been moving slow. Hurting a lot. More than I cared to let on, but I've been watching. Josh Henderson is a lousy campaign manager. You have got to take some initiative yourself, if he doesn't come up with these ideas."

She frowned, looking straight ahead. "He's all I have, Matt. He'll have to do the job." She felt a hand on her shoulder.

"Well, he isn't." Matt resisted moving his hand to touch her hair. This was a business discussion. If he touched more of her, it was liable to take another turn. And he was too confused to risk that right now. "Isn't doing a good job, anyway. And I owe you more than I can ever repay. I tell you what. Let's go official with my unofficial advice. If you don't think it'll put Josh out too much, I'd like to take over."

She almost slammed on the brakes. "I can't fire him, Matt."

"Why not? He's not doing squat for you."

She had no response to that. It was almost the truth.

But not quite. "I have to live here," she said. "You could be a wonderful help this time around, but there will be other campaigns. You won't always be there. Josh will.

He'll learn. As time goes by, he'll pick up the tricks of the trade."

Silence. Then: "All right. When we get back, I'll ask him if I can work as his assistant at no charge to either of you."

She gripped the wheel, her emotions twisting and turning. Wanting to stop and confront him with her feelings.

Not daring to. It wouldn't be fair or right.

"Thank you," she said. "I appreciate the offer, and I know Josh will, too."

Matt said, "Umph." Then nothing at all.

A little later, Laurel woke from her nap, and they didn't talk business for the rest of the long drive. Things were too hectic. Allie had forgotten what it was like to travel a long distance with a very small child. Laurel's job was obviously to remind her of all the details!

THEY REACHED her family's ranch late at night, having decided to drive straight through. Although she yearned to hug them, Allie didn't wake the twins. She just looked in on them. Her parents, Bill and Fran Campbell, were still up to greet her enthusiastically and to welcome Matt. But she could tell they were uncertain about his role in her life.

Well, that made a crowd of them.

Her father helped Matt set up the baby's portable bed in the guest room, while her mom fixed a late snack. The four then spent a pleasant, companionable half hour, talking about nothing in particular, except local gossip. Matt begged off eating too much, saying his head was bothering him, so Allie wolfed down most of the meal alone.

After Matt went on to bed, she spent a little time longer with her folks, explaining about him, his accident and why he was living in her house. She wasn't sure she made all her points clearly, since she was tired and still confused about her feelings, but her folks accepted her explanations and choices without overt criticism. As they always did. Then, they said an affectionate and loving good-night to her.

Allie breathed a sigh of relief, once she was finally alone. Relief and happiness to be at the one place on the planet where she could feel real peace and security. She took Fred to her old, childhood room and fell into bed. She slept like a baby without dreams until sunrise. But with the break of day…

"Mom!"

"Momma!"

The twins burst into her room just as the morning sun turned the air gold. Fred barked in alarm and then started wriggling and giving the little yipping cries that indicated a state of deepest canine joy.

Allie sat up, tears in her eyes as her children flung themselves on her and into her arms and they hugged and kissed, yelled and laughed with happiness.

Sam pulled away first. "Mom," he said, his brown eyes solemn in his tanned face. "Where's the guy and the kid?" His tone indicated he had concerns, and at that moment, he looked older than his mere ten years. Older and uncertain, or maybe, untrusting. As usual.

"Yeah." Sally's eyes were brighter, anticipating rather than worrying. Also, as usual. "Is he cute?" She brushed her soft blond hair back from her little face. "What about the baby? Is the baby cute, too?"

Allie looked up. Matt, Laurel perched on his hip, stood at the open door. The two of them were staring at her and her children. "See for yourself," she said, pointing to the doorway. "Apparently, we've awakened them both."

The twins turned around and stared back, their movements almost mirror images. As usual. While they might be completely different in personality and world outlook,

Allie could always count on their bodies moving in harmonious concert.

Matt had on jeans and a T-shirt and his hair was uncombed. Clearly, he was having a hard time adjusting to the sight of the twins. He looked confused. Laurel looked even more so. Her little face screwed up and she cried, "Mmmaaamma."

And she reached for Allie.

IT TOOK a while that morning to sort everything out, but by noon *almost* everyone seemed to accept almost everyone else. It was a tentative sort of acceptance, however, Allie realized. Rather like her little animal family. Each time she had introduced a newcomer to the group, there had been a lot of sniffing and testing and wariness. And so it was with her human family.

She found herself thinking of Matt and Laurel as hers, she also realized. That was dangerous, but she could do nothing to change it. So, she just let it happen.

Sally and Laurel became friends right away. This didn't surprise Allie, since her daughter was much like she was—immediately trusting. Probably too immediately for her own good.

Sam, on the other hand, obviously regarded Matt as an interloper and a threat. That did surprise Allie.

Young as he was, it was clear Sam Ford was a man's man in the making. He liked being around the ranch men. He'd been bitterly disappointed when she had broken off with Mike, the cowboy. Sam was tough, rough and masculine to a surprising degree at times. Never adopting hers or Sally's gentler ways. He doted on his grandfather and on M.J., his uncle.

Though never particularly friendly to strange men, Sam was never actually rude to any of her men friends. Certainly not with the kind of venom he was showing now. Concerned about the boy's attitude, Allie gently suggested they take a walk together and have a chat. She sent signals to her father, signals Bill Campbell picked up immediately.

"We've jawed enough, don't you think," Bill said, standing up from his seat on the front porch and stretching. "I got some jobs for the lot of you lazy city folk. Sam, while you and your momma go for your walk, why don't you check out the alfalfa field fence for me. Matt, you and Sally and Laurel come on down to the barn." His blue eyes almost disappeared in the smile that crinkled his tanned, lined face. "Got to count this month's litter of barn kittens."

Sally yelled with delight at the prospect.

That brought happy sounds from Laurel, who was more content than Allie had ever seen the child. She had apparently switched loyalties from the now-neglected and abandoned Fred to Sally.

Sam seemed less than thrilled at the prospect of the walk Allie suggested. She could talk if she wanted, he told her, curtly. He would work. He wore dusty overalls, his pockets loaded with fence-mending tools. His hands seemed too big for his skinny arms, and they bore small scars from other working days. Her boy, Allie thought, was growing up.

Maybe that was part of the problem.

They reached the field and started walking the perimeter. "Okay," Allie said, starting right in. "You and I have always been straight with each other, Sam. What's the deal? Talk to me. You've all but spit in Matt Glass's eye. Why?"

"He your boyfriend?" Sam didn't look at her. He ran his hand down a length of wire fence. "Is he staying in your room?" His voice wavered a bit, indicating emotions that did not show on his face.

"No. And no. He's a friend who is a man. And he's sleeping in Sally's room *with* his niece in the portable baby bed beside him. *And* when we get back to Linville Springs, if he's feeling okay, he's going to move back to his own house. I just let him stay with me because he was hurt in an accident." She and Matt had mentioned the crash, but had given no one the gory details. She had not wanted her folks to have any cause to worry. Now she wondered if, in her silence, she had done more damage than good.

"Um." Sam bent down and inspected the wood at the bottom of one of the fence supports.

"Come on." Allie touched his head, feeling the silky blond hair on her palm. "You didn't get so ornery when you thought I was going to marry Mike."

"Mike's a man." Sam stood up and continued walking the fence. "This guy ain't, near as I can see."

"Oh?" Allie kicked at some dust, watched it puff up and settle back down. The summer air was still, and the day was promising to be a hot one. "You figured that out about him in just a few hours?"

Sam didn't reply. He found a split in the wire, raised it up, caught it in a special tool and twisted it so the break was bound together. His small muscles looked like ropes under his soft child's skin. Allie let him work in silence, marveling at her son's skill.

Then, she said, "He runs an adventure-tour business. I don't see why you think he's a sissy."

Sam shrugged. He reached in another pocket and pulled out a crumpled baseball hat. He settled the hat on his head, jerking the bill down on his forehead. "Anybody can run a business, Mom," he said. He stared at her from under the cap. Then, his face twisted. "Mom, he's a jerk. Any guy'd take care of a little baby, carry her around, feed her and talk to her like that's a jerk. He acts like you and Grandma."

"Oh."

Sam turned away and started walking again. "But I guess if he ain't..."

"Isn't."

"*Isn't* your boyfriend, and he's going to be gone when I get home, it's okay."

"Well, thanks very much." Allie thought a moment and made a decision. Sam's chauvinist attitude bothered her quite a bit. Maybe she hadn't noticed it before because she had sympathized with the fatherless boy. She needed to help Sam see men in a more realistic light.

"Sam, just because a man can take care of a baby, doesn't mean he's a jerk. Laurel has no parents and Matt is trying to help her. He hasn't always run a business or had a little child to care for," she said, casually, as if they were just chatting now, the major part of the discussion already over. "I heard he rescued a bunch of people down in South America a few years ago. They were all so grateful, they've made a movie about it. It'll be on television this fall. He didn't tell me about it. Other people did. He doesn't brag about his life, but it's been extraordinary from what little I know. For sure, about those people, he did something no one else could or would do. He's a hero, Sam. He found them, and he saved them."

Her son stopped and looked at her. "He *found* them?"

"Yes."

"Did you tell him about..."

"About your father?" A chill crept up her back. "Yes."

"Could he find...?" Sam left the question unfinished, and Allie couldn't say a word. If that terrible telephone call had never happened, she could have been able to respond and set Sam's mind at ease as she had done in the past when he'd asked about his real father. But now...

"Find what?" Matt's voice made her jump. Allie turned to see him coming over to them. He was alone.

"Find my father." Sam's voice was clear, the tones ringing a challenge. He took off his cap and stared up at Matt.

"My mom says you're a big hero and you rescued some people. Okay. Find my father."

Allie felt caught. Unable to say or do a thing.

Matt stared back at the boy, admiring the strength of will he saw in young Sam Ford. "Why?" he asked. "Why would you want him, Sam?"

Allie smothered a gasp.

But it was exactly what Sam needed to hear. His tough pose softened and he shrugged. "Dunno. Just thought if you were such a big hero and all..." He scuffed the toe of his boot in the dust. "Dunno."

Allie was sure she saw a glint of tears in her son's eyes.

Matt cleared his throat. Looked away from them. "I don't know where my father is, either," he said. "I guess he's probably still alive, but that's about it. I figure, he knows where I am, and if he wants to see me, he can come to me."

Sam digested that, his smooth young face a mask and only his eyes showing emotion.

Allie turned away. There were tears in hers.

But after that, the atmosphere between Sam and Matt began to improve.

THEY STAYED at the ranch until the following Sunday. Everyone thoroughly enjoyed the Independence Day celebration held on Saturday, and she even gave a short patriotic speech at the ranch's barbecue dinner. It was only for practice, since none of the attendants would be voting in the election she was involved in. Matt approved, saying she couldn't get enough practice speech-making if she was truly intent upon a political career.

By then, Matt seemed to feel his old self. He had stopped complaining of headaches and was active and cheerful. He was also willing to discuss some of the problems he was having with the custody case. But mostly, he seemed to be unwinding. He went riding and fishing with Sam and Bill, listened to her mother talk about the best ways to handle two-year-old girls and generally made himself popular with everyone who met him. He spent enough time with Sally for the girl to develop an embarrassing crush on him, and even Mike, Allie's old flame, who dropped by one afternoon, approved of him, saying if he had to lose her, it was good to lose her to a "real impressive kind of guy."

No one seemed to believe she and Matt were just friends.

Allie was no longer sure what the truth was. If she hadn't loved him before, she would have at that special moment when he'd made such deep contact with her son.

But she knew there was no future with this man. Like Paul, he'd be gone from her life eventually. Any anger she had, she hurled at the fate that had sent her two such men. Matt, she would forgive. She knew about and understood his need to leave. Paul, she probably never would forgive, since there had been no warning, no explanation, and therefore, no understanding.

They left around ten in the morning on Sunday, planning to get home the same day. Laurel whimpered when she realized she was leaving her new friends, but when Fred flopped down next to her and put her furry head on Laurel's leg, the little girl smiled and relaxed.

"I have got to get a Fred, I think," Matt said, watching the child. "She's just great with Laurel."

"Years of practice." Allie steered along the straight stretch of open highway. "Remember, she's had the twins to learn on. She's a pro with little kids, Fred is."

"So're you." His hand stroked her shoulder with a touch so light, she almost couldn't feel it. "I have never in my life seen anything so wonderful as that first moment when I saw you with your children in your arms."

Her eyes stung. She blinked. "Well, they're great kids, and I do miss them. But it's important for them to spend time with their grandparents. You could see how good Dad is as a surrogate father."

"Uh-huh."

"You were terrific with Sam, too," she added, unable to help herself. *And I love you for that,* she thought. Along with all the other things about you that...

"He's a great kid. Going to be a great man. I can see it in his eyes. He's very mature, Allie."

She laughed, feeling things she didn't want to show. "Whereas Sally..."

"Is sweet and gentle, like her mother. Not a softy, though. She's as strong as her brother, in her own way." His hand settled on her shoulder. "She's what you would be, if life hadn't kicked you in the gut so hard. Sweet steel, capable of anything, but first and foremost, capable of great love."

Allie's throat hurt, the tears were so close. "I appreciate..." she started to say.

"I love you, Allie," Matt said.

She looked at him. He stared straight ahead. She returned her gaze to the road. "What?" she asked. "What did you say?"

"I said, I love you. Actually I realized it some time ago, but the accident put it out of my mind," he said, still not looking at her. "It hit me that I loved you just before the dump truck did. But somehow that circuit in my brain got jarred when I concussed. Then, when I saw you with your children..." His hand curled over her shoulder and tightened. He was trembling, just slightly.

"It all came back to me. But I couldn't tell you until now, though. I was afraid or I needed to keep it to myself for a while longer or I just couldn't find the right time. I honestly can't explain it myself. Isn't that odd? You'd think a man'd just have to blurt out a thing like that." He sounded bemused.

She swallowed hard against the tears. "What does it mean to you, Matt?"

She felt him shrug. "I honestly don't know yet." He pointed. "There's a side road. Pull over. I can at least show you, even if I can't tell you yet."

Without thinking about it, she obeyed.

And the moment the brake was set, her seat belt was off and she was in his arms.

CHAPTER TEN

THEY KISSED. Hard, clumsily and roughly at first, full of unfocused energy and wild physical need, but gradually settling into a slow, searching and tasting of each other. Allie lost herself in the wonder of it, and also lost all sense of how much time passed while she held this man, this special man. Desire swept through her, making her dizzy with its sweet power.

Predictably, Fred and Laurel put a halt to their activities. Fred barked, and Laurel said, "Maaa? Daddy? What doing?" The anxiety in her little voice was enough to cut through the sensual fog.

But Matt released Allie only slightly and continued to hold her while he smiled at her and then spoke soothingly to Laurel. "It's okay, sweetheart," he said. "We're kissing. That's all."

Laurel looked puzzled. Fred settled back down.

"Kissing," Allie said, looking at the little girl. "You know." She made exaggerated kissing noises. "Kiss, kiss, kissy."

Laurel giggled and imitated her.

Matt stroked Allie's hair. "What now, my love?" he quipped. "We can't exactly consummate our passion right here on the highway with a child and dog as witnesses."

Allie started to laugh, though she felt more like crying, so intense were her emotions. Until this moment, she'd been able to hide her own deep feelings and feel noble about it. But Matt had confessed his. Should she? Was she a coward to keep quiet?

Or just smart.

"I agree. This is insane," she said, drawing back from him a little more, trying to regain some degree of composure. "Silly, even. Kissing right here with Laurel watching. Now I know how married people must feel when they..." Suddenly realizing what she had been about to say, she blushed.

But Matt touched her cheek, gently. "I know what you meant. To be married, in love and have children together. With all the joys and problems of that condition. You never had that chance, did you?"

She could only shake her head.

"You know I can't promise you any kind of future like that, don't you?"

"Of course, I know that." She found strength to speak. "And I wouldn't ask it. The kind of life I live is so opposite of yours, that it would be foolish to even imagine that we..."

He put his finger on her lips. "Don't say it. It's foolish to predict anything, Allie. Let's just live this from day to day and see what happens."

They kissed again. It was sweet and exciting. But their passion was now blunted by the daunting presence of reality.

Reality in many forms, but mainly in the form of a giggling child who shouted, "Kiss, kiss, kiss, kiss, kiss," for the next hundred miles or so.

But as they drove, they talked.

"I lost out a lot on what it means to grow up with family ties, as you know," he said. "Ties and responsibilities were concepts my father never understood. So, when I say I love you, I'm not sure I can explain what I mean."

"It's okay." Allie glanced at him. "Right now, it means

you like being with me, enjoy my company and want to go to bed with me." She smiled. "I can sure relate to that."

"Sometimes," he said, touching her shoulder with a tap of his finger, "you are too plainspoken. How will you ever succeed in politics, if you just give them what's right up front in your mind?"

"Is this politics?"

"No."

"Then don't criticize."

"Point taken."

She drove on. Then: "Tell me how it was, growing up, never knowing what the next day might bring."

He made a soft sound. "It's not a terrific story, believe me."

"But I want to know. See, until I lost... Until Paul disappeared, I was always so sure of everything. That was unwise, I see now. But I still *believed* everything would be all right."

"You still do, Allie."

She shook her head. "I don't think so."

"Yes, you do." Another touch on the shoulder, gentle, brief, as if that was all he dared allow himself for the moment. "At heart, you are a person of faith. A believer. Trusting that things and people won't fail or betray you."

"I do not..."

"That's why you get so angry and upset when they do," he interrupted. "Me? I just shrug and figure the worst is going to happen eventually, anyway, so why get in a twist about it."

She absorbed that truth, somberly. "We are a pair, aren't we?"

"Indeed. Indeed we are." He paused, then began to talk again. Much of the time, he talked about his youth with his father. As she listened, Allie began to realize that Robert Glass was quite a celebrity. He was an explorer and adventurer of long standing and definite renown. He'd done landmark work for the National Geographic Society, among others, and he was praised widely for his bravery and intrepid spirit. This had had the expected influence on his son. Being in the shadow of the great adventurer, Robert Glass, had meant many things to Matt, but mostly had given him the need to excel himself—to do as much or more than his famous father. "It's not uncommon," he added, "for the son of a well-known man to strive to do his old man one better or more."

"Did you?"

"Sometimes."

BY THE TIME she pulled into her driveway many hours later, Allie knew a great deal more about the life of Matt Glass.

Enough to convince her he would leave her eventually. When the call to travel, to adventure became too strong for him to resist, he would simply take Laurel and go.

Just like his father had done with him.

Tom, Dick and Harry greeted their return with studied indifference. M.J. had come by daily to feed and water the three felines, and so their physical needs had been taken care of. Allie carried the sleepy Laurel, and the little one just sighed happily when they walked in the door.

She thinks she's home, Allie thought.

"I know this is about as romantic a pass as you've ever heard, but I have to be with you tonight," Matt said, as he carried the portable crib into Sally's room. "And I don't want to upset Laurel by leaving her alone. Any ideas how we can manage?"

"I do have a plan," Allie confessed. "I gave the logistics of our situation some serious thought on the drive down."

The look in his eyes was warm and admiring. He finished setting up the bed and took Laurel from Allie's arms. The child was half-asleep, calm and limp in his embrace. "But she seems so relaxed, maybe..."

"We let Fred sleep here," Allie said, pointing to Sally's bed. "I'll bring in her special blanket, and she'll stay put with the proper command from me. She sleeps with Sally from time to time, anyway, so it's no big deal. If Laurel wakes, she can see Fred in the glow of the nightlight. Fred represents security to her. Somehow, I think..."

"*I* think that if you run your political life half as sensibly and well as you do your personal one, you'll be president someday." Matt laid Laurel on the clean sheet and pulled a light cover over her. He patted her little head and kissed her good-night.

Allie looked at him. In the soft light of the small bedroom, he looked about as domestic as a man could look, bending over his niece and tucking her in for the night. But he was not domestic. She would be asking for trouble if she ever forgot that.

She was asking for trouble, as it was, anyway. She might be in love with him. That was unavoidable. But, if she let him make love to her, she wondered if she would be able to stand the inevitable loss.

Now was her last chance to back out.

"Get Fred's blanket," he said, straightening and gazing at her with a fierce heat in his eyes. "I can't wait much longer to be with you."

That did it. No chance at all. She ran to grab the blanket.

Matt stood by the door, watching her set things up and order Fred to stay with Laurel. He knew he was making a mistake, that to take her to bed was probably not a good move and would certainly put a spin on their relationship that neither one of them was capable of dealing with well.

But he had no choice. None at all. His desire for her had only increased as time had passed, and he was just too selfish to deny himself the fulfillment of loving her completely. Her face showed her own inner turmoil, her questioning of the wisdom of what they were about to do, but he made himself ignore it. He could see her hesitation now. But, too late. Love for her drove him... Need for her blinded him... Whatever it was, it was too strong for him to resist.

She continued to fuss over the dog and the baby. "Come on, Allie," he said, holding out his hand to her. "They'll be fine."

"I know," she said, stepping away from the bed. "But I'm scared." She turned out the light.

"Don't be." His voice caught in his throat, and he had to clear it. "I won't hurt you, Allie."

"No." She came closer, keeping her voice low. "I'm not afraid of you."

"What then?"

She didn't answer. They stood in the doorway, and in the diffused light from the living room, he knew he'd never seen a more beautiful woman in his life. She was tired from the long drive and totally devoid of makeup. Her blond hair hung limply, but it glowed with a radiance that came from deep within the woman.

The woman...

He hooked his hand behind her head and tipped her face up to his. *No more waiting. No more denial.*

Allie felt his passion as his mouth covered hers. He was fairly shaking with it, and it fueled her own desire to a white-hot degree. Her mind took one last shot at telling her to stop, but by then it was far too late. Her body and heart took over. She wrapped her arms around him and pushed herself against him. Hard!

"Out of these clothes," he whispered, hoarsely. He pulled at her shirt. "I want you now, Allie."

"Down the hall," she whispered back. "To the bedroom.'' She grabbed him and led him, both of them stumbling as they tore off clothing on the way.

They fell onto her bed. Pulled off the rest of their clothes. Naked, they touched each other, hands moving with eagerness and need, trembling with passion. Moments later, he was inside her, filling her and bringing her almost immediately to a climax. She forced back her screams of pleasure, remembering just in time the child asleep right down the hall. They had forgotten to shut the door.

Matt watched her, amazed she could be so quiet when he could sense the inferno raging within her. He forced himself to ease back, to give her time to recover.

He was determined to love her as no other man had ever done. Determined with a perverse kind of love-fury to brand her so she'd never want another man. Never need another. Never have another lover but him... Never!

Allie felt the wildness surging in him and welcomed it. Silently, she met his strong passion with strength of her own, matching him, sometimes surpassing him, but always in physical harmony.

The kind of harmony that would make a symphony soar to the highest heaven.

Matt took her through several more climaxes, but eventually, he could no longer control himself and spent his passion in her body. The relief of release was almost overwhelming, and he only managed to stifle his shout of joy by burying his face in the sheet at her neck.

Finally, Matt rolled to one side, his arm over his head, his breath still coming in deep gasps. ''I don't know about you,'' he said, hoarsely. ''But I think I might be able to sleep soundly tonight.''

Allie laughed and rested her body on her elbows while she looked down at him. ''Think I'll let you? Now that you're in my clutches?''

He rolled his eyes. "God, Allie. Have pity. I'm only human."

She traced the line a drop of sweat left on his chest. "You could have fooled me."

"It was all an act." He shut his eyes. "I find you completely undesirable." His smile belied his words.

She regarded him for a long moment. "Let's be serious," she said. Tears filled her eyes. "You know, I love you, too, Matt."

"I wasn't sure until now. Come here," he said, drawing her back down. His body showed that sleep was the last thing on his mind.

THE NEXT MORNING, he woke before she did, and he spent a few minutes looking at her. She was utterly beautiful. Passionate, intelligent, ambitious...nur- turing. A mother, a caregiver by her very nature. Look at all the animals she'd taken in, for goodness sake!

Why couldn't he stay with her? Why wouldn't it work? He surely would never find another woman quite like her. One that combined so many delightful qualities...

Maybe, just maybe, he needed to rethink his own life. Was returning to Los Angeles really that vital? Would Laurel be any happier growing up there than she would be right here where she was born?

After all, they could travel. Leave from time to time and go exploring...

But Allie was rooted to the land here. She wouldn't be happy anywhere else. He tried to picture her in L.A. and grimaced.

No way. He'd have to be the one to relocate if...

The phone rang. Laurel cried out, and Fred barked.

Allie sat up, her hair spilling in her face, a feeling that something monumental had happened. Then, she saw Matt, reaching for the receiver.

She felt her heart rate accelerate, wondering if this might be a repetition of the venomous call of two weeks ago, but when Matt shook his head and smiled at her reassuringly, she breathed in relief. The call apparently was for him. She reached for her robe and got out of bed.

Laurel smiled when Allie walked into the bedroom. Smiled and held up her arms. "Momma," she said, clear as a bell.

And Allie lost her heart for the second time.

MATT GRIPPED the receiver tightly, anger growing in him like a living fire. "Can they do this, M.J.?" he asked, wondering if the fury he felt would make his voice shake. Make him sound weak. "Is it legal?"

"So far," the lawyer replied. His tone was unemotional and professional. Almost unfriendly, Matt decided. "They do have some strong arguments going for them. They're a family. Settled. Related to John Essex. The wife kept in frequent touch with your sister and brother-in-law over the years, even though they live out of state while you..."

"While I was off, chasing adventure around the world." Matt swore. "I won't let them have her, M.J. I want to fight this."

"It's your decision, Matt. But I recommend you think about it."

"Who the hell's side are you on?" Matt yelled, finally losing his temper. "Think about it? What do you think I've been doing?"

"Cool down," M.J. said, his voice never changing pitch or attitude. "Talk to Allie about this. See what she says. I'll be in the office in about an hour. Call me there."

Matt slammed down the receiver. "Yeah," he muttered. "I'll call all right." He swore again, softly, heatedly. "The hell I will!"

"What is it?" Allie's voice made him turn. She stood in

the doorway, Laurel in her arms, Fred at her feet. Her beauty completely took his breath away. "Matt, what's wrong?" Her expression convinced him she really did love him. That her declaration the night before had not been out of physical satisfaction. Allie Ford loved him!

He felt panic rising now. How could he stand to lose all this? Allie? Laurel? The kind of peace he had found with them?

Simple answer! He couldn't lose it! He'd fight!

"That was M.J.," he said. "Laurel has a second cousin, a Mrs. Turner or somebody, who is going to challenge me on custodial rights. She's married and able to provide a normal home." His lips twisted on the last phrase, making it almost another curse.

Allie regarded him. "And?"

"And what?" He got up, pulling the sheet with him. "There's no question about what." He ran his hand through his hair. "I'm going to take a shower, get dressed, and then I'm going to fight to keep my child." He went into the bathroom and shut the door.

Allie shivered. His expression was exactly like the one she'd seen on his face the night she'd had dinner with him. A dangerous, angry expression. One that boded ill for anyone who opposed him!

Things got worse. After she fed Laurel breakfast, she opened the paper and got another unpleasant shock. One of the letters to the editor questioned Allie's qualification as a political candidate, since, the writer stated, she was obviously living in sin with a man who had a child that wasn't legally his. The latter point was emphasized. The letter was signed, but it was a name she did not recognize. Until she remembered the last name of the woman disputing Matt's claim to Laurel. Turner. One and the same? She reached for the phone, intent on calling the paper and asking to make a statement on her relationship to Matt and Laurel, but thought better of it.

Might stir up waters she wanted left quiet. After all, since last night, she *was* "living in sin." She certainly did not want to cause Matt further problems in his quest to keep Laurel. She cared too much for both of them to do that.

Matt came into the kitchen. "Your cousin sounded less than supportive," he said, his tone near a growl. "I don't know if he's the best lawyer for the job."

Allie bristled. "If M.J. sounded strange to you, then you need to ask him about it. Don't go flying off in a rage just because things have gotten tough. Who is this Turner woman? Do you know her?"

Matt scowled, obviously not happy with her comments. "Never heard of her. Didn't know she existed until now." He poured coffee and sat down at the table.

"Is this her name?" Allie asked, laying the newspaper with the acid letter in front of him. "Turner? If it is, she's playing dirty. Using our private situation to advance her own cause."

Matt read. The veins in his neck and temples stood out. "Son of a bitch," he said, so softly she barely heard him. He looked at her, and all she saw in his eyes was hate and anger. Allie shrank back.

He swallowed the rest of his coffee and stood up, apparently unaware of the effect he was having on her. She could see he was shaking with suppressed rage. His eyes were like steel. She'd never seen a man look quite like that.

He put the mug down and took a deep breath. "I have to go out," he said. "Please watch Laurel. I'll be back." He left the kitchen, not even pausing to touch Laurel, who reached out for him and whimpered when she was ignored.

Frozen, Allie listened as the front door slammed, shaking the house. She heard the grinding of gears and the screeching of tires as he left the driveway in her car.

And then, Matt Glass was gone.

Just like Paul.

She spent the next hour in a fog. She tended to Laurel, readied herself for the working day and set up a play area for the little girl in the basement where Allie could watch her and work at the same time. When the twins had been small, she'd done the same thing. The rules were simple. Keep the kid in view, and don't get too immersed in work to miss any sound of trouble brewing. She even handled a visit from one of her clients with no hitches. Business as usual.

About eleven, Josh called. "We seem to have a little problem," he said. "I think you might want to reconsider your living arrangements, Allie. It's terrible press."

"I understand." She dug her nails into her palms. "I'm working on the problem, Josh. Can you think of any way to do damage control?"

"Kick him out, or marry him."

"Thanks."

"Sorry, Allie. But you know how conservative folks are around here. It just doesn't look good."

"I understand that. But it's a bit more complicated than just my good name."

"What do you mean?"

Allie hesitated. Matt's situation was really not Josh's concern. "Let's just say that the writer of that letter has a personal ax to grind. You might want to look into that."

"Can you be more specific?"

"I'm sorry. I can't tell you any more right now."

"All right." Josh cleared his throat. "Let me see what I can do. By the way, I think I forgot to tell you, I've made arrangements for you to ride in the parade week after next. Keep that Tuesday morning clear."

"I will. Thanks." Feeling a little better, she hung up the phone. At least Josh wasn't the flop Matt claimed he was.

About eleven, M.J. called. "We need to talk," he said, curtly, without even greeting her. "Now."

"I can't, M.J. I'm taking care of Laurel."

"Bring the kid. Come down to the office. Is Matt there?"

"No, he…"

"He's in a pretty scary state of mind right now, Al. If you see him, play it really cool. Promise me."

"What're you saying? Do I need to be afraid of him?"

M.J. hesitated. "I honestly don't know. He's a volcano looking for a place to erupt, and I don't want you or the little girl anywhere near him when he does. Come down to the office."

Allie pushed her chair back from the desk. "I don't have a car. Matt took it. M.J., what happened?"

"Um." Silence. Then: "He was here this morning. I told him he might want to consider giving Laurel up to the other people. They have a home out in Lade, Nebraska. Husband has a good job with a local bank there, a good reputation, and they want several kids. Have one, but the wife can't have any more of their own. They're high on several adoption lists, but now that Laurel needs a home, they want her, instead."

"You met them?"

"No. But Penny Jackson, the lawyer for the Essex estate called and…"

"M.J., she doesn't like Matt. He doesn't know what he did to put her off, but I don't think her opinion is unbiased. What're these people's names?"

M.J. told her. "Frank and Joan Turner."

"Have you read the paper this morning?"

"No, I didn't have time."

"Get it."

"Hold on."

Allie held. She leaned out the door to check on Laurel. The child was banging away on some wooden blocks with a small plastic stick. The three cats observed the action from a respectful distance. Fred sat closer, her tongue hanging out, ready to pounce on a block if it was thrown.

The sound of newspaper rattling. Then: "Oh, damn." More rattling. Then: "I see."

"J.F. Turner? Couldn't be a coincidence."

"No. Most likely it's the same Turner's using some odd idea of putting pressure on you in order to get Matt to cave in." M.J.'s tone was thoughtful. "Now, I begin to understand his anger."

"But it's not going to help, is it?"

"No. Listen, babe. You stay put. I want to make a few phone calls. But tell me one more thing."

"What's that?"

"How do you really feel about the guy? I mean, long-term?"

Allie swiveled her chair around to face a blank wall in her office. "How do I feel? I love him. Long-term? No hope for us." Tears, up to now unshed, rolled down her face.

He sighed. "I guess an explanation would take too long. I'll have to be satisfied with that."

"M.J., for all I know, I still have a husband somewhere. I can't just up and marry again. No matter how I feel."

"Legally, you know you're free, babe."

She shut her eyes. "Legally has nothing to do with it. You should know me well enough to know that. Until I have absolute proof Paul is never coming back, I can't... I just can't, that's all."

"Okay. I guess I understand. Take it easy, Al. I'll get back to you. And, cousin..."

"Yes?"

"I think you're out of your mind."

"How reassuring. Thank you very much." They both laughed, to relieve tension more than anything else. Then

Allie said goodbye and hung up. She sat, thinking for a few minutes.

Then, the sound of Laurel's laughter brought her back. The sound of laughter and the cry of joy she gave. "Daddy!" she called out. Allie sat very still, feeling the hairs rise all along her arms and up the back of her neck.

It was Matt. "Come on, honey. We're out of here."

Allie burst from her office. Matt had gathered Laurel up in one arm. He had a duffel bag in his other hand. He wore an outfit similar to the one he'd had on the first time she'd ever seen him—khaki shirt and pants.

But this time, she could tell it was a working outfit. The boots were high, paratrooper style, and laced. A sheathed knife hung from his belt. When he turned, she was sure she saw the shape of a holster tucked in the small of his back at his belt. He was armed and dressed for a fight. He looked like a modern warrior on the way to battle.

"What are you doing?" she cried, not daring to move closer. She was too frightened to think for the moment.

"None of you want to help me," he said, lifting his chin and staring down at her. "So, I'm helping myself. Goodbye, Allie. It's a real damn shame, because I think I could have loved you the rest of my life."

And suddenly, with those words, it all became clear to her. She understood, at long last, what she had to do.

CHAPTER ELEVEN

"YOU'RE A LIAR!" Allie stood her ground, even though a warning surge of fear went through her. She'd slept with this man, made love to him, but she did not really know what he was capable of doing when desperate. Would he use violence to get his way? Was that, ultimately, the only thing he really understood?

Or was love a strong enough force to calm him down and make him listen to her? For now, she knew he loved her, and she knew she loved him. Wasn't that worth the danger? Worth the fight.

You bet, she thought, crossing her arms and glaring at the man in front of her. If it was a fight he wanted, then that was what he was going to get.

"I'm not lying when I say I love you," Matt said, a defensive, vulnerable look appearing in his eyes, contrasting with his belligerent stance. Laurel clung to him, silent and somber, as if somehow she understood how important this moment was for her own future as well as theirs. The very air was charged. Not even the four animals watching the scene dared to move. "No matter what happens or what I do, I meant every word I've said about my feelings for you."

"Sure you did." She sneered, deliberately baiting him. "Just like Paul did."

Matt lost some of his aggressive stature. "That's not a fair assessment of the situation, Allie. And you know it.

I'm trying to save what I have. If you really love me, you'll stand aside and let me do it."

"Wrong! You're so wrong. If I really love you, Matt, I won't stand aside. Ever. I'll stand *with* you." She started crying, angry at herself for displaying weakness. "I...I don't want to lose you, too."

"Allie." He took a step toward her, longing in his eyes. "Come with me. Or come when I send for you. When I get somewhere safe."

She shook her head. "There is no place on earth that's safe, Matt. Not from what you're running away from. Not from selfishness. Don't you see? If you do this now, one day you'll find yourself running from Laurel. Running from me, if I was stupid enough to go away with you. It's a pattern your father taught you, and if you don't break it now, you probably never will."

He took a partial step back. "Maybe you're right about me, but I can't lose you, Allie," he said, his voice almost a whisper, but fierce and strong. "And I can't lose Laurel. Maybe running is wrong, but I don't know how else to deal with this situation."

She moved toward him. "Then listen to those who do, Matt. Listen to M.J. To Miranda. Listen to me! We know this land and these people, and M.J.'s probably the finest lawyer in the region when it comes to hard legal work and intelligent courtroom maneuvering. If there's a way under the sun to get justice done, he'll do it!"

"But..."

"I know." She relaxed a bit. He *was* listening to her. "I know it seems the deck's stacked against you. Against us. But the game's just begun, Matt. The other side has fired their first shots, and all they've done is embarrassed and frightened us. Look." She held up her hands. "Am I bleeding?"

A faint smile turned his lips. A wry smile. "No. You're

tough and strong as ever.'' Matt bent down and put Laurel back on the floor. He kissed the child's head and patted Fred, who moved in to sit close to Laurel. The poodle was trembling. Matt patted the dog, calming her, and then he whispered something to both child and dog. Then, he looked up at Allie.

"I just told them both that we weren't going anywhere," he said, his tone soft. "At least not for the time being. Allie, I can't count the number of times my father and I ran to escape trouble when I was a kid. Sometimes, it was for a good reason. Other times... I suppose it was just because Dad wanted out of an uncomfortable situation. I guess it's just in my bones so deeply that I think only of doing that first. But I'm willing to listen now. If that's what it takes to keep you. I'm making no promises, but I will listen. I will wait.''

She felt all the strength go out of her in a wave of relief. "I love you, Matt. And I love Laurel.''

"You can't have any more children, can you, Allie.'' He stated it, rather than asked. No pity in his voice, either. Just a factual tone.

That surprised her. "That's right. When I had the twins, the birth was difficult and damaging to my reproductive system. How did you know...?''

He shrugged. "I didn't know for certain. Just a guess, really.''

"I wish I could have your baby, but it isn't possible.''

"I know, and it's all right with me. We have three kids between us. That's enough. We have more than enough, Allie. In every way.'' He straightened and stood up, smiling at her with a truly tender expression on his face. "I realized that last night. Confirmed it this morning when I watched you sleeping.''

Her heart nearly burst with emotion. She had never— would never—love anyone else the way she loved him right at this moment. "Matt, don't leave me," she cried. "We'll work it out, somehow. *All* of it!"

He reached for her and embraced her, wrapping her with his strengths and giving her his weaknesses and entrusting her with his future.

And then and there, Allie made a momentous personal decision. Her future and his would fuse. No matter what the cost!

BUT, a few hours later, it seemed the cost was going to be very high. Higher than she had even feared.

After she called M.J. to explain about Matt's change of attitude, her cousin called in the other troops. A hastily convened, informal strategy session with Josh, Miranda, M.J., Matt and herself only emphasized the weakness of their position.

They were all seated in the meeting room at M.J.'s office. The area was small and dominated by a long, polished mahogany table. The walls were lined with law books in wooden bookshelves. Windows in the south wall let in the summer sunlight, giving freshness and life to the somewhat gloomy room.

The lawyer acted as chairman. "I asked Josh to come," M.J. explained, "because as I explore this, I'm beginning to think that there are many strings in the tangled web of the lives we're dealing with here." He rubbed his forehead with his fingers, indicating to Allie that he was deeply troubled. "Ugly strings," he added. "Ones you two don't deserve and certainly a little child like Laurel does not need in her life now or ever."

Matt nodded agreement, saying nothing, but thinking how close he had come to throwing all this away. This...comradeship. This opportunity finally to join the human race.

He would have blown it, too, sure as he was now sitting

here. His temper had rarely flared hotter than it had this morning in this very place. If it hadn't been for Allie's strength in opposing him...

Well, that didn't bear thinking about. It was over and done with as far as he was concerned. He smiled to himself. *The education of Matthew Glass is about to begin,* he thought. How to be a social human, not an isolate like he'd been all his life.

He hoped to hell it would work. Otherwise, he'd be forced to try the old way. And somehow, he'd get Allie to go along.

"First," M.J. said, "we have Allie and her political campaign. She's perceived as a real threat to Rita, the party's candidate. She's a threat despite the fact she's operating on a shoestring budget with an inexperienced manager."

Matt glanced over at Josh, who was avoiding his gaze. Josh reddened slightly, but said nothing. That was a good sign, Matt decided. If he'd gotten defensive, Matt was prepared to chop him into little bits.

Figuratively, of course. The knife was back in his duffel bag along with his gun and his trekking clothes. For this meeting, he'd changed into a suit and tie. There was a time and place for one kind of weapon and a time and place for another. Now, his weaponry was his love for Allie and Laurel.

And, hopefully, his brains and courage.

M.J. held up two fingers. "Second, we have Matt and his desire to take care of Laurel. His legal position as the closest blood relative should be strong. But the problem is, he's a single male with a less than domestic background." The lawyer cleared his throat and looked down at the table. "Then there's the further disadvantage of his morally questionable relationship with Allie."

No one said a word. No one breathed. Most important, Allie realized, no one interrupted. M.J. was playing the devils' advocate and everyone seemed to realize and appreciate that. Especially Matt.

Another finger. "Then, there's the phone call Allie got week before last. Supposedly from her long-vanished husband. A verbal and emotional threat. Devastating in its own horrible way but stopping short of being a physical attack. Clearly, though, it was intended to weaken and frighten her.

"But Matt Glass made a more difficult target. His emotional fears, if he has any, are unknown. So they decided to play hardball. Miranda found out that Teddie Baker, who was humiliated publicly by Matt, worked a few months ago for David Benning, Rita Morely's political mentor. Now, that may seem like coincidence to you, but I wonder. The accident Matt had was no accident and no coincidence, in my estimation and..."

"You really think they're interconnected?" Allie was sitting on her edge of her chair. The confrontation with Matt had left her weak and shaky, but she was ready to deal with the devil himself, if she had to. "Could Teddie Baker and Rita and these Turner people have cooked up some kind of conspiracy? It seems farfetched to me. They're working together? How could that be?"

"We don't know yet, but we've now got an angle that M.J. didn't have this morning when he and Matt tangled," Miranda answered Allie. "It could be all tied into one thing." She smiled. "Or rather, into one person. Little Laurel Essex."

"What about her." Matt spoke. "Is she in danger because of this situation? This complex network of evil?"

His voice was soft, gentle, but at the core of his tone, Allie heard solid steel. She crossed her fingers under the table, praying that Miranda wouldn't say something to set him off again.

But Miranda hastened to reassure him. "No, Laurel's not in immediate danger. At least not physically. She represents a goal, though. It's her money, folks, that's sweetening this hornet's nest. I'll bet good money of my own on it. Old-fashioned greed. Pure and simple.'' She set some papers down on the table. ''Matt, are you aware of the extent of her estate?''

''Yes.''

''Then you know what the stakes are in this custody fight you face,'' M.J. interjected.

Matt frowned. ''I didn't think anyone would be able to touch her estate. A guardian would just manage it till Laurel was older. So I can't imagine...'' A calculating look came into his eyes. He leaned forward, elbows and forearms resting on the wooden tabletop. ''Wait a minute,'' he said. ''What does this Turner guy do?''

Miranda smiled approval. So did M.J. ''You got it, baby. Investment advisor at the bank he works for,'' she said. ''Small potatoes, but you know how that can be. Can grate on a guy for years, watching others make big bucks when he's in no position to take any chances...'' She let the statement trail off, implying rather than saying what she suspected, Allie realized.

And Matt realized it, too.

''Ah.'' Matt sat back. ''He can't touch Laurel's money directly, nor could I, because it's in a trust. But, there are other possibilities. As administrator, he could use Laurel's money to test investments without risking his own cash. Then, if something proved out, he'd pour in his own money. So, I see. Then we're dealing with something here other than the heartfelt desire on the part of the Turners to have a big happy family, aren't we?'' he asked, his tone now edged again, his anger showing only by the tension around his eyes and mouth.

''I'd say so,'' Miranda said.

''But,'' Allie added, ''there's absolutely no proof of any of this, is there? We're pulling things out of thin air.''

"For now," Matt said. "But at least we're aware of the enemy or enemies. And I don't believe they're as good at this kind of thing as they might think they are."

"Excuse me," Josh said, speaking up for the first time. "But I feel really out of my depth with all this. I mean, conspiracy's an ugly word, people. Are you sure you...?"

"Sure enough, Josh," M.J. said. "This is a strange situation, believe me. Don't take it to the bank yet, but there'll likely come a time when you can."

Josh squirmed. "I...I'm not really a very brave man, you know. I..." His voice took on an odd tone.

"Josh, you want out? All the way out?" Matt regarded him. "I'll take over Allie's campaign if you've no stomach for this."

"N-no." Josh shook his head, and the strange expression on his face made Allie wonder what his problem was. "I don't want to quit." He smiled weakly. "But I'd sure like your help, Matt. That is, if it's all right with Allie."

"Fine with me," she said. "In fact, we were planning to talk to you about it even before the crisis. Not that I don't think you're doing a good job. But Matt is..."

"A fighter," Josh finished. "I'm not. And it sure looks to me like you've got a fight on your hands, even if this conspiracy thing is all smoke." He got up. "I expect the rest of this meeting won't directly concern me, so I'm going to go. Allie, give me a call later, please."

She agreed, and Josh left.

"Well." M.J. adjusted the position of some papers in front of him. "Where do you want to go from here. Matt? I think the next move's yours."

"I do want to fight. Take it all the way." He reached in his pocket and took out a written check. "Here's your retainer. Your fee and Miranda's are of no concern to me. I don't need Laurel's money. I'm wealthy enough in my own right. Following my father around the world during my youth did have one advantage—I made business contacts that have paid off in my adult life. My investment portfolio is extensive and more than enough to serve my needs for the rest of my life. I don't need Laurel's money,'' he repeated, firmly.

"We know that," Miranda said, softly. "We checked."

"Good." Matt nodded approval. "I'd have been disappointed if you hadn't."

Allie sat back and listened as the three outlined legal strategy. They had managed to agree very quickly, and while that was good, she thought, it also made the alliance potentially unstable. She'd had enough political experience to know that. Matt seemed satisfied to play by the rules for now, but she was sure that all it would take to make him jump the traces was one threat to Laurel or herself. He was, in many ways, a very simple man. Out to protect what he loved and cherished, no matter what the cost.

That wasn't all bad.

But it wasn't good, either, when the future depended on his holding back, and trusting people he didn't know. She was going to have to watch him carefully.

She looked away from the three of them. Her eyes clouded. Not with tears but with thought and a hard decision.

Decide, she told herself. And, she did.

It didn't take too long for M.J. to outline his preliminary plan. He intended to file for custody rights on the bases of Matt's financial security, which was more impressive than the Turners' and on Matt's closer blood relationship to Laurel.

Other factors, such as Matt's immediate response to Laurel's need and his avowed declaration to be her adopted father would also weigh in his favor, he said. After that, he warned, the game would depend on the steps the other side took. How ruthless they were willing to be. No one mentioned the problem of Matt and Laurel's continuing to live with Allie, and Allie wasn't about to bring it up. She had no intention of letting them leave.

Also, no one brought up what steps they would take if another act of telephone terrorism or physical violence occurred.

Allie could only hope that the incidents had been one-time shots and that, if indeed there was a conspiracy against her and Matt, the enemy had decided to abandon those methods and move on to a more "civilized" confrontation in a court of law. The thought, put that way, made her glum and unusually quiet. In some ways, Matt's more dramatic, direct approach seemed cleaner. Fight or flight. It was a basic human response to danger, after all.

Matt noticed her silence, but said nothing until they left the law office. "You were awfully quiet in there once you had your say," he said, getting into the driver's seat of her car after opening the passenger door for her. They had agreed he would drive now that his headaches were over. They were sharing the one car until he had a chance to buy himself another. "No other ideas or opinions?"

"Plenty." Allie fastened her seat belt. "But none that are pertinent for now."

"For when, then?" He started the car and pulled out into the street.

"I'll let you know," she said. She slumped a little in the seat. "One thing, though. I do want to apologize to you."

"For what?" He chuckled. "If anyone needs to apologize around here, it's got to be me."

"I accused you of terminal selfishness, when I'm just as guilty."

"You?" Matt laughed. "Not a selfish bone in your lovely body, near as I can tell. And I have had a chance to check," he added.

His tone promised a great deal, and Allie was tempted

to reach out and touch his body and let the magic between them start again. But she wasn't willing to drop the issue. "No, Matt. I've lived alone almost all my life. I was an only child. I had things pretty much my way until Paul deserted me. But even after that, I managed to steer my own course."

"But, your children..." He sounded puzzled.

She shrugged. "Are mine. I don't have to deal with a co-parent in the business of raising them. They're terrific kids. I've been able to be quite independent, even though I've taken good care of them in the process. So, as I see it, I have no business casting any stones at you." Then, she gave in to her earlier temptation and she reached over and touched him. "You're just a bit more impressive about getting your way than I am," she said.

"Hmm." He turned a corner. "I think you have a point, though I can't see where it's taking you." He glanced at her. "And I can tell it's taking you somewhere. The wheels are obviously turning, my love."

She looked away, "Like I said. I'll let you know."

BUT SHE DIDN'T. Allie knew that if she told Matt exactly what she had in mind, he'd throw a monkey wrench into her scheme, just as sure as the sun came up in the morning. No, it was better to do what she had to do quietly and without fanfare.

She was right, this time, and she knew it.

But Josh argued, surprising her with his vehemence. "Allie, you cannot throw away everything just because of that man and his problems." He slapped a stack of papers on his desk. "Look at this," he said. "You've really got a chance to make a good race of it. My informal poll indicates you have a better than even chance of beating Rita despite the scandal of..."

"Living with Matt," she finished. It was the afternoon

of the day following the conference in M.J.'s office. Allie had left Matt at home with Laurel and had gone to confer with Josh.

She was giving up her race for office.

"I don't want to just drop out," she explained. "If I do that, it's likely to affect Matt's situation negatively. Kind of an admission of guilt. What I want to do is slip, lose energy, make it seem that I wasn't a contender, after all." She stared at her manager. "I'll declare my campaign over shortly after the first of September when the polls can show I've no chance at all. Can you do that for me?"

Josh shook his head. "I don't want to, but if you insist, I don't know that I have any choice."

"Thanks." She patted his hand. "After the dust settles, I'll make sure every one knows it wasn't your fault."

Josh shrugged. "I doubt they'll believe you." He put his hand on his desk and slid a piece of paper under a file. Then, he picked up a pencil and tapped it on the file.

"Trust me."

Josh nodded, not meeting her gaze.

She left, thinking of betrayal and what it meant. Why people did it to other people. Wondering if she was doing that herself by dropping out like this, and thinking she wished she was clever enough to think of an alternative that would make everything right for all of them. Josh's position especially bothered her. She was setting him up for yet another failure, and that was unfair.

It wasn't until she had left the office and was driving home that she wondered what had been on that sheet of paper he'd hidden from her sight. By the time she got home, however, she'd put it from her mind. She had far too many other things to think about.

Matt met her at the front door. "I need to use the car," he said. "Mind?"

"No." She lifted her face for a kiss, but he breezed past,

grabbing the keys. Allie sighed and went inside. Sharing her car was getting to both of them. Coordinating their plans was a real problem and she wished he'd buy himself a new one. Laurel greeted her with a cheerful, "Momma," that quickly changed to a cranky, whiny tone that demanded she give the child her total attention.

Allie sighed again as she complied. She and Matt might be the cause of gossip, but for all the wild and crazy illicit love they'd had a chance to make in the past forty-eight hours, they might as well just be an old married couple. Laurel did not contribute to an atmosphere of sensual indulgence. Not a bit! "Don' wanna," she whined when Allie tried to interest her in building blocks. "No!"

Sighing again, Allie reached up on the coffee table for a book. Even Fred and the cats had deserted her, undoubtedly the victims of Laurel's bad mood already. "How about a story?" she asked.

Laurel pouted, then nodded and settled into Allie's lap. Her thumb went into her mouth, and she fingered the silky slip that peeked out from under Allie's skirt. Her eyelids got droopy almost immediately.

Ah. "Did Daddy give you a nap?" Allie asked, only realizing after she said it that she had once more referred to Matt as the child's father. She'd been doing that much too frequently. If things didn't work out for them, she was liable to cause more grief for the little girl by imprinting Matt in her mind as the child's father.

Well, Laurel called her momma. So what harm would it do that hadn't already been done?

"No nap." Laurel made the statement emphatically. She scowled as only a sleepy, cranky child can. "No nap," she repeated.

"Yes, I think so," Allie stood up, lifting Laurel in her arms. "I think you need a nap in the worst way, my tiny little dear."

"No nap!"

"Sweetie, I'm afraid so."

"Nooooo!"

And the battle was on.

She hoped if she let Laurel rage for a few minutes, the child would cry her anger and frustration out before she went to sleep. But Laurel had no intention of giving in so easily. This was a big one. Allie had forgotten the extent and determination of toddler fury. Laurel screeched into Allie's ear until Allie was sure she would go deaf. She was also convinced the roof was going to cave in.

And then, in an unexpected way, it did.

Coming in the house as she had, mildly upset about the car situation and Matt's lack of attention to her, she had left the front door open, with only the screen door shut. When she walked past it on the way to the bedroom with the struggling child in her arms, she noted that the front stoop was occupied. Five people, at least, crowded at the door. Allie stopped, startled by the intrusion.

And was even more startled when a bright light hit her.

"See?" A shrill female voice called. "See. What did we tell you? It's child abuse, I say, plain and simple. Horrible, horrible child abuse! Get this. All of it! You have to get this on tape so we can have someone arrest that woman and take that poor, sweet, innocent child to a safe place!"

CHAPTER TWELVE

ALLIE STOOD STILL, dumbfounded by the words and confused by the blinding light. Laurel stopped struggling and crying. She tried to shrink into Allie and her little arms wrapped tightly around her neck. "Momma," she whimpered, burying her face in Allie's bosom. "Daddy? Daaad-dyyyy."

Allie held her closer, cuddling her and trying to give comfort. "Who are you people?" she cried out to the group at her door. "Go away. Please. You're frightening this child."

"Mmmaaamma," Laurel wailed, hiding her face against Allie.

But the people didn't leave. Instead, one of the women on the front porch barged straight in, slamming the screen door open. The sight of Allie holding Laurel seemed to enrage her. Laurel's wailing went on, but the stranger yelled over it.

"No, no no! *She's* not your momma, honey. I'm gonna be!" She glared at Allie. "She's mine, you bitch," she snarled, her hands grasping claws. "Give me that child! I want her now, before you can harm her anymore."

Allie continued to stand still, holding her ground with an effort of will. All her instincts shrieked at her to back up, protect Laurel and to retreat in the face of such naked aggression. But she stood firm. "Get out of my house," she said, amazed her tone was so quiet and calm. "Now," she added. "Before something bad happens." Her body was starting to tremble from anger and outrage.

The woman was short, but wide and built with a sort of female heaviness that indicated muscle as well as fat. Her complexion was ruddy with fury. She had black hair cut in a Dutch-boy bob and black eyes that radiated flat hatred. She was also vaguely familiar. Allie was trying to remember where she had seen that face before when the woman lunged. She grabbed for Laurel. "I won't leave without the child!"

Laurel screamed, and Allie swung the child away while striking out at the same time with her foot. She caught the intruder right on a pudgy kneecap with the sharp heel of her dress shoe. The woman went down, howling.

The door banged open again. "Hey now, here." This time it was a thin man addressing her, his finger wagging in the air. "You stop that brutality, woman," he yelled. "My wife's done nothing to you!"

The bright, unnatural light continued to shine on the scene, disorienting Allie almost as much as the unexpected violence. "She's invaded my house," she yelled back. "So have you. All of you! Get out!" Tears started to roll down her face, more from frustration and anger than fear. Fear, though, was a factor. The woman on the floor was now trying to grab at Laurel's dangling, kicking legs. Laurel's cry was one of pure terror. Now, she suddenly remembered where she'd seen the pair—it was the night she and M.J. had had dinner at the Chinese restaurant. They had been spying on her! A sense of nightmare closed in on Allie, pushing her toward actual panic.

Then Fred dashed in and barked, her little teeth showing in a snarl. An amazingly vicious snarl, Allie realized, for an animal as naturally friendly and mild-tempered as Fred. That brought her back to a sense of security and control.

Only someone who didn't know dogs would be fooled into believing Fred was really dangerous.

The attack had the desired effect, however. Both strangers screamed and backed away, yodeling about a mad dog. Allie bent down and scooped the poodle up, resting Laurel on one hip and Fred on the other. "Get out of my house!" she shouted. Fred punctuated this with a rapid string of barks, which caused her small, tense body to shake.

Allie waited, every nerve on edge. At first, she thought she was going to be challenged. The woman rose to her feet, but stayed bent in a crouch as if she was readying herself for another launch at Laurel. The man had his fists balled, too. But then, the bright light from the porch went out, and a quiet voice spoke from beyond the screen door. Allie felt her heart leap. It was Matt! She couldn't see him, but his voice was unmistakable.

"I think you should listen to the lady," Matt said. "Because if you don't, I'm going to have to physically remove both of you from her property. And I won't guarantee gentleness."

"Matt!" The cry came from Allie's heart. "They've been spying on me. On us. She tried to hurt Laurel! They're trying to kidnap her!"

"You lying bitch! I..."

The short woman's invective was cut off by a dueted shriek and then the sound of breaking glass and metal. From outside came the cries of another man and a woman, complaining about broken video equipment.

"I asked you to leave," Matt said. "Sorry you stumbled on that first step. You should look where you're going," he added. More crunching of metal and glass.

The man and woman in the house were now looking decidedly apprehensive. Fred, safe in Allie's grasp, continued to bark and snarl at them.

"You had both better go away right now," Allie said.

"I don't think he's in any mood to deal reasonably with you, whoever you are."

The screen door banged open. Matt, looking like an avenging angel, stood framed in the afternoon sunlight.

"That was a pair of unlucky and unwise news vultures out there," he said. "They're gone. And these birds are the Turners, Allie." He spoke softly, his tone conversational, a flick of one hand indicating the couple. "Joan and Frank Turner. My sister's husband's second cousin and her husband. Here to challenge my right to Laurel." His lips turned in an expression approximating a sneer of contempt.

No one else said anything. The air seemed to shimmer with tension and hatred. Laurel, silent now, huddled closer to Allie. Even Fred quieted.

Matt gazed at them in a clinical, detached manner and then looked back at Allie. "Now, can't you just see them as the proper parents for Laurel?" he asked, his tone still mild. Only deep in his eyes could the depth of his feelings be seen. "I was warned by Miranda that they might be coming here, so I cut my business meeting with her short and decided to swing by the house and check. Glad I did."

Allie shuddered with combined relief and dread. He was hanging on to self-control by a mere thread. She had already seen what harm he could do to an opponent when he was in control of himself. What would occur if he lost that control? Her heart thudded even harder.

What would happen if he lost it right now?

The Turners seemed unaware of the danger. "You can't keep her," the woman said, her tone much subdued. "We have the law on our side."

"Odd you should say that." Matt regarded her once again, his expression cold and set. "I understand the same thing applies to us. Until a court rules differently, Laurel's ours...mine." He opened the door. "Furthermore, you've violated that law by entering this woman's home. Now, leave before I call the cops.''

''You wouldn't dare...'' the other woman began. Hatred danced deep in her dark eyes. Her hands curled into claws. It looked as if she was ready to attack both of them.

Allie didn't wait to see what would happen next. Still carrying the child and the dog, she raced for the phone and punched the emergency call for 911.

''WHILE I APPLAUD your quick thinking, cousin,'' M.J. said a few hours later, ''I do believe you might have overreacted a teensy bit. Were fire trucks and ambulances really necessary?''

''Overreacted, hell!'' Allie set down her glass of iced tea. She, M.J. and Matt were seated in the kitchen that evening, hours after the Turner episode, sorting out events and discussing possible consequences. One problem was that when she called 911, every emergency agency in the city had responded, drawing unavoidable public attention to the situation.

''Matt had just trashed a video camera with his bare hands and sent two reporters scurrying for the high country,'' she said. ''That Turner amazon was looking for blood to shed. And I'm absolutely sure they were the same people who were listening in on our conversation that night at the Chinese restaurant. They've been plotting and planning this for a long time, I tell you. Matt was ready to fight, too. I wasn't about to wait and see which of them decided to try for the gold first. I figured the sound of sirens would get everyone's attention, and I was right. It did.'' She paused to catch up with her breath, remembering. The Turners had scurried away like large insects as soon as the police and fire trucks arrived.

''I wouldn't have hurt her or her husband,'' Matt said.

"I just intended to make sure they left, quickly. Before they did any more damage."

Unlike Allie, who couldn't seem to stop talking, he'd been very quiet since the dust had settled. Quiet like a volcano before an eruption or a fault line before an earthquake. The air around him seemed charged with energy and tension.

Negative energy and unhealthy tension.

"I was not looking for trouble," he added.

"I hope not," M.J. said. "I hope you'd have better sense. That would give the woman just the kind of excuse she would need to go to the authorities with a genuine complaint." He shut his eyes and rubbed his face. "As it is, I had to do a lot of smoothing of ruffled feathers to get those reporters to agree not to press charges."

"They were on my front porch," Allie protested, defending Matt again, as she had been doing for the past few hours, first to the police, now to M.J. "Trespassing on my property. Invading my privacy."

M.J. nodded. "They were. That's why they won't do anything about the destroyed equipment." He turned to Matt. "By the way, what did you do to that camera? Run over it with a truck?"

Matt shrugged. Laurel, who was sleeping on his lap, stirred. "I just stomped on it once or twice," he said. "Sometimes, when I'm really angry, I can get a little carried away."

M.J. nodded again. "Just don't let it happen again, okay?"

"I understand." Matt stroked Laurel's head. Leaned his cheek against her hair. "I understand," he repeated, so softly, Allie scarcely heard him. She certainly didn't catch the emotion in his tone.

But M.J. did, and the lawyer seemed to read into the words far more than Allie had. "Matt, I mean it," M.J.

said. "If you do anything else that smacks of violence, you'll blow your case right out of the water. You'll ruin any chance you have of keeping Laurel. This is no jungle where you can get away with doing as you please. In the eyes of the authorities, a man who uses violence to solve his problems is not a fit parent."

"How can you say that to him when they were the ones who started it?" Allie asked, still feeling defensive about Matt's action. He had, after all, saved her from a dreadful confrontation. Even if he had taken things to extremes by trashing the camera. Matt said nothing.

M.J. looked at them both, his expression sober. "It is their word against yours about that, since the tape in the camera was destroyed. Matt's anger worked against you, because he removed the only sure record of Joan Turner's aggressive behavior. While the two reporters are eye witnesses to her breaking into your home, they are also hostile witnesses. Angry at being run off and upset about the equipment being trashed. I wouldn't look to them for any support."

Matt stood up. "I'm going to put Laurel to bed," he said. "You're right, M.J. I was way out of line, and I'm sorry. I acted out of pure instinct. Gut reaction. I won't do that again."

"I don't think you need to apologize for your behavior," Allie said, folding her arms and glaring at M.J. "There's a time and a place for caution and thought. This afternoon, action was in order."

Matt shifted the sleeping child in his arms. "Yeah, but you were the one who called 911 and pulled the plug," he said, watching her carefully. "You knew the consequences of serious trouble, you could see where things were going, and I was part of the problem."

"Matt, no, you were not...," she protested.

But he had left the room.

Resisting the urge to follow him and continue the conversation, Allie turned to M.J. "What are we facing now?" she asked. "It's clear to any reasonable person that the Turner woman is nuts. Maybe her husband, too. I didn't get much of a chance to hear from him."

M.J. looked worried. "They were revved when they confronted you. Out of control, just like Matt. I think the fact that they were staking out your home with reporters in tow, just watching and waiting for an incident, indicates cleverness, however. I wouldn't put it past them to clean up their act when it comes to a custody hearing. If they can keep a lid on their emotions, they just might look better to a judge than Matt does."

"How about me?" She asked the question before she thought.

"What about you, Allie?" M.J. rested his elbows on the kitchen table. "Are you really in this, or are you just a bystander?"

She stared at the tabletop, unable to meet M.J.'s steady gaze. "Good question," she conceded finally. "I thought I was sure, but this incident has really shaken me. I need some time to think about it."

M.J. nodded. "I suggest you do that. *Strongly* suggest you do."

And she knew it was the lawyer, not the cousin, who was speaking to her. Warning her, really.

MATT SAT in the near darkness and watched Laurel settle into deep sleep. She had been more traumatized by the afternoon's events than anyone realized, he thought. She'd had no nightmares in all the time they'd been living with Allie, but tonight, he was taking no chances on not being right by her side if she should wake up with one.

That was the least he could do for her.

There was more, however. Much more, and he needed

solitude to think about that. He leaned back on the bed and shut his eyes.

The darkness took him away to a night when he'd been in real trouble for the first time in his life. Trouble that could have brought disaster not only to himself, but also to the one person in the world he knew well enough to love at that time—his father.

It had been a silly thing. A dumb thing. Quixotic. They were in the Middle East then. Nothing modern about the place, especially in social attitudes. Ten years old, nearly eleven, he didn't know yet what girls were all about, but had become interested in one who claimed to be fourteen. As a friend, only. They'd started meeting secretly, whispering to each other through the crack in the wall that ran between her home and the next-door villa his father was renting. Matt smiled, remembering the dry, gritty feel of the rock wall and the sweet smell of the flowers that blossomed along its base.

Then, one evening, she asked him to help her run away. Her father, she said, was going to make her marry an old man she didn't love. Matt believed and aided.

And was very nearly caught. When he ran to his own home with the authorities right on his tail, his father had taken the news with his usual *élan,* packed up their few personal belongings and had fled with his outlaw son into the desert night.

Forget any attempt to explain, he had said. Forget that the girl had lied to Matt. Had been using him to rendezvous with her real lover, with whom she had escaped, leaving Matt to face the music alone. The best thing to do, his father had said, was to run when you were outnumbered, and also when the other side had the cops with them.

"Dad," Matt whispered, "you were almost right." *Almost.* Just close enough to seem correct all the time.

Laurel whimpered in her sleep.

Matt lay very still.

His father was a coward.

He sat up, the realization coming at him like a slap across his face. His father. The great, intrepid Robert Glass, adventurer extraordinare, was a coward.

Not a coward in the sense of being physically afraid of pain, but a moral coward, who wouldn't face up to responsibility. And he'd taught Matt by example to do the same thing. Run. That was the way to handle difficult or dangerous moments in life.

A cold sweat suddenly covered his skin. He looked over at Laurel who now slept peacefully, Allie's daughter's baby blanket drawn over her small body. If Allie hadn't had the courage to stand up to him the other day, he'd be running away, too. Just as his father had. Even now, knowing what he did about himself, the temptation was strong.

Run. Hide. Avoid the danger... Wait out the storm...

He lay back down and thought of old Kelly McClean and his storm cellar under his shack of a house. Hiding. Waiting out the storm. Other men did that, too. Not just his father. Had Allie's missing husband tried it? Had he succeeded? Or failed? He thought about what McClean had said that day they had been waiting out the storm down in his cellar.

Paul Ford treated some important politician fella.

Hmm.

ALLIE WENT to her bed alone later that night. When she'd looked into Laurel's room, the little girl was sleeping peacefully and Matt had been sound asleep, too. He was curled on his side on top of the covers, still fully clothed, but with one hand hooked into the bars of the crib, as if he wanted to make sure no harm would come to the child. She hadn't wanted to disturb that protective pose, so she shut the door softly and went into her own room with Fred at her heels. The dog seemed unhappy about returning to her old bed, but once the light was off, she settled down.

That was more than her mistress could do. Allie tossed and turned, dealing with the problem of Matt and Laurel in her mind and heart and trying to come to some kind of solution to the dilemma.

M.J had gently and tactfully suggested she and Matt either decide to get married or return the fledgling household to its original status. Matt at his place and Allie at her home, alone. They could still date, of course. Just not live together.

But what if the Turners had gone to Matt's place when he was gone and Debbie was baby-sitting? Would she have been secure enough in her own authority and strong enough to fight them off while safeguarding Laurel?

No. That was too much to ask an outsider.

Well, M.J. had all but said that she, Allie, was essentially an outsider in Matt's situation. Uninvolved, technically.

Was she?

Should she be?

She turned over and lay on her back, staring up at the ceiling. The only way to be involved technically was to be legally tied to him.

Married.

Her stomach rumbled, indicating the onset of nervous indigestion. She tossed around, pulling at the sheet and disturbing the sleeping poodle. Fred sighed and rearranged her position on the bed.

Married. Again. Unimaginable. She couldn't do it. No matter how she felt about Matt or Laurel, she could not do it.

And that was that. She just couldn't live with the sword of uncertainly hanging over her head for the rest of her life. Until the day she knew for an absolute fact that Paul Ford was dead, she just could not take the risk. Tears filled her eyes and poured down the sides of her face. After a while, she fell asleep. Her dreams were fleeting and unpleasant.

In the small hours of the morning, however, a strange low sound woke her. Allie sat up, listening. Fred stirred and woofed softly, indicating that there was indeed something, but nothing dangerous. When Allie got up and reached for her robe, the dog's ears pricked forward. Her tail wagged.

"What is it, Fred?" Allie asked, whispering. "I wish I had keen senses like yours." She moved into the hall and Fred followed, tail awag, still indicating no danger.

The noise sounded again. This time, Allie knew what it was. Matt. He was talking or at least making sounds. A muffled groan. She hurried to Sally's room and opened the door.

Matt was sitting up on the bed, his face in his hands. Laurel still slept quietly. The room was dimly lighted by the glow of the moon coming in the window. The shade had not been closed. He looked up and saw her, standing in the doorway.

"Nightmare," he whispered. "An old familiar one. Nothing at all to worry about. Go back to sleep." His face looked strained and haggard.

"All right, I will," she said. Allie came into the room. She shut the window shade, dimming the room to almost darkness. She went over to the closet and took out a cotton comforter. Pulling it over her, she laid down on the bed next to him. Fred jumped up and arranged herself on top of the comforter. She sighed contentedly and closed her little eyes. Allie sighed, too. She smiled at Matt and patted the other pillow, inviting him.

Matt looked at the two of them for a moment. Then, without saying a word, he eased himself under the comforter, put his arms around Allie and rested his head on the pillow beside her. She could see the smallest gleam of moisture at the edges of his closed eyes, and her heart went out to him.

Soon, they both fell into a dreamless sleep, which lasted until morning. It was a time of peace for everyone.

Morning brought a fresh batch of trouble, however. Over coffee, Allie studied the newspaper, giving Matt a rundown on the essentials while he helped Laurel with breakfast. The little girl was practicing tossing food this morning.

They had made the headlines in the Police Report section. "According to this," she said, "my home was a scene of domestic violence yesterday." She looked up at Matt. "How the heck do they figure that?"

He shrugged. "You called 911, didn't you? They have to give out some reason, I suppose."

"Yeah. But the violence was not domestic. That makes it sound like you and I were in a physical fight." She snapped the newspaper. "That's a lie."

Matt retrieved a slice of pear before it hit the floor. Fred trotted over to sit nearer, looking disappointed at having missed a snack opportunity. "It's the right of the press to print the truth as they see it," Matt said. "You know that. You're also a public figure, having declared for office. That makes a libel suit difficult, if not impossible. Not to say, stupid. Does the editor have a political bias?"

"Oh, yes." Allie slammed a fist down on the offending rag. "She endorsed Rita a while ago."

"Well." Matt stood up and started to towel Cream of Wheat off Laurel's face. "We'll just have to see that the paper is used for carrying out the trash and little else. That it's of no real value when it comes to predicting political winners, won't we."

"Matt, I…"

"Don't argue with me this morning," he said, interrupting her. "I'm still in fighting mode, and that nightmare I had last night didn't help my temper. I want to turn my aggressions onto a useful target, such as getting you elected.''

"My campaign isn't important…"

"It is to me." He tossed the dirty towel in the sink and bent down to help Laurel out of her high chair. "I want you to succeed with your ambitions and dreams."

"But, Matt. You…" She ran down, unable to finish.

"I what?" He turned and looked at her. "I'm in your way, aren't I? If I stay here with you, the bad publicity's going to kill you. If I go…"

She stood up and went over to the sink. The window above it looked out onto the backyard and the prairie beyond. The high grass was still light green, but it was beginning to fade to summer gold. "If you go," she said, "who will sleep with you when you have nightmares?" She turned around to face him. "Or watch out for Laurel when someone tries to harm her and you aren't there?"

Matt stared at her. He set Laurel down, and she toddled off after Fred. "What are you saying to me, Allie?" he asked.

"I…I don't know," she replied, hugging herself nervously. "But I do know I don't want you to leave."

"I don't have a choice. Not if I consider what's best for you."

She shook her head. "I'm not sure I know what's best for me anymore." Tears came into her eyes, and this time, she didn't fight them. "Matt, I haven't known you two months yet, but you…"

"Allie, would you marry me?"

She bent over the sink, crying hard now. "I…can't. I never will be free. Oh damn!" She hit the counter with her open palm. "Damn, damn, damn."

"You *are* free," he said. "You're just using that as an excuse." He moved nearer, but didn't touch her. "Throw off the past, Allie. Let it go."

"I...I *want* to, but..."

He stepped back. "But it's a great excuse, isn't it."

She wiped her eyes. "It's no excuse, Matt. Don't push at me on this."

"Why not?" He folded his arms and frowned. "Do you want to know what my nightmare was about last night?"

"I... It's your..."

"No. Listen to me. It was about being lost and alone. Lost from you, from Laurel, from everything I've come to hold precious in my life."

Allie sobbed once more, then began to gain control of her emotions. This was a two-way street, after all, she reasoned. "What you're doing is not fair, Matt," she said. "You're asking me to forget about my past while you keep your future." She glared at him, wanting him to see the need and anger in her heart. "I don't believe you can stay here for the rest of your life, and that's what I need from a man I'll be willing to marry. I need a commitment I can trust."

He jerked his head back as if she'd slapped him. "Don't put it on me. I'm willing to compromise. Are you?"

"How can you compromise? How can you promise me you won't leave me someday, just like Paul"

"Oh, damn it all, Allie! Don't..."

"Don't what?" She put her hands on her hips, unreasonably angry now and knowing it, but unable to stop the words. "Don't say what's really in my heart? Oh, forgive me. I forgot for a moment that you..."

"Momma?" Laurel came toddling into the kitchen. Fred followed close behind. The little girl looked upset. "Momma crying?" She stared at both of them. "Daddy?" Her question and woeful expression acted like a sharp pin on Allie's puffed up sense of outrage. How could she carry on this way with Matt where Laurel would hear her? It was wrong!

Allie knelt down. "It's okay. Momma's okay, darling," she said, holding out her arms. Laurel giggled and ran to her. Allie embraced her and looked up at Matt. "What are we going to do?" she asked. "This isn't just about you and me anymore, you know." She stroked the child's hair. "Not by a long shot."

"You're right." His wide shoulders slumped. "If it was just you and me, maybe we'd see... But..." He rubbed a hand over his face. "Damned if I know what we should do," he replied. "Damned if I..."

The shrill, chilling sound of screeching brakes interrupted him. Allie straightened up, still holding Laurel. Fred stiffened, her ears perking forward, but her body rigid and trembling. She moved closer to Matt. From their hiding places, the three cats suddenly appeared at Allie's feet, tails atwitch. "What is that. Who...?" she asked.

Matt shook his head. "I don't..." he started to say. Then, he was silent. Listening... Put his hand on her shoulder...

Shouted a warning... Pushed her and Laurel to the floor...

And the world exploded in a series of thunderous roars.

CHAPTER THIRTEEN

SHE COULD HEAR glass shattering, wood splintering with each horrendous blast. Blasts that went on and on. Then, tires squealed again, the sound menacing and evil. Allie struggled against a terror so deep it made her numb. Matt's weight on her body pressed her down, forcing the air out of her lungs just as quickly as she struggled to breathe it in. She began to feel faint. The view at the edges of her sight started to fade to black. From somewhere far away, she heard Laurel crying, Fred howling and the cats yowling all at once. They needed her! She fought to regain her senses.

"Allie! Can you hear me?" His weight lifted. His hands touched her, brought her back from the darkness. "Allie? Say something! Please!"

She blinked, clearing her eyes. Took a deep breath and coughed. The kitchen was full of smoke and dust. A ragged hole gaped in the wall dividing it from the living room. A hole that look like a giant fist had punched it, through wallboard and inner insulation. Electric wire sparked and fizzed and smoked in the ruin. "What happened?" she asked, her tone amazingly normal. "Was it a bomb?"

Matt studied her for a moment, as if satisfying himself she was all right, then he stood, Laurel now in his arms. "No. Close, though. I think we've been shotgunned. Professionally. Get up and see if the phone's still working. Call the cops. 911. This time, we need them all!"

"But, who...?" She got slowly to her feet, her muscles

trembling and threatening to give way. Looking around, she saw all her animals, eyes wide with terror, but safe. Fred literally flew into her arms. "Who did it?" Sudden fear and a sense of deep horror at the close call they'd all had made her nauseated. "They tried to kill us! Are they still out there?"

"No." Matt narrowed his eyes against the dust. "I think they ran just as soon as they emptied the gun. I heard tires squealing just after the last shot." He looked at Laurel, at Allie and at the animals. "Listen, forget the cops." He bent down and picked up two cats, holding them securely, even as they struggled to get down. Laurel, silent, watched the two felines, but made no attempt to touch them. "Let's get out of here. Now."

"But…"

"Listen to me, Allie. For once, just do as I say and do it now without asking questions. Get in the car. We're going up the mountain to my place."

"Matt, are you sure?" She shifted Fred and picked up the remaining cat. Tom growled once, then quieted.

"I am." He herded her toward the back door, the one that led from the kitchen directly into the garage. "We've been attacked by someone who doesn't care who they hurt. A pro with a job to do. Well, I'm a pro, too. *This* I know how to deal with."

His words disturbed her, but she was too shocked by the attack to question him.

The few neighbors who were still home at this time of day surrounded the car as they started to pull out of the garage. Questions flew, but Matt dealt with them easily, asking everyone to get back in their own homes and to let the police know what they'd seen and heard. He asked her next-door neighbor to tell the police he was taking them up to the Essex home and could be reached there, but that anyone who wanted to talk to him had better call first, because he was intent on protection. The woman, a retired teacher, nodded.

As soon as possible, they were on their way up the mountain. As they had backed out of the garage, Allie had glimpsed the wreckage of the front of her house and had cried out in anger and horror. The shotgun blasts had destroyed the picture window in the living room and had left large holes in the wall. The window in Sally's room was gone, too. If Laurel had been playing in there... If her own children had been home...

Allie wept, softly, all the way up to the Essex house. She felt sick and weak. More frightened than she'd ever been in her life. Even more so than the day she had finally realized that Paul Ford was not coming back. What was going on? What had she done to have this happen to her? Threats. Harassment and verbal abuse. Now, real violence. A nightmare with no end in sight!

She was, she realized, in a mild state of shock. She let Matt bundle her and the animals and Laurel into the Essex house and let him get things organized. Her four pets seemed just as stunned as she was, content to huddle close to her where she sat with Laurel on the couch in the big living room, staring out at the peaceful mountain scenery. She almost smiled when she realized that the dog and cats weren't squabbling for what was probably the first time in their furry lives.

Almost smiled, but not quite. A smile would mean happiness and there was no joy in her for the moment.

She heard Matt on the phone and thought he must be calling the police. She closed her eyes. Laurel snuggled close, her little face resting on Allie's chest, and her thumb in her mouth. Allie listened to the cats purring, anxiety rather than contentment driving their humming. Listened to Fred panting. Listened to Matt, taking care of their problem...

"I don't care how much it costs, man," he said. "I want every damn one of you up here a.s.a.p. And get the weapons on the road yesterday..."

Allie's eyes opened wide. *Weapons*.

What about weapons?

"I want trained troops, Chico," Matt said, his tone harsh. "Ones that don't mind trouble. I don't know any around here, that's why I'm relying on you. I want you to get the old team together, my friend. I'm calling in old debts. You guys owe me, and you know it." Pause. "Okay."

She shifted position on the couch and set Laurel to one side. The little girl whimpered until Fred cuddled close. Then, she seemed to fall asleep with the dog nestled next to her. Allie got up. Found her knees shaky, but capable of carrying her up the three stairs into the dining room and kitchen area. Matt was hanging up the phone. He sat down at the kitchen table and made some notes on a pad of paper.

"What are you doing?" Allie asked.

He looked up at her. A new Matt regarded her. One with the hard glint of ruthlessness in his brown eyes. "Taking care of you. Of Laurel. Of...things."

She pulled a chair out from the table and sat down. "How?"

"Allie, just let me handle this."

"How?" She put her hands on the wood surface. "How are you planning to handle this? How are you planning on handling me?"

"By protecting you."

She started to reply, but the phone rang. Matt picked it up. His gaze became even more remote and distant. He mumbled a comment, then said, clearly, "Mercs are fine, but no hit men. Try any of the guys who worked with us before. I trust them. I don't want professional killers, understand me?"

Allie froze in place.

Matt replaced the phone after speaking for another few moments in Spanish.

"Who are you?" she asked, more frightened now than she had been when the shotgun was blasting away at her home. She shook her head. "I don't know you."

"Yes, you do."

"Mercs?" She stood up and began pacing around the kitchen. "Mercenaries? Hit men? *Killers?* Matt, I don't know you. I can't imagine…"

"How do you think I pulled off that kidnap rescue in South America?" he asked. "With a troop of Boy Scouts? Come on, Allie. Smell the coffee. I'm the same man you've known since the day Laurel smeared jelly on you. But please remember that I had a different job before becoming her surrogate daddy. I was an adventurer. I know people who have specialized talents. Some of them owe me. I'm just calling in a few markers. To save you…"

"Don't you dare use me as an excuse, Matt Glass." She stopped pacing and pointed her finger at him. "I had no trouble with this kind of horror and violence before I met you and I…"

"You want me to disappear?" He gazed at her with no warmth in his eyes. "I can do that."

"I…" She stopped pacing. Tom, the biggest and oldest of her cats, came into the kitchen and sat down, curling her furry tail around her feet. Watching.

"No," Allie said. "I don't want you to disappear. We've been through that. I love you. That's the problem. Because I'm not sure who it is that I love anymore. Who *you* are."

Matt stood up. "If you don't think you know, I can't tell you. Only show you. Please just trust me for now. Until you do feel you know me again."

"I…I don't know if I can, Matt."

His smile was wry, lopsided. "I guess that's honest enough."

"I'm very frightened." She hugged herself, not daring to go to him yet. He *was* a stranger. A mystery.

"You should be. So am I. I have fears just like anyone else. And, remember, you didn't have a nightmare last night so bad, you woke up crying out. *I* did. And you came to me and comforted me. Made me feel safe and secure." He held out his hand. "What you did for me last night, I can do for you today. Even if you disapprove of my methods. Don't turn from me, now Allie. I love you, too. God help me. I *need* you. And, frankly, you need me, as well."

Still, she hesitated. "I've never needed anyone else before. I...I always made my own way. I don't know how to deal with dependence."

"That makes two of us."

She touched his hand.

And came into his arms. She cried, and he held her close, comforting her. Their embrace was warm, and his kiss burned her doubts away. For now.

IT TOOK the rest of the week to sort out her life as best she could under the circumstances. To rearrange her schedule, canceling those appointments and putting off those clients that she could, to bring many of her belongings up the mountain, and to deal with the new reality of being a target of violence.

Because that's what they were.

After the official investigation, even the police agreed with Matt that they had been attacked by a professional terrorist. Or, at the very least, a local tough who had been instructed by one. She and Matt were advised to be on guard at all times, though no one encouraged Matt to go as far as he actually did.

"The cops can't provide bodyguard service indefinitely," he said, several days later. "We have to deal with this ourselves," he added, his tone indicating he would tolerate no argument.

She had none to give him. The county sheriff, who had jurisdiction on the mountain, was providing only drive-by security in the form of a patrol car passing the house now and then. It was not enough, given the calculated violence of the attack on them, she thought. The city police were conducting an investigation, but were clearly out of their league already.

No one had seen the car, though the neighbors had certainly heard the shots. No evidence, no suspects, no pending arrests. Whoever had done it, whoever was behind it was still free to act against them. So, she had finally agreed to Matt's style and plan of action. It all went against the grain, but for the most part, she kept her opinions to herself.

She had said nothing when some large, mysterious packages had started arriving by private delivery service to the house. Hadn't commented when Matt had installed an elaborate security system around the house, except to make sure he allowed for Fred's bathroom excursions.

Matt had agreed with that. But he had limited Fred to a leash and an adult human companion when she went outside. This made sense, because the property wasn't fenced, so Allie accepted it. Fred was less sanguine about the situation, but seemed prepared to tolerate the conditions for the time being. The three cats weren't allowed out at all and had to be watched closely each time a door was opened. They were not happy with the new rules and spent most of their time looking for messes to make in the new and unfamiliar environment of the Essex house.

Further, Laurel was showing all the signs expected from fear trauma and another change in environment. If there was trouble around that the cats missed, she found it and made it worse. With relish, it seemed to her "Momma" and "Daddy." And, with Matt so concerned with building his electronic fortress for their well-being, most of the supervision of Laurel fell to Allie.

It all made for a full, exhausting day, every day, and when night came, she and Matt fell asleep without even thinking of making love, though they did sleep together. But it was in the same room with Laurel and the four pets. Matt had done an extra-special job on the master bedroom with his security techniques and made certain every living being he cared for was safely inside that system before he finally allowed himself to sleep. A fly would likely set it off, Allie was sure.

But, she did sleep soundly and securely. Even knowing Matt had a loaded gun under his pillow. And though they didn't make love, something special was happening every night as they slumbered, exhausted, in each other's presence.

She was getting used to him, and he to her under far less than romantic conditions. If she'd had time to think about it much, she would have been pleased. Thinking about good things, however, was not a high priority. Too many negatives were still out there, unaccounted for.

On Monday morning, they were on the way out to the airport to pick up Matt's friends. The ones he had phoned a week ago. Until now, Matt hadn't let Allie or Laurel out of his sight for more than a moment or two and insisted on taking then both with him whenever he had to leave the house.

This trip was a small exception: Laurel was staying for the afternoon with Miranda while Allie went to the airport. There wasn't room, Matt had said, for the three of them and the men he was picking up, and he wanted Allie to meet them without having to worry about the child. Allie's patience was wearing thin. But she was still shook up enough to accept having some hired gun watch out for her.

Hopefully, Matt's buddy, this Chico person, would help her get on with her life.

When she saw him in the crowd getting off the plane, however, those hopes fell flat to the floor. "Your buddy's actually the Terminator, right?" she asked Matt.

Matt's grin was wide. "Don't joke about it," he said, speaking softly. "He's real sensitive about the scars on his face."

"It wasn't the scars that clued me," she replied. "It was his size." But she was speaking to herself. Matt had run over to the giant and was being caught up in a crushing bear hug, which he was returning with glee. The two looked and sounded like a mismatched pair of professional wrestlers, as they exchanged happy insults. Allie sighed. Male bonding. Who could understand it?

Three other behemoths arranged themselves around the newcomer, and she heard growled greetings in at least two languages besides English. Then Matt summoned her with an imperious wave of his hand. Hating it, she trotted over anyway. She even managed a smile. They were a truly scary bunch.

"This is Mrs. Ford," Matt said, repeating the words in Spanish, then German. "She's the client. She and a two-year-old child you'll meet later on." He paused. "The good news is, the lady will follow orders," he added, not looking at her. "Allie, this is Gunther, Christian and Manuel. And, of course, Chico."

"Hi." Allie managed another smile. *Follow orders?* Well, only if she agreed with them! "Thanks for coming," she added.

This greeting brought no comment from the men. They all just stared at her, as if she was nothing more than an interesting bug. Allie blinked. Pinched herself to see if she was in a bizarre nightmare. But she was wide-awake.

When they picked up the luggage, she could see why

Matt had decided to leave Laurel behind. Not only was her Eagle packed to the ceiling, but Matt and Chico strapped baggage onto the roof, as well. As they worked, the men said nothing. They had obviously done this before, Allie realized. They moved and behaved as a team.

A team aimed at what goal? Her safety? Laurel's?

Was Matt actually constructing some sort of private army with the aim of going after whoever was behind the terrorism aimed at them?

And, just what did she, law-abiding citizen that she thought she was, think about that?

She wasn't sure. Yet.

They drove to town, Allie squashed between Matt and Chico. No one said a word until they reached the section of the city that held "car row," the avenue of the automobile dealers. Then Chico pointed to a dealership. Matt slowed and turned in.

"Why are we stopping?" Allie asked, unable to bear silence any longer. "Shouldn't we be getting home? It's near Laurel's nap time. I don't want to impose on Miranda any longer than necessary."

"Be patient," Matt said, scarcely noticing her, she thought. "This is important. We're buying these guys a proper car."

She had to bite her tongue to keep from replying in the manner she felt most suited his attitude and the occasion.

But, they did buy the guys a car. Actually, what they drove out in, after paying the astonished and delighted salesman in cash, was more of a modified tank. It was an off-road, all-terrain vehicle designed for rigorous use, one of the knockoffs of the military Hum-vee that had captured the American imagination a few years before. Chico's guys seemed happy as clams in sand, Allie though glumly. And Matt had paid for it without counting the cost.

Or asking her to kick in. Somehow, that bothered her

more than anything else that had happened that afternoon. It was her neck, too, on the line, wasn't it? She ought to be a contributor to the effort.

Right now, she was angrier at Matt than she was at the person or persons behind their troubles.

In spite of her hidden rage, however, on the way to pick up Laurel at Miranda's house, a strange thing happened. While the other three men had abandoned the crowded back seat of her Eagle for the rarer joy of the ATV, Chico stayed in the front, again wedging her close to Matt. She could feel the play of Matt's muscles pressed against her arm as he drove. Felt his strength and control. Sensed his competence. Her awareness of him expanded.

The physical sensation began to stir her sexually, and by the time they pulled up to Miranda's house-office, she was so aroused, she could hardly get out of the car.

And she was embarrassed beyond belief by the combination.

Laurel greeted the two of them with sublime indifference and paid absolutely no attention to the big stranger with them. She was in the middle of some sort of playtime with two other small girls and clearly did not care to be interrupted. Miranda apologized.

"She's been having great fun," the private detective explained. "I invited my two little nieces over for a few hours, and they've gotten along really well, considering their ages." She stared up at the gigantic Chico. "Hi," she said. "Who're you?"

As Allie watched, the newcomer underwent an astonishing transformation. From a sullen, rather frightening, dark-visaged giant, he became a smiling, charming man. "My name is Chico Roderigez," he said, taking her hand and bowing over it, brushing his lips near the skin. *"Señorita."*

Miranda Stamos actually blushed. And giggled. She looked younger than her thirty-plus years, all of a sudden.

Allie thought briefly of M.J.'s thwarted lust for Miranda and sighed. "Mr. Roderigez is here to help Matt," she said. "They've done stuff together before."

"That South America thing?" Miranda glanced at Matt. Chico still held her hand.

Matt nodded. "Chico was my right arm in that operation." He picked up Laurel, who protested loudly. "Come on, sweetie. Time to go home. Say goodbye to your new friends."

"No home! Want stay 'Randa!"

Matt grinned. "It seems you've made a conquest, Miranda."

"Ah, then that makes two of us," Chico intoned.

Allie glanced heavenward. Laurel yowled. Matt looked embarrassed at his niece's behavior, and Chico and Miranda looked at each other. This was all getting far too complicated for her, Allie decided. She felt a yen for the quiet, simple life she had been leading up until a few short weeks ago.

When she first saw Matt Glass pushing a grocery cart and thought he was so good-looking.

It took some time to extract Laurel from the two other children, but they finally got her into the Eagle and headed up the mountain to the Essex house. The other men had gone on before them with directions from Matt and instructions from Chico. Since they had left the car seat out to make more room, Allie sat in back, holding the child, leaving Chico and Matt up front to talk about security measures.

And countermeasures.

They talked in rapid-fire Spanish, with German on the side, obviously thinking she couldn't understand them. Well, they were almost right. But she could make out enough of the Spanish words to get the general drift. Matt was not content only to protect. He and Chico were plotting an attack strategy. She was sure of it.

And, she found, she approved.

Events in her life were now so far out of her control that she welcomed anything that would start to set things back in order. Even a risky... Her attention was suddenly riveted on the conversation. Her thoughts tumbled, emotions whipping them into a whirlwind.

Matt had mentioned her husband's name.

He'd rolled it along in with a lot of other stuff she didn't catch, but she definitely heard Paul's name. Why? She hesitated to ask. Thought about it, but... What could Paul have to do with the current crisis? She ought to ask, she knew, but...

Then, they were home. And there was no time for questions. Matt and Chico piled out and started unloading equipment and luggage. The three other men were already at work around the grounds, apparently adding extra goodies to Matt's security system. Allie didn't ask about that, either.

Instead, she took Laurel and went inside. The animals were there to greet her, and Laurel came out of her pout when she saw Fred. *Just like home,* Allie thought.

Except, it wasn't home. She had to leash Fred up to take her outside. She had a whiny two-year-old to feed and put down for a late nap. She had virtually no privacy, what with the men coming in and out, ignoring her and going about their business. She had no chance at all to get any serious work done, even with Laurel out of the way for the time being. No one said anything about it, but she was also sure that she was expected to feed the four new faces as well as provide dinner for herself, Matt and Laurel.

Well, why not? Weren't all these guys here to help save her from enemies? Some weird, twisted sickos who'd frightened her and threatened her and destroyed her peace, her future and her home. She went into the kitchen and made coffee. Then, she sat down at the table and started to cry.

Matt found her few minutes later. Without saying anything, he brought over a box of tissues, then poured them both a cup of coffee. Allie sniffed and tried to regain some self-control while she hung her head over the steaming mug. "I don't know..." she started to say. "I just..."

"I'm glad to see you crying, finally," he said softly. "It's a normal reaction to all this."

She looked at him. "Give me a break, Matt. I'm being a wimp, and you know it. Don't patronize me. At least grant me that much."

He didn't seem impressed. "I'll grant you anything you want, Allie. But you are entitled to bawl some. All you want, in fact. Your world's been turned upside down. Anyone'd cry. Or wish they could."

She stretched her arms out on the table and rested her forehead on them. "I feel helpless."

"And you're not used to that, are you?"

"No."

He sat back, folding his arms. "You didn't feel that way when your husband disappeared?"

She shrugged. "Sure, but..."

"But, you took the bull by the horns, so to speak, and did things about your situation."

"Of course, I..."

"You're doing that now. You just don't know it," he said.

She started to reply, but the phone rang.

"I'll get it." Matt stood, went over to the phone and lifted the receiver. He frowned.

Allie tensed.

He glanced over at her and shook his head. "It's nothing. Don't worry," he said. "Just testing the wiretap system, that's all."

"Wire...tap?" She rubbed her sore eyes and took a sip of coffee. "Is that legal?"

Matt spoke in Spanish, then hung up the phone. "No," he said. "It isn't."

"But *we're* doing it anyway."

"That's right. If anyone calls now trying to put a scare into you, we'll be on them like flies on...honey."

She whistled through her teeth. "I'll never get to the governor's mansion by this route, that's for sure."

He threw back his head, finishing the rest of his coffee. "Allie, I'm doing this so you have a chance to stay alive and well enough to run for office."

She regarded him. "Why did you speak to Chico about Paul?"

Matt hesitated.

"Why, Matt? I have a right to know, I believe."

He was silent, but he nodded.

She sighed. "The truth, please. All of it."

"I have to take things one at a time, Allie," he said, looking past her at the wall of the kitchen where his sister's family pictures still hung. "First, I intend to find out who's been harassing us, you in particular, and who's behind it. Then, I..."

"What? What then?"

He paced the room a moment. Rubbed the back of his neck and looked at her. "I want to find out what happened to Paul Ford. I want to know. I want you to be free. I want us to have a chance at happiness together. Whatever we decide about the future, I want that decision to be based on our love for each other. Not fear."

He couldn't succeed, she knew. She had tried for so long and in so many ways herself. It was a rainbow chase. A doomed cause. But he was willing to do it. For her. For them.

Allie thought about that for at least one second. That was

all it took for her depression to disappear and for her strong sense of purpose to reestablish itself. She puffed out her cheeks and blew out air and made another decision.

"Matt."

"Yeah?"

"Is there any chance you and I can have a few minutes of privacy any time soon?"

He looked around. "This is private."

She shook her head. "Not private enough. Not for what I have in mind."

He stared, then a smile spread slowly across his face. "I can't make any guarantees."

She stood up. "Well, we're not likely to get them any time soon, are we, so we might as well..."

He moved toward her. "Allie, I'm doing all this because I love you."

She grabbed his belt and pulled him toward her. "Show me, then," she said, passion and need making her voice low and fierce. "Don't talk about it. Show me!"

CHAPTER FOURTEEN

BY THE TIME she dragged him down into the basement to the one room in the house where she was sure they could bolt out the world, she was so intensely aroused, she felt she would scream like a wild thing the moment he touched her. They went into the laundry room, turned on the overhead light and Allie locked the door.

And she did yell, at least, when their clothes came off. Softly, a female howl of primitive need. The passion she had kept buried for so many days and nights came boiling to the surface.

Matt's desire matched hers. He pushed her against the wall, his strong hands moving over her body. When he entered her, they both groaned with a delicious combination of relief and tension. Their mating was fast and furious and satisfying, and when it was over, they were both gasping for breath and damp with sweat, in spite of the cooler air of the underground room.

Allie held him tightly, her arms around his neck. Her body tingled all over from union with him. With this man who had crashed into her life and torn her careful plans for the future into shreds. This man she knew she loved more than any of those plans, now. Not exactly sure what she wanted to say to him, she chose to discuss the immediate and banal. It was silly and cowardly of her, she thought, but she wasn't yet ready to deal with truly serious matters.

"Do...do you want me to fix dinner for the crew tonight?" she asked, panting rapidly between every other word. Making love standing up against a wall was not exactly easy work. She was standing on one leg with the other still hooked around his body, as if she wanted to keep him close as long as possible.

Matt laughed, the sound shaky to his own ears. Their erotic exertions had surprised him with the intensity of feeling that had assailed him. For a second there, he thought he understood what it meant to be an actual extension of another person. He lost sight of the boundaries and differences between them and saw only unity. It was far more than sex, he knew. Even more than love. But just what else, he couldn't say. He, too, wasn't certain enough of himself right at the moment to discuss anything of any depth. So, he went along with her.

"Sure, that would be great," he said. "But you don't have to wait on them. They're here to take care of you, not the other way around." His fingers were still gripping her waist and hips, digging in, tightly, as if he didn't ever want to release her.

She relaxed, putting the other leg down for support. "I know that," she said, running her fingers over his warm, sweaty skin. "I want to help, though. And I can cook, even if I don't get much opportunity to do it for a large group."

He laughed again, his voice firmer. Control and common sense returning. "You're one in a million, Allie. I can't believe I found you."

She moved, gently but deliberately, and his eyes closed in pleasure. "Believe it," she whispered. "*I* do."

And desire overtook them again.

A WHILE LATER, she was back upstairs in the kitchen, humming to herself and working over a steaming kettle of stew. Laurel, rested from her afternoon outing, sat at the kitchen table, copying Allie's moves and banging small saucepans with a big wooden spoon.

"I cooking," she announced, slamming a pan on the table. Her expression was calm and serious.

Allie smiled. "That makes two of us, honey," she said. Fred ambled in and sniffed the air, hopefully. "Forget it," she said, addressing the dog. "This is people food."

"I making Fred food," Laurel said. "Fred, c'mere."

Fred went over and sniffed the little hand, licking the skin and making Laurel giggle. Allie moved over to the sink, wondering how, in the midst of so much turmoil and disaster, she could feel so happy. It had to be temporary, but it was there, nevertheless. She gazed out the window, relishing the breathtaking view of the city down on the plains. This house was ideally suited, she thought, for just living and dreaming and...

Loving...

Her eyes teared suddenly, thinking of the couple who had built it. Behind her, their little daughter played, chatting with her doggie about dinner, happily oblivious for the moment to the loss of her parents. Oblivious, because someone else had stepped in to take their place and give her the love and security she needed. Matt had done this for his sister's child.

Was he doing the same for her? Allie brushed away the moisture on her face. It wouldn't do to let Laurel see her cry. She moved back to the stove and stirred the stew. A bell dinged, and she opened the oven. She heard the front door open and close. Matt was here. The rolls were ready. Almost time to call in the...

"Are you out of your mind!"

Allie whirled. M.J. stood in the dining room area, his face red and his expression angry. "M.J.," she said. "What are you doing here?"

"No." He advanced into the kitchen. "What are *you* doing here?" He gestured with both arms. "Look at yourself! You look like a ranch wife preparing dinner for the hired hands. Fixing grub for your man's boys. Matt Glass is really something if he can turn you into a hausfrau just like this! My God, the man has his own personal army out there! Do you know the local TV stations are running this little fortress as prime-time news tonight? Your political career is…''

"On hold."

"It sure as hell is." M.J. turned redder. "Do you know what that big ape your boyfriend calls his buddy did to me? He searched me, damn it! For weapons, before he'd let me in the house, and I'm your damn cousin!"

"M.J., settle down. You're upset. I'm sure Matt…"

"Matt was standing right there watching! He's lost it, Allie. Lost it and taken you with him. Allie, I don't think I know you anymore."

"I'm not lost, M.J.," she said, calmly. "Not lost at all."

"Lost!" Laurel said, banging the saucepan on the table. "Lost it. Find it."

"Hi, kid," M.J. said. He sighed, deflated and sat down beside Laurel. "I think I know what you're talking about," he added. "Does your new mommy?" He rested his chin on his hand and regarded Allie. Then, he smiled, letting her know he wasn't really angry at her.

She smiled back, wanly. Went to the refrigerator and got out two beers, cracked them open and handed one to her cousin. "No," she admitted, taking a seat across from him. "Maybe I'm not exactly lost, but I have no idea what I'm doing, what's going on or even where I want it all to end up." She raised her beer can. "Here's to total confusion."

M.J. lifted his beer. "May it also infect our enemies."

"I'll drink to that." She took a sip. "What's this about the newspeople? I can't imagine Matt's allowed them on the grounds."

"He hasn't. They've got a van out there on the highway, and they're filming your commandos at work. Allie, this is the finish of your campaign, your entire political future, if you don't…''

"I don't care about my campaign." She set her beer down. "M.J., I've found a few new priorities recently. Getting shot at in your own house does that to a person.''

He nodded. Scratched his head. "I guess I can try to understand. But it seems like such a waste." He put his face in his hands and rubbed it. "I heard about all this when Miranda called to tell me about the storm troopers. She thinks the big guy is cute. Then that woman from the news desk called and…''

"M.J., are you put out because Miranda…?"

"Oh, hell yes. I'm put out, and I'm not happy about it." He lowered his hands and looked at her. "But I'm not cut up because she thinks Godzilla out there is tasty-looking. She's a free agent. I like her, but I don't love her, and that's a fact. Now, you…''

"We've had this talk before, remember. I told you, I don't know what I want or expect…''

"I know what you said, dear." M.J. leaned forward. "But your actions are shouting otherwise. You've made your choices clear. You're not just Allison Ford anymore. You're Matt Glass's woman. Aren't you?''

Allie looked away. At Laurel. "I'm caught up, M.J. This is bigger than I ever imagined it could be. I never dreamed I'd let myself get swept away from the path I chose. But here I am. Letting the flood take me right along, and I…'' She stopped, hearing a door slam.

"You what?" Matt came in. He put his hand on her shoulder. "Go on. I think I have a right to know what you mean by being carried along. Are you willing or unwilling?'' He pulled out a chair and sat down, giving Laurel's head an affectionate pat in the process. She looked up at him and grinned, then went back to banging her spoon around, in and on her pans.

"I'm willing," Allie said. "If I wasn't, I wouldn't be here." She pushed her beer over to Matt. "Tell the guys that dinner will be ready in a few minutes. M.J., do you want to join us? There's plenty."

Her cousin eyed her. "I wouldn't miss it for the world," he said. "Count me in."

Matt reached over and slapped his shoulder in a comradely manner. "Welcome to the Glass Castle, then, M.J.," he said. "We may look like we'll shatter, but we're strong as steel, believe me."

The Glass Castle? Allie wasn't surprised at the phrase. He was quite serious in using that term, she realized. It reflected his attitude, his fortress mentality. She had no argument with it, either.

At supper, Allie played her role as hostess while the men talked. It was what she wanted to do, and it was extremely instructive.

M.J., who had already met Chico, was introduced to Gunther, Christian and Manuel and his credentials as Allie's relative were established. Matt, sitting at the head of the kitchen table beside an unusually well-behaved Laurel in a high chair, accomplished this task. "He and Mrs. Ford are like brother and sister," Matt concluded. "You may all trust him with your plans."

Gunther frowned. *"Ja,"* he said. "A *bruder* is to be trusted. Usually. But dis one is a lawyer."

"It's all right," Allie interjected. "He's one of the good ones." She smothered the urge to smile. M.J. hated the poor image lawyers had in this day of unlimited and unrestrained litigation.

"Justice is important," Christian said. "But some lawyers…"

"*This* lawyer believes in the Constitution of the United States," M.J. said, his face reddening. "If any of you guys have a problem with that…"

"Ease up, M.J.," Matt cautioned. "We're just testing water here."

"All right." M.J. sat back. "Test away."

"Let's eat first," Matt said.

Allie served huge bowls of stew. It wasn't her best offering, but it seemed to do. The men ate quickly and with relish. They drank large glasses of lemonade and iced tea. No one drank beer but M.J. Not even Matt.

When the eating slowed, he began to speak, in English, talking slowly. "This is the situation. We have three known sources of trouble. Any one of them could be behind the incidents against Mrs. Ford and myself. They could be acting alone or in concert." He paused here and translated rapidly into German and Spanish, then went on.

"It's unlikely that the Turner couple are the primary villains. I don't see enough intelligence in them, though I may well be wrong. They're certainly full of cunning."

"But their lawyer, Penny Jackson, is the one who's handling Laurel's estate and who dislikes Matt so much," M.J. said. "And Penny's a long-time political supporter of Rita Morely. Don't discount the Turners, Matt."

Chico leaned over to the others, and now he translated while Matt waited. Matt knew they would understand most of what he said but he wanted every detail exquisitely clear. When there was silence again, he went on.

"I'm not discounting the Turners or Penny. I'm just putting them low on the list. For all their eagerness to get hold of Laurel and her money, I don't think they have the capacity for the kind of violence it took to blast Allie's house."

"What about the *hombre* whose arms you nearly broke defending your lady?" Chico asked. "You seen him again? Anywhere?"

Matt shook his head. "Not a hair, Chico. But someone

ran me off the road, and I'm sure in my bones it was Baker. Even if I can't prove it.''

''Miranda should be here,'' M.J. said. ''She's been tracing Baker's movements over the last month.''

''We'll hold a real war council tomorrow,'' Matt said. ''Miranda will have a lot to tell us then.'' He glanced over at Allie. ''She's been doing work for me on a number of projects.''

Allie didn't say anything, but she did raise her eyebrows. She continued to remove dirty dishes and then to serve ice cream and cookies while she listened carefully.

And thought about what she was hearing and learning.

Matt outlined the security structure. Chico was assigned to guard her, Gunther to watch out for Laurel with Christian and Manuel as backup and property patrol. The men would sleep outside in tents they had brought, but would take their meals in the house as long as Allie was willing to fix food. This even slight deference to her startled and pleased her, as such consideration was unexpected from such macho men.

''All the people who come to see you must pass through a search routine,'' Matt said, not looking directly at her. ''Every single one, regardless of how long you've known them or how much you trust them. One of the reasons I didn't prevent the TV folks from filming us at work today was to prepare your clients. To prepare the public for the kind of security you'll be under for I don't know how long.''

''Wyoming's not used to this sort of situation,'' she agreed. ''It's just as well I don't intend to campaign, then.''

Matt didn't respond to that immediately. He looked over at M.J., who shrugged. Then Matt spoke. ''You'll continue to campaign, but you'll do it my way,'' he said. ''For instance, when you ride in the parade next week, we'll have you in a bullet-proof vest and...''

"She is a political?" Christian asked. "Dey never listen to orders, Matthew. What you gonna do wit her?"

"She'll listen," Matt responded before Allie could speak. "She's smart, Chris. Not driven just by her ambitions."

"She should drop out of the race altogether," M.J. said, his expression indicating his reluctance to say that. "I think, for her safety, she..."

"She will continue to campaign," Matt interrupted, his face stone. "She *will* win."

M.J. cleared his throat. "Allie, you know you don't have to, if you..."

"It's okay, M.J.," she said, taking Laurel out of the high chair. "I've made my own decision about things. I'll tell you after I've talked with Matt."

"Well." M.J. shifted position to face Matt. "At least you're right about the television coverage. When I think about it, actually, it's a possible bonus. They had a field day with Allie's house. Now, seeing you enclose her in this place with guards around won't be such a shock. The public *knows* someone's out to hurt her. And that might be a benefit, politically." He turned back to Allie. "Most people hate the thought of violence, so this should get you a lot of sympathy."

"Fine for now." Allie smiled. Strangely, everything was fine with her right then and she was reluctant to spoil the mood. Laurel sat in her lap quietly regarding the strangers. Fred, who was napping by the refrigerator in hopes of a later handout, raised her head for a moment, then relaxed. The smallest cat, Dick, had jumped up on Manuel's lap without an invitation and was being treated to a gentle stroking. Tom and Harry, still unsure, sat by the back door, awaiting a chance to break for outdoor freedom. Allie kept on smiling, wondering at her own feelings.

She was safe, here with these strange, wild men, with

her man, and her heart was happy for what she was certain was the first time in her life! Her carefully planned future lay in pieces before her, but she was content. And she would tell Matt as soon as she could.

Contentment, however, wouldn't solve Matt's problems. She had plans for tackling that on her own.

They talked into the evening, tossing around ideas about who might have made the phone call pretending to be Paul, who might be the mysterious couple in the Toyota, who was behind the outright violence and if all these matters were connected. At one point, Allie announced that Laurel needed to go to sleep, and Gunther came with her to learn the ropes about dealing with the child. With all the security around, they had decided it was safe to put her back in her old room, and Laurel seemed to be happy about that.

"Matthew chose me," the big blond man said, "because I haf two little daughters." His command of English was halting, but adequate.

"Really?" Allie regarded him more closely. "I thought that you all were...soldiers or something."

"*Ja.* We are soldiers." Gunther said no more on the subject.

But Laurel liked him. She had a short period of testing this new adult in her life, being cranky and fussing over going to bed, but Gunther showed patience. If he was a father, as he said, he'd learned his lessons well. Laurel didn't get a trick past the man without him seeing it coming. He was gentle, but firm, gaining Laurel's trust and respect almost immediately.

And he handled her well, so Allie relaxed. The less she knew about Matt's men, probably, the better, she decided. Better for them, better for her. She went back to the kitchen and announced she was heading for her makeshift office to do a little work before going to bed. The men hardly looked up from their discussion and planning to acknowledge her.

Not even M.J., who, she reasoned in a wry way, should know better. Well, these were extraordinary times, weren't they?

They'd better be, she thought, walking slowly back down the hall to her office. There were quite a few lives at stake. She hadn't even considered her own kids, yet. What were they going to think, with their mom a target of some evil, violent intent and guarded by men who seemed almost as dangerous as the person or persons after her and Matt....

Fred followed her as she went into her new office and settled herself at the desk. The dog took up her old place underneath, sighing and seeking the most comfortable position before falling asleep. Oh, to be a poodle, her owner thought. With nothing more vital to worry about than which cat to bother at a given moment. Well, she wasn't a poodle. Nor was she anyone's doormat. This was Matt's fight? Men's business? Not by a long shot. It was hers, too!

Allie spent the next half hour typing up a letter to her children and another one to her folks. She tried to explain things so that they wouldn't worry, but so that if they saw *more* stuff about her on the news, they would be prepared. She had, of course, called them immediately after the shotgunning incident and let them know where she was, that she was safe and that Matt was doing the best possible job of keeping her safe. They had seemed to accept that, but she wrote now to add to their sense of security. In case the news made it look like she was still in jeopardy....

The news. She glanced at her watch. Five of the hour. She probably ought to give it a look, just to see what interpretation the local press was putting on Matt's activities. Spin was everything in the news game. She knew she could expect almost anything, from fear about a private army to sympathy for her situation. She shut down the computer and went across the hall into the den. The television and

VCR setup was state-of-the-art, so just for the heck of it, she popped in a fresh tape and recorded the news.

And the special editorial after the regular news.

Too stunned to believe what she had seen and heard, she was removing the tape with hands that trembled when the phone rang. From down the hall, she heard Matt yell that he was getting it. She stayed hunched in front of the television, waiting. In a minute, he was at the door.

"It's Josh," he said. "Did you catch the news?"

She held up the tape. "Better than that. Here it is. I taped it."

Matt whistled, low and admiring. That, and his smile, was all the reward she needed.

They all watched the tape. Allie wanted to view the rerun just to make sure she really believed what she had seen. The presence and reaction of the men helped establish the reality.

"My God," M.J. said. "They're making you out to be some kind of latter-day Western heroine, Al. Cattle Kate, Annie Oakley, Calamity Jane... According to this, you're a darn legend already. Heck, Joan of Arc's got nothing on you, babe."

"It's the victim thing," she replied. "Newsies love that."

Matt said nothing. The newscaster had reported the facts. Allie's house had been shotgunned and her "friend and campaign director, Matthew Glass, was attacked and run off the road a few weeks earlier in a deliberate attempt on his life." Allie and Matt had appealed to the proper authorities for protection and help, but had been forced to resort to their own resources, finally.

It was a positive approach, and one he had not expected. But, there was more. Much more. The woman went on to give an on-the-air editorial. That's what had stunned Allie.

The violence against Allison Ford, the reporter said, is

part of a conspiracy against her as an independent, womens'-issue candidate. Rita Morely's backers, particularly David Benning, have too much political capital invested in their pet female candidate to risk allowing a newcomer with no obligations or connections to gain the office. The focus of the report was radically feminist, but also underscored Allie's position as a reformer and a potential ally of the people in the street, male *and* female.

The program also ran clips of Allie's political past to emphasize this last point, showing her working on the school board and the city council, speaking to groups of children and mothers about financial planning and working as a volunteer on a project directed at displaced home-maker-single mothers without the ability to support themselves. She came across as an activist, dedicated not just to women's issues, but to the family and the home. Matt could not believe how well it was done. If he'd tried, he couldn't have put together a more positive campaign advertisement. And since it was presented as an editorial newscast, it had the trappings of real news.

It was the best thing that could possibly have happened for her, politically.

It also gave him another suspect. David Benning. Matt cursed his carelessness in not doing a deeper investigation into the political web in the county and state. If he had, surely he could have turned up this information on his own. The old spider was a bigger factor than he had guessed, and that was important data. He should have had it sooner.

But, it didn't matter. He had it now, and he knew what to do with it. "Josh wants you to call him back," he said. "He's got some ideas on how to capitalize on this immediately, and I want you to..."

"Matt, I need to talk to you about this." Allie looked around the room. Every male was watching her. New respect in the eyes of Chico and his crew. M.J. was just beaming with pride. "In private, please," she added.

Later, when M.J. had gone home and the other men were settled around the grounds, she told him. "I'm not going to run for office," she said, looking up at him from her sitting position on the bed. "I've made a decision. You and Laurel are more important to me than any political campaign. Our staying together is more important than any other dream I've ever had, and I won't give it up."

Matt stared at her. "You're kidding me. After seeing that show?" He frowned. "I mean, I appreciate what you're saying about us and that's great, but..." He rubbed the back of his neck. "Look, I've gone to a hell of a lot of trouble to make sure you can run and win, Allie. I won't accept this."

"Don't. Don't accept it. But *I've* made up my mind."

He sat down on the bed. "Why? Just tell me, unemotionally and logically, why you should give up a dream that was driving your life before you met me. If you can convince me it's the right thing to do, I'll back you all the way."

"Okay. Um. I..." She felt frightened, suddenly. All the convincing words she'd thought of earlier were gone. A cold kind of fear gripped her insides and made chilly sweat trickle down her sides. "Uh..."

"That's what I thought." Matt leaned over and took her hand. "You don't have this worked out in your head yet. Just in your heart. You're reacting and not thinking."

Anger replaced fear. "What does it matter *where* I have it worked out," she replied, jerking her hand away. "I have the right to choose for myself."

Matt shook his head. "Not anymore. Not when your decision will affect at least four other people directly."

She frowned, puzzled, then. "You, Laurel, Sam and Sally?"

He nodded. Took her hand again. "If it's humanly possible to do it," he said, gazing directly into her eyes, "I'm going to see us become a family." He covered her hand with his, encasing and caressing it. "Your kids and mine, you and me, the five of us. A family unit."

"Matt," she said. "When I spoke of giving up the campaign for our relationship, I didn't include marriage in the deal. You know how I feel."

His expression hardened. "I know I can't ask you to consider marriage until you know the truth about Paul. We've kicked that ball around enough already, and you must know that I..."

"I know that you are beginning to give up a great deal for me, and I don't think you have a corner on that market. If I choose to drop out of the political race in order to concentrate on my relationship and future with you, then I believe you ought to respect that decision, just as I..."

"God, you are stubborn!"

She smiled at him. "No. I'm just in love."

Matt started twice to argue but could find nothing to say in response.

Love, as strong as it was getting to be between them, did change everything. He sighed, temporarily defeated, as she reached over and began to unbutton his shirt. To stroke his chest. And he then reached to unbutton hers.

THE NEXT MORNING, he started in again, however. Laurel slept late, giving them some more private time together. They made love and afterward showered together, then went into the kitchen. There, Matt seemed to think it was all right to talk business. "Your obligation to run isn't just to me or yourself anymore," he said. "You've got voters out there who are counting on you. Call Josh, Allie. At least talk to him."

"I told you last night what I..." She was interrupted by

Chico, who came barging into the kitchen where she was preparing breakfast for all of them.

"Many cars outside, Matt," he announced. "Lots of people. They all want to see her." He pointed at Allie.

"Me?" She dried her hands on a dish towel and went over to the dining room area. The road past the house was partly visible through the trees. Cars and pickup trucks were lined along the roadside. She heard some honking and shouting. "Why?"

Chico shrugged. "Don't know. What we gonna do, boss?" He looked genuinely worried for the first time since Allie had seen him trundle his muscled bulk off the plane. "They insisting on seeing your lady. Say they want to hear a speech or something. We can't search all of them."

"No need." Matt controlled his expression, but he wanted to smile broadly. Things were beginning to work out, at long last! The public was taking care of the problem of Allie's stubborn unwillingness to get on with her dreams. *He* would deal later with her problem about marriage. "Just get her a bullet-proof vest, and let's get her out there." He turned to Allie. "It's show time, sugar. Smile!"

CHAPTER FIFTEEN

WHAT COULD she do but go along?

Suitably, safely vested in snug body armor under her shirt and armed only with her wits, a mug of coffee and a smile, Allie sallied forth, Matt on one side of her, Chico on the other. Allie knew both men were armed and ready to protect her. The July morning sunlight was warm, the summer air soft on her face like the caresses Matt had given her when they made love.

And love was the reason Allie was about to betray Matt. Or, at least, to betray his hopes for her political career.

She stood out on the deck, using the microphone setup that Christian had produced from the home entertainment center in the house, and greeted the crowd, acknowledging special friends.

"I really appreciate that all of you came over to see how I was doing. As you can see, I'm doing just fine. I've got terrific people protecting me, and I'm truly grateful for everyone's concern. But, because of what's been happening, I've decided to withdraw from the legislative race. This has gotten too dangerous. It's in the best interest of those I love for me not to run..."

That was as far as she got. The first to shout was Walt Resner, the young cop who had warned Matt about Teddie Baker after their confrontation weeks before. "Allie Ford, you can't let us down. We're the people who need you. The ones without a lot of clout. I've got a list of police officers who're willing to help guard you in off-duty hours," he added, holding up a sheet of paper covered with signatures. "We all couldn't come out here this morning," he explained. "But you've got to know folks are really behind you." He rattled the paper. "Look and see, if you don't believe me!"

"Allie, you've got to run," June Watson yelled up at her. The big woman had on a T-shirt that declared Allie's candidacy in bright, bold letters. "We've made up thousands of these!" She pointed to her impressive expanse of chest.

Josh Henderson appeared. "I've got the same number of bumper stickers in boxes in the back of my car," he said. "A whole raft of folks came over last night after the newscast and helped me. Allie, we've got volunteers like you wouldn't believe!"

"But I..."

"But what?" yelled up Tim Swensen, the manager of Safeway. "I've planned a fund-raising barbecue for you day after tomorrow. I'll provide the meat, the volunteer committee will bring side dishes and we'll charge ten bucks a plate. You have to make a speech, Allie."

"I..."

"Give up?" Matt spoke softly so that only she could hear him.

"Someone shot at me," she said, talking into the microphone. "Shot at us, in my house. Friends, I can't go out in public and take the chance they'll hurt some innocent bystander just because I'm there."

"Hell, let 'em," a creaky old voice bellowed from the center of the crowd. Kelly McClean raised a fist. "If they do, we'll string 'em up like the scum they are. Come on, Miss Allie. You can do it! Fight, girl!"

The crowd roared. A large group from her church loudly informed her they were praying for her and her family, as well.

Allie gave up. "Okay, folks," she said. "You have your-selves a candidate. Good luck!" And then she dropped the mike and embraced the cheering, laughing Matt Glass. He hugged her, made her pick up the mike and told her to give the people a rousing speech.

Which she did.

THE NEXT FEW WEEKS were busy ones for Allie. Having decided to run again, she plunged in with a vengeance. Confidence in Matt and his people, as well as the growing awareness of how much of the community was behind her, gave her the strength and the faith to do this. In the few moments she had to herself to reflect, she realized that her friends and neighbors had always been there for her. She had thought she was on her own. Now, when she needed their help and support, they thronged.

It was good.

And, for a time, it seemed the good would triumph.

Her kids and her parents called a few days after the newscast and after receiving her letters, worried about her and wanting to know what they could do to help. Allie restated her desire that Sam and Sally remain up at the ranch, out of harm's way, until the danger was over, even if it meant going to school there for the first part of the fall. Her parents agreed. Sally thought it was okay. Sam did not.

"I want to be home, Mom," he said. "You need me there, don't you?"

A plaintive note in his voice alerted her immediately. Her son needed to be needed. Allie thought quickly. "Yes," she replied. "I do. But if you two were here, I wouldn't be able to campaign as well, because I'd be too worried about you. That's the fair and honest truth, Sam. If you don't like it, I'm sorry, but that's how it is."

He was silent for a moment. Then: "That Laurel kid's with you."

"She would suffer a lot if she were separated from Matt, Sam. She's too young to know why it would be safer to be up with you all. She has her own bodyguard. I don't have to keep a constant watch over her now. I know if you were here, you wouldn't like having a guy hanging around you all the time. Never being able to get off and do what you wanted, alone. Think about it."

He was quiet for a time. Then he said, "Let me talk to Matt, Mom. Please."

She handed Matt the receiver. "He's feeling left out," she whispered. "From up there, this must seem exciting."

"Well?" Matt smiled at her. "It is exciting, isn't it? You're a celebrity." He took the phone. "Hi, Sam. Listen, your mom is okay, but she doesn't think the same way we do about things. You know and I know you'd be fine and a big help, but all she can see is the trouble and danger. So, give her a break, man. Stay put and take care of your sister, will you?" He listened for a moment. "You have a deal," he said, his tone different. Determined. "I swear it, Sam." He handed the phone back to Allie.

"What he said is okay, Mom," Sam said to her. "You stay out of trouble, you hear me?"

They talked for a little longer about ordinary matters. The horses and cats at the ranch, how Fred and the home cats were doing at Matt's place. Simple, everyday mom-kid talk. After she hung up, she turned to Matt. "What was that last part between you two all about?"

He didn't look directly at her or answer right away. But when he did, it cleared up a few more questions in her mind and answered a few more doubts in her heart.

"I was a twin, remember, Allie," he said. "I had a sister. And I had a mother and father who never lived together. Sam and I talked about that a lot while we were up at the ranch. He just made me promise again that I'd see to it he had some answers about his real dad."

"Matt, I... You don't..."

"And that he won't have to live without a father for much longer," Matt added, pulling her close and kissing her protests away. "I'm not blowing smoke at him, and he knows it," he added, solemnly. "Sam and I are too much alike for me to dare to try that. I made a promise, and I'll turn over every rock between here and hell if I have to in order to keep that vow."

Allie knew she couldn't argue with that kind of resolve. She hoped to high heaven he didn't dash himself to pieces on any of those rocks. Fortunately Allie had enough on her mind to keep her fears about Matt at bay.

THE TURNOUT for the barbecue Tim sponsored was good and the event got terrific media coverage. Allie gave another speech, then invited questions from the audience. In addition to the hundred or so volunteers who provided food, about five hundred curious and hungry voters showed up, and the woman who had done the editorial on Allie's problems made it look like a major political rally.

Which, in turn, inspired more people to get involved and volunteer their help and their resources to her campaign.

"Success breeds success," Matt declared one evening when she expressed wonder at the way things seemed to be snowballing. "Everyone loves an underdog, but they love a winner more." He hugged her. "And, honey, you are a winner."

"Maybe," she conceded. "Maybe I am. But I'll tell you one thing, I've grown a lot politically in the last few days. I have to admit I was pretty naive when I started out, but I'm learning as I go. People seem to agree, too. Support's growing each hour, literally. I wonder what that's doing to Rita's blood pressure these days?"

She spoke jokingly, almost sure, now that her campaign was on the move, that the forces against them had withdrawn their strong-arm tactics. Not even the strident Turners had appeared publicly to continue their pursuit of Laurel and her estate. It was peaceful, Allie believed, because the good guys were winning, finally!

Matt became intent. "It's too damn quiet out there to suit me," he said. "It's like being stranded in shark-infested waters and just waiting for the fins to break the surface."

Allie shuddered, her good mood dimmed slightly. "Maybe the bad guys gave up?" she said.

"Fat chance." He looked at her, put his arm around her and drew her close. "They're just waiting until we let our guard down." He kissed her hair. "Please, promise me you won't forget that."

"I promise." Allie kissed him back, praying that he was only speaking out of an inflated sense of drama.

HER RELUCTANCE to take him seriously controlled her actions on the day of the parade. The event began bright and early on a promising hot July morning. The county fair parade kickoff started at ten o'clock sharp, and Matt had planned for her to ride in the now fully armored ATV he had purchased weeks ago. With the rear section enclosed with bullet-proof Lexan, she knew she would be safe enough, if a little like a goldfish in a bowl.

Chico proudly informed her that the ATV would take a direct hit from a small missile before it would be brought to a halt. The very idea of such an attack made her break into a nervous sweat. The vehicle was air-conditioned, however, so she wouldn't steam-bathe while being driven at three to four miles an hour along the parade route, she was told.

But she could not bring herself to do it. She had made her own set of plans.

"I can't ride the parade route in a thing that looks like

a bad science fiction movie prop," she said to Matt. "I appreciate what you've done, all of you, but I won't be the first candidate in history to hide from the people."

"You have to." Matt was tinkering with a video camera he intended to use to film her en route. "It's common sense."

"Matt, even the governor's riding a horse, for crying out loud! I show up in the Batmobile, and I'll be laughed off the ballot."

"No, you won't. People understand your situation."

"They understand that weeks ago someone shot at my house. Nothing's happened since. Matt, the public memory for that sort of thing is short."

He set the camera down. "Mine's not. You're riding in the ATV."

"I'm riding a horse," she said. "Lois Lepo's palomino mare. Lois called M.J. the other day and offered her, saying I'd look terrific on the horse because our manes are the same color." She laughed, hoping to lighten the atmosphere. "Isn't that cute?"

"It could be deadly."

Allie settled in. "Matt, listen to me. I know you're right about a lot of this security stuff. You've been terrific. I haven't even had a hint of trouble since we moved up here and brought in the troops. Everything's gone our way because of what you've done. But this time, I'm asking you to listen to me. The people around here will not be amused at my riding behind Lexan in the parade. It'll be an insult. Like I don't trust them."

Before Matt could reply, Chico came into the den. "Boss," he said, pointing toward the front of the house with his thumb. "There's a guy with a horse trailer waiting out at the gate. Says he's got Mrs. Ford's ride for the parade." His shaggy black eyebrows pulled together, and concern puckered the spiderweb pattern of scars on his left cheek. "I tell him to take a hike?"

Matt looked weary. He rubbed his face. "No, Chico," he said. "Let him in. Allie, I strongly advise you against this, but I won't force you to change your mind. You've proved to me already that you know your future constituents better than I." Worry showed deep in his eyes, but he managed a small smile.

"Good," she said, standing up and kissing him. "Because I'm right."

As HE WATCHED HER later that morning, Matt had to admit she probably was right. No one else in the parade seemed to give a darn for any kind of security. Even the governor rode unprotected except for a small group of nervous sheriff's deputies. This was not a community used to or likely to be tolerant of candidates who were afraid of the people. Any hopeful who hid from the voters behind a bullet-proof shield was probably going to be unnoticed at the polls, as well.

And, damn, but she looked magnificent!

Her horse was a big-muscled mare with a coat of pure gold and a mane and tail that was silky, long and white-blond like Allie's hair. She had chosen to wear a simple costume—plain Western-cut jeans, an oversize embroidered shirt over the bullet-proof vest, and cowboy boots. Her hair flowed free, unbound by any band or barrette for a change. And she was showing off like a little kid, her smile as wide as all outdoors. She wore no makeup and needed none. In the hot sunlight and the excitement of the moment, her cheeks glowed with color and her blue eyes shone like sapphires. If he hadn't been in love with her before, he would have been smitten right where he stood, Matt realized. She was a picture to treasure forever!

The mare was a special animal, trained to perform in

dressage, she had told him. She knew some of the rudiments, she confessed. Rudiments! Matt smiled to himself as he watched her walk the horse from one side of the road to the other, letting just the tiniest touch direct the moment when she would stop and rear back, lifting her front hoofs into the air. Then, Allie would wave and whoop, encouraging the crowd to join in.

And they did. They *loved* her. Matt felt the burn of pride deep in his chest. The people loved his woman!

But not as much as he did. He followed her progress with the camera, intending to use some of the footage for political commercials later on, nearer the November day of reckoning. Beside him and on the other side of the street, Chico and Manuel ranged, watching the crowd for any sign of trouble or danger. Matt relaxed. She was quite safe. This was no time for anyone to strike against her. It would only infuriate the people and bring further support to Allie's cause.

The parade moved through the city streets, which had been cordoned off from traffic for the event. People lined the road, standing or sitting on lawn chairs. Casual and relaxed attitudes were the order of the day. Everyone was out for fun. Simple, old-fashioned good times. Friends greeted old friends. Children frolicked around or sat on the curb, staring in delight and wonder at the passing parade. Marching bands from the city and county schools, elaborate floats put together by local businesses or interest groups, a fleet of vintage automobiles, including an ancient fire truck that sprayed water on the laughing crowd... Matt felt he was experiencing an event from America's more innocent past. It was healthy and good.

And he'd missed it as a kid, because he'd been traveling all over the rest of the world. He stopped, hit by the sudden thought that *this* was what he wanted for Laurel. This life in the slow lane. Growing up in the town and the land that her mother and father had chosen for her.

Standing there, Matt came to a decision. Tomorrow he'd phone his office in L.A. and prepare them for a move of Glass Attacks, Ltd. to Linville Springs, Wyoming. With modems and faxes everywhere these days, he could keep in close touch with the world of adventure travel easily enough from anywhere on the planet. He didn't need an office in the city anymore. He didn't need the city anymore, for that matter.

How could he have dreamed of taking Laurel back to L.A.? She'd be one of millions there. Here, she was one *in* a million. *This* was her home, where she was supposed to be raised. *This* was her home, and that was her mother… He raised the camera to his eye again.

And saw the gun aimed at Allie.

ALLIE WAS READYING her mount for another pass at the left side of the street when the sledgehammers hit her in the back. *Pow! Pow!* Two blows that almost knocked her from the saddle. She slumped forward, striking her solar plexus on the saddle horn, and the breath went out of her. Only the training of a lifetime on horseback and the skills of Lois's grand horse kept her from falling to the pavement. She struggled to get her breath and held on to the animal's heavy mane.

People began to scream. Dizzied from the shocks of being hit and winded, she couldn't understand why they were yelling. She was battered and out of breath, but she wasn't really injured. She tried to sit upright.

And was slammed in the back again. This time, the blow caught her off balance and she lost her seat. As she slipped from the saddle, she heard the sound of a siren yodeling disaster in the distance.

I wonder who's hurt, she thought.

She hit the ground, ready for the impact, and was stunned, but didn't lose consciousness entirely. Strong hands grabbed her and a vaguely familiar voice murmured soothing things. She blinked, trying to get her sight focused. Where was Matt? He wasn't the one talking to her. Where was Chico? Surely, the big man would be right by her side...

But strangers lifted her and carried her along, past the people who stared and screamed. Allie tried to smile and wave and indicate to someone out there that she was all right, but no one seemed to notice her feeble gestures. "Matt? Where's Matt," she called, the sound a soft wail. No one heard.

Then she was set on a stretcher of some kind and lifted into the back of an ambulance. She blinked again, looking for someone in white, someone in charge, someone who would listen to her. Someone was there and turned to her. The doors shut.

And she saw who it was and tried to scream, but the wet cloth covered her face and as she struggled and fought and gasped, the overpowering fumes filled her lungs and Allie knew no more.

MATT DROPPED his camera and ran toward her, but the crowd seemed to close in, preventing him from getting close. Across the street, Chico was also struggling to reach her. When they finally forced passage to the street, Allie's horse was standing there, her head down and her skin shiny with sweat, but Allie was gone. Just the red stains on the pavement marked where she had fallen.

"What the hell happened to her?" Matt grabbed Chico's arm, swinging the man around to face him. "Where is she?"

"I couldn't see, man," Chico replied, his face strained

and his muscles bunched. "Somebody took her away." He knelt down on the street and touched the red liquid.

"It was a paramedic," a woman said, pointing up the street. "They're taking the poor girl right to the hospital."

Matt started to move.

"No!" Chico grasped his leg. "Boss, look here." He held up his fingers. Red dripped from them.

Matt fell to one knee. If Chico had something to show him, it paid him to pay attention. He touched the red. Sniffed. "It's paint!"

"Damn straight. Not blood."

"Then what…?" He got no further than that. The sky darkened. Matt looked up. He and Chico were surrounded by men on horseback. Men with drawn guns aimed at them.

The deputies who had been guarding the governor were now covering them. One snarled an order to lay down their guns. At first, it didn't register. Then, Matt realized both he and Chico had their own weapons in their hands. He looked at Chico, who nodded, and very, very slowly, they both lowered their guns and set them on the street.

M.J. FELT LIKE screaming and throwing chairs through windows and beating the hell out of someone. Preferably Matt Glass. Matt and Chico had been arrested immediately after the shooting. He was here to interview his client while his law partner did his level best to get the idiot and his friend released on bail.

"You had to do it your way!" he yelled. "All the macho trappings. Guns and goodies. Did they help?"

Matt said nothing.

"Hell no!" M.J. ran his hand over his hair. "They didn't help her at all!"

Matt stared at the lawyer. His eyes were like dark coals in the hollows of his eyesockets. M.J. relented a bit. The guy was clearly suffering the torments of the damned. "I can get you out of here, Matt, but you..."

"They've got her," Matt said. "She wasn't taken to the hospital. No one knows where she is. She's been kidnapped, M.J., and you know it as well as..."

"I don't know that!" The lawyer flung his hands up. "All I know is someone apparently shot Allie with one of those fantasy game pistols that splashes paint on the target. She fell and someone hauled her into a fake ambulance. If I were a cop, it'd look a hell of a lot like a publicity stunt to me, so I don't really blame these guys if that's what they think, too!"

"It's no stunt, and you know it. She couldn't even think of something that twisted."

M.J rubbed his head again. "I know, Matt." He deflated and sat down. "But that's not how the authorities see it. The fact that the governor was just about five yards away when she was 'shot' doesn't help. His boys are livid. They're all sure it was Allie's way of grandstanding. They want to nail you and Chico to the courthouse door by your ears, if not by something far more sensitive."

Matt's smile was grim. "I know. They weren't exactly gentle when they booked us for public disturbance and concealed weapons." His smile faded. "Get me out of here, M.J. I'll find her. I can do it. Just get me some freedom!" His clasped hands strained together, whitening the knuckles.

"I'm working on it." M.J sat back. "Once I get you out, what can I do to help? She's my blood kin, as well as my best friend. I *have* to help."

Matt studied the lawyer for a moment. Then, he told him.

AFTER THEIR RELEASE, hours later and on exorbitant bail, they returned to the Essex house to plan their strategy. Gunther was waiting there, guarding Laurel. And Manuel met them up at the house, as Matt knew he would. When Matt and Chico had been taken, Manuel had stayed low, out of the sight of the cops, waiting for the dust to settle. So had Christian. Then, they'd gone over the scene. Most of the evidence had been trampled by milling people and horses, but Manuel had recovered one special treasure. Something that might provide a clue to Allie's fate.

He had Matt's video camera.

ALLIE STRUGGLED against the chains on her arms and the silver duct tape that covered her mouth. She needed to scream. It might have helped with the overwhelming fear. But all she could do was make strangled, squealing sounds, so she gave up. The drug had nauseated her, too, and she was afraid she would be sick. If she was, with the gag on, she was liable to suffocate. David Benning tapped the syringe he held and smiled at her.

"That's right, Allie, dear, Save your strength. You're going to need it for your long journey," he said. "Long, dark journey."

Allie snarled at him inside her gag.

"Now, now." David set the syringe down on a piece of white gauze. "Must keep that temper under control. What will Paul say, if you swear as you go to meet him?"

Allie screeched, a little sound, but one from deep in her heart.

"Yes, Allison, dear." David leaned forward and patted her cheek, his touch gentle, almost fatherly. "I'm here to see you united with your true love. Your husband, Paul."

She stared at him.

He smiled, and his grin was a death's-head rictus. "Yes, I made those calls to you. To remind you how much of an obligation you have to him. How evil you were to let another man into your bed. How wrong you were to think you could change things to make women as well off as men are. Such terrible thinking! Rita could never think like that. Well, that's done with. You have an eternal duty to Paul. It's almost time to fulfill that obligation. Too bad you have to die to do it.'' He chuckled. ''But, that's life, isn't it!'' And then, he threw his head back and laughed and laughed and laughed as if he'd made the funniest joke in the whole universe.

Allie shrank inside, closed her eyes and determined to spend her last minutes alive thinking not about the insane man who held her prisoner but rather about her children, about Laurel and about Matt.

About the man who she knew really was the true love of what was left of her life.

It helped her control the fear.

CHAPTER SIXTEEN

MATT SLIPPED the video cassette into the player and turned the machine on. The den had become a conference room. A war room, really. Six men sat stone-still and watched the show. The only movement came from Laurel, who was playing quietly with a coloring set over by the window. Fred slept on the floor near her in the only patch of sunlight. Gunther watched her more than he did the television. She was his job; Allie was theirs.

Allie came on the screen. Matt's heart nearly broke looking at her. So alive and radiant and happy on the palomino mare's back. He pushed fast-forward.

"What we're looking for," he said, "is the face of the guy who blasted her with those rubber pellets. They were like paint pellets, but with more impact capability. That's what knocked her off the horse. I know I got him for at least a moment in my viewfinder, so we ought to be able to pick him out."

"And when we do?" M.J. asked. "What then? How're you going to find a face with nothing else to go on? Sounds like a needle in a haystack to me."

"It is." Matt stopped the fast-forward. The tape was almost at the place he wanted. "But that's what Miranda does best, isn't it? Find that particular needle." The doorbell rang. Matt turned to Chico. "Want to get that, please."

Chico grinned and rose.

M.J. glowered, but said nothing. He'd long since abandoned hope of recovering Miranda's physical affections.

They could be friends, he reasoned, but the lover potential was out. Chico was probably more her kind of guy. M.J. harbored no illusions about himself when it came to brains verses brawn. He was definitely not in the latter category.

In a moment, Miranda and Chico came into the room, the private investigator in the lead. Her expression was calm, but deadly serious. "I've got a list of all the properties in the state that Rita Morely or David Benning own," she said, handing a computer printout to Matt. "Since I'd been doing some investigating about their financial activities before this, it was easy to get the data. If they took her, and I really believe they did, it's likely she's stashed somewhere on the land they can control access to. Some place they know well enough to feel secure in or at. At any rate, it's worth checking into."

"Thanks." Matt took the printout. "Have a seat. We're about to see your next quarry."

"'Randa!" Laurel spoke up, startling everyone. She had been so quiet, most of them had forgotten her presence. "'Randa, where my mommy?" She stood up and toddled over to Miranda, holding up her arms for an embrace.

The woman bent down and picked the child up. When she straightened, tears shone in her dark eyes. "Don't you worry, sweetheart," she said, softly. "Your mommy's going to be here soon."

"Mommmaa..." Laurel rubbed her eyes.

Matt tensed, but Laurel seemed content with that answer and didn't start to cry as he had feared she would. She stayed with Miranda, however, sitting on her lap and crooning softly to herself.

He thumbed the remote and the video played on. Soon, the final scene appeared, and he froze the picture. "There he is," Matt said, pointing. Christian came forward with some special camera equipment and took some still pictures. "Any idea who he is?" Matt asked M.J. and Miranda.

M.J. studied the face. He shook his head. "I don't think so," he said. "Just a generic local lowlife, but I've never…"

"Well, *I* recognize him. He's one of Teddie Baker's cronies," Miranda said. "I'll be darned…"

"Get me some still shots," M.J. stood up. "And some depositions and I'll take this right to the governor. He's a fair man, Matt. You just pissed him off with the guns and ruining the parade. I think he was real frightened for a moment, too. Thinking someone was shooting at him."

"An understandable reaction," Matt said, dryly.

"I think we can get some speedy legal action on this." M.J. tapped the television screen. "Even I can see the gun in this guy's hand. With this kind of evidence, I can have a warrant issued…"

"By the time you have that in hand," Matt said, "Allie may be…" He glanced at Laurel. "Well, let's just say we can't wait for the wheels of the regular judicial and legal process to turn. Manuel. Chico. Christian. You know what to do. Gunther, you're still assigned to Laurel. Keep her safe." The men nodded. Gunther picked up Laurel and held her. He would, Matt knew, die for the little girl, if necessary.

As he, Matt, would do for Allie!

Matt stood up. "Let's get going." He turned back to M.J. "Those legal wheels need to be moving at the same time we are, M.J. Get it all going. We're taking down everyone who dared touch her! Understand me?"

M.J. nodded. "I do," he said, firmly. "Yes, I do, indeed!"

SHE WAS SO TERRIFIED, she'd become emotionally numb. Actually, it helped her to think, being numb like that. Fear, worn-out, had receded to the back of her mind. So, she thought, considered and even dared to hope a little. Allie couldn't believe she was still alive. Didn't understand why she could still hear and see and breathe and feel. She ought to be dead, but she wasn't planning on doing anything to bring that condition to a reality. David Benning was just crazy enough to kill her at any moment, once he decided to finish his game.

That "game" had been going on for a day and a half now, as near as she could tell. Maybe longer. Her sleep periods were so disordered, she had lost track of time. David would sit by the rude cot where she lay imprisoned, chained by wrists and ankles to large metal staples in the floor, and he would talk. Talk and talk for an hour or more about his past, his political career. His successes, both real and imagined.

Then, he would ask her questions. Like a professor giving a quiz after a lecture. If she answered correctly, she was allowed a small privilege—a trip to the outhouse, a bite to eat or even an hour or so of blessed sleep.

All privileges delivered, of course, with a loaded gun at her back or head. He gave her some privacy at the outhouse, but not much.

He was as insane as they came, she realized. Completely out of his mind, and dangerous as a rattler or a cornered cougar. She was going to die eventually, she feared. She had no chance with a man like this. He was going to kill her. It was just a matter of when.

And she was determined to grasp at life as long as possible, even if it meant putting up with his mental torture for weeks. She had little hope of being rescued. She wasn't sure where they were, but she did know it was far away from civilization. She'd heard no sounds but those of birds and insects since she'd regained consciousness. No cars or other indication that people were nearby. No, she was alone with David, isolated in a hell of his making. All she could expect was that David would be caught eventually. She knew that Matt and M.J. would see to that.

She only wished she could be around to hug them both and thank them for avenging her. That was, however, most unlikely. She felt tears rising and fought against the weakness of crying. It wouldn't do any good now. She needed to think and rest, not weep!

For the moment, she was alone. David had just finished a grueling session involving his years as chairman of an important Senate committee on Central America, and her answers to his questions had been sufficiently ego-supporting for him to offer her some sleep time. In fact, he'd been downright delighted with her, saying she'd earned a full night's rest. But she wasn't sleepy.

She surmised, from watching the sunlight in the small room, that afternoon had come and gone. The light was gold, not white, so it was late—probably five or six in the evening. David might be needing sleep himself by now, and she could be alone for some time. Allie leaned over the cot as far as she could and regarded her chains.

They were steel links, a common type he must have bought in a hardware store. New and shiny. No way to break them. The staples were old, though. She jerked an arm. A small puff of dust rose into the air.

Allie felt a jolt of hope so strong she nearly screamed aloud. She might not free the chains, but the staples were another matter entirely. She jerked her arm again.

And again...

"WHERE'S JOSH?" Matt asked. It was less than forty-eight hours since the kidnapping. He heaved the last load of equipment and weaponry into the rear of the stripped-down ATV. "Wasn't he supposed to meet us here an hour ago?

He promised to act as backup driver last night. You told him the time, didn't you?''

"I did. He was," M.J. replied. "Don't know about him, though. Josh's no hero. Of course, neither am I, but I have a very personal stake in this...mission. He doesn't, and he knew he wasn't absolutely necessary. Maybe he just got cold feet."

"Maybe." Matt stared out across the city. Dawn was just beginning to pearl the sky to the east, and lights were on here and there in the urbanscape below. Since it was still July, the morning began around four a.m. Early as sin, Matt had complained. He had wanted to strike during the dark, but they had run out of night, getting ready.

He and M.J. and the others were all dressed in battle fatigues and had smeared their faces with black paint. The three blondes, Matt, Gunther and Christian, had tied dark bandanas over their light hair, Vietnam war style. Only M.J. was unarmed. He'd been offered a pistol, but had claimed total unfamiliarity with weapons and declared he'd be more dangerous to his friends than his foes if he carried one. Miranda, who did know how to use a gun, wasn't in the group. She had elected to stay with Laurel, taking over Gunther's job. Her hunting was done.

And done well! She had found where Allie was imprisoned. By sifting through the property locations, she'd come up with the most likely places. And when Matt had looked at a map, he'd picked out Allie's prison as easily as if it were marked by a street sign. Secluded and easy to defend, the spot was perfect—or would have been if Matt and his men were ordinary hunters.

Matt looked down the road to town once more. Josh was supposed to come with them. His absence was troubling. He had called the day before and earnestly begged to be included, his fervor so strong that Matt had been unable to deny him. His absence was not a good sign. Josh knew part of their plans, and had been assigned a role that would now have to be filled by another. Matt looked at M.J. The lawyer looked uncomfortable and nervous.

"You know what you have to do," he said. "It's going to be riskier without Josh."

Now M.J. managed to look grim. "Yeah. I know," he said. "So much for what I learned in law school."

In spite of the deep fear for Allie's safety, Matt had to chuckle. "This is another kind of school," he said. "And I'm a good teacher, so relax."

"I'm so relaxed I might faint," M.J. replied, his painted face twisting in a kind of smile. "Just leave me where I fall, if I do."

"We will." Matt turned away.

And M.J. knew he wasn't kidding.

They drove up the road and over to the back side of Linville Mountain. As the sun began to stain the sky reddish orange, they pulled onto a large, wide meadow and parked under the shelter of a stand of pines. Matt spoke, and they got out and assembled around the hood of the vehicle. He took out a topographic map of the mountain and spread it for all to see.

"Here it is," he said, pointing with the blade of a knife. "Benning's cabin." He traced a pattern on the paper with the knife tip. "Here's how we do it."

M.J. stood back a little, listening. Matt spoke softly, calmly and repeated every sentence in three languages. But it was clear the five trained men had no trouble communicating. They acted, spoke and thought as a unit, now, relying on past experience. They had done this before in another land for another cause when they had rescued the movie crew.

But he had no such experience, and he was scared to death. Not so much for himself, although that was definitely a factor! His true concern was for Allie. If he messed up his part, she could die. Others could die. Hell, *he* could die. Nothing he'd ever done before had prepared him for this moment of truth.

Did he have the stuff to make it?

Matt turned around and looked at him. "You okay, M.J.?"

"Not really."

"Good." Matt folded the map and sheathed his knife. "If you thought you were, I'd be concerned. Stay scared. It'll help keep us all in one piece."

That helped. Some.

They moved out, entering the forest just as the morning sun hit the meadow. M.J. swallowed hard against a rising nausea, fought the urge to stop and go to the bathroom and forced himself to press on behind Matt. The bigger men moved through the forest like they were smoke. M.J. was sure he was stepping on every single dry leaf and crackly branch. He felt like an elephant.

But soon they reached the cabin. M.J. crouched in the shelter of the trees surrounding the clearing while Matt and the other men moved forward, scouting, sensing, preparing. He heard the sound of birds greeting the new day, the chattering fuss of a squirrel disturbed at nut-hunting, the sigh of the slight breeze in the tops of the lodgepole pines, and…

The nasty popping sound of a gun being fired inside the cabin. A scream.

Allie!

Another scream, a yell, really. Male. Enraged.

M.J. stood up and started to run toward the cabin. Matt grabbed him and managed to throw him to the ground. "Behind me," Matt snarled at him. "Stay behind me!"

M.J. nodded. His heart felt as if it were going to pound its way out of his chest. He stood and brushed himself off. Then he took a deep breath and prayed. Calm returned.

He followed Matt as the men fanned out, covering all

sides of the cabin. Weapons at the ready, black paint jagged across their faces, M.J. thought they all must look like demons from hell.

The view got worse the moment they burst into the cabin. M.J. stayed right on Matt's heels, but crouched down to avoid any gunfire that might come their way. He saw the room clearly. It was a madman's den, full of trash, books, magazines, newspapers and other paper, all strewn around garbage that had piled into stinking heaps. The odor was almost unbearable.

But more horror awaited. From a room in back came an ear-piercing howl like that of a wild, insane animal. Allie's voice sounded, yelling at someone. And a man's voice replied.

Josh Henderson!

Matt checked behind him to make sure M.J. was safely out of the way and then moved quickly to the doorway of the next room. He paused at one side of the door, his back pressed against the hard wood wall, his gun raised and ready to fire. Manuel slipped into the cabin through the front door and signaled to him that there was no window to that back room. He could only guess how many were in the room. Matt nodded.

Then, he stepped from hell into Hell.

The room was tiny. A cot against the far wall. No other door or window. Josh Henderson, his eyes wide with fear, a gun held in both trembling hands, was pressed back against the wall to Matt's right. On the cot...

Allie was on a cot and was chained to the floor. By three chains. The fourth, she had somehow managed to free from the floor, though it still hung from her wrist.

And she had wrapped it around David Benning's neck and appeared to be trying to choke the man to death. They were wrestling on the cot. She had the chain around his throat and her knee in his back and was hauling for all she was worth.

She looked like a Valkyrie or an Angel of Death. But it wasn't the sight of her that froze Matt in his tracks. Josh had his gun on her. Not on Benning.

Allie saw him first. "Matt," she cried. "Watch out for Josh. He's in with them."

Josh whirled, his weapon now aimed at Matt. "Stop!" he yelled. "I'll shoot. I swear it!" He wavered, then steadied. "I know how. You'd better believe me!"

Matt lowered his own gun. Behind him, he heard the sound of stealthy movement, a phrase murmured in German, then Spanish. "I believe you, Josh," he said. "Look. I'm putting my gun down." He set the pistol on the floor and straightened, his hands in the air. "You don't have to be scared of me, Josh."

"I am scared," Josh cried. "Of you, of her, of that madman there. Allie, let him go! Do it, or I swear I'll shoot Matt."

She released the chain. David fell to the floor, coughing and retching and gasping for air. "Don't hurt Matt, Josh. Please," she begged. "Come on. You've got the gun. He's unarmed. You can get out now. Run away from this. We'll let you go."

"I...I can't." Josh was trembling and sweating, gritting his teeth. His demeanor was one of both fear and arrogance, a dangerous, volatile combination. He kicked at Benning's supine form. "He's been my boss all along. Has evidence I was spying on you and reporting to him." He looked at her. "Allie, I was sure you'd lose. Everybody said..."

"You little piece of..." David growled from the floor. "I'll *ruin* you..."

"It's too late for that, David," Josh said, his voice suddenly much more steady. "I guess I know what I have to do now." He glanced at Allie. "I have no choice—I've got to shoot all of you." He paused, thinking, his expression turning sly. "If I burn this place down, no one will ever know what really happened, will they? I'm no killer, myself, understand. Not like David here, but there's no choice, as I see it." He wiped sweat from his face. "It's the only way I...ahhhggg!"

His words were cut off suddenly as the back wall of the cabin splintered inward, exploding under an enormous force. As Matt had expected, his troops had taken the initiative and they had chosen to attack right through the wall, punching at it with just enough explosive to cave it in, but not enough to endanger the people inside. Matt had been ready for anything, but this was even better than he had hoped. His men were absolute geniuses with *plastique*. The noise and dust and debris of the small blast distracted Josh just long enough for Matt to move.

But he didn't go for Josh and the gun. There wasn't time, and he wasn't near enough. Instead, Matt flung himself forward toward Allie. He covered her with his body as screams and shouts and gunshots filled the air. He heard Josh snarl a death threat at him and turned to face his fate....

And saw M.J. rise out of the dust and debris and lay a truly inspired roundhouse punch on Josh's astonished face, connecting with the other man's jaw. Josh went down with a sigh and was out for the count. M.J. grabbed the gun and stood over his foe, holding the weapon as if it were a rattlesnake about to strike.

"Good vork!" Gunther was the first to reach the lawyer. He slapped M.J. on the back and took the gun gingerly from his trembling grasp. "That vas some punch, *ja!*"

"Thanks," M.J. replied in a steady voice. Then, he sat down on the floor, crumpling as his legs gave way. "It felt great. I think my hand's broken, though." Gunther, still chuckling congratulations, bent over to check the injury.

Matt looked down at Allie, who lay under him on the cot. "You all right?" he asked, examining her quickly for serious injury. He found nothing wrong that he could see, but she had been a prisoner for over two days. "What did they do to you? Are you...?"

"I'm okay, but frankly, you look like the very devil himself," she said, grabbing his neck with her free hand and dragging his face down to hers. "And am I glad to see you!" The kiss she gave him told him almost everything he needed to know.

There was one more detail, however. "I can't wait for this answer," he said, holding her tightly and making her more of a prisoner with his arms than the chains had. "Will you marry me?"

She smiled. "Let me loose, then..."

"No. Now. Before I unchain you."

Her words went right to his heart. "Matt, yes, I'll marry you. I decided while I was sure I was going to die that if I did somehow manage to survive, the past would have no more hold on me. I don't care what happened before I met you. Now is all that matters. Now, and us. I believe we were meant to be, so... Yes!"

"As soon as possible?"

"Yes!"

He kissed her again, wondering at the miracle that was their love.

IT TOOK A WHILE to free Allie. While Matt worked the chains loose, the other men dug the now-babbling Benning out of the rubble and secured him with stout ropes to a tree in the front section of the clearing.

As they all waited in front of the ruins of the cabin for the sheriff to arrive, Josh talked. Bragged, rather.

"You were a born loser," he sneered at her. "Everyone knew it, and made their plans around it. Rita contacted

David who agreed you were the best possible candidate for her to face, since she would undoubtedly trounce you at the polls. She's his creature, you know. I've worked secretly for her for years, and I could tell you stories that would curl your teeth! Would do anything he asked. He needed her in office.''

"But it didn't wash that way." M.J. rubbed his hand. "And so the lousy lot of you panicked.''

"Not exactly.'' Josh regarded him balefully. "Taking Allie out permanently was Plan B. Or C. I can't remember. But we did discuss it. When Baker failed to get you both with the shotgun, we had to make fresh plans.''

"But David was supposed to kill me right away, not keep me alive to mock and torture me,'' Allie interjected. "Right?''

"Right.'' Josh glared at the raving older man. "He lost it a long time ago. We just didn't realize how much until a few days ago. He really got off on pretending to be Paul Ford when he called you.'' He smiled at Allie. "You know he knew what happened to your husband, don't you?''

Allie felt chilled clear through. "I know from what David said that there's some connection between Paul's death and David's activities on the committee dealing with Central America. I assume from what he said to me that...''

Josh laughed. "You'll never find out now. Too bad. David's mind is mush.''

Matt stepped in. "If you know, Henderson, I'd recommend you tell me. Or when the sheriff finally gets here, there might not be as much of you to deliver to him as there is right now.''

Another cold smile. "I have no idea,'' Josh replied.

Matt moved closer. He drew his knife and looked at the tip, speculatively.

"Really! I swear!'' Josh shrank back. "M.J., tell him he can't touch me! It's...it's illegal!''

"Hey." M.J. turned around to face the trees. "I don't see a thing, Josh. Can't hear you any too well, either. What'd you say?"

After a bit more carefully orchestrated intimidation, Matt finally decided that Josh honestly didn't know the truth.

But David Benning did. The facts were there, somewhere. His mind might be gone, but somewhere, the man must have kept a record of his evil triumphs and of material he could use against his opponents and enemies.

Matt turned to his men, ordering them to clear out all signs of their highly illegal private army action. Gunther, Manuel and Christian melted into the trees, hauling with them the high-powered weapons and the rest of the explosive that had torn down the back of the cabin. Chico stayed, guarding Josh closely, knowing his presence would show the authorities that Matt and M.J. hadn't done the job all by themselves. No one would have believed that. But the full truth would always be their secret. The cops, Matt decided, would just have to work the rest of it out for themselves without his help.

As the sheriff's helicopter sounded overhead, Matt turned to Allie. "I want one quick look through the cabin before the cops take over," he said. "Can you delay them? I hate to ask it of you, but it's important." He touched her wounded wrist. "Maybe make them take care of this, first?"

She looked into his eyes. "I'll try," she said, her tone firm and confident. "I love you," she added.

"I know." Matt touched her face, not trusting himself to do anything more. "But you don't love me as much as I love you. You just can't. It's humanly impossible." He let his hand fall to his side. "I was ready to die for you, Allie. Now, I intend to live for *us*. Get going. They're landing."

Allie felt joy bubbling up inside her and she yearned to

forget everything else just to hold him tight, but she turned away from him and faced the clearing where the helicopter was touching down. Branches whipped in the breeze created by the roters, and men spilled out. Clutching her wrist, she ran over to the leader.

And gave the performance of her life.

At first M.J was astounded. The bad guys were wrapped up and tied like Christmas presents, yet here was his cousin, having an apparent case of female hysterics. She'd been brave as a lioness, but now she was weeping and moaning and showing off her hurt wrist and insisting on getting medical treatment immediately before anything else....

Wait. Where was Matt?

M.J. headed back to the cabin. Sure enough, there was Matt ferreting through the mess, that would soon be a police crime scene, off-limits to all but licensed professionals. "Can I help?" he asked, stepping over a stack of old magazines and a pile of dirty dishes.

Matt looked up. "Dig in," he said. "Look for anything that might have to do with Benning's activities regarding Central America ten years ago. His insanity and his treatment of Allie had something to do with that. I know it!"

M.J. rifled through a stack of papers. "How do you figure?"

"Well, let's assume Benning had something to do with her husband's death. He was certainly fixated on it, so I think the assumption's a fair one. Let's say he knows his tracks are fairly well covered—after all, Allie did try to find out the truth years ago and came up empty. I've had Miranda on the case, myself, and she's turned up very little." Matt dropped the stack of books he was searching through and moved over to a small pile of jewelry-type boxes.

"Very little? But something?"

"Right. Seems Benning was the good Dr. Ford's first

patient when he opened his office in Linville Springs a
decade ago. Brought a bunch of other folks to the doc's
door. Made him seem like an important new physician on
the scene. Don't you think Ford might believe he had a
debt to the great politician?''

"You mean Benning recruited Paul for…"

Matt opened and tossed boxes. All were empty. "It's just
a guess. I need proof. But why else would Benning get so
hot about Allie's winning the election if he wasn't scared
that someday she'd be in a position to discover the truth?
Evidence has to exist somewhere.''

M.J. whistled low. "Man, you're going too deep for me.
I'm just a simple small-town lawyer. This high level stuff's
too rich for my…" He stopped talking and stared at the
papers in his hands. "My God," he said, whispering the
words. "I think you're right. Check these out.''

"What have you got?" Matt moved over to him. Took
the papers from his grasp. Looked at them….

"Bingo," said Matt Glass, softly. "Home run.''

CHAPTER SEVENTEEN

"IN MANY WAYS," Allie said, "it's poetic justice that David's gone around the bend, mentally. Lost touch with the real world, probably for the rest of his life. According to what you've found, in a way the same sort of thing happened to poor Paul, ten years ago. He lost his vision of reality, which was us, his family, and he followed a strange dream of adventure and heroics."

She paused and took a deep breath. "That was his fate and his finish," she added.

Matt nodded. "It could easily have been mine, too," he said, touching her hand. "If you hadn't come into my life, I can't say where I'd be today. Certainly not tomorrow. I know I'd have lost Laurel."

Allie didn't reply, but she squeezed his hand. Words were not needed. Now, it just took a touch to communicate. A touch, a look. Love…

They were all back in his living room three weeks now after the rescue. Allie had delegated her house to the four commandos, who had been required to stay around until the possibility of legal problems arising from the raid on the mountain had been dismissed. Now, finally, the many facets of the case had been resolved or otherwise dealt with. The publicity surrounding the rescue had been incredible. It had been an exhausting and yet invigorating period of time.

Today, Allie had called all the troops together in one place for the first time since that eventful July morning. All being the eight adults who knew everything that had transpired in the case. They had carried out individual assignments and investigations since the day of her rescue, of course, but this meeting she intended to serve as a forum for tying up any loose ends she had not already snipped.

Miranda moved some papers around on the coffee table. "Your husband was duped," she said. "Deluded. Apparently, he had a weakness for heroics that you never realized, and when Benning discovered that, he exploited it. Paul Ford followed Benning's orders to go down to Central America and work with an underground political group that needed a physician. He thought he'd be gone less than a week." She held up an old, yellowed envelope. "He thought he was striking some sort of blow for freedom and democracy. Being a hero, in other words. His letter to you makes that clear."

"A letter that was never delivered," M.J. said, his tone almost a growl. "Entrusted to David Benning and stuck inside an old magazine to be forgotten and never seen again."

"Your husband was a good man," Chico commented. "Whatever his reasons for being down there, he died trying to help people like mine in a small village where the floods had washed away many things and had brought disease."

Allie felt calm. And peaceful. All the tears and regret in the world wouldn't bring Paul back. But the file M.J. had found contained the letter Paul had written to Allie as well as Benning's notes on the coverup he had engineered to keep his role in Paul's death a secret. Now it was time to let go of the past. Allie's heart belonged entirely to the quiet, strong man sitting beside her. But still, it was good to know she hadn't been mistaken in her judgment of her husband. He had intended to come back. He hadn't really ever deliberately deserted her and the kids.

They knew that now, and both Sam and Sally seemed to

have a new center of peace, just like she did. Their father would have loved them, if he had known them, and now they could hold that knowledge for the rest of their lives. They knew also he'd been a hero of sorts, saving people, and that made themhappy.

"All of this stays secret, of course," she said. "I'll tell my kids everything in due time, but no one else will know. We just don't have enough concrete proof to bring any charges in the case, and the real villain is paying for his crime by losing his mind. It's a justice I can accept."

Matt made a sound. "You're pretty damn forgiving," he said softly, covering her fingers with his and moving a bit closer. "The bastard was going to pump you full of dope and leave you up there to die of an overdose."

"I know." She put her hand on his thigh. "But it didn't happen. And now Rita's completely discredited personally and politically. The media's seen to it she'll never show her face in politics again. Josh is up on conspiracy-to-murder charges. Teddie Baker's facing criminal charges on the house shooting, and for trying to run you off the road, and attempted murder..."

"Mom. Laurel's awake." Sally appeared on the balcony overlooking the living room. "Debbie says she's asking for you. Can you come?"

"In a second, honey." Allie turned back to her group of special friends. "Duty calls," she said. "Will you all excuse me for a while?" She kissed Matt. "Carry on, darling."

Matt held her hand, then let her go. The house was full with the twins back from Montana. Debbie Preston had taken up the offer of a full-time job as nanny for the three kids. *Their* three kids. Laurel was now Matt's, indisputably. While the Turner's role in the main conspiracy was vague, they had dropped their suit once they realized that Matt was considered a hero by everyone.

ONE WEEK LATER, Matt and Allie stood at the altar. By keeping the wedding trappings and extras to a minimum, Allie had limited the number of "outsider" people in town in the know to six. Including her parents, who drove down from the ranch, that made eight. Of course, there were the four soldiers. Gunther, Chris, Chico and Manuel had insisted on staying on for the wedding. The rest of the wedding party consisted of Miranda, M.J., Debbie, Sam, Sally and Laurel.

Real friends and family. She smiled to herself as she listened to the words of the ceremony. An announcement in the paper tomorrow or the next day would take care of the rest of the world....

The minister spoke on. "...any reason this man and woman should not be..."

She could feel the warmth of Matt's body next to hers. She would be safe and secure with him. She could trust him. He was the real thing—a genuine hero. He had proven that to her the morning he'd saved her life on the mountain.

Listening to the minister's voice, she realized that they were at that one part of the ceremony she had had nightmares about for ten years—she was about to marry again and in the middle wedding ceremony, Paul returned and demanded a stop to it... She relaxed. It would never happen, because the mystery was finally solved.

"...joined together, speak now or..."

"Hold it!"

Allie nearly fainted. A strange male voice rang out, demanding that the wedding halt. She turned around, her muscles almost frozen with fear....

But the handsome elderly man striding down the aisle with a big smile on his face was not the ghost of her late husband. It was...

Someone who looked amazingly like Matt! Matt as he might be thirty years from now.... Silver hair where Matt's was blond. Deeper character lines in the face. The same brown eyes and sturdy build, though the older man's back seemed a little bowed under the weight of those extra years....

"Dad?" Matt tightened his arm around Allie's waist, pulling her closer to his side. "Dad, what are you...? How did you...?" He saw Chico blush and knew how his father had found out.

"Hello, Son." Robert Glass walked all the way up to the altar and threw his arms around Matt, including Allie in the bear hug. "I couldn't just let you go and get yourself married off without showing up to watch, could I?" He grinned at the astonished minister. "Mind starting this over, Rev? I'd like to see the whole show, if you all don't mind?"

After that, the ceremony went off without another hitch.

EPILOGUE

FINALLY, election day arrived. Matt woke up early and found himself alone in bed. The house was dark and cold. Uneasy, he pulled on jeans, moccasins and a sweatshirt and left the bedroom, looking for Allie.

She wasn't in her office. Lately, she'd been spending long hours pouring over charts and poll results, determined to know her fate before the fatal day, though it had done her no good, as far as he could tell. The race was just too unpredictable, given all the dramatic and emotional factors involved in her campaign. She wasn't with the children. The kids were still asleep. He checked each bedroom. But she wasn't in any of them.

Neither was Fred.

Matt hurried down the hall, opened the front door and...

Sighed with relief. She was at the door, ready to come inside.

"Hi," Allie said. She wore a heavy coat and jeans. Fred, on her leash, jumped up on Matt's leg for a pat. "Or rather, good morning. We were just out walking," she said. "I couldn't sleep, so I went into the girls' room, kidnapped Fred and..."

"I love you," Matt declared, taking her face in his hands. Her skin was cold, but her mouth was warm when he kissed her. "You're going to win, darling. Don't let this get to you."

She smiled wanly. "Matt, whatever happens today, I

know I'm very lucky. I have you and the children. Is it selfish of me to want more?''

"You, selfish? Never.'' The indignation and love in Matt's voice brought tears to her eyes. She put her arms around her husband and thought, for at least the hundredth time, how much he'd changed. How different he was from the man she had met at the supermarket months ago. Then, he had been scared of his role as a family man. Now, he was very much at peace with that role. He and his father had both learned the true meaning of home and family. Robert Glass had become a wonderful grandpoppa for all three children. He had moved into her old house when Matt's four compadres had left. And he seemed perfectly content to stay.

"I know. Let's have a party.'' Matt's voice interrupted her thoughts.

"What?''

"A party. An old-fashioned election-night blast. That way, no matter what happens, you'll have a good time.''

"Oh.'' She looked up at the ceiling and groaned. "I just couldn't. It's too much work, and I don't have any extra energy right now. Too nervous, like I said. I...''

"*You* don't have to,'' he said. "I'll do all the work. You just enjoy!''

Allie started to protest again, but she couldn't think of a really good reason why he shouldn't do it if he wanted. Besides, she thought, if she was occupied with company all around, maybe she wouldn't stay glued to the television, her nerves screaming at each prediction. "Okay,'' she said, shrugging. "I suppose it's a good idea. At least it'll take my mind off the whole thing.''

She was wrong. By seven o'clock, when the polls closed, their house was jumping with friends and family, company all out to cheer her through the tension of the final hours of vote-counting. But Allie found herself in the kitchen, unable to watch the television. "I'm being ridiculous," she said to Fred, who seemed to have sensed her need for comfort and was curled up on her lap.

M.J. came into the kitchen and tried to hand her a beer. "Drink up, cousin," he advised. "You look like you need it."

She shook her head. "No booze for me. Not tonight."

Miranda took the beer from M.J. "What about the celebration champagne?" she asked, taking a healthy swallow of beer. "When you win, are you going to let us drink it all?"

Allie managed a smile. "If I win, I'll drink."

"Okay." M.J. walked off, his arm around Miranda's waist. Allie smiled again, but to herself. Apparently, now that Chico was gone, Miranda and M.J. were reestablishing their friendship.

A little later, Sally came over and leaned against her, disturbing Fred, who shifted position but did not leave Allie's lap. "Mom," she asked. "What's going to happen if you win? Will you go away?"

"Oh, no, honey." Allie embraced her daughter, spilling Fred to the floor. "I won't leave you all. Ever! What it means is that I'll go down to Cheyenne for a few weeks in the winter to attend legislature. But Matt will be here with you and Sam and Laurel."

Sally considered this. "I'd rather you not go anywhere."

Allie picked Fred back up. "What does your brother think?" she asked.

Sally frowned. "He says you want to be the boss of everyone. So…"

"I see." Allie put her arm around her daughter. "Honey, I didn't realize you still had questions." She stood up. "Where's Sam?" she asked.

A few minutes later, she and Matt were seated at the

kitchen table explaining to the twins what Allie's commitment to public service entailed.

"So," Sam said. "Mom'll really be working for *me* if she goes to Cheyenne?"

"That's right," Matt said. "Working for you and Sally and me. Even for your Grandpa Robert. Looking after our rights and our needs. That's what being a boss really means."

"Oh." Sam nodded and seemed satisfied.

Sally was quiet for a few seconds. Then, "I guess it's okay, Mom, if you have to be gone for a little while to help out other people and us. Long as you always come home."

"Honey, I always will come home. No matter where I go. I promise. And I think you have the right idea now. I…" A rising chorus of voices cheering interrupted her.

"Babe!" M.J. rushed into the kitchen. "Allie! You won!"

Miranda was right behind him. "A landslide victory, Allie. Nobody figured that, but you did it. Congratulations!" She opened the refrigerator and took out a bottle of champagne. "Celebration time!" She popped the cork.

But as Allie and Matt looked at each other, Allie realized that an even bigger victory had been the one she had scored right here at the kitchen table a few minutes before. She and her husband and her children had sat down, discussed a problem together and come to an understanding.

Matt took two glasses and filled them. He handed one to his wife. "To you," he said, lifting the glass. "And…"

"No," Allie said. "To *us*." She included her children. "To our new family…to…us all!"

As she hooked her arm with Matt's and drank, Allie realized that was a toast she could honor for the rest of her life. She and Matt were the real winners. And always would be!

The little girl is homeless and frightened. And Flynn McCallister is all she has. Is he up to the task?

TELL ME A STORY

Dallas Schulze

Chapter One

The pile of newspapers was moving. Flynn peered at it carefully to make sure. Yes, it was definitely moving. This seemed odd when he thought about it. Everything else was rather foggy at the moment, but he was positive that newspapers did not move on their own.

Therefore, there must be something moving them. This piece of brilliant reasoning burst into his alcohol-soaked mind with the force of a lightning bolt. He nodded slowly, pleased with himself. And to think that he'd taken a cab because he thought he was too drunk to drive home. This proved how wrong he had been.

He slumped against the wall that held him upright and considered the problem. If the papers were not moving themselves, which he had decided was the case, he should know why they were moving. After all, this was his alley; he ought to know what was happening in it.

His eyes narrowed. *Was* it his alley? Now there was a point for him to bring up with the lawyers. Since the family owned the building, did that mean they owned the alley, too? That question ought to keep them busy for at least ten minutes. They might as well do something to earn the retainers they were paid.

The newspapers stirred again, drawing his wandering attention. He wet one long finger and held it up waveringly.

Wind. That could be the cause. He was proud of this brilliant thought and rather irritated when he could feel no breeze on his damp finger.

When his gaze returned to the papers there was a definite frown drawing his black brows together. The papers shifted more violently this time and Flynn's frown deepened into a scowl. That was an arm. Thin and pale and amazingly fragile against the dark macadam, but still, it was definitely an arm.

Now he was going to have to investigate. No question about it. Whether it was technically his alley or not, he felt a proprietary interest in it. He couldn't just walk off and leave it in the possession of these animated and possibly dangerous papers.

Actually, he wasn't sure he could walk at all, he admitted with a flash of honesty. But that was neither here nor there. The point was—and he seemed to be having some difficulty in sticking to the point—it was his civic duty to find out exactly what was going on. What if this was the first wave of an invading force from another planet? This could be an alien pod looking for some innocent human to take over their body.

It didn't occur to Flynn that he was the only human within striking range of the potential pod, nor did he think that the alley behind a luxury apartment building in Los Angeles seemed an odd starting point for an interplanetary invasion. At five o'clock in the morning, after drinking all night, anything seemed not only possible but logical.

The ground showed a disconcerting tendency to tilt when he moved away from the wall but, filled with pixilated patriotism, Flynn managed to cross the space between himself and the suspicious papers. With some vague thought of protecting his back, he leaned against the concrete wall next to his target and slid bonelessly down it until he sat on the pavement.

His landing was not quite as clean as it could have been. The lump under his right thigh jerked alarmingly and the papers cascaded in all directions. This startling activity was accompanied by a muffled shriek of pain that settled into a high, childish voice.

"Hey! Get off my foot, you big ox." The foot in question was yanked out from under him.

Flynn found himself gazing into a small heart-shaped face, fine sandy brows drawn together in a fierce scowl. He smiled at the face in a friendly way. "Sorry about your foot."

The two studied each other in the gray predawn light that oozed between the high walls of the alley. Flynn's gaze was clear and alert. Only someone who knew him well would have seen the faint glaze that dulled the vivid blue of his eyes.

"Are you a pod?" His tone was interested, but not particularly concerned. "And if you're a pod, are you male or female, or doesn't it matter?"

The scowl on the little face returned in triplicate. "I'm not a pod. I'm a girl."

"Are you sure?" Flynn was vaguely disappointed. He'd been looking forward to telling his father that aliens had landed and they'd chosen McCallister property as their landing site. The old man would have had an apoplectic fit at their effrontery.

"Course I'm sure. There's no such thing as pods. That was only in a movie. If you're too drunk to know that you must be *really* drunk."

Flynn gave up the pleasing image of his father telling the aliens to get off his property and looked apologetic. "Plastered, I'm afraid. But then I didn't expect to be called on to decide matters of national importance. Are you sure you're not a pod?"

"Course I'm sure."

He sighed. "That's a relief. I'd really rather not have the fate of the world in my hands right now. If you're not a pod, what are you doing under that pile of papers?"

"I was trying to sleep," she told him with heavy sarcasm.

His brows rose. "Sleeping? Why were you sleeping under those papers? Wouldn't a bed be more comfortable?"

"Course it would, but I don't have a bed." The statement was flat, leavened with a touch of scorn.

Flynn's brows shot up until they almost met the heavy fall of black hair that drifted onto his forehead.

"No bed at all?" he asked. She shook her head and he echoed the gesture. "It doesn't seem fair. I have more beds than I know what to do with and you don't have one at all." He sat pondering the inequities of this for so long that the child leaned forward to see if he was still awake.

She jumped when he spoke suddenly. "Tell you what, you can use one of my beds. Help me up and we'll go to my 'partment and find you a bed. Bound to be a spare or two lying around the place."

He struggled to his feet, leaning one hand on his companion's shoulder once he achieved his goal. He frowned down at her. "You're not very big, are you?"

She drew herself up straighter, almost unbalancing him as she did so. "My mom says that being tall isn't important. Short people can move mountains, too."

He nodded, impressed by the profundity of this remark. "Very true. Come to think of it, I'm six-two and I've never moved a mountain. Just goes to prove that being tall isn't everything."

"Just a minute, mister." The piping voice interrupted his forward move, and he turned to look down at her, weaving slightly with checked momentum. "Are there any strings attached to this?"

He gave the question some consideration. "I don't think so. What kind of strings did you have in mind?"

She shook her head. "I don't know, but my mom always said that men don't make offers without strings."

"You know, the more I hear, the more I think your mother is a singularly intelligent woman."

She frowned a bit. "Well, I don't know about that, but she's real smart."

She guided his erratic footsteps across the alley and stopped in front of the door he indicated. He fumbled with the knob for a moment and then remembered it was locked. After a lengthy search for his keys, which turned up in the pocket of his gray slacks, his companion took the key ring from him and tried each key until she hit the right one.

The door closed behind them with an expansive whoosh of air. Flynn blinked rapidly in the sudden glare of light, though the short corridor was actually very softly lit. A bank of four elevators lined one wall. With a great deal of concentration, he managed to punch out a short combination of numbers that opened the doors on the elevator. The two of them entered the thickly carpeted cubical and the doors swished shut. Flynn grabbed for the nearest wall as the floor surged upward, leaving his stomach somewhere beneath them.

"Are you okay, mister?" He closed his eyes in exquisite agony as the elevator stopped and the doors slid open, revealing a wide foyer and two beautifully carved wooden doors on either side.

A small hand tugged on his pant leg. "Are you gonna be sick, mister?"

He opened his eyes and looked down into her concerned little face. "I am never sick," he announced firmly, the words directed at least as much to his churning stomach as to the child.

Using her shoulder as a brace, he steered her out of the

elevator and then stopped, trying to remember why he was here. A small voice recalled him to the task at hand.

"Which door, mister?"

Flynn turned slowly and then pointed to the door on the left, with a gesture worthy of Lady Macbeth. He shook his head with equal drama and then had to wait a moment for it to stop spinning.

"Don't go near that door. A dragon lives there."

"There's no such thing as dragons." The pragmatic statement did nothing to further the atmosphere Flynn had thought he was creating. He pulled his gaze from the door and looked down at his companion, his chin setting stubbornly.

"*I* live here and I happen to know that there is a dragon living there. We meet occasionally in the elevator. She has red hair and cold green eyes and she can freeze your bones with one look."

"A dragon wouldn't fit in a elevator."

"She's a very small dragon. Besides, I thought you said that there couldn't be a dragon because they didn't exist."

His new acquaintance shook her head, her small face twisted in an expression of adult exasperation.

"You're drunker'n a skunk."

Flynn frowned. "We have already established that point. I see no reason to belabor it."

He followed her lead to the other door and watched while she sorted through the key ring, trying each one in turn. He could have told her which key to use, but he was in no hurry. There was a pleasant buzzing sensation in his head. Sooner or later, the alcohol was going to catch up with him and he was going to regret the night's debauchery, but for now, he had no objections to standing outside his door.

The quiet snick of the lock interrupted his thoughts, and he reached out to push the door open. They stepped onto thick, soft carpeting and the door clicked quietly shut behind them. Flynn walked a few feet before realizing that something was wrong. He stopped and thought about it for a moment. He couldn't see anything. That was the problem. He spun on one heel with more enthusiasm than sense and stumbled against a narrow table. There was a faint thud as the table rattled beneath his weight and something fell to the floor.

His groping hands cleared the table of the remainder of its contents as he felt his way along the length of it, searching for the wall. He had just succeeded in finding it and was preparing to start the arduous task of locating the light switch when brilliant light suddenly flooded the hall.

He turned more slowly this time, then leaned back on the table and studied his companion. She stood on the opposite side of the hall, her hand just dropping away from the switch. He gave her a smile that had been known to make little old ladies swoon with pleasure.

She was not impressed. Her eyes took in the destruction he had left behind, and when she looked up at him her small mouth was pursed in stern disapproval.

"You're drunker than a skunk." It was obvious that his condition disgusted her, and Flynn tried his smile again, adding just a bit of coaxing apology to it. His new mentor only scowled deeper. "Look what a mess you made."

He cast his eyes on the scattered bric-a-brac that lay on the thick carpet, and shuddered. "Good grief. It looks like a miniature massacre." Small soldiers lay in positions suggestive of death and destruction. He gasped and clutched his chest theatrically. "Oh, my God! He shot me! The short guy in the gray suit shot me."

She giggled. "They're all short and there's lots of them in gray suits."

"Well, obviously, one of them recognized me as a Yankee through and through." He poked one of the little figures with an expensively shod foot. "My father's chess set.

Trust him to have a chess set based on the Civil War.''
There was an old bitterness in the words.

He cocked his head, listening to the mellow chimes of
the grandfather clock that stood in the living room. ''Six
o'clock. The whole night is gone.'' He threw off the brief
melancholy that had seized him and lurched away from the
wall. ''Come on. We've got to be in bed by six-thirty.''

''How come?'' The words were brought out on a yawn
as she followed his unsteady path. He stumbled down the
two steps that led into the living room and almost sprawled
onto the carpet. Some rapid and surprisingly graceful foot-
work kept him upright, and he turned to grin at her tri-
umphantly.

''Fred Astaire, eat your heart out,'' he exclaimed expan-
sively.

She studied him critically. ''Fred Astaire did things deliberately. *That* was an accident. Besides, you're not wearing a fancy black coat.''

''How do you know he did things deliberately?'' he
asked mulishly. ''I bet a lot of his best routines were ac-
cidents. And what's wrong with my clothes?''

He tilted his head to look down at himself. Gray slacks
and a blue silk shirt that matched his eyes were topped by
a suede jacket. He had thought the outfit looked fine when
he'd put it on earlier in the evening.

His companion ignored his question and returned to a
more important issue. ''How come we've got to be in bed
by six-thirty?''

He blinked at her as if trying to remember where he was
and then gave a sudden gasp. ''Six-thirty. Oh, my God!
We've got to hurry.'' He reached out to grab her shoulder
and steered a weaving path across the living room. He
stopped in the hall and gave her an intent look, bending
down to look her in the eye.

''If I'm still up at six-thirty, I turn into a vampire.''

Her eyes widened. "Really?"

He nodded solemnly and straightened up, grabbing onto a convenient doorjamb when his head spun. "It's an old family curse," he said sadly. "Every morning at six-thirty, we all turn into vampires."

She eyed him suspiciously. "Everybody knows that people turn into vampires at night and if they're caught out in the *sun*, they die."

"They do?" He seemed impressed with this information. "Do you mean to tell me I've been doing it wrong all these years?" He shook his head. "I might have known I'd screw it up."

She caught the twinkle in his eye and giggled. "You're very silly." The words were obviously a compliment, and Flynn accepted them in the spirit intended.

"Thank you. I do my best." He stood away from the wall, swaying for a moment before regaining his balance. His lips twisted in a rueful smile. "I'm afraid my night of wicked carousing is catching up with me." He blinked to clear his foggy vision. "We'd better get you settled before I collapse."

He set his feet down with neat precision, each step carefully planned and executed as he led the way through one of the doors that faced onto the hallway. The bedroom was beautifully done in shades of brown and slate blue. Plush blue carpeting and drapes formed a background for the rich mahogany furniture.

He stopped in the doorway and swept one hand out in invitation. Slowly, the little girl moved into the room, staring around her with wide gray eyes.

"Wow."

The soft exclamation drew Flynn's wandering gaze back to her. The pain that had darkened his vivid eyes softened and disappeared as he took in the wondering little face. In her childish eyes, the room was reflected as a palace and, for an instant, he saw her vision, pushing aside the hurtful memories that tainted it.

"Not bad, huh?"

"Wow." That one word expressed absolute awe. She tiptoed across the thick carpet and reached out to touch the heavy bedspread, drawing back before her hand made contact. The gesture spoke volumes. A stab of anger cleared Flynn's foggy mind for a moment, and he crossed the room in a few quick strides and grabbed hold of the bedspread, jerking it off the bed and tossing it carelessly on the floor.

She gasped as if he had committed a sacrilege, but he ignored her, pulling down the crisp linen sheets to poke a careless hand into the already fluffed pillows. When he turned to look at her, she was staring at him wide-eyed, sensing a difference that even he didn't quite understand.

He sat on the foot of the bed and smiled at her. "They're only things," he said softly.

"But it's so beautiful." She bent to touch the discarded bedspread reverently. His eyes followed her hand and, for a moment, he could almost imagine that he heard laughter and saw Mark winking at him, his eyes almost the same color as the spread. He blinked and the moment was gone.

"It's beautiful, but it's only a thing. It's all right to admire things but don't ever become obsessed with them." Silence filled the beautiful room for a minute as he looked around, seeing everything the same as it had been all those years ago. "Maybe it's time to make some changes," he murmured softly.

He shook his head and got to his feet, looking down at his diminutive companion. "Make yourself at home. This is a good room. It used to belong to my brother, but he doesn't need it anymore. Still, the room must remember him," he said whimsically.

She watched him silently, only speaking when he would

have pulled the door shut behind him. "Hey, mister, could you leave the door open?"

He stuck his head around the door and grinned at her. "You bet, and I'll leave the hall light on, too. My bedroom is two doors down on the right. If you need anything, just come in and poke me. Good night, urchin."

Flynn walked the few feet to his bedroom, deliberately encouraging the alcoholic fumes to cushion his mind. Once in the room, he collapsed on the wide bed, oblivious to the richly masculine surroundings. He shrugged out of his jacket and tossed it in the general direction of a chair and then tugged off his shoes, letting them fall where they would.

He leaned back on the thick pile of pillows and put his hands behind his head, staring up at the ceiling and seeing his brother's face mirrored there. The features marked them as brothers but the coloring set them apart. Mark had inherited their father's reddish-brown hair and dark eyes, and Flynn was a throwback to his mother's grandfather. With his black hair and bright blue eyes he was altogether too flamboyant to be a staid McCallister. Mark's imagined eyes crinkled with amusement, and Flynn could hear his brother telling him that self-pity never did anyone any good. He blinked and the image was gone.

He groaned softly. God, he was drunk. He hadn't been this badly smashed in years. Not since he and Mark... No. He didn't want to remember that. Not now. Not when his defenses were at an all-time low.

The memories faded and were replaced by tiny features capped with a mop of raggedly cut sandy hair. His mouth tilted up. Cute little thing. Who was she? Good Lord, he didn't even know her name! Oh well, in the morning he could find out her name and find her parents and get her back where she belonged.

The mists of drink and exhaustion gradually thickened,

creating swirling pockets of peace in his tired thoughts. The faint lines beside his mouth smoothed out as his breathing deepened and slowed, his long body relaxing into the cozy comfort of the bedspread.

He stirred once a few minutes later, some half-buried sense telling him that something was different. But he didn't wake even when the door closed quietly behind a tiny figure.

She froze just inside the door as the man on the bed stirred, and then breathed a silent sigh of relief when he relaxed again. Small bare feet moved quietly across the plush carpet until she stood at the edge of the bed. Moving ever so slowly and quietly, she turned back the corner of the bedspread and eased onto the bed.

The other room was pretty, but it was awfully big and lonely and, for the moment, this strange man offered safety in an unknown world.

She curled up against the pillow, one thin arm encircling a battered toy giraffe, the other hand tucked up under her cheek.

By the time the grandfather clock struck seven, man and child were fast asleep, the arms of Morpheus holding them both safe and secure.

Chapter Two

Flynn's nose twitched and his eyelids flickered. A muffled groan was smothered in the pillow as he buried his face deeper in the soft down. If the pillow were just a little bigger, he could find a way to sink his whole body into it and pull it shut behind him.

He was dying. That was the only possible excuse for this much pain.

His head hurt with a relentless, pounding throb that moved from the top of his skull all the way down his body. Even his toes ached. It was unfortunate that amnesia didn't go along with the ache. Then he wouldn't have been able to remember drinking himself into a stupor. At least he'd had the sense to take a taxi home.

He was getting too old for this kind of nonsense. At thirty-three he ought to know better than to try and lose himself in a bottle. It didn't make the memories go away and it didn't bring back the dead. Well, Mark's birthday had come and gone. Another year past and he still hadn't managed to put his brother's death behind him. But then, maybe that kind of thing was never really behind you.

His head hurt too much for philosophical questions. Right now he wasn't sure he could deal with the present problems, let alone the past. Present problems... There was something nagging at the back of his mind. Something he should remember about the previous night.

He frowned and then wished he hadn't. Changing expressions only made the pain worse. He could remember paying the taxi off, and then he'd wandered into the alley and there'd been something there.... The newspapers—and the little girl.

He gathered what little strength remained in his body and rolled onto his back. For the moment, he didn't try to open his eyes. His nose twitched again. What was that smell? Acrid and smoky. Was the apartment on fire? The thought forced his eyes open. No sign of smoke. The soft light hurt his eyes and he had to narrow his eyelids. He sniffed again. What was that smell?

"Are you awake, mister?" He rolled onto his side toward the voice. The little girl from the night before was perched on the edge of a chair she'd pulled next to the bed.

"I'm awake but I'm not sure I'm alive." His voice came out in a scratchy growl, which pretty much described how he felt.

"I made you some coffee. Mom always wants coffee when she has a hangover."

"Bless you." He dragged himself into a sitting position, propping his back against the headboard. His clothes seemed to crackle when he moved or maybe that was his bones. He really was getting too old for all-night binges.

The child got up, lifted a cup off the night table and handed it to him, holding it carefully with both hands. Flynn took it from her the same way, hoping the tremor in his right hand would counteract the quiver in his left.

He lifted the cup to his mouth and took a sip. If the synapses in his brain hadn't been so saturated with alcohol, they would have had time to warn him. As it was, by the time the message had gotten from his nose to his hands that the acrid smell was coming from the cup he held, he'd already taken a hearty mouthful of the liquid inside.

As a method of waking someone up, the brew was probably unequaled. Flynn's eyes sprang from half-mast to wide open. He sat up straighter in bed and, for an instant, he forgot about his headache.

The substance in his mouth might have been a primeval predecessor to coffee, but it bore only a vague resemblance to the smooth brew usually associated with the word. The acrid, smoky scent that had led him to wonder if the apartment was on fire was amplified in the taste. The liquid was thick, slightly rancid in flavor and so strong that it threatened to dissolve the enamel on his teeth.

He was about to spit the foul liquid back into the cup when his eyes fell on his small houseguest. Wide gray eyes peered from beneath ragged, sandy bangs. Their expression reminded him of a puppy who'd just performed a difficult trick and was hoping for a reward. Without another thought, he swallowed the liquid, praying that his stomach lining was tougher than it felt. He smiled, wondering if his teeth had actually been etched by their contact with the alleged coffee.

"It's wonderful."

His companion smiled. The beaming expression changed her from waiflike to almost angelic. Just for that look, it was worth the suspicion that his stomach would never be the same.

"Mom says you can't start a day without coffee."

"I...ah...feel the same way." Flynn tried to look casual as he held the cup in his lap, as far from his nose as possible. Would the stuff eat through the porcelain? "Could you get me a damp washcloth, do you think? The bathroom is through there."

"Sure." She hopped off her chair and trotted away. Flynn looked frantically for a place to dispose of the cup's contents. He didn't dare drink the stuff. He might survive a swallow, but a full cup would certainly be fatal. Water was running in the bathroom. He had only a moment. A quick tilt of his wrist dumped the liquid into the base of the philodendron that sat under a plant light next to the bed.

Was it his imagination, or did the plant shudder with the impact of the brew?

His guest came back into the bedroom carrying a dripping cloth, and Flynn set the empty cup down, trying to look as if he'd drained it and felt much better for the experience. He held out his hand, trying not to grimace at the icy cold, sopping wet cloth that landed in his palm. With an apology to the innocent philodendron, he wrung the cloth out in the pot before wiping his face with it.

The cold cloth didn't help much. His head still pounded and his eyes were still gritty. But his miseries were going to have to wait.

"I don't think we were properly introduced last night. I'm Flynn McCallister."

"I'm Rebecca Antoinette Sinclair."

Flynn's brows arched, meeting the black hair that fell onto his forehead. "Good grief. That's a mouthful. Do I have to use the whole thing every time?" He looked so appalled that she giggled.

"You can call me Becky." She picked up the empty cup and peered into it. Flynn wouldn't have been surprised to see that the bottom had been eaten away. "Do you want some more coffee?"

"No! I mean, it was delicious but one cup is my limit." He hoped his smile wasn't as sickly as it felt. The pounding in his head had returned a hundredfold. All he wanted to do was roll over in bed and die. Barring that, he was willing to try a long, steaming hot shower. He looked at Becky and knew that both plans were out of the question.

"I was not quite myself last night...."

"You were drunker than a waltzin' pissant." She said it so firmly that Flynn gave up any thought of arguing his condition.

"All right. I was drunk." He caught her eye and amended the statement. "Very drunk. But that's neither here nor there." He hurried on before she could argue the point. "I seem to recall that you were sleeping in the alley. Now, it's been a while since I was your age, but I'm sure I'd remember if sleeping in alleys was normal. Where's your mom and dad?"

"I don't have a daddy." Her chin thrust out, defying him to say anything. "He left when I was real little, but Mom and me don't need him. We do just fine on our own."

"Okay. What about your mom? Where is she? She must be worried sick about you."

The tough little chin quivered. "I don't know. She was s'posed to come home a couple weeks ago. Only she didn't."

Flynn swung his legs over the side of the bed and sat up. He wished his head would quit hurting. "Where did she go?"

"She went away with one of her boyfriends. She's real pretty and she has lots of boyfriends. She was supposed to come back on Monday. Only she didn't."

"Don't you think you should have stayed at home, so she'd know where to find you?"

"I did for a while. But then Mrs. Castle said she was going to report me to the welfare people 'cause I'd been left. But Mama didn't leave, and if the welfare people take me away, I'll never see her again. Mama told me all about them. And I'm scared that somethin' may have happened to her. Only Mrs. Castle wouldn't listen to me. She told me I was just a kid and I didn't know nothin'. But I know Mama wouldn't leave me."

"Who is Mrs. Castle?"

It took a while and some judicious questioning but eventually Flynn pieced together what he thought was a fairly accurate picture. Apparently, Becky's mother frequently left Becky on her own for the weekend while she went off with one of her many boyfriends. This was an established pattern, and Becky saw nothing wrong with it. She was very good at taking care of herself, she informed him.

Two weeks ago her mother had left as usual. To Becky, the boyfriend was just a faceless man named John. This, too, was normal. Becky never met her mother's escorts, which made Flynn wonder just what kind of boyfriends her mother had. This time her mother hadn't come back from the weekend trip.

Mrs. Castle managed the apartment building where Becky and her mother lived. She'd become alarmed by the mother's continued absence. Flynn couldn't help but wonder if her alarm hadn't been sparked by the fact that the rent had come due. She told Becky she was going to call the welfare department, and Becky packed a paper bag with her most important belongings and ran away. The welfare people and the bogeyman were apparently much the same in Becky's young mind. She'd been living on the streets for the past three days, and Flynn shuddered to think of what could have happened to her.

"You know, you can't just disappear like that, Becky. What's going to happen when your mom goes home and you aren't there? She's going to be worried."

Becky's brows came together. "I know. But I couldn't let the welfare people take me away. They'd never let me see her again."

Flynn rubbed a hand over the stubble on his chin. He felt unwashed, unkempt and unfit to handle this problem. He closed his eyes, half hoping Becky would turn out to be a figment of an alcohol-soaked imagination. But when he opened them again, she was still sitting there, her eyes fixed on him.

He sighed.

"You won't call the welfare people, will you, Mr. Flynn?"

He looked at her, wondering what imp of fate had chosen to drop her into his lap. Was fate testing him or her? Of the two of them, she was probably getting the worse bargain.

"It's just Flynn. And, no, I won't call the welfare people."

"What are you going to do with me?" She looked at him with absolute trust, clearly depending on him to make the best decision about her future. Flynn wanted to scream. Instead, he thrust his fingers through his hair and stood.

"The first thing I'm going to do is clean up and then we'll consider our options before we make any rash decisions."

"Does that mean I can stay here for a while?"

"That means you can stay here for a while."

"Do you think I could have something to eat?"

Flynn was almost to the bathroom door and the nirvana of a hot shower when the question reached him. He stopped and turned to look at his small guest. She was so independent and self-sufficient that it was hard to remember she was only a child. He swallowed a surge of self-directed anger.

"Didn't you get something while you were making coffee?"

"I wasn't sure if it would be okay. Mom says you should always wait to be invited."

"Consider this a permanent invitation. My home is open to you, madam. Feel free to avail yourself of all its facilities." He bowed low, and the sound of her giggle almost made him forget that his head was threatening to fall off his shoulders.

"Let's go see what the cupboard holds."

Luckily for the state of his stomach, Becky opted for cold cereal. Unfortunately, the remains of her coffee-brewing venture still sat in a pan on the stove. Flynn approached it cautiously, half expecting a scaled monster to rise up over the rim of the pot. Surely, the primordial goo from which life sprang must have smelled something like this.

Nothing lunged at him and, once he got a look in the pot, he could see why. No life form could possibly survive in the sullen black murk in the pot. He thought of the philodendron and winced. Not even a plant deserved a death like that.

"How did you make the coffee, Becky?" He grasped the handle of the pot with two fingers and inched it off the burner in the direction of the sink.

Becky looked up from her cereal. "Well, I couldn't find the regular stuff. But there was this jar in your 'frigerator and it said coffee. I can read," she interjected, clearly proud of this fact. Flynn made an appropriate noise and tilted the pot's contents into the sink, half expecting the stainless steel to melt on contact.

"Anyway, it didn't look like coffee but it said coffee so I tried to make some like I always make Mom. I boiled some water real careful 'cause Mom says you always got to be careful with stoves. And then I put some of that stuff in a cup. It was all in big lumps instead of powdery like real coffee. I tried to mash it with a spoon but it didn't work so I poured the water over it. I thought maybe the lumps would melt. Only they didn't and it didn't look right so I dumped it all back in the pan and boiled it for a long time. Those lumps never did go away but it turned the right color. You really ought to buy some new coffee, Mr. Flynn. I think that stuff's gotten old.''

Flynn thought of the twenty-five-dollar-a-pound Jamaican Blue Mountain coffee beans that she'd massacred. The laugh started deep in his belly and worked its way out. Becky looked up from her food as Flynn leaned against the counter and gave in to the laughter, clutching at his pounding head. She looked at him for a moment and then shrugged.

It was several minutes before Flynn regained control. ''I'm going to pick up the paper and the mail and then I'm going to take a hot shower. Then we'll sit down and talk about what we're going to do with you.'' She nodded, more interested in trying to find a way through the maze on the back of the cereal box.

Flynn left her to the puzzle and went to the front door. His mouth was still curved in a smile. Sometimes it took a child to put things into clear perspective. He unbuttoned his shirt. As soon as he picked up the paper, he was going to spend at least an hour under steaming hot water.

He stepped into the hall just as the elevator slid to a halt. Since he wasn't expecting any visitors, there was only one person it could be—his neighbor. His smile took on a wicked edge.

Ann Perry had lived in the apartment across from him for two years. She was young, attractive, single, and she sternly disapproved of him. She made that clear every time their paths happened to cross. She was a doctor at a local hospital, and the fact that he was sometimes arriving home just as she was going to work obviously offended her sensibilities.

It was unkind, but he could never quite resist the urge to reinforce her image of him as a worthless, womanizing playboy. When those green eyes looked at him as if expecting him to sprout horns and a tail, it brought out a particularly wicked streak. He stopped short of throwing an orgy just to confirm her opinions, but he doubted that she needed any additional proof of his worthlessness.

He turned toward the elevator and leaned one shoulder against the doorjamb. He knew exactly the picture he presented. It was four o'clock in the afternoon. He was unshaven. His hair was tousled. His feet were bare. His shirt was unbuttoned to the waist and his belt was unbuckled. He looked the very picture of worthless masculinity. It was perfect.

The elevator doors slid open, and Flynn felt a twinge of guilt. In the instant before she saw him, she looked tired. There was a vulnerable droop to her shoulders that made him want to offer her a place to rest her head. But it was only a momentary illusion. The moment her eyes fell on him, her shoulders stiffened into a military stance and her eyes turned a frosty shade of green.

Flynn slumped against the wall, letting his eyes trail insolently over her, from the tips of her neat black pumps—the heels a sensible two inches—over the gray suit—still crisp after a day spent at the hospital—to fine-boned features set in rigid disapproval and finally stopped on fiery red hair pulled into a smooth chignon.

When she'd first moved in, he'd had more than one fantasy about seeing that hair spread across his pillow, but it hadn't taken long for the message to come across that the fire in her hair didn't melt the ice in her eyes.

"Ms. Perry. Home from a day of saving lives?"

She tilted her head, her shoulders absolutely rigid as she stepped out of the elevator. "Mr. McCallister. Home from a night of drinking?"

She stalked to her door, stopping to pick up her mail and the newspaper. Flynn admired the line of her back. She really was a very attractive woman. If she'd just show some signs of humanity, he'd be able to resist the urge to live down to her opinion of him. He allowed himself a mental sigh of regret as she opened her door. Oh well, a dedicated doctor probably wasn't his style, anyway.

Right now the only female he had to worry about was about three feet tall and made a deadly cup of coffee.

Ann was aware of Flynn McCallister's eyes following her every move. Hands that were solid as a rock holding a needle suddenly felt remarkably quivery gathering up her mail. He didn't say anything more, but he didn't have to. Just his presence was enough to unnerve her.

She fumbled with the key before getting it in the lock. The door opened and she stepped into the haven of her home. She resisted the urge to slam the door. She wouldn't give him the satisfaction of knowing he disturbed her. The door closed with a quiet snick, enclosing her in the safety of her apartment and shutting him out.

"Ridiculous. You're acting like a child." Only there was nothing childlike about the feelings Flynn McCallister stirred.

The muttered reprimand didn't make her feel any less relieved, but it did bring her housemate running. She saw him coming across the living room and quickly dropped her mail and the paper on the hall table, emptying her arms. She was just in time. Three feet away, he launched himself into the air. Ann braced herself against the impact as seventeen pounds of gray fur landed in her arms.

It was Oscar's preferred method of greeting. It had been cute when he was a kitten. If he got any bigger, it was going to become life threatening, but Ann didn't have the heart to discourage him. It was nice to have someone excited about seeing her at the end of the day.

She carried the huge tomcat into the kitchen and set him on the floor. He jumped up on a stool and sat down to watch her make a snack. It was a ritual they carried out every afternoon. Oscar never begged for scraps, but if Ann happened to be fixing something he particularly liked, he was not above an occasional moan of hunger. He was judicious in his use of this technique. But roast beef was well worth the effort.

"Moocher." Ann chose a pink slice of beef and cut it into Oscar-size bites. He waited politely until she'd set the saucer on the floor before launching himself toward the treat. The meat was gone before Ann had finished making her sandwich, and Oscar returned to his stool to keep her company while she ate.

She set the plate down and then poured herself a glass of milk. Before she sat down to enjoy her snack, she slipped off her jacket and unbuttoned the first three buttons of her blouse. Her shoes had been abandoned on the way to the kitchen. She sat down but didn't reach for the sandwich. For just a moment she savored the stillness of the apartment. It wasn't that the hospital was noisy, but it was filled with such self-conscious quiet that there were times when she would have welcomed some healthy noise.

"I saw McCallister in the hall. He looked like he'd been up all night. Again. It's a good thing he doesn't try to hold down a job. It might interfere with his love life."

Oscar looked up from the paw he was washing and murmured sympathetically. He was familiar with the problem of McCallister. Ann smiled at the cat and took a healthy bite of her sandwich. Oscar was a great audience. He always agreed with her.

She chewed slowly, her eyes focused on nothing in particular. What was it about Flynn McCallister that never failed to irritate her? When she'd first moved in, she'd been prepared to be a cordial neighbor. Her father had pointed out that the McCallister family was wealthy and old power. Ann wasn't terribly interested in her neighbor's antecedents as long as he was quiet and didn't expect to borrow a cup of sugar at two-thirty in the morning.

At least that's what she thought before she'd met Flynn McCallister. He seemed to fit her simple criteria for neighborly behavior. He didn't throw wild parties. He was always polite. He'd never asked to borrow a cup of sugar at any time of day or night. In fact, they didn't run into each other very often. Sometimes it was a week or more between sightings.

Considering how little she saw of him, he took up an inordinate amount of room in her thoughts. Most of it hostile. It was the way he looked at her. Every time they met, those electric blue eyes seemed to strip her naked. And it wasn't just her clothes he was seeing through. It was as if he could see right through to her soul. Not that she had anything to hide, Ann told herself. It was just that she didn't like feeling naked in front of a total stranger.

And it didn't help at all to know that it was deliberate. He knew exactly what he was doing. He enjoyed flustering her. It annoyed Ann that he could read her so easily, and it annoyed her even more that she couldn't control her reaction to him. She was a doctor. People's lives rested in her hands every day. Control was essential in her work, and it carried over into her private life. With nothing but a look and a quirk of an eyebrow, Flynn McCallister managed to weaken that control, and she resented it.

It was resentment that made her feel so flushed and breathless when he looked at her. It was simple curiosity that made her wonder what it would feel like when he kissed someone. Not her, of course. She had no desire to kiss a man who couldn't even hold a job. It was just that he'd probably kissed a lot of women and she'd never been kissed by an expert. It was natural that she was curious.

"But we know where curiosity gets you, don't we, Oscar? Look what happened to the cat." Oscar blinked at her and then hopped down off the stool and trotted into the living room. "Oh dear. Maybe I shouldn't have mentioned it."

His tail disappeared around the corner with an indignant flip and Ann giggled. It was a girlish sound that would have surprised a lot of people who thought they knew her. Her colleagues at work had never heard Dr. Perry giggle. It was rare for her to bestow so much as a smile on anyone but a patient.

Despite the fiery warmth of her hair, she had a reputation for being icy cold. She did her work with a slightly feverish dedication that earned her respect, but she kept too much distance between herself and her colleagues to earn anything more than respect.

When Ann took time to think about it, she told herself she preferred it that way. She didn't really have time for all the foolish machinations that seemed to go along with friendships. Her work was too important to her. It filled her life quite nicely. If there were times when she saw two nurses laughing together and felt a little wistful, it was only when she was tired.

The phone rang, startling her out of her thoughts, and she jumped. It rang again, but she didn't move immediately. It would be her father. He would want a progress report. How did she tell him that a medical career wasn't like being a corporate executive where every day she could report some deal closed, some new advance toward a vice presidency? The triumphs of helping a patient didn't interest him in the least. He wanted to know where her career was going. He thought she was progressing too slowly.

The phone rang again, and she got to her feet. If she didn't answer it now, he would only call again later. Besides, it was wonderful that he was so interested in her career. It showed that he loved her.

Twenty minutes later she put down the phone, feeling more drained than when she'd left the hospital. Why couldn't she make him understand that medicine was usually a day-to-day grind with occasional advances? You didn't start out as a medical student and work your way to head of staff in ten days or less. Why couldn't he be proud of what she *had* accomplished instead of demanding to know why she hadn't done more? She suppressed the question before it had a chance to take root. He *was* proud of her. He just didn't know how to show it. He wasn't a demonstrative man, that's all.

She wandered back to the kitchen table and picked up her half-eaten sandwich. The food didn't look as good as it had a few minutes ago. She wrapped the sandwich in plastic wrap and rinsed out her milk glass. She was just tired. That's why her father's call was upsetting. That's why Flynn McCallister had seemed particularly dangerous.

She'd planned to go out and do some shopping, but maybe it would be a good idea to take a long hot bath and spend the evening with a book. She could use the time to unwind. She had the next two days off, and a relaxing evening at home would be a nice way to start her small vacation.

She left the kitchen and headed toward her bedroom, but she was sidetracked by Oscar who was sprawled flat on his back in the middle of the living-room floor. She stopped to scratch his ample tummy, and he took it as an invitation to play, wrapping his paws around her arm and chewing on her hand. His teeth sank gently into her fingers, careful not to bite too hard, and Ann responded by twisting her hand back and forth.

The sudden pounding on the door interrupted the playful wrestling match. Ann jumped, jerking her hand away from the cat so suddenly that she inflicted a scratch on her arm when his claws sprang out in automatic reaction to the sudden noise. Oscar rolled to his feet and streaked for the safety of the bedroom.

Ann stood up, staring at the door warily. No one had rung up from the lobby. Her father had just called her from the other side of town, and he was the only person she'd given the elevator code to. Of course, there was no telling how many people McCallister had handed out the code to. Maybe it was a friend of his who was too drunk to realize he had the wrong door.

The pounding started again. She would direct whoever it was to the correct apartment and then she'd make it a point to complain to the management company. McCallister couldn't just go around giving out security codes.

She grasped the doorknob, full of righteous indignation. This time he'd gone too far. It was one thing for him to be out at all hours of the day and night, and it was none of her business how many bimbos he brought home with him, but this was a matter of her own personal safety. She couldn't have him giving privileged information to all and sundry.

She yanked the door open, ready to give whoever it was her iciest look—the one that had been known to cow junior nurses at a glance. She'd make it clear that she didn't approve of his intrusion on her time. Her lips parted to deliver a scathing put-down, but not a word emerged. Instead of the inebriated sot she'd expected to see, she was nose to nose with a masculine chest. Broad, muscled and matted with hair. She knew it was matted with hair because it was bared to her gaze. In fact, there was not a stitch of clothing in sight. Her eyes dropped automatically to find that the only apparel her visitor was wearing was a towel—a rather small one—knotted carelessly around his hips. Her eyes jerked upward, and she took an automatic step backward.

The last thing she'd expected to find on her doorstep was Flynn McCallister, clad in nothing but a towel and a panicked expression.

Chapter Three

She was so disconcerted by this unexpected apparition that it took her several seconds to make any sense out of his words. Despite her best efforts, her eyes kept falling to his chest. There was something about that expanse of masculine skin that put a catch in her breathing and made her feel flushed.

She blinked, forcing her mind to function again. He was saying something. She dragged her eyes from his chest and looked at his face. Something was wrong. What was he saying?

"...in the shower and she fell. There's blood all over. I don't think a Band-Aid is going to do it. Maybe she needs stitches. You've got to come and take a look at her."

The doctor in her took over at the mention of blood. "I'll be right there. Keep her quiet and apply firm pressure to the wound. I'll get my bag."

Flynn disappeared in a flurry of blue towel and Ann hurried back into the living room. She grabbed up her bag, her mind working a mile a minute. The doctor in her was speculating on what the medical situation might be, wondering if it would be necessary to call for an ambulance. The woman, shoved well to the back, was speculating on other things, like whether or not her neighbor lifted weights. That would explain those sleek muscles that had rolled so easily under his skin.

In the shower and she fell. Flynn's half-heard explanation popped into her head, and her lips tightened in disapproval. Obviously, he had been cavorting in the shower with a woman, and she'd fallen. Probably hit her head, which would explain all the blood. There was a small, nasty part of Ann that muttered that she probably deserved it.

None of these frantic thoughts slowed her pace as she hurried out of her apartment and across the carpeted hall. She entered his apartment through the open door. She didn't have to look far for her patient. Flynn was kneeling on the floor next to one of the sofas, his naked back blocking Ann's view.

"She's a doctor and she'll know just what to do." His voice was soothing and full of confidence. A good bedside manner, she noted absently.

"But you said that a dragon lived next door." The voice was definitely feminine and just as definitely under ten years of age.

Ann tripped on the steps that had almost been Flynn's downfall the night before. Her recovery was not as graceful as his had been, but she didn't have the advantage of eight hours of steady drinking under her belt.

Flynn glanced over his shoulder, his face expressing his relief at her presence in the moment before he turned back to his companion. "I was kidding about that. She's really very nice." He didn't sound in the least embarrassed at having it revealed that he'd called her a dragon. Ann filed the words away to examine at some other time. Right now, what mattered was her patient.

Stepping around Flynn, she knelt by the sofa. Other than being female, the child bore no resemblance to her hasty image of a woman who'd been cavorting in Flynn's shower. She was small-boned and fragile with a mop of badly cut sandy hair that was matted with blood on one side. Her gray eyes were swimming with tears and an occasional sob shook her thin frame. She examined Ann solemnly without releasing her hold on Flynn's left hand. His right hand held a kitchen towel to the side of her head.

The scenario was not quite what Ann had been expecting, but the injury was exactly what she'd expected. Head wounds were always frightening, but they had a tendency to bleed out of all proportion to their seriousness.

"Becky, this is Ann. She's going to take care of your head for you."

Ann smiled at the little girl, unaware of the way her face lit and softened with the smile. "Hi, Becky. It looks like you smacked your head pretty good." She eased the towel away and was relieved to see that the actual wound itself was not too bad. A small cut at the end of Becky's eyebrow still oozed blood sullenly, but it wasn't enough to warrant stitches.

"Are you going to stick a needle in me?" Becky's lip quivered at the thought.

"I don't think we need to do that. A bandage should take care of this."

"I was in the shower and I heard her fall. I don't know what happened. She was looking at magazines when I went into the bathroom." Flynn's voice was tight with concern.

"I was just trying to get a closer look at that picture on the wall, Mr. Flynn. I stood up on the sofa, but I slipped on a book and hit my head on the table." Ann glanced over her shoulder at the coffee table. It was a massive affair of glass and wood. Becky was probably lucky the damage was as minor as it was.

"Is she going to be all right?" Flynn hadn't moved from his position beside Becky, but he managed to give off an aura of hovering that made Ann want to swat him like an obnoxious fly.

"She's going to be fine. Why don't you go boil some water?"

He seemed relieved to have something to do, and he hurried off to the kitchen. Ann watched him leave, trying to convince herself that he looked ridiculous in the barely decent towel. It didn't work. In fact, he looked distressingly sexy. She dragged her mind and her eyes back to her small patient.

Becky's eyes met hers solemnly, more than a trace of uncertainty in their depths. Ann smiled and the look faded a bit, but it wasn't replaced by trust. Ann had a feeling that this was not a child who trusted easily.

"What's the water for?"

"Nothing. He was making me nervous."

The little girl's eyes widened. "You mean you don't really need any water?"

"Nope. I don't need it at all. Men aren't very good at coping with things like this. They get all upset. I thought it would be a good idea if we got him out of our hair."

"Won't Mr. Flynn be mad?"

"I don't think so." Ann set the bloodstained towel on the glass-topped coffee table. Becky winced when Ann tried to cleanse the wound, and Ann gave her a reassuring smile. "This may sting a little bit, but it won't hurt much, I promise."

"Mama always says that but it hurts a lot."

"Well, maybe your mother doesn't have the right stuff so it hurts more than she thinks it will. But I'm a doctor and this is a special cleanser that doesn't hurt a lot. Okay?"

The gray eyes studied Ann for a long moment, weighing and considering in a very adult manner. Ann didn't try to rush the decision, letting Becky take her time. It was much easier to work with children if they felt they had some control over what was happening to them. Becky finally nodded, apparently making up her mind that she'd trust Ann this time.

She dabbed the cotton against the cut, feeling the tension in Becky's frame. "Is Flynn a friend of your mom and dad's?" The question had two purposes. One was to distract Becky. If she had something else to think about, she wouldn't have as much time to worry about what Ann might be doing. The other purpose was to find out what Flynn McCallister was doing with a little girl in his apartment. Over the past two years, she'd seen him with a number of women, but none of them looked the type to be mothers.

"I don't have a dad. Me and Mom do just fine without him."

"I'm sure you do. Then Flynn must be a friend of your mom's?" What kind of woman would leave her child in the care of a playboy like McCallister?

"Nope."

Ann's hand stilled a moment. "Well, then, how do you know him?"

"I found him last night."

"You *found* him?"

"Yup."

"How did you find him?" Ann's hand continued to move automatically.

"He sat on me."

"Sat on you?" She was beginning to feel like a parrot, repeating everything Becky said.

"Uh-huh. And then, he said it wasn't fair that he had lots of beds and I didn't have any so I could use one of his beds."

"Wait a minute. He sat on you and then offered you a place to sleep? Where did you meet him?"

"In the alley."

"What alley?" This was starting to sound like a vaude-
ville routine.

"The one back of this building."

"What were you doing there and what was Flynn doing
there?"

"Well, I was sleeping and Mr. Flynn was real drunk. I'm
not sure what he was doing there, but after he sat on my
foot we came up here. That's when he told me a dragon
lived next door, only I don't think you're a dragon. I think
you're pretty nice."

"Thank you." Ann applied a small butterfly bandage to
the wound, tugging the edges of the cut together. "There.
I think you're just about fixed up. We need to wash the
blood out of your hair and you'll be just as good as new."

Becky sat up, cautiously fingering the bandage on her
head. "It doesn't feel very big." There was an element of
disappointment in the words, and Ann hid a grin as she
repacked her medical bag. Was there a child anywhere who
didn't relish the idea of a big bandage to show off once
they were sure the injury itself was taken care of?

"It really wasn't a very big cut, just a nasty one. Don't
tug on the bandage and don't get it wet. In a few days we'll
take it off and you'll hardly be able to tell that you were
ever hurt."

She lifted her head and was surprised to find that Becky
was holding out her hand, her small face very solemn.
"Thank you, Miss..." Her face scrunched up in thought
and then she shook her head. "I can't remember your
name."

"Ann. Ann Perry." Since it seemed to be expected of
her, Ann took Becky's hand and shook it, biting the inside
of her lip to hold back a smile at the quaintly adult gesture.
"You're very welcome. I'm glad I was here."

"I've got the water ready. Should I put it in a bowl?"
Flynn stood at the top of the steps, his expression anx-

ious. He looked like a tousled satyr. Three-quarters naked, his hair mussed, his face unshaven. Becky knelt to look over the back of the sofa at him and then she turned to look at Ann, her eyes sparkling with mischief. Ann couldn't help but grin.

"You can put it in the sink."

Flynn frowned. "The sink? That's not very sterile, is it?"

"It doesn't matter."

"Doesn't matter? Shouldn't things that contact an open wound be sterile?"

"It's not going to contact an open wound. We're all done."

"All done? Then what's the boiling water for?"

"You were hovering. I had to give you something to do."

"You mean I boiled that water for nothing?"

"You could make tea."

Becky giggled at Flynn's indignant expression. He glared at Ann a moment longer, well aware that she was enjoying this. Ann gave him her most bland smile, the one she reserved for pushy salesclerks. She was relieved when his eyes shifted to Becky.

"Well, urchin, you certainly look a lot less gruesome than you did a few minutes ago."

"Ann says that in a few days I'll be good as new."

"Why don't we rinse that blood out of your hair and get you a change of clothes and then it will be hard to tell that you've endured a terrible ordeal."

He stepped down into the living room and then grabbed for the towel as it threatened to fall. He flushed, but Ann's face turned scarlet. She was a doctor, she'd seen plenty of naked men, but she had the feeling she wasn't going to be able to put Flynn McCallister in the same category as her patients. She stood up, hoping he wouldn't notice the color in her face.

"Why don't I take care of Becky and you can get some clothes on?"

Flynn hesitated a moment and then looked at Becky. The little girl didn't seem to have any objections to Ann's suggestion. He smiled, and Ann felt her pulse pick up at the sheer beauty of the expression. When he smiled like that, he looked almost angelic. But she doubted that angels had muscles like that.

"Good idea. This towel isn't really the best thing for entertaining. Becky can show you her room. Her clothes are in there and there's a bathroom right next door."

He disappeared into the hallway. Ann and Becky followed more slowly. The room he'd given Becky was, like the rest of the apartment, beautifully decorated. Everything was of the highest quality. The McCallisters were hardly hurting for money so that wasn't surprising. What was surprising was the empty feel of the room. Not just empty because no one lived there, but empty like something that had once held life and was now drained. Ann felt a shiver run up her spine.

"It's pretty, isn't it?" She looked down at Becky and forced a smile. The word that came to mind was dead, but she could hardly say that to a child.

"Very pretty. Now, where are your clothes? We'll get you cleaned up."

Becky lifted a worn shopping bag onto the bed and carefully took out a stuffed giraffe and set him on the bed. Next came a well-thumbed book and a scuffed jewelry case. The final layer was clothing, folded as neatly as childish hands could manage.

Ann's heart twisted when she realized what she was seeing. This was clearly everything Becky owned in the world. She sat down on the edge of the bed and picked up the giraffe, keeping her head bent over the toy so that Becky wouldn't see the tears in her eyes.

"That's Frankie."

"He's very nice."

"I've had him since I was a baby."

"Did your mother give him to you?"

Becky hesitated a minute and then shook her head. "I think Daddy gave him to me."

Ann fingered the distinctive button in the toy's ear and filed away that bit of information.

"Daddy gave me this book, too."

Ann set the stuffed toy down and picked up the book. It was *A Child's Garden of Verses,* a beautiful leather-bound edition, old and much worn, showing the love of more than one generation.

"Was this your daddy's when he was a little boy?"

"I don't know. Mama doesn't much like to talk about him." She took the book from Ann and set it next to the giraffe, clearly saying that the subject was closed. Ann accepted her lead, knowing that you didn't win a child's confidence by pushing.

"Is this all your clothes?"

"Most of 'em. When Mama comes home we're going to go shopping. She says I'm growing like a weed."

Ann nodded and picked up a pair of jeans and a long-sleeved blue shirt. There wasn't a whole lot of choice. Other than the garments in her hand, there was one other pair of jeans with the knees worn out and a short-sleeved pullover that looked too small.

"Well, let's get you changed and your hair washed."

Becky chattered confidently while Ann rinsed her hair, careful to keep the wound dry. There was a hair dryer in the bathroom cabinet, and it took only a few minutes to dry the little girl's hair. Ann borrowed a bobby pin from her own hair and pinned Becky's fine bangs back away from her face.

Looking in the bathroom mirror, she was aware that her neat chignon was beginning to look more than a little scruffy. She pushed at a few straggling strands, but there wasn't really much she could do. Not that it mattered what she looked like. Becky didn't care and Flynn McCallister's opinion was less than important.

Ann and Becky were in the living room, standing by the balcony doors when Flynn entered from the hall. He'd taken time to finish his interrupted shower, but he hadn't bothered to shave. Wearing a pair of jeans that were just snug enough to be interesting and a blue chambray shirt that he was still buttoning, he looked distressingly attractive.

It was pure dislike that made her feel slightly breathless. It had nothing to do with an urge to lay her palm against his chest and see if the hair felt as crisp as it looked. It had nothing to do with the way his shirt clung to his damp skin, outlining every muscle. It was nothing but dislike.

"Becky, why don't you go out and take a look at the plants on the balcony. I want to talk to Flynn."

Flynn stopped a few feet away and looked at her, one dark brow arching in question. Becky looked from one to the other and her pale brows puckered.

"Are you going to fight?"

"No."

"Maybe."

Ann flashed Flynn a quelling look that didn't appear to faze him in the least. "We're not going to fight, Becky. We're just going to talk."

Becky looked at Flynn, clearly more willing to trust his judgment than Ann's. "Go on out, urchin. There's some hand tools in the box next to the door. Why don't you dig in one of the empty planters. I promise we're not going to come to blows.''

The late summer sun was low in the sky, but it would be another hour or more before the light was gone. The upper floor of the building was smaller than the floors below, allowing for a large roof garden for each apartment. Ann hired professional gardeners to care for her garden. It was lovely, not a leaf out of place, and she seldom paid any attention to it. Flynn's garden was considerably less neat. Plants sprawled wherever their fancy took them. Some of the planters were empty, while others held such a wealth of vegetation, it was hard to distinguish one plant from another. It was the perfect place for a child to play. She watched Becky disappear into the jungle of growth, trowel in hand.

The smile that softened her mouth disappeared when she turned to look at Flynn. ''I think we need to have a talk, Mr. McCallister.''

That irritating brow arched. ''Call me Flynn. It's much easier to get out when you're yelling at someone.''

''I have no intention—''

''Sure you do. I recognize the look. My mother tried calling me Mr. McCallister when she was angry. She thought it might have more impact but then my father would think she was yelling at him and he'd get mad at her and...well, you can see how much simpler it is if you just call me Flynn. Would you like some coffee? Don't tell Becky, but her coffee is a potential weapon.''

He moved toward the kitchen, leaving Ann no choice but to follow. She wasn't quite sure he'd done it, but somehow he'd managed to take control of the situation from her.

In the kitchen, he began making coffee and Ann made an effort to bring the conversation back to where it belonged.

"I don't want any coffee, thank you. I want to talk about Becky."

"It's your loss. I make an excellent cup of coffee."

"I don't care about coffee. I want to talk about that little girl." When he glanced at her this time, his mouth had quirked to match the eyebrow, making Ann aware that her voice had risen. She wasn't shouting but she was perilously close. She took a deep breath, drawing on her considerable self-control and forced her voice to a calm level.

"I think there are some questions that need to be answered."

"Ask away." Since the invitation was punctuated by his turning on the coffee grinder, Ann had doubts about his sincerity. She waited until the machine had stopped running and then continued as if the interruption hadn't occurred.

"I'd like to know just what Becky is doing here."

He poured the coffee into the filter and turned to look at her as if he questioned her sanity. "She's playing on the balcony."

Ann ground her teeth together. The man was being deliberately obtuse and infuriating. She knew he was doing it deliberately, but it didn't seem to curb the rapid climb of her blood pressure.

"Mr. McCallister, I'm willing to stand here all night and play word games with you but it's not going to do either of us any good. I'm concerned about that child and I am going to get the answers I want."

Flynn poured water into the coffee maker and then leaned one leg against the counter and studied her. Ann felt a flush come up in her cheeks. She didn't have to look at herself to know what he was seeing. Her hair was coming down around her ears, her suit jacket was gone, her blouse was undone at the throat, her skirt was probably wrinkled and, to top it off, she wasn't wearing shoes. She made a less than imposing figure and she knew it.

Whether it was the determined set of her chin or something else that only he saw, Flynn seemed to make up his mind to cooperate, at least up to a point.

"I haven't said thank-you for what you did for Becky. I'm not sure who was more frightened, her or me. I really appreciate the way you came over here and patched her up."

"You're welcome. It is my job."

"Not when you're off duty. I'm truly grateful."

"It really wasn't that big a deal." *Damn the man!* Just when she thought she had control of the situation, he did something to throw her off balance again. Did he have to sound so sincere?

"It was a big deal to Becky and me." The coffee maker pinged, and he turned and got two cups down out of the cupboard. He filled them with coffee and handed one to Ann. "If you don't want it, I'll drink it. Let's go into the living room and get comfortable. We can keep an eye on the balcony from there."

Once again, she found herself trailing after him, not quite sure how he'd managed to turn the situation around. Somehow, the edge of her anger had been blunted. She settled onto an off-white overstuffed chair and then realized it was a tactical error. The chair didn't just invite you to sit back and relax, it insisted that you do so. The huge puffy cushions practically swallowed her. There was no way she could use any effective body language in this chair. On the other hand, she couldn't change seats without looking like an idiot. She shot Flynn an annoyed look, wondering if he'd done this deliberately, but he'd settled into an identical chair and managed to look completely in command of himself, the furniture and the situation. Ann felt like a little girl sitting in her father's chair. She could barely move to set her coffee cup down on an end table—the coffee she hadn't wanted, she remembered irritably.

"What did you want to talk about?"

"Becky."

"What about her?" His eyes were cool and watchful.

"I want to know what she's doing here. And don't tell me that she's playing on the balcony. She said that you found her in the alley last night and offered her a bed. Is that true?"

"Pretty much."

"How could you!"

"You think it would have been better to leave her in the alley?"

"That's not what I mean!"

"Then what did you mean?"

"Mr. McCallister—"

"Flynn. It's much easier to spit out."

Ann ground her teeth together. "Flynn. Didn't it occur to you that her mother would be worried about her? You should have contacted her immediately. I've always known that you were irresponsible but I wouldn't have believed that even you would do something like this. That poor woman must be out of her mind with worry."

"You've always known that I was irresponsible? You must have amazing powers of observation, Ms. Perry. Considering that your only contact with me over the past two years has been a few barbs exchanged in the hallway. On what do you base this sweeping judgment?"

Ann opened her mouth but he cut her off with a sharp gesture. "I don't really want to hear it. Your opinion of me is neither here nor there. Becky's mother disappeared two weeks ago. The landlady was about to turn Becky over to Social Services. Becky is terrified of them so she ran away. She's been living on the streets for the past few days. No matter how irresponsible I am, I think I'm a better bet than the streets."

"That's not the issue."

"Just what is the issue, Ms. Perry? Do you think I'm going to corrupt her?"

He was backing her into a corner and she didn't like the feeling. Somehow, he'd managed to put her in the wrong. She felt trapped—physically and verbally.

"She says you were intoxicated last night."

"Smashed to the gills."

"You can't possibly think that's a good influence for a child."

"I don't think it's going to put a permanent warp on her psyche to see a man drunk."

"The fact that you drink to excess doesn't make you a particularly good guardian for a child, even temporarily."

"I do not drink to excess on a regular basis."

Ann flushed angrily at the prissy tone he used to repeat her words. "I suppose last night was a special occasion."

"In a manner of speaking. It was my brother's birthday."

"And that's supposed to make it all right? The two of you go out and—"

"Not the two of us. I was alone. Mark died three years ago."

Ann wondered if it were possible to coax the huge chair into swallowing her completely. "I'm sorry."

There was a moment of silence and then Flynn ran his fingers through his hair. The crooked smile he gave her was half apology and wholly charming.

"I'm the one who should be sorry. I know you're concerned about Becky and I shouldn't be giving you such a hard time."

"She can't just continue to stay here. You've got to let someone know where she is. Maybe the Social Services people *should* be called." The suggestion was made without force.

"No. Becky's terrified of them. Probably with good reason. There are some pretty flaky sounding circumstances surrounding her mother. They just might take Becky away from her.''

''Then, what are you going to do?''

He rubbed his forehead and Ann noticed his pallor for the first time.

''Either I'm getting too old to drink like that or hangovers are getting worse. I'm not sure what I'm going to do about Becky. I thought I'd take her out to my parents' home tomorrow. They may have some ideas. You're welcome to come along just to make sure that I don't sell her to the white slavers.'' He grinned to show her that there was no rancor behind the words.

Of course she wasn't going to get involved any further. It was none of her business what happened to either of them. She'd done all that could be expected of her. Naturally, she would turn down his invitation. She was going to get out of her chair and say a polite good-night—she'd even wish him luck—and then she was going to go back to her own apartment and her simple, uncomplicated life. The only male she wanted to deal with right now was Oscar, who didn't have any of the dangerous seductive qualities of Flynn McCallister.

''If you wouldn't mind, I'd feel better seeing this a little farther. I don't know why. I hardly know Becky.''

''There's something about her that sort of gets under your skin.''

Ann nodded, suppressing the thought that Becky might not be the only one.

Chapter Four

"Are you sure you don't want another piece of pizza, Mr. Flynn?"

Flynn stared at the slice of pizza Becky was holding out and swallowed hard. Red with tomato sauce and dripping with cheese, it couldn't have looked more deadly to him if it had been laced with cyanide.

"No thanks. You two go ahead and split it." One thing he'd forgotten about hangovers was that, no matter how bad you felt when you woke up, you could count on it being the best you'd feel all day.

He pushed his chair back from the table, as much to get away from the food as to get more comfortable, and studied his companions. Twenty-four hours ago, he'd never have believed that he'd be sitting across the table from one small refugee and one hostile neighbor. To tell the truth, the refugee was easier to imagine than Ann. Who would have believed that the dragon across the hall would have such a pretty smile?

He looked at Becky, his face softening. She'd lost the wary look she'd had just a few short hours ago. She seemed completely at home. Tomorrow he'd have to figure out what to do with her, but for tonight, he just wanted her to be a child. He had the feeling that she'd spent too little time doing that.

"Parcheesi." Ann and Becky looked at him. Becky looked intrigued; Ann looked suspicious. He grinned at them both. "What we need is a nice game of Parcheesi before bed."

"I don't think—"

"I love Parcheesi."

Ann swallowed the rest of her protest and managed to look enthused. Board games were right below jogging on her list of fun things to do. She'd never understood why people thought it was fun to move little pieces of plastic around a sheet of cardboard. In her experience, it led to arguments and irritation and hurt feelings. But then she'd never played with Flynn McCallister.

Over the next two hours, she learned that not everyone was like her father, who went about playing a game the way he went about life—you were there to win and nothing else mattered. Flynn didn't seem to think that winning was all that important. His only goal was to have fun, and he took just as much pleasure in losing as he did in winning. He coached Becky, he coached Ann, and he didn't seem to care that they trounced him every time.

It was a novel experience and one that wasn't entirely welcome. She didn't want to like Flynn. Not only had she grown accustomed to their antagonistic relationship over the past two years—she felt safe with it. Something told her that Flynn McCallister might be dangerous if he got any closer than arm's length. She wasn't quite sure just how he'd be dangerous, but she didn't doubt that the danger was real.

After four games of Parcheesi, both adults called a halt to any further games. Becky looked as if she'd like to protest, but didn't feel confident enough of her position to argue. Flynn ruffled her hair as he put the lid on the game box.

"We'll play again, urchin. And next time, I won't go so easy on the two of you."

"Does that mean you're not going to lose every game, Mr. Flynn?"

Ann couldn't help but grin at the way the little girl got straight to the point. Flynn gave her a stern look but she could see the laughter in his eyes. She couldn't remember ever knowing someone who could laugh at themselves so readily. Was there anything that he took seriously?

"That means I'm not going to lose every game." He slid the game onto the top shelf of a cupboard and Ann tried not to notice the way his jeans molded to his thighs. The man was just too attractive to be safe.

"Time for a bath, I think." He rubbed his forehead as he spoke and, for the first time in hours, Ann remembered that he'd spent the better part of the previous night drinking.

Against her will, she felt sorry for him. She'd never had a hangover herself but it couldn't be pleasant. No matter how much she disapproved of his drinking, she couldn't help but take pity on him. If his head was hurting as much as she suspected, he could use a short break from his role as host and baby-sitter.

"Why don't I help you with your bath, Becky? I want to be sure you keep that bandage dry."

Ann ignored the grateful glance Flynn threw her. She didn't want him to get the idea that she was doing this for him. When she and Becky returned to the living room, Flynn was looking a little less pale, but Ann told herself that she only noticed because her medical training made it impossible to ignore.

He smiled at Becky, but his eyes skimmed over her and Ann knew he'd seen the threadbare condition of her pajamas. He didn't say anything that might hurt Becky's pride.

"Ready for bed?"

"I'm not tired." A yawn punctuated the end of the sentence and Ann saw Flynn bite his lip against a smile.

"Well, Ann and I are very tired so why don't you humor us and hop into bed. You can sleep in the room you had last night."

"Okay." She turned away and then looked over her shoulder at him. "Are you going to tuck me in?" The question was hesitant, as if she were afraid he'd refuse.

"I wouldn't miss it for the world. We'll both tuck you in."

Lying in the huge bed, the covers tucked under her chin, Becky's youth and fragility were more apparent than ever. She was such a plucky little thing that it was easy to forget just how young she was.

Flynn sat on the edge of the bed and brushed the hair back from her forehead. "Tomorrow, we're going to go visit my parents and we'll decide what to do about you."

"You won't give me to the welfare, will you?" Her thin fingers came up to clutch his hand.

"I won't give you to the welfare people. I promise. But we've got to decide how to go about finding your mom. She's going to be worried about you when she gets home and you're not there."

Ann moved to sit on the other side of the bed. "I'm going to go with you to visit Flynn's parents."

"We'll have a great time." Flynn brushed the hair back from Becky's face and smiled at her. Ann was stunned to feel a twinge of envy. She wanted that smile turned her way. The realization was so surprising that she almost got up and ran out of the apartment, as if getting away from him was the only way to protect herself. But protect herself from what?

"Could you tell me a story, Mr. Flynn? Mama always tells me a story 'fore bedtime."

Ann barely listened as he began to spin a story full of

the requisite number of dragons and princesses and hand-some princes. She didn't want to hear the soft rise and fall of his voice. She didn't want to see the way his eyes soft-ened when he looked at Becky. She didn't want to like him. It wasn't safe.

She was so absorbed in her thoughts that she jumped when he touched her arm. Her eyes focused on his face and then quickly shifted away, afraid that he might be able to see her confused thoughts. Becky was fast asleep, her lashes lying in soft crescents against her cheeks. She didn't stir as the two adults eased themselves off the bed and tiptoed out of the room.

Flynn stopped in the middle of the living room and turned to look at her. He ran his fingers through his hair, ruffling it into thick black waves.

"You can stay the night if it would make you feel better. There's plenty of room."

"No." The word came out too stark, too revealing. She cleared her throat and tried again. "I don't think there's any need for that. I'll just come over in the morning." She edged toward the door. "What time are you thinking of leaving?"

"Sometime after I get up and I have a feeling that, with Becky around, that's not going to be terribly late." He smiled crookedly. "I suspect she's an early riser."

"Probably. Most children seem to be." She edged a little closer to the door. "Well, I guess I'll go home now."

Flynn followed her to the door and Ann was vividly aware of him every step of the way. He reached around her to flip the lock, and it took all her control to keep from shying away from him. If he noticed her tension, he was polite enough not to mention it.

Ann stepped into the hall, feeling as if she were escaping some fatal temptation. "I'll see you tomorrow, then." Reluctantly, she turned to look at him, resisting the urge to run for the haven of her own apartment.

He nodded, stifling a yawn. "Sorry. I guess I'm getting too old for all-night binges. I'll come knock on your door around ten. That should give us plenty of time to get out to my parents' house by lunchtime. My mother puts on a great spread."

"That sounds fine." Ann was aware of him watching her until she opened her own door. She turned, lifting her hand in what she hoped was a casual gesture. "Good night."

"Good night."

She shut the door as quickly as seemed polite, slumping back against the sturdy wood. Oscar looked up from his favorite spot on the hall table, his yellow eyes full of polite inquiry.

"Oh, Oscar. What have I gotten myself into?"

BY THE TIME FLYNN'S CAR pulled into the long driveway of his parents' estate outside Santa Barbara, Ann had convinced herself that her nervousness of the night before was a product of an overtired mind and an overactive imagination. Flynn McCallister was attractive, there was no denying that, but he was also a playboy who seemed to be content to drift through life. She could never be seriously drawn to a man like that.

And, if her heartbeat showed a tendency to accelerate when he was near, that was just hormones. Easily understood and easily controlled.

"Is that where your mom and dad live?" Becky's awed question broke the silence in the Ferrari.

Flynn nodded as he pulled the sleek car to a halt in front of the door. "This is where I grew up."

"It's beautiful."

Flynn studied the building, trying to see it through

Becky's eyes. The house was built along the lines of an antebellum mansion, complete with a wide veranda and sturdy pillars across the front. When he was growing up there, it had just been home.

"I suppose it is."

The door to the house opened as Ann got out of the car and lifted Becky off her lap and onto the gravel drive. The woman who came down the steps was short and elegantly slim. Her dark hair was going gray without any pretensions, and her blue eyes were a much paler reflection of her son's.

Flynn came around the front of the car, his long strides covering the distance between them, catching his mother around the waist and lifting her off the bottom step. She laughed, a girlish sound that made Ann smile. "Put me down, hooligan." He obeyed, his wide smile matching hers. She examined her son with maternal eyes, finally reaching up to pat his cheek.

"We don't see you often enough, Flynn. Your father thought you might call this week."

"Because of Mark's birthday?" His smile twisted. "I celebrated in my own way."

"I know but your father was a bit upset."

"So what else is new? Mom, I want you to meet Ann Perry, my neighbor, and this is Becky Sinclair. I told you about her on the phone. Ann, Becky, this is Louise Mc-Callister, my mother."

The smile Louise turned on Ann and Becky was warm and full of welcome. "I'm so pleased to meet both of you. We're having a late lunch today so you'll have time to rest a bit after the drive from L.A. You must have been crowded in that little sports car. Why didn't you drive the Mercedes, Flynn?"

"Becky preferred the Ferrari, Mom."

"Actually, it wasn't very crowded at all, Mrs. Mc-Callister. Becky doesn't take up much room."

"Call me Louise. Come in and meet my husband."

Ann followed her hostess up the steps, aware of Flynn following behind with Becky. Becky seemed a bit awe-struck by the elegant house, and her hand clung to Flynn's. The interior of the house was as polished as the exterior. Dark mahogany floors and creamy wallpaper created a rich background for the beautiful antiques that filled the hall-way.

Ann's father was a wealthy man and she'd grown up around money. But there was something different here, some indefinable essence. The McCallister home smelled of old money—lots of it. The walls seemed permeated with quiet elegance. Some of the antiques were one of a kind pieces—all of them were exquisite. Despite the decor, it wasn't difficult to imagine Flynn and his brother growing up here. Beneath the rich beauty, the big house felt like a home. A place where two growing boys could have laughed and played without restrictions.

Louise led the way across the hall and into the study where her husband awaited them. The man who stood to greet them was not at all what Ann had expected. She hadn't given much conscious thought to what Flynn's fa-ther would be like, but she'd had a vague image of an older version of Flynn—tall, lean, with elegantly masculine grace.

She hadn't expected a stocky man a few inches short of six feet. His features were blunt, his eyes a clear, sharp gray rather than electric blue. The only resemblance she could see was the thick black hair, now heavily streaked with gray.

His handshake was firm, his look direct, lacking the lazy charm that made his son so fascinating and so exasperating.

"Thank you for allowing me to come, Mr. McCallister."

"I don't blame you for not trusting Flynn with the child. My son isn't known for his sense of responsibility." Ann blinked, wondering if she'd misunderstood him, wondering what she was supposed to say in reply if she hadn't.

"Hello, Dad. Nice to know that some things never change. It's great to see you again, too." There was an edge to Flynn's voice. "Ann, this is my father."

David McCallister nodded to his son, his eyes cool. "Flynn. I thought you might call this week."

"So Mom told me. You know how I always hate to do the expected. Besides, we would have quarreled and that seems like a hell of a way to honor Mark's birthday." His tone closed the subject and there was an uncomfortable silence in the room.

It was Louise who broke it, her expression determinedly cheerful. "Becky, I think the cook was making some cookies this morning. Why don't I take you to the kitchen. I don't think one or two cookies is likely to spoil your lunch."

Becky pressed tighter to Flynn's leg, her eyes wide and uncertain. "I'd like to stay with Mr. Flynn, please."

Flynn sank down to her level, meeting her eyes. "It's okay, honey. Go ahead and go with my mom. I promise I won't disappear without you. We have some things we need to talk about. Grown-up things."

"Are you going to talk about me?"

"Yes. But that's nothing to worry about. We're just going to decide what to do about finding your mother."

"You won't call the welfare, will you?"

"I already told you I wouldn't do that, didn't I? Now, go have some cookies but make sure you save some for me."

He stood up, ruffling her hair. Becky hesitated a moment longer, looking from Flynn to his mother's outstretched hand, and then she moved forward and tentatively placed her small fingers in Louise's palm.

"Are they chocolate chip cookies?"

"I don't know. Why don't we go see?" Ann watched Louise lead the little girl from the room and swallowed an unexpected lump in her throat. No matter what else he was, there was no denying that Flynn was very good with Becky. He showed an understanding of her fears and uncertainties Ann had to admit she couldn't have matched herself.

The door shut behind Louise and Becky and silence descended. At first it wasn't uncomfortable. Ann had never felt that every second had to be filled with talk. She looked around the room, admiring the walls of books, most of them leather bound. One shelf held trophies, another—family photographs. It was a warm room, full of leather and wood. There was a huge bowl of flowers on a table near the door, and the brilliant colors were a perfect accent to the muted tones of the room.

Having looked at the room, she began to notice how the silence had lengthened. She looked at Flynn, who sat in a chair, his long legs stretched out in front of him. His expression was brooding, his attention all for the toes of his sneakers.

His father sat in a chair not far away, but Flynn might not have been there for all the attention the man paid him. He was staring out the window, his face set in bitter lines, his stocky body held rigidly upright against the soft leather of the chair.

Since no one seemed interested in speaking, she moved over to the photos, studying them with an interest that surprised her. It wasn't hard to identify the family members. A younger Louise, her expression as warm as it was now. Her husband, his face a little less stern, his eyes softer. There was a stocky young man who showed up in most of the photos, which must've been Mark. She examined his face, liking the warmth and humor that lit his eyes. There seemed to be a vague melancholy in his eyes, but that could have been her imagination.

And there was Flynn. His lean body lanky with youth and then gradually filling out but retaining that graceful look that was so much a part of his attraction today.

She looked at the photos again, a little uneasy with what she was seeing. There were numerous photos of Mark as football captain in his uniform, at the beach and in almost every other setting. Flynn was in some of the pictures, sometimes in the background, sometimes with his arm over his older brother's shoulder. But there were no photos of Flynn alone. The realization sank in gradually and Ann turned away from the pictures, not wanting to think about the implications of what she was seeing. She didn't want to feel sympathy for Flynn McCallister. He was dangerous enough without adding that emotional complication.

The silence had stretched out behind her, making an almost visible presence in the big room. She cleared her throat.

"You have a lovely home, Mr. McCallister. Flynn tells me he grew up here."

His eyes snapped to her, dark and fierce. "He and his brother Mark both grew up here. Did he mention his brother?"

Ann glanced at Flynn, but he didn't shift his eyes from his shoes. She was on her own. "Flynn told me that his brother died three years ago. That must have been a terrible time for all of you."

"My son Mark was a wonderful boy. He was a police officer. Did Flynn tell you that? Died in the line of duty."

"I didn't know that. You must have been very proud of him."

"I was." He glanced at Flynn without speaking, and his son's eyes came up to meet his. From where Ann sat, there was absolutely no readable expression in his face. Father and son stared at each other across an abyss that had obviously been there for a very long time. Flynn smiled, the insolent smile that Ann had seen so often the past two years, the smile that said he didn't give a damn about the rest of the world.

"Hey, Dad, don't feel too bad. One out of two ain't bad."

The older man's face darkened, and Ann braced herself for the explosion that was sure to follow. She'd seen that look in her own father's eyes too often to mistake it. Why had Flynn provoked him?

The explosion didn't come. She didn't even know if it would have come, because the door opened and Louise stepped into the room. Ann felt as if she'd been thrown a life jacket in the midst of a stormy sea. The older woman's eyes took in the situation immediately, and Ann caught a glimpse of her distress before she set about pouring oil on the waters.

"Are you two at it again? Can't you see you're embarrassing Ann? She's going to think you're a pair of ill-mannered fools. Would you like some lemonade, my dear? Becky is settled in the kitchen and Maggie is teaching her how to bake cookies. I think lunch may be a little late.

"What a charming child. I'm so glad you brought her to see us, Flynn. Exactly what would you like us to do for her?"

The next few hours passed on a more calm note, though Ann had the feeling that the hostilities lay just beneath the surface, ready to break out again. Even when the McCallister men agreed on something, it was grudgingly, as if each were reluctant to admit that the other might have had a good idea. By the time Becky's immediate future was hammered out, Ann felt as if she'd witnessed a battle between the superpowers.

It was agreed that Becky's terror of the welfare department eliminated the possibility of calling the authorities. On the other hand, something had to be done about finding her mother. It was Flynn's suggestion that they call a private detective and, very reluctantly, his father agreed that it seemed like a reasonable alternative. The major disagreement came when the discussion turned to what to do with Becky while the detective searched for her mother.

"Obviously, the child will stay with your mother and I." David McCallister's bluff voice said there would be no argument. Ann felt herself quail at the tone. It was so familiar. Just the way her father always sounded when he was laying down the law.

Flynn did not seem impressed.

"I don't think so. Becky is doing just fine at my place. I don't see any reason why she shouldn't just continue to stay with me until her mother is found."

"Don't be ridiculous. You've got no business being in charge of a little girl. What do you know about children?"

Flynn eyes were sapphire blue and just as hard. "I know that you have to give them room to grow and you have to love them for what they are, not for what you want them to be."

"That's enough, Flynn." Louise's quiet voice discharged the explosion that was building. Flynn pulled his gaze from his father's angry face and glanced at his mother before looking at Ann. He lifted his shoulders in an apologetic shrug, his mouth a cynical line.

"Sorry. We shouldn't drag you into old family quarrels."

"That's okay." But it wasn't okay. She could see the pain in his eyes and she was surprised to find that she ached in sympathy. She had the strangest urge to stroke the tousled hair back off his forehead and hold him close until the pain left his eyes. She dragged her gaze away from him, frightened by the strength of the urge.

The thought slipped into her mind that it was safer to be

hostile to Flynn McCallister. He was a dangerous man to care about.

Once again, it was Louise who brought the conversation back to a more comfortable level.

"We're discussing Becky's welfare here and I think the least we can do is keep that in mind." Her stern gaze took in both her husband and her son. Her husband grunted and looked away. Flynn gave her an unabashed grin.

"You're quite right, Mom. *We* do need to keep that in mind. So what do you suggest?"

"Why don't we ask Becky?" Ann made the suggestion hesitantly, wondering if perhaps she was sticking her nose in where it didn't belong. But she was supposed to be here to help decide Becky's future.

The three McCallisters looked at her with varying degrees of surprise. Louise spoke first.

"What a wonderful idea. I don't know why we didn't think of that right away. Thank you, Ann."

"I love a woman who can think in the midst of battle. Remind me to kiss you first chance I get." Ann flushed, uncomfortably aware that the idea of him kissing her was not as unpleasant as it should be. In fact, it wasn't unpleasant at all.

"You can't expect a child to make a decision like that." David McCallister was the only dissenting voice.

"Why not?" Flynn's question held insolent challenge, all the laughing approval he'd shown Ann gone as if it had never been. His mother rushed into speech, intent on averting a scene.

"Becky seems like a very levelheaded little girl. I think she has a right to have some say in her future. I'll go get her now." She got up and left the room with quick steps, cutting off the possibility of further argument.

The three left behind sat in silence for the short time she was gone. Flynn's father stared into space. Flynn looked at

Ann and Ann looked at the toes of her shoes, unwilling to meet those bright blue eyes, uneasy with the way her pulse seemed to respond to the warmth of his gaze. It seemed as if hours had gone by, but it was no more than a minute or two before Louise returned with Becky.

The two of them had barely entered the room before Becky tugged her hand loose from the older woman's and ran to Flynn's side. Flynn slid his arm around her waist as she leaned against his knee. Looking at the two of them, Ann already knew Becky's answer.

"How were the cookies, urchin?"

"They were great and Maggie let me help her take them off the pan. Could we make cookies when we get home, Mr. Flynn?"

"Sure. But first, we've got a question to ask you." She caught the serious tone of his voice and stared at him, gray eyes wide with uncertainty.

"We're going to hire someone to look for your mom but, until they find her, you need a place to stay."

"Can't I stay with you?" Her voice quivered slightly and Flynn hugged her reassuringly.

"Sure you can, honey. But my parents have said that you can stay here if you want. There's lots of room to play here and I could come out and visit you." He was scrupulously honest in his presentation of the choice but it was clear that, as far as Becky was concerned, there was no choice to be made.

"Do you want me to stay here, Mr. Flynn? Am I too much trouble for you?"

"Of course not, Becky. I'd love to have you with me. But my parents would love to have you here, too. The choice is up to you."

"I want to stay with you, please."

To his credit, Flynn did not give his father a triumphant look. "I'd like that, too."

"MARK AND I USED TO PLAY on those swings. I bet they haven't been used since we were kids." Flynn waved at Becky who was happily absorbed in pumping herself as high as possible.

Lunch had passed without incident and they had been invited to stay to dinner. It was clear that Flynn hadn't wanted to stay but had agreed for his mother's sake and he'd escaped outside as soon as possible, taking Ann and Becky with him. Ann wasn't sorry to get away from the tension that stretched between the men in the family.

It was a beautiful day and the grounds that surrounded the house invited casual strolling. Flynn bent and picked up a stick, tossing it to the elderly retriever who'd followed them from the house. She sniffed at the stick and then looked at Flynn as if to say that he was very foolish if he didn't realize that she was long past the age to chase sticks. "Sorry, Bessy. I forgot."

She yawned once and then turned to make her way toward the house, her steps slightly stiff with age but her dignity unruffled. Flynn watched her cross the wide expanse of lawn that lay between them and the house and then turned back to Ann.

"I can remember when Bessy would beg me to throw sticks for her. I guess I haven't gotten home much these last few years. I tend to forget how old she's getting."

"You and your father don't get along very well, do you?" Ann hadn't planned on asking the question. It was none of her business, and she didn't want to become any more involved with Flynn and his family than she already was. Nevertheless, there the question was and, once asked, she wanted to hear his answer.

"A masterpiece of understatement if I've ever heard one." Flynn's voice was heavy with sarcasm. "My father thinks I'm a playboy and a wastrel. I haven't done any of the things a McCallister is supposed to do. As far as he's concerned, I haven't done anything right since I was born.''

Ann stared at Becky without seeing her. Flynn's words brought back her own childhood too vividly for comfort. "It must have been hard to please him."

Flynn shrugged. "I never tried. At least I quit trying so long ago that I can't remember it ever being different."

"How can you not try to please your father?" The concept was so foreign to her that it was as if he were speaking another language.

"I suppose I might have been more inclined to try if it hadn't been for my older brother. You see, Mark was perfect. My father didn't just *think* he was perfect, he really was." His smile twisted with memories. "He was captain of his football team, captain of the debating team. I swear, in kindergarten, he started out as captain of the clean-up squad. He got straight A's right from the start. He was intelligent, polite, handsome and had a great sense of humor."

He reached out and tugged on a pendulous eucalyptus branch, methodically stripping it of every leaf.

"The awful thing about Mark was that it was all absolutely sincere. He was truly the greatest older brother any kid could want."

"But you couldn't compete." Ann's voice was soft. She knew just how he felt, though her competition had been the ideal of a son who'd never existed outside her father's dreams.

"I couldn't compete." He finished with the branch and reached for another one. "I gave up trying even before I got into school. I don't know, I sometimes think I became a rebel just to give myself an identity. At least Dad noticed me as something other than Mark's shadow. But maybe that's making myself a little too sympathetic. I can't say I don't enjoy doing exactly what I'm doing. The fact that it irritates Dad is just a side effect.''

"Just what do you do?" He slanted her an amused look and Ann flushed, realizing how critical the question sounded. ''I mean, you don't seem to go to work or anything....'' She trailed off, aware that she hadn't done a very good job of explaining what she meant. Maybe it was because she wasn't entirely sure herself.

''That's okay. Not many people recognize my profession.''

He released the branch, letting it snap back into place. The smile he turned on her was brilliant. Ann blinked, not wanting to notice how her heartbeat accelerated under that look.

''Your profession?'' She was barely aware of speaking. Was it possible to get lost in a man's eyes?

''I'm a professional playboy. There aren't many of us left in the world. Our numbers have been decimated by increasing social pressures to be useful and develop careers. I'm one of the last of a dying breed. The truly useless man about town.'' He bowed low before her, and Ann had to bite her lip to hold back a giggle.

''I think you're too hard on yourself. Nobody is completely useless.''

''I am. And proud of it.''

''Don't you get bored?''

''No. There's so much to see in the world. I travel quite a bit. There's never a chance to get bored.''

She shook her head, unable to imagine a life without the limits of work or school to frame the days. ''I can't imagine not having a job.''

''That's the trouble with the world today. Nobody can imagine life without jobs.''

Silence fell between them, not uncomfortable but full of an awareness Ann didn't want to acknowledge. There was something about him that disturbed her in ways she didn't understand. He was so...different. She'd never known anyone like him.

"Hold still." His voice was hushed and Ann froze as he reached toward her. She felt his hand in her hair and when he pulled away, there was a ladybug resting on the tip of his finger. "She was tangled in your hair."

He held his hand up and blew gently. The tiny insect hesitated a moment and then flew away. The shadow of the big eucalyptus wrapped around them. The late summer air was still warm. The scent of the rose garden drifted on the air, a faint hint of perfume.

"You know, for a dragon, you're pretty nice." Flynn's hand came up to tug at a lock of hair that had escaped from her braid, but he lingered, his finger twisted the fiery strand as if tangled in the warmth of its color. "I've always wondered what your hair would look like down." The tone was causal, but there was nothing casual about the way he was looking at her.

"It just looks like hair." Ann told herself she was imagining the breathlessness in her voice.

"I bet it's beautiful."

His head was lowering toward hers, that brilliant blue gaze on her mouth. Her lips were suddenly dry and her tongue came out to wet them, a nervous flicker of movement. She saw his eyes darken and then his hand was slipping around the back of her neck, holding her still. But Ann couldn't have moved if her life depended on it.

His mouth touched hers and her eyelids fell shut as if attached to weights. She stood as if turned to stone, her hands clenched into fists at her sides, her head tilted to accept his kiss.

His mouth was warm and dry. She could smell the faint tang of after-shave. Her lips softened under his coaxing and his hand tightened on the back of her neck, tilting her head farther up. Ann's breath caught as his teeth sank gently into her lower lip. Her mouth opened the smallest amount and the kiss deepened. Their breath mingled until it was impossible to tell where one began and the other ended.

Flynn's free hand settled on her lower back as he stepped closer, and Ann's fingers unclenched, her hands creeping up to rest on his shoulders, her movements tentative.

There was a warmth in the pit of her belly. A warmth that had nothing to do with the weather. Her toes curled inside her shoes as his tongue brushed ever so lightly against her lower lip. She could feel something waiting just out of reach. Something exciting and dangerous and full of promise. Something she wasn't sure she was ready to reach for.

"Mr. Flynn."

The voice seemed to come from a long way away. At first Ann couldn't even make sense of what it was saying.

"Mr. Flyyynnn."

Her eyes opened slowly as Flynn's mouth left hers. In his eyes she could see some of the same surprise she was feeling. Her hands dropped away from his shoulders but he was slower to release her. They stared at each other for a few seconds, neither of them quite sure what to say.

"Mr. Flyyynnn." Becky's high-pitched call wafted toward them and Flynn's hands dropped away from Ann. She took a step back, dragging her eyes away from his face. Whatever had just happened, she wasn't ready to examine it.

"Becky wants you. I...ah...I think I'll go see if I can do something to help your mother with dinner. Set the table or something."

She walked away before he could say anything, but she was aware of his eyes following her until she turned a corner and was shielded by the bulk of the house.

Louise McCallister looked up as Ann all but scuttled into

the room. Her face was flushed and there was a distracted expression in her eyes as if she weren't quite sure where she was or how she came to be there.

"Flynn is with Becky. I thought I might be able to help you with dinner."

Louise bit her lip to conceal a smile and bent her head over her needlepoint. "That's very sweet of you, my dear, but I think Maggie has everything well in hand."

"Of course. How foolish of me."

"Not at all. Why don't you join me in a cup of tea?" She poured the fragrant liquid into a Limoges cup, setting it on the edge of the tea table as Ann sat in the chair across from her.

"Did you enjoy your walk?"

"Yes, the grounds are lovely." Ann picked up her tea cup, and Louise politely pretended not to notice the faint tremor that made the delicate cup rattle in its saucer.

"My husband's mother started the landscaping but I've added to it over the years. It's an ongoing job, of course, but I enjoy it. Have you known Flynn very long?"

The cup rattled but Ann's voice was calm. "I live across the hall from him. We don't really know each other that well. Becky fell and hit her head yesterday and Flynn knew that I was a doctor so he came and got me."

"A doctor. I didn't know that. So you don't know Flynn all that well. I'm surprised. The two of you seem quite comfortable with each other."

"Comfortable? I'm not sure that word applies to Flynn." She realized that her comment might sound like a criticism because she continued hurriedly. "I mean, he just doesn't seem the type—"

Louise laughed. "Don't worry. I know just what you mean. And you're right. The word comfortable and Flynn don't really go together. Now Mark was a different story. He was so easy to get along with. Flynn was always too restless and full of questions. I think that's why he and his father have always had a hard time getting along.

"Mark was a strong boy but he was willing to bend in the direction his father wanted. Flynn is just too much like his father. Neither of them knows how to bend. It's a shame. They have so much to give each other. Flynn especially has so much to give to those he cares about."

She didn't lift her head from her needlepoint. Ann could either take the point or not as she chose. Louise had seen the way Flynn looked at Ann and her maternal instincts were telling her that Ann could be exactly what her son needed in his life. She didn't want to be a pushy parent, but it wouldn't hurt to nudge just a little.

Chapter Five

If Ann had seriously believed that her involvement with Becky and Flynn was going to end after the visit to his parents, she was doomed to disappointment. Over the next few days, the focus of her life seemed to shift.

Ever since graduating from medical school, her life had centered on her work and, before that, it had centered on school. When she took a vacation, she used the time to catch up on medical journals; her visits with her father were spent discussing ways to advance her career.

When she'd thought ahead, she'd never really considered whether or not things were always going to be that way. She'd never given much thought to a husband or children. There'd never been any room to think about them. Somewhere in the back of her mind were the usual dreams of a home and family, but they'd never been given any room to grow and solidify and they'd remained vague, nebulous images without real focus.

Now, in the space of a few hours, her life had been turned upside down. Whether she wished it or not, she was caught up in Becky's life. Through her, Ann was caught up in Flynn McCallister's life. It wasn't that either Flynn or Becky asked her to spend her free time with them. There just didn't seem to be anything else to do.

The morning after the visit to Flynn's parents, she woke

up and told herself that she was not going to go across the hall. This was her day off and she had things to do. Things that didn't include a little girl and a dangerously attractive man.

"Not that *I'm* attracted to him, of course." Oscar stirred and raised his head to blink at her. Ann stared at him in the mirror, aware that she was taking a great deal of time with her makeup, considering that she was planning on relaxing at home. "One kiss is nothing these days. It was a pleasant kiss but no big deal. Flynn McCallister is a playboy. Maybe he's got a heart of gold when it comes to children but he's still a playboy. The man doesn't have a job!"

Oscar yawned. "I may just go over to make sure that Becky is doing all right but then I'm going to come right back here and catch up on my reading. Besides, Flynn probably hasn't been up this early since he was in high school. It might be amusing to see how he's coping with a child in the house."

Oscar yawned again and put his head back down. He knew an excuse when he heard one.

As a matter of fact, Flynn was coping quite well. Self-preservation had led him to get up early and make his own coffee before Becky could bring him some of her deadly brew. When the doorbell rang, he was showered, shaved and fixing breakfast for himself and Becky. Becky was drawing pictures at the table.

"Answer the door, would you, honey?"

"Sure, Mr. Flynn. Should I tell them that we don't want to buy anything?"

"I doubt if it's a salesman. Not if Joe's doing his job."

"Who's Joe?"

"Joe is the man downstairs who's paid to tell salesmen to go away."

"Gee, that sounds like an easy job."

She hopped off her chair and trotted out of the kitchen while Flynn was turning the bacon. He knew it was Ann even before he heard her voice. After all, who else could it be? Everyone else had to ring through from downstairs.

Though his back was to the door, he knew the moment she stepped into the room. It was amazing to think that they'd lived across the hall from each other for two years. Two years and he'd only kissed her yesterday. He'd had his fantasies about his uptight, disapproving neighbor, but none of them had come close to the reality of the way she'd felt in his arms.

He set down the fork and turned to look at her, letting his eyes skim over the emerald-striped top and white pants to settle on the deep red of her hair. He could still remember the feel of it against his hands, and he wanted to cross the room and pull the pins out and let it spill through his fingers.

"Good morning."

Ann felt herself flushing under the look in his eyes, though she couldn't quite put her finger on why. He didn't leer, he didn't ogle, but he made her feel intensely aware of her femininity in a way that was really rather pleasant.

"Good morning. I didn't mean to interrupt your breakfast."

"That's okay. Have a seat and I'll stir up a couple more eggs and you can join us."

Ann protested politely. She never ate breakfast. She detested greasy bacon and equally greasy eggs. The fat and cholesterol content of the average American breakfast was enough to give a person instantly hard arteries. If she ate anything at all, it was a cup of yogurt with a few fresh berries.

"I'm really not hungry."

"There's always room for bacon."

Ten minutes later, she found herself sitting down to a breakfast of bacon, eggs, potatoes and toast and enjoying every bite. Becky ate with the healthy appetite of a growing child, and Ann found her enjoyment of the meal tangled with her enjoyment of the company.

Flynn pushed his plate away and poured himself a second cup of coffee. Ann thought about pointing out the hazards of caffeine and then decided that it was none of her concern. Besides, he didn't look as if caffeine had done any damage to his nerves so far. If anyone had ever been the personification of a laid-back Californian, it was Flynn McCallister.

"Becky and I are going shopping today. Her wardrobe needs updating. Want to join us?" His tone was casual, as if it didn't matter to him one way or another.

Of course she wasn't going to go. She had other things to do with her time. But Becky did need clothing, and could a man—a bachelor—really be trusted to buy suitable clothes for a little girl? Still, it wasn't her problem. The mental argument took only a few seconds and was still waging when she heard herself say, "Sure, I would love to go shopping with you."

Shopping with a man and a little girl was a different experience for Ann. She was a very organized shopper. When she went to a store, she had a specific need in mind and she purchased exactly that need or she bought nothing at all. The only exception to this rule was shoes. She couldn't resist shoes and she had several pairs that she'd probably never find an occasion to wear.

Flynn, on the other hand, didn't try to resist anything. Rather than going to an exclusive children's store and asking a buyer to help them choose a wardrobe for Becky, they drove to a nearby mall. On a Monday afternoon, the stores were reasonably free of crowds, but Ann wasn't sure that this was an advantage. Maybe crowds would have curbed some of Flynn's enthusiasm. As it was, there was nothing to deter him as they swept through the stores, much like Sherman marching through Georgia. Instead of leaving fire and destruction in their wake, they left charge slips and checks. In return, they received promises of immediate delivery.

By the time Ann managed to convince him that Becky had a wardrobe any little girl would kill for, Flynn had thought of toys. Ann shuddered as they invaded the toy store. Within minutes, she'd lost her companions in the high-walled aisles, and she retreated to a bench in the mall to rest her feet and hope that Flynn would remember that Becky would probably prefer a doll to a race car. She needn't have worried. He bought both.

It took Becky and Flynn an hour to come out, loaded down with packages. Clothes could be trusted to be delivered, but toys were another matter altogether. It was hard to tell who was more excited. The last of Becky's reticence had vanished beneath the excitement of being able to buy just what she wanted, and she chattered happily about the Barbie doll Mr. Flynn had bought her, complete with a wardrobe.

"Shoes and everything, Ann." They were on their way to the car to leave off the packages, and Becky's childish voice echoed in the cavernous parking structure. In her excitement at describing every detail of every small garment, Becky slid her hand into Ann's, skipping happily. Ann was unprepared for the rush of feeling the simple gesture brought.

Becky's hand felt so small, so vulnerable. Looking down, Ann was struck by the absolute trust Becky had given to her and to Flynn. She had literally put her life in their hands. Her work at the hospital occasionally took her to the children's ward, and she'd always been awed by the confidence a sick child had in the doctors and nurses who treated them. They didn't question, didn't doubt, they simply accepted that the adults were there to help them.

Becky was doing much the same. She wasn't ill but she was vulnerable, and she was trusting that Ann and Flynn would take care of her, find her mother and put her life back together again. Ann's fingers tightened slightly over the little girl's. She was as committed to Becky's needs as Flynn was, whether she liked it or not.

"...red with black stripes and Mr. Flynn says it will go just like a real one." Ann shook off her preoccupation in time to hear Becky's last words. They had stopped next to Flynn's Mercedes and Flynn had opened the trunk.

"Flynn bought you a toy car?"

"It's not a toy, it's a working rep...reptile."

"He bought you a snake?"

"Becky means a replica." Flynn took the packages that Becky had handed to Ann, his eyes not meeting hers. "Let's go get something to eat. Are you hungry, Becky?" If he'd hoped to distract her with the offer of food, he was disappointed.

"Sure. I'm starved. The car isn't for me, Ann. Mr. Flynn bought it for hisself."

"Himself." Ann made the correction automatically, her eyes on Flynn's back as he shut the Mercedes's trunk a little more forcefully than was necessary. "So you bought a toy car."

Flynn turned to look at her, his brows raised, as if amazed that she would question such a thing. It was difficult to be sure in the dim light of the parking garage, but Ann was almost positive that his face was flushed. Flynn McCallister? Blushing? What an incredible idea.

"It's a remote controlled replica of a Jaguar XKE."

"That's different than a toy?" Ann took Becky's hand as they turned to go back into the mall. Flynn took Becky's other hand as she skipped between them, oblivious to the byplay going on between the two adults.

"It's a sophisticated piece of engineering."

"But not a toy?"

"It's a very educational piece of equipment. It teaches good eye-hand coordination." Ann didn't say anything. The look she gave him over Becky's head said it all. Flynn threw her an exasperated glance.

"They didn't make them when I was a kid." He sounded so defensive that Ann had to bite her cheek to keep from laughing out loud.

"Well, I hope it helps your eye-hand coordination."

The look he gave her was all male. "I think my eye-hand coordination is pretty good. I haven't had any complaints so far. I could demonstrate."

Ann felt the color surge into her cheeks at the blatant invitation. She could only hope that the dim light was as kind to her as it had been to him. "I don't think that will be necessary."

"I was afraid you'd say that."

The regret in his eyes was only half joking, and Ann felt a twinge of purely feminine pleasure before she looked away. Flynn's eyes lingered on her a moment longer before dropping to Becky.

"Well, Rebecca Antoinette, what would you like for lunch?"

"Corn dogs and French fries with catsup."

Flynn shuddered, his eyes closing for a moment. "Sounds terrific."

Ann laughed and wondered if it was foolish to be so happy over nothing.

"LOOK AT IT GO, Mr. Flynn. I bet it could go clear to the moon."

"It just might if you don't hold onto the string really tight."

Flynn reached out to steady Becky's small hands on the spool of string and then leaned back on his elbows, staring up at the bright scarlet kite that floated high above them. Since it was a weekday, the park was uncrowded. The weather was perfect. Becky had informed him that there was no temperature at all, and he knew just what she meant. The air felt neither warm nor cool. The sky above was a warm blue, a shade that Los Angeles didn't see very often. The residents had learned to savor it as long as it lasted.

"How high do you think it is, Mr. Flynn? One hundred miles?"

Flynn squinted at the kite. "Not an inch over ninety-nine miles." The kite kicked in the wind, swooping back and forth, weaving dancing patterns against the blue sky.

Flynn closed his eyes for a moment, savoring a feeling of peace like he hadn't known in years. Not since Mark's death had he felt so relaxed. He shifted one hand, touching Becky's slim back affectionately. It felt so right to be here with her. He'd never thought of himself as a family man, but Becky was making him reconsider. And Ann. Ann was making him reconsider a lot of things.

It was hard to believe that they'd spent the last two years across the hall from each other and barely exchanged a civil word. Like Becky, she'd become an integral part of his life. It was hard to imagine a time when she hadn't been there.

Dangerous thinking, McCallister. Next thing you know, you'll be thinking about rings and babies.

And why not?

The thought was so surprising that his eyes flew open and he sat up, oblivious to Becky's startled look. He'd begun to think of himself as a confirmed bachelor. He hadn't thought about marriage and children in years. Now, suddenly, the idea seemed not quite so alien. Appealing almost.

"Something wrong, Mr. Flynn?"

He shook himself and gave Becky a smile. Time enough to consider the implications of his thoughts later. "Not a thing. Come on, let's see if we can get your kite to go even higher."

Becky scrambled to her feet as he stood up, her fingers clenched around the spool. "I don't think it can go higher. It's awful high now."

"If we've got more string, we can get it higher."

She looked from him to the kite scudding across the sky above them. Her expression was cautious, doubtful. "What if it goes so high we lose it?"

"We'll buy another one." He grinned down at her. "Where's your spirit of adventure?" She eyed him cautiously before handing him the spool of string. Flynn took it from her with one hand and reached out to ruffle her hair with the other. "Don't look so worried, urchin."

It was clear that Becky had never learned how to be a proper child. She worried too much. Who better to teach her the fine points of childhood than someone who'd never grown up? He grinned and began to unreel the string, watching the kite dip and sway as it climbed higher.

"Let's see if we can set a world record in kite flying."

"Okay." Becky's eyes were wide as she stared up at the kite, picking up his enthusiasm. "I bet Ann will be impressed when she gets home and we tell her how high we got our kite."

When Ann gets home. Flynn repeated the phrase in his mind. It made the three of them sound like a family. It was rather frightening to realize how right that sounded.

ANN LEANED AGAINST the padded wall of the elevator and closed her eyes. It seemed as if her work schedule was getting more and more hectic. From the moment she arrived at the hospital, one thing after another claimed her attention. She used to tell herself that it was exhilarating, but today it had been near to drudgery. She'd always thought she knew what she wanted out of life. She'd become a doctor, work her way up the staff hierarchy in a good hospital and sometime before she grew too old to hear him, her father would tell her that he was proud of her.

Somehow, since letting Becky and Flynn into her life, her goals seemed skewed. Medicine suddenly didn't seem as interesting or exciting. Becoming chief of staff someday held no interest at all. She shook her head. It was a temporary state. She'd wanted this for too long, wanted to prove herself to her father. Once Becky's mother was found, her life would get back to normal and her future would fall into place again.

Ann tried not to think of how impossible the day had seemed. Her heart hadn't been in the job, and that was a dangerous thing for a doctor. She'd gone through all the motions and done all the right things but, in the back of her mind, she'd wondered what Becky and Flynn were doing. She'd wished she were doing it with them.

She was getting too involved.

But it's only for Becky's sake. As soon as her mother is found, I'll be out of the picture.

But what about Flynn? Are you going to back away from him?

Of course. I'm only seeing him because that's where Becky is. It's nothing to do with him personally.

And if she just kept telling herself that, she might believe it. The mental argument came to a halt with the elevator. She opened her eyes as the door slid open. Never had the peace and quiet of her own apartment held more appeal. She wouldn't even go over to see Becky tonight. She'd give Flynn a call and make sure that the little girl was all right, ask if there was any progress toward finding her mother and then she'd hang up. That was all anyone could possibly expect of her.

Ann stepped out of the elevator, the decision firm in her mind. And then nearly jumped out of her skin as a small red object hurtled toward her across the smooth carpet. She had only a moment of panic before she recognized it. This must be the infamous sophisticated piece of engineering. The toy car that Flynn had bought the day before.

It came to a halt inches from her feet as if to invite her to admire its shiny red paint. Ann had to admit that it looked remarkably like the real thing. It scooted a little forward and then back, reminding her of a small child shifting from one foot to another, impatient with adult slowness. Then she saw the piece of paper threaded onto the antenna. She bent and slid the paper loose, her fingers hesitant. It would be just her luck to break Flynn's new toy. Nothing broke, however, and she looked at the note, finding her name inscribed in a bold script that had to be Flynn's.

Ann,
Becky and I would love to have your company at dinner. No corn dogs. I promise. Becky wants to show off her new dolls. I just want to show off.

Flynn

The signature was a huge scrawl, as fascinating and unconventional as the man himself. Ann stared at the note and then looked down at the little car. She wasn't going to go, of course. She glanced at Flynn's door, which was open a crack. It didn't take a genius to figure out that he was crouched behind the crack, controlling the car. The image was so silly, so appealing that Ann found herself smiling for the first time all day.

She scrambled in her purse for a pen. Balancing the paper on her purse, she scribbled a reply.

Am disappointed at the thought of no corn dogs but will try to bear up. Expect me in half an hour. Looking forward to seeing your and Becky's new toys.

Ann

She threaded the note back onto the antenna and watched as the car made a quick reversing turn and spun for Flynn's door. The door opened just wide enough for the little car to shoot through and then shut, leaving Ann alone.

"So much for being strong-minded and spending a quiet evening at home." But there was no real regret in the muttered words.

Flynn kept his promise. There was not a corn dog in sight when the three of them sat down to dinner. Fried chicken with all the trimmings covered the table to the groaning point. Ann took one look and gave up trying to count the cholesterol content. It was a meal chosen to appeal to a child and yet offer something substantial for an adult.

"This looks fabulous." She could say the words with absolute sincerity. In fact, she couldn't remember the last time a meal had looked quite so good. Unless it was the breakfast Flynn had prepared the morning before. "You're a wonderful cook, Flynn."

"Thanks. My father thinks it's a wimpy occupation for a man but I enjoy it. I get tired of restaurant food. Becky helped tonight."

"I made the biscuits."

Ann looked at the lumpy, misshapen masses of dough and forced a smile as she took one. It seemed to weigh a great deal in proportion to its size and, when she tried to cut it open to put butter on it, it took quite a bit of hacking and sawing to get it apart. She stared at the grayed dough inside and swallowed hard.

"They look wonderful, Becky." Her eyes met Flynn's, bright blue with amusement.

"Becky believes in kneading all doughs thoroughly."

"Oh." There didn't seem to be anything else to say. "Aren't you having a biscuit, Becky?"

Becky shook her head, her mouth full of chicken. "I don't like biscuits. They always taste like old rocks when Mama makes them."

"I see." She set the biscuits aside, hoping that Becky would forget about it. There was no way she was going to risk thousands of dollars in orthodontic work by attempting to bite into that ominous mass.

"So what did you two do today?"

"We went to the park. It was a great day for flying kites."

"Mr. Flynn got a big kite and we flew it for a long time only then he got it caught in a tree."

"I prefer to think of it as the tree got in my way."

Ann answered his grin with a smile, surprised to realize how right it felt to be sitting across the table from him. She pushed the thought away. She didn't want to look too closely at where her relationship with Flynn was heading. For once in her life, she didn't want to look at the future. She just wanted to enjoy the present.

After dinner, Ann loaded the dishwasher with only a few token protests from Flynn. She insisted that it was the least she could do, and he didn't argue long. She was afraid to run the biscuits down the disposal. They looked far more deadly than the chicken bones, so she threw them in the trash, burying them deep in the hope that Becky would never find them.

She wandered out into the living room to find Flynn and Becky sitting on the sofa, their attention on a box on the table in front of them. Or at least Becky's attention was on the box. Flynn's attention was on nothing in particular unless Becky was talking to him. Ann crossed the soft carpet and sank onto the sofa on Becky's other side.

"What have you got?"

"Pictures." The succinct answer came from Becky. Flynn appeared to be half dozing.

Ann reached for a handful of the photographs that were scattered across the table. She expected to find family pictures, and she admitted to a mild curiosity to see what Flynn had looked like as a child. But the photos she held weren't your typical family shots.

The first was a picture of the park across the street. A light drizzle gave the background a gray look that could have been depressing. But the focus of the shot wasn't the weather. It was a little boy wearing a bright red raincoat and hat with incongruously bare feet. The camera had caught him in the act of jumping into a shallow puddle, his face ecstatic with anticipation. Leaning drunkenly against a bench nearby was a pair of red rain boots.

The picture made her smile, but it brought back the feeling of being a child—the intensity with which children lived every minute of every day.

The next photo was of an old woman. Ann assumed it was downtown Los Angeles, but it could have been any city. The woman's clothes were ragged but clean. Her face was weathered with decades of hard living, but there was pride in the set of her chin, in the clarity of her eyes. Pride that wasn't dimmed by the shopping cart of belongings that sat next to her. Her gray hair was pulled back into a bun, and stuck in the thin strands was a bright red carnation, its jaunty color a defiant denial of the circumstances.

Ann blinked back tears and moved to the next picture. Each photo touched the emotions, some happy, some sad, but all of them evocative. They spoke to the heart, more than the mind.

She had no idea how long she'd been looking at them

when she looked up. Becky had disappeared and Ann could hear her somewhere behind the sofa, talking to her dolls. Flynn was sitting just where he had been, his long body relaxed back into the deep cushions, only his watchful eyes telling her that he was still awake.

"Did you take these?"

"It's a hobby."

"They're beautiful."

"Thanks. I've got a small darkroom and I enjoy playing with it."

"You've done a lot more than play with these. They're full of emotion. Have you had much published?"

He laughed and leaned forward to gather up the photos scattered on the table, laying them back in the box. "I've never submitted them."

"Never submitted?" Ann looked at him as if he'd just confessed to murder. "How could you not submit them?"

He cocked an eyebrow at her appalled expression. "It's a hobby."

"But they're so good."

"It's still a hobby. Everything in life doesn't have to have a goal, you know."

No, she didn't know. He could see that the very concept was foreign to her. She sat there staring at him as if he were an alien from Venus. There she was on his sofa, her hair pulled back in the inevitable chignon, her green eyes wide with confusion, her chin set with what he suspected was a determination to argue with him. All he wanted to do was pull her across the few feet that separated them and kiss her senseless.

He sighed inaudibly. This was a hell of a time to discover a lust for his uptight neighbor. With Becky playing only a few feet away and Ann ready to chastise him for his worthless life-style, it was unlikely that she'd be receptive to what he really wanted to suggest. But it never hurt to dream.

"These photographs are good, Flynn. Really good. I know you could get them published."

He took the pictures she still held and put them in the box with the others. "I probably could. But I don't want to."

"Why not?"

"Ann, if I sold some photos, it would cease to be a hobby and become a career. I couldn't play with it anymore. People would expect me to take wonderful photos according to their schedules. It wouldn't be fun anymore."

"But you can't just take pictures like that and not do something with them."

"Why not?"

The simple question seemed to stymie her. She stared at him blankly for a moment. "You just can't."

Flynn sought for another way to explain it to her. "How would you feel if one of your hobbies suddenly became a job?"

"I don't know. I don't have a hobby."

It was his turn to stare at her in stunned silence. "You don't have a hobby? Everybody has a hobby. Do you sew? Crochet? Knit? Paint? Grow African violets?" Ann shook her head in answer to every suggestion and his suggestions became more outrageous. Becky came to lean on the back of the sofa and threw in a few suggestions of her own.

"I've got it. You're a closet taxidermist."

Helpless with laughter, Ann shook her head.

"What's a taxi...taxipermist?" Becky's question came out on a yawn, making Flynn realize how late it was.

He stood up, abandoning the subject of Ann's hobbies for the moment. "It's someone who gives permanents to taxi drivers. Time for bed, urchin." He ignored the inevitable protests and herded her toward the bathroom with instructions to wash her hands.

"I'll supervise." Ann followed Becky into the bathroom and he could hear the two of them talking. He turned down the sheets on Becky's bed and then looked around the room. It was funny how just a few nights with Becky sleeping here and already the room felt lived in again. Mark's presence was fading to pleasant memories.

He turned as Becky and Ann entered the room. Becky was tucked into bed with Frankie the giraffe snuggled beside her.

"Tell me a story, Mr. Flynn." Flynn told her a story about a frog who became a prince and the princess who loved him even when he was a frog. Behind him, he could hear Ann moving around, quietly putting away the last of the day's purchases. It felt so right. It felt like…home.

He finished the story and reached up to tuck the covers under Becky's chin. "Good night, Becky."

"Mr. Flynn? Do you think I'll ever see my mama again?"

Flynn was aware of Ann coming to stand behind him, but he knew the question was his to field. What was he supposed to say? Life didn't offer any guarantees. Not even to children.

"We've got a man looking for her, honey. He's very good at finding people. All we can do is cross our fingers that he'll find her soon."

"What's goin' to happen to me if he don't find her?"

Flynn brushed the ragged bangs off her forehead, telling himself not to promise too much. Behind him, he could feel Ann's tension. He looked at Becky, seeing the uncertainty in her eyes, the hint of a quiver that shook her stubborn chin and the absolute trust she gave him. And suddenly the answer was very simple.

"I'll take care of you, Becky. Whatever happens, I'll take care of you."

The uncertainty faded from her eyes. If Flynn said he'd take care of her, she believed him. She yawned. "What are we gonna do tomorrow?"

"Tomorrow, you and I are going to find a hobby for Ann."

"That'll be fun."

"I think so. Now, go to sleep." He dropped a kiss on her forehead and then waited while Ann did the same. They left the room, leaving the door partially open behind them.

"That's an awfully big promise." Ann's voice was carefully noncritical.

Flynn ran his fingers through his hair. "I know, but what else could I say to her? Besides, I meant it."

"I'm sure the detective will find Becky's mother."

"I hope so. But whatever happens, I'm going to make sure Becky doesn't suffer for it."

Ann reached out to touch the back of his hand. "I know you will."

ANN DIDN'T GIVE any more thought to Flynn's threat to find her a hobby. She knew he was just kidding. After all, nobody could choose a hobby for another person. She might have known that this was another rule that Flynn McCallister had never heard of.

The next evening when she got home, she didn't even bother to pretend to herself that she wasn't going to go to Flynn's apartment. Like it or not, she was involved. As long as he had Becky, Ann was involved in his life.

She changed clothes and fed Oscar, giving him some extra attention to make up for the fact that she was leaving him alone again. An hour after arriving home, she was knocking on Flynn's door. Becky answered the door.

"Ann! Mr. Flynn is making tacos. He says there's lots

if you want to eat with us." Becky took Ann's hand and pulled her into the apartment. Ann was surprised by how much it felt like coming home. "We got you a hobby."

"You did what?"

Flynn came to the kitchen doorway in time to hear her exclamation. He gave her his most devilish grin. "Ann! How nice to see you. Becky, why don't you go get Ann's hobby. I'm sure she must be wild with excitement. Are you going to be joining us for dinner?"

"That depends." She checked to make sure that Becky was out of earshot and lowered her voice to be safe. "Did Becky cook any of it?"

Flynn's grin widened. "She made the instant pudding for dessert."

"Then maybe I'll join you for dinner."

Becky ran back into the room, a gaily wrapped package in her hands. She was a far cry from the ragged little girl Ann had met less than a week ago. Her hot pink cotton play pants and matching T-shirt gave color to her rather pale face. Her hair still needed a good cut, but Flynn had pulled it back from her face and clipped it into two pink barrettes. She looked like a normal, healthy child.

"Here." She thrust the package into Ann's hands, her face glowing with excitement. "Mr. Flynn and I picked it out together."

"Bring it into the kitchen so I can keep an eye on the tacos." Ann and Becky followed Flynn into the kitchen, and Ann couldn't help but sniff appreciatively at the spicy aromas that filled the room.

She set the package down on the table and tugged off the ribbon. Becky stood beside her, hopping back and forth with excitement. "Do you need help getting it open?"

It was clear that Ann's usual methodical procedure was not going to do. She nodded and Becky's small fingers made short shrift of the wrapping paper. When the contents were revealed, Ann didn't know what to say. Lying in the tattered remnants of the wrapping was a paint-by-numbers kit. A picture of a bowl of flowers.

She looked at Flynn who looked back at her with a totally bland expression. "Becky and I thought you'd enjoy it."

"It's wonderful. Thank you." She hoped the comment sounded enthusiastic enough for Becky. She didn't worry about Flynn. After all, he had clearly bought it as a joke. He didn't really expect her to do anything with it. Paint-by-numbers. How silly could you get?

She could never quite explain to herself how it happened. She took the kit home, planning to throw it away, but it seemed a shame to throw it out without at least opening it. And then those little pots of paint looked kind of interesting. It couldn't hurt to dab a few colors on the canvas. And before she knew it, it was midnight and she was still hunched over the table, dabbing little bits of paint into numbered segments on the picture.

And damned if she wasn't having a thoroughly good time!

Chapter Six

"I'm sorry, Mr. McCallister. I wish I had more news for you. We'll keep looking but, frankly, we're beginning to run out of directions to go."

Flynn nodded, his eyes on the rather bilious floral print that hung over Leon Devoe's desk. Leon Devoe fit neither his name nor his profession. Everyone knew that private investigators were either tall and stunningly handsome with a slightly world-weary attitude, or short and slimy and out to cheat every client who came within reach. Leon looked like an ad for Mr. Average. Average size, average looks, average honesty. But he came with high recommendations.

"Perhaps if I could talk to the little girl. She might be able to tell me something that would help me to locate her mother."

"No." Flynn shook his head. "I don't want to involve Becky any more than we have to. She's scared enough without having someone asking questions. I've told you everything she knows about her mother's disappearance."

Leon shrugged and shuffled the papers on his desk. "I don't suppose it would do much good anyway. Frankly, there are a number of odd things about this woman. I can't find any record of her or the child past about three years ago. It's as if they fell out of the sky and into Los Angeles."

"That might have been about the time that Becky's father took off. She's a little vague on the dates."

"Well, if her mother wanted to hide the two of them from the child's father, she did a remarkably good job of it. I'm sure I'll be able to trace them but it could take quite some time."

Flynn leaned forward in his chair. "I'm not all that interested in their past. I want to know where the woman is now. I want to know why she didn't show up when she was supposed to."

"I understand, Mr. McCallister, but as I told you, we're running into walls. Beyond the fact that she left with a man, just as the little girl said, we haven't been able to find out much more. No one remembers the car, except that it was brown or possibly tan or maybe black. No one remembers the man except that he was tall or possibly short and he might have had brown hair, though one of the neighbors distinctly remembers that his hair was red."

Flynn stood up, his movements tight with controlled impatience. "Didn't anyone pay any attention at all?"

"Not really. Apparently, it wasn't at all unusual to see the woman leaving with a man. It was a normal occurrence. There was no reason for anyone to take special note of the child's mother going off for a weekend trip."

"Except that she didn't come back from this trip."

"Exactly. But there was no way of knowing that ahead of time."

"Have you managed to find out anything at all that might tell us where she went?"

Leon shook his head slowly. "I wish I could say otherwise, but so far we've found very little of any use."

"Let me know if anything changes. You've got my number."

Leon stood up, coming around the desk to open the door for Flynn. "Rest assured, Mr. McCallister, that you will be the first to know if we find out anything helpful. But, frankly, I can't hold out much hope.''

The two men shook hands and Flynn stepped out into the hall, listening to the door shut behind him. He didn't move away immediately. He wasn't looking forward to going home and telling Ann that he hadn't found out anything at all. As time passed, it was beginning to look less and less likely that Becky's mother was coming back. How was he supposed to tell a little girl that her mother might never return?

CHILD AND CAT STARED at each other with equal intensity. Each waiting for the other to make a move. Oscar's paw darted out, catching hold of the old sock and jerking it from Becky's hand. With a triumphant lunge, he was off and running, Becky hot on his trail.

Ann looked up from the medical journal she was reading and smiled. She'd been concerned about introducing Becky and Oscar, uncertain of how the big tomcat would take to having his territory invaded by a small human. After some initial caution, Oscar had apparently decided that Becky had been imported solely for his pleasure. When he was tired of playing, Becky was content to sit beside him and pet him. Oscar was in cat heaven.

Ann looked at the clock and frowned. It was only five minutes since the last time she'd looked at the clock. This was ridiculous. Flynn would return as soon as he could. He'd only been gone a little over an hour. As soon as he'd talked to the private detective and found out if there were any leads to Becky's mother, he'd come home. There was no sense in watching the clock.

When the doorbell rang fifteen minutes later, Ann practically flew to the door, Becky hard on her heels. Oscar watched them from a safe perch on the sofa. Ann flung open the door, hoping that she'd be able to read something

from his expression. They'd already agreed not to tell
Becky where he'd been, so until they could get Becky out
of the room, they wouldn't be able to talk openly. But
surely he'd find a way to let her know if there was, any
news.

"Flynn—"

"Mr. Flynn—"

Both sentences came to an abrupt halt. The man standing
outside the door was definitely not Flynn. He was short,
stocky and balding, and the expression on his face bore no
resemblance to Flynn's lazy charm. His eyes traveled from
Ann's face to Becky.

"Dad." Ann knew her tone fell short of enthusiasm and
she repeated the word, trying to sound less like she'd just
discovered an encyclopedia salesman on her doorstep.
"Dad."

"Ann." He nodded. "Obviously, you were expecting
someone else."

"That's okay. Obviously, you aren't someone else." He
didn't bother to smile at her weak attempt at humor.

"May I come in?"

"Of course. I'm sorry. I didn't mean to keep you standing there." She stepped back, aware of Becky retreating to
stand next to Oscar. She shut the door behind her father
and followed him into the living room. "Dad, this is Rebecca Sinclair. She's staying across the hall and I'm taking
care of her for a little while. Becky, this is my father, Mr.
Perry."

He acknowledged the introduction with a short nod.

"Staying with the McCallister fellow, is she? I thought
you were steering clear of him."

Robert Perry believed that children should be seen and
not heard. He also believed that they should be treated as
if they were part of the furniture, which included not only
silence, but deafness.

Luckily, the doorbell rang again before Ann had to find an answer for her father's comment. Her pace was much more subdued this time, and she waited until the door was fully open before greeting her visitor.

"Flynn." They had only an instant in the semi-privacy of the hall. There was no time for Ann to ask any questions about his visit with the private detective. Her eyes met his and he shook his head slightly, the only thing they had time for before Becky clutched Flynn around the knees.

"Hi, urchin." He bent and scooped her up, holding her casually under one arm. Her giggles drew a smile from Ann, a smile that died when she looked at her father.

"Flynn, this is my father, Robert Perry. Dad, this is Flynn McCallister."

The two men nodded. Robert Perry's face expressed his disapproval of both Flynn and Becky. "I understand Ann has been baby-sitting for you."

"I suppose you could call it that."

"My daughter is a very busy woman. I hope you don't plan to intrude on her time like this again."

"Dad!" Ann could feel the color coming up in her cheeks. She looked at Flynn, half-expecting him to stalk out in a rage. But, of course, Flynn McCallister never did the expected thing.

One black brow arched upward, and his mouth twisted in a half smile that brought an angry flush to Robert Perry's face even before Flynn spoke.

"I think Ann can take care of herself. She's never hesitated to speak her mind in the past. Of course, you have to be willing to listen to hear what she's saying." His words fell into a little pool of silence. Ann held her breath, waiting for the explosion.

Flynn seemed oblivious to the tension. He shifted Becky from one arm to the other, holding her against his hip as if she weighed nothing. "Ann, we're having chili dogs tonight if you want to join us."

He turned and left without another word to her father, tugging the door shut behind him, cutting off the sound of Becky's giggling pleas to be put down. Ann stared at the door for a long moment, surprised by the strength of the urge to follow him.

She had to force herself to look at her father, pinning a determinedly cheerful expression on her face. Maybe he would just ignore Flynn's comments. One look at his purple complexion told her that he wasn't going to ignore anything. It was going to be a rough visit.

"HAVE A GLASS of wine."

Ann shook her head. "I really shouldn't stay. It's late and...thank you." She took the glass he handed her and sipped the pale red contents.

"You'll sleep better after a nice glass of *pinot noir*."

Flynn sank into a chair at right angles to the sofa and propped his stockinged feet on the glass coffee table. He looked absolutely boneless, slouched in the chair, a wineglass in one hand, the other hand relaxed on the wide arm of the chair. He had nice hands, long fingers and neatly clipped nails. Artistic hands.

Ann took another sip of wine and felt some of the tension seep out. She slid farther back on the sofa and leaned her head against its back. It was so peaceful here. Becky was asleep; the city was quiet beneath them. No one was demanding anything of her. How had it happened that, in the space of a few short days, Flynn McCallister had gone from being a thorn in her side to being an oasis of calm?

Of course, it was only temporary. As soon as Becky's mother was found, she and Flynn would go their separate ways again. Not that they'd go back to being antagonists, but they'd certainly have no reason to do more than nod politely in the hall. Why wasn't that thought more reassuring?

"What did the private investigator have to say about Becky's mother? Any luck?"

Flynn shook his head. "Not much. He's found out quite a bit about her but nothing that tells us where she might have disappeared to." He swirled the wine in his glass, his expression uncharacteristically serious. "She doesn't sound like your average mother who belongs to the PTA and bakes cookies every second Tuesday."

"So? Most women don't fit that pattern anymore."

"True. But most women don't have a different boyfriend every weekend and no visible means of support."

"You think she's a..." Ann cleared her throat, her eyes going toward the room where Becky was asleep.

"I don't know." Flynn took another swallow of his wine, his frown deepening. "She must love Becky or she wouldn't have bothered to keep her. Maybe she is earning her living in the oldest profession. Maybe she doesn't have a choice."

"Still, that's not going to be very good for Becky, especially when she gets old enough to understand what's going on."

"It would explain why her mother has instilled a fear of the 'welfare people' in Becky. I imagine they would take her away if her mother's doing what I think she's doing."

"What are we going to tell Becky?" She used the plural without thought. It was no longer possible to pretend that she wasn't involved in this situation.

"Nothing. At least not until we have some news of her mother. She's happy here. I'm just going to let her stay that way."

"What if her mother's never found?"

Flynn downed the last of his wine and stared broodingly at the glass. "We'll cross that bridge when it gets here."

Ann took another swallow of wine, feeling the warm glow of it settle in her stomach and then ease its way through her body.

"Did Becky get to sleep all right?"

"No problem. I told her a story and she went out like a light before I even got to the punch line. She asked where you were."

Ann tried to ignore the pleasure the words gave her. She was getting too emotionally involved here. She was going to get hurt. "What did you tell her?"

"I told her that you'd asked me to give her a kiss for you and that you'd see her tomorrow."

"That was nice."

"I thought so. Of course, you owe me a kiss now." Ann's eyes flew to his face. He gave her a lazy smile that set up a fluttering in her stomach. "I'll collect later."

"Oh. Fine." Fine? Had she really said fine? It had to be the wine. Maybe he'd drugged it.

"How did the visit with your father go?"

In her current relaxed state, not even the mention of her father could seriously dim the warm glow Ann felt. He seemed so far away.

"The same as usual. I'm not doing well enough. I should be further along in my career. I don't attend the right gatherings. He doesn't like my cat, my apartment, my lifestyle."

"And he most especially doesn't like Becky and me."

It had to be the wine. She wasn't even upset that he'd hit the nail on the head with such unerring precision.

"It's nothing personal. He just worries that I'll let things get in the way of my career."

"Things like personal relationships?" The question was unanswerable, but he didn't seem to expect a reply. He leaned forward and picked up the wine bottle, filling his own glass before leaning forward to fill Ann's.

"I really shouldn't. It's late."

"You've got to try it now that it's had time to breathe."

She sipped obediently. It didn't taste any different to her, but she nodded and made an appreciative noise. She really should go home, but the sofa felt so wonderfully soft.

"You know, I've found that you can't always fulfill your parents' dreams for you. Sometimes, you just have to do what *you* want to do, even if it disappoints the people you love."

"I *am* doing what I want to do."

"Then you've got nothing to worry about."

Ann frowned into her glass. "It's not that my father isn't proud of me. It's just that he has very high standards. He wanted a boy, you know."

"Well, I, for one, am glad he didn't get what he wanted. You're much too beautiful to make a good boy." He raised his glass in a toast and Ann felt that disturbing tingle of pleasure again.

"Thank you. I don't think that's any consolation to my father."

"I wasn't trying to console him."

"You know, I wish I was more like you." Ann was almost as surprised by her words as he was. Amazing what a couple of glasses of wine could do.

"Like me? I wouldn't have guessed that you harbored a secret desire to be a worthless playboy, as my father so succinctly puts it."

"No, I don't mean that. I mean, I wish I didn't care so much what other people thought. You just go through life doing what you want to do. You don't let what your father wants control your life."

Flynn's mouth twisted ironically. "Oh, I don't know. In some ways, I am what I am just to spite my father. Nobody is completely free of their parents' influence. You've just got to keep it in perspective."

"Perspective." Ann yawned. "Did you know that I wanted to be a veterinarian when I was a kid?"

"Why didn't you?"

She swallowed the last of her wine and set the glass down with a thump. "My father thought it was dumb. Doctoring people is more important than animals." She yawned again. "I'm sorry. I should have warned you that wine makes me sleepy."

"That's okay. Do you ever regret it?"

"That wine makes me sleepy? It doesn't cause me much trouble." She blinked at him owlishly.

He smiled, his eyes bright with amusement. "Do you ever regret becoming a people doctor instead of an animal doctor?"

"Of course not. People doctoring is much more important." Her eyelids felt so heavy. "I really should be going home."

Flynn watched as her head slipped slowly to the side, her eyes shut, her mouth the slightest bit open as she slid into sleep. There was a funny ache in his chest. She looked so vulnerable. He set his glass down and stood up. He should probably wake her up and send her home. She wasn't going to be happy about falling asleep in front of him. It was too big a chink in the wall she kept between them. He looked at her a moment longer and then left the room.

When he returned, he was carrying a pillow and a blanket. Ann didn't twitch when he tucked the pillow under her head, easing her down to lie on the sofa. He lifted her feet up, slipping her shoes off.

He covered her with the blanket, and she cuddled under its light warmth, snuggling her face into the pillow. Her hair was still pulled back in a loose bun, but a few rebellious strands had escaped the pins to curl around her face.

He brushed them back, letting the soft warmth curl around his fingers.

He wasn't entirely sure what was happening between them, but he knew it was a lot more than just concern for Becky. Thirty-three was a hell of a time to fall in love for the first time. He'd almost begun to think it would never happen. He tucked the blanket more firmly around her shoulders and moved away, scooping up the glasses and the half-empty wine bottle on his way to the kitchen.

THE JANGLE OF THE PHONE was an unexpected intrusion and Ann jumped, splashing red paint onto a portion of the picture that was designated for blue.

"Drat!" She dabbed at the errant paint and succeeded in smearing it a little farther. The phone rang again, and she dropped the rag and got up. She hesitated, staring at the phone indecisively. What if it was Flynn? In the two days since she'd awakened on his sofa, she'd managed to avoid much contact with him. She saw him only when Becky was present to act as a buffer. A buffer from what, Ann couldn't have said. All she knew was that Flynn threatened her carefully planned life-style. The wine had made the evening a little fuzzy around the edges, but it hadn't blocked out what had been said.

What had gotten into her that she'd said such things to him? She never talked to anyone like that. Not even to herself. There was something about him that made it all too easy to reveal things she didn't want revealed, say things she didn't even want to think.

The phone rang again, and she took a deep breath and reached for it. It wasn't likely to be Flynn and, even if it was, there was certainly nothing to be afraid of. Maybe he was calling to suggest that they leave for their picnic early.

"Hello?"

"Ann?"

"Oh, hello, Dad." The relief was only temporary. Her father hadn't been entirely happy with her when he left two days ago.

"I wanted to let you know that I've taken matters into my own hands."

"What matters?"

"When we talked about that child that McCallister is keeping, I told you that the only thing to do was call the Social Services. After giving it careful thought, I felt it would be best for all concerned if someone did the right thing so I called Social Services this morning and explained the situation to them."

"You did what?" Ann hadn't thought it was possible to be so angry so quickly. Her voice came out on a breathy note. She was surprised she could get it past the tightness in her throat.

"I know you'll agree that this is the best solution. McCallister is clearly unfit to be taking care of a child and—"

"How dare you?"

"What?"

"How dare you interfere like this?"

"There's no need to get hysterical, Ann."

"I'm not hysterical. I'm mad! Damn it! You had no right!" She slammed the receiver down in the midst of his angry protests about her tone. She stared at the wall for several long seconds, taking deep breaths, suppressing the desire to scream with rage.

Flynn. She had to warn Flynn. Barefoot, paint on her fingers, she flew out of the apartment and across the hall. She knocked, hurting her knuckles with the force she put into the simple gesture. It seemed like hours before the door began to open.

"Flynn, I'm so sorry. My father called—"

"Come in and meet Ms. Davis, Ann. She's here about Becky."

Ann dragged her eyes from the rage that glittered in his and looked past his shoulder to the woman who sat in the living room.

Flynn took her arm and pulled her into the hall, shutting the door behind her with a snap. Ann stretched her stiff facial muscles into a smile and hoped she didn't look as sick as she felt.

"YOU HAVE TO UNDERSTAND, Mr. McCallister, this is a very unusual situation. If you'd reported Rebecca to us when you first found her, she would have been placed in appropriate foster care until her mother was found. Now, the child has had a chance to form an attachment to you. And, of course to you also, Ms. Perry. It will make it much harder for her to settle somewhere else."

Flynn gave the woman a coaxing smile. "Then why move her? You can see that she's doing just fine here. Why not let her stay until her mother is found? I realize that I'm not, perhaps, a typical foster parent but I've done a pretty good job so far. Becky is happy here. Ann keeps an eye on her health and well-being."

"I tell you what. I can't promise anything but I'll see what I can do to allow you to keep Rebecca." She held up her hand to forestall Flynn's thanks. "It will only be temporary. If her mother isn't found soon, more permanent arrangements will have to be made."

Jane Davis got up, gathering up her briefcase and purse. Flynn and Ann rose with her, both of them smiling with relief. She held out her hand. "I'll call as soon as I've talked to my superiors."

Flynn took her hand, but instead of the expected handshake, he raised it to his lips, kissing her fingers with a courtliness that brought a flutter even to a heart toughened by years of social work.

The door shut and Ann turned to Flynn, wanting to offer some explanation, some apology, some excuse for her father's behavior. Before she could speak, Becky's voice interrupted.

"Is she gone?" The adults turned to find her peering into the living room, her eyes wide and uncertain.

"She's gone."

"She's not going to make me go away with her?"

"Nobody is going to make you go anywhere." Flynn bent to catch the little girl as she flew across the room to him. He swept her up easily, accepting her arms around his neck and returning the hug. Ann swallowed a lump in her throat.

"She wanted to take me away, didn't she?" Becky's voice was muffled by Flynn's shoulder.

"She wanted to make sure that you were all right."

"Is she going to let me stay with you?"

Flynn stroked the back of her head, offering her physical reassurance as well as verbal. "She's going to let you stay with me. She was just worried about you and she wanted to make sure Ann and I were taking good care of you."

Becky snuggled her head deeper into his neck. "What about Mama? Are they going to take me away from Mama?"

Flynn's eyes met Ann's in helpless question. His answer was very carefully phrased. "I'm sure they'll want to talk to your mom when we find her but when they see how much she loves you, everything will be all right."

Apparently that was all the reassurance Becky required. If Mr. Flynn said it was going to be fine, she'd believe him. Her arms loosened around his neck, her world set right again.

Flynn set Becky down and pointed her in the direction

of the bedroom. "Go get a jacket and I'll get the picnic."
She skipped off, confident that all was right with her world
as long as Flynn was in it.

Ann shifted toward the door, her eyes settling on a point
somewhere beyond Flynn's shoulder. "I guess I'll let you
two get on with your picnic. I...I'm sorry about what my
father did."

"Where are you going? I thought the three of us had
planned this extravaganza of hot dogs and indigestion."

Her eyes flickered to his face and then away. "I didn't
think I'd be welcome."

Flynn caught her arm as she moved closer to the door,
pulling her forward until she stood right in front of him.
There was nowhere to look but at him. She stared at his
collarbone, too ashamed to meet his eyes.

"Ann, you can't possibly think I blame you for what
your father did? It had nothing to do with you. I know
that."

His voice was so gentle that Ann had to blink back tears.
It had been a long time since anyone had used that tone
with her. It made her want to lean her head on his chest
and let him take care of her.

"How can you be so nice about it? If I hadn't told my
father about Becky, he wouldn't have called the social
worker and you wouldn't be about to lose Becky."

"Don't be silly." He gave her a gentle shake that
brought her eyes to his face. "You couldn't have known
what your father was going to do. And I'm *not* going to
lose Becky. *We're* not going to lose Becky. Hey, you've
got to cultivate a more positive attitude."

Ann managed a shaky smile, but she couldn't prevent
the single tear that slipped down her cheek. Flynn's eyes
darkened, his expression softening almost magically. His
head lowered, and Ann closed her eyes as he kissed the
tear from her cheek. It was a gentle gesture, a comforting

gesture and yet, somehow, comfort was not exactly what it achieved. With the touch of his mouth on her cheek, the atmosphere was charged with sexual awareness. As if the awareness had been there all along, just waiting for an excuse to break through.

He hesitated, his mouth against her skin, and Ann forgot how to breathe. His lips shifted, trailing along her jaw, drawing closer to her mouth. Ann's mouth softened, anticipating the touch of his. He was so close. So close.

"Are you kissing Ann?"

Flynn jerked as if slapped. Ann's eyes flew open as he stepped away. Was it her imagination or was his breathing a little uneven, his color a little high? His eyes locked on hers for an instant, but it was impossible to read their expression. And then he looked away, and Ann could almost believe that she'd imagined the entire incident.

"Becky. You got your jacket."

"'Course I got my jacket. I thought we was going to the park." The look she gave him made it clear that he was acting slow-witted. Flynn flushed.

"We are. But Ann has to go and get her shoes and I've got to get the picnic."

"You said you was going to do that when you told me to get my jacket."

"Well, yes, I got distracted."

"What's 'stracted mean?"

"How DO KIDS MANAGE to ask so many questions?" Flynn's tone was exaggeratedly weary, and Ann hid a smile.

"How else are they going to learn?"

"It just seems like they try to learn everything all at once."

Ann looked to where Becky was playing with a group of other children.

"I think that's the first time I've seen her with kids her age."

Flynn's eyes followed hers, settling on Becky's brightly clad figure. "I think she and her mother moved a lot. According to the investigator, they've had six different addresses in the last two years. I doubt if Becky's had a chance to make any friends."

"Has she ever talked about her father?"

Flynn shook his head, reaching for a bite of cotton candy from the cone Ann held. "She hasn't said much. I get the feeling her mother didn't want to talk about him."

"She told me that Frankie was a present from her father and that book she has was his. That's not a cheap edition of Robert Louis Stevenson and it's part of a set. And Frankie isn't a dime store stuffed toy. He's Steiff."

"Steiff? What's Steiff?"

"They make toys. Expensive toys. Collectible toys. The tag is gone but they always put a button in the animal's ear. If her father bought her Frankie, he probably wasn't on the dole line."

"Maybe he stole him."

"Maybe. I can't help but wonder where he is. I can't imagine what kind of a man would abandon his own child."

"Happens all the time. Here." Ann opened her mouth automatically, her thoughts on other things. She was unaware of the intimacy of Flynn feeding her a bite of sticky cotton candy, or of the way his eyes watched her tongue come out to lick the sugar from her lips.

"You're very good with her."

"With Becky? She's easy to get along with." He shrugged off the compliment, pulling off another length of spun sugar.

"You'd make a good father." His eyes went to Becky again.

"At least I know what not to do. You don't pigeonhole your kids from birth. You don't expect a kid to be perfect. I watched what that did to my brother. Always striving to be exactly what Dad wanted, never feeling like he'd quite measured up."

"What about you?"

"Me? Well, there are advantages to being the black sheep of the family. No one expects anything but trouble out of you." His smile took on a wicked edge. "I was pretty good at living up to those expectations."

He held another bite of cotton candy up to her mouth, and Ann hesitated a moment before taking it from him. They were slipping into dangerous intimacy. His fingers brushed her lips.

Ann felt the sticky sweet melt on her tongue, her eyes never leaving his. It wasn't fair that he should have such blue, blue eyes. It was too easy to get lost in them. The sounds of the park faded into the background. His fingers shifted but didn't leave her face. His hand cupped her cheek, his thumb brushing across her skin.

"You have the softest skin."

Any second now, she was going to make some light remark and draw away. Any second now. But she couldn't seem to move. "I do?"

"Umm." His eyes dropped to her mouth and Ann felt her pulse pick up. It wasn't fair. He shouldn't be able to do that with just a look. "Did you know you have cotton candy on your mouth?"

"I do?" The words were breathy. She couldn't get enough air. His head was lowering and she should be moving away. She didn't want this. Didn't want it at all. Which explained the quivery sensation in the pit of her stomach when his breath touched her mouth.

Her eyes fell shut. His tongue came out, delicately licking the sticky sweetness from her mouth. The touch was so intimate, so hungry that Ann forgot all about not wanting it. Forgot all the reasons she couldn't get involved with him. Forgot everything but the surprising hunger in her own body. She was the one who moved closer. Her hands came up to rest on the front of his light jacket.

Flynn groaned, a low rumbling sound that Ann felt in every pore of her body. Her mouth opened, inviting him inside, and he took the invitation, sweeping her breath away as his mouth closed over hers, his tongue sliding inside, hot with demand.

They were standing under the huge branches of a live oak, the ancient tree sheltering them, giving the illusion of privacy. Ann wasn't sure how it happened but suddenly she was pressed against the tree, the bark rough against her back, Flynn's body a sensual weight against her.

Her hands slid around his neck, pulling him closer. She felt as if all her life she'd been only half alive and suddenly he'd awakened the sleeping half of her. She'd never known such a rush of urgency, of need. Of hunger.

The passion that flared between them was instantaneous, catching them both off guard, leaving no room for pretense, no room for anything but each other.

"Mr. Flynn, you've got cotton candy in your hair."

Ann felt as if she'd just been pushed out of an airplane without a parachute. The return to reality was so abrupt that she was disoriented. Flynn's head came up, his eyes meeting hers for a moment before he stepped away, leaving her to lean limply against the tree. If it hadn't been for its support, she would have simply slid to the ground. There didn't seem to be any stiffening in her knees.

"How come Ann put cotton candy in your hair?" Becky's piping question was another rude introduction to reality. Ann stared at the little girl for a moment, and then her eyes dropped to the crushed paper cone in her hand. The pale pink confection was almost gone but she'd forgotten all about it when Flynn kissed her. He ran his hand over the back of his head, drawing it back with a grimace.

"I think I need a shower."

Ann nodded, still dazed. He wasn't the only one. She wondered if there was a shower long enough and cold enough to slow her pulse down to normal.

Chapter Seven

"How come the water comes out hot?" Ann looked from Becky to the stream of water splashing into the tub and tried to organize her thoughts. It had been like that all afternoon. No matter how she scolded herself for letting one little kiss throw her off balance, she couldn't seem to get back to the real world.

Of course, calling it "one little kiss" was rather like calling King Kong a spider monkey. A little kiss didn't send shock waves to your toes. A little kiss didn't leave you tingling hours later. A little kiss—

"Ann?" She blinked and smiled at Becky.

"They heat the water in a big tank and pump it up to the faucet." As basic explanations went, it was about as basic as they came but she wasn't up to trying to explain the miracles of modern plumbing, even if she understood them, which she didn't. Becky seemed satisfied and she climbed into the tub without asking another question.

Becky was quite capable of taking a bath without a supervisor, but it had become a nightly ritual for Ann to sit in the bathroom with her. It was hard to say who enjoyed the ritual more. Ann tried not to think about what was going to happen when Becky's mother was finally found. She couldn't pretend anymore that life was going to go back to the way it had been before she'd opened her door to Flynn's towel-clad, panic-stricken presence.

She reached out to tuck a strand of Becky's hair out of the way of the washcloth. Becky smiled at her, revealing a gap where a tooth had come out two days ago. Ann smiled back, hoping the little girl wouldn't notice the shimmer of tears in her eyes. Flynn had been so nervous when Ann had checked the loose tooth and announced that it was time to pull it.

He'd let her do the honors, telling Becky that since Ann was a doctor, she'd know how to do it just right. When the moment finally came and the tooth was pulled, Ann thought Flynn might cry right along with Becky. But the tears lasted only a moment, more from fright than actual pain. Afterward, they'd made a ritual out of placing the tooth under Becky's pillow for the tooth fairy. Becky had explained that there wasn't really a tooth fairy, but the pragmatic words didn't quite match the excitement in her eyes.

Ann's smile widened as she reached for the washcloth to scrub Becky's back. It had taken her almost ten minutes to convince Flynn that a dollar was enough for a tooth. If she hadn't been there, he would probably have left the Ferrari under Becky's pillow.

"Are you and Mr. Flynn going to get married?" The washcloth slipped and Ann almost fell into the tub.

"What?"

"Are you and Mr. Flynn going to get married?" Becky wound the spring on a toy boat and set it sailing across the tub.

"What on earth would make you ask that?" Ann hoped the amusement in her voice sounded light and not hysterical.

"He was kissing you today."

"Becky, you know people don't get married just because they kiss each other."

"Why do they get married?"

"Well, they get married because they want a home and a family, something to come back to every night. Somebody who'll love them no matter what and be there when they're happy or when they're sad."

"Don't you want those things?"

Ann stared down at Becky, meeting the innocent question in those clear gray eyes. "I don't know. I guess I've never really given it much thought. I've had to work very hard at my job. I guess everybody wants those things but it's not easy to find them."

Becky rubbed soap over the washcloth, lathering it up until the cloth all but disappeared in bubbles. "Mama says that if you really want something, you've got to go out and get it. She says you can't sit around waitin' for stuff to come to you." She scrubbed the soapy cloth over her face.

Ann watched her. Out of the mouths of babes. Surely that statement had to have been designed for Becky.

HALF AN HOUR LATER, Becky was dressed in a long cotton nightgown and tucked into bed. Ann dropped a kiss on her forehead, trying not to think of how much she'd grown to care for this small scrap of humanity.

"Tell me a story, Mr. Flynn." This, too, had become a nightly ritual. Ann moved quietly around the room putting away the day's accumulation of clothes and toys, while Flynn's voice spun a quiet story about elves and princesses and beautiful moths that flew them through fairyland.

The story was only half over when Flynn's voice stopped, and Ann turned to see that Becky had fallen asleep, her lashes making dark crescents against her flushed cheeks. Flynn eased himself off the bed and dropped a kiss on Becky's forehead. They tiptoed from the room, leaving the door open just a crack.

In the living room, the atmosphere was suddenly awk-

ward. The early autumn temperature had dipped low
enough that Flynn felt justified in lighting a fire, and it
hissed quietly in the fireplace. One lamp burned next to the
sofa, casting a pool of brilliance that seemed too intimate.

"Join me in a glass of wine?"

Ann glanced at him and then looked away. He was altogether too sexy. He'd washed the cotton candy out of his
hair, and it now fell onto his forehead in a heavy black
wave that made her fingers twitch with the urge to push it
back. His jeans molded his thighs, just snug enough to tan-
talize anyone with the least imagination. His shirt was plain
blue cotton, but the top two buttons were undone, allowing
a glimpse of curling black hair.

It would be foolish to stay for a glass of wine, and one
thing Ann had never been was foolish.

"That sounds nice."

Ten minutes later, the two of them were seated on the
thick carpeting in front of the fireplace. Huge pillows bolstered their backs. It was a warm, intimate setting and part
of Ann couldn't believe that she was here, courting disaster
like this. But that was the practical Ann, who'd spent her
life working toward certain goals.

There was another Ann, the Ann that was beginning to
realize how much she'd given up to ambition. The Ann that
wondered about all the things she'd told Becky that went
into marriage. That was the Ann sitting here. Besides,
where was the danger in sharing a simple glass of wine?

She stared into the fireplace, afraid to look at Flynn,
afraid to look too closely at what she was doing. Afraid to
stay and even more afraid to go.

Flynn's hand came out and took the wineglass from her
fingers. Ann watched him set it on the hearth. The pale
liquid picked up all the colors of the fire, bending them into
new displays of light and color. Flynn's glass joined hers,

the two of them sitting side by side. And still she sat there, her hands lying in her lap, her eyes on the two glasses.

She felt his hands in her hair, pulling out the pins one by one. She should say something. She couldn't just sit here and do nothing. She couldn't just let him... The last pin came out slowly, as if he were dragging out the anticipation. She closed her eyes as her hair tumbled onto her shoulders.

He didn't move, didn't speak until, at last, she could bear the tension no more. She opened her eyes, turning her head until she could see his face. She needed to know what he was thinking.

His eyes were on her hair, deep red waves that made the fire pale in comparison. The flames cast shadows over his features, making it difficult to read his expression.

"You are so beautiful." His voice was husky, soft. "I wanted to see you with your hair down the first moment I saw you. You looked so cool and disapproving but there was such fire in your hair." His fingers slid into the thick waves and Ann shut her eyes again. His thumb brushed her earlobe and she shivered. She felt him shifting closer. Her lips parted, anticipating, needing, wanting.

And then he was there.

His mouth claimed hers hungrily, with none of the tentative searching that had been in his other kisses. They both knew the time for questions was gone. There might be new questions tomorrow, but tonight there was only the two of them.

The spark that had been kindled earlier had lain waiting, needing only a touch to burst into life. Flynn's fingers slid deep into her hair, cupping the back of her head, tilting her mouth to his.

Ann moaned low in her throat as her lips opened, welcoming the invasion of his tongue. He tasted of wine. He tasted of madness. He tasted of all the things she denied herself for so many years. Things she'd only dreamed of. Her tongue came up to meet his, as hungry as he was. They tangled in erotic love play, testing, teasing, savoring.

She was barely aware of his hands shifting to her shoulders, lowering her to the thick carpeting. His mouth left hers but only to taste the delicate skin along her jaw. The firelight created dancing red shadows against her closed eyes. Flynn's mouth slid down her throat, his tongue tasting the pulse that beat frantically at its base.

His fingers teased open the buttons on her blouse, spreading the thin cotton fabric out around her body. When he lifted himself away from her, Ann's eyes fluttered open. She should have felt self-conscious, lying beneath him with only the fragile lace of her bra shielding her breasts from his gaze. But the look in his eyes was warm, melting away her inhibitions, her fears, leaving her feeling wanted, loved.

"You are so beautiful." He breathed the words out as if he could hardly believe that she was lying here beneath him.

Her fingers came up to smooth the hair back from his forehead. It promptly slipped back down again, but her hands had moved to other things. His shirt buttons slid apart easily, baring his muscled chest. Ann could feel him watching her but she kept her eyes on her fingers, concentrating on sliding each button loose. If she looked at him, she might lose the fragile courage she'd found.

The shirt at last fell loose and she set her palms against his chest. The crisp curls tickled her palms. He was warm, so warm. She slid her hands up his chest, feeling the shudder that ran through him as her fingertips grazed his flat nipples. She felt powerful. For the first time, she realized the power of her femininity. Flynn actually trembled when she touched him. It was a heady feeling. But she didn't have long to savor the feeling, because Flynn soon showed her that it worked both ways.

His fingers mastered the front clasp of her bra and Ann's nails dug into his chest as she felt it slip loose. Her eyes swept up to meet his and were caught and held in the brilliant blue fires that burned there. He kept his eyes on hers as he opened the lace garment, brushing it aside without really touching her.

His hand rested between her breasts, unmoving, so close without touching. The tension grew as she waited for him to move. Her palms tingled where they touched him, her breathing was shallow. *Why didn't he move?* Just when she thought she would surely explode, he moved.

His eyes never left hers as his hand shifted slowly, so slowly, his fingers hovering over her for an instant before his thumb stroked ever so gently across the tip of her breast. Ann hadn't even realized that she was holding her breath until it left her in a sigh that came perilously close to a sob. Her eyes fell shut, her entire being concentrated on that one tiny point as he captured her nipple between thumb and forefinger and tugged lightly.

"Please." The word was a whisper, almost lost in the crackle of the fire. Her back arched, begging, demanding. And the demand was answered. His head dipped and her fingers buried themselves in his hair as his mouth closed around the swollen point. He seemed to know just what she needed, far more clearly than she herself knew. She felt the tugging at her breast but she felt it more deeply, setting up pulsing waves low in her stomach.

Her hips moved in unconscious invitation, seeking something to fill the aching void that had settled inside. Flynn continued to suckle at her breast, his free hand sliding across the satiny skin of her abdomen. The snap of her jeans popped loose, and then the zipper rasped downward and his fingers were sliding beneath the stiff denim. His hand came to rest over the very heart of her need, only the satin of her panties separating them.

Ann stiffened as his fingers stroked her dewy flesh through the thin fabric. His touch was so intimate, the feeling so intense, it was almost painful. He seemed to understand, because he didn't move to deepen the caress until he felt the tension ease.

When she relaxed beneath him, his fingers moved again, stroking, probing, teasing, all with that frustrating layer of cloth between them. His mouth nuzzled between her breasts and she arched upward against his hand, a moan escaping her. He was so close. So close. She felt him smile against her breasts and a sudden spurt of rage made her dig her nails into his shoulders.

He laughed, the merest ghost of masculine triumph brushing her skin. Before the sound could fan her frustration higher, his hand lifted, sliding beneath the waistband of her panties. Ann's breath came out in a sob as he touched her at last, stroking the delicate folds.

Her body arched as he fanned the flames inside her higher and higher, pushing her toward some goal she was half afraid to reach. But, where he'd made allowances for her uncertainties a moment ago, now he was ruthlessly determined to push her forward. His mouth closed over hers, his tongue stabbing within at the same time that his finger slipped inside her, his thumb pressing on the most sensitive part of her.

Ann felt as if she were suddenly spinning apart. The pleasure caught her, lifted her and then dropped her to fall endlessly through space. She was blind, helpless, with nothing to cling to except Flynn's broad shoulders. He held her tight, his mouth and hands gentle on her trembling body, easing her back down from the heights.

She opened dazed eyes as he stood up, bending to lift her in his arms. The fire continued to burn on the hearth, the flames lower now. Her eyes met Flynn's, reading the hunger that still burned in him, and she buried her face against his bare shoulder, oddly shy in the face of his need.

He carried her easily, kicking the door of his bedroom shut behind them. He set her on the bed and then returned to the door, flicking the lock shut, reminding Ann that they were not alone in the apartment. Her cheeks warmed when she remembered her total abandonment of a few minutes ago. The possibility of being interrupted had been the last thing on her mind.

The room was lit only by one small lamp that burned on a table near the bed. In the dim light, Flynn looked intimidatingly large. She could feel his eyes on her, but she couldn't bring herself to meet them. She stared at his chest as he shrugged out of the loosened shirt and let it fall to the floor. His fingers went to his belt buckle, and Ann felt the color come up in her cheeks at the sight of his arousal blatantly pressed against the heavy denim. She shut her eyes as his jeans hit the floor.

Flynn hesitated, staring at her. She was so still. Was she having second thoughts? He left his shorts on and crossed the room to kneel in front of her.

"Ann?" Her eyelids fluttered but didn't lift, and he cupped her chin, tilting her face to his. "Ann? Look at me, love. You're not afraid of me, are you?"

Her lashes lifted slowly, and he felt as if he could lose himself in the smoky green depths of her eyes. There were so many emotions in her face. Uncertainty, desire and a slumberous look that made his muscles tighten. He bent forward to kiss her and her mouth softened instantly, welcoming him, reassuring him.

Need burned in him. He wanted to bury himself in her, soothing his aching body in the warmth of her. He contented himself with kissing away the tension he could feel, easing her clothes away so slowly she was hardly aware of them going.

When she at last lay naked beneath him, he thought he would surely explode with hunger. He'd had fantasies about how she would look in his bed. The reality far surpassed anything he could have imagined. Her skin was creamy pale, like the finest satin, cool to look at but hot beneath his touch. Her hair spread like fiery silk across his pillow. And her eyes. Her eyes seemed to burn into his very soul.

He could feel her uncertainty as his hands stroked her body, stroking the slumbering fires to new life. If she'd thought it was impossible to want again so soon, he was determined to prove her wrong. He heard the surprised catch in her breathing as his fingers worked magic. She arched beneath him, tangling her fingers in his hair.

The pleading tug of her hands stripped away the last of Flynn's fragile control. He fumbled in the drawer of the nightstand, thinking of her protection though he knew she was long past any clear thoughts. He slid his body over hers, feeling her stiffen and then melt as she felt the heat that burned in him.

Her legs opened, cradling him, welcoming him. He tested himself against her, resting his weight on his hands so that he could watch her face. Her eyes reflected wild uncertainty and her body stiffened for a moment as he slid inside her. He shuddered as she sheathed him. She felt so good, so right. The uncertainty left her eyes, replaced by surprised pleasure and her body softened beneath him. Flynn groaned, lowering himself so that his chest was a sensuous weight on her breasts.

He began to move, slowly, savoring the feel of her tight warmth. Ann matched his movements, clumsily at first, gradually picking up the rhythm, drawing another groan from him. The hunger had been building for so long that the fulfillment could not last long. Flynn felt the delicate contractions grip her body and he moaned a protest. He wanted it to last forever and then his own climax took him, sending him spinning after her into a place where the only reality was each other.

The return to earth was slow. Flynn lifted his head, feeling as if the entire world had been rearranged in the last few minutes. Ann lay still beneath him, her body lax, her face utterly peaceful. He kissed her, tasting her satisfaction in the softness of her mouth. He made to move away and her hands tightened on his hips.

"Don' go." The protest was slurred.

Flynn smiled, kissing her again. "I'll smash you."

He pulled away, seeing the faint moue of discomfort as he withdrew. His brows drew together as a vague suspicion began to form.

"Ann?"

"Umm?" She didn't open her eyes, didn't shift from her sprawled position.

"I have this funny feeling that you've never done this before."

He couldn't have gotten more results if he'd dropped a bomb in the middle of the bedroom. Her eyes flew open, her body tightened, all the lazy pleasure leaving her. She scrambled to pull the sheet over her, tucking it around her breasts defensively. He almost regretted the question. Her reaction gave him his answer even before she spoke.

"What makes you say that?"

He leaned on one elbow next to her, drawing one finger down her bare arm. "It wasn't an accusation, love." He smiled, coaxing her to relax again.

"I'm thirty years old. It isn't likely that I'd still be a...a..."

"Virgin? Ann, it's all right. Why are you so defensive about it?"

Her eyes shifted away from him. "It's ridiculous."

"It's surprising but not ridiculous. Nothing about you could ever be ridiculous."

"You don't think that I'm...frigid or repressed or something?"

"Haven't you heard? There's no such thing as a frigid woman. Only an inept lover." His mouth brushed her shoulder and she shivered. He felt some of the tension ease from her.

"It's not that I have anything against sex, you know. It's just that I never had time for it. I don't mean that exactly. It's just that I've always felt like I had to prove that I'm worthy and I've worked so hard that I've never really had time to get close to other people."

Flynn's mouth cut off the tangled explanation, kissing her until he felt her soften, her hands coming up to clasp his shoulders. He wanted to go out and find her father and beat him to a pulp. Though the name hadn't been mentioned, he knew who it was that Ann was trying to prove her worth to. But he said nothing to her.

When he finally let her up for air, he was pleased with the slightly glazed look in her eyes. She looked like a woman who'd been well and thoroughly loved. The look pleased him.

"You don't owe me any explanations. But you should have told me sooner. I might have taken more time."

The look she gave him was half-shy, half-bawdy and all female. "If you'd taken any more time, I'd have exploded. You made it wonderful for me, Flynn. Thank you."

Flynn felt the color rise in his face. Blushing! She actually had him blushing. He laughed self-consciously. "Don't thank me. Believe me, the pleasure was all mine."

He slid his arm beneath her shoulders, pulling her to his side. Ann's head snuggled into his shoulder, feeling so right that he wondered how he'd ever slept without her small body tucked against his. She was asleep within minutes.

It wasn't quite that easy for Flynn. Lying there, staring into the dimly lit room, he wondered at the changes that had overtaken his life. Three weeks ago, he'd had nothing more important on his mind than whether or not to fly to Switzerland for the ski season. Now, here he was with a little girl who looked to him to take care of her and Ann.

Just what was he going to do about Ann? He didn't even know what he *wanted* to do about Ann. Somehow, she'd gone from being his beautiful but hostile neighbor to feeling so right in his bed that he couldn't imagine doing without her.

He turned his head, inhaling the faint herbal scent of her hair. Making love to her had been like nothing he'd ever experienced before. She'd felt so good. He'd never found such total satisfaction in a woman. He reached up to shut out the light. Nothing could be decided tonight.

Tonight, he just wanted to savor the closeness, the warmth of her in his bed.

Chapter Eight

Ann woke up suddenly, with the feeling of panic that comes of knowing that you're not in your own bed but not knowing where you are. Realization came quickly but it did little to slow the pounding of her heart. She shifted gingerly, easing away from Flynn's hold until she could sit up.

Flynn continued to sleep as she gathered up her clothes and dressed. Her movements were furtive, as if she were a thief in the night. She snapped her jeans and jerked her shirt on, thrusting buttons through buttonholes without paying much attention to whether she was matching the right button with the right buttonhole.

She stole quick glances at Flynn, terrified that he would wake up before she could slip away. She couldn't face him right now. It was foolish, childish even, but she just needed to get away.

Once dressed, she hesitated for a moment, unable to resist the chance to study him when she didn't have to worry about those brilliant blue eyes watching her. In sleep, he looked younger than his thirty-three years. His mouth was softer, more vulnerable. His hair fell onto his forehead in that tantalizing black lock, and she clenched her fingers against the urge to push it back off his forehead.

The sheet lay draped across his waist, exposing the mat of curling dark hair that covered his chest. She flushed, remembering the feel of those crisp curls against her body. Her breasts tingled at the memory. Her eyes followed the line of hair as it tapered across his stomach and disappeared beneath the sheet. She flushed again as the line of her thoughts moved beyond what the sheet revealed.

Part of her wanted to climb back into bed and wake him. She wanted to find out if it was possible to know the kind of pleasure she remembered from the night just past. Surely, she must have dreamed the total satisfaction she'd felt. She backed away, physically resisting temptation. She hurried from the room, carefully shutting the door behind her.

It was early. The light outside the balcony doors had the watery quality of dawn. The fire had burned to ashes on the hearth, not even a glowing ember to show what had been the night before. Ann picked up her shoes, trying not to think of what had begun here and ended in the bedroom.

Letting herself into her own apartment, she had a feeling of unreality. Oscar trotted toward her, meowing low in his throat, a questioning greeting. Ann wondered if he could see that something was different about her and then scolded herself for the foolish thought. The only thing Oscar could see was that she was home and it was morning and he was ready to be fed.

Ten minutes later, she stood in front of the mirror in her bedroom. Oscar was happily devouring his cat food and the apartment was still. The Ann who looked at her from out of the glass wasn't the Ann she'd known for thirty years. There was a new knowledge in her eyes. An awareness that hadn't been there before.

She looked away from her reflection, uncomfortable with what she saw there, unwilling to deal with the changes just yet. She'd get dressed and go to the hospital. It was early but there was always work to be done. And, right now, she wanted to lose herself in work.

FLYNN CAME AWAKE SLOWLY, feeling at peace with himself and the world in general. His hand went out but found only empty space. He opened his eyes, knowing that Ann was gone. A hint of her shampoo clung to the pillows, bringing vivid memories of how soft she'd felt in his arms.

He was disappointed that she was gone but a little relieved, too. This would give him a chance to figure out what he was going to say to her when they met again. Were they now lovers in the full sense of the word, or was she going to see last night as something that happened once but never again?

He wanted to be her lover. It surprised him to realize how badly he wanted that. He wanted her back in his bed, in his arms. He wanted to wake up next to her in the morning.

He got up and walked into the bathroom, turning the shower on full force and stepping under the warm spray. Becky would be up soon, if she wasn't up already. One thing he'd learned over the past weeks was that children didn't understand the idea of sleeping late. Mornings were for getting up, no matter what had gone the night before.

Becky. She'd been the catalyst to bring him and Ann together, but it was no longer possible to pretend that she was all that connected them.

Half an hour later, he left his bedroom and walked, barefoot, into the living room. Ann's shoes were gone but the pillows still lay on the floor in front of the fireplace and their wineglasses still stood on the wide hearth. He picked up the glasses and then turned at a sound behind him.

Becky stood in the hall doorway, her eyes stern with disapproval. "It's awful early to be drinking, Mr. Flynn. Are you going to get plastered again?"

Flynn grinned at her, not in the least put out by her scolding tone. "I haven't had a drop, urchin. These are from last night. Hungry?"

"Starved."

"Well, go comb your hair and I'll see what I can do about finding you some breakfast."

WHEN THE KNOCK ON THE DOOR CAME, Ann jumped, spilling milk on the counter. She grabbed a sponge to mop up the puddle, grimacing at the fine tremor in her hand. She'd known that she wouldn't be able to avoid Flynn forever. In fact, she'd known that she wouldn't even be able to avoid him all evening. But she hadn't expected him to come knocking on her door when she'd been home less than twenty minutes.

He was going to want to talk about last night and she wasn't ready to talk about it. She wasn't sure she'd ever be ready. This was one problem she hadn't been able to put aside by going to work. It had nagged at the back of her mind all day, like an aching tooth that couldn't be ignored.

The knock came again, and she dropped the sponge into the sink.

"I'll just tell him that I don't want to talk about it. After all, what's to discuss? We made love. People do it all the time. No big deal."

Oscar gave her a dubious look, as if he didn't believe her words any more than she did.

She pulled open the door to find Flynn's hand raised to knock a third time. All her carefully selected phrases flew out of her head when she saw his face.

He looked old and tired. Deep lines bracketed his mouth, and there was a dull hurt in his eyes. He was far removed from the man she'd left sleeping only twelve hours ago.

"My God, Flynn. What's wrong?"

"They found Becky's mother. She's dead."

"You're sure Becky is all right alone?" Ann handed Flynn a cup of coffee.

"Thanks. Becky is plugged into a tape of *Return of the Jedi*. I don't think she'll come up for air for another hour, at least. I left the door open and she knows where we are if she needs something."

He took a swallow of the coffee, staring into the cup broodingly. "I just don't know how to tell her."

"I know." Ann sat down across from him with her own cup. "Tell me what Ms. Davis had to say."

"She came by this afternoon. I sent Becky out onto the balcony so we could talk. She said that they'd found Becky's mother. At first, I didn't know whether to be glad or sorry. I mean, I was glad for Becky's sake but I figured it meant that I was going to lose her and she sort of grows on you."

"I know." She did know. The thought of Becky going out of her life was a painful one.

Flynn set the cup down and leaned his head back against the chair, his face so weary that Ann wanted to smooth the lines away.

"Anyway, before I could say much of anything, she told me that Becky's mother had been found dead."

"Oh God. Poor little Becky. What happened to her? Do they know?"

He shook his head. "It's too soon to know much yet. All I know is that they found her body in one of the aqueducts. I guess they'll have to do an autopsy."

"Are they sure it's her?"

"The identification in the purse is hers and the landlady went in and gave positive ID just a couple of hours ago."

"Poor Becky."

There didn't seem to be anything else to say. After a long silence, Ann stirred, trying to gather her thoughts into some practical pattern.

"What did Ms. Davis say about Becky staying with you? They're not going to take her away now, are they?"

"No. She said that, under the circumstances, she thinks it would be cruel to remove Becky from our care. Becky feels safe here."

"That's something at least."

He stirred restlessly. "Not much in the face of her mother's death. And it's only temporary. They're going to try and find some record of Becky's father and contact him. If they can't find him or he doesn't want her, then she'll be put in a foster home."

Flynn surged to his feet, his long strides eating up the distance between sofa and door and then back again. Ann watched him, uncertain of what to say to reassure him.

"You know, it isn't like the days of Jane Eyre. A lot of foster parents are really wonderful people."

"Sure. But what if she gets foster parents who aren't wonderful people? You know, she acts real tough on the outside but she's still just a little girl."

"I know." She watched him pace back and forth, his strides quick with pent up frustrations. "Maybe you could be her foster parent."

Flynn stopped and spun to face her so suddenly that Ann jumped. His eyes pinned her to the chair, bright blue with emotion. "Do you think I haven't thought of that? But what do I know about kids? I'm a bachelor. I don't even have a respectable job. Besides, a little girl needs a mother. And it wouldn't matter anyway because Davis made it clear that she had to work very hard convincing her superiors to let Becky stay with me. The only reason that they aren't taking her away immediately is because my parents have spotless reputations and she told them that Becky and I would be spending most of our time with them.

"Even that wouldn't have done it if she hadn't implied that the rest of the time you'd be around to protect Becky's impressionable young mind from any bad influences that I might exert. You'll be pleased to know, Dr. Perry, that your reputation is impeccable. Good thing they don't know that you spent last night in my bed.''

The apartment was absolutely silent as they stared at each other. Color flooded Ann's face and then drained away, leaving her ashen. She stared at him for a long moment, hurt in her eyes before she looked away, gathering her defenses around her like a cloak.

''I think—''

''Oh, God, I'm sorry, Ann.'' He covered the short distance between them in one long stride, dropping to one knee and taking her hands before she had a chance to draw away. ''I'm sorry. I shouldn't have said that. I don't even know *why* I said it.''

Ann looked anywhere but at his face. She felt very vulnerable and she didn't want him to see that vulnerability. ''It's okay.'' She tugged on her hands but his fingers tightened over hers, denying release.

''No, it's not okay. I didn't mean to sneer about last night. That's the last thing in the world I meant to do. It was special.'' Unwillingly, her eyes were drawn to his face, reading the absolute sincerity there. Some of the ice that had settled around her heart melted.

''Was it special?'' Ann hadn't meant to ask that. It sounded too young, too vulnerable.

His face softened magically, leaving Ann breathless. ''It was incredibly special and I had no business throwing it in your face like that.''

''It's okay.''

''No, it isn't okay. It's just that it was pretty frustrating to realize that the only reason Becky was being allowed to stay with me was because you were around to make me look respectable. I've never thought of myself as quite that much of a rake and roué. I mean, I'm not a dedicated banker or lawyer but I'm hardly Don Juan, either. By the time Ms. Davis was through explaining all the half-truths she had to tell to get them to leave Becky here, I felt more like Jack the Ripper.''

Ann's fingers tightened over his before pulling away. This time, he let her go. ''It's all right. I know how worried you are about Becky.''

''How do you tell a little girl that her mother is dead? That she'll never see her again?'' The agony in his face made Ann's heart twist. Without thinking about it, she reached out to smooth the unruly lock of hair back from his forehead.

''We'll do it together. Becky's strong. She'll be okay.''

''I just wish there was some way I could protect her from this.''

''I know you do, Flynn. I know you do.''

JOHN WILLIAMS'S MUSIC BLARED out the finale as Princess Leah, Han Solo, Luke Skywalker and their assorted furry and metallic companions accepted the accolades of the rebel forces. Flynn stared at the screen over Becky's shoulder, wishing that George Lucas could arrange for real life to work out as neatly as it did in the movies. He picked up the remote control and shut the television off as the credits began to roll.

''I love *Star Wars*. When I grow up, I want to be like Han Solo and fly through space. Wouldn't you like to do that, Mr. Flynn?''

She turned to look at him, her face still lit up with the magic of the film, and Flynn had to swallow hard. He dreaded being the one to snuff that light.

''Becky, I need to talk to you.''

She stared at him and then her eyes dropped away. Her face closed up, reminding him of the way she'd looked when he'd first found her.

"It's about that lady from the welfare."

"Sort of."

"Are you gonna send me away?"

"No. Of course I'm not going to send you away." He reached out to pick her up, setting her on his lap, feeling the rigidity of her small body, as if she were afraid that if she relaxed, someone would hurt her. "Didn't I promise that I wouldn't send you away?"

"People don't always keep their promises." It was said in such an adult, resigned way that Flynn could only stare at her downcast face. He looked at Ann, seeing the tears swimming in her eyes.

"Becky, I'm not going to send you away but I've got some bad news about your mother." She said nothing, only continued to stare at her hands and Flynn went on, feeling as if he were stumbling hopelessly but not knowing what else to do. "Your mother is dead, honey."

The words sounded so bald, but he didn't know how else to say it. In the quiet that followed his words, the video tape hit the end of its travel and began to rewind, the quiet hiss sounding unnaturally loud.

"You mean dead, like when Charly the cat died?"

"I…yes, like when Charly the cat died."

She lifted her head, looking at him out of clear gray eyes. "She won't be coming to get me?"

"She won't be coming to get you."

He waited for the tears. She dropped her head again, her small fingers picking at a spot of lint on her corduroy pants.

"Can I stay here?"

"You can stay here for as long as you'd like." Later, there'd be a time to try and explain about foster homes and adoption. Now, what she needed was some security.

"Can I watch *Jedi* again?"

Flynn stared at her and then looked at Ann. She

shrugged, clearly at a loss. "Sure you can, sweetheart. Do you want us to watch it with you?"

"If you want." She slid off his lap and picked up the remote control, pushing the button to turn on the screen and then starting the tape over again.

"Ann and I will be in the kitchen, if you need us."

"Okay."

Once in the other room and safely out of earshot, Flynn turned to look at Ann. "What's wrong with her? Do you think we should call a doctor or something?"

"I *am* a doctor."

"Of course." He thrust his fingers through his hair, ruffling it into wild disarray. "Why didn't she cry or something?"

"She's just a child, Flynn. Death is still a bit abstract to her. It may take a little while for her to realize that her mother is really never coming back."

"I suppose." He raked through his hair again. "I keep thinking there's something I could do to make this easier for her, something I should say."

"You've done the best you can. Now all you can do is be there for her when she needs you."

FLYNN HAD NO IDEA what time it was when he came out of a light sleep, aware that something was wrong. He hadn't been asleep long. He was surprised that he'd fallen asleep at all. After tucking Becky in and telling her the obligatory story, he and Ann had shared a glass of wine and then she'd gone back to her apartment, leaving instructions to call her if he needed her.

Looking in on Becky, he'd experienced a feeling of total unreality. She slept so peacefully, as if this night were no different than any other. Was death really such an abstract concept to a child that she didn't realize what it was going to mean in her life?

But then who was he to question her reaction? Death had been an abstract to him until that night three years ago, when the police had called to tell him that Mark was dead and ask him to identify the body. Staring at his brother's face, forever wiped of emotion, death had ceased to be abstract and had become very real. If it had taken him three decades to understand the reality of death, why should he expect Becky to understand it in less than one?

The sound that had awakened him came again and he slid out of bed, slipping on a black silk robe as he left his bedroom and padded down the dim hallway. Pushing open Becky's door, the sound was clearer, easily identifiable. She was crying.

He crossed the room, easing himself onto the edge of her bed and gathering her shaking body into his arms. Her arms came up to circle his neck and she buried her face in the thin silk over his shoulder.

"It's all right, honey. It's all right."

"Mama. I want Mama." The words were muffled by sobs but Flynn felt them like tiny knives in his heart. "Mama."

"I know you do, sweetheart. I know you do. Cry it all out, honey. I've got you safe."

He had no idea how long she cried. He held her, rocking her, brushing the tangled hair back from her face, murmuring soothingly and wishing that there was something he could do to take her hurt away.

She cried herself to sleep and, even in sleep, her breath came in shaken little sobs. Flynn lifted his long legs onto the bed, easing her into a more comfortable position across his lap and settled his back against the headboard.

He studied her face in the light from the hallway. Her lower lip still quivered with each breath. Her lashes made spiky little patterns against her pale cheeks. She looked like exactly what she was—a frightened little girl whose world had been turned upside down.

Looking at her, he was struck by how right it felt to have her small body cuddled so trustingly against him. His arms tightened and he brushed a kiss against her hot forehead.

He'd never given a whole lot of thought to the matter of fatherhood. If he'd thought about it at all, he figured that being a husband would come first and children would be a much later consideration. But then he'd gotten drunk and stumbled into an alley and come up with a whole new perspective on life.

He didn't want to give up Becky. He didn't want to lose her small presence in his life. He wanted to keep her with him and watch her grow up. And, it wasn't just Becky that he wanted in his life. He wanted a woman to share it with.

He leaned his head back against the headboard and closed his eyes, feeling exhaustion creep over him. It had been one hell of a day.

"MR. FLYNN, what does being dead mean?"

Flynn dropped the spoon into the pancake batter and then reached in to fish it out, stalling for time. Becky had been unusually quiet this morning but, other than that, nothing seemed to have changed. Of the two of them, he wondered if he wasn't having a harder time coping with her mother's death than she was. And then a question like that came out of the blue.

He set the spoon in the sink and turned the heat off under the griddle. Wiping his hands on a towel as he moved over to the table, he sat down opposite the little girl. How was he supposed to answer a question like that?

"Well, when someone dies, they go out of our lives forever and we don't see them anymore."

Her eyes met his solemnly and he wondered if he'd explained it clearly enough. Should he tell her that her mother was in heaven or would that confuse her more than ever?

"You mean like when Yoda dies in *Return of the Jedi*?"

"Well, yeah, I guess so."

"Will Mama come back and visit me like Yoda visited Luke?"

"I...well..." He thrust his fingers through his hair, wondering how to explain that Yoda was make-believe and that make-believe and real life didn't always work out the same. He moved around the table to the chair next to hers, lifting her onto his lap.

"You won't see your mom like Luke can see Yoda. At least you won't see her standing in front of you and talking to you. But when you think about her and remember her, you'll see her in your mind and that will be sort of like having her there again."

Becky leaned her head against his shoulder, her fingers twisting a button on his shirt. "But, she won't really be there, will she?"

Flynn swallowed hard, his eyes stinging. "No, honey, she won't really be there. But that doesn't mean that she doesn't still love you." He brushed the hair back from her forehead, wishing it were easier to read her thoughts. "You know, it's okay to cry. You can even get mad because we all get mad when someone we love leaves us behind even when we know it wasn't their fault."

He didn't know if he'd said the right things. He felt woefully inadequate for explaining death and how to deal with it. He'd offered her the simplest of comforts. Surely there was something more to say.

He waited a long time to see if Becky would say anything else, ask any more questions, but she seemed content with his clumsy explanation. When she slid off his lap, he didn't try to hold onto her. Perhaps everyone had to deal with death in their own way, no matter what their age.

Flynn went back to the counter and turned on the griddle again. The last thing in the world he felt like doing was eating breakfast and he wasn't sure if Becky had any interest in food, but it seemed like a reasonable thing to do. He stirred the batter and decided it was too thick. A little milk would help. Turning toward the refrigerator, he bumped into Becky who'd been standing right behind him.

"Sorry, urchin. Would you get the milk for me?"

She went and got the milk carton and handed it to him. He watched her out of the corner of his eye as he splashed milk into the batter and stirred it. Instead of going back to the table, she stood right next to him, watching every move he made.

Without comment, he hooked his foot around a stool and pulled it over to the counter, lifting her up onto it so that she could watch what he was doing.

"Hungry?"

She nodded, watching him flick water onto the griddle to test it. The droplets danced on the cast iron and disappeared instantly. Flynn reached for the bowl and ladle.

"Mama used to make me teddy bear pancakes for breakfast."

It was the first words she'd spoken in several minutes. Flynn hesitated with the ladle in midair. It hadn't been a request but still....

"Teddy bear pancakes?"

She nodded solemnly. "They taste better than regular pancakes."

"Teddy bear pancakes." His tone was flat and resigned. He studied the batter and the griddle, seeking some inspiration. Why hadn't his mother ever made teddy bear pancakes? She should have known that it would be an important skill in his life.

It took numerous failures and most of the batter but, with Becky's coaching and Flynn's imagination, they eventually turned out a credible facsimile of a teddy bear in pancake form. Flynn eyed his masterpiece with great pride as he settled it on the plate in front of his small judge and watched her devour a half hour's work in a few bites.

It was worth the burned knuckles and wasted batter to hear Becky giggle over his clumsy efforts. He dried his hands, watching as she consumed the teddy bear pancake, carefully cutting off first one ear and then the other and working her way down to the legs. Clearly, there was an established pattern to eating a teddy bear.

He stroked his hand over her head and she glanced up, smiling through a mouthful of dough. There was a shadow in the back of her eyes but for now, her world was safe, as long as Flynn was within reach.

Flynn only hoped he could keep it that way.

Chapter Nine

"Dr. Perry to emergency please. Dr. Perry to emergency." The tinny voice echoed over the PA. Ann scribbled her signature on the bottom of a chart and handed it back to the nurse before hurrying down the hall to the elevator.

This had possibly been the worst week of her life. Just when her personal life was demanding more emotional energy than she had to give, her professional life was seeing a surge of unwanted business.

The elevator was empty for once, and she allowed herself the luxury of leaning against one wall and closing her eyes. If she was honest, it wasn't so much that she was any busier than usual. It was just that her heart wasn't really in it these days. A part of her wondered if it ever had been.

She pushed the thought away but it refused to be ignored. It wasn't that her work wasn't important, and it could be very rewarding. It was just that...just what?

Just that she had the feeling that she was living her father's dreams and ambitions instead of her own. He'd been the one to direct her toward medical school and she'd done just what he wanted, pushing aside her own desires to please him. Now she was beginning to wonder just how much she'd given up in an effort to make him love her.

She straightened as the elevator came to a halt and the doors slid open. Now was not the time to try and analyze her entire life—past, present and future. She'd think about it later.

The next chance she had to sit down and think of anything wasn't until late that afternoon. Seated in the staff lounge, a cup of lukewarm coffee in her hand, Ann leaned her head back on the worn sofa and shut her eyes, closing out the buzz of conversation coming from two doctors across the room.

She was so tired. Not physically tired but mentally tired. Tired of thinking, tired of trying to decide what was right, tired of worrying about what her father wanted. She wanted to get up and walk out of the hospital and never come back. She wanted to go home to Flynn and Becky and shut the door and not come out for a month.

Home to Flynn and Becky? Was that how she was beginning to think of it? Dangerous thinking. What were they doing right now? Had they gone to the park, or maybe Becky was watching a movie on the VCR and Flynn was doing more of his endless research on the subject of schooling. The new school year had started two weeks ago, but Ms. Davis had agreed that it might be best for Becky to stay home. It was a difficult time for her. Unspoken was the thought that, when they placed her in a foster home, she probably wouldn't be in the same school district that she was now, anyway. Flynn refused to talk about foster homes.

Flynn. Another subject she'd been avoiding examining. She wasn't sure just what her feelings were, and she was afraid that if she looked too closely she might not like what she found.

They'd made love. It wasn't something that she could ignore or forget. Once in a while, she would look up and catch Flynn watching her and she knew that he hadn't forgotten, either. Just the memory of that night was enough to make her knees feel quivery. What would have happened between them if Becky's needs hadn't taken precedence?

The alarm on her watch pinged discreetly and she sat up, downing the last of her coffee and forcing her mind back to her job. Soon, she was going to have to have a long talk with herself. There were a lot of things she needed to think about. Like the direction her life was going; did she want to spend the rest of her life in medicine; and what would it be like to fall in love with Flynn McCallister?

The next afternoon, she was no closer to answering any of her own questions, but the questions themselves had been pushed aside by more pressing matters. Sitting on Flynn's sofa, she watched him pace back and forth across the living room, his strides full of coiled energy.

"What time is it?"

"It's five minutes later than it was the last time you asked. Flynn, she isn't even due for another five minutes."

"I know. But she might get here early."

"So you're wearing a path in the carpet for her?"

He stopped abruptly, staring down at his feet as if he'd only just realized what he was doing. The smile he gave Ann was rueful. He came and sat down in a chair beside the sofa.

"I'm a little uptight."

"No kidding."

"It's just that Ms. Davis didn't give me any idea of why she wanted to see us."

"Maybe she just wants to check and make sure Becky is all right."

He shook his head. "She was here three days ago."

"Did she say anything then that might give you a clue?"

"Just that they were still looking for Becky's father." He frowned. "I don't know why they're going to all this effort to find him. What kind of a jerk abandons his kid?"

Ann shrugged. "Maybe there's extenuating circumstances."

"Ha!" Before he could expand on his opinion of extenuating circumstances, there was a knock on the door. Their eyes met, each wanting some reassurance that neither of them could give. Flynn grinned and lifted his thumb in a cocky gesture of reassurance, but he didn't feel in the least bit secure.

As he walked to the door, he felt as nervous as if he were walking down the gray corridors leading toward death row. He'd told Joe to send Ms. Davis up when she arrived. Now, he wished he hadn't. If Joe had called first, it would have given him a minute to prepare for whatever she might have to say. None of his feelings showed in his face as he opened the door.

"Come in, Ms. Davis. It looks like you beat the rain here."

She smiled as he took her light jacket and hung it in the coat closet. "Early in the season for rain but it does look like we may get a storm before nightfall."

Flynn followed her into the living room, wishing that he could read something from her face.

"Dr. Perry, I'm glad you could be here. I hope it hasn't put too much of a crimp in your schedule at the hospital."

"Not at all." Ann smiled at the older woman and she wondered if Flynn felt as nervous as she did.

"Would you like some coffee?" He had to force himself to make the polite offer when what he really wanted to do was demand why she was here.

"No, thank you. I'm sure you're both anxious to know the reason for this visit." She sat down, arranging her skirt over her knees.

Flynn forced himself to sit down when every muscle in his body demanded action. "Actually, we were wondering. Was there a problem with your visit Monday?"

"No problem at all, Mr. McCallister. Personally, I've seldom seen any two people more suited to taking care of a child. You've done wonders with Becky."

Flynn smiled, feeling as if his face might crack with the effort that went into the gesture. "Becky is a terrific kid."

"All kids are wonderful. Where is Becky?"

"My mother has her for the afternoon."

"Good." Ms. Davis smoothed her skirts. "I'm afraid I have some good and some bad news."

Flynn smiled slightly. "I've always had a healthy distrust of conversations that start out on that note."

"I'm afraid it won't be possible for you to adopt Becky, Mr. McCallister."

Flynn kept the faint smile pinned in place, aware of Ann's head jerking toward him. He should have told her what he had in mind. But there was no time to explain it to her now. "I didn't expect a decision so quickly. I can't believe that my reputation is so bad that it would earn me an immediate rejection as parental material."

"It really has nothing to do with your reputation, Mr. McCallister."

He leaned forward, his eyes pinning her to her chair with their intensity. "What if I were to get married? Would that help at all?"

His eyes shifted to Ann. She stared at him, feeling her own eyes widen with shock as she realized what he was thinking. If they were married, it might make it possible for them to adopt Becky. She sat back against the cushions, unable to drag her eyes away, unable to believe what she was thinking.

He was suggesting that they marry for Becky's sake. It was a ridiculous idea. Gothic. After all, people didn't marry just for the sake of a child that didn't belong to either one of them.

It was amazing that he could even consider such a thing.

It was amazing that she wasn't leaping up and denying any such implication. But what was most surprising was that it hurt to think that he'd be willing to marry her for Becky's sake.

She wanted him to want her for herself.

The thought was so stunning that Ann jerked her eyes away from his, afraid that he might read it in her expression. She stared down at her linked hands, unwilling to even consider the implications of the thought.

"Your bachelorhood really doesn't make any difference, Mr. McCallister. Adoption simply isn't possible. Becky's father has been located and he wants his child."

The words fell into a pool of silence, as if each were a small stone, sending out ripples as they hit the water.

"Her father?" Flynn's voice was dazed. He'd never seriously thought that they'd find the man. "Her father wants her now? Where was he for the last three years? You can't just be a parent when the mood strikes you and then drop it! What's going to happen the next time he decides he doesn't want to be a father? Is Becky going to be sleeping in alleys again? I thought you people were supposed to be concerned that Becky get a good home. And now you're just going to hand her over to some flake who couldn't be bothered with her for the last three years." By the time he finished speaking, he was on his feet, glaring down at the social worker.

Ann wondered how Ms. Davis could look so calm. Flynn was a more than slightly intimidating figure. The clouds had thickened, leaving the apartment lit with a thin gray light. In his anger, Flynn looked enormous, as if the force of his emotions had given him added size. Electricity seemed to crackle around him. Ann was thankful that his rage wasn't directed at her. Ms. Davis was apparently made of sterner stuff.

"I understand your concern, Mr. McCallister. And your

disappointment. I know that you wanted to adopt Becky yourself and I can tell you that I would have given you my recommendation if Mr. Traherne hadn't turned up."

"Who's Mr. Traherne?"

"Becky's father."

"Traherne? Becky's last name is Sinclair. If this Traherne couldn't even be bothered to marry Becky's mother, how can he lay any legal claim on Becky?"

"They were married, Mr. McCallister. You see, three years ago Becky's mother left Mr. Traherne and took their child with her. Mr. Traherne has been looking for both of them since but, until our department started a search for Becky's father, he had been unable to locate his wife or his daughter. He did not abandon them."

Flynn sat down slowly, searching for some flaw in her words. "Why did she take Becky and run? She must have had a reason."

"According to Mr. Traherne, they had a misunderstanding. His wife disappeared before they could clear the misunderstanding up."

"She must have been afraid of him to run like that."

"Mr. Traherne's reputation is impeccable. He's a doctor, the Traherne family has been in Denver for over seventy-five years and they are all respected members of the community. We feel that it's in the best interests of the child if she can be with her natural father."

Ms. Davis glanced at her watch and reached for her brief-case. "I have another appointment in half an hour. I assume it's all right with you if Becky stays here until her father arrives. He should be here day after tomorrow."

Flynn roused himself at her words. His smile was strained but he stood up to show her to the door. "I want to thank you for the work you've done on Becky's behalf, Ms. Davis."

"It's my job, Mr. McCallister." Her fingers were warm

and dry as they shook hands. "You've done wonders for that little girl. She's very lucky to have met you."

"Oh, I don't know. I feel like I'm the lucky one."

"You'll make a wonderful father when you have children of your own."

He smiled and shut the door behind her. Behind him, he could hear Ann neatening the stacks of children's books that were scattered over the coffee table. He stood in the dim hallway and looked at the wreckage of all his plans.

He was losing Becky. No more horrible coffee, no more trips to the park, no more bedtime stories. The thought brought a hollow ache to his gut. She'd wound her small fingers into his heart and it was going to hurt like hell to pull them loose.

With Becky gone, what was going to happen to his relationship with Ann? Becky was the catalyst that had brought them together. Most of their time had been spent with Becky in tow. They'd had so little time together. He didn't have to close his eyes to remember the one night they'd spent together. The feel of her in his arms, the scent of her on his pillow, those were things that were with him every minute.

When Becky left, would Ann still want to be with him or was he going to lose her, too?

THE NEXT TWO DAYS were strained. Flynn and Ann had decided not to tell Becky about her father. If there was some mistake, there was no sense in getting her hopes up only to have them dashed. There'd been enough disappointments in her young life.

Every time Flynn looked at Becky, he was reminded of how little time was left. Every time he looked at Ann, he saw so many questions that he was afraid to ask.

There was so much left unsettled between them, things that had nothing to do with Becky. Where was their relationship going to go once Becky was gone? They'd made love and then circumstances had parted them as firmly as if they'd been on different continents. Since the death of Becky's mother, there'd been no opportunities to think about the two of them.

Ann had never mentioned his oblique suggestion that they marry in order to adopt Becky. Flynn wondered if she had been mortally offended or if she'd understood and shared his desperation. He wanted to ask her about it, but there never seemed a moment when they could really talk. Or, perhaps, they were both afraid to find out what would happen when they finally didn't have Becky to serve as both link and barrier between them.

But she wouldn't be there much longer. What then?

THE DAY BECKY'S FATHER was supposed to arrive, Ann stayed home from the hospital. The sudden showers that had drenched southern California had given way to more typical sunshine. It was the kind of weather that made visitors to L.A. wonder why anyone would ever live anywhere else. Flynn was not impressed.

All he could think about was the meeting with Traherne. Father or not, he wasn't turning Becky over to the man until he was sure she'd be cared for. Ann occupied herself in the kitchen, baking endless batches of cookies and burning every other panful. Becky had opted to play on the balcony, losing herself among the greenery.

When Joe buzzed up from the lobby to say that there was a Mr. Traherne here, Flynn felt as if the world had come to a halt. He hadn't realized how much he'd been hoping the other man wouldn't show up until this moment.

"Send him on up, Joe."

He turned from the intercom and met Ann's eyes, reading the same uncertainties that he was feeling. He forced himself to smile, wanting to ease some of the tension from her face.

"Hey, how bad can he be?"

The knock on the door came before she could say anything. Flynn gave Ann a thumbs-up and went to answer the door. Ann couldn't make herself follow him. What if Becky's father turned out to be a blustering, obnoxious creep? How could they let Becky go with someone like that? How could they let Becky go at all?

There was a murmur of male voices as Flynn answered the door. Ann had only a second to offer a garbled prayer, not even sure what she was asking for.

"Ann, this is Rafferty Traherne, Becky's father."

Ann offered her hand to the man next to Flynn, trying to keep her surprise from showing in her face. She wasn't sure what she'd expected. Someone not quite so large and... She reached for the right word to describe him and finally came up with solid. Rafferty Traherne was definitely solid.

The first surprise was his hair. For some reason, she'd expected him to share Becky's pale gold coloring. But his hair was gray. Not sprinkled with gray but solid steel. The color was unexpected, the more so when it was easy to see that he was still in his early thirties.

At six foot tall, he had none of Flynn's lean whipcord strength. He was built like a bulldozer. Broad shoulders and hands that swallowed her own fingers. There was nothing here that reminded her of Becky's delicate bone structure. Nothing to show that he was related at all until she looked into his eyes. They were the same clear gray as his daughter's. And they gave her that same feeling that they could look right into her soul. Something told her that this man would not be easy to lie to.

"How do you do, Mr. Traherne."

"Please, call me Rafferty. I understand you've been taking care of Becky.'' His voice matched his body. Deep, dark and strong.

"Well, between the two of us, Flynn and I have been looking out for her.''

"I appreciate it.'' His eyes flicked away from her, and Ann knew immediately what he was seeking.

"Becky is outside. We thought it would be best if we had a chance to talk to you before the two of you met.''

"Of course.'' If he was impatient to see his daughter it was impossible to read it in his face, but Ann suspected that Rafferty would never be easy to read.

"Why don't we have a cup of coffee. I know you must have a lot of questions.'' She looked at Flynn and he nodded.

"Good idea. Have a seat, Traherne. I'll get the coffee.''

He disappeared into the kitchen, leaving Ann alone with their guest. She led the way to the fireplace grouping, seating herself on the sofa and watching him sink into one of the chairs. Like Flynn, he dominated the overstuffed piece of furniture without effort.

"How is Becky? All they told me was that she was in good health.''

"Becky is wonderful. She's bright and very mature for her age.''

Flynn came in, setting a tray of cups on the coffee table. "Becky is a great little girl. She deserves a solid home.''

Ann flushed at the edge of hostility in his voice, but Rafferty seemed to take it in stride. "I never intended for her to have anything else. I can understand your concern. From what Ms. Davis told me, you've done an awful lot for Becky.''

Flynn picked up a coffee cup and settled into the other chair, stretching his long legs out in front of him. He was the picture of total relaxation, and Ann wondered if it was her imagination that made tension seem to hum around him.

"I found Becky sleeping in the alley behind this building. She'd been on the street for three or four days and she'd been alone for two weeks before that. She's a hell of a gritty kid."

Rafferty's mouth tightened at the recital of what Becky had been through. "I can't believe Maryanne would just leave her alone like that. She's just a baby."

"From the sounds of it, Becky was the more mature of the pair. I don't think your wife had a whole hell of a lot of common sense."

Rafferty stiffened and Ann held her breath. Flynn was deliberately trying to antagonize the man. Even if what he said was true, couldn't he have found a more tactful way to say it? Slowly, the tension eased from Rafferty's broad shoulders. His mouth turned up in a rueful smile.

"I can't blame you for speaking your mind, McCallister. You've done a lot for Becky, things I should have been there to do. I guess that gives you the right to ask a few questions.

"You're right. Maryanne didn't have much common sense."

Flynn set his coffee cup down and leaned forward, all pretense of relaxation gone. "What I'd really like to know is why your wife felt it necessary to take Becky and run away from you. I've had Becky in my care for over a month now and if you hadn't turned up, I was going to adopt her. The government may be satisfied with the fact that your name is on her birth certificate but, until *I'm* satisfied, Becky is staying right where she is."

The two men stared at each other, weighing and measuring in some way that Ann couldn't follow. Whatever he saw apparently decided Rafferty in Flynn's favor. He nodded slowly.

"I'd feel much the same in your position."

"Good. Then you wouldn't mind telling us why your wife took Becky and ran away."

"Maryanne was a very high strung, very sweet girl. And I use the word 'girl' deliberately. She just didn't seem to know how to grow up. I thought maybe she'd grow up when Becky was born but she didn't. She was a good mother but I'm not sure she ever really figured out that this wasn't a doll to play with. She'd dress the baby in fancy outfits with little ruffled hats and take her out in the stroller to show her off. When Becky was two, Maryanne bought matching mother and daughter outfits. They looked like something out of a magazine."

He was silent for a moment, lost in memories. He shook himself, coming back to the present with an effort. "I'm a doctor and my hours aren't all that regular. Maryanne wanted someone who could be there to pet and hold her, someone to take her out to dinner so she could show off her clothes. I wanted someone who understood how important my work was to me."

He shrugged. "It was a classic case of two people who didn't have enough in common. We quarreled a few times but never anything major. I wanted her to grow up and she wanted me to be a father figure. There was no middle ground."

He reached for a coffee cup, turning it absently. His hands were huge and Ann had a hard time imagining them holding a scalpel or anything smaller than a tractor.

"Maryanne…did something that she thought was going to make me very angry. She was right. I was furious. But she'd been told that when I lost my temper, I was downright dangerous." He set the cup down, linking his hands together loosely, elbows braced on his thighs. "I'll be the first to admit that I've got a nasty temper but I've yet to hit anybody, much less a woman. But she didn't know that and she thought… Hell, I don't know what she thought."

His fingers tightened on each other until Ann was sure that knuckles would crack. "We quarreled and I stormed out of the house. I went for a walk and ended up spending the night on a friend's sofa. I went straight to work from there. I figured we could both use the time to cool down. When I got home, she was gone and she'd taken Becky with her.

"I hired investigators but no one could turn up a trace of Maryanne or Becky. For all I knew, they were both dead, until I got the phone call from Ms. Davis."

He stopped speaking and no one else seemed inclined to say anything right away. Rafferty had told the story without fanfare or dramatics. He might have been talking about something that had nothing to do with him. But Ann had watched the way his fingers knotted over one another and she knew just how much it had cost him to dredge up the old memories. She looked at Flynn and could see that he was impressed despite himself.

"It's going to be awfully hard on Becky to just pack up and move. To her, you're a total stranger."

Rafferty nodded. "I know. She's just lost her mother. You two are the only security she knows right now. How did she take Maryanne's death?"

"Pretty well, I guess." Flynn took a swallow of coffee, his eyes on the cup. "I'm not sure she's completely grasped the reality of it. I think there's a part of her that still expects her mother to come back but we've done what we could to help her."

"Does she know how her mother died?"

"We decided to tell her that her mother fell and hit her head. Which, for all we know, is the truth. The coroner said that she died from a blow to the head but they don't know whether it was murder or an accident. She might have fallen accidentally and the guy she was with panicked and left her body in an aqueduct."

"Or he could have killed her." Rage rumbled in Rafferty's voice and Ann spoke quickly.

"We don't know that."

"And we never will." He thrust his fingers through his hair, tousling it into waves of gray. He gave her a quick, strained smile. "Don't worry. I'm not going to go hunting for this guy. There's nothing I can do for Maryanne. I've got to concentrate on Becky. I want to get to know my daughter again. You two know her a lot better than I do. What do you think would be the best way to tell her who I am?"

It was clearly not easy for him to ask for help, and Ann could not help but respect him for putting Becky's need above his own pride. She glanced at Flynn, but he appeared willing to let her take the lead.

"We thought that if Becky had a chance to get to know you before you leave, maybe even before she knows who you are, it might take a lot of the pressure off of her."

Rafferty stared at her for a long moment and then his eyes dropped to his hands. "You mean I should just hang around and let her get used to me and then tell her who I am? Seems like a hell of a way to get to know my own daughter, sneaking up on her?"

Flynn answered the pained question. "Becky's been through a lot lately. If we just drop it on her that her father has arrived, it's going to be pretty hard on her. You can stay here. There's plenty of room and it will give her a chance to get to know you without any pressure."

Rafferty ran his fingers through his hair and Ann held her breath, waiting for his decision. It couldn't be easy for him to rely on the advice of a pair of strangers for how to deal with his own child.

"Isn't she going to wonder why I'm staying here?"

"We can tell her that you're a friend of mine." Flynn's

offer was made without expression, and Rafferty studied him for a long moment before nodding slowly.

"All right. I appreciate the offer."

Ann allowed herself to relax for the first time since hearing of Rafferty's existence.

"Now, I'd like to meet my daughter."

"I'll take you out and introduce you." They all stood up, but Ann caught Flynn's arm when he would have led Rafferty out to the balcony.

"I think Rafferty might appreciate a chance to meet Becky without an audience. She's out in the garden." She gestured to the sliding glass doors.

Rafferty gave her a grateful smile. "Thank you."

Flynn said nothing, but the muscles in his arm were rock hard beneath Ann's fingers as he watched the other man open the door and step out, sliding the glass shut behind him.

Chapter Ten

Rafferty threaded his way between wide planters, some
overgrown with vegetation, some full of bare soil. The sun
seemed stifling after the Indian summer he'd left in Colorado. He stopped next to a planter that contained a small
jungle of ficus trees and unbuttoned his cuffs, rolling them
up his forearms. It was a delaying tactic.

What was he going to say to Becky when he was finally
face-to-face with her? How could he resist the need to pull
her into his arms and hold her close? He had to remember
that he was a total stranger to her, less welcome in her life
than the two people in the penthouse behind him.

He walked on, feeling the rhythm of his pulse throbbing
in his temples. Three years. Three years since he'd seen
her. What would she look like? Did she look like her
mother?

He came around the corner of a planter that contained a
tangle of unidentifiable vegetation and stopped abruptly,
feeling his heart almost stop also.

She was kneeling by a planter just a few feet away, digging in the bare soil with a small trowel, mounding the dirt
carefully to one side. She was wearing bright purple jeans
and a purple-and-white striped top. Her hair was pulled
back in a ponytail, a bright yarn bow slightly askew.

He swallowed hard, his hand going out for an instant

before he jerked it back. He pushed both hands in his back pockets to control the tremors that shook them. He'd done surgery, knowing the patient's life depended on the steadiness of his fingers, and his hands had been rock steady. He drew in a quick breath. He had to remember that he was supposed to be nothing more than a friend of Mc-Callister's.

"Hello, Becky." He hoped she wouldn't notice the way his voice shook.

He moved forward as she turned to look at him and Rafferty sank onto the edge of the planter, as much to give himself support as anything else. The move put his face almost level with hers.

"Hello. This roof belongs to Mr. Flynn, you know. Did he say you could come out here?"

"I'm a friend of his."

She studied him for a long moment, her expression solemn. Rafferty took the opportunity to study her, his eyes devouring every inch of her. She'd changed so much. The realization hurt. She wasn't the plump toddler he remembered. This was a little girl on her way to growing up. She was taller, of course. He'd expected that. But he hadn't expected her to look so different. She was slim, with none of the chubbiness she'd had as a baby. And her eyes, her eyes looked so much older and wiser than her years.

He felt a flash of anger. She'd had to grow up too quickly. Maryanne had robbed her of part of her childhood.

She looked like Maryanne. The same delicate features, elfin in a child, changing to beauty in a woman. But he could see himself in her face. The same stubborn chin, and her eyes weren't the pale blue of her mother's. Her eyes were gray, uncompromisingly gray.

"I guess if you're a friend of Mr. Flynn's, it's okay if you're out here."

Rafferty smiled, hoping she wouldn't notice that his eyes were too bright. "Thanks. I'm Rafferty."

"I'm Becky." She held out her hand and he took it.

The first time he'd been close enough to touch his daughter in three years. Her hand felt so tiny in his.

"I'm digging for gold."

He dragged his eyes from her face and looked at the hole she'd dug. "Have you had any luck?"

"Not yet but Mr. Flynn says you got to keep at something to make it work. And Ann says that pers...perst...."

"Persistence?"

"That's it. Ann says you got to have that to get anywhere."

"Sounds like you've had some pretty good advice."

"Mr. Flynn and Ann are my best friends in the whole world. They know everything."

Rafferty's mouth kicked up on one side. "Well, I hope you and I can be friends, too."

"We'll have to see if we like each other." Becky picked up the trowel and returned to her digging.

"I think we're going to like each other a lot, Becky."

He sat there, with the hot L.A. sun beating down and watched her dig in the soil. He'd missed so much of her life. Years that he could never regain. But he wouldn't miss any more of it.

IT WASN'T THAT he wasn't pleased for Becky's sake, but did Rafferty Traherne have to be so damned perfect?

Flynn picked up the dice and shook them before tossing them onto the table. A full house stared back at him. The fourth full house he'd had in a row. He stared at the Yahtzee score sheet, wondering what else he needed. Nothing that the dice were offering. He picked up the dice and threw them all again. At the end of his turn, he was forced to scratch his Yahtzee.

"You're not having much luck tonight, are you, Mr. Flynn?"

He smiled at Becky. "Not much. But you're making up for it, urchin. It's a good thing we're not gambling or I'd have lost the farm to you by now." She giggled.

Rafferty threw next and, of course, threw a Yahtzee on the second toss of the dice. Becky squealed with excitement and Ann laughed. Flynn smiled, but what he really wanted to do was throw the dice out the window.

No, if he was honest, what he really wanted to do was throw the man out the window.

No. He didn't want to do that. There was nothing wrong with Traherne. In fact, that was what was wrong with him. Couldn't the man have a few flaws? Bad breath. Bowlegs. Anything would do. But there was nothing.

He was absolutely perfect father material. He was patient with Becky but not above being firm. He had a good sense of humor; he was a polite house guest. He was good-looking, but not too good-looking. He probably loved God, America and apple pie, not necessarily in that order.

It was impossible not to like him but Flynn was trying.

He watched Ann smile across the table at Rafferty and felt a knot in his stomach that had nothing to do with the biscuits that Becky had made for dinner. Jealousy. Plain, old-fashioned jealousy. He was honest enough to admit that he felt it, but that didn't change the feelings.

In the last two weeks, Becky had come to adore Rafferty. Which was just as it should be. Flynn was doing what he could to loosen the ties between himself and Becky. It hurt but it had to be done. She needed to transfer her dependence to her father. He was glad that she was doing so.

He wasn't so glad that Ann seemed to think Rafferty was the greatest thing since sliced cheese. Did she have to smile at him quite so often?

He picked up the dice when his turn came and threw

again, barely noticing when he had to put the results down on chance. His eyes caught Ann's as Rafferty picked up the dice. She gave him a flickering smile and then looked away, her fingers toying with her pencil.

She'd barely looked at him since Rafferty's arrival. In fact, come to think of it, they'd barely spoken since the night they made love. It seemed as if something was always taking priority. First there'd been the death of Becky's mother, then finding out about Rafferty and then Rafferty himself showing up.

Flynn wondered if he was the only one to feel the tension between them. There was so much left unspoken. Their relationship had taken a giant step and then been frozen in time. They couldn't go back to what they'd been before, but there was no saying what might lie in the future.

"Your turn, Flynn." He looked up, startled out of his thoughts. Ann was holding the dice out to him, her expression quizzical.

"Sorry. I guess I wasn't paying much attention." He reached out to take the dice from her, their fingers brushing. Their eyes met, and Flynn knew he wasn't the only one to feel the sparks that resulted from the casual contact.

Soon, he promised himself. Soon, they'd have time for each other.

"GOOD GAME. Not that the Raiders can compare to the Broncos, of course." Rafferty's grin took the sting out of the words.

Flynn lifted his hand, signaling for another round of beers before settling back in the booth and looking at his companion. "I haven't been to a football game in years."

"I thought you had season tickets." Rafferty emptied his mug as the waitress set another round down in front of them. He reached for his wallet, waving off Flynn's attempt to pay for them. "My treat. The tickets were yours."

"Thanks. But the tickets weren't exactly my treat. The family always has season seats. We just haven't used them in a while. My brother and I used to go almost every game."

"Did he switch to hockey?"

"He died and I guess I just got out of the habit." Flynn took a long swallow of the frosty beer, surprised by how little it hurt to mention Mark.

In the background, a country song twanged out the miseries of divorce. Two would-be cowboys played a desultory game of eight ball at a pool table near the jukebox. It was broad daylight outside but the bar was dusky, as if light never quite penetrated the shabby wooden walls. The bartender polished glasses with a rag that looked like it had been used to polish an engine.

"Must be tough, losing a brother. Was he younger or older?"

Flynn dragged his gaze away from the surroundings. "Older. Older and perfect. In fact, you remind me of Mark."

Rafferty raised an eyebrow, his skepticism clear. "I do? Doesn't seem likely. Perfect is hardly a word likely to be associated with me."

"Not perfect, maybe, but you're so damn upright. Mark was like that. It was impossible not to like him but it was hell living up to him."

"Upright? I don't know that I see myself that way."

"Sure you are. You're a doctor. You're a great father. You probably own your own home and I bet you contribute to an IRA every year."

Rafferty laughed. "Guilty. Are those the only criteria for being upright?"

"Just about."

"Then I guess I have to confess to the crime."

Flynn smiled. "It's not exactly a crime. What do you think of Becky?"

Rafferty's face softened, answering the question even before he spoke. "She's terrific."

"Yeah. I thought so myself."

"I'll be telling her who I am soon."

Flynn nodded. "I figured. I'm going to hate to lose her but there's no sense in dragging things out forever."

"I think..." Whatever Rafferty thought was destined to remain unspoken. While they were talking, Flynn had been vaguely aware that the bar was filling up. Urban cowboys, construction workers and an assortment of women, accompanied and otherwise. The jukebox had been turned up and one or two couples were rocking back and forth on a tiny strip of space that could optimistically be called a dance floor.

It was the dance floor that was the source of the sudden trouble. Apparently, three men were claiming the privilege of the same dance with one woman. The disagreement had escalated into a shouting match. It was only a moment before the first punch was thrown.

Rafferty and Flynn slid out of the booth, both of them with the same thought in mind. To slip quietly and unobtrusively out of the bar. Unfortunately, things were not destined to work out quite that neatly. The fighting in the middle of the room seemed to have a ripple effect. Every man in the place remembered a grudge against the man next to him. Before they'd gone more than three steps from their booth, they were involved in a full-fledged brawl.

Flynn ducked under a punch thrown at him by a man in a cowboy hat and buried his left fist in the man's overfed belly, coming up with his right fist against the cowboy's chin. The man staggered back and Flynn spun to check Rafferty's progress. Rafferty was holding his own, using his sheer bulk to force his way toward the door and using his fists when he had to.

A journey that had taken a matter of seconds earlier in the day took closer to ten minutes in the midst of the brawl. Flynn could feel the adrenaline pounding in his temples as he ducked flying fists and flying bottles, always keeping the door in sight. He jumped forward, pulling a man off Rafferty's back and spinning him into the melee around them. Rafferty turned.

"Thanks."

"Don't mention it." Rafferty's eyes went past him, widening. Flynn spun around. He caught only a glimpse of a stop-sign red shirt, a black beard and an upraised hand. He threw up his arm. The bottle that would have landed on his head and removed half his face, shattered against his forearm instead. He was aware of pain but there was no time to worry about it now. Rafferty came around him like a freight train. Red-shirt didn't have time to react and Flynn saw the startled look on his face as Rafferty's fist connected with his chin, rocking him back on his heels. A second blow sent him crashing to the floor.

Rafferty turned, his eyes bright. "You okay?" He had to shout to be heard. Flynn nodded. "Let's get the hell out of here."

They were only a few feet from the door, and seconds later they ducked through into the relative quiet of the street. Both men collapsed back against the building. Inside the battle raged on, shouts and obscenities mixing with the shatter of breaking glass.

Flynn rolled his head to look at Rafferty, their eyes meeting in the dusky light. They were both disheveled. Rafferty's lip was split and oozing blood sullenly. His jacket had been left behind in the bar, his shirt was torn and his jeans were covered with beer. Flynn knew he looked at least as bad. He could feel blood soaking the fabric of his shirt. He had no idea how bad the cut was. He only hoped he wasn't bleeding to death. Every muscle in his body ached.

He grinned, feeling more alive than he'd felt in years. "Hell of a fight."

Rafferty grinned back, wincing as the gesture tugged at his split lip. "Hell of a fight." He dabbed at the blood on his chin. "How bad is your arm?"

Flynn shrugged, still grinning. "I have no idea."

"Ought to check it out." The wail of sirens punctuated his remark and their eyes met again. "We'll check it out later."

Flynn nodded. "I can't imagine Ann's reaction if I had to call and ask her to bail us out of jail."

"Think we can make it to the car before the cops get here?"

"We can try." Flynn pushed himself away from the wall and sprinted the half block to the Ferrari, aware of Rafferty right behind him. They arrived at the car just as the first squad cars came around the corner ahead of them. Flynn skidded to a halt by the passenger door, tossing the keys to Rafferty.

"You drive. I don't think my arm is up to it."

Rafferty walked around the end of the car, glancing up as if mildly curious when the police cars hurried by, lights and sirens going. He opened the car door and slid inside, flicking open the lock for Flynn. Flynn slipped into the dark interior and shut the door.

"Wonder where they're going."

"I have no idea." Their eyes met and they both grinned like a couple of teenagers. Their friendship was cemented in those moments.

An hour later, Flynn turned the key in the apartment door. "Ann's not going to be happy."

"We could lie and tell her we were rescuing someone from a fate worse than death."

"Just what is a fate worse than death?"

Rafferty shrugged his huge shoulders. "I don't know."

Flynn hesitated, the key still in the lock. "She'd never believe it."

He withdrew the key and opened the door. Inside, a peculiar acrid smell assaulted their noses, and Flynn stopped dead just inside the hall.

"Becky's cooking again."

Rafferty had had some experience with his daughter's cooking and he winced, both at the smell and at the thought of what might have caused it. "I wonder what's she's made."

"I don't want to know."

"Me neither. Let's go back to the bar. It's probably safer."

Flynn grinned at Rafferty's suggestion. He pushed the door shut behind them but he didn't take off his coat. The black leather served to conceal the blood that soaked his arm. With luck, he could get into the bathroom and deal with the wound without Becky or Ann being any the wiser. If it needed medical attention, he could call on Rafferty's expertise.

"Hi, Mr. Flynn. Hi, Rafferty. I'm making a cake." Becky greeted them as they stepped into the living room. Her small form was swathed in an apron, but it hadn't prevented flour from coating every exposed surface. "Did you have fun?"

"We had a lot of fun, pumpkin." Rafferty came around Flynn and scooped Becky, dropping a kiss on her flour-dusted hair. "What kind of cake are you making?"

"Spice. Ann says she thinks I may have added too much cinnamon."

Flynn inhaled, finally identifying the acrid scent as burning spices. He had the feeling that Ann was right. Ann came out of the kitchen, also apron-wrapped. She had flour in her hair and a slightly harried expression on her face, and Flynn thought she'd never looked more beautiful.

"How was your..." Her eyes, more critical than Becky's, went over the two of them, seeing the bruise starting to show on Rafferty's cheekbone, his swollen lip and torn shirt, Flynn's disheveled hair and clothes and the careful way he held his left arm.

"What happened?"

"Nothing. We stopped and had a drink after the game."

"A drink? That's all?"

Rafferty looked from Ann to Flynn and took hold of Becky's hand. "How would you like to go to a movie?"

"Yeah!"

"Coward." He shrugged without apology in answer to Flynn's quiet accusation.

"Sorry. I don't think it's good for Becky to see bloodshed and I have a feeling that's what's about to occur."

"Who's going to blood?"

"Bleed, sweetheart. Nobody's going to bleed. I was just kidding. Why don't you come help me find a new shirt and we'll go out to the movies."

"Is Mr. Flynn and Ann going to come, too?"

Becky's ungrammatical question was the last sentence spoken until she and Rafferty returned a moment later. Rafferty was shrugging into a clean shirt. Becky was carrying a jacket.

"Okay if I borrow a car?"

"If it wasn't for Becky, I'd make you walk to the theater. Take the Ferrari. I just hope you can sleep tonight after abandoning a friend in need."

Rafferty grinned, not in the least disturbed by Flynn's dark warning. "Ann's too nice to do more than minor damage." He looked at Ann's set face. "It really wasn't our fault."

The door shut, leaving Ann and Flynn in the quiet apartment.

"What happened?"

Flynn shrugged, wincing as the gesture shifted his arm. "Nothing much. A little fight broke out in the bar and we got involved in the edges of it while we were trying to get to the door."

"How badly are you hurt?"

"Not bad. A few scrapes and bruises. It really wasn't that bad a fight."

"Then why are you favoring your arm?" She was wearing a pink apron that clashed with the fiery red of her hair, her feet were encased in bright blue socks and he knew exactly how her jeans molded her firm body. She looked absolutely feminine, except for the stern line of her mouth.

Flynn didn't want to talk about his arm, or the fight. He didn't want to talk about Rafferty or Becky or the fact that soon they'd be going away and he'd be alone again. He wanted to pull Ann into his arms and kiss the stern expression from her face. He wanted to feel her soften against him.

"Do you realize this is the first time we've been alone in a month?"

Awareness flickered through her eyes for a moment before being sternly pushed aside. "Let me see your arm."

"It's really not that big a deal."

"Then you won't mind me taking a look at it, will you?"

To tell the truth, his arm was beginning to throb like the devil. Besides, if he wanted to seduce Ann, it would be nice if he weren't bleeding all over her.

"All right. I would appreciate it if you took a look at it. To tell the truth, I haven't looked at it since it happened."

If she was suspicious of his abrupt capitulation, he couldn't tell it from her expression. He led the way into the huge bathroom off his bedroom and then stood there, looking as helpless as possible. All was fair in love and war. He wasn't quite ready to call this one or the other. All he knew was that he wanted Ann in his bed again and, if he could accomplish that by playing on her sympathies, then he wasn't above doing that.

Ann pulled a wicker stool over next to the sink. "Sit down and we'll see if we can get that coat off."

He sat down and shrugged the coat off his uninjured arm, letting Ann ease it off the other arm. He didn't have to pretend to a pained silence when the fabric stuck to the wound. In fact, by the time Ann was through fixing him up, he felt worse than he had before she started.

She took one look at the cut and announced that it would require stitches. Flynn's protests were ignored as she fetched her medical bag and proceeded to scrub the wound with what he would have sworn was pure lye. She stitched the arm without local anesthetic, announcing that he was big enough to handle the pain. Flynn thought of suggesting that he might prefer not to handle the pain, but her disapproval was so palpable that he decided not to risk her ire any further.

As it turned out, she wielded the needle so carefully that he barely felt the four stitches she put in his arm. He watched her as she worked, her head bent over him, her attention on the job at hand.

"There. That should do it." She picked up a roll of gauze and began to wind it around his arm. "If you can just stay out of barroom brawls for a while and give it a chance to heal."

"I'll see what I can do." He lifted his free hand and tugged loose the pins holding her hair.

"Don't." But her protest came too late. His nimble fingers found the last pin and her hair tumbled onto her shoulders. She tried to ignore him, concentrating on taping the gauze bandage shut. But it was hard to ignore the way his fingers burrowed into her hair, finding the tense muscles at the back of her neck.

"You're too tense. You should relax more."

"Flynn..." She tried to back away but his hand tightened, pulling her closer. Seated on the wicker stool, his eyes were just level with hers, but she didn't want to meet his eyes. "Let me go."

"Look at me." He was so close that his breath stirred the hair that curled against her temples. Slowly, her eyes came up to meet his and she felt her knees weaken. It wasn't fair. How could his eyes be so blue, so full of need?

"Flynn..." He stilled her whispered protest with a quick kiss, stealing away her voice.

"Stay with me tonight."

"I can't. I..." He kissed her again and she forgot what she'd planned to say.

"Stay with me. I just want to hold you."

She started to shake her head but his mouth stopped the movement. The kiss was longer this time. His mouth molded hers, stealing not only her breath, but the ability to think.

"Please, Ann. I want you with me tonight."

"Flynn..." She wasn't quite sure how they'd gotten from the bathroom to the bedroom. Sometime during that drugging kiss, he must have eased her in here. She didn't remember walking but he certainly hadn't carried her. He kissed her again, his fingers untying the frilly apron.

"We can just sleep. I won't push you into anything more." He tugged the apron off and his attention moved to the buttons on her cotton shirt. For a man with full use of only one hand, he didn't seem to be having any trouble getting her clothes off.

Before Ann could marshall her thoughts, she was standing in front of him clad in a lacy camisole and tap pants, not quite sure how she'd come to be there. He reached around her to turn down the covers on the bed.

She hesitated, aware that this was a crossroads in some way that she couldn't quite define. Once in that bed, she would have taken a step toward... Toward what? She wasn't sure, but she knew it would change her life.

Flynn unsnapped his jeans and then waited. He could feel Ann's hesitation and he held his breath. He wouldn't pressure her but, if she walked away now, he felt as if something inside him would die. She looked up at him, her eyes bright green with questions he couldn't read, and then she turned and slid onto the bed.

He released his breath in a rush, unzipping his jeans and slipping them off. He left his briefs on as he climbed into bed beside her. He'd said that he just wanted to hold her and that was all he'd ask of her.

He reached out, pulling her close. Ann snuggled against his side, her small body seeming made to fit his, her head resting on his shoulder. Flynn reached up to shut out the light, plunging the room into darkness.

He rested his cheek against her hair, feeling complete for the first time in a very long time.

Chapter Eleven

Flynn came awake slowly, aware of feeling completely rested. He'd slept heavily but he didn't feel groggy. He didn't have to open his eyes to know the source of his contentment. Ann was snuggled against his side, one arm thrown over his chest, one leg nestled intimately across his thighs.

He kissed her forehead, brushing aside a bright curl to find the soft skin beneath. She stirred, tipping her head back. He didn't know if the invitation was deliberate or not, but he wasn't going to turn it down. He kissed his way down her face, planting soft kisses at the corners of her eyes, on the tip of her nose, on the delicate skin just under her jaw.

She stirred again and he knew she was awake. His lips teased the corners of her mouth and her lips parted, inviting him. His mouth settled over hers. It was a sleepy kiss, warm with passion that didn't need to be rushed.

Flynn's hand slid up her side, beneath the hem of her camisole, finding sleep-warmed skin that heated to his touch. Ann moaned against his mouth as his hand cupped her breast, testing its weight, finding the soft peak that hardened with the stroke of his thumb.

Still without speaking, Flynn shifted her until she lay on top of him, her breasts pressed against his chest with only the thin silk between them, her thighs lying between his. He brought his knees up, cradling her.

His hands burrowed into the thickness of her hair, pulling her face to his. The sleepy passion took on an edge of urgency. The kiss was a little harder, a little more demanding, and Ann met him with demands of her own.

His hands tugged impatiently at the camisole and she lifted herself so that he could tug the garment over her head. His hands caught her around the rib cage, lifting her higher, sliding her up his body. He heard her pleasure as his mouth closed around her nipple, stroking the pale pink tip to hardness. He held her helpless, suspended in his hands while he took his pleasure of her. He took his time, painting each breast with tongue strokes, covering every inch of soft flesh, feeling her desire in his hands.

He lowered her slowly, reluctant to give up the tender territory he'd conquered but needing the taste of her mouth. The kiss was explosive, the impact of it rolling through both of them. Suddenly, all the patience was gone. His hands fought the silk tap pants, hearing the fine silk tear but not caring. All that mattered was that her skin be bare to his touch. He couldn't stand anything that kept him away from her.

She struggled with the stretchy fabric of his briefs, her breath leaving her in a frustrated sigh when her hands couldn't master the task. Flynn brushed her hands aside and suddenly there was nothing between them. He rolled, putting her beneath him. Her legs parted, cradling him. His mouth caught hers, his tongue plunged inside at the same moment that he sheathed his aching hardness in the damp warmth of her body.

Flynn swallowed the keening moan that left her throat. The emptiness was filled, but the hunger was still there. He moved, feeling her body shift to accommodate his, tasting the response she gave so willingly.

He wanted to drag the moment out forever. But the need was too strong, the hunger too long denied. Ann shivered beneath him, her body contracting around him, and Flynn groaned, following her to the culmination of their passionate love.

Not a word had been spoken, but they communicated as fully as was humanly possible.

RAFFERTY WOKE SUDDENLY, aware that he was no longer alone. He was lying on his stomach, his face near the edge of the bed. He opened his eyes to find Becky seated on the floor next to the bed. She was still in her pajamas. Clutched in her arms was the tattered brown giraffe he'd given her for her second birthday. Her eyes were wide and solemn on his face.

"Good morning." He blinked, clearing the last remnants of sleep from his eyes. He rolled onto his back and pulled himself up until he could lean against the headboard. A glance at the clock told him it was barely six o'clock.

"You're up early. Did you have a bad dream?"

"No." She continued to stare at him and Rafferty's eyes narrowed, studying the intent expression on her face.

"What is it, Becky? Is something bothering you?"

"Are you my daddy?" The question was so totally unexpected that Rafferty had a moment of wondering if he was still asleep and dreaming this confrontation. But, looking at Becky's serious little face, he knew this was no dream.

"Would you like it if I was your daddy?"

She shrugged, her eyes dropping from his face. Her fingers twisted an ear on the battered stuffed toy. "I don't know. I guess it would be okay." She stopped but Rafferty didn't say anything. He knew there was more.

"If you're my daddy, how come you left me and Mama? How come you left us?"

He chose his words carefully, knowing that what he said now could affect their relationship for a very long time to come. "Your mother and I had an argument a long time ago. She thought I was very angry with her and she thought I was going to stay angry forever. So, she took you and she left."

"Were you mad?"

"I...was angry for a little while but I got over it. Your mother just didn't realize that I'd get over it. After she left, I looked for the two of you but I couldn't find you. I never stopped looking, Becky."

He waited a long time, hardly breathing. Had he said the right things? Was there something more he should have told her, some other way to say it?

"Did your mother ever talk about me?" It was taking a chance to ask the question, but he had to know what Maryanne had told her.

She shrugged without looking at him. "It always made her cry when I asked about you."

He closed his eyes, and for an instant, it was as if Maryanne was standing in front of him. She'd been such a sweet pretty girl. It wasn't her fault that she just hadn't known how to grow up. Yes, he could imagine that she'd cried when Becky asked about him. He'd never doubted that, in her own way, she'd loved him.

"We used to have a lot of fun together when you were little. You probably don't remember much of that."

Her eyes flickered up at him and then away. "I remember you used to throw me up in the air. And sometimes you'd tell me a bedtime story. Only you'd read it out of a book. You didn't make one up like Mr. Flynn does. Mama had a picture of you that she'd show me sometimes only your hair was all streaky. Not one color like it is now."

Rafferty ran his fingers through his iron-gray hair. "When your mother left, my hair hadn't gone completely gray yet. It runs in my family, you know. Your grandfather's hair was gray by the time he was thirty.''

"Grandfather? Do I have a grandfather?''

"Sure. And a grandmother, too. And you've got two aunts and three cousins.''

Her eyes widened at this bounty of relatives. "All those?''

"All those. That is, if you want me to be your dad.''

She stared at him for a long time. "I think I'd like that.''

Rafferty blinked, swallowing the hard knot in his throat. If his smile was shaky around the edges, he didn't think she'd care. He reached out one hand, careful not to expect too much too soon. Becky stood up and reached out to take his hand, her small fingers engulfed in his huge palm. She hesitated a moment, as if weighing him in some balance in her mind, and then she threw herself forward.

Rafferty's arms closed around her and he buried his face in her sandy hair. She smelled of soap and baby powder. His chest ached as her arms went around his neck.

He'd lost so much time with her. Three years gone never to be regained. He'd never lose sight of how lucky he was to have her back with him.

IT WAS AFTER NINE when all the inhabitants of the penthouse met up. Rafferty and Becky were in the kitchen cooking pancakes when Ann and Flynn showed up. Rafferty had his own theories as to who had slept where the night before, which was why he hadn't let Becky wake Flynn to announce that she'd found her father. When Flynn wandered into the kitchen, Becky pounced on him.

"Guess what, Mr. Flynn. Guess what.''

"It's too early to guess anything, urchin. Are you helping Rafferty cook breakfast?'' He eyed the pancakes cautiously. Rafferty grinned and waved the spatula.

"Becky is only supervising this morning.''

"That's nice. Now, what is it I'm supposed to guess?"

He sank into a chair, leaning his elbow on the kitchen table, his expression indulgent as Becky hopped up and down in front of him.

"Rafferty is my dad. My real live dad. He and Mama had a fight and she left but he never stopped looking for us. Isn't that neat?"

Flynn's smile was twisted as he reached out to ruffle her hair. There was a sharp pain in his chest as he looked at her. Just in the few weeks he'd known her, she'd grown so much. It hurt to think that he wouldn't be there to watch her grow and see her change.

"That's great, Becky. I'm really happy for you."

Rafferty flipped a pancake and then leaned one leg against the counter. "I've got reservations on a flight back to Denver late this afternoon."

"So soon?" The protest came from Ann who'd come to stand in the doorway. It was clear that she'd heard Becky's news. Her eyes shimmered with quick tears, and Flynn had to resist the urge to go to her and put his arms around her. It wasn't as if they hadn't known that this moment was coming. It was just that it was difficult to let go now that the time had come.

Ann looked from Becky to Rafferty. He shook his head, his eyes understanding.

"I don't see any sense in dragging things out. Goodbyes are best said quickly."

"You're right, of course." Ann blinked, clearing her eyes. The smile she gave Becky shook around the edges but not enough for Becky to notice.

"I'm really excited for you, Becky. I know you're going to love living with your dad."

"Yeah. He says there's snow and everything." Clearly, the 'everything' wasn't nearly as interesting as the snow.

"Denver isn't that far away. You guys should come visit us this winter. We'll go to Aspen for the skiing."

"Sure we will." Flynn looked at Ann, wondering if she'd noticed the way Rafferty automatically paired them. Wondering what she was thinking.

NO MATTER HOW QUICKLY SAID, the goodbyes were still painful. Becky had been part of Flynn's life a relatively short time, but she'd wound herself deep into his emotions. It wasn't easy to say goodbye.

Rafferty refused Flynn's offer of a ride to the airport. A taxi was expensive, but it would save them all a painful parting in public.

"You've got Frankie, don't you?" It was the second time Ann had asked the question, but Becky answered it again.

"He's in Daddy's purse."

Rafferty winced. "Carry-on luggage, pumpkin, not a purse." Ann smiled but her mouth shook and she had to bite her lip, half turning away until she controlled her expression.

"Don't cry, Ann. You and Mr. Flynn will come see us soon, won't you?"

"You bet we will, urchin." Flynn crouched next to the little girl, his eyes going over her face. "You take care of your dad, okay? And don't go getting lost in any snowbanks." He ruffled her hair, keeping his smile tacked in place. He stood up and held out his hand to Rafferty. "Take care of her. She's a pretty special kid."

"I will." Rafferty shook hands with Flynn and then took Ann's hand, pulling her close to brush a kiss over her cheek. "Come and see us soon."

"We will." Ann's smile was shaky but intact and she bent to hug Becky. "See you later, Becky."

"Okay. Say goodbye to Oscar for me."

"I will."

Flynn leaned against the edge of the door as they walked to the elevators. Behind him, Ann swallowed a sob. His chest ached as the elevator door slid open. Rafferty stepped in but Becky hesitated. She turned around and Flynn smiled, lifting his hand in a casual wave. She stared at him for a long minute and then tugged her hand loose from her father's and ran back.

Flynn dropped to one knee, catching her as she flew toward him, burying his face in her hair, breathing in all the sweet little girl smells that he'd grown to love.

"I love you, Mr. Flynn." It was as if she'd only just realized that she was really leaving him behind.

"I love you too, Becky." His voice broke on the words and he held her tighter. They stayed that way for the space of several slow heartbeats and then Flynn drew back. He smiled at Becky, reaching up to brush a tear from her cheek.

"I'll come and visit you soon. I promise."

"Will you tell me a story before I go to bed?"

"You bet. But I bet your dad tells a pretty mean story himself." Becky looked over her shoulder at Rafferty, who was standing just outside the open elevator. She looked back at Flynn, torn between the excitement of a father and the security Flynn represented.

"Go on. You're going to miss your flight and then the two of you will have to walk all the way to Colorado."

He turned her around and gave her a gentle push toward Rafferty. She took two steps and then hesitated, looking back at him. He smiled, hoping she wouldn't notice the unnatural brightness of his eyes.

"Scoot, urchin." She looked at him a moment longer, her gray eyes full of uncertainty and then turned and ran to her father. Rafferty caught her hand in his and stepped into the elevator. Flynn stood up, watching as the elevator doors slid shut, closing Becky from sight.

He shoved his hands in his back pockets, staring at the blank panels for a long time, blinking rapidly against the burning in his eyes. Behind him, Ann sobbed quietly.

He turned at last to find her leaning against the wall, her eyes brimming over, one fist pressed to her mouth as if to hold back the sobs. He put his arm around her shoulders, leading her back into the apartment and shutting the door.

"Come on. It isn't like we'll never see her again."

"I know."

"And it isn't as if she wasn't going to have a good home."

"I know." She let him lead her to the sofa and settle them both onto the soft cushions.

"Rafferty is a terrific guy."

"I know."

"So why are you crying?"

"I'm going to miss her so much." The words came out on a hiccoughed sob and Flynn's heart twisted.

"I know, love." He pulled her head to his shoulder and Ann collapsed against him, one hand curling around the edge of his shirt. "Go ahead and cry."

She cried for a long time, crying out her grief over losing Becky, but also crying out the confusion that seemed to have taken over her life. Nothing fit into the neat patterns she'd devised for herself. Most of all, Flynn McCallister didn't fit into any pattern.

When she lay still against him, he brushed the tangled hair back from her face. He dropped a kiss on her flushed forehead, tilting her face back to place another kiss on her still trembling mouth.

"I must look awful." It was a measure of her exhaustion that she didn't try to hide her tear-streaked face.

"Actually, you do look pretty terrible." Ann's eyes flew open in shock.

"What?"

"I said you look pretty terrible. Your eyes are red, your nose is red, your face is red. Actually, now that I think about it, your hair is red, too, so you look kind of coordinated. Everything matches. Think you could do it in purple?"

Despite herself, Ann laughed, which was exactly what he'd been trying for. He ducked the pillow she swung at him.

"Fiend."

"*Moi?* I was simply agreeing with you. My mother always told me to agree with a lady." His face was the very picture of injured innocence and Ann laughed again.

"What am I going to do with you?"

"I could think of several possibilities." He waggled his eyebrows in a lascivious manner. She chuckled again but it died out on a sigh.

"I really am going to miss her."

"I know. I am, too." She settled back onto his shoulder, and he wondered if the position felt as right to her as it did to him.

"I've never spent much time around children. I wonder if they're all as neat as Becky."

"I doubt it, but Becky does tend to put parenthood in a new perspective."

"Yeah." Ann sighed.

They sat in silence for a long time, staring at the empty fireplace, their thoughts drifting. The grandfather clock chimed and Flynn cocked his head, counting each mellow bong.

"Six o'clock. Their plane left fifteen minutes ago."

There was another long silence. Flynn suddenly sat up, dislodging Ann from her comfortable position.

"Where are you going?"

"There's no sense in sitting here moping all night." He stood up as Ann pulled herself upright on the sofa, tugging her shirt back into place.

"You're right. Becky is happy. We should be happy for her. I guess I'll go home. Oscar probably thinks I've died."

Flynn felt a surge of panic. She couldn't go home. Not now. Not yet. He had the feeling that, if she went home now, they might never find each other again. Ridiculous, of course, but he never argued with a gut feeling. Becky had been the tie that bound them together. Now Becky was gone. Did they have anything left?

"Dinner."

Ann looked up at him, startled by the way the word came at her so forcefully. "Dinner?"

"Dinner." He smiled crookedly, bowing low. "I would consider myself honored if you would dine with me this evening."

"Like this?" She pushed her tangled hair back and stood up, looking down at her jeans and shirt. "I look like I've been dragged through a knothole backward."

"How about if we meet in the hallway at eight. I know a great restaurant where the lobster is slathered in butter. I'll call and see if I can get reservations."

TWO HOURS LATER, Ann stepped nervously out of her apartment. She felt like a sixteen-year-old going out on her first date. It had been years since she'd spent so much time fussing with her appearance. She'd tried on every garment in her closet, finally setting on an emerald-green silk sheath and matching silk pumps that added inches to her height. She'd brushed her hair ruthlessly, finally pinning it into a soft Gibson girl style, leaving tendrils loose to caress her neck.

The time she'd spent was immediately forgotten when

she saw the look in Flynn's eyes. He'd been waiting for her, leaning bonelessly against the wall. He straightened as she stepped through the door. Ann froze, feeling the butterflies in her stomach jump nervously. His eyes went over her, starting at the top of her head and working their way down to her elegantly shod feet and then reversing the journey.

When his eyes finally stopped on her face, Ann felt her toes curl inside the narrow pumps. He was looking at her as if she were the most exquisite thing he'd ever seen. The blue of his eyes seemed to penetrate deep into her soul, leaving her weak and trembling.

They stared at each other without speaking for a long, still moment. At last, Flynn walked toward her, his stride deliberate, his eyes never leaving her face. He stopped in front of her and Ann looked up at him. The dark suit made his shoulders seem wider than ever. Caught between his bulk and the thick door at her back, she felt vulnerable, deliciously feminine, excited and scared at the same time.

"You are so beautiful."

He reached for her hand, lifting it to his mouth, but turning it at the last minute so that his kiss landed in her palm. His mouth felt warm and dry against her skin and then his teeth closed over the fleshy area at the base of her thumb, nipping gently, sending a shiver up her arm. Ann closed her eyes, leaning back against the door when her knees threatened to give way.

His lips touched lightly on the inside of her wrist, and then he placed her hand in the crook of his arm. She opened her eyes, wondering if she looked as dazed as she felt.

"Your carriage awaits, madam."

The Ferrari wasn't quite a carriage, but it served just as well. Closed in the intimate interior, they might have been alone in the world. They didn't speak much on the way to the restaurant. There didn't seem to be any need.

The evening seemed to have a fairy-tale quality to it
The table was tucked in a dimly lit corner. The service wa
exquisitely unobtrusive; the food was beautifully prepared
The wine was smooth, slipping over the tongue like warm
velvet. And Flynn's eyes couldn't seem to get enough o
her.

Never had Ann felt so cherished, so wanted. He mad
her feel as if she were the only person in the room. The
talked about impersonal things: food, wine, books and mov
ies. He listened carefully to her opinion on the least o
subjects, making her feel that what she had to say wa
important to him. It was an amazingly seductive feeling.

Ann ordered medallions of beef and Flynn ordered th
lobster. When the meals arrived, he caught her looking
longingly at his plate.

"You should have ordered the lobster."

Ann cut into her beef, finding it meltingly tender. "It'
impossible to eat lobster neatly and I don't want to end th
evening with butter on my chest." She took a bite of bee
and then looked up to find Flynn's eyes on the décolletag
of her dress.

"I'm sure I could think of some way to get it off." Hi
eyes swept up to hers, and Ann forgot how to chew when
she saw the hunger he made no attempt to conceal. Sh
was grateful when he looked away. She swallowed withou
having the slightest idea what she'd just tasted.

Flynn concentrated on his lobster, giving her a chance t
slow her pulse. But it picked up again when he dipped
bite of his entrée in butter and held it across the table t
her.

"You can't possibly get butter on your dress this way."

Feeling self-conscious, Ann leaned forward and took th
proffered tidbit. Her teeth sank into the succulent white
flesh and she closed her eyes in ecstasy, savoring the but
tery richness of it. When she opened her eyes, she foun

Flynn staring at her. The need there made her feel like a siren. Her eyes never leaving his face, she let her tongue come out, licking the butter off her lips with slow deliberation.

Flynn's eyes blazed electric blue, making her wonder if she was starting something she wasn't going to be able to finish. She looked away, reaching for her water glass, though it was going to take more than water to quench the fire they were starting.

"I should have brought the Mercedes."

"Why?"

"Because then I wouldn't have to wait until we got home to make love to you."

The water glass hit the table with a thump as her eyes flew to his face. "What?"

"You heard me. As it is, we'll have to wait till we get home. I'm a little old for the contortions the Ferrari would require. But once I get you home, I'm going to strip that sexy dress off of you an inch at a time and I'm going to taste every single inch until you beg me to make love to you."

His tone was conversational, almost casual, and Ann wondered if she was hearing things. Then she saw the look in his eyes and knew that she hadn't dreamed the things he'd just said. She could feel the color start at her toes and creep over her body like a slow red tide until it reached her face. She stared at him a moment longer, and then her eyes dropped away and she busied herself with her meal.

There was silence for a few minutes and then she looked up again, her eyes mischievous. "Are you sure you're too old for the Ferrari?"

His expression promised retribution of the sweetest kind.

Though she knew the food was exquisite, Ann couldn't really say that she tasted much of it. All her attention was for the man across from her. They said very little during the meal, but she could feel the tension building to a boiling point.

They both refused dessert and Flynn paid the bill. He put his hand against the small of her back as they walked from the restaurant, and Ann wondered if the sparks that seemed to shoot from that light touch were visible to the other patrons.

They didn't speak as they waited for the elevator to arrive. Another couple got off and Flynn nodded politely to them as he ushered Ann into the luxurious cubicle. He pushed the button to take them to the parking garage and the doors slid silently shut.

In an instant, Ann found herself pinned to the wall, Flynn's body a heavy weight against her. Startled, she looked up but she caught only a glimpse of his eyes, dark with passion; then his mouth came down on hers. She melted instantly, her body flowing into his, her arms snaking around his neck.

She forgot where they were, forgot who she was, forgot everything but the feel of his mouth on hers, the scent of Aramis tickling her nose. She moaned a protest when Flynn eased his mouth away. Her lashes felt weighted as she opened her eyes.

"The elevator has stopped." It took a minute for the words to sink in. She looked around, still dazed.

"Elevator?"

Flynn's grin was pure masculinity. He wrapped an arm around her shoulders and led her out of the elevator and to the Ferrari, tucking her into the seat as if she were the rarest of treasures.

Neither of them said a word on the drive home. The tension inside the low-slung sports car was so thick, it seemed to be almost breathable. He pulled the car into his parking space, his movement controlled. Ann could feel every breath she took as they walked to the elevator, not touching, not speaking. The doors closed behind them and she was in his arms, their bodies melding hungrily.

Ann didn't notice when the doors slid open on their floor. She wouldn't have noticed if the doors had slid open on Wilshire Boulevard. Flynn bent without taking his mouth from hers, his arm catching her behind the knees, lifting her off her feet and into his arms. Ann's fingers worked their way into the thick blackness of his hair as he carried her to his apartment, kicking the door shut behind them.

He carried her through the silent rooms to his bedroom, laying her on the bed and following her down, pinning her with the sensual weight of his body.

She couldn't have said if it was hours or days later when they at last fell asleep. She was conscious of nothing beyond the warmth of Flynn lying next to her, his ragged breathing slowly steadying. He'd kept every promise he'd made her in the restaurant.

Chapter Twelve

When Ann awoke the next morning, she knew immediately that she was alone. She rolled over in the huge bed, burying her face in Flynn's pillow and breathing in the mixture of scents that she knew she would always associate with him.

She opened her eyes and sat up, feeling more alive than she had ever felt before. She cocked her head, listening, but the apartment was quiet. With a shrug, she swung her legs out of bed. She had to be at the hospital in an hour. It was probably just as well that Flynn was gone.

Her clothes were neatly folded and stacked on a chair and she flushed, remembering how quickly they'd been discarded the night before. Lying on top of her silk slip with a folded piece of paper. She picked it up, feeling as quivery as a school girl.

Ann,
Sorry I'm not there to kiss you awake but I'd probably end up making you late for work. I had to go out to my parents'. Some papers Dad needs me to sign. Let's have dinner again tonight. Maybe, this time, I'll manage to taste some of the food. I'll pick you up at eight. Wear the green dress again. I had such fun peeling it off of you.

Love, Flynn

Ann hugged the note to her chest, her cheeks pink with the memory of their lovemaking the night before. Her smile widened. She might have waited a long time to take a lover, but she'd certainly picked a winner. She threw on a robe of Flynn's and gathered up her clothes before hurrying to her own apartment. There would be time for basking in a rosy glow later. Right now, she had to get to work.

But, as the day wore on, some of the glow faded to be replaced by a host of uncertainties. What was she getting into? Never in her wildest dreams could she have imagined that she would be attracted to a man like Flynn McCallister. He was exciting and she'd certainly learned that he had a warm side, which she'd never have expected. But he seemed to drift through life without any real thoughts of the future. She sometimes wondered if he ever thought of tomorrow at all.

Yes, he'd been wonderful with Becky, but there was more to life than being kind to small children and animals. There was dedication and ambition and... Well, weren't dedication and ambition important enough? And he didn't have a trace of either one.

And what was it that he wanted from her? Was he looking for a brief affair? A long-term affair? He couldn't be thinking in terms of marriage, could he? Because she certainly wasn't thinking in those terms. Flynn was the dreamer. Ann Perry was a very practical woman who knew better than to think that love alone could support a marriage.

Love?

A slip of the thought. She wasn't in love with him. Or was she?

By the time eight o'clock rolled around, Ann had argued with herself until her stomach was tied in knots. She wanted to crawl into bed and pull the covers over her head and not come out until all her problems had been magically solved.

But she also desperately wanted to see Flynn. She was becoming addicted to his smile, to the way his eyes could laugh while his face stayed completely solemn. She wasn't yet ready to put a label on all the things he made her feel, but she craved being with him.

The evening started out well enough. She'd worn the green dress as he requested. She chose it as much because she was incapable of making even the minor decision of what to wear as to please him.

Flynn's eyes warmed when he saw her, melting some of the nervous ice from around her heart. And when he kissed her, she could almost forget all the fears that had plagued her day.

He took her to another quiet restaurant. This time, they were seated in the center of the room, but there was so much space between the tables that the atmosphere remained cozy and private.

Flynn tasted the wine and nodded to the waiter before turning his full attention to Ann. "How was your day?"

"It was okay." She shrugged, feeling tension creeping into her shoulders. This felt too good, it felt too right. But she knew it wasn't right. It couldn't be right.

"It must be an incredible feeling to save someone's life."

"It is."

He leaned back as the waiter set spinach salads down in front of them. "Do you ever think about what your life might have been like if you'd become a veterinarian?"

"No!" His eyes jerked to her face and Ann flushed, realizing how abrupt the word had sounded. "I mean, why would I? I'm very fulfilled in my career. I can't imagine my life without it. Being a doctor is important work and I'm very proud of what I do."

"You should be."

Ann picked at her salad without interest. Why did the

words ring so hollow? What was it about Flynn that made her feel like somebody's uptight maiden aunt? He had no right to make her feel like that. Everybody didn't have to have hobbies and take brilliant pictures that they never showed to anyone. Some people wanted to make a difference in the world. Some people had ambition.

"How was your visit to your parents?"

"Pretty much the same as always. Dad wants me to take an active role in the corporation. I don't know why he should care. He's retired now and it's running itself just fine but he feels there should be a McCallister on the board." He half laughed and, at another time, Ann might have heard the pain in the sound. "I don't know why he can't get it through his head that I'm not like Mark."

"Was Mark involved in the company? I thought he was a police officer."

"He was but he had a great head for the business. Dad always figured Mark would quit the force and join the company after a few years and he's probably right. But I don't have the least interest in the company. And I've got a lousy head for business."

"Maybe it disappoints him that you don't have more ambition."

Ann leaned back to allow the waiter to take her untouched salad plate and pretended not to notice the way Flynn's eyes widened at her tone.

"We can't all be ambitious. I'm fairly content the way I am."

"Are you? I can't believe that." Ann didn't know where the words were coming from. She just knew that she was suddenly brimming with anger and frustration that had to find an outlet.

Flynn half laughed. "Why do I have the feeling that I've done something to upset you? Is it my tie?"

"I just hate to see waste, that's all."

"One man's waste is another man's life-style," he murmured, still trying to keep the conversation light.

"You can joke all you want but you're wasting your life and you're wasting your talents."

His mouth tightened and his eyes glittered with the beginnings of temper. "It's my life to waste and they're my talents."

"You're copping out."

"Where the hell is this coming from? When I left this morning, there was a warm, responsive woman in my bed. Now, I'm sitting across the table from an uptight, driven yuppie."

The waiter approached their table with the entrées and Flynn sent him away with a flick of his hand and a look that probably seared the food on the plates.

"I'm neither uptight nor driven. I'm a reasonably ambitious woman who's chosen to make something of her life."

"Fine. Have I complained? You be ambitious and I won't be and we'll do just fine."

"It just seems to me that you're a little old to still be defying 'Daddy.'"

"I beg your pardon." The tone was icy, warning her to back off.

She gestured angrily, oblivious to the fact that the other diners were becoming aware of the altercation taking place in their midst.

"Everything you do is done to prove to your father that he can't tell you what to do. You're like a little boy, shouting defiance and hurting yourself more than anyone else. Isn't it time to grow up?"

Flynn's knuckles whitened around the delicate stem of the wineglass. His eyes glittered furiously as he looked at her. His tone was level, absolutely calm and brimming with anger.

"At least I haven't let my entire life be run by my father like you have. You've spent thirty years trying to be the perfect little girl for a man who neither notices nor cares."

"That's not true!"

"I thought you wanted the truth tonight, Dr. Perry." He continued ruthlessly. "The truth is that your father doesn't give a damn about you as a person. All he cares about is that the things you do reflect well on him.

"Sleeping with me is probably the first thing you've ever done that you didn't ask Daddy's permission for. Or did you call and check it out with him first?"

The crack of her hand against his cheek echoed in the quiet room. Flynn's head jerked slightly with the impact of the blow, but he didn't lift his hand to check the injury. His eyes seemed to burn into her.

Ann drew her hand back, pressing it against her mouth, her horrified eyes on the red imprint of her palm that was slowly darkening his lean cheek. "Oh, my God."

There was a sharp ping and she looked down to see that the stem of his wine glass had snapped in his fingers. The bowl fell to the table, spreading white wine across the table. On its heels came the darker tint of blood.

"Oh, my God."

"I believe you said that once." Flynn barely glanced at his bleeding hand. He raised his hand to the waiter, who was staring at them in stunned silence, along with the rest of the restaurant. Ann reached for his hand, responding instinctively to the sight of his injury. "Don't!" He didn't raise his voice, but something in the tone stopped her instantly.

She watched in miserable silence as he pulled a snowy handkerchief from his pocket and wrapped it around his palm, stemming the bleeding. The waiter crept up to the table, as if half-afraid that his bizarre customers might intend him some bodily harm.

"The lady and I will not be dining tonight after all. Please tell Mike to put the meal on my tab and add a healthy tip for yourself."

Flynn stood up, dropping his napkin on the table. "I think we should go now."

Ann stood up, miserably aware that every eye in the house was on them. Flynn walked behind her without touching her. She had never in her life caused a scene. Never in her life been involved in a scene. She wasn't sure which was worse, being involved in a scene or knowing that it was completely her fault.

Flynn didn't say a word as they walked out into the street. He gave the valet his ticket stub and then stood next to her, hands in pockets while they waited for the Ferrari. Ann glanced at him once or twice. She wanted to say something but she didn't know what. He was so close but he looked a million miles away.

He saw her seated, his hand completely impersonal on her elbow. Seconds later, he was sitting beside her and the car's engine growled as he pulled away from the curb.

Ann could feel the temper that simmered in him. She half expected him to drive like a maniac, and she made up her mind to say nothing, no matter what he did. But he stayed well within the speed limit, steering the powerful car at an almost sedate pace. It was worse than if he'd speeded.

"Flynn—"

"Don't. Just forget it."

"But I—"

"Drop it." There was such command in the simple words that Ann subsided into her seat. She wasn't sure what she'd planned to say anyway. How could she apologize for the things she'd said? How could she explain all the turmoil that had built up inside her, seeking some exit and that he'd just gotten in the way.

The Ferrari came to a halt outside their building. Inside, she could see Joe sitting at his desk, his eyes registering the familiar car before going back to the book he was reading.

She glanced at Flynn but his eyes were focused out the windshield, staring at the empty street. "Aren't you coming in?"

"No. If you didn't bring your key, Joe can let you in."

"I have my key. Flynn—"

"Goodbye, Ann."

He didn't look at her. It was as if, in his mind, she'd already ceased to exist. Ann blinked back unwanted tears and reached for the latch, stepping out onto the sidewalk. Flynn leaned across the seat and pulled the door shut, putting the car into gear immediately.

Ann watched the sleek black sports car disappear around a corner, the well-bred howl of the engine sounding loud in the quiet night. The air was still warm but she shivered. She felt as if she'd just lost something incredibly important. She stood there a long time, half hoping that he'd return, that he'd give her a chance to explain the inexplicable.

But he didn't come back.

Ann let herself in, gave Joe a strained smile and went upstairs to her quiet apartment. Oscar greeted her with a meow of inquiry, clearly pleased to see her, but the cat's pleasure couldn't begin to fill the aching hollow that was opening up in her chest.

For the first time since she was a child, Ann cried herself to sleep.

THE NEXT FEW DAYS were an exercise in torture. Ann could not stop going over the disastrous evening in her mind. The events replayed themselves like a broken record: each word, each gesture, had to be taken out and examined again and again.

She'd deliberately set out to pick a fight with Flynn. There was no other possible explanation. She'd been looking for a reason to break off their relationship, looking for some terrible flaw in him. She'd found a flaw, but it was in herself, not in Flynn.

One thing she'd always prided herself on was her ability to face reality. She tried never to lie to herself. Yet, she'd buried her head in the sand when it came to Flynn McCallister. From the moment she'd moved in, she'd used hostility to camouflage a powerful sexual attraction. Even then, she'd sensed that he could be a threat to her neatly ordered world, and she'd done everything she could to keep him at arm's length.

Then Becky had dropped into their lives and she'd been forced to look at the real Flynn, not the mythical, womanizing creation of her imagination, but the real man. The man who took in a little girl who had no one else and gave her a home. The man who captured such sensitive images on film. The man who'd taught her about passion.

The man she'd fallen in love with.

Ann leaned her head back against the wall of the elevator and closed her eyes. It was not exactly the most romantic of locations to realize that she'd fallen in love. No—she couldn't really say that she was just now realizing it. She was just now admitting it to herself, but some part of her had known it for a long time. That's why she'd been so frightened. That was why she'd struck out at him, pushing him away because she was afraid to let him get any closer.

The elevator came to a halt and the doors slid open. Ann stepped out, her head bent over her purse as she searched for her keys.

"Excuse me." Her head jerked up, her heart pounding. Flynn was standing not two feet away. It had only been three days since she'd seen him, but Ann drank in the sight of him as if it had been months.

He was wearing tailored slacks and a blue shirt that echoed the brilliance of his eyes. His hair was combed into neat black waves and Ann couldn't imagine anyone had ever looked more handsome.

"Excuse me." He repeated the polite phrase and she realized she was blocking the elevator. A hundred words surged to her lips but she didn't speak any of them. This came too close on the heels of her realization of her love for him. She felt too raw, too vulnerable.

She stepped out of the way without a word. Flynn nodded, his eyes as cool and distant as the Sierras. His shoulder almost touched hers as he stepped into the elevator. Ann didn't move until she heard the doors slide quietly shut behind her.

She saw him twice more in the next three days. Each time she ached with the need to say something—anything—to break through the terrible wall that lay between them. But she said nothing, did nothing. Just looking at him seemed to paralyze her vocal cords.

A week after the disastrous dinner date, her father came to see her. They'd spoken very little since he'd called the Social Services department to report Becky. Typically, he'd never apologized, apparently not seeing the need to do so.

Ann was seeing him in a new light. Flynn's words might have hurt but they had sunk in. She didn't want to believe that he was right. Of course her father cared about her.

"I understand that little girl McCallister was keeping is gone now." Robert Perry leaned back in his chair and sipped at the coffee his daughter had just handed him. Not the instant she usually made for herself but freshly ground, freshly brewed coffee. He didn't believe in instant.

"Becky is with her father now."

"Good. Best for all concerned. Gets McCallister out of your life, lets you concentrate on your career."

Ann sipped her coffee, trying not to be irritated by the

cavalier way he dismissed Becky. She looked at Oscar who was lying on the back of the sofa directly across from her father. Oscar was staring at him, his golden eyes unblinking.

Robert Perry looked at him and then looked away and then looked at him again. Ann took another sip of coffee, hiding her smile in her cup. Her father shifted uneasily beneath the cat's steady regard.

"Does he always stare like that?"

"Not always." She could have gotten up and shut Oscar in her bedroom but she didn't move.

"Animals. Never could understand why anyone would want to have one."

"Oscar keeps me company." She kept her tone mild.

"Animals belong in a barnyard, not in a house. Keep them where they belong and everybody would be happier."

"I'm afraid Oscar is spoiled. I don't think he'd like a barnyard at all."

Oscar continued to stare and her father shifted again, apparently looking for a position that would shield him from the cat's impassive gaze.

"Animals. Don't know why you like them. Nasty, dirty things."

"Actually, Oscar is extremely clean." Ann set her cup down with careful deliberation. "I've been thinking about giving up my practice and going back to school."

"School! What on earth for? You've had all the training you need."

"Not to be a veterinarian." The words could not have had stronger results if she'd just announced that she was going to become a terrorist.

"Veterinarian!" He made the word sound like an obscenity. "Don't be ridiculous!"

"Dad, I'm not happy with my work. It's not that it isn't worthwhile. It just isn't what I want to do. I love animals and I love medicine. I'd like to combine the two." Her tone pleaded with him to understand. She might as well have been talking to the coffeepot.

"I forbid it! I don't know where you got this asinine idea but I absolutely forbid it."

"Dad, I'm not happy where I am. I want to try something else. There's nothing wrong with that."

"There's everything in the world wrong with it. A veterinarian. Hah! Do you think I spent all that money for your schooling just to watch you throw it all away on a whim?"

"This isn't a whim. I've given this a lot of thought and I think this will make me happy. Don't you want me to be happy?" There was a little-girl-lost quality in the question, but it was lost on him.

"Happy? What's happy got to do with it? People these days think that's all life is about. Well, it isn't. Life is about getting somewhere, accomplishing things, making something of yourself.

"I see where you get this stupid notion. It's that McCallister boy, isn't it? He's filled your head with a lot of twaddle. The man's a bum. He may not be in the street but that's only because his family has money. What's he accomplished in his life? Nothing, that's what. And he never will accomplish anything because he's a bum. Look at him. Is that the kind of life you want to live? Nobody respects him, nobody knows his name."

"*I* respect him."

"Just shows how far he's turned your head. I should never have let you move in here. Should have stopped it the minute I found out he was living across the hall. You'll move out immediately. You can move home and we'll get these stupid notions out of your head."

Ann stared at him, not wanting to believe what she was seeing. "Dad, can't you hear what I'm saying? This has nothing to do with Flynn, though he's the one who made me see how foolish it is to waste my life. *I'm not happy. I want to do something else with my life. Don't you want to see me happy?''*

''I want to be proud of you. I want people to know that my daughter is a success. I can't be proud of someone who's wasting their time on a bunch of filthy animals.''

He glared at her, and Ann looked at him over an abyss so vast that there was no crossing it. Later it would hurt, but right now she felt numbed by the weight of all the years she wasted trying to please him.

''You don't care about me at all, do you? Not about me as a person.''

''Don't be melodramatic. Of course I care. You're my daughter.''

''But I'm not a person to you at all, am I? I'm just an extension of yourself. Something that you can point at for people to admire.''

He stood up. ''I think it would be best if I left before you say something you'll regret. I've always had your best interests at heart, Ann. When you've calmed down, you'll see that I'm right about this, too.''

''I don't think so.''

She listened to the door close behind him and waited for all the pain to come crashing down on her. But the only feeling that emerged was a tremendous relief. As if she'd known all along, and getting it out in the open had lifted the burden from her.

Ann didn't know how long she sat there thinking. All the turmoil of the past few weeks was suddenly gone and her mind was working clearly. She knew exactly what she wanted out of life. It was so clear that she couldn't understand how she could have let herself get so muddled about it.

And the first step was to find Flynn. Nothing else in her

life could be right until he was back in it. Flynn was the key to everything. Why hadn't she seen that from the start?

She stood up so abruptly that it startled Oscar, almost making him lose his balance. He dug his claws into the linen of the sofa to keep from falling and gave her an indignant look as she hurried by. But Ann didn't notice. She had more important things on her mind.

She knocked on Flynn's door and waited impatiently for him to answer. She wasn't exactly sure what she wanted to say but she knew the words would come once she saw him. He would understand. He had to understand.

She knocked again, waiting for a long time before finally admitting that he wasn't home. She leaned her forehead against his door as if she could will him to be there.

"I've got it all straightened out now, Flynn. Where are you?" The whisper went unanswered.

Chapter Thirteen

"That was terrific, Mom." Flynn pushed his plate away and dropped his napkin beside it.

"You hardly ate enough to keep a bird alive. Are you sure you got enough?"

"I think that theory has been proven false. Didn't I read somewhere that birds have to eat twice their weight every day? If I ate enough to keep a bird alive, you'd have to roast another chicken or three."

His mother smiled but he read the worry in her eyes. He looked away. He knew that she could sense that something was wrong but he wasn't ready to talk about it. Not yet. The hurt was too new, too raw.

He reached for his wine, sipping it slowly. The crisp chardonnay was a far cry from the things he'd been drinking this last week. Stupid. It shamed him to think of how much time he'd spent drinking since the fight with Ann. There were no answers to be found at the bottom of a bottle. He knew that, and he hadn't really been looking for answers. He'd been looking for oblivion. Only that wasn't to be found, either.

It didn't matter how drunk he got, he could still remember his losses. Mark, who'd died much too young, leaving so many unanswered questions and leaving Flynn with a burden of perfection he felt woefully inadequate to carry.

Becky, darting in and out of his life and changing it completely. And Ann. God, how could he describe that loss? She'd given him a glimpse of heaven and then snatched it back.

Maybe she was right. Maybe the fault was his. He should have more ambition. Maybe if he'd tried harder to please his father, Mark wouldn't have had to carry the whole burden. Maybe he wouldn't have died.

Flynn shook his head. Stupid. He was what he was just as Mark had chosen his path. He couldn't make himself something he wasn't, just as his brother hadn't been able to be something he wasn't.

"Flynn!" Flynn's head jerked up at his father's sharp command and he realized that he'd been staring at the tablecloth, completely absorbed in his thoughts. David McCallister frowned at him sternly from across the table. "Your mother is speaking to you."

"I'm sorry, Mom. What were you saying?"

"Your mother shouldn't have to repeat herself. Have you been drinking? You act like you're only half awake." His father jabbed irritably at a steamed carrot and Flynn wondered if he was wishing it was his son he was poking.

"I haven't had anything today but I could change that if you'd like." The smile he gave his father was designed to make the older man's blood pressure rise. Their eyes fenced in an old challenge, one that neither of them had ever won.

"Flynn. David. Stop it, both of you." The look Louise gave her husband and son could have controlled an entire army. It served quite well with her family.

"Sorry, Mom."

David muttered into his coffee cup. The words might have been an apology or they might have been a curse. His wife chose not to ask for clarification.

The rest of the meal passed without incident. No one was in the mood for the chocolate pie the cook had made and left for the meal. The three of them adjourned to the study and, with a worried look at her husband and son, Louise left to make coffee.

When she returned, they were exactly where she'd left them. Her husband was seated in his favorite chair, his gaze focused on the wall opposite. Flynn leaned one shoulder against the mantel, his eyes on the snifter of brandy he held. It was raining outside, the first big storm of the season and a small fire crackled in the fireplace, more for psychological warmth than to supplement the heating. But it didn't seem to have done much good. The atmosphere in the room was chill with old hurts.

Louise sighed faintly as she wheeled the coffee tray into the room. She settled herself in a chair across from her husband, near the warmth from the fireplace. David accepted a cup of coffee from her but Flynn lifted the brandy snifter in silent refusal. She caught David's eye on his son and hurried into speech before he could comment on Flynn's drinking.

"Have you heard from Becky?"

"I got a letter yesterday." His face softened in the first real smile she'd seen since his arrival. "The spelling was a little shaky but I gather that she's happy. Rafferty took her into the mountains to see the snow and she's pretty impressed with it. They had a snowball fight and she won. The house is great and there's a huge backyard with a big tree. Rafferty has promised her a swing this summer."

"It sounds like she's happy. I'm so glad. She's a sweet child."

"Yes, she is. I miss her but it helps to know that she's happy. I know Rafferty is going to be a great father."

"It could have been such a tragedy. I think it's wonderful that everything worked out so well. How is Ann? She must be missing Becky, too."

Flynn's smile faded and his eyes dropped back to his

drink. "I'm sure she is. Ann and I aren't seeing each other these days."

He said it casually, but his mother could hear the pain underlying the words and her heart went out to him. Mark had always been the serious one, but Louise knew which of her sons felt pain most deeply. Flynn had always been so good at hiding his feelings, but his emotions ran deep.

"I'm sorry, Flynn."

He shrugged, his smile twisted. "So am I, Mom."

"Figures. Thought the girl had too much sense to be seeing you."

"David!" Louise's shocked exclamation brought a flush to her husband's face.

"No, that's all right, Mom. It's not like Dad's opinion of me is anything new, is it, Dad? Families should be honest with one another."

David's flush deepened at the sweet sarcasm in Flynn's tone. "The trouble with you, Flynn, is that you've got a chip on your shoulder. You're always looking to blame someone else for your troubles."

"I don't blame anyone for anything, Dad."

"And you lack sense. Any half-wit could see that Ann was a woman worth keeping. What do you do? You let her go."

"What do you suggest I should have done? Chained her in the basement?" Flynn's smile stayed in place but his knuckles whitened on the brandy snifter. "She seemed to think that one of my major flaws was that I was too much like my father. Amusing, don't you think?"

David McCallister didn't see the humor. "Like me? Ha! Thought the girl had more sense. I can't imagine two people less alike."

"For once, we agree on something." Flynn lifted his glass in a mock toast.

"The trouble with you, Flynn, is that you lack any real

direction. A man needs a career, something to focus his energies on.''

"Dad, I focus my energies on enjoying life. That's enough of a career for me.''

"Stop it, both of you." Louise's voice interrupted the budding argument. "I don't want to listen to this. Honestly. I don't understand why the two of you can't get along.''

"Bad blood, Mom." Flynn shook his head mournfully. "I've inherited bad blood from your side of the family. No McCallister could ever be so worthless. You'll just have to live with the fact that you've tainted the McCallister line.''

"Hah! What McCallister line?" Flynn winced at his father's barked comment. "There is no McCallister line anymore and there's not likely to be. Now, when your brother was alive, there was some hope for it. *He* had some sense.''

"David.''

He stood up; his frustration was too great to let him stay still. His eyes were on his younger son, anger and confusion in their depths.

"Don't 'David' me, Louise. It's not as if I'm saying something that we don't all know already. Mark would never have wasted his life the way his brother is doing. Mark had ambition. He had pride—in himself and in the family name.''

"Mark didn't give a holy damn about the family name. Mark wanted to please you and he spent his whole life trying to do it." Flynn stopped with an effort, setting his jaw against the urge to say more.

"And what's wrong with wanting to please your father? Seems to me to be a worthwhile thing to do.''

"There's nothing wrong with it. Look, Dad, why don't you just give up? I'm never going to be the model son Mark was.''

"Don't think I don't know that." The older man's tone

was bitter and Flynn whitened at the bite in the words. He set the brandy snifter down on the mantel. The faint ping of the crystal hitting the marble sounded too loud.

"Mark was a son a man could be proud of. If he hadn't been killed in the line of duty, he'd probably have presented me with a grandson by now. Instead, I'm left with you. A playboy." His tone made the word a curse. "A man who hasn't amounted to anything and never will."

Flynn felt something snap inside. It was as if he were suddenly standing outside himself, watching this confrontation. "I don't think that's too likely." The words seemed to come from somewhere outside himself.

"You don't think what's too likely? That you'll amount to anything? I know it's not likely."

"I don't think it's too likely that Mark would have presented you with a grandson by now."

"Flynn, no!" He heard his mother's hushed protest, but it didn't penetrate the wall of pain that seemed to be tearing him apart.

"Mark was gay." Father and son stared at each other across a gap that had been there for more years than either could remember. As soon as the words were said, Flynn wanted to call them back. He'd never planned to say them. Never wanted to hurt his father with them.

The older man stared into his son's horrified eyes, reading the truth there. He seemed to shrink and age in a matter of minutes. He groped behind him for his chair, his movements shaken.

Flynn took a quick step forward, his hand coming out, but his father waved him away with a look of loathing so intense it seemed to burn into his soul. He sank into the chair, his hands gripping the arms, his knuckles white.

The stillness was thick, almost a presence in itself. Outside the rain poured down, splashing onto the brick terrace. Inside the fire popped, sending sparks shooting up the chimney. The sound, like the sparks, was swallowed instantly.

"You're lying." David McCallister's voice sounded old and feeble. There was no trace of his usual blustering tones. Flynn didn't hesitate. He'd have done anything to take the shattered look out of his father's eyes.

"You're right. It was a lie. I'm sorry." He backed away, picking up his brandy, his hand clenched over the crystal snifter.

"You're sorry? You're sorry?"

"David, please..." Louise might as well have remained silent.

"You impudent bastard!"

Flynn shrugged, staring at the glass he held. "I'm sorry, Dad. I shouldn't have said it."

"You were jealous of him. You were always jealous of him." David's voice rose with each sentence. "He was everything a man could have wanted in a son. I couldn't have expected to have two sons like him but I can't believe I fathered a sniveling bastard like you."

"Don't feel too bad. It happens in the best of families." Flynn's flippant remark cracked at the end, but his father was too enraged to notice.

"Get out. Get out of this house. I don't ever want to see you again." Flynn whitened, his eyes burning in his face as he stared at his father. "Do you hear me? Get out!"

Flynn lifted the snifter and tossed the last of the fine cognac down his throat, feeling it burn all the way down. His smile was twisted, his eyes empty.

"To happy families." He set the snifter down on the mantel and strode from the room.

Louise looked from her husband's shattered face to her son's rigid back. In the space of a minute, her family had been torn apart. If it was ever to be put back together again, it would be up to her. She rose from her chair and hurried after Flynn. He was tugging his leather jacket off the coat rack when she caught him.

"Flynn."

He turned and tears filled her eyes at the shattered look in his eyes. He shrugged into his jacket.

"You should be with him. He's pretty upset."

"I'll go to him in a minute. I wanted to talk to you."

"Don't worry, Mom, I'm not going to wrap my car around a telephone pole."

She caught his hands in hers. "Flynn, give him some time. He didn't really mean it. He'll come around."

He pulled his hands loose and touched her cheek, his fingers gentle. His smile broke her heart; there was so much loss there.

"Some wounds not even time can heal. Don't worry about me. I'll be all right."

He was gone before she could say anything more. There was a moment when the door was open to the rain-swept night and then it shut, closing her inside and shutting him out. She stared at the blank panel a long time, hearing the growl of the Ferrari's engine disappearing down the drive.

She turned slowly, walking back into the study. Her husband was slumped in his chair, his features old and worn. She hardened her heart against his suffering. Flynn was suffering, too. And had suffered for a long time.

"It's not true. How could he say something like that about his own brother?" The words were muttered, his eyes shifting away from hers.

Louise knew what David wanted. He wanted her to say that he was right, that Flynn had lied. He wanted her to right his world for him. But she couldn't do that.

She sat down, reaching out to take his hands in hers, stilling their restless movements. "David, the only thing that's important is that Mark was a wonderful son. He was good and kind and we were very lucky to have him with us for as long as we did.''

"I know that! I just don't know how we could have ended up with a son like Flynn. He's a changeling, that's what he is.''

"No, David. Flynn is as much your son as Mark was. More perhaps.'' Her fingers tightened over his, stilling his indignant protest. "You and Flynn are too much alike. Neither of you knows how to give an inch. Mark was willing to bend. He let you shape him. But Flynn knew just who he was from the time he was a baby and he never let you bully him into anything.''

"I never bullied Mark!''

"You didn't have to. Mark was content to do what you wanted. But Flynn wanted to go his own way. Just like his father always did.''

She paused, letting that sink in, seeing the way his eyes shifted away from hers, as if trying to avoid the truth in her words.

"He's pigheaded and shiftless.''

"He's no more pigheaded than you are. And he's doing exactly what he wants to do. How can that be shiftless?''

"He doesn't show proper respect.''

"Have you ever shown him any respect?''

He glared at her for a moment and then looked away, staring into the fireplace. "I never knew what to do with him. He'd look at me with those bright blue eyes, listen to what I said and then do exactly what he wanted.''

"Are you any different?''

He grunted, unwilling to agree, unable to argue.

"David, we've already lost one son. Mark is gone and we can't ever get him back. I don't want to lose my other son and I don't think you do, either. Flynn has tried all his life to be friends with you. Don't you think it's time that you tried just a little? If you don't reach out, we're going to lose him. *You're* going to lose him. Just as surely as we did Mark.''

He didn't say anything, only continued to stare into the flames. With a sigh, she squeezed his hands and moved away. She'd tried all she could. She could only pray that she'd gotten through to him. Time would tell.

Chapter Fourteen

The rain poured down with a steady persistence that said
it was here to stay for a long time. Ann stared out the
sliding glass door on to the neatly tended rooftop garden
and wondered if it was possible to feel any more depressed
than she did at that moment.

It was after one o'clock in the morning. She'd been
knocking on Flynn's door every half an hour since eight.
At one point, she'd even gone down to the garage to make
sure he wasn't home and just refusing to answer the door.
But the Ferrari was gone and so was Flynn.

Where was he? She tried not to think of what she would
do if he arrived home with a woman on his arm. She
couldn't bear to lose him now. Not when she'd finally realized that he was what she needed. How could she have
been so blind? Why hadn't she seen weeks ago that she
was in love with him?

She stepped away from the window and drew the cur-
tains shut, closing out the stormy night. What if he'd had
an accident? With the storm soaking the streets, the roads
would be dangerous. She could stand anything, just as long
as he was safe.

She sat down on the sofa, staring into the fireplace. She'd
built a fire earlier but it was down to embers now, a sullen
red glow that seemed more dark than light. Oscar was

asleep on a chair, there was not a sound in the apartment except for the occasional crackle of the dying fire and the steady drone of the rain.

Ann leaned her head back, closing her eyes. She had to talk to Flynn. It couldn't be too late for them. It just couldn't.

She had no idea how much later it was that she was startled upright. She hadn't been aware of falling asleep until she was shocked awake. Oscar was crouched on the back of the sofa, his fur on end, obviously disturbed by whatever it was that had awakened his mistress. The knock on the door came again, sounding loud in the quiet night.

Ann stumbled to her feet, groggy and disoriented. She tugged at her loose shirt and pushed her hair out of her face before reaching for the doorknob, her mind still blank with sleep. She pulled the door open and all her thoughts shifted into instant focus.

Flynn stood outside. A Flynn she'd never seen before. He was soaking wet, from the black hair that molded his head to the snakeskin boots that glistened with water. Water dripped off of him, creating little puddles before soaking into the thick carpeting. All of this, she noticed peripherally. What caught her and held her was his eyes.

Their brilliant blue was dulled to steely gray. His skin looked pale and his face seemed much older than his years. He looked like a man who'd seen the death of all his dreams and had nothing left inside. He looked absolutely shattered.

She stared at him in stunned silence, her shocked eyes taking in his condition. His mouth quirked in a frail ghost of a smile and his eyes dropped from hers to stare at the damp floor.

''I know it's late. I...didn't know where else to go.'' His voice was hollow, lost. Ann felt as if her heart were breaking. Whatever he'd been through, it had drained him of all the vibrancy she'd come to associate with him.

She reached out, taking his hand, feeling the chill of his skin. "Come in." He stumbled as he stepped in, catching himself against the wall.

"Sorry."

"You're frozen. Come in by the fire. I'll throw a couple more logs on and get it stoked up."

He let her strip the ruined leather jacket off his shoulders. "I didn't know where else to go." He repeated the words as if it were the only coherent thought in his mind.

His shirt was as wet as the rest of him. "What happened?"

He stared at her blankly and she expanded on the question. "Why are you so wet?"

"The Ferrari ran out of gas. I've been walking."

"How long did you walk?"

"I don't know. I just walked."

"Well, you're soaked to the skin. I want you to go get in a hot shower. I'll go to your place and get you something to put on."

He seemed to come out of his fog somewhat. He ran his fingers through his hair, only just then realizing how wet he was. "I'm sorry. I'm probably ruining your carpet. I should go home."

"Don't be ridiculous. Go take a shower. I'll go get some dry clothes and make some coffee." She gave him a push in the direction of the bathroom, waiting until she heard the shower start before getting the key he'd given her when Becky was staying with him and letting herself into his apartment.

By the time Flynn got out of the shower, Ann had made coffee and sandwiches and thrown enough logs on the fire to create a roaring blaze. Flynn looked a little less like the walking dead when he stepped out of the bathroom. She'd brought him fresh jeans and a heavy flannel shirt and, if it hadn't been for the dampness of his hair, it might have been possible to imagine that the two of them had been sitting in front of a fire all night.

"I didn't know if you'd be hungry."

He sank onto the sofa and glanced at the coffee and sandwiches. "The coffee looks great but I'm really not hungry. It was nice of you to fix them, though."

She handed him a cup of steaming coffee, her eyes going over him carefully. He looked better. There was still that rather frightening emptiness at the back of his eyes but his skin was not quite so gaunt.

The silence grew between them. Oddly enough, it wasn't an uncomfortable silence. The rain continued to pound down on the roof tops outside, filling the void with its hypnotic rhythm.

"What happened?"

Flynn had been staring into the flames and it was a moment before he dragged his gaze to her, his eyes reflecting the fire. He was quiet so long, his eyes looking almost through her, that Ann began to wonder if he'd even heard her question.

"I went to visit my parents. My father and I had a fight."

Ann waited, but he didn't seem to have anything else to say. "I thought you and your father quarreled pretty often."

"We do." He stirred abruptly, his eyes dropping to the mug he held. "This time was…different. This time I don't think we're going to be able to forget it."

Ann hesitated, wondering if she had the right to probe, her instincts telling her that he needed to talk about whatever it was that was eating into him.

"I know I may not seem like the best candidate but I've been known to lend a sympathetic ear."

Flynn glanced up, smiling briefly. "I know."

Silence settled between them again. Ann waited, knowing that the next move had to come from him. He finished his coffee and reached forward to pour a fresh cup, settling back against the cushions and staring into the fire, his expression brooding.

"I suppose we quarreled about you indirectly." He spoke so abruptly that Ann jumped.

"Me? What about me?"

"He thinks you were smart to get rid of me. He agrees with your opinions. He thinks I'm a worthless, ambitionless playboy."

"Flynn, I didn't mean those things I said." Her fingers knotted around her cup, her heart breaking at the thought that she could be the cause of his misery.

He glanced at her again, his smile sweet. "You know what's funny? It hurt when you said it but I knew you didn't mean it. Not like he meant it. You were right about a lot of what you said. I do still do some things just to prove that my father's opinion of me is right. And I suppose I don't have a whole hell of a lot of ambition but then, I've never seen ambition as being the be-all-and-end-all of life."

"Flynn, what did your father say to you?" She had to know what had put that look in his eyes.

"It wasn't what he said to me. It's what I said to him." His mouth twisted bitterly, his eyes on the fire. "I broke a promise. I broke a promise and I did it because I was hurt and I wanted to lash out and hurt back. Not a very good reason."

"What promise, Flynn?"

"My father was riding me about my life, my personality, my future. All the usual stuff. I should be used to it by now." He set the cup down and stood up, moving to crouch by the fire and pick up the poker. He jabbed at the logs, sending flames shooting up the chimney.

"And then he started telling me how, if Mark had lived, Mark would have given him a grandson by now." He stood up, leaning his forearm against the mantel and staring down into the flames. "I told him that wasn't likely. It's the truth but, God help me, I had no right to say it."

Ann stared at his taut figure, a vague suspicion forming in the back of her mind. "Why wouldn't Mark have given him a grandson?"

He turned his head to look at her and she almost cried out at the self-loathing in his eyes. "Mark was gay. Mr. Captain-of-the-football-team, tough-cop. God, how he hated himself. He hated himself for being what he was. He said Dad would never be able to stand the shock if he found out and I kept his secret for him. I kept it all these years until tonight. Tonight, I blurted it out like a child. Just because I was hurt. My father called me a bastard. I can't even blame him." He put his head down, resting his forehead on his arm, his shoulders slumped in absolute defeat.

Ann got up and went to him. All the hurt that lay between them was forgotten. This was the man she loved and he was in pain. All she wanted was to ease his hurts. He resisted her arms when they slid around his waist but Ann ignored him, pressing her forehead against his taut back, holding him.

"Flynn, you're only human. I'm sure Mark would understand what you did. And your father will come around. Just give him some time. He was hurt and shocked but he'll come around."

He held himself away from her a moment longer and she thought she'd lost, that he wasn't going to take the comfort she offered, that he wasn't going to be able to let down the barriers he'd built up over the years.

He turned suddenly, almost throwing her off balance, his arms going around her and clutching her convulsively tight. Ann lifted herself on her toes, circling his neck with her arms as he buried his face in her loose hair.

They stood that way for a long time. Ann stroked his

hair, wanting to soothe away years of hurt. Beside them the fire snapped and popped. Outside, the rain poured down on the city, washing clean the summer's accumulation of dirt.

Inside, there was just the two of them. No past, no future, nothing but the present. Ann felt the dampness of his tears on her neck and her arms tightened. She wanted to tell him that everything was going to be all right, but she couldn't get the words out past the lump in her throat. She could only hold him, offering the only comfort she could.

Inside, a part of her was singing with elation. He'd come to her. In his misery, he'd come to her. That had to mean that he cared. He wouldn't have come to her if he didn't care for her.

She didn't know how long it was before he moved, his arms loosening around her. He backed away, wiping self-consciously at the dampness on his cheeks. His eyes looked anywhere but at her.

"It's late. I shouldn't have kept you up so late."

"It's all right."

He glanced at her and then looked away. "I should go home."

It was Ann's turn to look away. "You could stay here tonight."

The silence seemed to stretch out endlessly. Neither of them looked at the other, but it was in both their minds that they'd reached a major turning point.

"I'd like that." Ann let out her breath in a rush, only then aware that she'd been holding it.

They didn't turn on lights in the bedroom. They undressed in the dark, without speaking. They weren't ready for words. Ann slipped on a silk sleepshirt and slid onto the cool cotton sheets. A moment later, Flynn joined her.

They lay apart for a few moments, each uncertain of the other's expectations. So much had been said but there was so much left to say. Flynn's hand slid across the inches that separated them, seeking her arm. It was all the invitation Ann needed. With her head nestled securely against his shoulder, the strong beat of his heart beneath her palm, she felt as if she'd come home.

Within minutes, he was asleep, his breath stirring her hair. But, even in sleep, his arms held her securely. Despite the late hour, Ann lay awake, staring into the darkness. He needed her. The realization slipped into her mind with the softness of a whisper, but the impact was much greater. With that realization came another. All these weeks, she'd been so afraid of falling in love with him, terrified of being vulnerable. She finally knew why.

Flynn seemed so complete in himself. He'd never seemed to need anyone. In his own flip way, he'd always been invulnerable. It was frightening to need someone so much and feel that the need was one-sided.

But, tonight, she'd seen the vulnerability in him. She'd seen what she had to offer him. An unconditional love. Someone who accepted him with all his faults and all his good points. Someone who'd never compare him to another and find him wanting.

Someone who'd love him just as he was.

WHEN FLYNN WOKE, he was alone. He rolled over in bed, his arm sweeping out in search of Ann's warmth, but the bed was empty and the sheets were cool. He opened his eyes, feeling strangely empty. He stared at the ceiling, exploring his emotions, seeking the source of the emptiness.

Mark. For the first time in three years, he was not carrying the hard knot of pain that had been there since his brother's death. He called his brother's face to mind and was surprised to find that it had grown slightly fuzzy around the edges. The warmth in the eyes, the smile, those were still crisp and clear, but other details were blurred. Softened.

Softened. That was how the pain felt. It was still there. He'd never stop missing Mark. The loss would always be with him. But the pain had softened, become bearable. It was as if, in talking about him, really talking about him, the memories had fallen into their proper place.

He sat up, his eyes skimming over the room. It was the first time he'd been in Ann's bedroom, and he found it looked just as he'd expected it to look. Neat and tidy, almost like a motel room except for the occasional touches that showed the woman lying beneath the career.

Her closet was partially open, and he grinned when he saw the tangle of shoes that covered the bottom. He would have expected her to have her shoes neatly lined up on shelves, carefully paired and labeled with the days of the week. There was an extravagantly feminine vanity in one corner, its surface covered with delicate perfume bottles. Funny, he'd never associated Ann with perfume.

His curiosity aroused, he slid out of bed and walked over to the vanity to pick up an exquisite crystal flagon. It was empty, as were all the other bottles, and his grin deepened. She collected perfume bottles. He remembered their discussion about hobbies and wondered why she hadn't told him about this. Funny, how she seemed almost ashamed of the frivolous side of her.

He set the bottle down and walked into the bathroom, picking up his clothing on the way. He took a long shower, wondering what he was going to say to Ann when he saw her. He'd never opened himself up to another person like he had to her. Not even to Mark. He wondered what she'd say. She loved him. He was sure of it. Or maybe he was only sure of it because it was what he desperately wanted to believe.

She had to love him. If she didn't, he didn't know what he was going to do.

Ann was making coffee when she heard the bedroom door open. She spilled grounds onto the counter and quickly scooped them up, trying to control the shaking of her hands. What was he going to say? How was he going to act? Was he going to pretend that last night had never happened?

She turned, hoping her smile looked more confident than it felt. He was standing in the kitchen doorway and she couldn't imagine how it was possible for a man to look so gorgeous. He was wearing the same jeans and flannel shirt she'd brought over for him the night before. He'd rolled the sleeves up on the shirt and his feet were bare. His hair looked like he'd combed it with his fingers and his jaw was shadowed with beard. He'd never looked better.

"Good morning." His voice was husky but whether from sleep or nerves, Ann couldn't guess. "Looks like the storm's over."

She nodded, glancing over her shoulder at the sunshine that spilled in through the window over the sink. "Looks like a beautiful day."

She tugged at the hem of her loose cotton sweater, wishing she'd taken time to put on more makeup, wishing she was wearing something more flattering. Wishing he'd say something to break the tension.

"I love you."

The words dropped into the tense silence like a boulder into a pond. There was the initial splash and then ripples rushed outward, throwing Ann off balance. Her head jerked up, her eyes meeting his. He was still leaning in the door in the same casual position, but now she could see the tension in his shoulders, the tautness of his body.

"Oh God." She slumped back against the counter, her knees shaking.

His brows shot up. "Oh God? Is that horror or pleased surprise?" The question was flip but she knew him too well now. She could see how much her answer meant to him.

"I've been trying to figure out how to apologize for the awful things I said to you at that horrible dinner. I've been agonizing how to go about carefully building a relationship. I've been…" He was across the kitchen in an instant, his arms going around her, holding her close.

"You've been talking too much. Do you love me or do I go jump off the balcony?"

She rested her head on his chest, feeling the way his heart pounded beneath her cheek. Her mouth turned up in a smile. Never again would she fall for his flippant, I-don't-give-a-damn act.

"I love you." His arms tightened, drawing a squeak of protest from her.

"I still don't have any ambition."

"I know. I've always wanted to live with a bum."

"I will probably never have any ambition."

"That's okay. I've got enough for both of us."

"I—"

"Will you just shut up and kiss me, for crying out loud."

His hand slid into her hair, tilting her head back until he could look into her eyes. The look of love he read there wiped away the last traces of pain. Years of loneliness melted in her love.

"What did I ever do to deserve you?"

She smiled at him, her eyes sparkling through a film of tears. "I don't know. It must have been something pretty terrific."

"It must have been."

His mouth came down on hers, smothering any reply she might have made.

Oscar trotted into the kitchen and studied the two humans for a moment. It was time for breakfast, but the cat could see that they weren't going to be thinking of anything practical for a long time to come. Being a tactful feline, he turned and left the room.

the floor. However, I've given up work on Ms. Wallington
until I'm lamp base, or some sitting around table, for
carpet and just too much.

Epilogue

"What do you think you're doing?"

Ann jumped at the barked question, jerking her head out of the box she'd been packing and spinning around to face her husband.

Flynn looked at her sternly, a look not in the least softened by the fact that his hair stood on end and his face was streaked with dirt.

"I'm packing a box. What did it look like I was doing?"

"You're not supposed to be doing things like that."

"Things like what? Flynn, I was packing some china, not a cast-iron stove."

"I don't care. You're supposed to be sitting back and watching me work." He picked his way through the turmoil of packing boxes until he reached her side. Taking her by the arm, he led her to the sofa, shoving stacks of linen onto the floor to make room for her.

"Flynn, I'm two months pregnant. I'm not sick. I'm not injured. Pregnancy is a perfectly normal function of the human body and there's no reason to treat me like an invalid."

He crouched in front of her, reaching up to tuck a stray lock of hair beneath the scarf she was wearing. "Indulge me. I've only been a father to be for a week. I'm still in the crazy stage."

She reached out to smooth his hair, feeling her love well up inside. "You're always in the crazy stage. You're going to make a great father."

"I like to think so. Ouch!" He gave her a hurt look, reaching up to remove her fingers from the strand of hair she'd just tugged. "What was that for?"

"To keep you from getting overconfident."

"I think I've got something to be overconfident about. After all, we decide we want a baby and you get pregnant the first month of trying. I think that says something about my manly prowess."

He looked so smug that Ann couldn't help but laugh. "It says more about your appetites. Considering how many times you ravished me, it would have been more amazing if I *hadn't* gotten pregnant."

"I don't remember you kicking and screaming."

She smiled, running her fingers over a streak of dirt on his cheek. "No. I suppose I wasn't. Are you really, truly happy about this baby?"

"Ann, I am really, truly happy about everything. You. The baby. Moving. My life couldn't be more perfect."

Her eyes grew dreamy. "We'll have to start thinking of names. If it's a girl, we could name her Rebecca, after Becky."

He shook his head. "No. There's only one Becky. Besides, since we're going to be moving into her neighborhood, it would get confusing with two little girls named Becky."

"I suppose. Rafferty called last night. He says he's got all the real estate ads marked for us. Becky's looking forward to helping us pick out a house."

"Just as long as she doesn't cook dinner for us. Are you sure this is what you want to do? We're making a lot of changes all at once. You quitting your job, moving to a new state, trying to get into school and having a baby. It's a lot to take on.''

"I'm not pushing any of it." She smiled at him, feeling contentment fill her. A year of marriage hadn't softened the intensity of their love. Flynn had become her champion, her companion, her lover. She'd never thought it possible to be so happy. He'd supported her through the difficult decision to leave her job and apply to a school of veterinary medicine. He'd stood by her when her father all but said she was no daughter of his. When Flynn found out that the school she wanted to go to was in Colorado, he'd suggested that they move there, confident that she would be accepted.

He believed in her more than she believed in herself.

"I love you, Flynn McCallister."

"I love you, too, but I'm still not going to let you do any of the packing. I'll do the china and we'll let the movers do the rest."

"Okay. But you're being overprotective."

"I like being overprotective."

She watched him move over to the box she'd been packing and start wrapping the china in tissue.

"Have you called your parents to tell them about the baby?"

"I talked to my mother. She was very excited."

"Did you talk to your dad?"

"Ann, forget it." His tone held a gentle warning. The subject of his father was off-limits. He said he'd accepted the rift between them, but she knew it still bothered him. Still, there was nothing she could do about it.

A knock at the door interrupted her thoughts. She started to get to her feet but Flynn waved her back. "Sit there and relax. It's probably the guy from the moving company. I told Joe to send him up when he got here."

Ann stood up as he walked to the door. It was nice that Flynn wanted to take care of her, but she wasn't going to act like Camille and greet visitors lying back on a sofa. She heard him open the door and then there was a long silence. Curiosity drew her forward.

Her eyes widened as Flynn stepped into the living room, his face absolutely expressionless. Behind him were his parents. Not just his mother, who had visited them on a number of occasions, but his father, too.

Ann came forward, holding out her hands. "Louise. How nice to see you." The two women hugged with real affection and then Ann was left facing her father-in-law. It was the first time she'd seen him in over a year. He hadn't even come to the small wedding. "Mr. McCallister. It's nice to see you." She held out her hand, not quite sure it was the right thing to do but needing to make some gesture.

He took her hand, his grip a little too tight, his eyes reflecting his uneasiness. "It's good to see you again, Ann. I...it would make me very happy if you would call me David. No need to be formal."

"Thank you, David." She looked at her husband, but Flynn was looking at one of the packing boxes. She could see the muscle that ticked in the side of his jaw and she knew how nervous he was. There'd be no help from him.

"Why don't you both come in and sit down. I think I've got some coffee in the kitchen and there's probably some banana bread left."

"That's all right, Ann. We had coffee before we left home." Louise followed her into the shambles of the living room, leaving the two men to trail behind, not speaking, looking anywhere but at each other.

The two women sat on the sofa and the men remained standing. Flynn leaned against the empty fireplace, his boneless slump making it clear that this visit meant nothing to him. His father stood next to the window, his blunt fingers shoved in the pockets of his suit coat.

Louise and Ann looked at each other and then looked at

their respective husbands, letting the silence stretch. David met his wife's stern look and cleared his throat awkwardly.

"Your mother tells me that you and Ann are going to be having a child."

"Yes, we are."

"That's wonderful. Wonderful." David took his hands out of his pockets and stared at them for a moment as if not quite sure who they belonged to and then shoved them back into hiding.

"You're...ah...moving to Colorado, I understand."

"That's right." Flynn would have left it at that but he caught Ann's eyes, reading the plea in them. "Ann's going to be going to school there."

"Good. Good." The silence stretched again. "We... ah...that is, your mother and I thought we'd like to maybe help out with the...house. We...that is...I didn't get you a wedding present and it would mean a lot to us if you were to consider the house a wedding gift."

Ann held her breath, waiting for Flynn's answer. He had to see how difficult this was for his father. Surely, he wouldn't turn him away. Flynn glanced at her and then looked at his father.

"Thank you. Ann and I would be happy to accept your gift."

Ann let her breath out in a rush, feeling Louise do the same next to her. "Thank you, David. The house will mean even more to us, knowing that it comes from the two of you." David McCallister shifted uneasily beneath the warmth of her words.

"You know, Flynn, you've got a real treasure here. I hope you know how lucky you are. Marrying Ann is about the smartest thing you'll ever do. Just like marrying your mother was for me."

Flynn's face relaxed in a half smile. "You don't have to tell me how lucky I am. I know."

"Your mother tells me that you're quite a photographer. I never knew that. She says you've even submitted some things to a few magazines."

"That was Ann's doing. She can be pretty stubborn." His smile was so loving that Ann had to swallow the lump in her throat.

"Well, good luck with them. I'm...I'm proud of you, son."

Flynn's eyes widened as he stared at his father. "Thank you..." The two men stared at each other across the years, across a lot of hurts. The distance couldn't be wiped out in one short visit, but the first steps had been taken. "It means a lot to me to hear you say that."

Ann sniffed, unashamed of the tears that filled her eyes. David looked at his son for a moment and then looked away.

"Well, we can't stay long. You've got a lot to get done."

Ann didn't urge them to stay longer. Perhaps it was best to keep this first visit short. At the door, she hugged Louise tightly and then hesitated a moment before tentatively putting her arms around her father-in-law's stocky figure. He patted her on the back, the gesture awkward, as if it had been too long since he'd shown anyone any softness.

Flynn hugged his mother and then faced his father. After a moment, David held out his hand and Flynn took it. More was said in the fervency of their grips than could have been said with words.

"Keep in touch, Flynn. Losing one son in a lifetime is enough for any man." He was gone before Flynn could reply, the door closing quietly behind him and his wife.

Flynn stared at the door for a moment and then turned to see Ann watching him, tears running down her face. His own eyes were suspiciously bright.

He held out his arms and she stepped into them, linking her arms around his waist, pressing her face to his chest.

She could feel the strong beat of his heart beneath her cheek. It felt so right.

"I love you so much." His voice broke on the words and he buried his face in her hair.

Her arms tightened around his waist. As long as she had him to hold on to, everything in her life was right.

HARLEQUIN SUPERROMANCE®

...there's more to the story!

Superromance. A *big* satisfying read about unforgettable characters. Each month we offer *four* very different stories that range from family drama to adventure and mystery, from highly emotional stories to romantic comedies—and much more! Stories about people you'll believe in and care about. Stories too compelling to put down....

Our authors are among today's *best* romance writers. You'll find familiar names and talented newcomers. Many of them are award winners—and you'll see why!

If you want the biggest and best in romance fiction, you'll get it from Superromance!

Available wherever Harlequin books are sold.

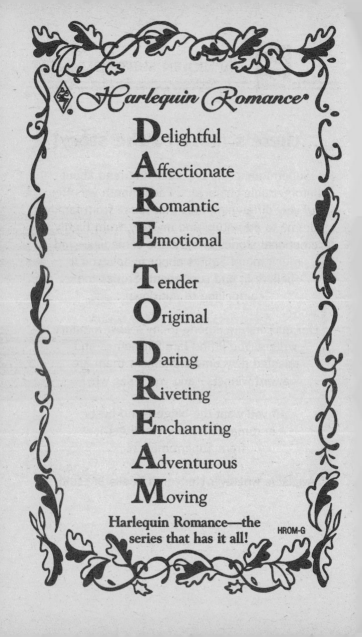

Harlequin Romance

Delightful

Affectionate

Romantic

Emotional

Tender

Original

Daring

Riveting

Enchanting

Adventurous

Moving

Harlequin Romance—the
series that has it all!

HROM-G

Harlequin® Historical

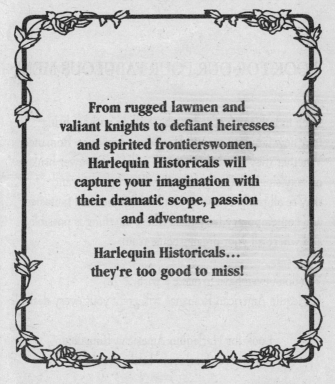

From rugged lawmen and
valiant knights to defiant heiresses
and spirited frontierswomen,
Harlequin Historicals will
capture your imagination with
their dramatic scope, passion
and adventure.

Harlequin Historicals...
they're too good to miss!

HHGENR

LOOK FOR OUR FOUR FABULOUS MEN!

Each month some of today's bestselling authors bring
four new fabulous men to Harlequin American Romance.
Whether they're rebel ranchers, millionaire power brokers
or sexy single dads, they're all gallant princes—and
they're all ready to sweep you into lighthearted fantasies
and contemporary fairy tales where anything is possible
and where all your dreams come true!

You don't even have to make a wish...
Harlequin American Romance will grant your every desire!

Look for Harlequin American Romance
wherever Harlequin books are sold!

HARLEQUIN PRESENTS®

HARLEQUIN PRESENTS
men you won't be able to resist
falling in love with...

HARLEQUIN PRESENTS
women who have feelings
just like your own...

HARLEQUIN PRESENTS
powerful passion in
exotic international settings...

HARLEQUIN PRESENTS
intense, dramatic stories that will keep you
turning to the very last page...

HARLEQUIN PRESENTS
The world's bestselling romance series!

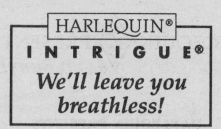

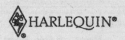

Not The Same Old Story!

 Exciting, glamorous
romance stories that take
readers around the world.

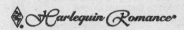 Sparkling, fresh and
tender love stories that
bring you pure romance.

 Bold and adventurous—
Temptation is strong women,
bad boys, great sex!

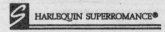 Provocative and realistic
stories that celebrate life
and love.

 Contemporary
fairy tales—where
anything is possible
and where dreams
come true.

 Heart-stopping, suspenseful
adventures that combine the
best of romance and mystery.

 Humorous and romantic
stories that capture the lighter
side of love.